**DIARY
OF THE
CUBAN
REVOLUTION**

DIARY

OF THE CUBAN REVOLUTION

CARLOS FRANQUI

Translated by
GEORGETTE FELIX,
ELAINE KERRIGAN,
PHYLLIS FREEMAN,
HARDIE ST. MARTIN

A Seaver Book

The Viking Press   New York

Diario de la revolución cubana

© Editions du Seuil, 1976
English-language translation Copyright © Viking Penguin Inc., 1980
All rights reserved
A Seaver Book/The Viking Press
First published in 1980 in a hardbound and paperbound edition by
The Viking Press, 625 Madison Avenue, New York, N.Y. 10022
Published simultaneously in Canada by
Penguin Books Canada Limited

Library of Congress Cataloging in Publication Data
Franqui, Carlos, 1921–
    Diary of the Cuban revolution.
    Translation of Diario de la revolución cubana.
    "A Seaver book."
    Includes index.
    1. Cuba—History—1933–1959—Addresses, essays, lectures.
2. Cuba—History—Revolution, 1959—Addresses, essays, lectures.
3. Cuba—History—1933–1959—Sources. I. Title.
F1787.5.F7313   972.91063   78-12300
ISBN 0-670-27217-5 (hardbound)
        0-670-27213-2 (paperbound)

Printed in the United States of America
Set in Baskerville

The editors of Seaver Books wish to thank Mr. Raúl Chibás for his precious help.

THE DIARY AND THE DIARIES

Underground, in prison, in exile, or at war I was always able to participate in the events in two different ways.

One, participating in the action; the other, from afar, as an observer.

Like a strange animal who looks around and yet sees himself from the outside.

Coldly.

Moreover, history is *made,* and told later. But when history is recounted it is inevitable in a different way. It is then remade.

I always felt that a diary was too personal and too limited a vehicle with which to narrate collective events.

What I did find most genuine in the collective struggle was precisely that, by participating in it, I transcended my personal needs and conflicts. I became integrated.

I refused to be a hero, a leader; I refused to be separated from or placed above the group.

I became integrated. I disappeared into the whole.

Anonymity fascinated me, and the underground was just that: anonymity.

The struggle was a collective creation and by necessity it guaranteed revolutionary freedom and creativity.

My responsibilities within the struggle gave me the means with which to narrate history in the broadest manner possible.

As editor-in-chief of the underground newspaper *Revolución,* in charge of public information for the national leadership of the 26th of July Movement, and as director of Radio Rebelde in the Sierra Maestra, I received and was entrusted with all that was to be written: letters, war communiqués, reports, articles, statements, recordings, interviews, publications.

I could use a variety of materials for our revolutionary press.

We knew that the battlefront of ideas offered another effective means with which to wage war: Che, Fidel, Frank País, Armando Hart, and myself, among others, agreed that propaganda, or public information, was a decisive weapon in our struggle.

We defeated Batista's army and his forces of repression with a minimum of physical destruction and a maximum of psychological penetration.

Part of our battle was waged by breaking through censorship and liberating the people's will to rebel—a will that had long been held in check and controlled by the use and technique of a gigantic propaganda network, extending to radio, television, and the press.

And, if we prevailed then over tyranny and domination, it was because the people joined in the struggle and became its real protagonist.

Thus my diary was unique; I recorded what to me seemed worthiest: the problems and development of the struggle as they occurred, written by many of those, including myself, who participated closely in the battle.

If I thought something essential was missing in a story, I would inquire further.

What was written down was later supplemented with recorded conversations. I always tried to discover the inner core and humanity of all or most of the participants.

Their words here are as they were spoken in the early days of combat.

My main concern was to know the limitations of history: the people who were actually *making* it had no time to relate it.

That history was so anonymous and collective that it would not register and endure in mere words.

Each word recorded here, however, is the history of thousands of anonymous fighters and guerrillas who fought and died for freedom, in cities and in mountains.

This is by no means an all-embracing diary—an unrealistic and impossible task—but a selective-collective account.

It is the word of many and of the principals in the struggle, as they spoke then about each event in which they participated.

Thus what I am presenting here is an authentic source for the history of the Cuban insurrection.

—Carlos Franqui

THE ISLAND OF CUBA

The brief but intense history of Cuba presents two constants and a single movement.

There was the world's invasion of the island and the island's struggle to repel it, to know and project itself on the world, to re-create itself at home and abroad.

The constant is movement. The island is a dance, a cyclone.

Its character and destiny are those of an island crossroads: a ship. It looks toward its neighboring or distant continental shores, a tradition inherited from its founders, who never stayed long in port.

Cuba is an adventure without fear of the unexpected, the magical, the impossible, or the unknown.

Cuba is not Indian. Cuba is not white. It is neither black nor yellow. Cuba is mulatto, mixed, whitish black, and tobacco-hued. Together with Brazil, it is one of the blackest countries in white America. One of the whitest of black countries as well.

Cuba, like the United States—which is geographically so near and yet so remote and different in everything else—is one of the newest nations of the world. One is a continent, the other is an island. One is Anglo-Saxon Protestant in character, and based on the industrial revolution, power, and wealth. The other is Latin, Spanish, black, and Chinese.

If Venice was Europe's door to the Orient and Florence symbolized the end of antiquity and the coming of the Renaissance, Cuba is the beginning of America's new world, yesterday embodied in today. There, everything began. All travelers paused there. The island was a bridge, a crossroads, and a base for continental expeditions in the New World.

The Spanish presence in America lasted from 1492 to 1899—four centuries in which Spain remained untouched by the Reformation, the industrial revolution, and the bourgeois upsurge.

And so there remained the prehistoric and the feudal establishments: adventure, religion, absurdity, dreams of grandeur, madness, impracticality, genius, caudillism, militarism, and the lack of laws and institutions and other establishments which accompanied the development of the bourgeois world. What did remain were the features of a world which preceded the industrial, machine civilization. And that ancient world was merged with what was left of the Indian world and the black world.

The slowgoing, predominantly Spanish population of Cuba was engaged mostly in agriculture and in cattle-raising until the industrial development of sugarcane and the gigantic slave trade it generated upset the balance of a more developed agricultural economy—cattle, coffee, cocoa, minor products—and created a violent shock in the colonial community.

Thousands of Chinese and Canary Islanders arrived later, most of them expert farmers, artisans, and merchants.

In the first half of the nineteenth century, an educated class, the Creoles, began emerging in Cuba. Its members studied in France and England, or in the fine schools of Havana founded by Varela and Luz y Caballero.

Cuba's Wars of Independence—1868–95—were caused fundamentally by the development of nationality, the economic and political clashes with Spanish colonialism, the great English, French, and American revolutions, and the impact of the struggles of Simon Bolívar and others inspired in Latin America to achieve liberation from Spain.

The first books, printing press, and newsprint to reach Spanish America came in through Cuba. Later, José Martí, the liberator, poet, and first anti-imperialist known in America, initiated the revolution known in literature as *modernismo.*

Thus mulattoes and mestizos, burghers, peasants, workers, intellectuals, and revolutionaries began appearing in that exuberant island paradise, "the most beautiful land that human eyes have ever beheld," as Columbus called it, a violent island with a rebellious Caribbean to the south and a placid lazy shore on the north, an island without frost and seasons, abounding in lush greenery, in sugarcane and tobacco but lacking in great wealth.

A good Cuban is one who possesses the rhythm of the black, who dances well, and is as delirious as a Spaniard but a bit more graceful; one who thinks like a Frenchman, believes in gambling luck as the Chinese, is as much of a Don Juan as if he were an Italian, does not like the gringos, is a chatterbox, and is also capable of embarking on *anything,* be it a ship, a plank, a rubber tire, a war, a fiesta, a ball, a love affair, a drinking spree, or a scientific experiment (the first rocket was invented by a Cuban—only on a postage stamp); capable of embarking even on a revolution against the Yankees or on socialism.

The Cuban always has time for anything. Nothing is impossible to him. He is always on the move; "the only thing one must not do is die," he says. Child or adult, he emphatically dislikes being ordered about.

The Cuban says no, and means it, to all authority; to bosses, kings, generals, presidents, colonels, commanders, doctors. And no to empires, too. Spanish, American, or Russian. He wants none of them.

Sí, señor, that's how it is.

Cuba has everything; there everything starts and nothing is finished. And so . . .

In that world without norms, without logic, without classicism, bourgeois culture or an industrial world, all myths are real. Things exist before they are invented. The only requirement is to search for the origin of things—the real, not the supernatural—learn, and then re-create them.

Therein lies the story of the men who represent our Latin American world. Where did Bolívar learn the art of war and the philosophy of revolution he needed to launch Latin American independence? In Europe, of course.

And José Martí, how did he discover that the problem was the United States, not Spain; and then start the anti-imperialist war right within the monster itself, while living in the United States?

Bolívar and Martí balance Marx. To his revolutionary analysis of the German capitalist world, Bolívar and Martí added the continental unity needed in our feudal world and gave it a permanent anti-imperialist outlook. And that unity and that outlook still constitute the revolutionary political thought of our Latin American world.

Cuba could be called the Island of Beginnings. The Spanish conquest began there. The Indian rebellion began there.

Cuba was the beginning of the end of Spain's power.

The rebellion against the United States began in Cuba.

Three rebellions are struggling simultaneously in Cuba: the anticolonialist, the anticapitalist, and the antibureaucratic.

Cuba is an island of immigrants and émigrés. In constant movement and danger. Coveted by the great powers. Invaded by buccaneers and pirates. Occupied by Spaniards, Britons, North Americans. An island of sugar and tobacco, of misery and slavery: rebellion itself.

—C.F.

GENERALS GÓMEZ AND MACEO

MASTERS OF GUERRILLA WARFARE

Cuban wars of independence were not waged in the manner of classical battles, such as those of North America or Bolivia, which were led by academic officers of middle-class origins and education, under the influence of European military models. The Cuban wars were guerrilla wars waged by the people.

Intuition and popular peasant wisdom, a fountain of inventiveness, made revolutionary warfare possible in Cuba. A long, narrow island, rather small in total territory, Cuba formed part of no continent and fought its wars of independence by itself.

During the Bolívar epoch, Spain was forced to fight simultaneous battles over immense territories. During the Cuban wars, forces could be concentrated within a limited territory, surrounded by seas, without running the risks of spilling over into other countries, or of running into conflicts with other European powers, as in the earlier period.

The Cuban wars were the fruit of an existing organized political movement, and the last one, the war of 1895, was the offspring of the Partido Revolucionario Cubano [Cuban Revolutionary Party], formed by José Martí.

Cuba offered natural protection for guerrilla forces: its woods and jungles, fields without great mountains or raging rivers, ferocious beasts or deadly ills. In fact, the fields furnished animals and plants fit for human consumption, and, above all, they were populated by a rebellious people.

These special characteristics—geographic, social, and human— joined to our historical tradition, constitute a factor worthy of serious study, for all guerrilla warfare in Latin America, since it is one necessary for a revolution; the technique for transferring it to the field of action (guerrilla warfare is an offspring of organization and not its begetter) is one of the decisive hurdles to be overcome.

In our wars of independence we made use of the jungle, the element of surprise, ambush, long marches, sieges of the cities, carried out from the surrounding countryside; we also used the tactics of machete attacks, quick and ruthless, to balance and overcome the firepower, which was both heavy and deadly. Terrifying charges and furious counterattacks alternated with feints and retreats, and the enemy was attacked where he least expected it.

The destruction of the country's riches and setting fire to property were important factors. The last war, the War of 1895, was spread by Cuban invasions of the island from east to west, from Oriente Province to Pinar del Río. While the invading forces advanced, small guerrilla units operated throughout the island. Some great battles were waged, and cities were taken, but only as alternative actions, for our strength lay in quickness of movement, the element of surprise, and use made of the terrain which was unknown and hostile to the Spanish.

Controlling the fields and mountains, destroying the wealth, eluding the Spanish firepower, the outnumbered Cuban guerrillas proceeded to wear down, smash, and demoralize the enemy, thus ensuring the conditions necessary for victory.

Máximo Gómez, born of humble stock on the island of Santo Domingo, was a master of guerrilla warfare; he was able to count on the intelligence and imagination of the Cuban populace and on that of the mulatto Antonio Maceo, also of humble birth, whose epic machete charges, bravura, and popularity were one of the principal inspirational assets in that war.

The tactics invented in 1868 were mastered by the chiefs and the combatants to the point of becoming a collective form of warfare, in which tens of thousands of Cubans and hundreds of Hispano-Americans and Europeans distinguished themselves.

In this kind of combat the protagonist was the populace and not the heroes.

The guerrilla war against Batista drew on this historic tradition.

CUBA

Iguara
MORÓN
CIEGO DE ÁVILA
SANCTI SPÍRITUS
Jíbaro
Júcaro
Piedrecitas
Minas
CAMAGÜEY
x El Jigüe
Guáimaro
VICTORIA DE LAS TUNAS
Naranjo
Uvero x
Soledad
HOLGUÍN
Palo Seco
Guaro
Cauto
BAYAMO
MANZANILLO
Yara
Bueycito
Baire
PALMA SORIANO
Jamaica
GUANTÁNAMO
Sierra Maestra
El Cobre
Mount Turquino
SANTIAGO
DE CUBA
La Plata

CONTENTS

CONTENTS

CONTENTS

1959

1921-52

1. THE GENERATION OF 1953

FIDEL CASTRO

CHILDHOOD AND YOUTH   Interview by Carlos Franqui

From all indications, I was born to be a politician, to be a revolutionary. When I was eighteen, I was, politically speaking, illiterate. Since I didn't come from a family of politicians or grow up in a political atmosphere, it would have been impossible for me to carry out a revolutionary role, or an important revolutionary apprenticeship, in a relatively brief time, had I not had a special calling.

When I entered the university, I had no political background whatsoever. Until then I was basically interested in other things, for instance, sports, trips into the countryside—all kinds of activities that provided an outlet for my unbounded natural energy. I think that is where my energy, my fighting spirit was channeled in those days.

At the university, I had the feeling that a new field was opening up for me. I started thinking about my country's political problems—almost without being conscious of it. I spontaneously started to feel a certain concern, an interest in social and political questions.

All the circumstances surrounding my life and childhood, everything I saw, would have made it more logical to suppose I would develop the habits, the ideas, and the sentiments natural to a social class with certain privileges and selfish motives that make it indifferent to the problems of others.

I was born into a family of landowners in comfortable circumstances. We were considered rich and treated as such. I was brought up with all the privileges attendant to a son in such a family. Everyone lavished attention on me, flattered, and treated me differently from the other boys we played with when we were children. These other children went barefoot while we wore shoes; they were often hungry; at our house, there was always a squabble at table to get us to eat.

This tends to make boys grow used to a privileged situation and take on the attitude that whatever they receive is rightfully theirs. And yet, one circumstance in the middle of all this helped us develop a certain human spirit: it was the fact that all our friends, our companions, were the sons of local peasants.

I'm trying to remember the first time I wrote dates on a blackboard; it must have been sometime between 1930 and 1931, when I was about four.

I spent most of my time being fresh in school. Maybe because of my family's position, or my age, I remember that whenever I disagreed with something the teacher said to me, or whenever I got mad, I would swear at her and immediately leave school, running as fast as I could. There was a kind of standing war between us and the teacher. Whenever we would curse at the teacher, with dirty words we had picked up from the workers, we would get out of her way as fast as our feet would carry us.

One day, I had just sworn at the teacher, and was racing down the rear corridor. I took a leap, and landed on a board from a guava-jelly box with a nail in it. As I fell, the nail stuck in my tongue. When I got back home, my mother said to me: "God punished you for swearing at the teacher." I didn't have the slightest doubt that it was really true.

I learned to read and write very fast in that school.

I can say that I had one teacher after another, and my behavior was different with each one. With the teacher who treated us well and brought us toys, I remember being well-behaved. But when pressure, force, or punishment was used, my conduct was entirely different.

My parents lost patience and sent my sister and me to Santiago. I don't know whether it was because I caused too much trouble at home or because my teacher convinced my family that it would be a good thing to send me away to school. When children are of that age, especially if the family has money, people like to say that the children are intelligent, and they usually use this as an argument in their own favor. We went to Santiago by train. I had never been there. It all seemed extraordinary to me: the station with its wooden arches, the hubbub, the people. In the city, we stayed in the home of a cousin of the schoolteacher's. I remember that I wet the bed on the first night.

One of my first impressions of political events goes back to that stay in Santiago. I was standing opposite the high-school building when I saw a group of students come out and walk past some sailors who were carrying guns. I was standing there in the doorway, across the street, about thirty yards away, when the students passed. They must have muttered something to the sailors, because they had walked only a little way when the sailors followed them into the building, brought them out, and took them off to jail, hitting them with their gun butts. This left a lasting impression on me.

The first time I ever visited a jail was with a terribly unhappy countrywoman who had come to see her husband. He was a mechanic by the name of Antonio and he had been arrested for being a Communist. I went with her into the prison, and the sight of the jailers impressed me very deeply. I still remember Antonio in his cell.

Then came the struggle, when the fight against Machado was fiercest and bombs were set off every night. In a way, I took part in the period of terror: I used to sleep on a small sofa near the back door, and at night the bombs exploding close by would wake me up. I was awakened several times when the bombs went off in the neighborhood, near the high school. This must have been in '32 and I couldn't have been more than six.

By then I was in the first grade at the school run by the La Salle order. I knew all about being ill-treated from previous experience and, in a way, I was on my guard. I was a day student, and felt that I was worse off than the boarders. They were taken to the beach or out for walks on Thursdays and Sundays; my life was very dull. My guardians were constantly threatening to enroll me as a boarding student, and since I was unhappy with them, I decided that I'd like to board. All this happened one day when I was given a whipping at home; I don't remember why my godfather, who was my guardian, gave me a couple of good whacks on my rear end. I made up my mind then, and proceeded to rebel and insult everybody. I told them all the things I'd been wanting to tell them for a long time. I behaved so terribly that they took me straight back to school and enrolled me as a boarder. It was a great victory for me. I was finally going to have the same kind of life as all the other kids.

On our first holidays, we went home for a three-month vacation; I don't think I've ever been happier. We hunted with slingshots, rode horseback, swam in the rivers, and had complete freedom during those months.

One day, when I was in the third grade, I was talking with one of the officials who was in charge of us. He was commenting on how much money that boy's father made, how much the other one's father made, and I remember that I told him some of the things I had heard at home. I explained to him that sometimes the lumber cut for my father, and all the other business interests he had, brought in 300 pesos a day. This really astounded the official, and from that moment on, he began acting in a very special, civil, friendly way toward us. So, then, in school we could already notice, even among students from wealthy families, that we were treated according to our family's income. After that day, in my third year, they invented a special fourth grade for the three of us, for myself, and my brothers, Ramón and Raúl, because Raúl was four or five years old by then, and I was eight. That's how we were skipped from third to fifth grade.

Every Thursday and Sunday we went to the island of Renté, which was then owned by a very rich family—the Cendoyas from Santiago de Cuba; the La Salle brothers ran a recreation center there. We used to go in a little launch, called *El Cateto*. It took about an hour to cross the bay from the Alameda to Renté. We would spend the afternoon there, playing, fishing, and swimming; and then we would come back.

Going back from Renté at night, we would go up one of the streets leading from the Alameda to the La Salle school and we would have to pass through a section, near the market, that was filled with bars and prostitutes. The people around there used to taunt the brothers, who wore cassocks. We walked in two rows, one on each side of the street, and some of the prostitutes would always come to the windows of the houses to tease the boys as well as the priests. I would get angry when I saw the hostile attitude of the passersby toward the men in cassocks. One day on our way back from Renté I had an argument on the launch with a boy, Iván Losada, the priest's pet. The boy and I had a fight out there, right in the middle of the water. The minute we got back to the school and were alone, we battled it out. It turned out badly for him, because he got a black eye. I knew that would bring a storm down on me. That evening, there was what they call benediction, a religious service, and we all went to the chapel in the sacristy. In the middle of the service, which was very solemn, the chapel door opened and the priest called me. He led me down the hall and asked me what had happened between Iván and me. I started to explain, but he gave me a slap that just about stunned one side of my face. I spun around, and he caught my other cheek. When he let me go, I was in a complete daze. I felt painfully humiliated.

Another time, I don't remember if it was that same year, we were marching in single file and he struck me again, this time on the head. Then, I promised myself not to let it happen again.

We were playing ball one day. The kid who was at the head of the line always had the best position, and I was half arguing over first place with somebody else, when the priest came up to me from behind and hit me on the head. This time I turned on him, right then and there, threw a piece of bread at his head and started to hit him with my fists and bite him. I don't think I hurt the priest much, but the daring outburst became a historic event in school.

During our vacation at home, our parents got a bookkeeper to make us practice math. We didn't like being forced to study at a time when we should be playing and having fun. We struck back: we had gotten hold of an answer book at school, and when we were given the math problems to do, we copied the answers, finishing quickly, and went out to play.

That same year, I remember, our father would complain to anybody he ran into that they had told him at the school that his sons were the three biggest bullies who had ever gone there. It was an unfair report but they believed it at home, and it was therefore decided that we should stop studying. It was a decisive moment in my life; I can't explain how I could have such good intuition, under the circumstances—but I think I was really convinced that I was right about school and they had been unfair to me; and although a boy wasn't supposed to like studying at that age, I felt that taking me away from school was a punishment I didn't deserve and I was being hurt, unfairly hurt.

And so, when January 7, the date for going back to school, rolled around, Ramón was kept out, and he was happy because he liked machinery, trucks, and things like that; he was delighted not to go to school anymore. Raúl was packed off to a military school run by a country teacher, a sergeant, who also gave him a hard time. They were going to keep me out of school too. But I remember going to my mother and explaining that I wanted to go on studying; it wasn't fair not to let me go to school. I appealed to her and told her I wanted to stay in school and that if I wasn't sent back, I'd set fire to the house.

Our home was a large, two-story frame building on piles, partly Spanish in style; the cattle were below, the dairy barn was under the house. I really threatened to set the whole place on fire if I wasn't sent back to school. So they decided to send me back. I'm not sure if they were afraid or just sorry for me, but my mother pleaded my case.

I was taken to school by my father, who was involved in a political campaign at the time. A friend of his was running for office and my father was helping him out. I remember what politics were like in those days: when election time rolled around, some men, called political captains, would run for office. Each of them would say he controlled some four hundred, two hundred, or a hundred votes. And so my father was helping out this friend, who in turn did business and had close dealings with him. Politics were controlled by money back then, and I remember people going in and out of the room where the safe was kept at home. Some mornings I'd be awakened by the first activities at the safe. Eight or ten thousand pesos were spent on each political campaign.

I formed a very poor opinion of all this, constantly hearing my mother protest against it. I always heard her complaining about politics, because it cost a good deal of money, money thrown out the window, and my mother was thrifty. She also complained about journalists, who were always coming to our home to collect money for newspaper articles and other things. She suffered at seeing so much money wasted on politics and journalists, when she, my father, and everyone else worked so hard.

In the fifth grade we were sent as day students to the Dolores Jesuit school.

I always had plenty to eat, but for pocket money I received twenty cents each week: ten for the movies on Sunday, five for ice cream afterward, and five to buy a comic book called *El Gorrión* [The Sparrow], which I bought every Thursday.

I registered very late at the Dolores school, which was a school that set very high standards. I had trouble keeping up with the others.

All my life, ever since I was a young boy, I was aware of all the injustices, wrongs, and rough treatment boys have to go through. I'd say I've had a lot of experience with the way boys are exploited, having seen how self-interest prevailed over any kind of human consideration. Wherever we went, we were the instruments of business. I personally suffered from the lack of the most elementary perception about teaching and about the psychology of educating boys. I'm not blaming my parents, who were ignorant people without a proper education; they left us in the hands of others they believed were treating us properly, but we had a hard time of it.

My guardians in Santiago had three grown-up children. My sister had also been sent to their house. If I didn't get the highest marks because I wasn't in the right frame of mind or hadn't done the necessary preparation, they would cut off my twenty cents' allowance. I decided to take steps to protect my interests. I said to myself: "Well, now, what will happen if the notebook with my school marks should get lost?" And one day in school I told my teachers that I had lost the notebook and I was given another. From then on, I would put my grades in the new book and take that one home to be signed—with very good grades in it, of course. The other notebook, the one they put the real marks in at school, I signed myself and returned to school.

I never had good marks in math, grammar, and other subjects—except for history, a subject I like a lot, and in geography.

The semester finally ended, and there was the school celebration, with lots of excitement, and we got all dressed up in our best clothes. All the relatives and all the boys were there. Prizes were announced with special ceremonies, recitations, and so on.

When the fifth grade's turn came, I still hadn't worked out the story I'd have to tell when my guardians would discover I hadn't had the best marks. There I was, cool and waiting for them to say: "Fifth grade, first prize, Enrique Peralta. . . ." I started to look shocked, as if I couldn't figure it out. They began to read off the prizes for each subject and I won absolutely nothing. And I went on looking more and more shocked. Then I said, "Oh, darn it!" And I remember I said, "I know what's happened. I started very late, in December, that's why they haven't counted me in, I was three months short, so my grade totals are less than the others', and that's why I'm not getting any prizes."

When September came, I got appendicitis. They took me to the Colonia Española Hospital and I was operated on; I was there for three months, because I developed problems with the healing of the scar.

I remember that at that time, shut up in the hospital, I was practically alone, and I made friends with all the other patients. I am telling this because I think it shows I already had an ability to relate to other people; I had a streak of the politician.

When I wasn't reading comic books, I spent my time visiting other patients. I made friends with everyone, except those in the contagious ward. At the time, some people thought I might make a good doctor, because I used to play with lizards and a Gillette razor blade. I had been impressed by operations like the one I'd been through. I think that few sanitary measures were taken at my operation, and that's why the wound opened up and I had to stay in the hospital three months. After that, I would "operate" on lizards—lizards that usually died, of course.

Then I would enjoy watching how the ants carried them off, how hundreds of ants working together could carry the lizard and move it to their heap.

I went back to school in the sixth grade. I was sick of the house I was staying in, and the lack of understanding and the bad treatment I received. I'd get home from school after a day of classes—when all any boy wants is to come home and do nothing, listen to the radio or go out—and they would shut me up in a room for hours so I'd have to study. I did stay there for hours, but without studying anything. How did I pass the time? My imagination would fly off to places and events in history, and to wars. I liked history very much, and particularly the stories of battles in the first history books I read. I even used to invent battles. Those hours I was forced to spend locked up were a kind of military training. I'd start off by taking a lot of little scraps and tiny balls of paper, arranging them on a playing board—it was one of those silly things we sometimes like to do—and setting up an obstacle to see how many would pass, and how many wouldn't. There were losses, casualties. I played this game of wars for hours at a time.

But I had had enough of that place, and one day I stood up to the lady of the house; I told her off about the way they treated me, I told them all to go to the devil, and entered school as a boarder that very afternoon. This was the second time, or the third, fourth, fifth, I can't remember which, that I had to take it upon myself to get out of what I considered an unpleasant situation. I had to do it so that I'd be sent to La Salle as a boarder, I had to do it at La Salle, I had to do it at home so I'd be sent back to school, and now in that house so that I'd be put back into a boarding school once more.

From then on I definitely became my own master and took charge of all my own problems without advice from anyone.

I played soccer, basketball, jai alai, all kinds of sports. All my energy went into them.

We would go on outings in a school bus. We'd arrive at El Cobre and often I would decide to climb the mountain, keeping the bus waiting for two or three hours. Or we would go somewhere near El Caney, and I'd also go climb the tallest hill there. One of the things I also loved was to take off along the rivers when they were swollen, cross them, and hike awhile before coming back. The bus always had to wait for me.

The priest in charge of us, our prefect, was a Father García; he never scolded me for this. It's odd—disappearing for two or three hours was considered a breach of discipline. Of the whole group, I was the enthusiast, the mountain climber par excellence. I did not imagine that mountains would one day play such an important role in my life!

I was twelve or thirteen. The year after that was my last year in grade school. The new atmosphere made me study and that year I was one of the best in my class. I passed the entrance exam and entered high school.

Shortly after that I decided to change schools on my own, because I didn't feel at home surrounded by older boys, and went to another Jesuit school.

I remember that I had a different attitude toward people who understood me and treated me kindly. My conduct could be entirely different, depending on the treatment I received. There are really few people who I can remember understood me as a child.

In Jesuit schools I found that the educators were better prepared than those in other schools. They were carefully selected, and had had to study for many years. There was a spirit of discipline. This doesn't mean that I approve entirely of their educational methods. The separation of boys and girls, the lack of contact, made us look forward eagerly to the lines of girls that came from other schools. Kept away from girls, we couldn't take our minds off them. That separation seems utterly wrong to me. It tends to create repressions, and makes boys think of nothing but women. The same goes for religious teaching in which sexual problems were posed as problems of sin, with woman as an instrument of sin, an instrument of temptation used by the devil. I do, however, feel that creating habits of discipline and study was good. I am not against that kind of life, Spartan to some degree. And I think that, as a rule, the Jesuits formed people of character.

Once we had a poetry contest, sponsored by a radio station. All the students took part in it, and the parents voted for the best poems. Mine weren't the best, but I had made friends with all the boys, which I think again reveals perhaps a political streak in me.

So I wrote my verses and almost all the kids asked their parents to vote for me; as a result, letters were sent in—there was a boy named Elpidio Estrada, who wrote very pretty poems, much better than mine— letters that went something like this: "Elpidio's poem to mothers is very beautiful and very touching, but our vote goes to Fidel. . . ."

FIDEL CASTRO   Taped interview by Carlos Franqui

The Bogotá affair took place in April 1948.

In those days I was quixotic, romantic, a dreamer, with very little political know-how but with a tremendous thirst for knowledge and a great impatience for action. I could not yet foresee distinctly the great enemies I would have to fight against, but I was already beginning to detect them. The dreams of Martí and Bolívar, as well as a kind of utopian socialism, were vaguely stirring within me.

I found it hard to understand why the America conceived by its great and extraordinary emancipators had drifted so far toward the painful reality exemplified by almost twenty divided, weak, impoverished republics.

I had read many biographies of Bolívar and was deeply drawn to the life and work of that extraordinary man. Of course, I could analyze this phenomenon only in very simple terms, according to an extremely idealistic concept of history. I imagined history to be the result of betrayals, human treachery, corrupt politics, and military ambition; in a way, I was automatically viewing the situation in other countries in the light of politics in my own country, where there were many examples of this. I could not yet understand the bitter reality of the imperialist phenomenon or its decisive influence in the fate of our Latin American nations.

And yet, reading and studying the writings and speeches of Martí, whom I never tired of reading in those days, as well as accounts of the recent military interventions of the United States, not only in our own country but in many other Latin American countries, in order to defend the most bastardly interests, I came to realize more and more clearly that the policy of the United States, and its wholly disproportionate development with respect to Latin America, was the great enemy of the unification and development of the Latin American nations; the United States would always do its utmost to maintain the weakness and division on which it based its policy of directing the fate of our peoples as it pleased.

I attributed this to the evil nature of man, not to the consequences of a historically determined social system. I felt very close to the people of Puerto Rico, frustrated in their hope for independence; I regarded the construction of the Panama Canal as an act of piracy and plunder against Colombia and the people of Panama; I felt a deep revulsion for the brutal policy that had stripped Mexico of a huge and very rich portion of its territory.

What's more, some European powers still had colonial possessions here. A number of our countries were under the yoke of military despots who reminded us of the dark years of Batista's first eleven years of power.

As a student, I believed we had to start doing something; students could play a significant role in the struggle against all that. In those days this was a kind of crude revolutionary program that was just beginning to take form.

I proposed to a group of student leaders that our Federación Estudiantil Universitaria [FEU, University Students' Federation] should organize a congress of Latin American students to coincide with the opening of the foreign ministers' conference of the Organization of American States in Bogotá.

I had the impression that those meeting there would be the representatives of corrupt governments like ours, common looters, political schemers who could be bought, or just errand boys of bloodthirsty satraps. The contempt we felt for the government of [Ramón] Grau San Martín,* which was a perfect example of an unbelievably frustrating and disorganized administration, gave us an idea who would be meeting there in the name of the people of Latin America. That's why we believed that the students, who had a much better right than they to speak for all the people, should also meet there.

The hostility of the United States toward the Peronist movement in Argentina made us instinctively see Perón and his followers in a rather favorable light. Many pamphlets with Perón's speeches to the workers, his nationalist declarations, his appeals to the masses, and his attacks on oligarchies were circulating among the students around that time. We were impressed by those speeches, but had qualms about them because they leaned toward concentration of power in one man supported by the military, a fact that most of our newspapers, following the lead of the United States, had been drumming into us for years; this clashed with the fervent constitutionalist and democratic feeling we students had.

Democracy was still a magic word for us. In its name, the blood of millions had been spilled on battlefields in a war we read about with the passionate interest boys can show for historical as well as current events. Horrified by the savagery of Nazism, all our sympathies were on the side of those fighting for democracy. In its name, innumerable exiles from all corners of the continent rallied around our student committees.

We had been reading the highest praise of Greek democracy in all the history books in our elementary and secondary schools, and no one had ever thought of mentioning that it had been sustained on the shoulders of slaves whose numbers ran into the tens of thousands and on the labor of masses of citizens without the right to participate in public assemblies. And we hadn't yet realized that the so-called democracy of our time also rested not on the shoulders of tens of thousands but of millions of people reduced to common slavery in cities and fields, whose rights to

* President of Cuba, 1944-48.

equality and freedom existed only in the doctored-up texts of our bour-geois-democratic constitutions. As a matter of fact, we were ready to give our lives for that democracy.

We got in touch with some delegates from the Peronist movement visiting Cuba at the time and they became interested in the program we were drafting for the student meeting; it called for a struggle against the vestiges of colonialism, including, among others, the Falkland Islands, in which the Argentine government was interested. We therefore worked together with them to organize the congress. They promised to mobilize student centers in areas where they had connections and, in turn, we sent delegations to Central America. Then we left for Colombia, going by way of Panama and Venezuela.

In Panama, we got together with the students at the university, who were up to their necks fighting for Panama's right to the canal; there had been victims, among them a young fellow, crippled by a bullet, who had become a fighting symbol for Panamanian students.

I was amazed by the strong anti-imperialist sentiment expressed at the university student center, politically so far ahead of our own. We got their support for the congress.

What impressed me most in Panama were the streets near the naval base leading to the Canal Zone. They were an endless succession of brothels, nightclubs, and other lurid amusements—a depressing and un-forgettable sight.

I walked around those streets and, in the midst of what seemed to me a perfect picture of what U.S. bases and installations signify for a people, in the midst of those shocking surroundings, I heard something that weighed our heavy hearts down even more: since Cuban women were looked on as the most beautiful of all, many women of other na-tionalities passed for Cuban, adding to the hundreds or perhaps thou-sands of real Cuban prostitutes there, dragged into that painful profession by international white slavers, who transported boatloads of them to Panama from our island. The famous Panama Canal Zone was the final destination of women from humble families, turned into pros-titutes by the Cuban bourgeoisie and its system of corruption, unem-ployment, hunger, and despair!

I was profoundly troubled when I realized that this was the only reason that Cuba was so well liked and well known beyond its frontiers! These same women who, later, during the Cuban Revolution, would give such extraordinary proof of their enthusiasm, patriotism, and moral virtues!

From Panama we went to Venezuela, still in the throes of the revo-lutionary movement that overthrew the tyranny; the university students gave us their support for the Bogotá student congress. The distinguished novelist Rómulo Gallegos had recently become president. We thought very highly of him and decided to speak with him. To ask for the interview, we went directly to his family, to a house they owned in La Guaira, and I was very favorably impressed by the absence of guards, protocol, and formalities. We were received very simply by the members of his family, who telephoned him, because he was in Caracas. He agreed to an interview for the following day, but we couldn't see him then because we had to catch an early plane for Colombia at the Maiquetía Airport.

In Colombia, we met right away with the university students. Eighty percent of them were active members of the Liberal Party, headed by Jorge Eliécer Gaitán. The atmosphere was openly progressive as well as anti-imperialist. The Communist Party, with only some ten thousand members, was in an uphill battle and did not have any influence to speak of.

The idea of holding the congress while the OAS conference was in session was welcomed enthusiastically, and preparations for it got under way immediately. Delegates from other universities began to arrive; we had several preliminary meetings to discuss our program, which covered all these points I have mentioned: the struggle against military dictatorships, Puerto Rico's independence, the internationalization (or the nationalization, I can't remember which) of the Panama Canal, the end of all colonial territories in Latin America, and the organization of a Latin American student federation.

At this point a small question of jurisdiction came up. Though I was president of FEU in the University of Havana's Law School, not of the Cuban FEU, the delegates at the preliminary sessions in Bogotá elected me chairman. But while we were there, the president of the Cuban FEU arrived. He was a colorless young guy who had shown absolutely no interest in what we were doing until then, joining us only when he saw how successfully it was turning out.

A rather embarrassing situation had now developed, because he ranked higher than I among the students of Havana. The question was: Would I continue to preside over the meetings? I explained to the various delegates that I had no interest in this; that all I cared about was the ultimate success of what we were trying to get done; that I knew the history of America well and how those men who had fought hardest—and had infinitely greater merit than any of us could possibly ever deserve—had ended their lives in obscurity; and that I didn't expect any kind of honor from the job: that was not what I was fighting for. My sincerity must have been obvious from my words, because it was unanimously decided that I should go on presiding over the congress.

Our enthusiasm grew when the Colombian student delegates told us we might be able to get Gaitán to open our congress with a public statement in the Plaza de Cundinamarca, on the same day that the OAS conference was to begin.

The students asked me to go with them to Gaitán's headquarters to meet him and invite him officially. He received us in his private office on

April 7; he was very friendly during the interview and spoke with deep interest of our undertaking. He gave us pamphlets with his speeches, among them an eloquent one called "Oración por la Paz" (Words for Peace), which he had delivered a few weeks before, after an enormous mass parade, to protest against the murders of his followers in all parts of the country.

I read this speech with very great interest. In addition, the reports about the strength of the Liberal movement, Gaitán's victory by a sweeping majority in the recent congressional elections, the importance of his actions in behalf of the people and his popularity among them, his plans for legal and social reforms, convinced me that here was a true progressive and that he would defeat the oligarchy in Colombia.

Gaitán had asked us to meet him again two days later, at 2:00 p.m.—three hours after his tragic and despicable assassination.

Gaitán was not only enormously popular among the masses, he also had many supporters in the Colombian army. He had come to the defense of a lieutenant who had killed a policeman (or someone like that, an official or a policeman, I don't really remember), apparently in self-defense.

Since this officer had a background as a liberal and the political situation seemed to influence the trial, the hearing was soon converted into a matter of tremendous importance. Gaitán was counsel for the defense; the hearings were broadcast on the radio and heard in virtually every barracks in the country. The students invited us to attend a session of the trial. Gaitán defended his case with such extraordinary skill, from the penal as well as the political point of view, that the accused became more or less the Dreyfus of the Colombian army.

It's not strange, then, that the Colombian oligarchy, already finding itself riding on a wave of blood, should plot the murder of its formidable opponent.

On April 9, we left our hotel to go sightseeing and have lunch before going to our meeting with Gaitán that afternoon. Around 11:00 a.m., we saw people running wildly through the crowded streets and shouting, with a horrified look on their faces: "They've killed Gaitán! They've killed Gaitán!" The news spread like wildfire through the city.

Minutes later, an extraordinary commotion, an incredible wave of anger spontaneously arose; no one could have planned or organized anything like it.

I walked down a street to the park in front of the capitol building, where the foreign ministers' conference was in session. A cordon of police in blue uniforms with fixed bayonets had been guarding the building, but the crowd in the park was now converging on it, smashing the cordon, and entering the building, which must have seemed to the people a symbol of the power they hated.

I was in the middle of the park, where I could see what was happening. People were wrecking streetlights; rocks flew in all directions. Meanwhile, someone was trying to speak from a balcony, but no one listened or could have. Glass store fronts were shattering, and it was impossible to tell what would happen next, but a popular uprising was obviously under way.

I knew nothing about uprisings of this kind, except what had been engraved on my memory by accounts I'd read about the taking of the Bastille and the alarm bells of the revolutionary committees in Paris, rallying the people in the first glorious days of the French Revolution. But no one was in command here.

I joined the crowd headed for a police station several blocks away; I had no idea what would happen there. Dozens of men with guns were posted on roofs along the way, but not a shot was fired. We got to the entrance of the station and went inside. Hundreds of people rushed after us, and a desperate search for arms began. I was one of the first inside, yet all I could get my hands on was a tear-gas gun and several cartridge belts of ammunition, which I thought might come in handy. I went up to the top floor to see if I could find any other equipment, fighting arms or something better than what I had. I entered a room where I found a bunch of men looking demoralized and panicky. I realized that they were officers and asked if they had weapons or army fatigues. I'll never forget what happened next: I sat down on a bed and started pulling on a pair of army boots, and one of the officers started screaming at me, in the midst of all that chaos: "Not my boots! Not my boots!"

But I finally got out of there with boots, a military cape, and a cap. I heard a lot of shooting and went down to the courtyard, where I saw the first armed civilians trying out their guns by firing them into the air. In the center of the courtyard, an officer with a gun was trying to form a squad. I went over and lined up too.

Seeing me with so many rounds and the tear-gas gun, the officer, who apparently wanted to speed up things and move out, said to me: "What are you going to do with all that stuff? Look, you'd better let me have it and take a gun." I had to shove my way through all the other people who also wanted weapons, but I got the gun and sixteen bullets.

When I left the building, the crowd was on the move again, armed with guns, machetes, and iron bars. We headed for the Presidential Palace. Several streets farther on, the shooting started. The crowd fell back instinctively, then surged ahead again almost immediately, as if set in motion by a spring.

The unlikeliest things happen at times like this. When I reached the corner where the shooting had broken out, I saw two armed men halting people and heading them off in another direction, telling them that only military personnel could pass. I thought they were revolutionaries and started helping them. (I realized later that they were not revolutionaries but merely two soldiers trying to establish order.)

When I tried to find out what was going on, somebody told me that the crowd had been fired on from a Catholic university and there had been an exchange of fire. I must admit that I didn't believe it then, having spent so many years in Catholic schools; I couldn't imagine priests shooting at the people. As I stood there looking on, someone pulled me roughly toward a wall. Days later, after all I'd seen, I decided that there were clergymen reactionary enough to fire at the people without qualm.

After jumping back against the wall for cover, I went on to the next corner and saw students haranguing the people from cars with loud-speakers; they had put the bodies of their first dead comrades on the roofs of their cars for everyone to see. I recognized some students in one group and joined them. News filtered in that the army had attacked a radio station which had been taken over by some students and they needed help. So we headed that way.

As we reached the Ministry of War building, a tank and a company of helmeted soldiers were coming toward us from another street. They weren't firing their guns, and we couldn't tell where they were going or whose side they were on. There were six or seven of us together then. We crouched behind some benches in the huge square near the ministry and waited; the tank and the soldiers went on, ignoring us. We crossed the street and stopped in front of the ministry.

At this juncture, the army was still undecided, waiting to see which way the wind would blow, and I remember getting so carried away that I climbed up on a bench to harangue the soldiers going past. Then we went to where the students were being attacked. There was tremendous confusion everywhere.

We had almost gotten to the end of the block when we heard some gunfire; several soldiers had come out of the ministry and were chasing us. We saw them just in time, scrambled into an empty bus, and took off. We had only three guns for seven of us.

The bus pulled up at a corner of a wide avenue, and the three of us with guns got out and started walking. Two blocks away, a whole contingent of cavalry was attacking the station and literally sweeping the street with its gunfire. We took cover behind some benches once more, retreating as soon as we could to the street where the bus was parked. Then we decided to go see what was happening at the university.

There was nothing but confusion on the main campus, and no organized action anywhere, although the place was crawling with students who were stirred up but not armed. Someone came up with the idea of converging on a police station and we took off again. Our force still had three guns in all, but we were lucky: when we got to the station we were presumably going to capture, someone had done the job for us.

That's where I first saw anyone making an attempt to get people organized and lead the action. A police chief had come into the station and was trying to see how the revolutionary forces—made up of ordinary civilians and policemen—that had taken over the police stations could be utilized. I had a quick talk with him about how to start organizing and offered to help. He accepted readily, and we went in his jeep to the Liberal Party's headquarters in the center of Bogotá.

Several men at the headquarters were setting up plans for action, and my spirits rose when I thought that all those forces which had risen so spontaneously might be organized now that the first signs were there.

Night was falling when we took different jeeps back downtown. The chief was in the first and I in the other—I was practically his deputy now—but his jeep broke down and he was left without a car. When no one in my car got out to give the commander his seat, I gave him mine, letting the others see how outraged I was.

Two students stayed behind with me. We ran into a policeman with a machine gun who told us that Station 11 had also rebelled, so we set out to join forces there. (I won't waste time telling you how my wallet was stolen and I was left without a cent.)

It was night. Hundreds of men, mostly armed soldiers, were at Station 11, on the outskirts of Bogotá, near a hill that overlooks the city. Here the first real attempts at some kind of organization began. I joined a company forming in the central courtyard, a company in name only; it was posted in different parts of the building without being told what to do.

Time was passing and every few minutes word would go around that the army was about to attack us. I knew then how futile and suicidal that passive, strictly defensive tactic was. I got permission to speak with the station chief and I explained that I was from Cuba and knew, from what had happened there, that forces garrisoned like ours in a fortress were always crushed. I told him about armed incidents at Atarés and El Nacional in Cuba, and I suggested that, considering the mood of the people right then, and the five hundred men he had with him, he could form two columns. Why not take the offensive, lead the men out in columns, and set up positions at strategic points? My advice or my attempts to convince him were useless. He heard me out in a friendly, appreciative way, but couldn't make up his mind.

I went back to my post in one wing of the building, in a bedroom. I remember several things about that awful night, never knowing what was coming next. People were very jittery; we were constantly being warned of an attack, and they would all make a beeline for the windows. Tanks went past several times and were fired on, but nothing happened.

I also remember hearing, close to the bunk where I was resting, a man screaming that he was being beaten up. He was a policeman who had been discovered in his new uniform, the kind issued only to supporters of the regime. I interceded because the sight of a man who was paralyzed with fright being beaten up made me sick.

I spent the whole night patiently waiting. There was a moment, toward daybreak, when I took time out to ponder the situation. I knew that our troop didn't stand a chance: it would be wiped out in an attack; it was being led stupidly. A question rose in my mind: Should I stay? I thought of Cuba, my family, and many other things, and I asked myself why I should stay on this futile mission. I was in a quandary. I was completely cut off, no other Cubans with me. There was nothing tying me to the Colombian people and the students, except thoughts and ideas. Yet I decided to stay. I told myself: "Okay, the people here are just like those in Cuba or anywhere else; they are the victims of crimes, abuses, injustices; and these people are absolutely in the right, so I'll stay."

April 10 dawned. The hills behind us were stategic positions, but we were still waiting for an attack. I went to the commander again and made him see how silly it was not to set up a defense on those foothills, since any attack launched from there by the enemy would give it a powerful advantage. I convinced him to let me have a patrol and set up positions there.

Thousands of people from the poorest neighborhoods on the outskirts of Bogotá had started looting the night before. In the midst of that chaos, that destruction and death, endless columns of men and women, like ants, were carrying off everything: wardrobes, radios, packages and bundles of every kind. This unfortunate sight was an important lesson to me; later, during our Revolution, I constantly reminded Cubans not to do anything like that, even though I was sure looting could never happen in our case, with our people being more politically advanced than these.

I left my patrol that morning; I set up positions and assigned my men to their posts. The whole city seemed to be going up in flames; there was smoke and fire everywhere. We visited some huts, where we were treated hospitably and given food and wine brought from the city, where everyone was helping himself to anything he wanted. I went over the terrain of the hills, checking those points where the enemy was likely to attack. A car came speeding by, and I tried to flag it down; it wouldn't stop but I didn't want to shoot. Then it sounded as if it had crashed turning the corner. I started running and when I reached the curve, I saw some people scuttling from the car. I ordered them to halt, but they kept on going; I still didn't shoot, although they could have been spies. Later I found out from the peasants around there that it had been a man and two whores. A terrible tragedy was going on, Bogotá was virtually in flames, and here was this man having a good time in a car with two whores!

I spent the whole morning up there. Toward noon some planes began to appear over the city. The army's position hadn't become clear, and we were hopeful that the planes were with the revolution. Groups of men in army uniform were coming out of the station we had left. We asked them how things were going back there and they said that everything was lost. They were getting out. We tried to talk them into staying, but they wouldn't; some even threatened us with their rifles. We let them go.

We had been told that the station was being attacked from the city, but when we reached it, we found out it wasn't true. In fact, several patrols were coming out of the station to occupy other positions.

Night fell, and the situation was still uncertain. The first rumors began to circulate that a truce was being negotiated. Nothing happened that night, but the next morning the radio announced that both sides had come to terms: everyone was to lay down their arms. I really couldn't understand what was going on. Then the radio announced the cease-fire again, and a whole series of proclamations. So I decided to go back to the hotel where I had first checked in and wait for further developments.

The hotel was full of conservatives who had sided with the oligarchy; this put me in a tough spot. So I went over to the boardinghouse where some of my comrades were staying, with the intention of spending the night there. Only twenty-five minutes were left until the 6:00 p.m. curfew. The owner of the place, another conservative, began accusing the revolutionaries of terrible things. I was indignant and told him in no uncertain terms that he didn't know what he was talking about. He asked me to leave his house; it was a critical moment, almost fifteen minutes to six, when anybody found in the streets could be gunned down. With only five or ten minutes to spare, I set out for a hotel where other delegates were staying.

We met an Argentine there who had been at the congress, and he was petrified when he saw us. By now, false rumors were going around that the Cubans had organized the whole thing and had been seen leading the uprising, that it was the work of Communists and foreign agents, and so on. Anyway, the Argentine was frightened and I don't know why he picked on me, but he started telling me, "Some mess you've gotten me into!" And I said: "Okay, here's what: you'll give us a ride in your car right now." He had diplomatic license plates, and I ordered him to take us to the Cuban embassy. It was past curfew time, but we made it to our embassy, thanks to the diplomatic car. We explained our situation and we couldn't have been treated better.

I remember quite well the president of the Cuban delegation to the conference; he was a friendly man, very considerate about our plight. I told him where our other companions were, where they could be picked up, and the embassy took care of everything.

Strangely enough, the last name of the Cuban consul, in whose home we slept, was Tabernilla. He and his wife were very kind to us. Yet he was the brother of the Tabernilla who was later Batista's army chief of staff. In spite of the other Tabernilla's disgusting exploits later on, this man left me with the lasting impression that he was kind.

The Cuban delegation got us out of Colombia safely. We made the five-hour flight to Havana in a plane that had come over to pick up some bulls for a bullfight in Havana.

I had used only four of the sixteen bullets I had. But it's incredible, truly incredible, that we weren't all killed. When I was told that the station was being attacked and I set out to defend it with the few men I had, only to discover it was a false alarm, there were several patrols on their way to attack a building in which several "bloated plutocrats" had holed up; it was a religious building. It's true I went along to attack the place, but no one attacked it because it had already been taken. I didn't fire a shot then, but I had a different attitude the next morning. I recall that as our columns were advancing toward the building where the reactionary elements of the oligarchy had taken refuge and were shooting from, something happened that would be hard for me to forget.

We were going down the street and a little boy came up to me, weeping uncontrollably, and said to me: "They've killed my daddy! They've killed my daddy!" His cry touched me deeply; he might have been killed by a stray bullet, but this was the kind of thing that leaves painful memories—of war and of the sufferings of the people.

CHE GUEVARA

MEMORIES OF TWO CHILDHOOD FRIENDS

Alberto Granados: I was born in Hernando, a small town in southern Córdoba. I studied in the university in my province. In 1945 I received a degree in pharmacy, and three years later, one in biochemistry.

I met Che in 1941, when he was in high school with my brother Tomás. That year we had organized a strike at the University of Córdoba and it spread all over Argentina, protesting the violence against university students. I was arrested by the police in Córdoba. Tomás used to come with food for me—the prison did not give us any food—accompanied by his classmate, Ernesto Guevara.

I told Tomás and Ernesto that the high-school students should take to the streets, so that the people would find out that we were imprisoned. I was amazed at young Ernesto Guevara's answer. He said, "Alberto, why? Go out into the street so that the police can chase me with clubs? Not that way. I'll only go if they give me a revolver." In spite of his asthma, Ernesto was an athlete, a rugby player. While he was still very young, he was known for his courage and decisiveness. Sometimes he left the field to use his vaporizer. His asthma choked him.

An education alternating between Baudelaire's verses and sports tempered him spiritually and made him physically fit. From then on, he participated in trips and in action.

His father had a library whose principal user was Ernesto, and then myself. I still have books I took without asking permission.

Even as a child, Ernesto had the kind of mind that enabled him to excel in all aspects of life. He enjoyed going out with us on trips to the country, and he learned many of the things that would later prove useful during our motorcycle trip over the continent. Many years later, when he was a guerrilla, that experience served him well. He knew how to make a tent, a shelter, with few means. It was a healthy way of life, in the fresh air, escaping the routine of the student and the city.

Guevara spent his high school years in Córdoba. At the end of 1945 his family moved to Buenos Aires and there he began his university career. He used to do six hours of volunteer work in the Municipio Hospital, and four in the Institute for Allergy Research. Because of his ability in and knowledge of mathematics, we all thought that he would study engineering and we were surprised when he told us that he was going to major in medicine.

After 1945 I was appointed as a biochemist in a leprosy hospital 120 miles from Córdoba and more than 650 miles from Buenos Aires. Ernesto visited me there. After December exams he would gather his belongings, get a bicycle or a motorcycle or sometimes use his strong legs, and he would travel to different parts of the country, instead of staying in Buenos Aires studying for the exams in March. Those trips almost always coincided with a visit to my hospital.

He told his fellow students: "While you stay here preparing those assignments, I think I'll cover the province of Santa Fe, northern Córdoba, eastern Mendoza, and do some studying on the side so that I can pass with you."

To travel all over Latin America, to know its beauty and the misery in which its inhabitants lived, was a dream we long cultivated. During those weekend nights we spent in the mountains with Guevara and my brothers, the obligatory theme of discussion was our future trip.

One day Guevara came to visit us, taking advantage of September vacations. I spoke of my interest in leaving the country and using a motorcycle as a means of transportation.

Ernesto said: "If you wait until I pass some subjects in December, I'll go along with you." I waited for him.

On December 29, 1951, we mounted our motorcycle loaded with gear: shaving cream, an automatic pistol, and other things. We passed through Buenos Aires and said good-bye to Ernesto's family. In order to avoid the peaks of the northern Andes, we went south. Just before arriving in Santiago, when we had not even covered an eighth of the trip, the motorcycle broke down. Sadly, we had to leave it in the tent, in a corner, and continue on foot. We worked at different jobs to earn money and

continue traveling: moving merchandise, as raftsmen, sailors, stowaways, doctors . . . We also got to know the people this way.

Being two stowaways able to peel potatoes—one with a university
degree, the other almost a doctor—meant that the police was not hard
on us and even solved some of our problems. Wandering around penniless, we arrived at the doors of the Braden Company, which operated the
Chuquicamata mines in Chile.

In Peru, our stay was instructive and moving. We met the native
masses up close—the descendants of the ancient Incas, exploited and
nearly stupefied by the use of coca, which was provided to them like
food. These people did not trust anything. They ate corn or chewed
coca. The Quechua and Aymará peasant masses are more deceived than
in other countries. A Peruvian doctor, intelligent and able, made it possible for us to see the leprosy hospital in San Pablo, Loreto Province, on
the banks of the Amazon.

Before then we had visited another leprosarium, an unbelievable
thing, in the heart of the jungle, at an altitude of a mile or two. We were
interested in the lepers, the many aspects of the disease, and the ways of
curing it. We traveled on muleback to Huambo, where we met the physician who had founded this leprosy center in Peru.

At the heart of the Inca empire is Macchu Pichu, the fortress city,
constructed in the almost inaccessible peaks of the Andes, testimony to
Inca grandeur. We stayed there several days.

I remember being stretched out on the ruins of the "sacrificial" rock
one day while Ernesto was making maté for us. I commented on the
possibilities of our winning power through elections and making the revolution for all these poor people living marginal existences, and implementing agrarian and educational reforms. Smiling, Ernesto said:
"Make a revolution without firing shots? Are you crazy? . . ."

I remembered that day in '41, when he had said that without a revolver one couldn't do anything.

Assisted by the doctor, we went by boat to the port of Pucalpa, on
the Ucayali River, a tributary which, with the Marañón, forms the
Amazon. We stayed a few days in Iquitos. Guevara suffered an asthma
attack due to his allergy to fish, the only food there. He had to be
hospitalized.

When he recovered, we continued our voyage to San Pablo. We
worked in a laboratory, played soccer with the lepers, accompanied
them on their excursions, visited the Indians, hunted monkeys, and
amused the patients, who were full of gratitude for "the doctors" who
shared their time with them. With the help of the patients we made a
raft to cross the Amazon. We went a few miles by river until we reached
Leticia, where the Amazon joins three countries: Brazil, Peru, and
Colombia.

In Peru the tango was very popular then and we often played tangos in lieu of payments. Leticia is part of Colombia, which had given us visas, and they baptized our raft *Mambo-Tango*. When one speaks of traveling by raft on the Amazon, it seems impossible, but we had seen ten-year-old children and pregnant women with nursing infants on rafts. It was not as difficult as ignorance and the imagination make it seem.

The patients, cheering, saw us off at the bridge that separates the port from the leprosarium. It was a moving leave-taking. It was June 20, 1952.

We set sail for Leticia, excited by the vast Amazon. We were not very skilled in steering the raft and soon ran aground near a Brazilian island. There we traded the raft for a rowboat and returned upriver, against the strong Amazon current, to Leticia. We slept in a barracks. As Argentine soccer players, we played with the local team, which won, and as our share of the prize, they gave us two plane tickets to Bogotá.

In Bogotá, Laureano Gómez headed a fiercely repressive government. Foreigners were viewed with mistrust, and we were arrested. We were freed through the mobilization of the students. With their help and the money we still had, we went by bus to Cucuta, on the border of Venezuela. We encountered some difficulties and on July 14, 1952, the anniversary of the taking of the Bastille, we crossed the international bridge that connects Cucuta with the city of San Cristóbal, in Venezuela.

In Caracas, we met a friend of Ernesto's family. He had a small airplane for transporting racehorses. We agreed that Ernesto should return to Buenos Aires to graduate, as he had promised his mother, Celia de la Serna.

The plane flew from Caracas to Miami, where Ernesto spent a few days and went through some difficult situations, due to a conversation he had with a Puerto Rican who was being followed for having criticized President Truman. The plane had brought Argentine horses to be sold, and took on American horses, which would be sold in Maracaibo and Buenos Aires. Che took advantage of the flight because it was inexpensive. The trip, however, turned out to be complicated and long.

We had separated in July 1952. With his strange study methods and his ability and intelligence, Che passed his examinations in March 1953. Upon graduation he took a trip in a milk train, which made a run of more than 4000 miles from Buenos Aires to La Paz, Bolivia. He crossed Lake Titicaca, where we had been on our trip, and continued along the coast because he was in a hurry to arrive in Venezuela and talk to me about whether to continue the trip or to stay and do research in the leprosarium at Cabo Blanco, where I was working.

Upon reaching Guayaquil, Ecuador, he met the Buenos Aires lawyer Ricardo Rojo, exiled from my country, who had spectacularly escaped from prison and received asylum in the Guatemalan embassy in Buenos Aires. A Guatemalan diplomat had accompanied him to Ecuador. When Ernesto told Rojo of his intention to continue on to Caracas to meet me, and to work on something, the lawyer answered: "But, Guevara, why do you want to go to Venezuela, a country that's only good for making money? Come with me to Guatemala, where a real social revolution is in progress."

Rojo, who did not know Guevara, convinced him with these words to go to Guatemala. Because of that, I received a note from Ernesto that said, "I'm going to Guatemala. I'll write you later. Ernesto."

This is the last letter I received from him:

I do not know what to leave you as a souvenir, so I force you to plunge into the sugarcane. My itinerant house will have two paws again and my dreams will have no frontiers, when the bullets say so. I'll wait for you, sedentary gypsy, when the smell of gunpowder subsides.

I won't answer your cheap philosophy in the letter because for that we would need a few matés, a meat pie, and a spot in the shade of a tree. . . .

I hope that you do not expect to end your days without knowing the smell of gunpowder and the war cry of the people, an exalted way of having adventures no less interesting and more useful than that employed on the Amazon. . . .

José Aguilar: We came as exiles from Spain to Argentina in 1937. We settled in Alta Gracia. The same day or the next Che's father learned that we had arrived with my mother. My father, who was a physician, had stayed in Spain and sent my mother and us to America; we were four brothers. Che's father went looking for us four little ones so that we would make friends with his sons, who were the same age. The oldest of the Guevaras was Ernesto, then came Roberto, Celia, and Ana María, and then the fifth was born.

Our economic situation was very bad and the Guevaras helped us a lot. Alta Gracia was a summer resort in the Sierra de Córdoba. During the winter, it is a dead city. It had about ten thousand inhabitants.

The Guevaras lived in Villa Nidia. Alta Gracia has two distinct sections: the "upper" and the "lower." The upper one, the residential zone, had rows of houses that all looked alike and which belonged to the Englishmen from the railroad. Villa Nidia was in the residential zone.

Ernesto's parents were bourgeois—his father was of Irish descent and his mother was of Spanish descent. They had a large farm in Misiones, almost a latifundio, the property of Celia, and they lived off their maté crops. They sold it cheaply in '47.

His grandmother, who lived with his aunt Beatriz, was like Ernesto's second mother. That grandmother, whom Che adored, had the surname of Linch and was the daughter and granddaughter of Irishmen. They were left-liberals, with open sympathies toward the Spanish republic.

Che went to a school in Alta Gracia called San Martín, and, maybe for disciplinary reasons, he was transferred to the school where I studied, called Manuel Belgrano.

We saw each other almost every day. We practically lived together. The Guevara children were very daring in games, in sports, and we were terrified by them. Che liked risky games. Once Roberto jumped from the fourth floor of our house over to the next house, laughing at us for not following.

I remember that the teacher would give Ernesto spankings. Ernesto once put a brick in his trouser seat, which created a tremendous row when he was hit.

He was so rebellious, yet once when his parents had to go to Buenos Aires, they asked my mother to stay in their house in Alta Gracia to take care of the children; my mother says that he was the best behaved, the most obedient, the most helpful, and especially considerate of her.

They were a Catholic family, but not practicing Catholics. At that time we used to read a lot. Our favorites: Jules Verne, Dumas. And I remember that my father, who had been reunited with us, was amazed that at fourteen or fifteen years of age Che read Freud.

Che had a diary, from which I read some things about his first trip with Granados, during the motorcycle trip. I read it when he came to spend a few days at my house in Córdoba, and it fascinated me. He always kept up the diary. During the Sierra Maestra and afterward.

He had no musical sense. In order to dance, he would ask the musicians what they were playing, and when he was told, would dance steps he had learned by heart. Granados had taught him to dance the tango. One day they played a very soft *baião*—in style then—which reminded us both of a girl from Córdoba, Che's girlfriend, and Che, thinking that it was a tango, started dancing it in tango rhythm.

From Alta Gracia they went to Córdoba; Che was in high school. The Guevaras had an old car, which they called "the Catramina," a 1930 Chrysler roadster. It had only one seat in the back and we all piled into it when Ernesto's mother drove us to school. Che went to high school in the Dean Funes National Institute. We studied a little Spanish and Argentine literature. They taught English. Ernesto liked French and he learned it from his mother, who spoke it well.

He liked to read French literature and poetry. A lot of poetry. He would spend days reciting poems, Neruda, and a poem by a Spanish poet about the fall of Madrid: ". . . It was a lie and a lie changed into sad truth, that his footsteps were heard in Madrid which no longer existed." From hearing it as a child from Che, I've never forgotten it.

In Buenos Aires, Che, not very brilliantly but very quickly, completed his medical studies.

Our friendship continued in Buenos Aires. We were close, we felt as if we were related, and we continued to see each other daily, celebrate holidays together, including Christmas. But exchanging ideas took precedence later. Long conversations, like before his leaving for Bolivia by train. We left the going-away party at his house, and walked the length of Santa Fe Avenue up to the Plaza San Martín.

That summer of 1952 he was engaged to a beautiful and rich girl from Córdoba. When he returned, I was in Córdoba and he in Buenos Aires. When he came to Córdoba I read part of his diary: Peru, Macchu Pichu; indigenous architecture. Colonial domination of the indigenous culture through architecture: a church constructed over indigenous ruins.

Before that he was in a leprosarium. He was interested in leprosy and in allergies. In those days, he took medicine very seriously.

After his first trip, I noticed that he was becoming more interested in politics. It was during that trip and his stay in Guatemala that his course changed definitively. Che started the trip in second class, on a very slow train. The family's financial situation was no longer very good; the economy was deteriorating rapidly.

Che had worked since high school. He earned little; enough for his personal expenses. He told me that during that period he had been writing a philosophical dictionary for his own use. He used to do it in the office in which he worked in Buenos Aires; and this had earned him, inadvertently, a promotion. One day his boss arrived, everyone was supposed to be at work, but the only one there was Che. The boss praised him for his dedication to his job—not knowing that he was working on his philosophical dictionary.

As boys, we all would discuss Pérez, Galdós, and others. The Guevaras defended the French authors and we Aguilars the Spaniards. Che would say that "the viewer embraces a painting, and in embracing and confronting it, he puts in something of himself, creates a time. That is also true of literature, the reader participates in it."

From Mexico he wrote to his mother, before leaving in 1956, "It is like fighting against a wall."

WHO WAS ABEL SANTAMARÍA?

It was not until 1927 that the common struggle against General Gerardo Machado began. He was president of the republic, and had been elected in 1925 as the Liberal Party candidate, with the support of the Popular Party—in spite of the fact that from the beginning his aims were clearly evident. His political program can be summarized in the slogan: "Water, roads, and schools." For eight years, hunger, terror, repression; student and labor struggles; U.S. interference; economic crises, demagogy, frauds, thievery, and crime were rampant as the result of a policy dictated by the prevailing reactionary forces. And it was in the year 1927, in the town of Encrucijada, Las Villas Province, in a house on Jesús Rodríguez Street, on the corner of Máximo Gómez, at 7:00 p.m. on October 21, that Abel Santamaría Cuadrado was born, the son of Benigno Santamaría y Pérez and Joaquina Cuadrado y Alonso, both natives of Spain. The Santamarías were from Orense; the Cuadrados, from Salamanca.

And, to be sure, he was the typical Cuban sugar-mill boy, son and grandson of Spaniards, the student of a black country schoolteacher, who read, knew, and *lived* Martí and felt a passionate love for baseball, horses, swimming, and outdoor life; considerate in deeds and words, devoted to his family and to companionship, to true friendship, which he made a duty. But where was his rage, where his struggles, his conflicts, his anger, where was his nonconformity, his passion for learning, his concern with the social order, politics? The answer is there, in that minuscule office; two cubbyholes with small windows facing the porch, through which, hundreds of times, there filed dozens of ennobled faces and hands of lowly workers exploited perhaps to the most abject squalor. Of those men, who at times did not even earn enough to pay for a medical prescription, Abel would write to his father: "But when it comes to bad times and suffering disappointment, no one knows more than the working and struggling man who lives his whole life in perennial disillusion." From there came his social conscience. "Of course, I do not apply this to myself, because in reality I have not had any such problems, but I have had some and I observe the rest." He referred to other men, not to himself. That understanding, that love for his fellow human being, drove him to transform the reality he knew and loathed.

Benigno Santamaría was the foreman of the Constancia carpentry shop, an employee on the payroll, a man who could consider himself the possessor of a solid economic and social position.

Haydée Santamaría: In the Cuban sugar-mill hamlets, at least where I was born and raised, there are many class differences. They are very small places, and families live there for years. My family has lived there for more than sixty years. There, the children are born and have their children. Everyone knows each other. In school one studies with other children who have very little. There aren't even a dozen well-to-do families. They think they are rich, although they are nothing. They have a better little house, a little car, they eat all year round. That is why they look rich to the other families.

That is where one truly has to confront the great differences. For those few children, there are the Magi, there are clothes, there are shoes. When one is seven, eight, or nine years old, one begins to ask: "Why? Why do some have those things and others not?" And one begins to see that the Magi do not exist, because if they existed there would have to be Magi for everyone. One goes to church, to the chapel, and sees the benches where the owners and the few trustworthy administrative employees sit, and one begins to ask: "Is there a God?" From childhood, one begins to be a little materialistic.

I had that tremendous concern and used to ask, "Why?" I would go home and ask, but no one explained. Sometimes someone would say, "Well, because I work hard and the rest are lazy."

To that answer I had another, "But, well, what are the lazy like, if I see that they come here asking for work and you tell them that there isn't any. I heard them tell you, 'Santamaría, I want to cut cane for two or three days.' You answered that there was no work for them."

I believe that if I hadn't been born and lived in a sugar-mill town, perhaps I would have felt that concern not as a child but later. But if I had not seen those things in my girlhood . . . It seems to me that all of that woke Abel and me up. You will ask me, "And why not the others?" We were five children, well, four, because the other sister was too small. The other two were not worried so much by these things, Abel and me, yes. The others saw and felt sorry but in a little while they looked the other way.

When Abel earned enough—we didn't need much—he rented a little apartment that cost sixty-five dollars. One can still see it, a little bedroom, a little living room, and a little dining room; fifteen pesos for the electric lights. He took me there, but we never lost contact with the mill. We went there a lot, on weekends, Christmastime, and Holy Week. Abel had a car because he used to work for Pontiac. We were kids who had gone to Havana and now we would return home in a car.

We began to read Martí in depth. Abel was a devoted disciple of Martí. He found in Martí an answer to everything. All that was two or three years before Moncada.

We had connections with the Communist Youth, especially Abel, but we felt dissatisfied with everything. We were associated with the Ortodoxos.

Abel moved to Havana to liberate himself from the social and economic pressures of a work complex where capitalist exploitation inhibits the natural development of the country and its citizens. Nevertheless, he had to accept employment in the offices of Genio y Morro of Ariguanabo Textiles. He had to prepare himself for this new opportunity. Now he formed part of that new market made up of enterprising youngsters that the U.S. firms avidly value. The year 1947 is very significant for Abel Santamaría. He matriculates in a night school at the Manzana de Gómez, taking some subjects that will make it easier for him to enter the School of Commerce. In only a month and a half he enters the Institute of Secondary Education in Havana.

January 22, 1948, Jesús Menéndez is assassinated in Manzanillo.*
Abel arrives at work distressed. His indignation grows in response to the
indifference of some colleagues at work who excuse the crime, alleging
that Menéndez was a Communist. Abel knew Jesús Menéndez: both
were from the same place; both knew the misfortunes, the miserable existence of the peasant and the sugar worker. Abel confronts a colleague
and, careful not to hurt him, fervently explains who Jesús Menéndez
was. Perhaps it was that hour that pointed to the route of struggle he
would take to "liberate the slave from his misfortune and good Pedro
from his infamy."

Abel Santamaría will say that he was an Ortodoxo, not a politician.
He is an Ortodoxo because he believes in the policies of Eddy Chibás's
political party, which fights embezzlement, political scheming, administrative corruption, vice, sinecures, privileges, despotism, and force.

Together with his school textbooks, he brought to his room biographies of illustrious men, three volumes on the French Revolution, books
about political orientation, his closest friends, Díaz and Vázquez, recalled. One added: "I don't know if it was at that time or later, when he
was preparing for the struggle, that he read Lenin, I don't know if he
read Marx also."

On August 16, 1951, Eduardo Chibás commits suicide. Menéndez is
dead. Abel Santamaría does not sleep that night, or the following nights.
He concentrates on a destructive question, a gloomy word that answers
nothing. Why, why, why?

Abel now works as an accountant for Pontiac, 60 Hospital Street.
Haydée, the oldest of his sisters, keeps house.

The apartment fills up almost every night and weekend with Abel's
accountant friends and other friends; there they discuss and study the
country's situation. They read José Martí, they talk incessantly of
Eduardo Chibás.

On March 10, when Abel arrived home, I was in the apartment,
and he told me: "There's been a coup d'état, Batista." Batista was Guiteras's assassin. Guiteras had been our leader. We felt we were Guiterists,
although afterward Guiterism was converted into something very different from Guiteras.

When he told me that it was Batista, I was full of rage. I said, "And
you, what are you doing here? . . . Poor little one!" reproaching him a
little. And he replied, "I came to tell you."

We went to the university. We returned at night, waiting for them

---

* Menéndez was a member of the Chamber of Deputies and head of the
Sugar Workers' Federation.

to give us guns. And when, at two or three in the morning, I asked him, "Abel, why aren't you sad?" He said, "Because it is the best thing that could have happened."

CARLOS FRANQUI

CHILDHOOD AND YOUTH OF A WORKER

I was born in Clavellinas, a sugarcane region between Cifuentes and Sagua la Grande, at the end of 1921, the year of the depression. The bottom fell out of the sugar market, banks were closed, and a severe economic crisis began. For Cuba, a country dependent on one crop and the U.S. market, it was a catastrophe.

My father was a cane cutter. For six months he used to earn forty cents a day; the other half of the year—the "dead" period—he, like a half million other sugar workers, was unemployed. During the dead period one had to do something, anything, to keep from starving: work for a little food, sharecrop with some landowner for a third or quarter of the crop.

In my family there was a libertarian tradition. My grandfather's brother Eligio, a captain in the mambí army, died fighting in the Wars of Independence. Like my grandfather, he, too, was a rebel peasant and a balladeer. Eligio's body, pulled by horses, was dragged through the village and thrown in front of Father Tejo's church—he was a Spanish priest who fought the Cuban patriots with a rifle in his hand.

The region in which we lived had eight sugar mills, the property of wealthy owners, Creoles and North Americans. They lived in large houses with big grounds—near the barracks shared by cows and workers—and rode on horseback, revolver in the belt, through the countryside.

Large fires, lasting days and nights, burned cane fields. It was a spontaneous form of individual protest and a move to bring pressure against the landowners by making it easier to cut the burned cane, but lowering yields. When the poor peasants and tenant farmers could not pay their debts, the rural police would kick them out. My father, my mother, and I lived in a palm hut next to the highway, on which we could see the dispossessed families carrying their possessions on their backs. The workers' protests and the sugarcane burnings ended under the blade of a machete or in prison. Suicides were frequent; men hanged themselves from trees, women poured alcohol over their bodies and set themselves on fire.

Though I was very little, I had to help my father. I woke up very early, milked the cows, drank a cup of milk, picked up a cane cart, and around four in the morning would go to the village to buy bread and sell it in the cane fields. Night after night I had to cross the farm and the hill next to my house, where several people had committed suicide; I had known three of them.

They said that the dead reappeared mounted on a horse's rump or emerged in a light that came and went between the palms and the darkness. The country night is full of mysteries: owl calls, phantasmal trees, strange murmurs and sounds; solitude and fear; terror and fright, which I had to confront nightly. I tried to fight my fear by whistling a peasant song or improvising a ballad.

The smell of warm bread made up for my fear and as I left the small town of Cifuentes, daylight would break over the cane fields. I used to sell one hundred rolls to cane cutters and cart drivers. I earned five centavos, a roll for myself and two for my parents. Each roll was worth one centavo and with a little warm sugar water or guava paste, you had the cane cutters' breakfast. I would return home later, in midmorning, in time to learn the alphabet with my mother and then to go to school.

I had a premonition that I would not accept this kind of world. I watched the misery. My parents' life, the neighbors', the huts and barracks at the mill, where the workers and the blacks would sleep, not very distant from the large towers of the mill and the sugar growers' chalets and haciendas.

The only just and beautiful things were the flames of the fire razing the cane fields. Fires and firebreaks, rural guards on horseback who fled, terrified, between the paths and the burned cane. Do not cut the cane. Burn it. I knew nothing then, but I was sure that, when I learned to read and could study, I would be able to understand things.

My father encouraged me. At Christmastime, when I went to my grandfather's house, he would tell me stories about the Wars of Independence. My aunt Laureana, a teacher in Guayabo, would lend me Martí's books, which whetted my curiosity.

In La Duda public school I met an exceptional teacher: Melania Cobos. She explained the history of Cuba to me; she helped me to know its martyrs, its poets, its struggles. We put out childish newspapers. They would take us to student demonstrations, which the police or the rural guard on horseback would break up violently.

In Cifuentes, there lived a Spaniard exile, a Marxist, and a libertarian, who had a good library; there I read, for the first time, books about social problems, Marxism, anti-imperialism, and anarchism.

In town there was a loudspeaker facing the park and the highway, which broadcast a curious mixture of local sales announcements, songs, news, improvisations, ballads, and patriotic poems. On that loudspeaker, I launched my earliest salvos against Batista's first dictatorship. The little town was conservative. It had no factories, no unions, no traditions of struggle, only a few plotters for liberty.

When my first signs against tyranny and the Yankees appeared, painted on walls and bridges, the disconcerted police went after the phantom group of conspirators.

The 1933 revolution had lasted an instant. In only four months Guiteras's anti-imperialist decrees, the nationalistic measures, the eighthour work laws, the minimum wage, and other conquests had permeated and shaken the country's conscience.

Among themselves, Colonel Batista, the Yankee ambassador, and the army decapitated the revolutionary government, imposed an iron dictatorship, murdered anti-imperialist leaders, and violently repressed the strikes and protests of the workers and the people.

I was an apprentice freewheeling revolutionary: I distributed whatever clandestine propaganda fell into my hands; I searched for contacts; I went to demonstrations and protests.

One day, I think it was in 1936, I was leaving the village and carrying a package of the Marxist magazine Mediodía [Midday] under my arm. On the main street, the only one leading to the highway, I passed the rural guards' barracks and the post's chief, Corporal Felipe—well known for the brutal way he used his machete—saw me going by with my package. He had heard my salvos over the loudspeaker, and he arrested me.

It was my first imprisonment, and it turned out pretty well because I was a minor and because an old guard named Zacarías, who knew my father, interceded in my favor. They let me out, but my name was on file.

I finished public school and with the help of Melania, I got ready to enter high school. My parents wanted me to study but it was impossible for them to pay for my education. The only possibility, a scholarship. Difficult because of the competition, and because they were awarded according to one's pull with mayors, military men, or rich people.

To buy the first book required, which cost three dollars, I had to plant an onion field and sell many basketfuls of them in hamlets and small towns. I got the other books by entering children's literary contests sponsored by newspapers and magazines in the capital.

I read everything I could get my hands on—poetry, novels, economics, history. An essay by the French socialist Paul Lafargue, Marx's son-in-law, and above all The ABC of Communism, by Bukharin, opened my eyes.

The Spanish civil war began. The challenge to the republic was a shock and an awakening for Cuba. We understood that there were two Spains: the imperial one against which we fought for independence, now Francoist and fascist, and the other one, republican and for the people. The Cuban people identified with one of its two roots. The other one, the black one, deep, interior, unconscious, prohibited, subversive, would continue leading a subterranean existence.

The impact of the attack on the republic shocked the Cuban people.

Mass actions, thousands of volunteers fighting to join the international brigades. Committees of support were organized all over the country. For me, underage, isolated, with neither contacts nor resources, the hope of going to Spain did not get much further than some activities on behalf of the republic.

For three years in a row I had tried for a scholarship in provincial contests, but good grades were not worth as much as political pull. I was almost a loner. People did not understand me. The peasants said that to abandon the land was a tragedy, bad luck, almost treason. But it was not the land. It was those who owned the land. The rural guard, injustices, sugarcane, dependence on foreigners.

Nature was my world; the trees, my friends. I was pushed by a tremendous force. Slavery offers no alternative. Some laughed at me. More than one doubted my sanity. They sensed that I talked to myself when I walked. I used to talk to the mastic trees, mangoes, and palms along the highway. They were my old pals.

One day my father, in order to thatch the roof of the little house that we lived in, which the torrential rains wet more inside than outside, cut the tops off some palms. An old, forgotten law contained certain rules for cutting off the tops of the leaves, and a neighboring farmowner who wanted to earn part of the fine denounced him to the rural guard. My father was sentenced to pay a fine of 180 pesos or spend thirty days in jail. We didn't have a centavo, and for the first time in his life he was locked up in the Cifuentes jail.

Miguel Suárez, a childhood friend, worked at the jail. Each night, when it got dark, Suárez would give him a horse so that he could come to sleep in our house and return to the jail well before daylight.

A worker, a man of the people, my father had courage and stoicism; his way of handling himself in this situation and similar ones has been my best help in confronting life in its hard and difficult moments.

Not much later his neck became infected; a palm leaf had scratched him when he was again thatching the roof. He was sent to a dilapidated hospital in Sagua la Grande, and there, while he received a transfusion of my blood, he faced death with a clear mind; serene, counseling me, and reminding me of my obligations toward my mother and my people.

If Spanish bullets killed my great-uncle, misery and injustice murdered my father. I felt no hate—hate is for me an alien feeling—but I did feel an absolute necessity to rebel and fight against misery, injustice, and tyranny.

Everyone has his compass. Mine points to those villagers among whom I was born and of whom I feel a part. Anywhere in the world: here, there, in this place, or in some other, what matters to me is not the brutal or beautiful words of those in government but how my people live, and who is the boss who robs them of their strength, their work, their lives; if that boss is a military man, a bourgeois, or a bureaucrat, it means that the revolution has not yet been made, that we must continue the struggle.

My people are not those at the top but those on the bottom. Profound solitude has led me to seek the companionship of the workers, peasants, poets, youths, or revolutionaries who don't speak in the name of the people but who form part of it.

I won a scholarship to the high school in Santa Clara and began a new stage in my life. There, I joined the student movement, participated in struggles, read Marxist books. I joined the Jóvenes del Pueblo [People's Youth]. "I am fighting, I am a revolutionary; I think in Marxist terms," I would tell myself. My baptism of fire was in a sugar-workers' strike in the Covadonga mill in the Zapata swamp.

In 1939–40 a national student conference took place in Santa Clara's Caridad Theater. I was the only Marxist delegate elected in the province. It was a turbulent congress. The closing session was at the theater and I was expected to participate in it. It was summer and the heat was suffocating. I didn't have a suit of my own, and a companion had lent me a heavy, blue winter one.

At that congress I saw Rolando Masferrer for the first time. Back from fighting in the International Brigades for the Spanish Republic, he was now a Communist student leader; later he would be the head of Batista's "tigers."

Then the conflicts began among the Havana student groups, armed bands of youths, who as a consequence of the abortive 1930* revolution, embraced the happy trigger as a profession. They created the pistol feud, criminal assault, Molotov cocktails, corruption, threatening notes, and no-show jobs. They fought each other openly, imitating the Chicago gangsters, in shootouts in the street. The practice intensified later on, during the Auténtico Party governments of 1944–52, and it was one of the motives for the military support that Batista received for his second barracks coup.

When my turn came to speak on the dais, I was warned by the Havana bunch, who were two paces behind me and armed with pistols, that if I accused them of anything, they would shoot. On the opposite side of the stage, Masferrer and his group, also armed, were prepared to intervene in my favor.

Microphone in hand and fist raised, addressing the audience, I shouted: "Long live the Revolutionary Communist Union!"

The audience rose as one and began to repeat the slogan and to applaud frantically. Turning away from the microphone, I warned the gangsters: "There is going to be more than one corpse."

I began my discourse-denunciation, sweating profusely, partly with

---

* This was during the second term of President Gerardo Machado y Morales, 1925–33.

the heat from the blue suit and partly from fear that before long a bullet would hit me in the back. But the night proved calm. The skirmish came the next day in the park, in front of the institute. The consequences were mostly noisy.

Santa Clara, the capital of Las Villas Province, was a city with strong racist feelings. In the Parque Leoncio Vidal, whites strolled around inside and blacks, separately, outside. A white could walk among the blacks, but blacks were not permitted to mingle with the whites. The mascot of the town, the famous burro, Perico, went all over the city, accepting bread without letting anyone mount him, playing with everyone, and ending his circuit at the Condado Bridge.

Underneath flowed the waters of the Manso Belico. The red-light district was here: cabarets, and whorehouses where one could dance. A famous black flutist, from an orchestra from Cienfuegos, would receive a centavo per piece, another centavo for the "dancer," and three for the proprietor and the police.

At a bend in the river was Daniel's kiosk—he was a Communist veteran of the Spanish civil war—a meeting place for the comrades from the province, who came to bring money for Party campaigns.

Farther on was the marketplace. There a "blue-plate" dinner of rice, beans, and beef hash cost five centavos in the Chinese restaurant, and for just one centavo more they gave you a banana, crackers, and a glass of cane juice.

Close by was the baseball stadium, famous for the duels between the immortal Dihigo* and the black North American, Jabao Brown, and other stars of Cuban and black American ball games.

Santa Clara was famous for guava, bread with guava paste, brown sugar, and for the machete blade of Batista's colonels.

In three years of studies I spent more time outside school than inside, busy with student, union, peasant, and people's struggles. That was when I met a black sugar workers' leader, Jesús Menéndez, who engaged in epic battles with the mill owners. His independence and radicalism were well known; he concentrated on direct mass actions rather than the "arrangements" with the Ministry of Labor that the Party would have preferred. Years later he was murdered by an army captain.**

I had finished my high-school studies and should have gone on to the university. The top four students in the class had the right to a government scholarship in Havana, and I was one of them. But I was not given a scholarship because of my political activities. I left for Havana in a mover's truck, with a battered suitcase and five pesos in my pocket.

Havana was Mecca.

---

* Martin Dihigo, Negro League player elected to National Baseball Hall of Fame by special committee; active 1923–45.
** See p. 28.

I got off the truck near the Parque Central. Looking for a café and a men's room, I got to the Paseo del Prado. There, I discovered the orchestras made up of women, playing in the open air. Beyond the Prado, I walked up to the Malecón. Where the Spanish Prado ends and the U.S. Malecón begins. Farther on the old Morro Castle, and the magnificent sea lapping at the feet of Old Havana. Past the Malecón, the gods' park, called the park of love, with its old Greek statues, smeared and scribbled on. On Apollo's ass, one read: "My wife." Darkness, vagrants, couples making love, trees, and that magic atmosphere, that light, that enchantment which only Havana has.

I was getting ready to enter the university. I slept in a small Party room in Arsenal, a few steps from the Regalías El Cuño cigar factory. My bed was a long narrow bench that did not allow me to turn right or left without falling off. Afterward the people said: "Look how Havana has straightened him out." The comrades I lived with had one jacket for the four of us, several torn shirts, and a collection of collars that we tied down with a string under our arms. The jacket was used for elegant and romantic occasions. The trouble started when it got so hot that one had to take off the jacket. We ate when, where, and however we could. Panhandling or sponging off friends who made cigars or drove buses. We were the terror of the neighborhood's Chinese restaurants because of the ingenious techniques we used in order to eat without paying. The cleverest ruse was to put a cockroach into the Spanish bean soup.

When I wasn't studying, I would spend my time working for the Party in the district. Jesús María was one of the most authentic, popular, happy, and picturesque black sections of Havana. They spoke a black Spanish like music, which resounded through mulattoes, hot rumbas, and brothels. The police couldn't enter a house, even if the quarrels and parties ended amid conga drums and gunshots. That rebellious people lived by their own code.

The 1942 university term was about to begin and I was getting ready to enter it when one day I was ordered to go to the Central Committee of the Party, at 609 Carlos III Street. There, Blas Roca, Ordoqui, and Grovart told me: "A militant like you should dedicate his life to the Party. Then you will lead a more revolutionary life than if you go to the university and get a degree."

After all the effort I had made to go to the university and fulfill my dream, now that I had a foot in the door I was being asked to forget it.

But there is nothing more beautiful than a chance to change humanity.

I didn't hesitate for a moment. It was a dream come true. The Party sent me to take charge of the Fomento region, in the southern part of Las Villas, one of Cuba's most rebellious areas. With the old suitcase once again, a new suit, and 25 pesos in my pocket, I began the return journey.

I felt part of a marvelous universal family. It was a year of intense work. In Fomento, I met excellent militants: Merelo, Martínez, Lemus. . . . Strikes, organizing unions, workers' elections, fund-raising campaigns, incessant coming and going from sugar mill to sugar mill, from cane field to cane field, conflicts, struggles against fascism, against Azqueta, the sugar-mill king. And almost all these battles were won.

And afterward Trinidad—city suspended between past grandeur and present misery, isolated, without industry except for a few crafts-men, practically without natural resources. This was another Cuba to me, a city surrounded by tall mountains—the Escambray—by seas, near Casilda, where Hernando Cortes, fleeing the jealousy of Governor Velázquez, was aided by the people of Trinidad to escape and launch the conquest of Mexico. A city of stone streets and marvelous half-ruined colonial palaces. Romantic sounds of the guitar, voices singing at dawn to serenade girls who showed their heads or hands between the iron bars. A city that was not revolutionary like Fomento. The only city where Batista ever won an election. Only in the Trinidad sugar mill and in the tileworks and coffee farms of the mountains, where peasants were evicted from their lands by the earth-eaters, was there some will to fight. In those unforgettable places violent conflicts took place. My feet became accustomed to the manly profession, climbing mountains, as Martí said.

When I returned to Havana, I was twenty-two and had a wealth of experience as a struggling revolutionary. I had shared years with that marvelous family of the people: workers, peasants, militants. I had lived with their difficulties, rebellions, humanity, and hope. That was my world. Its spirit of justice and generosity had confirmed my conviction in an egalitarian and free Communism. Havana was another aspect of that truth.

For the next two years I would not live with militants. I was going to be with cadres and leaders. Their behavior and tactics—their bourgeois ways—had erased their revolutionary past, prison days, sacrifices. They had discovered the easy life and their private and public actions had nothing to do with the anonymous militants of the interior, with revolutionary morale, and with the Marxist doctrine they preached. The pact with Batista, subservience to the Soviets, participation in the government, had obliterated the Party's revolutionary spirit. Founded in 1925 by Julio Antonio Mella, then nourished with members who represented the best of the factories and the university, heir to the *mambí* and anti-imperialist tradition, an exponent of universal and humane socialism, that Communist Party had stood for the most radical aspirations of the Cuban people.

To fight for the social revolution in America is not the utopia of lunatics or fanatics; it is to fight for history's next step forward. Only the feebleminded will believe that the evolution of the American

peoples stopped with the Wars of Independence, which have produced these factories called republics, where the same men govern,
sometimes worse than the Spanish viceroys and captains general.

It is necessary to make the social revolution in the American
nations.

From prison, Julio Antonio Mella for weeks led a hunger strike that
shook the country and forced the tyrant Machado to taste defeat. Yet
Mella was accused by the regional delegate of the Communist International of petit-bourgeois and nationalistic methods, and the Party expelled Mella and forced him to go into exile in Mexico—where a hired
assassin's bullet took his life.

After that, the Party committed two monumental errors. The first
was negotiating with Machado during the strike of August 1933—thus
causing the defeat of the strike and nullifying the possibility of the people's taking power, permitting the army sergeants and the American embassy to maneuver and provide a substitute for Machado.

The second occurred a month later, when the provisional government—influenced by students, workers, the people, Antonio Guiteras,
and the Revolutionary Directory—enacted nationalist and anti-imperialist labor laws. But when ships with U.S. Marines appeared in Havana
Bay and Colonel Batista—supported by the army, the reactionaries, and
the American embassy—began preparing a new military coup, the
Party switched from a rightist position of negotiation with Machado to
an ultrarevolutionary one, declaring its opposition to the anti-imperialist national government and proclaiming workers' soviets; one was established in the Mabay sugar mill in Oriente Province.

Four months later, Batista and the American embassy carried out
the coup. A fierce repression drowned popular protests in blood. Thousands of revolutionaries were murdered—Guiteras and Aponte, and
many, many Communists.

Three years later, in view of the impossibility of creating a popular
front together with the Auténtico opposition forces as the Communist
International had asked, the Party veered again and made a pact with
Batista. In the Constituent Assembly of 1939, the six Communist delegates, distinguished by the brilliant oratory of the black leader Salvador
García Agüero, played an important role in drafting the new Constitution. The sessions were broadcast over the radio and created an enormous popular impact and sympathy toward the Party. Eddy Chibás and
the most radical wing of the Auténticos, plus the propitious climate for
new popular struggles, also played their part. Thus one of the most
progressive constitutions in Latin America and the bourgeois world was
approved.

The Communist Party, now legal, had ministers—Carlos Rafael
Rodríguez and Juan Marinello—in Batista's government. A Confe-

deración Unica de Trabajadores [United Workers' Confederation], created by the Party's influence in the Ministry of Labor, grouped together all the workers in the country, and won numerous economic advantages for the working class: minimum wages, a forty-four-hour week with pay for forty-eight, a month of paid vacation, an end to dismissals in the factories, and other advances. Although the majority of the people and the working class opposed Batista, the Party's progressive actions and the reforms it obtained earned it support in many popular sectors.

Those just and important gains had the stamp of the theoretical economist, rather than being the consequence of mass struggles organized from the bottom up; they were, instead, obtained with influence from the top, through the Communist ministers in the government. It was an artificial construction, bureaucratic and reformist, which later fell apart, but it had meanwhile established control over the workers' movement by the ruling party in government and ended with the total destruction of the revolutionary Cuban workers' movement.

The participation of the Party in Batista's government demoralized its leaders. On his return from Washington with the crumbs imperialism had given him, Batista was received by the Party as a popular hero: "The messenger of prosperity."

I returned from Trinidad after the defeat of the Batista supporters backed by the Party; Grau San Martín and the Auténticos were in power, and the Party began to maneuver in order to ingratiate itself with the new leaders.

I worked for a short time in the leadership of the Socialist Youth, I founded and edited the magazine *Mella,* but the continual discussions about Browderism*—a theory of the conciliation of classes inside the country and abroad—and the movement's bureaucratization were more conflicting every day.

I decided in 1945 to go to work in a factory in Luyanó, but I had an accident and lost the job.

I started to work as a proofreader for the newspaper *Hoy* [Today], run by Aníbal Escalante. There, I discovered a repressive, bureaucratic laboratory germinating into the Communist-Soviet type, and it froze my blood. It was a cemetery for the revolution and revolutionaries. Escalante was a despot. He imposed his political or personal caprices in an inexorable manner.

Professionally, the paper was well done. Cuban journalism was one of the most corrupt in the world. Escalante, who paid the editors starvation wages, allowed the reporters to take bribes from the ministers—as long as they gave 50 percent of their loot to the paper. Obviously, a minister who paid would not be denounced. Escalante's family—father, brothers, wife, etc.—received more than a thousand pesos a month from

---

* After Earl Browder, head of the U.S. Communist Party until 1945.—Ed.

the Party, while the family of an editor or Party employee would have to live on sixty pesos.

One had only to praise Escalante lavishly to obtain money, loans, a promotion, or whatever one asked; but let anyone who criticized him beware, because he would be fired. It was the atmosphere of a police state with Jesuit morals. The executives made love to the secretary, lived well, and drank cognac or whiskey. They were implacable with the militants. If someone drank some rum or beer in the corner bar, he was denounced in the collective meetings. It was so absurd that, in order to drink a beer on Sundays, a secret society called "the antifascist drunks" was formed, which met in the back rooms of bars.

I had been raised in the open-air Communism of the provinces, and I couldn't take that atmosphere. They promoted me. They respected me because I would speak my mind to anyone. I corrected the style and politics of the articles that the editor in chief did not see. The people who heard me speak thought of me as a rare bird who would not last long.

I thought: To be a Communist is to be free. I was wrong, I was wrong.

Comrades were spied on continually and were criticized in the collective meetings for the most unimportant actions. The directors were untouchable. There was such demoralization, not only on the paper but in the whole Party directorship, that at a national congress they had to forbid the directors to sleep with the wives of their comrades.

Here is one of the weekly criticisms (I am quoting from my diary of that period): "Read Mayakovski, Neruda, and Vallejo; have one of Bukharin's books; go to the symphony concert on Sunday to hear the music of Bach, Prokofiev, and Varèse; have Lam paintings and Picasso reproductions in the house; drink a rum in the corner bar; and go to the Malecón with the sister of a director...." The rest of it was fine, I won first place in the monthly praise for assignments for the Party and the paper.

My answer: "The poets I read, besides being good and my liking them, are Communists. Lenin recommended Bukharin, I like music as you like dominoes or chess. My date is a single girl and, as far as I know, is unattached, and I think that those who talk like Communists but act and live like the bourgeoisie are bourgeois disguised as Communists, or bourgeois Communists."

There were dramatic, or comic conflicts. The conflict between *j* and *g** was famous. Escalante wrote a daily column, a really cutting one, under the pseudonym Juan Simplón, and one day he declared war against the *g,* ordering that all words in his column be spelled with a *j.* Hence the same word was written with *j* in the editor's column and with *g* in the rest of the newspaper. It was a caprice that affected the print-

---

* In Spanish, as in French, *g* and *j* are pronounced the same before *e* and *i.*

shop's work and fast closings. The typesetters and proofreaders, between jokes and laughs, asked for G-men or Jiménez. We tried to put things in order, and as Escalante demanded the use of *j* in writing, they proposed that the matter be brought to the Royal Spanish Academy for consideration.

My last discussion was about Trujillo. Escalante wrote an article about "the progressive steps" taken by the Dominican dictator, who had at the time made a move to allow Communist exiles to return to Santo Domingo. Those who returned were murdered, naturally.

That was in 1946, and it was intolerable. On November 7 I left the newspaper and the Party, and started a difficult adventure with hunger, which ended, many months later, when I enrolled in an expedition against Trujillo, on which I saw Fidel Castro for the first time.

False hope is fatal to the revolutionary. A revolutionary should look reality in the face, and if the means with which he opposes a cruel world do not work, then he must not accept them. He must rebel again.

The future is composed of many presents made up of many pasts. The world will not change if one does not live, think, and behave as a Communist every moment of one's life. Only a continuous Communist present will arrive at a revolutionary future.

I had left the Party without saying a word, but it declared war on me. My name was on the black list. Unions refused to lend me support. And the capitalists offered me work on their newspapers, as they had done with other comrades, but only if I repented, attacked Communism, and served their interests. The Party's failings did not justify the misery, the injustice of capitalist reality and I did not accept them. I cut sugarcane, I worked with pick and shovel, sold postcards, slept in parks. Sometimes I slept in gangsters' haunts, but I did not get mixed up with them; I knew that their frustrated rebelliousness led to crime, jail, or the capitalist cemetery, but not to revolution.

I think it is easier to tolerate a lot of hunger than a lot of wealth stolen from the lives of others. For my part, I participated in whatever protest I considered just. I returned to Sitio Grande, to cut cane and milk cows. Now Prío Socarrás, not Batista, governed, but everything was the same: the sugar boss and the land, the rural guard, the misery of the workers and peasants.

I returned to Havana. Two poets, Tallet and Núñez Olano, got me work as a proofreader for the newspaper *Luz* [Light]. I earned twelve pesos a week and worked eight hours a night. There I saw Eduardo Chibás, progressive leader and creator of the reformist Ortodoxo movement. The newspaper was in the Colón section, famous for its thousands of prostitutes, who operated from houses in several neighboring streets.

It was 1947 and one day I learned that an expedition against Trujillo was in preparation. I sympathized with the cause, the Dominican people. Old General Máximo Gómez, who for almost thirty years directed the Cuban Wars of Independence, was a Dominican. I already knew hunger and struggle, but not war and adventure. I thought: If I lose, there's no problem; if I survive, maybe I can write something, see Europe.

But the expedition began and ended badly. One night I arrived at the port of Antillas. There I found the gangsters drinking whiskey, and conflicts, immorality, ambitions. The "papas" who looked for their sons, the prostitutes who exposed themselves. I realized that the expedition was lost. I thought of leaving immediately. I didn't do it because I couldn't turn back or maybe because sometimes one has so much more fear of saying no than saying yes, and also because among all those opportunistic adventurers and odd people, I found idealists and revolutionaries and I decided to share their fate.

After a few months of adventure the expedition was dissolved, and its 1500 Dominican and Cuban members ended up in prison in Havana's Camp Columbia, where after a hunger strike we were set free with a cheap suit, no money, and no work.

I would later meet some of the members of that expedition, while struggling against Batista: Fidel, the only one who escaped; Carlos Gutiérrez Menoyo, who directed the attack against the Presidential Palace, where he died; Daniel Martín, who fell in the Principe Prison; Pichirilo Mejías, helmsman of the *Granma,* murdered afterward by the Yankees in Santo Domingo; José Wangüemert; Julio César Martínez, who later printed all our clandestine propaganda; Juan Bosch, the Dominican progressive president deposed by the military, and many other Latin American, Spanish, and Cuban revolutionaries.

Again hard times, made somewhat easier thanks to the generosity of a revolutionary family from Oriente Province—the Cabrera Infantes— who then lived in one room, in a tenement in Havana, where there was always room for one more. Zoila, the mother, whose Communist spirit enlivened everything. In that room many dreams were born and many projects became reality. There the magazine *Nueva Generación* [New Generation] was born, so was the Nuestro Tiempo [Our Time] society; there too was forged what would later be the staff of *Lunes* [Monday], under the editorship of Guillermo Cabrera Infante.

We kept busy between comings and goings, attending theater performances in Havana's Parque Central, the first exhibition of Wilfredo Lam's paintings, and many other events.

We were in the midst of Prío's tenure. Depravity and demoralization were the order of the day. The hero of the moment was the one who stole the most, and already I felt the astringent voice of Eduardo Chibás lashing out against theft, cynicism, and corruption. The political gangsters filled the streets of Havana with shots and gunsmoke, with their sensational assaults right out of the movies.

Meanwhile Batista, in the United States, dreamed of returning to his Camp Columbia in Havana, through discreet contacts with his military and American friends.

The checkmate to Prío and his government was made by Eduardo R. Chibás. In a violent dialogue with Minister Sánchez Arango, in which he could not prove what everyone knew—that the Auténtico government was made up of a pack of thieves—Chibás shot himself during one of his daily radio talks, thus trying to make a last appeal to the Cuban people's conscience.

His agony, his death and burial—a gigantic mass act—gave the coup de grâce to the government and a guaranteed victory to the Ortodoxo Party in the next elections.

Elected senator while in exile, Batista returned, well aware that he would not win more than 10 percent of the votes for the presidency. And so he took advantage of the army's demoralization and disgust over the impunity with which the gangsters operated, and he began to conspire.

We lived then immersed in legalism; no one believed in the possibility of another dictatorship.

One March dawn, by surprise and without firing a shot, Batista entered Camp Columbia.

It was the first of a series of events that would change the life and history of Cuba and its people.

1952

2. DAYS IN MARCH

CARLOS FRANQUI   Havana, March 10

Ex-Colonel Fulgencio Batista announced today that he had taken over the government of Cuba. Army tanks, trucks, and patrol cars carrying soldiers with machine guns entered the Presidential Palace grounds, overthrowing President Carlos Prío Socarrás, who took asylum in the Mexican embassy.

Classes at the university were suspended early in the morning. Students thronged into the Plaza Cadenas up to the university steps; and speeches against Batista began. At noon, units of the army and the police surrounded the university. Shortly afterward, over the university loudspeakers, the leaders of the FEU began to urge the people to rise up against Batista: "Once more, we are the standard bearers of the national conscience. We are defending the constitution, the people, and the democratic process." The legislature was dissolved and the representatives of the opposition were taken to the Bureau of Investigation.

At the Presidential Palace, a parade in support of Batista began, consisting of bankers, big landowners, representatives of the Chamber of Commerce, industrialists, leaders of Eusebio Mujal's Confederación de Trabajadores de Cuba [Confederation of Cuban Workers, CTC]. Speaking for the Church, Cardinal Arteaga sent the following message: "Now that your government has been established, under your worthy leadership, it is only fitting for me, as archbishop of Havana, to pay my respects to you, who stand for order, justice, and peace throughout the nation." It was an official blessing.

By Sunday, March 17, a week after Batista's coup, nothing had happened. Students and revolutionaries went to the university but the arms still hadn't arrived. Prío, the president, went into exile. Nothing but manifestos came from the Ortodoxo Party and the Communists.

Rolando Masferrer and his CTC gangsters, Ramón Vasconcelos and his newspaper, all went over to Batista's side. Only Sergeant Sócrates Arteaga and a few comrades fired against one of the tanks from Camp Columbia as it attacked the Palace, killing one man from the garrison. The United States "recognized" the general, and the Latin American countries followed suit.

But the people are against Batista and the takeover. Why is nothing happening?

For a week, we young people, students and revolutionaries, kept going from the university to the unions, from the home of one opposition leader to another, from Ortodoxo headquarters on the Prado to the Communists on Carlos III, asking them to take a stand, demanding action, strikes, protests, and demonstrations. Nothing. Only the FEU loudspeakers from the campus on the hill started coming to life, calling on the people to put up some resistance. From then on we began considering the university as the true home of the revolution; the place where the fight against Batista would be launched.

Each of us tried to do something, in Santiago, in Havana, all over the country.

On the afternoon of Sunday, the seventeenth, we met with Emilio Martínez, a Linotype operator, and others in the printing industry; we decided to try and get on Station CMQ's "University on the Air" radio program, and went over there. It was the Sunday program about the history of Cuba, which always had a large audience. The host was Jorge Mañach and the guest lecturer was Raúl Roa.* The studio audience was the usual mixture of academics and snobs. At the end of the lecture, a live debate with the audience was also broadcast.

Some of our group in the front row raised their hands quickly and Cepero Brito, the announcer, came over with the microphone. I asked: "Doctor Roa, what can you tell me about Batista's new barracks coup and his military dictatorship over the Cuban people?"

Mañach sharply pressed his buzzer and declared the question out of order, saying that all questions must be limited to the period of history just discussed by the lecturer.

Roa was obviously annoyed at not being allowed to answer.

The microphone was handed to Martínez, who asked: "Doctor Roa, isn't this man who carried out the coup the same Batista who assassinated Guiteras in 1935?"

A violent buzz from Mañach stopped the answer to that one, but another question came from someone else in our group. After the fourth or fifth, the moderator announced that time was up and the broadcast was over.

---

* Then a university professor; later Castro's minister of foreign affairs.

There was much commotion in the studio, and an animated discussion started. Roa protested because he had not been allowed to answer questions. Mañach, a good professor who was against Batista but also a timid conservative, criticized us for jeopardizing his program and running the risk of its being taken off the air. We answered: "We'd rather see it closed down by tyrants than see it censoring itself."

We had lashed out at Batista on a program heard by at least a hundred thousand people. That was the important thing.

A completely different audience came to the studio on Sundays after that. Young members of the opposition began showing up: Armando Hart, Gustavo Arcos, Faustino Pérez, Silvio Castillo, and many others whose special target was Batista's regime. The program, the only one the opposition had, became a fantastic success. There were a million radios in the country and CMQ was our most powerful station.

A few weeks later Batista's paid assassins attacked the "University on the Air," beating everyone in the studio brutally with clubs, even Professor Mañach. The whole country heard about this. The younger generation had used the radio as an instrument for the first spontaneous offensives against the dictatorship.

That was when I personally began to use broadcasting as a weapon of revolution.

Our group was made up of Ortodoxos, Dominican exiles, students, intellectuals, and workers in the printing industry. We were Marxists of the left, activists; we were against imperialism.

We were at odds with everyone about the role of the military and about underground work. We criticized the Communist Party for fighting only to remain legal, for its elitism and its failure to act; we criticized the Ortodoxos for their passiveness; and the Auténticos for all their big talk. We agreed with the students about going into action, but their ideological vagueness worried us.

Since we were in no position to form our own organization and disagreed with the ones operating then, we decided to set up a secret printing press and work with those who most closely shared our ideas. We rented a house in the Vedado district of Havana and moved our equipment in: Linotype, cylinder, and an old, very noisy printing press that sounded like a gun. We ran off newspapers that looked like regular newspapers but contained things that frightened people.

It was called *Liberación,* and I'm almost sure it had the largest format of any underground paper ever known. We paid the rent and other expenses out of our salaries but paper was expensive, and Jorge Tallet raised a little money, thanks to his friend Raúl Roa. The pressman was a Dominican exile, Julio César Martínez, who printed almost all the underground propaganda published in Cuba.

With the first issue, we began to have problems with our financial "helpers." Roa was associated with Aureliano Sánchez Arango, a former minister of the Auténtico Party, who was in turn linked up with some gangsters, and we wouldn't have anything to do with the AAA.* So we took our press to the university and set it up in the Law School basement. Working with Manuel Carbonell and FEU, we began to print *Alma Mater,* the clandestine paper that the students, defying the police, sold on the buses and streets of Havana.

Two issues had great impact: "Hunger: Christmas under Batista" and one on the death of Rubén Batista Rubio, with pictures of the attack by the police on the demonstrators and of the political killers firing on Rubén.

The old political forces showed their ineffectiveness and their middle-class affiliation, but the younger generation threw itself into the fight. There was one student demonstration after another. It was a period of self-searching.

During 1952 Batista kept control over the police force and was able to avoid the shedding of blood. His prior experience as dictator had taught him that the Cuban people were opposed to crime and tyranny, and he had learned to be patient. But Rubén's death, in February 1953, showed the true character of the regime.

Demonstrations became more violent and the struggle more fierce. Student agitation began to spread over the country. Thanks to its rebellious spirit, its prestige, and its autonomy, the university was the laboratory of the revolution.

The demonstrations were getting us nowhere, and we started to think about other ways of organizing ourselves and taking action. A torchlight demonstration on January 28, 1953, marked a new starting point. Once again, the students went into the streets and mingled with the people; revolutionaries with students. The discipline, organization, and will to fight shown by the young Ortodoxos, led by Fidel Castro and Abel Santamaría were impressive.

VILMA ESPÍN   Interview by Carlos Franqui

Vilma: The first thing that happened in Santiago was the Bárcenas movement,** and it captured the imagination of professors and students at the university.

Frank País led all the actions. We worked there for a short while, till we saw we weren't getting anywhere. One day, my sister, Nilsa, said:

---

* Clandestine offshoot of the Auténtico Party.
** Rafael García Bárcenas was a philosophy professor at the University of Havana, a journalist, and a founder of the Auténtico Party. He was arrested in April 1953 for planning a coup to oust Batista.—Ed.

"Okay. I'm going to Havana to see what kind of people are running things there, because the situation here isn't clear at all." She took off for Havana, where she conferred with García Bárcenas and Mario Llerena.

After Bárcenas's arrest, I got in touch with Armando Hart and Faustino Pérez, and they talked me into continuing to work with them. They told me that things had changed and there were only good people there now.

Franqui: On May 20, 1952, the Bárcenas movement was organized at the university in Havana. There was a ceremony in the auditorium. I asked to be allowed to speak and explained a theory I had: in Latin America, you could never conspire with the military; every plot worked out with them always backfired. It was like something out of a movie—a terrific argument because I was challenging what was being cooked up there. I knew Bárcenas and really liked him as a person, but his head was always in the clouds.

Vilma: Well, you know that movement didn't last long. But Frank continued to be action chief, and everybody in Santiago began clustering around him. We had an action group, and we set up an organization like the one that would become the 26th of July Movement. I was working on finances, collecting money. Can you imagine, they gave us five cents only now and then. It was awful in the beginning.

That was only in Oriente. We were in touch with Armando Hart and Faustino Pérez, and through them, later on, with Fidel and the others, and Gustavo Arcos too. They began to attack small garrisons to get dynamite, rifles, and so on.

1953-55

3. THE ATTACK ON THE MONCADA BARRACKS

MELBA HERNÁNDEZ AND JESÚS MONTANÉ

Taped interview by Carlos Franqui

Montané: Abel [Santamaría] and I knew each other before Batista's coup. I was working for General Motors in Cuba, and he was with Pontiac. We always met for a bite, morning and evening, in a café on Humboldt Street called the Detroit. We both followed the Ortodoxo Party line—so closely that on March 10 we both went to the university, separately, expecting to find the long-overdue weapons, which never did come. We started the first revolutionary group. Almost immediately after March 10, we all began to meet: Abel, Raúl, Gómez García, and several Ortodoxo Party members from the Santos Suárez section. We began publishing a newspaper: *Son los Mismos* [They Never Change]. Mimeographed copies appeared sometime during the first two weeks in April 1952, and it was published for two or three months, until we met Fidel. On May 1, 1952, International Labor Day, there was a political rally at the Colón Cemetery. Fidel came to it; it was in honor of Carlos Rodríguez, who had been murdered by [Rafael] Salas Cañizares.*

I had met Fidel in 1951 when I helped him buy a car on credit from General Motors. Although we knew each other, I couldn't support him in the elections that were to take place in 1952; I don't remember who I was for—it was someone who was a protégé of Chibás. We talked to Fidel and then and there worked out our first attack on Batista. That was when Fidel told us that he knew a doctor in Colón called Mario Muñoz, who was an Ortodoxo Party member and very trustworthy, to whom he was going to give the job of building two radio transmitters to

---

* Batista's chief of police, who was shot by Israel Escalona in 1957.

send out secret broadcasts in Havana. We agreed to meet the following Sunday to go to Colón. Fidel suggested that we use Abel's car because his own was unreliable. The first Sunday in May we went to Mario Muñoz's house and asked him to build the two transmitters. Within a month we had both of them.

Melba: Abel impressed me tremendously from the start. Here was an idealistic and concerned young man who was in touch with another such young man unknown to us but admired by all who had heard him speak. One day Elda Pérez came and said, "Melba, I've found just the person we've been looking for. He is a young man from Las Villas, and he lives with his sister very near here. He's already mimeographed some underground material. I'd like you to meet him because I think you'll be impressed. He is in touch with another young fellow"—but she didn't know his name either—"who you'll realize is just what we need as soon as you hear him speak." So that evening after dinner we went to Haydée and Abel Santamaría's house. Abel was at home. He began giving us his view of Cuba's dilemma: it could be solved only by fighting. He talked about the problems of following the Ortodoxo Party line; he felt that it was up to the new group to find a solution. Haydée impressed me as much as Abel. They knew somebody who, according to them, was the only one capable of really getting the movement going. They invited me to come and see them again. They weren't expecting him that evening so I was to come back the next day to meet him—Fidel. From then on, I went to their house morning, noon, and night. Sometimes I went to listen to Abel, sometimes to Yeyé [Haydée]. The house was like a magnet, and I was attracted to it from that evening on. But I got around. I kept in touch with Juan Manuel Márquez, and together we supported the Ortodoxo movement. Juan Manuel was very restless and impatient.

Fidel and Abel began to organize meetings with other young people at the house on O and 25th: Boris Luis Santa Coloma, René Betancourt, Vicente Chávez, Pedro Miret, Carlos Bustillo, Orlando Castro, Raúl Martínez Arenas, Oscar Alcalde, Eduardo Granados, Gustavo Amejeiras, Ernesto Tizol, Nico López, and others.

Montané: We started our newspaper, *Son los Mismos,* before Fidel published his *El Acusador* [The Accuser]. We stopped publishing *Son los Mismos* when we joined Fidel.

Melba: I think we only published one issue of *El Acusador.* The newspaper's offices were seized August 16.

Montané: Fidel inspired *El Acusador,* Raul Gómez García ran it, and Tinguao, Abel Santamaría, Melba, and I were the editors. Except for Fidel, Abel Santamaría was the most mature of the comrades who made up the original 26th of July group. Although we all joined the group at the same time, everybody accepted Fidel as leader and Abel as his second in command.

Melba: Well, I don't like to talk about any of our comrades and even less about Abel. There was only one Abel Santamaría.

I remember that it was Fidel who got him started reading Marxist literature. I don't know exactly how it happened but I do remember that Abel turned up one day with a different kind of book instead of his usual Machiavelli and books about Cuban history—Cuba was his passion.

Montané: In Abel, Fidel had a right-hand man, who complemented him. From the start Fidel was the creative force, and during the struggle, he went after every detail. For example, he could send Abel to Artemisa or to Guanajay to reorganize the cell there.

On August 16, we printed a leaflet besides the newspaper. It read: "The Ortodoxo Party leaders are going to waste millions of pesos on their election campaign and yet they won't spend a cent on the revolution." We printed *El Acusador* in Joaquín González's house down in the Vedado district. About that time the police picked up one of our group, a telegraph operator—I still don't know why—and he told the police where we were printing the newspaper. They confiscated almost half the edition, but in spite of that, we still managed to take a pile of newspapers to the cathedral.

Melba: The Ortodoxo Party had organized a mass in the cathedral followed by a pilgrimage to Chibás's grave in the afternoon. Nico López, Calixto García, and other young fellows were in the large group representing the Ortodoxo Party. It was beginning to look like a real organization. When we got back to H Street in the Vedado, we noticed an unusual amount of activity. We drove on and while Abel was parking the car, even before we got out, there were two plainclothes policemen waiting to arrest us. That was the first time Abel was arrested. We were all arrested. Only Yeyé and Fidel got away. The rest of us were all caught—and our arrest files were useful later to Labastida, who was head of the SIM [Servicio de Inteligencia Militar; Military Intelligence Service] in Santiago de Cuba, for identifying those who took part in the attack on Moncada Barracks. The police also took over the secret radio station on Tamarindo Street because of a mistake on our part. The person who was operating the station went over to the enemy.

Another time, they searched the apartment. We had just taken a machine gun away from there. Pilar García's son, Leonardo, was making the search. Abel began to talk about why it was necessary to fight against Batista's military coup. Abel had such a strong personality that even though Leonardo was a soldier, he spent an hour in the apartment listening to him.

Montané: The first time we asked to take part as a group in a demonstration was on January 28, 1953.

Melba: Abel was a wonderful organizer.

Montané: Yes, Abel and José Luis Tassende organized us into several groups, and we joined the torchlight demonstration to make a show of force.

Melba: Abel worked in Pinar del Río. We mobilized all our revolutionary cells, so the movement was strong there.

(Raúl Castro: The rank and file of the Ortodoxo Party was like an army whose officers were in a permanent state of confusion, but the young people continued to take part in any antidictatorship street demonstration they supported while the new leaders were gradually emerging from the lower ranks.

A few months later, on January 28, 1953, the centennial of José Martí's birth, an impressive group of demonstrators set out from the main entrance of the university. Both blue- and white-collar workers took part, students, and the general public, but a group of several thousand young people stretching over six blocks, marching in well-disciplined contingents, stood out from the rest and caught everybody's attention. Fidel led them. These young people, mainly from the Ortodoxo Party, had at last found a leader and were now looking for new ways of tackling the struggle.)

Haydée: We were very organized and carried flaming torches. We had stuck a nail into each torch so that when it was hot, we could use it to fight the police. Melba and I were the only women in the group. I remember people saying: "Those are the Communists." I remember saying to Melba: "What are they talking about? We're only Fidel's group." People said we were Communists because we were so well disciplined. I used to say to Abel: "Why do they call us Communists when we're really Fidel's group?" And even the students who knew we weren't Communists kept saying: "How well organized Fidel's followers are! Have you ever seen anything like it?" But besides this, we clashed with the police. As soon as one of them attacked us, we brandished the nails. We were prepared to put up a fight to see how the crowd reacted. The students kept asking: "Where is Fidel Castro? There's Abel, there's Nico. . . ."

Montané: By then, there were about six hundred of us. It was around that time that we got down to work. Abel organized the group in Pinar del Río with Pepe Suárez from Artemisa.

Melba: San Cristóbal and Guanajay too.

Montané: Ramirito Valdés, Ciro Redondo . . .

Melba: Julito Díaz . . .

Montané: He started the movement in Santiago de las Vegas too.

Melba: Pepe Ponce, from Artemisa, set up cells. Fidel, using the knowledge he'd gotten through experience in the Ortodoxo Party, always paved the way for us, opened doors, set up contacts—that's what he did in Pinar del Río. Abel followed close behind, setting up the organization.

Montané: In 1952 we organized the Santiago de las Vegas cell; Pedrito Trigo and René Bedia Morales were in it also. Abel finally organized the Artemisa and Guanajay groups.

Melba: Abel often went with Fidel to Matanzas.

Montané: And to the group that Armando Mestre and Almeida belonged to, the Arroyo Apolo group. By December 1952 our organization was very tight and it was divided into two parts: one civilian and one military. Fidel, Abel, Boris Luis Santa Coloma, Mario Muñoz, Pedrito Miret, and I headed the civilian part. The military was led by Fidel, Abel, José Luis Tassende, and Pedrito Miret.

Melba: At that stage the members of the Auténtico Party kept warning us that one day soon . . .

Montané: The real showdown! Be ready for the zero hour!

Melba: That famous zero hour . . .

Montané: Which never came.

Melba: As soon as Fidel realized that we weren't going to accomplish anything by beating on the doors of the Ortodoxo Party leaders, he changed his tactics and got us in touch with the Auténtico cells. Not to get us closer with them for the zero hour, but to see what could be gained because they had so many weapons. On the twenty-ninth, Abel arrived at my house in Jovellar. He was worried and annoyed, and started telling me awful things about these people: "These Auténticos! They are liars, they'll never do anything." At the beginning of January Fidel decided that "we mustn't rely on anybody. We must concentrate on strengthening our own forces to solve the problem." So we tried to work out our finances, in order to be able to buy all the weapons we could.

Montané: So did Pardo Llada,* and I remember Abel and I went to see another man, Emilio Ochoa, who enjoyed playing revolutionary. He was a blabbermouth of the first order. I remember distinctly that Abel

---

* José Pardo Llada was Ortodoxo Party leader.—Ed.

and I kicked each other under the table as this guy openly dropped the names of all his contacts in the army. We didn't have much experience in uprisings, but we had enough common sense to realize not only that this kind of information should not be given to anyone but also that this man was not going to be able to help any revolution. The more we came into contact with these people, the more we realized that it was up to our generation to make the revolution. This we did from January 1953 on. Cells were organized, aimed at attracting young people. We told people: "This movement is going to end with an armed struggle, but for security reasons, we can't tell you when or where." We held rifle practice. It was a selective secret movement.

Everybody took part in rifle practice. I would say more than a thousand young people practiced in the university, at one time or another. There were ranges in Los Palos, Nueva Paz, and Pinar del Río. We had made special arrangements and when we were practicing nobody else could. The problem was that since we practiced on the university campus itself, Pedrito Miret, Léster, and José Luis Tassendre knew about it.

Melba: The practice at the university was at the first stage, when we didn't even have a rifle to practice with. Yeyé and I never showed our faces there after January 1953.

Montané: We continued testing people's reactions to the shooting and the problem of mobilization, and we analyzed our mistakes.

Melba: The struggle demanded so much courage and real determination that many people gave up.

Montané: Fidel had participated in all kinds of activity in 1952, making speeches, doing all he could, but after Rubén Batista's death, we didn't hear a word from him until Moncada. At first Raúl took part in the activities only occasionally. He was to have joined the Movement when he came back from a visit to the Socialist countries, but he was arrested on his return and they seized his diary. When I went to see him at the police station, he was very enthusiastic about his trip and told me all about it.

Melba: Antolín Falcón, the police chief, hoped to convince me that the whole business was mad by telling me the crazy things Raúl wrote about the trip in his diary. "How can you believe all that?" he used to say. "Look at the way this diary describes the Socialist world! As a heaven on earth! I've never come across a heaven here." You know, I was arrested several times and Falcón knew me very well.

Montané: On March 10, when Batista carried out the coup, Boris Santa Coloma sent Batista a letter saying: "You are as big a thief as Prío and a murderer besides." Boris belonged to the Ortodoxo Youth Movement. We got down to the job of finding money after the demonstration January 28, 1953. We held a meeting and I was named treasurer with a committee made up of Oscar Alcalde, Joaquín González, and the accountants. We collected about 22,000 pesos and bought guns and other weapons. One of the few remaining papers Abel left is a letter he wrote to somebody telling him that one day he would explain why he couldn't pay him back for some debt he owed.

Melba: At the end of May or the beginning of June, Abel left for Santiago de Cuba.

Montané: But we didn't even know he had gone. I'm telling you this to show you that the planning of the whole Moncada business was a model of secrecy and compartmentalization. Even Melba was in on it, and when I arrived in Oriente, I was amazed to find Abel, Melba, and Haydée there too.

Melba: And there was such discipline too. Not one of us would have dreamed of asking any of the others what he or she was doing there.

Montané: We practiced shooting on one of Hidalgo Gato's farms in Los Palos. Abel said to me in Santiago before the attack: "Well, Montané, I knew you were going to give me a 'Piedra,' so I brought an H. Upmann box to put it in." That's the last thing I can tell you about Abel when we were on the way to Moncada, except that before he separated from Renato Guitart's group, we stopped at ————'s house. I don't know if you remember that, Melba? And that was where Fidel and Abel spoke to each other for the last time. But I can tell you that Abel looked extremely happy. Honestly, Franqui, we really believed that we were going to beat the enemy and if the thought of defeat crossed our minds, it was only fleetingly.

JUAN ALMEIDA   Taped interview by Carlos Franqui

I worked as a bricklayer. We were doing a job in Ayestarán. Our foreman wasn't a bad fellow, at least, deep down he was all right, except when it came to working with him—he paid starvation wages.

One day I met Comrade Armando Mestre, who was studying for his high-school diploma at the La Habana Institute; he was an athlete and knew some interesting people, and he lived near me. We got along well, and we often went out together. He asked me if I was a student and I told him that I had left school in the fourth grade and never got the chance to study again. He offered to coach me, so that I could attend the institute too and have more of a chance in life and better job opportunities. I told him he was right but that my parents depended on the money I earned to help them support our family, which was very large.

We had been friends for years when he came to pick me up on March 10, the day of Batista's coup: "They're mobilizing everybody to try to resist the coup. Let's go and join them at the university." So we went, hoping to find weapons of some kind—but there weren't any. Someone was going to bring them, no one did; they were coming, they were not. . . . In the end, the first gun I ever saw in my life was the one Fidel brought to the university hill, to the Hall of Martyrs, for rifle practice—the Springfield rifle and the famous M-1, familiar to every student at that time: that M-1 with a collapsible butt that everybody got his hands on.

Those were the basic weapons we first used when we were learning to handle arms.

Pedrito Miret was in charge of rifle practice. Do you remember that T-shirt he used to wear with *H* stamped on the front and the way he greeted you, hand clenched, then open, and the famous kick?

That's where I met Fidel and we talked about the revolution and how the coup would delay it, how young people had to get together, and how he relied on people who had never been involved in politics before.

It was my first meeting with Fidel. He was carrying the book on Lenin that later turned up at Moncada. Fidel was wearing a gray suit and a threadbare shirt with a collar that looked as if it had been darned more than once—it suited his strong character.

"Something very great is going to happen that will awaken the people's consciousness."

—Abel Santamaría

RECOLLECTIONS

A witness: Seventeen cars left for Oriente. In Oriente, Renato Guitart was the only one there who knew what was being planned. This was the first truly secret operation ever carried out in Cuba. Renato and Abel were in charge of the detailed plans for Moncada and the work that was being done in Santiago. There were 165 people to attack the Moncada Barracks; 30 were to attack the one in Bayamo. By one o'clock that morning they were all gathered at the Siboney farm.

During the afternoon of July 25, Fidel and Abel met those who had come from all parts of the island to Santiago de Cuba to fight, and told them their plans for dawn on the 26. Nearly everybody went to the house on the beach that night to get a uniform and a gun. Renato, Melba, Elpidio, and Haydée cooked a chicken stew in the early evening. But Abel didn't eat that night because he had promised an old Spanish couple called Núñez, who lived opposite the Siboney house, to drive them to see the masqueraders. He couldn't let them down because they were very old, and there probably wouldn't be better carnivals for them in the future. Haydée thought that this might be the last one her brother would ever see.

Melba and Haydée ironed the uniforms. Renato was the first to get his on. The house was soon full of concentrated activity. Everybody moved in silence.

Haydée had great faith in Abel's cheerful, optimistic outlook. Even Abel had admitted to some of his friends that his optimism made him blind to problems. He would never admit that something he desperately wanted to happen, and had planned so smoothly, might fail. Maybe he'd been chosen to see it through, and the others had not. His self-confidence reassured her. She remembered how, just before he left for Santiago, he was trying to figure out how many days it would be before his dog had her puppies. He wanted to know if he would see the puppies when he came back. When they got to Siboney, he planted some mangoes and told a friend: "Just you wait: three years from now you'll see how many mangoes I'm going to eat!" That night, at Siboney, he laughed as he said: "Fidel is going to give people such a shock in Cuba, and I am really going to enjoy the way his revolution is going to shake them up."

Haydée didn't think Abel would die, yet she was sure Boris—her fiancé—would. And he must have thought so too, because he said: "Do you really know what it is like to die that way? Not everybody will have a death like this."

That night when Fidel came back to the farm, he called them all together. After the weapons were distributed, Haydée and Melba asked what he expected of them. He told them that they'd better wait at the farm until they found out what happened. But they insisted, so Fidel finally said that it was up to Abel to decide if the girls should go along.

Melba said: "As soon as Abel arrived, we rushed up to him to find out what he thought. But by then we had found a supporter in Dr. Mario Muñoz, who said we could go with him as nurses. He said we were indispensable. Abel and Fidel gave their permission and we began to get ready."

Fidel had told everybody there: "Comrades, tomorrow we may win or we may lose, but in the end this movement will triumph. If we win, tomorrow will fulfill what Martí aspired to. If we don't, the gesture will have set an example for the people of Cuba."

Then Abel spoke: "We must all believe that we will win tomorrow, but if fate is against us, we will have to bear defeat bravely because one day everyone will know what happened. History will record it, and all young Cubans will follow our example of dying willingly for Cuba. That will make our sacrifice worthwhile and help ease the sorrow of our loved ones and our parents. To die for one's country is to live!"

Haydée kept trying to think of reasons why Abel might die, but she couldn't. He couldn't die because he stood for life itself, he was the very soul of the struggle. That was exactly what Fidel Castro thought a while later when he said to Abel: "I'm going to the barracks and you're going to the hospital because you are the soul of the struggle, and if I die, you will take my place."

Abel argued with Fidel about going to the hospital: "I'm not going to the hospital—that's where the women and the doctor are going. If there is a fight, I must be there. Let the others do the disk-jockeying and distribute the leaflets."

"You are second in command," Fidel replied. "I have to lead the men and may not come out of this alive."

"We are not going to follow Martí's example," Abel argued, "by letting you go to the most dangerous place and get killed when you are the one we need the most."

But Fidel had the last word: "You must go to the hospital, Abel."

It was then about five o'clock in the morning and he gave the order to set out.

Ramón Paz Ferro: Since I had a rifle, I was sent to the first of the fifteen vehicles that made up the motorcade. The first car was driven by Abel, who as commander, gave us our orders. We were to occupy the local civilian hospital, Saturnino Lora, which was in a strategic position and would enable us to operate as snipers, covering our comrades as they attacked on the front.

Abel, dressed as a soldier, went up to the policeman guarding the main entrance of the hospital, and said: "The people are going to take over the hospital. We won't hurt you; we just want your gun. This is a doctor and two nurses. We don't want to kill or wound anybody, but if this should happen, they will be here to look after them."

Fidel Castro: The final mobilization of men from the most remote towns of the island was completed with clockwork precision and in absolute secrecy. The whole attack was amazingly well coordinated. In both Bayamo and Santiago de Cuba, it began simultaneously at 5:15 a.m. In both places the key buildings around the military camps fell within seconds of the appointed time. But for the sake of strict truthfulness, even though it may not enhance our image, I am going to tell for the first time about another fatal event: by a terrible mistake the best armed half of our troops was delayed at the city gates and so was not present at the vital moment.

Abel Santamaría and twenty-one men had gone to occupy the civilian hospital. Raúl Castro and seven others occupied the Courthouse. It was my job to lead the attack with the remaining ninety-five men. When the advance party of eight had stormed Post 3, I arrived with the initial group of forty-five. My car ran into a military patrol armed with machine guns, and the struggle began. Our reserve division, which had almost all our heavy weapons—except for those with the advance party—made a wrong turn, and completely lost its way in a city that was unfamiliar to them.

I must make it clear that I don't question the loyalty of those men at all: they were anguished and desperate when they discovered they were lost. It was extremely difficult to re-establish contact with them due to the nature of the fighting and the fact that both sides wore the same color uniform. They were imprisoned later, and many died a hero's death.

Everybody had received very clear instructions emphasizing the importance of humane behavior in the fight. No group of armed men has ever treated their enemies more leniently. From the very start they took a great many prisoners—around twenty. At one point near the beginning, three of those who had captured the guard post—Ramiro Valdés, José Suárez, and Jesús Montané—actually managed to get inside the barracks, where they held about fifty soldiers at bay for a time. Later, when these three appeared in court as prisoners, the soldiers all confirmed that they had been treated with great respect, without even a harsh word spoken. I am grateful to the district attorney for his handling of this side of things: in his summation, he recognized unequivocally that our behavior had been honorable throughout the fight.

The army's discipline, on the other hand, was rather bad. The decisive factors in its victory were that it outnumbered us fifteen to one and that it had the fortress as protection. The soldiers agreed that our men were better shots. We were equally matched in courage.

Apart from the terrible mistake I mentioned before, I think that the main reason for the failure of our tactics was that we should not have split our well-trained commando unit. We divided up our best men and most daring leaders by sending twenty-seven to Bayamo, twenty-one to the hospital, and ten to the courthouse. Maybe things would have turned out differently if we had distributed our forces in some other way. The incredible coincidence of bumping into the patrol (completely accidental, since, given twenty seconds either way, it would not have even been there) meant that the military camp had time to mobilize its forces; otherwise, we would have captured it without firing a shot since we already had Post 3 under our control. Another factor was that our artillery consisted almost solely of .22-caliber rifles. If we'd had hand grenades, they wouldn't have been able to resist more than fifteen minutes.

I began to pull my men out in groups of eight or ten as soon as I realized that we couldn't possibly capture the fortress. Pedro Miret and Fidel Labrador bravely led a group of six snipers, holding off the army so that we could retreat under cover. Our losses in the actual fighting had been negligible: it was the cruelty and inhumanity *after* the fighting that accounted for 95 percent of our dead. Only one of our group was killed in the hospital. The rest were cornered when the troops blocked the only exit from the building, and only laid down their arms when the ammunition ran out. Abel Santamaría, the most beloved and daring of all our young men, was with them. His glorious part in the resistance movement will find a place in the history of Cuba.

A witness: Shots were heard inside the building. Abel looked at the others and said, "What has gone wrong? Has Fidel died? We must fight!"

Paz Ferro continues the story: "I stood up at a window behind the blinds and began to shoot. Time raced past, but instead of hearing fewer answering shots, we heard more and more. This could only mean one thing—something had gone wrong. Then I realized that the 'guards' were aiming directly at our position."

Melba and Haydée left for the Moncada Barracks in the last vehicle. Julio Reyes, Raúl Gómez, and Dr. Muñoz went with them. They came across Boris's truck abandoned by the side of the road with its doors open. This terrified the women, and Haydée again had the uneasy feeling that she would never see Boris alive again. But he was the first person they saw shooting near the wall of barracks. He waved to them between rounds.

The battle was raging when they arrived at the hospital, and they had to go through the crossfire to reach the door. Their first patients were Batista's soldiers, but when they tried to lift them up, they realized they were dead. Then one of their comrades was brought in with a bullet in his stomach. Many more followed. Then the shooting became sporadic. It was a bad sign.

Haydée, Melba, and Dr. Muñoz, helped by one of the hospital nurses, began to bandage the arms and legs of the wounded who were inside the hospital. Melba told us that Abel took her and Haydée aside at eight o'clock that morning and said: "We've had it. You know what is going to happen to me, and perhaps to everybody: but it's more important not to risk you two. Hide in the hospital and just wait. You have a much better chance than anybody else of staying alive—do that, at all costs. Somebody has to survive to tell what really happened here."

He disappeared before we could think of what to say. Minutes later, down in the courtyard, we saw him being arrested and hit and kicked by soldiers as he was taken away. Haydée remembers that his face was bleeding.

Melba recalls: "Secretly we were both quite sure that Abel was dead but we felt that we could somehow keep him alive by not saying it out loud. Haydée never mentioned her brother once, afraid that her thoughts might kill him."

Haydée, now: "Boris had gone to Siboney in the meanwhile and met

Ramirito Valdés there. He asked Ramirito about us, and when he found out that Ramirito didn't have any idea where we were, he turned back toward Santiago de Cuba. He was already on the road to the hills, but he had turned around to come back, and that's when they caught him. When we were in the hospital, Abel kept saying: 'Okay, they are going to kill us, right here, but Fidel is the one who must not die. Why can't I be with Fidel? I wonder if the men with him will realize how important it is for him not to die?' His only thought was for Fidel's safety, even though he knew they were going to be killed."

That night, Melba and Haydée heard one soldier telling another: "That one with the two-tone shoes, he's in for it!" Then they knew that Boris had been caught and tortured.

As they went into the basement of the police station in Santiago de Cuba, Haydée said to Melba: "If Abel isn't here, that means that they've killed him." On their way down in the dark, they instinctively clutched each other's hands. Haydée looked for her brother among the men huddled together in the basement. Melba felt her grasp slacken as her gaze reached the last one. Abel Santamaría was dead.

Fidel tells how a sergeant came into the cell where Melba Hernández and Haydée Santamaría were imprisoned, carrying a bleeding eyeball. Going up to Haydée, he showed her the eye and said: "This belongs to your brother, and if you don't tell us what he refused to tell us, we'll gouge his other one out too." Although she loved her brother more than anything else in the world, she managed to answer: "If he didn't tell you anything when you gouged his eye out, you will get less out of me."

Later, the same man came and told her: "They have killed your brother." Haydée said afterward, "I felt Melba's hands on my shoulders. I saw the man coming over to me and heard his voice. Bullets shattered my mind again. I heard myself saying in a voice I didn't recognize, 'Was that Abel?' I looked at the man and he lowered his eyes. 'Is it Abel?' He didn't answer. Melba came close to me. She was there, her hands, keeping me company.

" 'What time is it?'
" 'Nine o'clock,' Melba answered."

Fidel Castro: Where were our wounded? There were only five in all Oriente Prison. Ninety killed and five wounded. Can you imagine anything like this in a war? What happened to the others? Besides, where were the fighters who were arrested on the twenty-sixth, twenty-seventh, twenty-eighth, and twenty-ninth? Santiago knows the answer. The wounded were dragged out of the hospitals and killed immediately, sometimes even before they were out of the hospital. Two wounded prisoners got into a hospital elevator with their guards and came out dead. Those who had been confined in the military hospital had air and camphor injected into their veins; one of them, an engineering student, Pedro Miret, survived this criminal treatment and told all about it.

Only five, I repeat, came out alive. Two of them, José Ponce and Gustavo Arcos, were protected by Dr. Posada, who wouldn't let the soldiers drag them away from the Colonia Española Hospital; three others owe their lives to Captain Tamayo, an army doctor, who in a gesture of professional honor, pistol in hand, transferred the wounded Pedro Miret, Abelardo Crespo, and Fidel Labrador, from the military hospital to a regular hospital. They didn't want even these five to live.

EFIGENIO AMEJEIRAS   Taped interview by Carlos Franqui

When I met Fidel—naturally, I, like many other people, had already heard of him, because he was well known, he was a student leader, and he also had a radio hour, where he talked a good deal, denouncing the crimes and robberies of the Prío administration, which preceded Batista's. But he was introduced to me for the first time by my brother Juan Manuel one morning, before Moncada.

The second time I saw him was two or three days before Moncada. I had just come back from a job I had at that time with a company that made radio towers; I was chauffeur for the company director. Fidel came to a house where my brother was.

We didn't see each other again until after what happened at Moncada—where my brother Juan Manuel was killed—because all our people were in prison. In Havana, we organized an Action cell, as we had promised to.

That's how we kept the flame of rebellion alive at 109 Prado, while the others were in prison. We started planting bombs, demonstrating in the streets, taking part in all the student rallies, until they got out of jail and Fidel decided to leave the country for Mexico, because we knew the regime was planning to kill him.

VILMA ESPÍN   Taped interview by Carlos Franqui

Vilma: When they attacked Moncada, I wanted to go to the hospital to see who was there. I met Asela at the university, and the next day, early on the morning of the twenty-sixth, we were very worried, because we could hear shots, which meant that they were still killing our men.

The police were afraid of the people! People were talking in the middle of the street, outraged; they didn't know who was inside, but they realized what was happening. They were murdering people there, and every few minutes the trucks would come out with bodies and take them to the cemetery. There was a wave of indignation in the streets.

I remember a man standing on the corner of San Félix and Enramada reading a paper and saying: "Just think, they didn't tell anybody! If they had let people know . . ." And the cops standing there. This wave of indignation, people wanting to save those boys—all this paved the way for what happened on November 30,* they didn't want what had happened on the 26th of July to happen all over again; so many boys had been killed then.

Yeyé [Haydée Santamaría] says that every time she goes by the back of the hospital, it upsets her to think that if they had gone that way, where there were people, they would have been saved—only they didn't think of that. But on November 30, the boys did go that way and were able to get rid of their uniforms and hide their guns, and the police couldn't tell who was who.

I remember the demonstrations you were in, Franqui, on December 7. You and that kid who went to Venezuela, right?** Yes, December 1953. I remember the posters vaguely; they said something like "Down with assassins of Moncada" or "Down with the dictatorship." I remember distinctly that one said something about the 26th of July. Yes, we were demonstrating against the Moncada killings. I hardly had time to read the posters because the police suddenly showed up and there was a fight.

You know that Frank País and our boys had made the posters; no one blabbed, they just hid them. Then the police came, remember? The police came to the door of the National Teachers' College and wouldn't let us leave. "No, but listen." "Okay, we're going to let you go, but only if you promise not to make trouble for us." We said we wouldn't make trouble, all we wanted to do was to get the posters, and that's when the trouble started. It didn't even last for two blocks, but we managed to give it to them with the fire hose.

Nilsa was there, and "Papito" Serguera, who spoke at the rally.

Do you remember that we put your movie camera in a banana crate and left it with a man selling bananas there in the square? And you showed the film on TV, it was great.

Franqui: Actually, the whole thing was a surprise to me, because the only ones I knew there were you and Nilsa, I think.

Vilma: You had gone to cover another story at the university. Frank was at the Teachers' College, when this happened. Then we came out and when we got to the second block, the shooting broke out. They started firing at us and we had to run for cover.

---

* November 30, 1956, the revolt at Santiago was led by País.
** Ramón Suárez, a photographer, who was filming the demonstration.

Franqui: I was clubbed by the police once but the padding in my coat was thick, and it didn't hurt me.

I remember that they got down on their knees and started firing up the hill at us. Then everybody scattered in all directions and I hid in a doorway, but you know how Nilsa is; she stood right there, saying: "Look, they're shooting at us!" I had to grab her and pull her inside.

Asa, who eventually was shot on the train by us later on, after he became a captain and chief of police, was there; he was only a deputy then. Anyway, he had caught Jossué País, and when we got to the Plaza de Martí, they captured Jorge Ibarra, who was our president; he was almost strangled by the police and the kids, pulling him from one side to the other, because he had on a leather jacket, zipped all the way up to his neck. Then the police started throwing the kids into their squad cars, till there was no more room.

At this point, the butchers ran out of the market with those huge knives they call *"calabozos,"* shouting that they weren't going to let them take away any of those kids. And the police let the boys go; you can't imagine how scary the butchers looked with those big knives!

Something else happened. A young kid, the youngest Griñán kid, stopped a policeman and the policeman stuck his gun in the kid's stomach; the boy punched the officer who was holding the gun against his stomach, but nothing happened. There were lots of incidents like that, and it was all like something out of a movie.

They were picking up boys, but they didn't touch us and we kept getting farther down the hill. Then the patrol cars came back and they started picking up the boys again.

When we got to the Emergency Center, Jossué País broke a street lamp with a rock; all the glass fell on a policeman guarding the door. There was a scramble because the cop grabbed Jossué, and I began to distract him by talking to him, while País managed to get away.

We reached the Maceo house, and I asked for a piece of paper to write something on and leave it as proof that we had been there and had held the demonstration. We put it inside an empty cartridge that one of the Maceo family had brought me and we left it in the hollow plaster bust of Maceo.

Franqui: I think the police came to break it but one of the old Maceo ladies wouldn't let them touch it.

Vilma: Yes, they always behaved magnificently. They stuck a fire hose out the door and kept the police out. And apparently the chief of police said: "Okay, leave them alone. As long as they stay in the house and don't do anything else, let them stay there."

Yes, that's right. We went with you to see Gustavo Arcos in the hospital. It was in December 1953. I'm sure of it because we had gone to Gran Piedra that day and it was very cold.

4. Prison—Amnesty

I know that prison will be tougher for me than it has ever been for anyone else; there will be no end to the threats, the vicious and cowardly attacks, but I am not afraid of it, or the rages of the miserable tyrant who took the lives of seventy of my brothers.

—Fidel Castro

FIDEL CASTRO

Letters   Oriente Prison

I have been in prison thirty-five days now, and they have really gone by quickly. The first days in jail, when there's still so much time ahead and you are becoming resigned to the endless waiting, are not so bad as the last days, when there is a short time left and you are impatient to be free. I felt the same way in boarding school; we could put up with September, but June drove us crazy. After all, prison is a good rest, and the only thing wrong with it is that it has been forced on me; where else would I be able to rest?

Life is what you make it. Usually, we are never satisfied. If we are free, we worry about other things, and if we are behind bars, we worry about getting out. It is an endless chain, and once we see that, we can accept things better.

Why do I find prison bearable? Because I know how to use my time. I read and study. Letters normally get here, but it is like boarding school, the mail is censored here too.

The small cigars are terrific. The last box is almost empty; I always have to give a few to some of the staff here. I am taking the vitamins; I hope I don't run out of them sometime.

I think I will write to my parents this afternoon. Will they understand that I am in jail because I have done my duty?

I like French literature very much, especially social and political writing. Reading Rolland's *Jean Christophe*, I get the same feeling I had when I read Victor Hugo's *Les Misérables;* I did not want it to end. They were written in different eras, but it's natural for Rolland's book to inspire us more; after all, he is a man of our times, and his pen defended the great causes of this century. He is in the same ideological group as José Ingenieros, H. G. Wells, Maxim Gorki, and other prose writers who hungered for justice. *Jean-Christophe* is a fascinating book; I read it every night for about an hour before going to sleep. I am particularly interested in the author's social ideas.

I have finished reading *The Keys of the Kingdom, The Story of San Michele,* Maurois's *Memoirs, Cakes and Ale,* and some other books. I received them at a very tough time, days of unending torture and lonely struggle when I had to draw on all my strength.

How many times during the seventy-seven days I spent in my solitary, isolated, and silent cell, on a distant radio I could hear a sad song— it's very popular now—which stirred up vivid memories. I felt as if I had died and was listening to faint echoes coming from the world in which I had once lived. Fantastic moments of strange emotions that would test the courage of any fighter, but I never wavered or lost faith in my ideas. What difference does it make if our bodies live or die? Sometimes, we give birth to ideas and feelings we cannot imagine will die with us, even if they follow us to the grave. Only someone who has sacrificed the best things in life to let a great idea live on can understand this.

Isle of Pines,*
December 18, 1953

In the last few days, I have read some interesting books: William Thackeray's *Vanity Fair,* Ivan Turgenev's *A Nobleman's Nest,* Jorge Amado's *A Gentleman of Hope: The Life of Luis Carlos Prestes, The Secret of Soviet Strength* by the Dean of Canterbury, Eric Knight's *Fugitives of Love,* Nikolai Ostrovski's *How the Steel Was Tempered* (a modern Russian novel, a stirring autobiography of the author as a young man taking part in the Revolution), and A. J. Cronin's *The Citadel.* I'll never regret reading them—they all have enormous social value.

I'm also studying Karl Marx's *Capital* thoroughly, five huge volumes on economics, researched and explained with scientific exactness. And I've begun studying the work of some Cuban writers like Félix Varela, Luz y Caballero, and others.

---

* Castro was transferred to prison here, after the court in Santiago sentenced him to a fifteen-year term.—ED.

Christmas is just around the corner. I won't celebrate it; I'm so weighed down by sad memories that even Christmas music is painful to me.

December 19

The human soul is an enigma. Like nature, it has calm and stormy days; like the earth, it has light and darkness; and like the sea it has fair and stormy weather.

This prison is a terrific classroom! I can shape my view of the world in here, and figure out the meaning of my life. I do not know if I will have a long or a short life, whether it will be productive or wasted. But I feel my belief in sacrifice and struggle getting stronger. I despise the kind of existence that clings to the miserly trifles of comfort and self-interest. I think that a man should not live beyond the age when he begins to deteriorate, when the flame that lighted the brightest moment of his life has weakened, and he does not have the strength to go on living to a dignified old age; that is when you see them going around depressed and repentant, like common criminals. Deep down, they become ashamed of the only noble thing they had in their life, the years when they were generous, altruistic, and did not care only about themselves; they are going downhill, doing the opposite of what they preach. Looking back on their youth, they begin to think they must have been naïve, mad, dreamers; they cannot see that they have become impotent, frustrated, deceived, submissive. They are a sad spectacle, on a wretched and ridiculous road back to a past they will never be able to recapture.

But there are many men who will rise from their ashes, like the phoenix; the strong beat of their wings will ring out in the skies over their homeland again.

December 22

At 5:00 a.m. on the dot, when you feel as if you have just shut your eyes, the shout: "Roll call!" followed by clapping hands, is to remind us that we are in prison, as though we had maybe put it out of our minds in our dreams. The lights, which were on all night, are more blinding than ever; your head feels like lead, but there's the voice again: "On your feet!" In less than thirty seconds, I am in my shirt, pants, and shoes. No more sleep for me until 11:00 p.m., when my eyes close while reading Marx or Rolland, or, like tonight, when I finish writing you this letter. Let me sum up: breakfast at 5:30, classes from 8:00 to 10:30, lunch at 10:45, classes again from 2:00 to 3:00 p.m.; recess until 4:00; dinner at 4:45; from 7:00 to 8:15, we have classes in political economy and read together; at 9:30 p.m., silence.

We live in a gallery some 120 feet long and 24 feet wide in one wing of the infirmary, a huge one-story building. White lime walls reflect the light from the three bulbs on the ceiling, and the floor is granite. The bathroom is at one end; at the other there is a small marble counter we use as a little kitchen for making coffee. From one end of the room to the other, there is a double row of beds set up in perfect formation: the twenty-seven beds, with their mosquito nets, look like tents protecting us from the army of flies and mosquitoes; until recently, they had us at their mercy. At 60-by-35-foot inner courtyard; there is a roomy porch, supported by pillars, all around the courtyard and a granite floor here too. On the porch, next to the door out to the courtyard, there are two long tables we use for lunch and dinner, and for our classes also. We can't see anything outside; all the windows are at least 9 feet high.

We are permitted to go into the courtyard from 10:00 to 10:30 a.m. and from 1:00 to 4:00 p.m. Every morning from 9:30 to 10:30, I give a talk—philosophy one day, world history the next. Other comrades give lectures on Cuban history, grammar, arithmetic, geography, and English. At night, I give a class on political economy and twice a week on public speaking, if you can call it that. Instead of holding a class on political economy, I read to them for half an hour—either a full description of a battle, for example, the attack of Napoleon Bonaparte's infantry at Waterloo, or else I read them an ideological text like Martí's address to the Spanish Republic, or something along that line. Right after that, different men, picked at random, or volunteers, must give a three-minute talk on the subject. It is a competition and prizes are given out by the judges. On every important date in Cuban history, we have get-togethers and talks on the subject. A party on the twenty-sixth of each month; on the twenty-seventh, mourning and acts of commemoration, reflection, followed by a discussion of what happened that July 26, 1953. Naturally there are no games or entertainment on the day of mourning.

The school week runs from Monday to Saturday noon. We call the school the Abel Santamaría Ideological Academy, and it does honor to his memory in every respect. The library now has three hundred volumes, but this does not mean we have three hundred different books or that they are all first-rate. The two wooden bookshelves are full; Lieutenant Perico had them, as well as the blackboard, made in the carpentry shop. The library is named after Raúl Goméz García; it is tiny now, but it will be large someday. The young men are all great. They have survived many trials and are now the elite. Those who learned to handle weapons are now learning to wield books for the important battles of the future. Their discipline is Spartan; their lives, their education is Spartan; everything about them is Spartan, and their faith and commitment are so unshakable that they too will rise to the cry "With the shield or on a shield!"

January 24, 1954

In his biography of Shakespeare, Victor Hugo says beautiful things; he is particularly eloquent when he talks about books: "The enormous human Bible made up of all the prophets, all the poets, all the philosophers, will blaze resplendently in the glow of that huge bright lens known as compulsory education." His words have been prophetic in the countries where compulsory education has been established, but in many countries, including our own, it is compulsory only in theory: suffering, incompetence, and outdated ideas are even more compulsory.

January 27

You ask me if Rolland would have been as influential if he had been born in the seventeenth century. A man's thinking is definitely conditioned by his time, and I would even say that political genius is totally conditioned by the age in which one lives. In the time of Catherine the Great, when the aristocracy was the ruling class, Lenin might have been a staunch supporter of the bourgeoisie, which was then the revolutionary class, or he simply could have been ignored by history. If Martí had been alive during the British takeover of Havana, he would have fought alongside his father for the Spanish flag. What else would Napoleon, Mirabeau, Danton, and Robespierre have been in the days of Charlemagne but humble serfs in some feudal castle? There would have been no reason for Julius Caesar to cross the Rubicon in the first years of the Republic, before the intense class struggles became serious enough to shake the foundations of Rome, and before the huge plebeian party developed, making Caesar's rise to power possible and necessary. Julius Caesar was a true revolutionary, and so was Catherine, but Cicero, so greatly revered in history, was the embodiment of the Roman aristocracy. That did not stop the French revolutionaries from condemning Caesar and praising Brutus, who plunged the dagger into Caesar's heart for the ruling class. Yet the revolutionaries lacked sufficient historical perspective to see that the Roman Republic was like the French monarchy, and that the common people fought against the patricians, as the French bourgeoisie was then fighting against the aristocracy. They never dreamed that a new Caesar who would indeed imitate the Roman emperor was about to come to power in France. While on this subject, I had always wondered why the French revolutionaries were influenced so much by the Romans until one day, reading a history of French literature, I discovered that Amyot, a sixteenth-century French writer, had translated Plutarch's Lives from the Latin; its accounts of the great men and events of Greece and Rome was used two centuries later as a guide for the protagonists of the great French Revolution.

But literary, artistic, and philosophical genius doesn't depend so much on the particular period. Rolland could have been born fifty years earlier and he still would have been as brilliant as Balzac and Victor

Hugo, and another fifty years earlier, he would have been equal to Voltaire, though their ideas would have been very different.

All ideas, even those of brilliant men, are conditioned by their time. Aristotle's philosophy is the culmination of the writings of earlier Greek philosophers, such as Parmenides, Socrates, and Plato; his work would not have been possible without them. Similarly, Marx's doctrines bring the efforts of utopian socialists to a culmination in the social field, and synthesize German idealism and materialism in philosophy. Yet Marx was not only a philosopher but a political genius as well, and, in that aspect, his role depends entirely on the epoch and setting in which he lived.

A genius like Cervantes or Shakespeare creates characters of universal value. Like Dostoevski, they knew about psychoanalysis long before Freud came along—not from scientific research but from penetrating with incredible acuteness into the deep workings of the human mind. Sometimes they are light-years ahead of their times.

Literary, philosophical, and artistic geniuses have considerably greater scope in time and history than political geniuses who are locked into the world of reality and action, the only setting in which they live.

February 12

I write quickly, and sometimes illegibly, partly because of the teachers I had when I was in my teens. They did not make me kneel, but they did make me write a thousand times: "I must not talk in class" or "I must behave in line." Instead of having me write the same sentence over and over, Brother Salgueiro (a Jesuit at the Dolores School in Santiago de Cuba, who was in charge of the boarding students) had me do division problems with six digits in the dividend and three in the divisor—usually twenty problems each time I misbehaved. Once he even had me do a hundred problems just "to give me a hard time"—that's what he said—on the morning of a holiday. He was a very short Spaniard, but with a terrible temper. Out of respect for the cloth, he never cursed when he got angry; he was proud of how he made us cringe, but he was not a bad person.

One time, when we came back after some holidays, my two brothers and I brought a parakeet from Birán for the father prefect, who really loved those birds. He set up a perch in the small garden next to the study where the dreaded priest watched over us. The first thing the parakeet, coached by the boarders, learned to repeat was: "Salgueiro, twenty math problems!" The parakeet repeated this over and over when we were in the study. All the guys really got a big kick out of this! And the expression on the priest's face! It was the prefect's bird, so the priest couldn't touch it. Finally, they gave the parakeet to the San José Sanctuary, where the nuns even taught it to pray and amazing stories were told about it.

March

I have been alone in a small cell for more than two weeks. Countless books have gone through my hands in that time, and I definitely prefer the novels of Dostoevski, who is certainly the greatest Russian writer. I will talk more about him some other time. *The Brothers Karamazov, The Insulted and Injured, Crime and Punishment, The Idiot,* and *The House of the Dead* are his best-known works. I have all of them here, plus his first novel, *Poor Folk,* and "Proarchin," a short story. I only have *The Brothers K.* and Balzac's *The Wild Ass's Skin* left to read. I have already read Stefan Zweig's biography of Balzac, which is primarily a self-portrait. Rómulo Gallego's *Over the Same Ground* is a charming book, and I liked *The Stars Look Down* very much for the light it throws on the social problem in England—though I do not agree with its skepticism of the end, without a word of encouragement for the defeated fighter. I am halfway through *The Razor's Edge;* it is so interesting that I have to keep myself from reading it all in one sitting.

Which book on Napoleon are you reading, Ludwig's or Hugo's? The Big one or the Little one? If it is the latter, we are both reading the same book right now. What a coincidence! It is so much like my own life that if someone were to make a movie about it, he'd have to emphasize in big letters that "Any similarity is purely coincidental." I am so excited reading Victor Hugo's *Les Misérables* that it is impossible to put it into words; and yet I am getting a little tired of his excessive romanticism, his wordiness, and his erudition, which is sometimes so tiresome and exaggerated. Karl Marx's *The Eighteenth Brumaire of Louis Bonaparte* is a terrific book, also on the subject of Napoleon III. Comparing these books, one appreciates the huge difference between a scientific, realistic conception of history and a purely romantic one. While Hugo sees only a lucky adventurer, Marx sees the inevitable results of the social contradictions and the conflict of interests prevailing in those days. For Hugo, history is a series of chance happenings, while for Marx, it is a process governed by certain laws. Hugo's lines bring back to mind our own talks, filled with a poetic faith in liberty, the righteous indignation against the outrages committed against it, and the hope that it will, in some miraculous way, be reborn.

I must also speak to you about Freud. I already have four of the eighteen volumes of his complete works and I hope to get the rest soon; they contain a world of interesting theories. I want to understand for myself their importance, and apply them to some characters of Dostoevski, who, in his art, preceded Freud's great scientific research into the secrets of the subconscious.

But my attention is really focused on something else. I have rolled my sleeves up and begun studying world history and political theory.

March 18

After drinking some piping-hot coffee the guys next door sent me in a Thermos, I lighted a cigar, and began writing to you with all the more pleasure because I had spent the day studying Kant's *Critique of Pure Reason,* and I needed a break.

I dozed off as soon as I finished reading the "Transcendental Aesthetic of Space and Time." Naturally, time and space vanished from my thoughts for a good while. Kant brought to mind Einstein and his theory on the relativity of time and space and his famous equation, $E \, \mathrel{\unicode{xBF}} \, mc^2$ (energy equals mass, times the speed of light squared); the possible connection between their ideas, perhaps the opposite of each other; Kant's conviction that he had definitive criteria that would rescue philosophy—beaten down by the experimental sciences—from its collapse, and the telling results of Einstein's discoveries. Descartes's ideas could not stand up against the facts of Galileo's and Copernicus's proved experiments—would this have happened to Kant? Kant does not try to explain the nature of things, but rather the means by which we arrive at knowledge of them: Whether it is possible to know something and, if it is, under what conditions is knowledge true or false. It is a philosophy of knowledge, not a philosophy of the objects of knowledge. That is why Kant and Einstein do not contradict each other. Yet his concepts of space and time do exist, they are the basic points on which he rests his philosophical system. Is there a contradiction? Obviously, it would not be difficult to find this out, but as I was asking myself this question, among many others, I thought of how little we know and of the immense ground man has covered with his intelligence and hard work through the centuries. Even so, the very relativity of those convictions makes me sad: so many theories, doctrines, and beliefs, now out of date, that long ago were like bibles of science. Man has had to pay dearly for human progress! Yet I never stopped wondering if it was worthwhile spending my time on such studies, if they would help me combat existing evils. Still, one can only feel a deep reverence for those men who gave their whole lives to thinking and finding ways to leave a legacy to humanity.

March 23

You can grow so fond of people that it seems as if you have always loved them; it is hard to imagine how it all started. It is worth it though, when we consider that we've built something solid and indestructible with something as delicate and tenuous as our feelings. Love is like a diamond, the hardest and purest of all minerals, able to scratch anything, but nothing can scratch it. But you cannot polish just one facet; it is not perfect until all its edges have been cut and shaped. Then it sparkles from all angles with an incomparable radiance. The metaphor would be perfect if the diamond, once buffed and polished, could grow bigger and bigger. A genuine love is based on many feelings, not just one, and they gradually balance each other off, each reflecting the light of the others.

Here is a quick rundown of my opinions on a few things. Robespierre was an idealist and an honest man right up to his death. The Revolution was in danger, the frontiers surrounded by enemies on all sides, traitors ready to plunge a dagger into one's back, the fence sitters were blocking the way—one had to be harsh, inflexible, tough—it was better to go too far than not to go far enough, because everything might have been lost. The few months of the Terror were necessary to do away with a terror that had lasted for centuries. In Cuba, we need more Robespierres; as Mira says in his chapter on the psychology of revolutionary behavior: "The moment the radicals carry the flag and direct the revolution to its climax, then the tide begins to ebb." This stage began in France precisely with fall of Robespierre. As someone has said: "Like Saturn, the Revolution devours its own children." Maybe I will be able to explain this better later on.

Giuliano* may really have been a kind of Robin Hood. Anyone who has taken from the rich and given to the poor has always won over the common people. There are some ages that justify more or less the means and conditions that favor or obstruct legend. Robin Hood belongs to the romantic, chivalrous Middle Ages, a time of individual feats; Giuliano belongs to our time, a time of great social revolutions, powerful nations, and mass movements.

March 24

Have you ever been able to imagine how alone I am in this cell? Since I like to cook, I sometimes keep busy by preparing some dish. The other day, my brother sent me a small ham from Oriente, and I made myself a steak with guava jelly, and today, some of the guys sent me a little jar of pineapple rings in syrup. All I have to do is think about something and, presto! it's here! So tomorrow I will eat ham and pineapple. How about that? Once in a while I also cook spaghetti, by different recipes of my own invention, or a cheese omelet. They come out great! Of course my repertoire doesn't stop there: I also filter my coffee, and it comes out delicious. In the last few days, I have been lucky enough to receive a box of H. Upmann cigars from Dr. Miró Cardona, two excellent boxes from my brother Ramón, and a handful from a friend, and finally, a very nice little box with books I'm very grateful for. I am smoking a cigar right now, but you're wrong, I am not chain-smoking, though my floor is strewn with butts.

Around 7:00 p.m., I turn on the light, and the war against the mosquitoes begins. When I'm writing, I keep them away with the heavy

---

* Salvatore Giuliano, a Sicilian bandit of the 1940s.

smoke from my cigars. If I am not careful, each time I go in and out of the mosquito net, they sneak in and I have to hunt them down one by one. And whenever I sit down to read, something always happens: I forget to bring in the colored pencil, so I go outside the net to get it; I open a book and I realize I have the wrong volume, or I forget the dictionary or my glasses and I have to leave the net again. It is a mess! That's why I have a small heap of things on the right side of the bed and another one on top of the bed to make it easier for myself. But I do take care of my things.

I try to read ten, twelve, or fourteen hours a day, till I can't keep my eyes open. The ants here eat everything: cheese, oil, bread; but oddly enough, they do not come near the condensed milk. A battle is always raging among the little creatures: the flies fight it out with the mosquitoes, the spiders catch flies, and the tiny ants carry off the leftovers like small vultures. The cell, cramped and narrow for me, is an enormous world for them. A hummingbird sometimes appears at the windows, way up. Seeing it happy and free makes me understand better than ever that it is evil to cage birds, and I also remember *The Story of San Michele*. A few oblique rays of sunlight come in from above at dusk and project the shadow of the prison bars on the cell floor for a few minutes.

The latest books are all terrific. Napoleon knew the French inside and out—his harangues and proclamations are genuine works of art! He plays on them in each phrase, strumming the most sensitive strings one by one. The little book is a stirring account of serious politics, government, and affairs of state. How generous Napoleon was with his enemies! I have read many books about him and I never get bored. As some forgotten author said, Napoleon was an Alexander without his doubts, a Caesar without his shameful vices, a Charlemagne who did not slaughter whole nations, and a Frederick II with a good nature and a heart open to friendship. I always thought Napoleon was the best. You have to keep in mind that Alexander inherited the powerful throne of Macedonia from Philip, his father, Hannibal was given an army seasoned by war by his father, Hamilcar Barca, the famous Carthaginian general, and Caesar owed a lot to his patrician ancestry. Napoleon owed nothing to anyone, only to his own genius and will. Napoleon would never have done what Alexander did—a man so jealous of anything clouding his own glory that he caused the death of some of his best men, like Philotas, head of the Macedonian cavalry, and later that of Philotas's father, Parmenio, his best general, a man to whom Alexander owed so many of his victories.

April 4

I take some sun for a few hours every afternoon, and also Tuesday, Thursday, and Sunday mornings, in a large, solitary courtyard completely enclosed by a gallery. I will end up forgetting how to talk after spending so many pleasant hours in it.

It is eleven and night, and I have been reading Lenin's *State and Revolution* since six, without a break, after finishing two books by Marx, *The Eighteenth Brumaire of Louis Bonaparte* and *The Class Struggles in France*. These three priceless books have a lot in common.

I am hungry so have put some spaghetti with stuffed squid on the boil. In the meantime, I have picked up my pen to write you a few more lines. I forgot to tell you that I cleaned my cell last Friday. First I washed down the granite floor with soap and water, then with scouring powder and detergent, and finally I rinsed it with creosote and water. I put my stuff in place and everything's spic and span now. The rooms in the Hotel Nacional are not this clean. . . . The heat "forces" me to take two showers every day; I feel great afterward! I pick up a book and sometimes feel kind of happy. My travels through the fields of philosophy have been very useful to me; after breaking my head over Kant for a while, Marx seems easier to understand than the Lord's Prayer. Marx and Lenin each had a weighty polemical spirit, and I have to laugh. It is fun, and I have a good time reading them. They would not give an inch, and they were dreaded by their enemies: two genuine prototypes of the revolutionary.

I'm going to dine on spaghetti with squid, Italian candy for dessert, a hot cup of coffee, and then an H. Upmann No. 4—don't you envy me? They take good care of me, each one doing a little bit; I am always arguing with them not to send me things, but they don't listen. When I sit outside in my shorts in the morning and feel the sun and the sea breeze, I think I am on a beach and later, here, in a small restaurant. They will make me think I am on vacation! What would Karl Marx say about such revolutionaries?

April 11

They took me to the courtroom a few days ago. It had been a long time since I had seen fields or open spaces; the landscape here is beautiful, sunny, brimming with light. I spent a good while talking about national affairs to some friendly clerks of the lower court. I felt uncomfortable and strange when I got back to my cell.

Oddly enough, I have no personal ambitions; I can fall back on moral resources, a sense of honor, dignity, and duty. The main contradiction in my life boils down to this: I am a man who is absolutely indifferent to punishment—physical or material, to biological existence; I can always take that with a smile, and my only prison or chains, the only thing that can bring me to my knees, is my sense of duty. I am very strong physically and I don't think physical force can ever sway me, because I am not afraid. Yet, the moral man within me makes the physical man give in. The natural rebel always fights against clear, cold logic, which has a strong moral basis. Don't you think that such a man is consumed like a candle in the fire of its own flames?

April 15

I want to find out as much as I can about Roosevelt and his policies: in the agricultural sector, raising the prices of farm products, conserving and increasing the fertility of the soil, ways of providing credit, canceling debts, expanding national and international markets; in the area of social programs, more jobs, reducing the workweek, raising salaries, social benefits for the unemployed, the aged, and the sick; and restructuring industry, new tax systems, regulating trusts, and banking and monetary reforms, in the area of the general economy. The U.S. economy was stagnant and on the brink of collapse when Roosevelt gave it a shot in the arm by stimulating and reorganizing the country's resources, reducing certain privileges, and attacking powerful interests. The prosperity that followed, after years dominated by poverty, was not the by-product of chance or the famous free play of supply and demand, but the result of the sound measures courageously taken by the government. He attacked the conservative spirit entrenched in the Supreme Court; he had to get rid of a few old men legally, by pensioning them off. Given the character, the mentality, the history of the people of the United States, Roosevelt actually did some wonderful things, and some of his countrymen have never forgiven him for doing them.

The similarity between the great social reforms of the past and those of the present is interesting. Many measures adopted by the Paris Commune of 1870 could be found in the laws of Julius Caesar. The problems of agriculture, housing, debts, and unemployment have been faced by all societies since the distant past. I love the magnificent spectacle offered by the great revolutions of history: they have always meant the victory of the huge majority's aspirations for a decent life and happiness over the interests of a small group. Do you know what I consider very moving? The revolt of the black slaves in Haiti. There was Napoleon acting like Caesar, as if France were Rome, when a new Spartacus appeared, Toussaint L'Ouverture. What a small place in history is given to the rebelling African slaves who established a free republic by routing Napoleon's best generals! I know Haiti has not progressed much since then, but have any of the other Latin American republics fared any better? I am always thinking about these things because I would honestly love to revolutionize this country from one end to the other! I am sure this would bring happiness to the Cuban people. I would not be stopped by the hatred and ill will of a few thousand people, including some of my relatives, half the people I know, two-thirds of my fellow professionals, and four-fifths of my ex-schoolmates.

They told me how enthusiastically you have been fighting; I feel very sad that I am not there with you.*

1. Our propaganda must not let up for one minute because it is the heart of the struggle. It should have a style of its own and adjust itself to the immediate situation. You must continually keep on denouncing all the murders. M.** will tell you about a pamphlet*** whose ideological thrust and unbelievable accusations will have decisive importance. I want you to read it carefully. The twenty-sixth of July must be commemorated with dignity. You must manage one way or another to hold a rally on the front steps of the university. It will be a terrible blow to the government; you should start planning now and plan it well. There should also be rallies in high schools in Santiago de Cuba and abroad. Contact the Ortodoxo Party in New York, Mexico, and Costa Rica. Gustavo Arcos should get together with heads of the FEU about the university rally.

2. We must coordinate the efforts of our people here and abroad. To do this, you should go to Mexico, as soon as possible, to meet with Raúl Martínez and Léster Rodríguez. Study the situation well and then decide what line to follow. Use great care when considering any proposal to align ourselves with other groups—they may just want to use our name as they did with Pardo Llada**** and his friends, that is, discrediting any other group that might overshadow them. Do not take a back seat; do not agree to anything that is not based on a clear, solid foundation, has a good chance of succeeding, and will definitely benefit Cuba. Otherwise, it is better for you to continue alone and stick by our high standards until these impressive young men get out of prison, where they are carefully readying themselves for the struggle ahead. "To know how to wait," said Martí, "is the great secret of success."

3. Keep your eyes open and smile at everyone. Use the same tactics we used during the trial: defend our viewpoint, without stepping on anyone's toes. There will be plenty of time later to squash all the cockroaches. Don't be discouraged by anyone or anything; we have proved before that we could take it. One last warning: avoid rivalries. When you have fame and prestige, mediocre people readily find causes or excuses to be touchy. Take any help you can get, but remember, don't trust anyone.

---

* Melba Hernández; she and Haydée Santamaría had just been released from prison.—C. F.
** Mirta Díaz Balart, then Fidel's wife.—ED.
*** *History Will Absolve Me*, rewritten by Fidel in the Isle of Pines prison.—ED.
**** See footnote, p. 53.

June

I am still isolated from my comrades, no doubt because they want to block the intellectual growth of these young men; they think of them as their diehard enemies of the future. I can't even trade books with them. But things are improving in other ways. They've brought Raúl here, and my cell (which you saw in *Bohemia**) is now connected to another room four times as large with a big courtyard kept open from 7:00 a.m. to 9:30 p.m. The prison staff does the cleaning, the lights are off when we sleep, we don't have any roll calls or lineups, we can sleep late—improvements I didn't really ask for.

We have all the water we want, electric light, food, clean clothes, and it is all free, even the rent. Do you think it is better on the outside? We can have visitors twice a month. It is very peaceful here now, but I do not know how much longer this "paradise" will last. There will be lots of grumbling and groaning after the elections, and the regime will have to declare an amnesty to ease tension in the country. What to do with political prisoners is becoming more of an issue each day—it is deplorable how they have been ignored. There's a big difference between the politicians' position and ours. Our hour is near: we were only a handful before, but we now must close ranks with the people; we must change our tactics. Those who see us as a small band will be badly mistaken—we will never think or act as a small group. What is more, I will now be able to put my heart and soul, all my time and energy, into the struggle. I will be starting a new life, and I plan to overcome all obstacles and wage battles whenever necessary. I see the road we must take and our goals more clearly than ever. Prison has not been a waste of time: I have been able to study, observe, analyze, plan, and shape men. I know where and how to find Cuba's best. I began alone; now we are many.

June 18

There are a few things I would like you to consider carefully:

1. The speech. At least 100,000 copies of the speech should be circulated within four months. This must be done according to an organized plan concerted throughout Cuba. Copies should be mailed to all news reporters, law offices, doctors, and regular and professional schools. It should be done as carefully as if you were handling weapons, to make sure that none of our caches is found or any of our men arrested. You had better use at least two different printers, the cheapest ones you can find; each run of 10,000 should cost no more than $300. You must all work together in this. The speech is extremely important; it contains our platform and ideology, and without them, we cannot accomplish any-

---

* The leading Cuban anti-Batista magazine.

thing. It gives a full report of the crimes committed; they have not been publicized widely enough, and that is our first duty to our dead comrades. It also talks about the part played by Haydée and Melba, which should be disclosed, in order to make their work easier.

2. Financial matters should be handled cautiously and coordinated. The cost of printing the speech should take preference over other expenses. I am sure many people will help you once they have read the speech, because it is the strongest statement yet made against the government.

3. Start a drive immediately to protest my being held incommunicado. It makes it harder for me to get things done.

4. Organize high-school rallies for the twenty-sixth of July. It will be difficult to set up a large rally at the university, but maybe a small one could be held in the Hall of Martyrs. Talk it over with the students and get together with the university rector. I will try and get *Bohemia* and the radio stations to talk about the anniversary. Don't forget to send a letter to Mexico concerning the events planned for the twenty-sixth and go see Conchita Fernández about contacting the Ortodoxo Party of New York about it. There should be no acts of violence that day; we have to save our energies for the right moment. We need propaganda now: without it, there will be no mass movements and without mass movements, no revolution. Don't forget that without Chibás's harangue, we would not have been able to gather 2000 men, and if we had had enough weapons, we would have been victorious.

June 19

It may be hard to believe but Abel and I often did not see eye to eye, although our ideas were very similar. I would often get an idea that he would disagree with from the start, but I was sure that he would end up seeing it my way once I explained my point of view. Though he was new to the struggle, his intuition and intelligence were exceptionally fine. I always had the fullest confidence in his judgment when there was no time for us to confer.

With things the way they are now, we can't discuss every issue as we once could, but we have a plan of action we must stick to. I told them in Santiago de Cuba that all of you had earned a spot in the leadership of the movement; I made that clear right after I got together with other comrades in prison, and we officially approved it. We also decided that the headquarters for the movement would be here on the Island of Pines, where the majority of the leaders and the self-sacrificing comrades who had voluntarily chosen prison were to be found. Any major decision should, therefore, be made from here. As part of the leadership in charge of the movement on the outside, you must obey our decisions to the letter with the zeal and discipline required by the duties and responsibilities of the positions you hold.

The notion of making a deal with the Auténticos is a serious ideological deviation. If we would not do it before—when they had millions and we were begging for pennies and denying ourselves everything to buy weapons—why should we do it now, defiling the memory of those who died for their untarnished ideas? We did not think the Auténticos had the ability, morale, or ideology to lead a revolution. If we were not fooled by their tall tales, fantasies, and boasts in the past, why should we believe them now?

The revolution cannot mean the restoration to power of men who have been utterly discredited by history, and who are fully responsible for the situation we are now in. Remember that our chances of success are rooted in the firm belief that the people will back up efforts of untarnished men whose revolutionary beliefs come before everything else. Those who have deceived or betrayed the people can never again expect their support.

Our mission, as I want to convince you, is no longer concerned with setting up revolutionary cells so as to have a few more men available— that would be a fatal mistake. What we must do now is to get public opinion behind us, make our ideas known, and win the support of the masses. Our revolutionary program is the soundest, our intent is perfectly clear, our history is marked by personal sacrifice; we deserve the support of the people, and without it—I will repeat it a thousand times—no revolution is possible. Once we pioneered these ideas in secret; now we have to fight for them in the open, with totally new tactics.

We can't worry about ten men: we have to create the conditions to be able to mobilize tens of thousands when the time comes. I know what this involves, because I had to fight against a million intrigues to find and organize our first men. Only solid ideas can defeat intrigues and mediocrity—we have to implant these ideas so that the men we recruit will not change their stand the way they change shirts.

We have to kick out anybody in our ranks who is trigger-happy and ready to make a deal with the devil just to get a gun. This must be done without qualms, just as there must be no qualms, when the time comes, about shooting cowardly turncoats, who are generally the ones that make a big show about wanting to fight. We do not want gangsters or soldiers of fortune, but men who are aware of their historical role and are willing to wait and work patiently for the future of their homeland.

If we are not on the right track, why is it that the people's support for us grows day by day, while groups that were once strong are slowly disappearing?

Because of our stand, we can count on the full support of the Ortodoxo Party, which is untouched by factions and represents thousands of citizens.

Why must we keep affirming our support for Chibás's ideas? The recording of his last appeal, which we brought to Santiago, is a formidable instrument to rouse the people. Wasn't the most radical position spelled out in that recording?

Our hopes lie with the people. Let us take our program, the one true revolutionary program, and our ideas out into the streets as soon as we can! Then we can organize the great revolutionary movement that will consecrate the ideals of those who have died.

I hope you will be able to live up to the faith and trust we have placed in you. It is going to be hard, but I will take care of any criticism as I did when we used to get together on Twenty-fifth Street. The new leaders must be able to take the place of those who are now gone.

July

A campaign should be organized at once to protest my being kept in solitary confinement. It has been 90 days now, and it is infinitely worse than it was in Boniato.*

July 5

I have just heard on the 11:00 p.m. CMQ news broadcast that "the secretary of the interior has fired Mirta Díaz Balart." Since I can't really believe she was ever an employee of that ministry, I have begun a libel suit against the secretary. If this is the work of her brother Rafael,** I will demand that he publicly take up the allegation with Hermida,*** even if it costs him his job or his life. He can't shirk his responsibility to his sister who is in a difficult position, with her husband in jail.

July 17

It's all a plot against me; it's the most vicious, cowardly, indecent, despicable, and intolerable act.

Only an effeminate creature like Hermida would go to such inconceivably indecent and unmanly lengths. Doesn't a political prisoner deserve some respect? Can a prisoner let himself be insulted like that? Can't a prisoner challenge someone to fight him when he gets out of jail? Does he have to taste the bitterness of disgrace while he is powerless and hopeless behind bars? I am ready to come to blows with my own brother-in-law when I get the chance. I would rather die a thousand times than have to put up with such an insult!

---

* The prison in which Fidel and the other Moncada attackers were held before their trial.—ED.

** Rafael Díaz Balart had been a classmate of mine at Havana University, and together we shared our first political awakenings as students—that is how I met his sister, who later became my wife. As time went by, he took a different road and joined Batista's party two years before the coup d'état; that is how he and his father rose to high positions in Batista's tyrannical administration. He was then under secretary of the interior, and he put her name on the payroll as an employee of the department; thus, the unpleasant incident.—F. C.

*** Ramón Hermida was secretary of the interior.—ED.

July 31

I was on my bed in my underpants, reading, around 1:15 p.m., when a guard came to my cell and told me to come to attention. Before I could do anything, the commanding officer and two men dressed in cotton twill came in. The officer said: "Castro, Gastón Godoy and Marino López Blanco want to meet you and say hello." I said: "Okay, but you could have let me know ahead of time." "We want to know how you're being treated," López Blanco said. I answered: "It hasn't been easy, but I never thought of prison as a tourist hotel or a palace." We talked for another five or six minutes about unimportant things and then they said good-bye. As they were leaving, the officer added: "Castro, the secretary of the interior is here and wants to say hello, but he's not sure how you will receive him." I answered: "Commandant, I am not a savage who is going to frighten him with vulgarity and curses. However, I am angry at some of the statements he has made, and if I talk to him, it will be to ask for an apology." The officer replied: "I think it would be best if you did not bring up that point." "In that case, sir, I think I had better not see the secretary," I said.

But five minutes later, I heard the call to attention again. The secretary of the interior came in and put out his hand in a friendly way. The first thing he told me was that he remembered meeting me at Cossío del Pino's funeral. And then he went on: "Castro, I want you to know that neither I nor the president is your personal enemy. I have nothing against you; I'm only doing my job as secretary of the interior. You are prisoners here because you were sentenced by the courts, and I'm here to carry out the president's wishes and see that the prisons are run smoothly." He added: "Batista is an easygoing man. In the twenty years I've known him, I've never seen him get nasty with anyone or even raise his voice. I know I'm not like that, and so people say that I'm rude." The commanding officer broke in: "Each time I see the president he asks about the political prisoners and says 'Treat them like gentlemen, because they are gentlemen.'"

I listened quietly and said: "I have never thought of our struggle as a personal quarrel; it is a fight against the ruling political system." I added: "Some of your statements questioning my moral integrity have hurt me very deeply. You have no right to smear my name simply because someone related to me, and to certain high government officials, was put on the payroll of some department; it was done without my knowledge or approval. I'm behind bars, I can't defend myself, nor even try to prove my innocence, or even put the blame on those officials who have taken advantage of family ties and treated me unfairly. If I can't be bribed with all the millions in the Treasury, why go to such lengths to try to impugn my moral integrity?"

The secretary then said: "Look, Castro, I know it's Rafaelito's fault—he's always acting like a spoiled brat. I swear on my honor that I didn't want to attack you; someone rewrote the open letter you're talking about, changing my words. No one doubts your honesty. There's no one in Cuba whose stand is clearer than yours. Be patient, I too was a political prisoner in 1931 and 1932; I stationed myself at the Country Club many times to make an attack on Machado and Ortiz. You're a young man; take it easy, these things happen all the time."

"Okay," I said, "I'll take your word for it now, but I still plan to get to the bottom of this when I get out of here. As for you, I realize that you've done the right thing in trying to correct the affront; as you well know, the only time there is no excuse for humiliating someone, or, worse, for attacking his family, is when he can't really defend himself; Cubans are a noble people and they hate that kind of intrigue from the bottom of their hearts."

August 14

The cutthroat personalities and ambitions of a few leaders and factions is one of the biggest obstacles in keeping a movement like ours intact. It is difficult to get each man to sacrifice his prestige and self-importance for a cause, an ideology, or a discipline, to put aside his pride and ambition. The first thing I have to do is organize the men of the 26th of July into an unbreakable front—those in prison, in exile, or free. There are more than eighty men who were involved in this step in history and made the same sacrifices. That well-knit, disciplined force will be invaluable in forming cadres for insurrectional as well as civilian action. A great civilian-political movement has to be strong enough to overthrow those in power, whether by peaceful or by revolutionary means; otherwise, it runs the risk of having victory snatched from it; that happened to the Ortodoxo Party two months before the elections.

Our first task is to unite all our fighters; it would be a terrible thing if failure to do this resulted later on in important defections from our ranks. My experience before July 26 has shown me that one trustworthy young man is worth a thousand others, and that the most difficult and slowest task is finding qualified men and preparing them well so their participation in the struggle can be effective from the outset. Apart from the men we already have, we can increase our numbers enormously, building up solid, strong, disciplined forces, ready to join others like themselves to defeat the ruling class. Ideology, discipline, and leadership are essential to build a true mass movement, but leadership comes first. I don't remember if it was Napoleon who said that a bad general on the battlefield is worth more than twenty good ones away from it.

A movement can't be organized when everybody thinks he has the right to make public statements without consulting anyone else; and you can't expect much from a movement made up of anarchists who, at the first disagreement with the others, take the easiest way out, splitting up and wrecking the machinery. The propaganda and organizational machine must be strong enough to crush anyone who tries to form factions or cliques or schisms, or rebels against the movement. Political realities should be firmly kept in mind. Our platform should be comprehensive, concrete, and courageous in dealing with the serious social and economic problems facing our country, so that the masses will be offered a truly new and hopeful program.

September 5

I would have preferred it if you had all put your energies into propaganda work, tying up the loose ends and oiling the springs, instead of spending so much time in clandestine meetings and going after new converts: I can never repeat too often that propaganda rallies the people under one flag. The 26th of July would never have come about if we had not organized those who had been swayed by Eduardo Chibás's teachings. The emphasis on action over propaganda is the result of the delusory atmosphere of rebellion that prevailed for so many months.

As I finish this letter, so many things weigh heavily on my mind: the house in Oriente where I was born and lived has recently burned down; I haven't heard a word about my son in months; my family life has gone to pieces, and soon nothing will be left of it; my feelings have recently been severely tested; with me behind bars, my enemies have been more vicious and more treacherous than ever.

October 3

I have thought long and deeply about where our Movement stands and what it can do for Cuba. For months, I have been under inhuman strain and grueling problems have sapped my strength; a fundamental sense of propriety, duty, and responsibility has forced me to make certain decisions I will put into effect as soon as I have the support of my fellow prisoners, in whose hands the chief ideological and tactical leadership of our struggle has rested so far.

The responsibility and revolutionary ethics those of us in prison here owe the Movement are not functioning right now. Several things have brought on this situation: the most important being our strict prison life and almost total isolation; another thing is the poor cooperation of our activists on the outside, which can be blamed in part on circumstances beyond their control and also on a lessening of a sense of personal responsibility.

Right now it is impossible to settle on a line of action that we can be sure all our comrades will support. We are in a crisis as serious as those brought on by false alarms that divided our ranks before July 26 and made many units abandon our cause. Having to endure hunger, hard work, and all kinds of difficulties, our exiled comrades can only despair. Their activities are determined by the financial help they get from those who have the money. I know that if we were with them in Mexico, they would join us, even if we had to swim back, and we would do it without letting anybody know about it. But here we are in jail, and to get back to their own country they will follow—even if the leader's orders mean death—not because he shares their ideals but because he has better financial backing. Their fate worries me, for they are good men and Cuba needs them. In the revolutionary plans they are making there, the 26th of July has been completely overlooked. I place most of the blame for this on our leaders in Cuba, who seem to be blindly headed for suicide. It is amazing that they did not see the vested interests fiercely plotting against the 26th of July, because our Movement was something altogether new in the history of Cuba; it was a display of faith and valor by a handful of young men without political experience, without any resources whatever, who didn't rob, attack, or kidnap anyone to collect funds. They skillfully eluded the watchful eyes of the dictatorship and threw themselves with unparalleled energy against forces more powerful and numerically superior to any seen during the wars of liberation; moreover, theirs was a precise battle strategy and a total revolutionary platform.

It was logical for the privileged classes and the political hierarchies to feel their lives threatened by the awakening of a new revolutionary generation. Never had political interests joined so closely together to try to crush and silence forever such a unique display of heroism, ideals, sacrifice, and love of country. Even some who have commemorated that date have tried, under the guise of praise, to deny its true significance. "It has been said over and over again that the Moncada Barracks attack was impulsive and rash, not coherently planned. Their greatest merit lies precisely in what they are reproached for. They did not go there to take power, but to die" (Aracelio Ascuy's* speech in the Spanish Atheneum). Instead of rejecting such words, people accept them as praise for us, but they deny us our true merit: we were willing to die for a greater cause, but they deprive us of our ideas, deny our revolutionary objectives, which means negating everything we fought for. Our duty was not to be the accomplices of the inertia generated by this conspiracy of silence and mystification that denied and vilified our struggle; our duty was to fight it with all the skills, intelligence, and perseverance we had. That should have been the first and principal objective of those on the outside, but you have not even tried, much less succeeded. What have you been doing with your time and energy? The police have tried to hide their crimes and make us look like a gang of thieves; the politicians have tried to silence our true merits. What have our friends done to stop them? I am not sure you know that whatever has been done to stop them out there was started by us in here. We believed you were paving the

* Ascuy was an Auténtico Party leader.—Ed.

way while we hatched an ideal revolution with persistent study and political education. We believed in vain.

All those pseudorevolutionaries are interested only in splitting apart the Movement and sharing the spoils like mangy vultures. They are common political schemers, incapable of rounding up and preparing men, and that's why they acted as if they were too good for the Movement; they only wanted to use their men as cannon fodder. Things would be different if we were free, and they know it! The 26th of July Movement would either be in the vanguard of a close-knit, orderly revolution or the Movement would carry it out on its own. But nobody cares if we are free.

I cannot put an end to the confusion and chaos of the Movement from in here, since I am almost totally incommunicado. I have also heard that some people are challenging the right of those of us here in prison to lead the Movement, urging that the organization be restructured in such a way that our group, the heart and soul of the Movement, will be left powerless. The orders, always given with their full consent, are either not being carried out, carried out badly, or totally ignored. We can't go on steering the Movement from here like that. Understand that, from now on, you bear the entire responsibility in the eyes of history.

I know that I have been criticized for talking about a revolutionary mass movement instead of scattering plans of rebellion to the four winds. My dear revolutionary experts, don't forget that a few days before July 26, I was sowing rice in Pinar del Río! Or do you think those of us in prison have stopped fighting because a more radical wing has sprung up?

I am very bitter about the way you have handled my speech. What was the good of my sacrifices and my killing myself with work? You have had five months to bring the speech to the people. Your indifference proves how pitifully little you know about the importance of ideas shaping history.

I want this letter to express how much I appreciate the full, exemplary loyalty given me at all times by Melba Hernández and Haydée Santamaría.

This letter has been approved by all the comrades who are prisoners on the Isle of Pines, and each will sign it; I will immediately send it on to you.

December 13

I'd like to have Villaverde's *Cecilia Valdés;* I haven't thought of it for years, but now I'm in a hurry to have it. I spent many happy days reading this wonderful book on Cuban history, fascinated, forgetting everything else; I was practically transported back into the last century by it.

The desire to learn more about our past, our people, our ancestors has been preying on my mind for some time. The enthusiasm, love, and interest I put into all my reading on this subject is a big help to me. This time, in my second reading of this book that depicts the age so accurately, I want to check up on a few aspects of the Cuban way of thinking, especially the problem of slavery. This problem is particularly interesting because I've been observing more and more that much of the confusion and indecision that marked Cuban political thinking up to the decade of 1868 was derived from it.

1955

I'm not asking, and will never ask for amnesty. I have enough sense of my own dignity to stay here twenty years or die of rage before that. But at least let me fly off the handle and once in a while tell a lot of people to go fly a kite, and send to the devil those loud-mouths who are always looking for a way to make me lose my patience.

To Luis Conte Agüero: March 15

I know I have to be patient and stoically bear everything calmly and bravely; it's a part of the sacrifice and bitterness demanded by every ideal. To be in prison is to be condemned to forced silence; to listen and read whatever is said and written without being able to comment, to put up with the attacks of cowards who jump at the chance to fight defenseless people and say things I would immediately challenge, if my hands were not virtually tied.

May 2

I thought of using one of the two apartments as a kind of office and the other one for the four of us to live in, since people are always barging into the house, making it impossible to have any privacy. It doesn't bother me that much, but Emmita and Lidia,* like all women, need a place to retreat into, to putter around in, to make a mess and straighten up, to put things down and then take them away, without having us men ruin everything. Otherwise, by the end of the day, one is fed up with people and the world. I've been in this life and struggle for enough years to know how many little snags occur when you turn a house into an office. I really regretted having my law office in Old Havana—what a feat it was just getting there! I was completely happy when I could lock myself in to study or attend to some work. It was the perfect place to see people with good grace, even when they came to pester me or bring me the cases of poor persons who were about to be evicted and needed a lawyer and who, of course, could never pay. I didn't feel so gracious

---

* Fidel's sisters.—ED.

when someone came to me just as I was leaving my home—not to take a walk, naturally—and detained me with something very trivial. There were times when very touchy people got angry because I couldn't pay as much attention to them as they wanted; but this hardly ever happened, because I'm a stoic man when I have to deal with demanding people. One can never totally avoid these little annoyances, but they must be reduced as much as possible by setting up routines and controlling one's schedule, and I'm no exception, even if I'm a bit of a bohemian and not orderly by nature. There's nothing better than having a place where you can throw as many cigar butts as you want on the floor without the subconscious fear that a housewife, watching you like a sentry, is waiting to place an ashtray under the falling ashes; or making you nervous about burning the sofa or the curtains. Domestic peace is at cross-purpose with the constant bustle in a fighter's life, and it's a good idea to keep them apart as much as you can.

As far as creature comfort goes, if I didn't have to keep up appearances just a little, I would be happy to sleep on a field cot in a room in a tenement, with a box to keep my clothes in. A plate of malangas and potatoes would seem as delicious to me as the manna in the Bible. Things are expensive, but I could get along on a well-spent forty centavos. I'm not exaggerating, I'm being quite honest. The more I come to depend on life's comforts and forget that I can be perfectly happy not owning anything, the lower I slip in my own estimation. That's how I have learned to live, and it makes me more fear-inspiring as a passionate defender of an ideal that has been reaffirmed and strengthened by sacrifice. I will be able to practice what I preach, and that will speak louder than words. The less I am tied down to the material wants of life, the more independent and useful I will be. Why make sacrifices to buy a shirt, a pair of pants, or anything else? I'll leave here in my worn-out gray wool suit, even if it is the middle of the summer. Didn't I return the other suit I didn't need or ask for? Don't think I am an eccentric or turning into one, but clothes make the man, and I'm a poor man, I own nothing, I have never stolen a penny or begged, and I have given up my career for a cause. Why should I be forced to wear linen shirts, as though I were a rich man, an official, or an embezzler? Since I am not earning any money right now, they will have to give me what I need, and I can't and won't be a burden on anyone. Since I have been here, my biggest struggle has been to insist and never tire of insisting that I don't need anything; I have needed only books and they should be thought of as spiritual possessions. I can't stop worrying about all the money you have been spending.

I can't have any weaknesses; no matter how small they might be today, you would never be able to count on me tomorrow.

I am wondering if the bill collectors will start dogging my steps as soon as I get out. I have put them off with so many excuses and promises! With all the everyday problems, maybe I will miss the peace I have in prison now. One is never satisfied anywhere, but here at least you're not hounded by bill collectors. Perhaps Balzac, who was hounded all the time by these people, would have felt very comfortable here. I hope that the feeling I have that I'll miss prison once I'm out doesn't come true!

FIDEL CASTRO

Interview by Carlos Franqui

May 15, 1955

It is 5:00 a.m., Monday morning. For the last few hours we have been staring at the dark sea from the Batabanó docks. The boat finally arrives from the Isle of Pines. The young men of the Moncada attack are coming back to freedom, and among the cheers, tears, and hugs of family, friends, and the people, we began this short interview with Fidel Castro for *Carteles* magazine, and continued it on the train ride to Havana.

C.F.:   Do you plan to stay in Cuba?

F.C.:   Yes, I plan to stay in Cuba and fight the government in the open, pointing out its mistakes, denouncing its faults, exposing gangsters, profiteers, and thieves.

C.F.:   Will you remain in the Ortodoxo Party?

F.C.:   We will struggle to unite the whole country under the flag of Chibás's revolutionary movement. Together with Bárcena, Conte Agüero, and other new leaders and groups, we will try to build a revolutionary front. I am an Ortodoxo. As to the positions I have been offered, I will first have to talk it over with my Moncada comrades.

C.F.:   How many men took part in the July 26 raid?

F.C.:   One hundred sixty-five in Santiago de Cuba and Bayamo.

C.F.:   How many died?

F.C.:   About eighty, around ten of them fighting.

C.F.:   Will those who attacked the Moncada Barracks go on working together?

F.C.:   We are joined by a close and complete bond, forged by our struggle and sacrifices for our ideas of justice and freedom.

The amnesty of the revolutionary prisoners is the first great victory of the Cuban people.

The regime has to live up to its promises now. We will have to go on fighting for our freedom without any letup. We will know how to make the right moves at the right time, and not play into our enemies' hands.

There is a growing national awareness again, and anyone who tries to snuff it out will bring on an unprecedented disaster. As for myself, in spite of everything, I still have not learned how to hate.

FIDEL CASTRO

Letter   Havana, July 7

I am packing for my departure from Cuba, but I have had to borrow money even to pay for my passport. After all, it is not a millionaire who is leaving, only a Cuban who has given and will go on giving everything to his country. All doors to a peaceful political struggle have been closed to me. Like Martí, I think the time has come to seize our rights instead of asking for them, to grab instead of beg for them. Cuban patience has its limits.

I will live somewhere in the Caribbean. There is no going back possible on this kind of journey, and if I return, it will be with tyranny beheaded at my feet.

1955-56

5. EXILE—THE SUGAR-MILL STRIKE

FIDEL CASTRO

Letters   Mexico, July 24, 1955

If our work is to succeed, not a single cog of the organization must be allowed to slip, and the ways and means of communication, coordination, and replacement must improve day by day. I am in real need of collaborators here. Here, as well as in Cuba, we need a group of the best-qualified comrades. Here you will find a terrain I am already getting to know inch by inch, and your days here will be less bitter than those I have had to live through, blazing the trail in a setting completely new to me and always worrying about what was being accomplished over there.

For me this city and this country will soon be like those I was in during the months before July 26.

You must remember that I am working against great odds because I do not have the necessary resources. We may even have to go hungry during the first few months. I had to pawn my overcoat in order to be able to bring out the first manifesto; the pawnshops here are run by the state and they charge very low interest. If the rest of my clothes were forced to go the same way, I wouldn't hesitate for a second.

Puerto Rico, July 28

The rally was started almost spontaneously by young Latin Americans from different countries under the heel of despotism. They have all adopted July 26 as their own anniversary. Sitting beside us and presiding with us over the rally was Doña Laura Meneses, the wife of Albizu Campos, the Puerto Rican nationalist leader.

August 1

I have the greatest respect for A.H.,* and for his ideas. It is an honor to have him in our ranks. You can't imagine how reassuring it is to have him and the doctor** with us in this new phase, when our best comrades have fallen and others have cowardly deserted us instead of facing the long period of sacrifices ahead of us. A.H. and F.P. have more than filled the vacuum left by the small group of deserters. "Renew yourself or perish." Perhaps that is our soundest principle: recognize men for what they are worth and assign them to their rightful place, without letting anyone rest on his laurels. Those two men now occupy the places of Abel, Boris, José Luis, and Guitart.***

I have great faith, not religious but rational and logical faith, because in this time of tremendous confusion we are the only ones who have a line, a program, and a goal—and the will to carry them through or die in the effort!

From all this, I can see that if Carlos Prío doesn't openly come out for nonviolent elections—when he least expects it, after the first police roundup and they discover the first cache of arms—he will find himself in the cells of the Castillo del Príncipe [the Prince's Castle] in the role of victim, and that will be all the revolutionary activity we can expect from him. Conspiracies are in the air, and if they were not, the police would be told to invent them; arms will continue to pass from hand to hand, and there will be trouble in the air. How long can Prío keep this up?

How long can they go on spreading this myth of insurrection?

From all this, and a whole series of political and economic circumstances, I suspect that the situation will go from bad to worse and that, in spite of the leaders, who are no longer masters of the situation, but merely puppets, Cuba's problem will get more and more tangled, like a Gordian knot that only a revolution can unravel.

In politics, our main enemy is the tendency to agree to partial elections; that must be fought tooth and nail in all our proclamations. Now we will come out with thousands and thousands of underground manifestos, every two weeks at least.

August 3

Someone you can trust will bring you the first Manifesto to the People. You'll have to print at least *50,000*. Get everything ready so you can start printing at once. It should be on the streets on August 16, the

---

* Armando Hart, a well-known student leader who had just joined the 26th of July Movement.—C. F.

** Faustino Pérez, a recent medical-school graduate, had been in prison for his part in a conspiracy and later was the main underground leader of the 26th of July Movement.—C. F.

*** Abel Santamaría, Boris Luis Santa Coloma, José Luis Tassende, Renato Guitart; all killed in the attack on Moncada.—C. F.

fourth anniversary of Chibás's death, and several thousand should be distributed at the cemetery.

The day will also be commemorated with a "Message to the Ortodoxos" that should be run off in mimeograph. I'll turn that project over to one of you in another letter.

You'll see how we'll rip through the curtain of silence and clear the way for a new strategy.

The second manifesto will criticize the tactics we have been using; it will carry the first call for insurrection and a general strike.

The third manifesto will appear in early September and will be a specific appeal for economic help, though I'll also mention that in those sent out before. By that time, all the cadres must be completed so that contributions can be made; that's why the appeal can't go out before. At least *100,000* copies must be printed of this manifesto which will be vital.

The fourth will be addressed to the armed forces, and so on.

I need to know how the work in each sector is progressing: workers, Ortodoxo youth, women, combat groups, underground-propaganda distribution, the printing setup, and the economic sections.

How are things going in the unions? Have you done everything you can on this point? Never forget how important it is. Has a group been set up in Havana to take care of this? What does our leader among the proletariat say about it?

Have you kept in touch with the Frente Cívico de Mujeres Martianas [Women's Civic Front for Martí]? We ought to try to bring this group into the women's section of the 26th of July Movement. The doctor and the lawyer* will be responsible for this mission.

August 5

I'm still busy recruiting the most trustworthy revolutionaries. Our friend from Marianao, J.M.M.,** has written me a beautiful letter from Miami, where he's back again. He is in the top leadership there, but is only waiting for word to join me here. He has contacted many Cubans who live in the United States.

August 29

The printing and distribution of propaganda must be foolproof. I think this is crucially important because the manifestos in themselves, secretly circulating throughout the country, not only keep morale up but also do the work of thousands of activists and convert each sympathetic

---

* Pérez and Hart.—Ed.
** Juan Manuel Márquez, leader of the Ortodoxo Party, exiled in the United States, where he organized a branch of the 26th of July Movement. He was with Fidel in the *Granma* landing and was wounded and killed by Batista's soldiers. —C. F.

citizen into a militant who will spread the arguments and ideas in the manifestos.

In contrast, we must maintain rigorous silence about weapons, and about those who have anything to do with them and about where they are stored. Above all, we will have to work hard and carefully to put all the weapons we get where they will be under our absolute control. Later we'll stow them away in convenient places, but nobody, regardless of his importance, should know where all those places are. If one of us gets to know too much, we'll have to take him out of the inner circle. We must be prepared for any emergency. I don't think more than fifteen or twenty people in all of Cuba should be in on this, and none of them should know about those outside his sector. Those persons and those caches must be controlled from here.

The three things, then, that must be handled with the greatest care, making sure only a handful of people are in on them, are: arms, the names of leaders, and the cell in charge of printing and distributing propaganda; in essence, our secret will consist of these three activities. Outside of this work, the more people we have working and conspiring, the greater will be the confusion and disorganization within the repressive forces. If they know that there are a hundred, two hundred, more or less known partisans in a factory, they won't be able to do a thing.

I insist that the activity in the workers' centers is decisive. Every time you give out propaganda, the largest share should go to them.

The Movement will have to have a centralized leadership that will hold all the important strings, but also a decentralized mass organization that will rally to specific goals; these will be passed on, in the same way, to members of the armed forces who sympathize with us.

These general aims of organization and effort will permit us to replace the better-known leaders slowly, without causing a breakdown of the Movement.

Going into details, I am not completely satisfied with the way our leaders are working together. I would like to know right now if there is complete harmony of goals and understanding among the members of the directorate. This is absolutely indispensable. The work program was drawn up clearly from the beginning. I insisted that it be followed to the letter. I know the enormous problems you have had with the recent desertion by the Prío group; in the future, there will be absolutely no excuse to justify any indiscipline or disorganization. We must impose absolute discipline now that we are the sole vanguard of the revolution; those who join us will have to respect our standards unconditionally.

Mexico, August 30

We are penniless; printing and postage have wiped out the little we had. I have received $85 so far, through Pedrito [Miret]. It was for personal expenses but I turned it over to the cause. Each of us lives on less money than the army spends on any of its horses.

September 21

We are all working hard. Juan Manuel Márquez has turned out to be brilliant and well qualified in every way. Those of us who are here feel like soldiers of the army of liberation and we can't wait for the time when we will all fight the last battle together.

September 25

Of all the support we have received, none is more encouraging than that of Acción Cívica Cubana [Cuban Civic Action], which calls to mind the unforgettable pages of our War of Independence; the spirit of the club of émigrés of 1868 and 1895 seems to inspire the ideas and actions of that group of Cubans living in New York, who so generously, spontaneously, and unselfishly concern themselves about the fate of their country and are prepared to serve it. They wish to complete what those other generations could not, to do what their republic has not done in its fifty years, to establish political and social institutions that will make Cuba one of the leading nations of America.

If it were not for this, if the purpose of the Revolution were only to restore power to those who have used it so disgracefully, to replace the dictatorship of reactionary and bloody bayonets with a dictatorship of corrupt politicians, who have also reviled and sacked the country, murdered Cubans and trampled on our laws, it would be meaningless to spill a single drop of generous blood.

New York, October 30

I live somewhere in the Caribbean and I can get along as well in a city like this as on a deserted and inhospitable key. I don't live anywhere permanently. I am dedicated to the struggle, and the inconveniences and sacrifices of this hazardous life are not important to me; the two years in a lonely cell prepared me well.

We all live modestly. There are no millionaires here. You'll never see any of us in a bar or nightclub. The first revolutionary manifesto was printed with what I got from pawning my overcoat, but that did not discourage us; we have faith in the justice and logic of our mission. In New York alone, there are thousands of Cubans who are willing to give a part of their wages every month. Besides, there are Cubans who are enthusiastically organizing themselves in Bridgeport, Union City, Elizabeth, Long Island, and other places. We are getting some things done among the émigrés here just as our Apostle Martí did in a similar situation. These thousands of families driven into exile by poverty, coming by the hundreds every month, sad and unhappy and forgotten, don't interest the politicians because they don't have a vote; they want to go home whenever they can live there with some dignity; they still love Cuba and are powerful bulwarks of national liberation. The Cuban people there and here will stand behind us. Just look at what is happening here in the Palm Garden: thousands of pesos collected in a minute. This struggle can only go on with the donations of the people.

I can tell you with complete confidence that in 1956 we will either be free men or we will be martyrs. That means that in 1956 we will be fighting in Cuba. For us, this struggle began March 10. It has been going on for almost four years and will end only with our death. One of our most illustrious liberators once said that whoever wants to take over Cuba will find its soil soaked in blood.*

The 26th of July militants will go to all the rallies in Cuba, regardless of what opposition party organizes them, to make one speech to the people: Revolution! Revolution! Anybody who gets a permit for a rally can be assured of a crowd. We also know how to use political maneuvers.

We are against the use of violence toward any people or any opposition party, and we are totally opposed to terrorist acts against persons. We don't kill dictators. When they tried to persuade Maceo to murder an enemy leader, he said: "The man who faces gunfire may kill his enemy on the battlefield but he does not stoop to treachery and the shameful act of murder."

The Cuban people want more than a mere change of leaders. Cuba wants a radical change in its entire public and social life. The people must be given more than an abstract ideal of freedom and democracy; every Cuban must be able to live a decent existence.

In Cuba today, we are the only ones who know where we are going and we do not wait for the dictator's latest edicts.

I said publicly to the Cuban émigrés at the Hotel Flagler in Miami: "Let's all get behind the idea of full dignity for the people of Cuba, and justice for the hungry and the forgotten, and punishment for the chief culprits. . . . Money stolen from the republic cannot start a revolution. Revolutions are made honestly. One cannot consider as combatants the thieves who pretend—and who have kept 10 percent of the money they stole—to have won the goodwill of the people. The embezzlers are not held in high esteem. The embezzlers can't turn against the dictator who protects their ill-gotten gains. The embezzlers prefer tyranny to revolution. That's why the embezzlers want the Sociedad de Amigos de la República [SAR, Society of Friends of the Republic] to make a settlement with the regime. It's the only way they can survive politically."

I would like to know which of those long-suffering Cubans—who have come to our meetings and who now make up the membership of the Revolutionary clubs of Bridgeport, Union City, New York, Miami,

---

* Antonio Maceo.—Ed.

Tampa, and Key West—which of these humble compatriots, who live by working hard, away from their homeland, which of them is a happy property owner? I have seen how they live in tiny apartments, where couples can't have children; where women, bone-weary after a ten-hour day at the factory, have to do their washing and cooking; where life is hard, exhausting, and sad; where you don't hear anything but "I would be happy to live in Cuba on half of what I make here." At one time, when one talked about exiles, they numbered only a hundred or so; many of them were doing all right; their children often had their pictures in the paper, but sometimes they got homesick for their friends and their native land. But nobody thinks about the poor children of the émigrés who have to live in subzero temperatures in the United States, where there are no schools to teach them their mother tongue, and doctors don't understand what their parents say. To call them happy property owners shows how much the politicians resent the emigration of Cubans, because these tens of thousands of families away from their homeland are a living and painful indictment of the corrupt governments the republic has had. The politicians say: "The Cuban problem will be solved when the exiles can come home." We revolutionaries say: "Cuba's problems will be settled when the émigrés can come home."

The evil that began in Grau San Martín's time was rooted in the resentment and hatred Batista sowed during the eleven years of his oppression and injustice. People who saw their comrades murdered wanted revenge; a government that was unable to enforce justice allowed them to exact it. You can't blame the youth, driven by natural restlessness, and by the legend of the heroic times of the underground, for trying to start a revolution at a time when it was impossible to bring it off. Many of those who were duped and died like gangsters would be heroes today.

To avoid repeating the mistakes of the past, we will make the Revolution when the time is ripe. There will be justice to keep people from taking personal revenge. When there is justice no one will have the right to set himself up as an agent of vengeance, and if he does, he will have to bear all the weight of the law. Only the people have the right to punish or pardon. There has never been any justice in Cuba; it is simply unjustifiable that a poor devil goes to prison for stealing a chicken while the notorious embezzlers are above the law. When has a judge ever condemned a powerful man? When has a sugar-mill owner ever been arrested? When has a rural guard ever gone to prison? Or is justice, in our society, merely a dirty lie used for the convenience of the vested interests?

They know I left Cuba without a cent, they know I haven't knocked on the doors of the embezzlers, but they are afraid that we are going to start a revolution; they know that the people will be with us.

The opposition's political machine is falling apart and nobody believes them. First, they demanded a neutral government and immediate general elections. Then they decided only to ask for general elections in 1956. Now they don't even say when; they'll end up stripped of their last stitch and go along with any deal the dictatorship offers them.

But it is not going to be as easy as they think! The people are waking up. The peasants are tired of speeches and promises of agrarian reform and redistribution of land, and they know they can't expect anything from the politicians. Half a million Cubans are out of work because of the incompetence, shortsightedness, and greed of the bad administrations we have had; they know they can't expect anything from the politicians. Thousands of sick people, who don't even have beds or medicine know that they can't expect anything from politicians who promise a favor in exchange for a vote, and who make it their business to see that there are always a lot of poor people whose votes can be bought cheap. The hundreds of thousands of families living in shacks, sheds, vacant lots, tiny rooms, or paying exorbitant rents; the workers on starvation wages, whose children have no clothes or shoes to wear to school; the townspeople who pay more for electricity than anywhere else in the world and wait ten years for a phone and never get it, and those who have had to suffer and still suffer the indignities of a miserable existence—they know they can't expect anything from the politicians.

People know that if it were not for the hundreds of millions drained by the foreign trusts, in addition to the hundreds of millions stolen by the embezzlers and the favors that thousands of parasites enjoy without working or doing anything for society, plus the large sums wasted in gambling, vice, and the black market, Cuba could be one of the most prosperous countries in America. We would have no emigrants, no unemployed, no starving or sick people without care, no illiterates or beggars. . . .

The people expect nothing from the political parties.

They expect to get everything from the Revolution, and they will get it!

CARLOS FRANQUI   December 1955–January 1956

A violent large-scale strike has broken out from one end of the island to the other. Twenty of the principal cities of Cuba are shut down, businesses and industries are closed, and the workers have occupied churches, town halls, and many buildings. Streets are strewn with nails, highways closed, and the railroads are at a standstill. Men and women are rallying in the streets. Two sugar workers were killed, more than twenty wounded, and more than a thousand jailed by the police.

Eusebio Mujal and José Luis Martínez* ordered an end to the

---

* Pro-Batista labor leaders.—ED.

strike, but the masses did not obey; the strike will not stop until the decree giving them a 4 percent raise is signed.

The beginning of the harvest finds the sugar workers in open rebellion. The limitations on the crop the year before, the loss of concessions to the workers, like a bonus for extra production, lower wages; the movement of people from one place to another, with long periods of idleness delaying the clearing of the fields and repairs to the refineries, have made it a year of poverty for five hundred thousand families that live from the production of sugar.

On the other hand, the decree setting the conditions for this year has not frozen wages as was claimed. What they have done is to maintain the pay cut the workers got last year. Furthermore, the harvest will be 4.6 million tons instead of the 5 million they asked for. They were not granted the right to produce any surplus or other basic demands.

EDITOR'S SUMMARY

The government settlement accepted by Mujal and the other officials of the CTC as well as the leaders of the Federación Nacional de Trabajadores Azucareros [FNTA, National Federation of Sugar Workers] has been turned down unanimously by the five hundred thousand sugar workers, and they say that they will not start harvesting until their just demands are granted.

Later, José Luis Martínez recalled that Batista had summoned him and Eusebio Mujal to the Presidential Palace and demanded that the strike be called off in order not to jeopardize sales of sugar to Europe. The government promised, in return, to agree to a raise. The workers, however, refused to obey the back-to-work order unless their jailed colleagues were released. Student and other anti-Batista groups demonstrated in support of the strikers.

Faced with rebellion in his ranks, Martínez suspended the leaders of the diehard strikers.

NICOLÁS SANTIAGO

Nobody could stop the strike once it started. They stirred up workers all over the country by telling them that they were being robbed of their raise. Nobody could stop the people once they took to the streets. There were too many hungry and poor, and the masses wanted to show how they felt. At the Punta Alegre mill, the workers wouldn't let those who had given the order to stop the strike come in. When I got to Baraguá, where I have been general secretary for many years and everybody likes me, they shouted: "Scab, double-crosser, rat!" Nobody paid any attention to the order from the FNTA and the strike went on.

FIDEL CASTRO

Statement   Mexico, March 19

The 26th of July Movement is not a tendency within the party; it is the revolutionary apparatus of Chibás's organization, a grass-roots movement, from which it emerged to fight against the dictator, while the Ortodoxo Party was lying helpless and divided.

From then on, our revolutionary thesis has been the thesis of our party's masses; they had expressed their feelings unequivocally; from then on, the masses and the leaders have gone different ways. When did the party militants shatter this unity? Perhaps at the mass meetings in the provinces, where everybody shouted: "Revolution! Revolution!" And who but us sustained the revolutionary thesis? And who could make it work except the revolutionary apparatus of the Chibás masses, the 26th of July Movement? That was seven months ago. What has the official leadership done since then? Defend their idea of dialogue and mediation. What did we do? Defend the revolutionary thesis and start putting it into practice. What was the result of the former? Seven months gone down the drain. And what about the latter? Seven months of productive work and a strong revolutionary organization that will soon be ready to fight.

Mediation has turned out to be a complete failure. We were strongly opposed to it because we found out it was a maneuver by the government, whose only purpose since March 10 has been to stay in power indefinitely.

Now it is the people's fight. The 26th of July Movement was organized to help them in their heroic struggle to regain the rights and liberties they had lost.

The 26th of July against the 10th of March!

To Chibás's followers, the 26th of July Movement is not different from the Ortodoxo Party; it is the Ortodoxo movement without landlords like Fico Fernández Casas at its head; without sugar-plantation owners like Gerardo Vázquez, without stock-market speculators, without industrial and commercial magnates, without lawyers for the big interests or local political bosses, without small-time politicos with no-show jobs. The best of the Ortodoxo movement are helping in this beautiful struggle; we offer Eduardo Chibás the only praise worthy of his life and his tragedy: freedom for his people. It is something that can never be offered by those who have done nothing but shed crocodile tears over his grave.

The 26th of July Movement is the revolutionary organization of the humble, by the humble, and for the humble.

The 26th of July Movement is the hope of redemption for the Cuban working class, who can hope for nothing from the political cliques; it is the hope of land for the peasants who live like pariahs in the country whose freedom their grandfathers won; it is the hope of going back home for the émigrés who had to leave their country, where they could not live or work, and it is the hope of daily bread for the hungry and of justice for the forgotten.

CARLOS FRANQUI   Havana, April

In April 1956 Batista's SIM uncovered a powerful conspiracy by a group of high-ranking career officers with important commands. They controlled the tank and the artillery corps, and several key positions in Havana. The conspirators were led by Colonel Ramón Barquín and Major Enrique Borbonet.

They were arrested and sentenced by a military court to several years in prison on the Isle of Pines.

It was a new generation of career soldiers; they were convinced of the army's specific role and opposed to Batista's crimes, graft, and the military in politics.

They were young, with middle-class backgrounds and university training, and had ties with people in the United States as well as in the traditional opposition sectors at home.

From then on they were called "the pure ones." Their rebellion had been premature; Batista still had complete control over the army, in the high command as well as in the lower ranks, where he was popular because he had once been a sergeant.

This episode had great repercussions, especially in the army. It was crucial because it prevented the usual replacement of one army man by another in the presidency.

Matanzas

On April 29, a group of young men led by Reinol García of Matanzas commandeered some trucks from a mine and attacked the Goicuría Barracks, headquarters of the Matanzas military regiment, with weapons they had salvaged from an Auténtico plot.

The camp's heavy machine guns were on the alert—no one knows if someone had talked or the guards just happened to be on their toes—and opened fire on the attackers when they entered the courtyard of the barracks. The attack was crushed and only the men in the trucks bringing up the rear were able to escape.

Colonel Pilar García, a cold-blooded killer who was the commander of the province, showed the press the horribly mutilated bodies before they had time to get cold.

A Cuban photographer managed to take some spectacular shots inside the barracks. In one, a prisoner was shown walking between two guards with his hands tied behind his back. In the second, the soldiers could be seen shooting him in the back. In the next, his body sprawled out on the ground with ten other bodies photographed earlier. The pictorial series appeared in *Life* magazine with the caption, "The mystery of the eleventh corpse," and caused a big stir in the United States, Latin America, and Cuba.

The Goicuría attack was an almost hopeless action.

At the end of 1955 and the beginning of 1956, during the "civic dialogue" between the regime and the opposition parties, Batista and Prío had made a coexistence pact. In exchange for certain guarantees for Prío and promises to work out solutions through the electoral process, the Auténtico Party surrendered up arms smuggled into the country. When Reinol García was ordered to turn in the arms Prío's men had given him, he refused and immediately got ready for action. For months, he had been preparing an attempt on Batista's life that was to be carried out at Varadero beach, one of Batista's favorite spots, but the enormous difficulties involved had held him back. Instead of giving up the arms, he risked everything and led the attack on the Goicuría Barracks.

The impact of the Moncada assault was vividly alive in the minds of the young revolutionary opposition.

Almost all those who escaped after the attack sought political asylum in the Haitian embassy, where they stayed, unable to leave the country for lack of funds. They were murdered there by the police months later.

The attack on the Goicuría Barracks was the first important event in 1956.

FIDEL CASTRO

Letters   Miguel Schultz Prison, Mexico, July 9

We are prisoners in a foreign country; we have been locked up for more than twenty days, without their having fulfilled the basic requirement of taking us before competent authorities.

I had received repeated warnings from Cuba, and sometimes sympathizers of ours had even pleaded with me to take extra precautions for my safety: they had heard from reliable sources that a plot against my life was being hatched.

For several months, certain persons in the regime had been toying with the idea of putting me out of the way, but it was only quite recently, as the dictatorship's position became more desperate and our Movement grew visibly stronger, that the plan obtained official sanction and they took the first steps to carry it out. They were faced with the problem of avoiding scandal, of not leaving any tracks. I must admit that they worked out their plan very meticulously, almost to perfection;

it was not brought off—partly because we got wind of it, but mostly through sheer luck.

The agent assigned the mission made two trips to Mexico in the past few months. He stayed at the Prado, the most luxurious hotel in Mexico City. The first time our men caught him snooping outside the house on Emparan Street. Evidently he became discouraged and went back to Cuba to report that his mission wasn't so simple. He returned some weeks later with two other agents. This time he was assured that the only one in Mexico who could do the job successfully was a Cuban known as Arturo "El Jarocho," a fugitive from justice in Cuba; he lives in Mexico City, but his identity papers are from Veracruz.* What's more, he is a Secret Service agent and right-hand man of General Molinari, the chief of police. But I understand that Molinari had nothing to do with the whole business. The Cuban agents made a deal with "El Jarocho" himself for 10,000 dollars; he would split this with another man who was coming from Venezuela, since "they didn't want any Mexicans mixed up in the deal." They knew I always had someone with me and meant to put him out of the way too. They planned to come up to us in police uniforms, in a squad car, arrest, handcuff, and kidnap us, and make us disappear without leaving a trace. I've been told they have a paper with my signature perfectly forged on it, which they intended to use for a letter they would mail from some foreign country to 49 Emparan Street, saying I had to leave Mexico urgently. They believed this crude ruse would sow confusion to begin with, especially when they started spreading various versions of my departure. Around June 10, the agents left for Cuba after checking all the final details.

We knew that a common murderer was getting ready to kill us for 10,000 dollars, but we had to sit back patiently waiting for the next step. We took simple precautionary measures, like seldom going out or never going to the same place twice.

I admit that we didn't think of all the possible dangers we faced. When they found out that we were armed and ready to defend ourselves, and how risky their original plan was, they took our license-plate number and sicked the Federal Judicial Police on us.

I was not arrested at the ranch, as the papers said, but on the street, and if the agents had not acted with extreme caution and identified themselves first, there could have been a serious accident. Maybe that's what the plotters had in mind.

There was a river of gold behind the whole plot. On the other hand, we had only 20 dollars in the Movement's treasury.

The Cuban embassy knew about the whole thing. They heard about it before anybody else and immediately began a propaganda campaign. It was all carefully worked out. They immediately gave the press a story

* "Jarocho" means native of Veracruz.—ED.

that "seven Cuban Communists had been jailed for conspiring against Batista," interlarded with details about the Moncada assault, the sentence, etc., things that only the embassy could know about, and followed that with the statement that I had come to Mexico "with a passport obtained thanks to the recommendation of Lázaro Peña* and Lombardo Toledano."** As if everybody did not know that you can get a passport in Cuba without having a recommendation from anyone; for the visa from the Mexican consulate, you just have to present a letter from your bank, and I wasn't even asked for that by the consul, who gave me the visa in a very helpful and friendly way.

Naturally the charge that I was a Communist was fabricated to get the U.S. embassy to add weight to the pressure they themselves were already putting on the Mexican authorities.

The press talks about an arsenal of guns and all the Mexican police seized were five old rifles and four pistols.

At first the press published only what they were told by the police and what they could get from the embassy. But when the truth was known, the honest press, the decent reporters who can also be found here, all came around to our side.***

CARLOS FRANQUI

The Movement sent me to Mexico twice, in June and in July 1956, to take Fidel 5000 dollars, the first issue of the underground newspaper I edited, and a report from Faustino on our work in Cuba.

Fidel and the others were in Miguel Schultz Prison, which had a center courtyard where visitors could be received.

Fidel was desperate. He paced back and forth like a caged lion.

Che**** had his shirt off and was playing ball with another prisoner. It was raining and his wife and small daughter, Hildita, were under an umbrella. These visits eased the strain on the prisoners and raised their spirits.

I had some lively talks with Fidel. He was desperate because money from Cuba trickled in so slowly; he was in prison and he had to keep his promise to land in Cuba in 1956; yet almost all his weapons had been seized and the cost of arming a hundred men, buying a yacht, and keeping it in Mexico for several months was enormous. He didn't think the Movement could muster sufficient force. To solve specific problems,

---

* Cuban Communist labor leader.—C. F.
** Mexican labor leader.—C. F.
*** Castro and most of his group were freed in July.—ED.
**** Ernesto Guevara, the Argentine who became Fidel's close associate, met him through Raúl Castro, in Mexico, in August 1955. Guevara was arrested with Fidel in June 1956.—ED.

especially financial ones, we would have to make an agreement with Prío and his Auténtico Party.

The Movement was something new and different in Cuba, uncorrupted by politicians; it consisted of young Ortodoxo members who were anti-Prío. Fidel's words in Miami about the embezzlers—"We shall knock on their doors after the Revolution"—were still fresh, and Prío was one of the biggest embezzlers. Right now the most important objective, in Fidel's eyes, was to go to Cuba and fight.

We agreed on that. But there was the question of principles and, besides, he had to consider the reaction of the Movement in Cuba, which would surely be against any agreement with Prío. Prison exacerbated Fidel's frustration; he felt as if everyone had deserted him.

He asked me to tell the National Directorate of the 26th of July Movement, in his name, about the agreement with the Prío forces; I didn't approve of it, but as he would not be there, he asked me not to meddle. It seemed only fair and I agreed not to interfere.

Fidel and Che slept side by side in prison. They were studying Stalin's *The Fundamentals of Leninism.* The three of us had a very serious argument. Che defended it and I attacked it.

Fidel's opinion was clear: "A revolution must have only one leader if it is to remain whole and not be defeated. One bad leader is better than twenty good ones."*

I proposed a plan that I thought had possibilities but he had little faith in it: a campaign in the Mexican and the international press to set the group free.

I could count on important help from the Mexican writer Fernando Benítez and his friends. Benítez was editor of the literary magazine *Novedades* [New Things]. He was instrumental in getting *Excélsior,* the biggest newspaper in Mexico, to do an exclusive interview with Castro in prison; the United Press picked it up and released it to the whole world.

A massive newspaper campaign got under way and continued for several weeks. Some editors hailed Fidel as "the new Martí."

Progressives in Mexico, the United States, and on the Continent went into action. Several days later the prisoners were freed.

From then on, Fidel showed faith in my propaganda methods, and I was given a free rein.

Running a newspaper was one of my specialties, but to start one in Cuba, to buy a Multilith, I had had to scrape up the money and overcome the rather childish objections that a fighter should put his ideas into the barrel of his rifle. Anyone could see it was better to put them into the brain of the man using the rifle.

We talked with Fidel about the underground press. He insisted it would be wrong to burn down the *Diario de la Marina,* when the tyranny

---

* See analogous statement, p. 83.

was eventually defeated. This paper was an evil that had lasted over a hundred years. It had fought against Cuban independence in the last century. It was reactionary, fascist, pro-Franco, and on the side of the great imperialist interests. It was hated by the Cuban people but it was protected by vested interests, and had held on during the republic and in the 1930s. We agreed with Fidel that it should not be burned, but nationalized.

From then on, our press and propaganda section was ready to take over the Batista press when the time came.

I remember some of the Mexicans who helped us; the Barbachano Ponces, "Fofo" Gutiérrez, Machado, and Benítez.

Fidel asked me to tell Faustino, Pedro Miret, and some of the others to go to Mexico and join the expedition; Frank País was to make the trip in order to talk about coordinating the time of the uprising in Santiago. I reminded him that the Dominican refugee Pichirilo Mejías was in Havana; he was an excellent sailor whom Fidel and I had met in 1947, during the Cayo Confites expedition against Trujillo. Fidel told me to ask him to become our pilot, which I did, and he accepted.

The second return trip to Havana was nerve-racking. After I got on the Cubana Airlines plane in Mexico, someone told me Batista's police were waiting to search it. I was carrying some manuscripts, letters from Fidel, and other important papers I couldn't let the police get hold of.

I knew two or three passengers—one was a Communist lawyer—and I asked them to help me out but they refused.

We were about to land at Boyeros, when I caught sight of Luz Gil, a Mexican actress. When she had weighed in at the airport in Mexico, she had discovered that her baggage was over the weight limit; I had almost no luggage, and I had let her put one of her bags on my ticket. I asked her to take my papers. She kindly agreed and they went through easily. She never knew what kind of papers she was carrying.

Shortly after this, the men Fidel had called for started leaving for Mexico. Frank País was the last to go.

When I got back to Cuba, Frank, Hart, Oltuski, and I completed and revised the draft of the movement's ideological thesis. In October, Oltuski took it to Fidel in Mexico to go over it with him and get his approval.

Fidel had vanished from Mexico City and Oltuski did not see him.

Later on, Felipe Pazos, Regino Boti, and Baudilio Castellanos* worked out a draft of a more moderate economic and constitutional position, which fared no better. Fidel disliked written programs, even those of an ideological nature.

---

* Felipe Pazos, first president of the National Bank of Cuba and an internationally known economist (his son, Javier, was a member of the 26th of July), had resigned when Batista seized power in 1952; Boti was also a distinguished economist, and, like Castellanos, a professor at the university.—ED.

If we insisted, he always fell back on *History Will Absolve Me*. As usual, Fidel made the right move.

Not even Raúl or Che could ever guess exactly what was on Fidel's mind. He was inscrutable.

EDITOR'S SUMMARY   Mexico–Havana, July 28

After Comrade Franqui's return from Mexico, the National Directorate of the 26th of July Revolutionary Movement met to hear his report on unity.

Comrade Franqui revealed the possibility of an understanding between the 26th of July Movement and the other revolutionary groups. A discussion of the unity proposal ensued, but it was agreed that since all the members were not present, no final decisions could be made. *

*To several, the notion of a pact with the Prío forces represented a sharp break with the past. Armando Hart and a number of the others saw it as an indication of Fidel's lack of faith in the Movement, or in its operations in Cuba. Nico López pointed out that "the pact was tactical and not ideological." As he saw it, Fidel did not believe that the directorate had failed in Cuba, but that it could not bring about the Revolution by itself. Faustino Pérez questioned whether it was proper to change course without consulting the directorate. Montané interposed that this was not a departure but a reflection of earlier decisions. The ideological basis of the Movement, he added, remained the ideas articulated in Fidel's manifestos, his writings in Bo*hemia, *and in* History Will Absolve Me.

At the end of July 1956, a committee consisting of Carlos Franqui, Enrique Oltuski, Armando Hart, and Frank País drew up this document. It was actually drafted by Franqui and subsequently approved by the entire committee.

Against a background of the political events of the Wars of Independence, the thesis traced the growing involvement and importance of the workers in determining Cuban history. The first workers' strike was held in 1902; by August 1933, the workers were strong enough to mount a general strike that was instrumental in the overthrow of the dictator Gerardo Machado. This marked the start of a collaborative effort between the workers and the students that has continued in Cuba.

After the Communist movement was organized by Julio Antonio Mella, in 1925, the Communists replaced the anarchists in the leadership of the workers' movement. During the 1930s, the Communists continued to struggle for improved rights and benefits for the workers, following instructions from the Communist International. When Batista came to power in 1934, "the savage military dictatorship wiped out all the social and national gains that had been made; it stained Cuba with the blood of students, workers, revolutionaries, and other Cubans, crushing the revolutionary movement and the unions."

---

* At Fidel's request, Franqui did not participate in the discussion; see p. 105.

In 1938, however, when Batista was challenged by internal and external pressures, "the Communists—always under the orders of the CI—took advantage of his desperate situation to make a pact with him; they got the Ministry of Labor to recognize the workers' organizations in return for their help in the elections; they would also agitate among the people—something they were experts at—divide the country, and sow confusion by joining forces with the extreme right.

"The results of this pact were dismal for Cuba, for the workers' movement, and for the Communists themselves." Gains obtained through pressure rather than real worker strength gave the unions an illusion of popular support, but in 1944, the Auténtico candidates won the election, the old union officers—good and bad—were thrown out by Eusebio Mujal and a new group of labor leaders, and the workers found themselves at the power of the bosses and the state. When the March 10, 1952, coup brought Batista back to power, Mujal proceeded to join forces with him. Democracy was dead inside the unions, and the government took "fascist-type military action" against the unions and the other organizations that opposed its policies.

Once again, the workers resorted to the strike as a weapon, this time against the wishes of the double-dealing labor leaders. It was the sugar-workers' strike that "was of historic importance because it united again all the revolutionary sectors of the country, which had fought side by side, since the last century, for independence and the founding of the republic. Workers and students, the youth and the common people joined the militant followers of the 26th of July Movement and the Revolutionary Directorate—one of whose members, Raúl Cervantes, was killed—and shook the whole country."

CARLOS FRANQUI

Programmatic thesis of the 26th of July Movement

Conclusions:

1. We believe work is the only source of wealth.

2. We are against the division of society into classes, because it is one-sided and unjust; forcing the majority to work for the few is the source of all social conflict.

3. We want the Cuban society of the future to provide everyone with a job and the income his ability and effort deserve. A society in which no individual or group can steal the product of another's efforts and this is possible only in a society without classes or privileges.

4. The Revolution can exist only if it protects the immense majority from the few who would exploit it.

5. Everyone who takes the revolutionary road must follow progressive aims.

The middle class, which led our country in 1868, began by setting the slaves free and taking them into the *mambí* army. We have seen how social progress advanced in 1895 and 1930.

The Revolution—and you, workers of our country, are the Revolution—calls on you to conquer everything through your own effort and work. Join the struggle.

The 26th of July Movement needs your participation in order to guarantee the success of the Revolution.

Fight for your Revolution!

FIDEL CASTRO ‧ Mexico, August 6

Now it's all over and I don't want the Cubans to harbor any ill feelings against the Mexicans. Jail and mistreatment are the wages of our job as fighters.

The persecution and calumnies came from the Cuban embassy. They are all lackeys in tails who spend the country's money persecuting its people.

August 26

What difference is there between the two tyrants? The Cuban and the Dominican peoples want to get rid of Batista and Trujillo. Cuba and Santo Domingo will be happy the day those two are ousted. Trujillo's administration was the first to endorse the March 10 coup wholeheart-edly. Batista always criticized the Auténtico governments for offering generous help to the Dominican revolutionaries.

Neither Batista nor Trujillo wants his country to have a democratic government.

Salas Cañizares cannot cast doubt on my firm democratic convictions or my unswerving loyalty to the cause of the Dominican people. Juan Rodríguez, Juan Bosch, and the rest of the exiled Dominican leaders know how hard I fought for Dominican democracy in the university and how I spent three months living outdoors on a sandy key waiting for the signal to leave;* they know how many times I was on the spot, ready to go into the fight against Trujillo. They can vouch for me. They know who their real friends are, and they are better informed than anyone else about the doings of the dictator who oppresses their country.

My attitude toward Trujillo now is the same attitude I had at the university and will always have.

I believe that in a revolution principles are more important than cannon. We fought at Moncada with .22-caliber rifles. We have never counted the enemy's guns; as Martí said, the stars on your forehead are what count. We would not swap a single principle for the arms of all the dictators in the world.

---

* Castro trained for the invasion of the Dominican Republic planned by General Rodríguez in 1947. The assault was never carried out.—ED.

Four months and six days before December 31, 1956, I calmly reaffirm that we will be free men or martyrs this year.

EDITOR'S SUMMARY   Mexico City, September 1956

The Mexico City Pact agreement, signed by Fidel Castro and José Antonio Echeverría, opened with a statement of aims:

"The Federación Estudiantil Universitaria-Directorio Revolucionario [University Students' Federation-Revolutionary Directory] and the 26th of July Movement, the two groups formed by the younger generation that have won the support of the Cuban people by their sacrifice and struggle, jointly address the following declarations to the people:

"1. Both organizations have decided to combine their efforts to overthrow the tyranny and carry out the Cuban Revolution."

Eighteen more points were listed, the first specific one being the refusal to support the limited elections Batista offered; they demanded free general elections instead. They warned of bloodshed if the elections were allowed to take place.

Alluding to Fidel's repeated pledge to make a landing in 1956, they asserted:

"We think the social and political conditions are right, and the preparations for the Revolution far enough advanced to offer the people their liberation in 1956. The uprising backed by a general strike will be invincible."

Several paragraphs dealt with support for Batista from General Leónidas Trujillo, dictator of the Dominican Republic. This had recently been reaffirmed at a meeting of Hemisphere presidents in Panama.

An overture was made to the armed forces by applauding the actions of anti-Batista conspirators Colonel Barquín, Major Borbonet, and others now imprisoned, and Castro and Echeverría promised that "Under the command of these honorable and prestigious officers serving the Constitution and the people, the army will have the respect and support of the Cuban Revolution."

Finally, calling on all sectors of the population to abandon the fruitless efforts at compromise, the pact concluded:

Now that the Revolution is faced with a battle to the death against the tyranny, victory will be ours, because history is on our side.

The Revolution will come to power free of commitments and selfish interests, to serve Cuba with a program of social justice, liberty, and democracy; a program of respect for just laws; and recognition of the dignity of all Cubans, without petty feuds against anyone. Those of us who lead the Revolution are willing to sacrifice our lives as a pledge of our good intentions.

FIDEL CASTRO

Interview in *Alerta** (Havana)   Mexico, November 19

If the country's problems are not solved two weeks from the publication date of this interview, the 26th of July Movement will be free to start the revolutionary struggle at any time; it is the only possible way out. We strongly reaffirm the promise we made for the year 1956: We will be free men or martyrs. But even then, if Trujillo forces should invade Cuba during our struggle, we are ready to make a truce and fight against our country's enemies.

ENRIQUE DE LA OSA   *Bohemia* (Havana)

When classes were suspended and there were clashes with the police, the students in Santiago poured into the streets. They demonstrated, called lightning meetings, tied up traffic, and stoned buses. People from all walks of life were arrested, and the government called out the army to "restore order."

The commander of the army, General Tabernilla y Dolz, said, "The landing announced by Fidel Castro can never come off. From a technical point of view, groups of undisciplined hotheads, without the military know-how or fighting equipment to carry it out, are bound to fail."

---

* The government newspaper.

6. NOVEMBER–DECEMBER, 1956: PREPARING THE LANDING AND THE *GRANMA*

FAURE CHOMÓN–ENRIQUE RODRÍGUEZ LOECHES

Report   Havana, November

The all-important Mexico City Pact sealed the ideological unity of Cuban youth and marked the start of a new phase in the fight against tyranny.

The Revolutionary Directory, which evolved out of the university in 1955, through the momentum given it by its main proponents, José Antonio Echeverría and Fructuoso Rodríguez, in those days worked fanatically preparing action and political cadres, making them function, implementing a plan of mass action with the help of the FEU, a plan that José Antonio and Fructuoso were ready to put into action; this was the first time that the revolutionary forces and the students were standing up to police aggression.

We came back from our meetings in Mexico with renewed spirit and the firm conviction that we could not lose. With the pact, we had established the unity of Cuba's fighting youth under one ideology, although it had not been possible to come up with a common strategy. The Directory and the 26th of July Movement had each opted for a different fighting front, and there didn't seem to be enough time for a solution acceptable to both. So we agreed to follow separate plans that would culminate in Frank País's uprising in Santiago, Fidel's landing in Oriente, and the Revolutionary Directory's attack on the Presidential Palace.

Our plans were set in motion the moment Echeverría, Rodríguez, Joe Westbrook, Juan Pedro Carbó, and José Machado stepped on Cuban soil again. The men of the Revolutionary Directory were not the kind to wait.

Following the example of their leaders, the students held a demonstration on November 27, braving Batista's dog pack. It was a terrifying encounter, but the students and the revolutionaries were not intimidated.

LUIS RICARDO ALONSO *   Havana, November

The authorities are faced with open hostility and sabotage. They live like an army of occupation, their fingers always on the trigger, their eyes peeled, because the daring revolutionary may strike around a street corner, in a silent house, protected by darkness, or anywhere.

Colonel Blanco Rico, chief of SIM, Marcelo Tabernilla, chief of the tank corps, and another officer were in the Cabaret Montmartre waiting with their wives for an elevator. It was 4:00 a.m., the nightclub show was over, and the gambling rooms had closed.

The officers were talking and laughing as two young, seemingly carefree men came down the corridor. One quickly drew a submachine gun and opened fire on the officers.

The sudden execution of the Commander in Chief of one of the repressive corps produced a state of anxious expectation throughout the country. The seriousness of events, in addition to the usual Sunday quiet, increased the air of solitude and silence hanging over the capital of Cuba. Traffic was light. Theater audiences were small. The movies and the stadium were practically empty.

The funeral for the chief of SIM was hardly over when Rafael Salas Cañizares, chief of police, and Colonel Orlando Piedra, head of the Bureau of Investigations, broke into the Haitian embassy to capture ten young political refugees, some of whom had been in the assault on the Goicuría Barracks in Matanzas.

Salas Cañizares and his companions rushed into the embassy courtyard with pistols drawn, knowing that the refugees were unarmed—that was the story told by journalists later. The refugees had been anxiously watching the police cordon set up around the embassy since early that morning, and, when the hated police chief burst in, they were determined not to let themselves be killed without putting up a fight.

The outcome of this one-sided encounter would have been the same if they had not put up a fight: ten dead revolutionaries; but before the regime had time to celebrate the massacre, General Cañizares received a charge of lead in the stomach—from the one refugee who had a weapon—that caused his death a few hours later.

---

* Journalist for the magazine *Bohemia* and an underground collaborator of Armando Hart.—C. F.

To counter the anxiety caused among the top military brass by the execution of two pillars of the repressive forces, Batista lost no time shaking up the high command and effecting a whole series of promotions. To make clear his support of the dictatorship once again, President Eisenhower reinforced Cuba's naval power with three fast, highly maneuverable patrol boats equipped with radar and powerful artillery. This gift coincided with Fidel's announcement that his plan to invade Cuba would soon be carried out.

In the latter part of November, Colonel Orlando Piedra presented an emergency court with a long list of charges indiscriminately leveled against Fidel Castro and José Echeverría, as well as Trujillo, Prío, and well-known gangsters such as Eufemio Fernández, Policarpo Soler, and several other political schemers of Machado's era.

Colonel Piedra charged that Trujillo's armed forces would attack various objectives in Oriente Province within the next twenty-four hours and that Trujillo and Prío had paid Fidel 200,000 pesos to help the landing by staging armed actions in Pinar del Río on the 26th of July.

At the same time, the U.S. Military Mission in Cuba advised Batista to hold military maneuvers to intimidate the people with a huge display of the war weapons and equipment he had at his command. During one of these "exercises," the commander of the tank corps, General Tabernilla, rode out of Camp Columbia at the head of an impressive column of Sherman tanks, which he led through the main streets of Marianao, Santiago de las Vegas, San Antonio de los Baños, and other sections of Havana Province.

The Cuban newspapers give wide coverage to the air force war exercises: night bombing and strafing of Santa Clara, simulated artillery attacks on Pinar del Río, mortar fire on Havana, while reinforcements were sent to the 7th Military District in Holguín. With equal fanfare, the U.S. ambassador in Cuba turned over to Batista a squadron of jets, field artillery, and a large shipment of arms for the infantry.

But in spite of all efforts by the United States to show its support of Batista's regime and by the regime to discredit Castro as the founder and leader of the 26th of July Movement, the cry of "Revolution! Revolution!" had reached the streets, and the Movement was beginning to make itself felt with its steady harassment of the repressive forces and other branches of the regime.

An objective picture of what was happening in Cuba: the revolt against Batista's corrupt and ruthless government has spread to the palatial homes of the privileged class but its real strength lies in student circles, workers' centers, in the fields and in the streets. There isn't a corner left on the island where the 26th of July flag doesn't wave at one time or another; everywhere bombs explode, cane fields are set on fire, and nails are thrown onto the highways to puncture tires, always to the rebel cry of "Revolution! Revolution!"

Student beatings extend beyond Havana to Matanzas, Camagüey, Victoria de las Tunas, and Holguín. Santiago de Cuba needs a chapter of its own.

FAURE CHOMÓN

The time was ripe for continued attacks. The Revolutionary Directory had received a cable with a coded message from Fidel in Mexico, saying that he would land on the Cuban coast the following day. The order to mobilize went out to the rest of the men in the group who had not been able to do it in those difficult days of persecution. The Revolutionary Directory's high command, which was in continuing session, informed the men of the war material we could count on and the number of men mobilized. We didn't have enough arms even to carry out the emergency plan we had evolved for this situation, since we had not expected it to happen until later on. Everybody was eager to do "something" to help those who would land the next day. Although it is not our plan, since we were resolved to assassinate Batista, we decided that the climate that we had created throughout the country, together with Fidel's landing, could be decisive in leading up to an armed uprising in Havana. With this in mind, two members of the directory, Julio García and I, got together that night with Pepe Suárez of the 26th of July Movement and with Alvarado and Blanco, who were Auténticos. We were surprised to find that the last two apparently did not know what was going on. We had to act quickly and decided to tell them what was going to happen, insisting on the urgent need to unite all the revolutionary forces in a joint action, since Batista's fate depended on this. They were against our plan, arguing that they had not been told about it, but we guessed what the real problem was: they had no weapons.

Pepe Suárez agreed that we had to pool our resources to get anything done in Havana, but at this meeting and others we had later on, thanks to the liaison of the Women's Civic Front for Martí, we discovered that in Havana the 26th of July Movement lacked the organization and the fighting equipment needed to carry out our plan. On the evening of November 29, 1956, the executive council of the Revolutionary Directory met and we reported the situation. We all realized that we were powerless to act. Then José Antonio Echeverría took the floor, and—with the composure that, despite his youth, he always showed when there was a crucial decision to make—he said: "I don't like José Wangüemert's idea of posting men, with the few arms we have, on rooftops and street corners, nor Julio García's plan to dig in with those arms at the university. We'd be sacrificing our men. I'm against both and accept full responsibility because we can't send a group of our comrades to certain death. We must not give up our plan to kill Batista. We'll need those men who would be killed in any suicidal action. But our original plan is worth any risk or sacrifice, because the dictatorship will end if we succeed."

CARLOS FRANQUI

Fidel's statement to the government newspaper *Alerta,* in November, that if Batista did not resign, he would land in Cuba within two weeks, stirred up a hornet's nest. Fidel knew he couldn't keep secret the fact that he was preparing an invasion in Mexico. Besides, he would inspire confidence in the people by saying and doing what others said but never did.

The RD's sensational killing of Colonel Blanco Rico and other officers in the Montmartre; the execution of Salas Cañizares, fatally wounded while he was murdering the attackers of the Goicuría Barracks at the Haitian embassy; the student demonstrations, the acts of sabotage and the protests, had shaken up all of Cuba and created the right climate for an insurrection.

In Mexico, Fidel issued a statement criticizing Blanco Rico's execution. He did not want to look like an enemy of the army. And although Blanco Rico had been the chief of one of the most hated repressive organizations, he had not been one of the worst killers.

The police reaction was severe, and we slept many nights among the dead in the Caballero funeral home. It was patronized by the rich; and hundreds of people attended the wakes there. It had a coffee shop and a bar on the ground floor. All we had to do to avoid calling attention to that safe hideout was exchange places with the bodies once in a while.

There was much disagreement among us about the role Havana should play in our plans. Oriente Province was a better place for the struggle, and we thought Santiago and the Sierra should be the main front. For the Revolutionary Directory, Havana and the university came first.

Fidel's choice was strategically sound, but he underestimated Havana's value. It had 2 million people and was the nerve center for Cuba's economic, military, and political affairs. But the 26th of July group maintained that the regime should be attacked in Oriente, where it was obviously more vulnerable, without, of course, neglecting the capital.

It had been a mistake to send Faustino, Hart, Miret, Haydée, Montané, Melba, and the other leaders to Mexico or Santiago, where they were less helpful to Fidel or Frank than they would have been in Havana.

Only a group of comrades who could not call the shots—Aldo Vera, Sergio González, Oltuski, Enrique Hart, Fontán, Suárez Gayol, Salado, myself, and a few others—remained to carry on the fight in a deserted Havana.

In contrast, the directory's power was centered in Havana, where it played an essential role but at too high a price; almost all its cadres were wiped out. Yet it balanced things by bringing the capital into the struggle.

Fidel sent three telegrams to say that he was leaving Mexico. One to Frank: "Book ordered out-of-print," addressed to Duque; another to a Havana hotel: "Make reservation," which its receptionist, comrade Pérez Font, was to deliver to Aldo Santamaría; and a third to Santa Clara. All reached their destinations safely.

It was November 29 and Aldo suggested that we meet at one of two places: the corner of Prado and Virtudes or at the *Carteles* magazine office, where I worked. It was here we decided to meet with the rest of our comrades of the Action section to complete our plans. I thought it best to wait for him there, before the others arrived, to avoid any slipups. But first Aldo was to meet a soldier, our only contact with the army at that time.

At five o'clock, when the meeting was to begin, Aldo hadn't shown up yet. Two hours later I realized that something serious had kept him from coming.

Joe Westbrook, a leader of the directory, waited as long as he safely could and then left. Pepe Suárez, a Moncada veteran, was the Action leader in Havana then. The only weapon his group had was a machine gun, and he didn't think we stood a chance. He was in touch with other groups and I thought it unwise to let him know that Fidel had sailed; they were not in the right frame of mind or in condition to do anything, and the news might leak out. I had no doubts about Pepe, but I hardly knew his companions.

That night we found out that Aldo had been tailed by the SIM on his way to meet the soldier and had been arrested after trying to escape through the Prado: he swallowed the famous cable from Mexico during the chase. We used our contacts in the newspapers to report Aldo's arrest; it was our only chance to save his life.

The action in Santiago and Fidel's landing would depend on Aldo's capacity to resist Batista's torturers. He was able to. I avoided two years in prison, through one of those freak accidents so frequent in the underground struggle, when I decided not to meet him at Virtudes.

Those were terrible days; we never knew what was coming next.

Pepe Suárez and the Movement in Havana were inoperative and might as well not have existed. They hid so well that no one believed they were real. We improvised a new Action group led by Aldo Vera; we were really unarmed and inexperienced when we carried out our first acts of sabotage.

We decided to blow up the main electric, gas, and telephone centers. Betloc, the electrical engineer, had obtained the plans.

On the night of December 4, Aldo, Sergio, Suárez Gayol, Oltuski, Machaco [Angel Amejeiras], Tabaco, Miralles, Juan Misterio, Marcelo Salado, Vera, myself, and a few others I can't remember went out on our first sabotage job. At nine o'clock, Pepe Suárez was to hit an electric tower with his machine gun and cause a blackout, but of course it didn't come off.

My group was assigned the Camp Columbia telephone exchange, which was in front of the park on Twenty-fifth Street and the Vedado institute.

With traffic all around us, we lifted the heavy manhole cover and used a cigar to light the wick of our homemade bomb; we had to hold it up to keep it from getting wet.

As soon as we had done it, we started yelling to the couples in the park: "Run, run, a bomb is going to go off!" They scattered like rabbits.

I hid about a hundred yards away, in Dr. Santamarina's house, to wait for the blast that never came. None of our bombs went off that night. Mine was recovered years later, still intact. No one ever knew whether the wicks or faulty dynamite was to blame.

The same thing happened when we tried to set fire to the main stores in Havana with lighted phosphorus—lots of smoke and small fires easily put out by the fire department.

But our will to fight surmounted obstacles and made up for inexperience and the lack of resources and arms. The action and sabotage group, started in those days under Aldo Vera's dogged leadership, later on put up a tough fight against Batista's henchmen, shaking up all Havana with its acts of sabotage.

FÉLIX PENA AND FRANK PAÍS
Conversation with Carlos Franqui

On November 23, the leadership of the Movement asked the chief of each group to choose his military objective and turn in a special report on it. Three days later we agreed that the key points were the maritime police, the national police, and the Moncada Barracks.

On the twenty-eighth, we met to go over our plans and check last-minute details. We had been notified that Fidel and his men had left Mexico on the twenty-fifth for Cuba; they would arrive in five days. On the twenty-ninth, we were hard at work preparing living quarters and distributing arms and uniforms.

We mobilized that night. The city seemed normal, but early the next morning, sons, husbands, and brothers were missing from their homes, and the whole city was tense, waiting for something to happen.

The attack had originally been set for 6:00 a.m. but it was moved to 7:00 to avoid coinciding with the changing of the guard.

For the first time we put on the 26th of July uniform, olive green with black armbands and red lettering.

Pepito Tey gave us a pep talk: "We're going to fight in Cuba for Cuba! Long live the Revolution! Long live the 26th of July!"

Our group consisted of 28 men; 20 in uniform, led by Pepito, would attack police headquarters from the front, and a surprise element of 8 men in civilian clothes, headed by Parellada, would be stationed behind the building.

We had submachine guns, rifles, grenades, Molotov cocktails, and a .30-caliber machine gun. We had a few vehicles but needed more; so we stopped several drivers going by: "The revolution is beginning in Cuba now. Your country asks you to give up your car. In the name of the 26th of July, we're going to fight the dictatorship."

Parellada's group entered the School of Fine Arts on the Padre Pico Street side, crossed the courtyard, and went up to the roof, which overlooks the rear of the police station, but a sentry saw us and fired, sparking off a one-sided battle: 28 revolutionaries against 70 policemen and 15 soldiers.

Those of us with Pepito were going up the hill toward the station house, when they opened fire on us with a machine gun they had placed on top of the building. This stopped us from reaching the door of the station in the cars we had commandeered. Pepito got out and urged us on, and we took up our positions and started firing toward the building.

The enemy answered our fire. Our comrades behind the station house managed to get several policemen who were running across the courtyard. The smoke and flames from the fire set off by Molotov cocktails were starting to shoot up, Pepito saw Tony Alomá fall, struck in the head by a bullet.

Pepito stood up and ordered us to charge on. He led the column protecting us, firing with his M-1. As he turned a corner, a spray of bullets hit him in the leg. He continued to advance, leaning against the wall and firing. Another burst of fire cut him down.

When Parellada saw that we hadn't been able to get to the main door, he tried to concentrate his fire and reach the courtyard, but he too was felled by a bullet in the head.

We had lost the element of surprise, two of our leaders were dead, and a hail of bullets was pelting us; we began an orderly retreat, protected by our .30-caliber guns. Three of our men and five of the enemy were killed.

A few minutes later, flames were gutting the station. If we had waited a little instead of rushing, we could have wiped out everyone defending the station house.

One policeman running away from the flames stopped to open the jail door to try to save some young people from Santiago who had been locked up the evening before. Lieutenant Durán, who had been thrown out of the army for his crimes and later reinstated by Batista, ordered him: "Stand back. Let them all burn; that'll stop them from starting any more revolutions!" Left behind by the policeman with the keys, the terrified prisoners were starting to burn, but they were saved in the nick of time by the fire department.

We fared better against the maritime police headquarters. Several armed comrades, dressed like workers, surprised and disarmed three posts. The others, in uniform, drove their cars right to the headquarters' door and went in. The guard on duty tried to open fire but was cut down by a barrage from our side. Two other policemen were killed, and the lieutenant in charge, who was hit, kept on screaming: "Don't shoot, boys, we're on your side. . . ."

We began collecting the artillery stores and the weapons they had there, about 20 rifles, and taking care of the wounded policemen. They had four dead, but we came out of this first clash unscathed. Then two trucks brought 70 soldiers from the Moncada Barracks with heavy equipment and a lopsided battle followed.

We finally managed to beat a retreat, protected by a screen of bullets, toward general headquarters in Moncada.

Since our mortar hadn't worked, and we had been seen by the enemy, we could not attack the Moncada Barracks.

We had planned to cut it off, set fire to it, and carry out other actions. The army tried to break our siege, and the exchange of fire between us was intense. Our men were driving back the soldiers.

Many refused to fight against the revolutionaries; 67 were arrested and later court-martialed.

We trained a .30-caliber machine gun on the frigate *Patria,* which was in the harbor, and she had to clear for action and retreat to the mouth of the bay.

Four comrades went to the Dolores hardware store and held up the owner: "We're sorry, but we need these weapons to fight for Cuba's freedom."

The city woke up under heavy fire. Weapons of every caliber were spitting fire and lead. The sound of sirens from fire trucks, from the Moncada Barracks, and from the naval headquarters filled the air. Airplanes flying low droned overhead. Fires broke out all over the city. The revolutionary forces controlled the streets, and Batista's army was making every effort to rout them. The battle cries of our comrades were taken up by the people.

The entire population of Santiago joined the revolutionaries and cooperated in every way. They took care of our wounded, hid our armed men, and looked after the weapons and the uniforms of those hunted by the soldiers. They encouraged us, let us take over their homes, and followed the army's movements from place to place, reporting them to us. In Guantánamo, our 26th of July comrades stormed the barracks of the Ermita sugar mill. Fighting lasted in Santiago from Thursday to Sunday.

FAUSTINO PÉREZ   Tuxpán, Mexico, November 25

I had no problem avoiding the police watchdogs in Havana. It was my third trip to Mexico. I was one of the last to arrive. I stayed in one of the houses where the future combatants were billeted. There were more than a hundred in military training, and I was impressed to see them all so well organized and diligent. I had to get up at 7:00 a.m. and after breakfast we went on long marches, rowed and swam in Lake Chapúltepec. In the afternoon we had classes in military theory and politics. Later we were transferred to a training camp six hundred fifty miles north of Mexico City. We lived outdoors in a sparsely wooded area crawling with rattlesnakes. José Smith, who was from Matanzas, supervised our strict training schedule: target practice, field exercises, attack and defense, river crossings, mountain climbing, long marches, hunting and fishing. We were constantly harassed in Mexico City. On Sunday, November 25, 1956, Smith told us: "We're leaving for Tuxpán tomorrow and we'll sail for Cuba at night."

Several days before, Fidel Castro Ruz, the leader of the Movement, had set the sailing date. The recruits had to leave the training camps ahead of time. Mexico City, Veracruz, and Tamaulipas were centers of secret mobilization. Except for a handful of leaders in charge of the men and arms, no one knew the exact destination. The vigilance of the police and the zeal of Batista's spies were a permanent threat. A valuable load of armaments and several key men had recently fallen into the hands of the police. We had to move with speed and caution to keep from losing something we had put together with so much effort and sacrifice. And there was a promise to keep; Cuba was anxious to fulfill Fidel's words: "We will be free men or martyrs." We assembled at night at Tuxpán, on the Gulf of Mexico, a city divided by the river whose name it bears. It was a dark, rainy night. Many "civilians" crossed the river that night in rented boats; their owners rowed slowly. The "travelers" gave generous tips hoping to cut down the chances of being turned in. One after the other, the groups came to the prearranged meeting place, using the darkest streets. We were totally convinced of the importance of our mission, and nobody asked questions, or even spoke. A silent embrace among the weeds at the river's edge was the only greeting between men who hadn't seen one another for some time. A short distance away, silent shadows moved toward the river; they were other comrades who were feverishly loading a small boat that could be partly seen in the lights reflected on the water—it was the *Granma*.

When the arms, ammunition, and other military supplies had been loaded, an orderly rush to get on board began. We were afraid that the last ones would have to stay behind. Some hadn't arrived yet. We waited. It was 1:00 a.m., November 25, 1956, and time to leave. As quietly as possible, with only one engine going at low speed and all her lights out, the *Granma* began to pull away. We were crouched so closely together that we were almost on top of one another. The helmsman followed the middle of the channel toward the river's mouth. On either side of us, the city slept on. It took half an hour to leave the river, and perhaps another half an hour to cross the harbor. No one had seen us, and we were now entering the gulf. And all at once, as if by prearrangement, we started to sing our national anthem, as one man. We were on course for Cuba, but the hardest part still lay ahead of us. Hours later, nausea, seasickness, and weariness assailed us. The storm warnings and Mexican navy had banned all maritime traffic in that part of the gulf. It was El Norte, the winds so frequent this time of year. The gale gathered strength as we sailed on, and the mountainous waves toyed with the small yacht. She seemed to be making no headway. She began to ship water and seemed in increasing danger of sinking. The bilge pumps were put to use, but the water was rising instead of going down. We grabbed buckets and started bailing, but the water kept on rising at our feet. I went to see the captain to ask how far we were away from the coast of Yucatán. Someone else told me, "Very far away." We're goners, I thought, and went to look for Fidel. He seemed worried and was helping the men who were running back and forth bailing out the water with buckets. I wanted to suggest that we all jump into the water and swim ashore, but I noticed that the water was going down. The deck's planks were beginning to reappear. The pumps were working and we all breathed more easily. The *Granma* was invincible. Forces other than purely physical ones had resisted the storm and were driving the ship to her destination.

The zone of the northers was left behind, but other dangers lay ahead of us. The sight of a ship or plane was enough to put us on the alert.

After crossing the gulf, early one morning, we went through the Strait of Yucatán. The coast of Pinar del Río was close and we were tempted to land, but Oriente awaited us and that was where the *Granma* was headed. Our radio picked up an important bulletin: events in Santiago de Cuba. The naval base and police headquarters had been attacked, and there was shooting in the streets. Mortars and machine guns had been captured at the institute. A general strike had paralyzed Guantánamo. There were waves of sabotage in Matanzas and Las

Villas. We realized their magnitude and what had sparked them off: news of our departure had reached our comrades. In Santiago, our brave and well-disciplined fighters, led by Frank País and Pepito Tey, had control of the city. Pepito Tey, Otto Parellada, and Félix Alomá were the first victims of the tyranny's forces. It was November 30, 1956.

Aboard the *Granma,* off the Cuban coast, December 1

Our impatience grew but the *Granma* was no more remarkable for her speed than for her size. We passed very close to the Caymans. A helicopter approached but spun around and left without bothering us. It was the last day of our long crossing, and we were all armed and ready for anything. Anything except being captured or killed without putting up a fight. We were in our olive-green uniforms and desert boots, and we had our knapsacks, cartridge belts, and flasks. We fought off hunger and illness. "The lighthouse at Cabo Cruz should appear any minute now," said one of the sailors. The horizon was dark, the sea rough.

Comrade Roque, an ex-navy lieutenant, climbed up to the *Granma*'s cabin roof, but there was no land in sight. Coming back down, he leaned on the antenna and fell into the sea. There was a cry of alarm: "Man overboard! Stop the engines, stop!" The helmsman, Pichirilo Mejías, did his best. We all wanted to pitch in and do something. We heard several desperate cries—"Here, here, here!"—which seemed to be drifting farther away. We strained our eyes but could not see or hear anything. The *Granma*'s searchlight was turned on for the first time, when it was more dangerous than ever. Nothing helped. Our comrade was being swallowed by the deep. Never willing to give up, Fidel ordered one more search. We heard the cry "Here!" again, weaker but inexplicably closer now. Pichirilo Mejías, our brave, efficient Dominican helmsman, saw him first and miraculously rescued him. His strength, his ability, his levelheadedness, as well as Fidel's faith and the efforts of his comrades had saved his life. It was some time before we saw the Cabo Cruz lighthouse flashes.

The first glimmer of day began to appear, and we still were not sure of our position. The tide was low and there was danger of running aground. We made straight for the coast, which could be glimpsed in the semidarkness. Our ship sailed until it could get no closer, less than a hundred yards offshore. The lifeboat was lowered and a reconnaissance party, led by Captain Smith, boarded it; but it was overcrowded and began to ship water. Everyone had to get out and wade through the muddy sea bottom. It was rough going, but we headed in search of solid ground. The sea reached in as far as the mangroves, which formed a thick, jumbled net that was hard to penetrate. Ahead of us, nothing but mud, more water, and mangroves. We pushed on. One comrade climbed the tallest tree and told us there was more water beyond the trees. We thought we had landed on a key in the middle of the ocean. We had to go on, Cuba had to be straight ahead. After endless hours in the enormous swamp, struggling through mud, mangroves, and water, we finally began to touch solid ground. Some of our men had to be carried out by the stronger ones. We lay down on the grass, exhausted, hungry, covered with mud, knowing that we were finally on Cuban soil.

Crespo, a country boy, climbed up a tree and saw a small house. He went there and found the surprised owner at home. Crespo brought him back to us. He was a poor peasant, on whom rested our fate. His name was Angel Pérez. Fidel talked to him, explained who we were, our mission, and our ideals. Pérez asked us to his hut and offered us what little food he had. We drank water and some of us started to scrape the mud from our uniforms. Others cleaned their guns. The peasant's family chased a chicken and ran after a pig. A lot of our comrades had not gotten there yet.

Suddenly, we heard a lot of shooting, blasts, explosions, from where we had left the *Granma*. We could not tell if it was the infantry or the navy, but we took cover in the nearest thickets, giving up our roast pig. Eight of our men were missing; we would find them two days later, far from here. We couldn't find a bite to eat the first day. We went into some thick woods, hoping to get some rest. It was December 2. We had landed at Playa Colorada. And, as Juan Manuel Márquez said, "It wasn't a landing, it was a shipwreck." Our plans had failed completely. Fidel looked angry.

We had originally planned to attack Niquero on November 30, at daybreak. Crescencio Pérez was waiting for us near there with a hundred men and several trucks. We would take Niquero, storm Manzanillo in our trucks, and go on to the Sierra, while the uprising raged in Santiago. From then on, a campaign of agitation, sabotage, and strikes would get under way.

We had landed behind schedule and in the wrong place. Everything had gone awry. That night we camped in a thick forest, without food or water. At dawn, we set out eastward, for the Sierra, and met some peasants along the way; we had our first breakfast in Cuba—cassava and bread dipped in honey. Airplanes appeared and we had to run for cover under the trees. On December 3 we had a discouraging day: no houses or people, no water, and we could not find any guides or farms. We saw a hut owned by a family of charcoal workers, who fled in fright when they saw us. We ate in their house and left 5 pesos. We slept in the woods. At daybreak a peasant and a scout we had sent out returned with the eight men missing since the day we landed.

Airplanes were strafing the area around us. To avoid the planes, Fidel ordered rest during the day and marches at night.

CHE GUEVARA   Alegría del Pío

Suddenly, there was a steady burst of fire. Bullets whistled right and left. Airplanes appeared and began strafing us.

Montané and I were leaning against a tree, talking about our children and eating our meager ration of half a sausage and two crackers, when we heard a rifle shot, followed, seconds later, by a hail of bullets. My rifle was not one of the best. I had asked for that one, because I was still in terrible shape after a prolonged attack of asthma. I remember all this vaguely. I recall that in the midst of the shooting Almeida came over and asked for orders, but there was no one there to give them. Fidel had tried unsuccessfully to get us all together in a cane field close by. The surprise attack had been overwhelming, the gunfire too heavy. My problem was to decide between my obligation as a doctor and my duty as a revolutionary. I grabbed a box of ammunition, leaving behind the knapsack with medicines, and crossed the clearing that separated me from the cane field.

Faustino was on his knees, at the edge of the field, firing his automatic. Near me, a comrade named Arbentosa was walking toward the cane field. A burst of fire got us both. I felt a hard blow on my chest and sharp pain in my neck. I was sure I had been fatally wounded. Blood spurting from his nose, mouth, and a gaping wound, Arbentosa shouted something like, "They've killed me!" and started firing wildly, since there was no one to be seen. Lying on the ground, I said to Faustino, "They got me." Faustino glanced at me and told me it was nothing, but in his eyes I could see the fatal verdict.

Stretched out on the ground, I fired into the woods, driven by the same dark impulse as the other wounded man. Everything seemed lost, and I suddenly started thinking about the best way to die. I remembered an old Jack London story in which the hero, knowing he will freeze to death in the cold wilderness of Alaska, leans against a tree trunk and gets ready to die with dignity. Somewhere behind me, Camilo was shouting: "Nobody surrenders here!" Ponce was dragging himself toward me; a bullet had apparently gone through his lung. For a moment, I just lay there, alone, waiting for death, but Almeida came over and encouraged me to go on. I did, in spite of my pain, and we went into the cane field. A group, which included Ramiro Valdés, Chao, Benítez, and myself, led by Almeida, crossed the last lane of the cane field and reached the woods safely, just as we heard the first shouts of "Shoot!" in the cane field.

Each brigade met its own fate.

UPI News Release

Government planes strafed and bombed the revolutionary forces to-night and wiped out 40 members of the 26th of July Movement's supreme command. Thirty-year-old Fidel Castro, its leader, was among those killed. The revolutionaries had landed successfully on the southern coast between the port of Niquero and Manzanillo, in Oriente Province, but they were caught out in the open and wiped out tonight, in a brief and bloody skirmish, by aircraft and ground troops. The revolutionaries, whose bodies were recovered by government troops, were wearing the olive-drab uniform of the 26th of July Movement and armbands with the Cuban flag's red star and the words "26th of July." Besides Castro, the most important leaders killed were his younger brother, Raúl, and Juan Manuel Márquez.

CONFIDENTIAL
ARMY COMMUNIQUÉ   Alegría del Pío, December 5

At approximately 0700 hours, Sunday, December 2, the undersigned received a confidential report: 200–300 men had landed at dawn this day from a yacht at Punta Colorada, about 16 miles south of Niquero. Contact was made immediately with the commander of Coast Guard 106 anchored in port and a full report made to Maritime Police Headquarters; the squadron commander was ordered to make a reconnaissance to determine the location, exact number of men, and fighting strength of the forces; reinforcements were to be sent from other ports.

The port captain sent a reconnaissance patrol to investigate and report the enemy's capacity and the name of its commander. Some hours later this patrol reported that it had not sighted the enemy but had learned from people in the area that it numbered approximately 200 well-armed men* commanded by Dr. Fidel Castro Ruz. . . .

[The report goes on to describe reconnaissance efforts by plane and on land, designed to cut off the enemy's access to the Sierra Maestra. Ambushes were set up at several sites.]

At Agua Fina, we picked up the enemy's trail and followed it over a path in the woods and across a sugar-cane field to a point south of Alegría, where we made contact with the enemy at 1645 hours, December 5. We fought while it was still light, although we could not actually see the enemy because of the thick vegetation and the hilly terrain. After approximately one-half hour of gunfire, they scattered into the woods, leaving behind four dead and one wounded, and almost all their military equipment, including knapsacks, weapons, ammunition, medicine

---

* There were only 82 men.

kit, etc. We proceeded to evacuate our wounded, and procure a better position to pitch camp. Our forces had 3 wounded, 1 of whom died due to the seriousness of his wounds. The following day we learned that the chief of operations had ordered the ambush at La Esperanza to pull back, which leads me to conclude that if Dr. Fidel Castro has escaped, he did it through La Esperanza, after it was left open.

Aquiles Chinea Alvarez
2d Lt., Squadron 12, Rural Guard
José C. Tandrón, Captain,
Squadron 13, Rural Guard

RECOLLECTIONS

Guillermo García: We had received our instructions, exactly five days before the landing and movement had started in the zone. We had assembled several trucks of various kinds in the Plátano area.

We expected the landing to be at Ojo del Toro, near Niquero, but no one was sure of the exact location and, from November 28 on, we had lookouts ranging the coast, mostly near Ojo del Toro.

Crescencio kept us informed of everything.

On November 30, we were told that they would arrive on the coast but nothing happened. The landing took place a little after 5:00 a.m. on December 2, 1956. We found out early the next morning, and there was already plenty of military activity in the area.

At noon on the third, we sent out patrols to organize the peasants and tell them that they should give protection to any armed men who might show up. At this point, the army began to close in tighter on all sides, and it became impossible to meet up with the expeditionaries; truckloads of troops were literally pouring into the area.

We organized all the young people. Many of them would soon die, among them an affectionate little mulatto, Godofredo, who was full of fun. He was in Lorenzo's squad and was killed in Las Mercedes.

We ran into Fidel on the night of the thirteenth, at 1:00 a.m., in Marcial Areviches's farm. Faustino and Universo were with him.

Manuel Fajardo: The first one I met was Nico López, who had organized the Movement in this sector back in the middle of 1955. I met Frank in May 1956 at Celia Sánchez's home. Then we received the call to insurrection on November 30.

The first member of the Movement to make contact with Fidel was Rubén Tejeda, a young peasant from around here, and he gave Guillermo the word.

We had organized a peasant militia for the Movement in the zones of El Plátano, Durán, and Sevilla Arriba.

Celia Sánchez: The 26th of July had been organized in Niquero, Pilón, and that whole zone.

Guillermo García: Celia did most of the work. I was with Crescencio Pérez. The Movement had been started in 1956 and was still very small. We had already grouped together to wait for the landing. We didn't know just where they would come ashore but we had made extensive preparations in the whole area.

Manuel Fajardo: Guillermo and I were the General Staff of the peasant militia. On December 14, when Fidel passed through Purial, Guillermo was sent to pick up more guns, because they had only two rifles. We collected ten that had been left behind, among them a Thompson machine gun I was to use.

There was one Mendoza and one Remington, the machine gun, a Johnson, and some telescopic sights. The army had closed in around us, but we knew every path by heart and could slip in and out anytime we wanted to. We moved around on horseback or on foot.

On December 14 Guillermo met Fidel and we took him to the home of Mongo Pérez, Crescencio's brother. Raúl showed up later with Ciro Redondo, Armando Rodríguez, Efigenio, and René Rodríguez.

Celia Sánchez: Before he came to my house in Pilón, I had already seen Frank with Pepito Tey at a meeting we had in Manzanillo, after Fidel got out of the Isle of Pines Prison. That was when the 26th of July was formed. Frank went to Pilón with Pedrito Miret, because we were making preliminary preparations for the landing, and we wanted to find out how deep the water was on that part of the coast and the possibilities of landing there. I studied the depths on some charts I borrowed in Pilón and never returned. I remember that they were found in the *Granma* later and taken to my father, wrapped in a girdle, to make him believe I had taken part in the landing.

We planned to wait for Fidel and see if we could get arms to him. We decided that Echeverría, who said he knew the area well, would act as Fidel's guide from Pilón, El Macho, or La Magdalena—all ideal landing places. From there, they could have taken trucks, buses, and other vehicles from Pilón or Niquero.

From the twenty-ninth on, we had trucks, jeeps, and barrels of gasoline everywhere in the area. There were groups from Manzanillo and Campechuela; people who knew the area were stationed all over.

We also kept in touch with Crescencio's family, the Acuñas, in case they disembarked on that side. Carracedo, who we called El Jabao [the halfbreed], was there too; and Crescencio's son, Ignacio, who was a cane cutter and was killed in action at Jiguani.

We sent the men from Campechuela into the woods to begin training without guns, because all we had were two M-1's.

When they landed, we were in the Sierra. We had reached Crescencio's house at daybreak on the twenty-ninth, and spent the next day waiting. When we got there, I said: "Wake up, Crescencio! Fidel is coming and you have to go wait for him with all your men—but don't let anybody know." "Just a minute," he said, calm as could be. He went into his bedroom and came out a little later, in his Sunday best! Wearing low shoes, *guayabera* shirt, lariat at his neck, and a felt hat, as if he was on his way to a party instead of the woods. But his gun was at his waist.

One group of men from the *Granma* could have attacked Niquero, and another could have attacked Pilón. At Pilón, they would have been one step away from the Sierra; it is right on the flank of the mountain. There would have been no problems. They couldn't have landed in a worse place than the swamp. If they had done it on the small beach, it would have been a breeze. They would have found trucks and jeeps with gas, and they could have stormed the garrison with the guns they had.

Universo Sánchez: After the rout at Alegría del Río, Fidel and I ended up alone. That was around 5:30 p.m. It was getting dark when Faustino joined us. The three of us walked through the cane fields for several days till we got to Mongo Pérez's house. We waited there for his brother Crescencio. They told us he had many rebels with him in the Sierra, and it was true.

Fidel Castro: We landed on December 2, 1956, with 82 men, and had our first setback. After a week at sea in a tiny boat, battered by storms, and with our supplies almost all gone, our expeditionary force landed, hungry and weak. First, we had the bad luck to come ashore in a terrible place, a real swamp; we took a beating, wading through mud for several hours to reach solid ground. Then, after three days without food, marching through strange country without a guide, we were surprised and routed by land forces far superior in number and by an aircraft squadron.

Only a few of our men were killed, but our group was completely dispersed. I had two men and two rifles with me; and eight men and seven rifles were with my brother Raúl. When we two managed to regroup, we had twelve men and eleven rifles. All the other weapons were lost or hidden. Several of our comrades, who had hidden their guns in places they couldn't remember at all, got together with us again. Others were captured by the army and killed.

Vilma Espín: From November 30 on, everyone in San Gerónimo was in on the conspiracy. The neighborhood people were told all about it.

In December, they made a search, but we kept on using our house for everything: contacts, hiding dynamite, loading the people to go to the Sierra, all the contacts with Havana Province, until April. Everybody in the neighborhood knew what the problems were. There were stool pigeons on the corners, but since we knew about them, we stayed there, because it was hard to get houses in the beginning. In spite of all that, we could still do everything, because the people would tell us: "Now the stoolie is coming over here, now he's over there." And from the other corner, someone would say: "Now the stoolie is having coffee. Take advantage of it." It was a real network.

Sometimes they said: "Something's going on. It looks like they're going to make a search," and we would shift all the boys to other houses in the neighborhood. The people were really fantastic.

Carlos Franqui: On December 10, there was great confusion in Havana. No one knew what had happened to Fidel and the *Granma* expeditionaries. The Batista press office had put out a report that government forces had killed forty of the 26th of July expeditionaries, including Fidel and Raúl Castro. We did not believe that Fidel was dead, but it was obvious that many in the landing force had been killed, others were in prison. There was no news from Santiago.

We had a meeting, and I was chosen to go to Santiago to see Frank, Vilma, Hart, and Haydée and find out what they thought. I was preparing an issue of *Revolución* to report what had really happened and give the Movement an idea of the work ahead of us.

I took the Havana–Santiago bus. We were almost in Matanzas when I noticed a group of men who were obviously policemen. They were in civilian clothes, but their attitude, their gestures, their faces, and the guns bulging underneath their jackets were a dead giveaway.

I moved closer to them and started talking with another passenger about José Pardo Llada, a well-known Ortodoxo Party leader and radio commentator, who was openly against Batista as well as against us for being rebels.

The policemen were listening and I told them I was a reporter on *Información*—a serious middle-class newspaper, where I had once worked as a proofreader—and was on my way to Oriente to do a story on Fidel Castro and his aborted expedition.

The chief police agent turned out to be Sergeant Calzadilla, one of the Bureau of Investigation's most notorious henchmen. He sat down next to me and started telling me some of his experiences on the police force. The trip took several hours and we drank beer after beer at each of the many stops.

He told me he was heading a mission to Santiago, because they had been tipped off that Hart and Haydée, as well as Frank País and Vilma

Espín, were hiding there; he knew the first two personally and would be able to identify and arrest them. He promised to let me have the story of the arrest before anyone else.

I told him I was interested in visiting the Moncada Barracks to talk with General Díaz Tamayo, chief of operations, and to interview some of the prisoners from the *Granma* and get the full story of their defeat.

Calzadilla told me he would clear the way for me; in fact, he himself would take me to Moncada to see the prisoners. He invited me to stay at his hotel and told me not to worry about the bill; it would be charged to General Batista.

The hotel was in the center of Santiago. Calzadilla got me a room next to his. He told me to be ready in two hours to go with him to Moncada.

I visited stores and other busy places to make sure I wasn't being tailed; and after calling up Vilma, I set out for her house, still keeping a sharp eye out. A few minutes later, I was with Frank, Vilma, Hart, Haydée, Pena, and other Santiago leaders, telling them of my luck in running into Calzadilla.

We decided which prisoners I should talk to. The most important and the ones who knew me best were Léster Rodríguez, who had been arrested on the night of the thirtieth, Mario Hidalgo of the National Directorate, and Echeverría, who had been sent to Manzanillo to act as guide for the men on the *Granma*. I was given an additional list, in case those men were not in prison.

I went back to the hotel and Calzadilla drove me to Moncada. He took me to see General Díaz Tamayo, who told me that Fidel and the other survivors still being hunted down would soon be caught.

On one wall there was a huge map sprinkled with red and yellow dots—and some in other colors; they indicated sieges, battles, and places where they had found stragglers—roads, rivers, and farm shacks; it had all the army units, camps, and garrisons in the area between Alegría del Pío and the spurs of the Sierra Maestra.

It was a major troop movement, but Fidel and a large number of the expeditionaries had obviously slipped through; however, their situation was still difficult.

I was then taken to the prison and allowed to talk with the inmates. They couldn't believe their eyes when they saw me, but we somehow managed to conceal our feelings. I had last seen some of them in Mexico, some on the island. I asked some preliminary questions to cover up, and then I was left alone with them. I found out that Che had been wounded and that Fidel, Faustino, Raúl, and others had slipped through the encirclements.

I said good-bye to the prisoners and to my friendly "protectors." Then I went back to Vilma's place and reported everything to Frank and the others. I had pulled off a terrific feat without any special merit on my part; the cockiness, the vanity, and the stupidity of the police sergeant had made it a cinch.

I stayed in Santiago a few days, during which Frank received the first message from the Movement, in Manzanillo: Fidel, Faustino, Che, Almeida, Raúl, Amejeiras, Universo, Ramiro, Ciro Redondo, and others were safe in the hands of Crescencio Pérez and the peasant militias. Guillermo and Fajardo were guiding them into the Sierra.

I returned to Havana. A few days later, Faustino arrived with instructions from Fidel to reorganize the Movement and get ready to help those in the Sierra.

Revolución appeared: twenty thousand copies filled with information, organization plans, and guidance for its readers. It explained that Fidel was safe and sound with the guerrillas and the peasant militia, and it played an important part at a moment of confusion, weakness, and hardships. It made the whole country sit up and take notice of the Movement. And it sparked off an all-out persecution campaign by the police.

FIDEL CASTRO   Purial de Vicana, December 25

About to set out again on our march toward the Sierra Maestra, where we shall go on fighting until we meet with victory or death, we want to express our gratitude to comrade Ramón Peréz Montané and his family, who helped us to regroup the first contingent of our detachment, fed it for eight days, and put it in touch with the Movement on the rest of the island. The assistance we received from him and many others like him during the Revolution's most critical days encourages us to go on fighting, confident that a people like ours deserves every kind of sacrifice.

1957

7. JANUARY–FEBRUARY: TO THE SIERRA MAESTRA

FIDEL CASTRO   Sierra Maestra, January

Just as we kept our promise to land in Cuba with an expedition and start an armed struggle, the Cuban people can be assured that we shall cease to fight only when we have overthrown the tyranny or have died fighting.

Sabotage and burning the sugar cane are preliminary steps to the general strike, which the people must carry out to help our drive to turn back the forces of tyranny. We are satisfied with the cooperation of the people; although the 26th of July Movement has few arms and resources, it has nevertheless been active, in one form or another, throughout the island. We have never intended to topple the dictatorship at one stroke but to launch a revolutionary campaign that, with agitation and sabotage, will culminate in the general revolutionary strike. We managed to land in Cuba and to keep the Revolution in action for three weeks.

RECOLLECTIONS

Guillermo García: After seeing Fidel, I went back to pick up seventeen guns, finding my way with the maps they made for me. I returned on December 30 with Fajardo.

I spent Christmas Eve near Bélice, looking for guns. Fidel and the others spent that evening in Mongo Pérez's home.

Manuel Fajardo: We started climbing up to the home of a peasant, Marrero, in a place called El Cilantro, and reached it December 30 or 31.

I'll never forget that we were going up a slope near Caridad de Mota with our guide, Lebrígido, on New Year's Day. Around five o'clock in the afternoon, Fidel asked him the name of a peak that looked close.

"That's Caracas," Lebrígido said.

And Fidel answered, "Batista will never win the war now!"

I looked at the troops. The men were exhausted, filthy, more dead than alive, and here was Fidel talking like that! It was January 1, 1957.

CHE GUEVARA   January 14

On January 14, 1957, a little over a month after the surprise attack at Alegría del Pío, we stopped on the banks of the Magdalena River. A strip of land reaching from the Sierra to the sea separates the Magdalena and La Plata rivers. We had target practice, then went in for a swim. We had 23 guns; 9 were rifles with telescopic sights. That afternoon we climbed the last hill and stopped not far from the garrison at La Plata. The next day, January 15, we sighted the garrison and at daybreak, on the sixteenth, we started watching it. The coast-guard boat had left during the night. At 3:00 p.m. we moved up the road, which runs beside La Plata, to the army camp, and at nightfall we crossed the shallow river and set up positions alongside the road. We were short of ammunition and it was essential to take the garrison to stock up on equipment. We sneaked up to within 120 feet of the enemy post. There was a full moon. Fidel opened fire with two bursts from his machine gun and all the available rifles followed suit. It was 2:40 a.m. The soldiers were practically defenseless and were being mowed down by our bullets. Camilo Cienfuegos was the first to go in. We took 8 rifles, 1 Thompson machine gun, and 1000 rounds; we had used about 500. Two soldiers were killed and five wounded (three died later); we took three prisoners but let them go. Not a scratch on our side. At 4:30 a.m. on the seventeenth, we set out for Palma Mocha, and reached it at daybreak, going through the steepest region of the Sierra Maestra. This was our first victory.

January 30

After our victory over Sánchez Mosquera's forces,* we had followed the banks of La Plata, crossed the Magdalena, and doubled back to the Caracas area, which we knew well. But things were no longer the same as the first time we had been there on the hill: everyone had been on our side then, but Casillas's** troops had since passed through, spreading terror throughout the region. The peasants had all gone, leaving behind

---

* Lieutenant Colonel Angel Sánchez Mosquera.—ED.
** Colonel Casillas Lumpuy.—ED.

their empty farm shacks and a few animals that we killed for food.

That was the situation on the morning of January 30. Eutimio Guerra had requested permission to go visit his sick mother, and Fidel had not only let him go but had also given him money for the trip.

We were just getting up, on the morning of the thirtieth, after a cold night, when we heard the drone of airplanes, but we couldn't see them through the trees. Our field kitchen was burning, some 200 yards below, near a small water hole, where we had set up our advance post. Suddenly, we heard a fighter plane diving, the rat-a-tat-tat of machine guns, and then bombs. We had very little experience at that time and we heard gunfire on all sides. Fifty-caliber shells exploded when they hit the ground, and when they struck near us, they seemed to be coming from the forest itself; we could also hear machine guns strafing from above. The sound was so close that we thought we were being attacked by the infantry.

It was a depressing scene: the kitchen had been hit with unusual marksmanship that, luckily, was never repeated during the rest of the war. The stove had been smashed to pieces by shrapnel, and a bomb had exploded smack in the middle of our advance post, but of course there had been no one there.

CARLOS FRANQUI

Letter to Frank País   Havana, January

Thinking back on our conversations and arguments in Santiago, toward the end of last year, and on the problems raised by the old "program" Oltuski took to Mexico just before Fidel's departure, and remembering the talks with you and Armando, I think we had better not put out too many decrees. In this country, even the Auténticos claim they are nationalists, anti-imperialist, and socialist; and after Grau's skulduggery, nobody believes in words anymore.

I know that you and Armando aren't frightened of radical ideas. Of course, after the coup, our group in Havana was sectarian and avant-garde in its position.

It must have seemed insane to many people. The influence of Lenin's decrees was evident, but we had adapted them to the Cuban situation. I know that wiping out capitalism and establishing a new socialism that is really free and humane is not really the job of a group like the 26th of July Movement. It is large and diversified and has almost become a national movement, but its young people and its militants are genuinely anti-imperialist and, under present conditions, as Guiteras said: "There can be no revolution in Cuba unless it strikes at Yankee imperialism."

The legal quibbling of Castellanos and Boti, two bourgeois professors at the University of Oriente influenced by Felipe Pazos, strips the Santiago Proclamation of its revolutionary character, and it is much less radical than *History Will Absolve Me*.

The conversations I had with Fidel last year in Mexico, and other things you know all about, have convinced me—other comrades feel the same—that Fidel does not want any kind of written program. It may have something to do with his personality and his short-range planning methods, and I know there is not much chance of changing him. But we must keep on fighting not so much for the program but to make him see that although he may be the leader, the organization now and the people tomorrow must also play an important role.

We could have published the program approved by the National Directorate, but it would not be a very responsible thing to do. It's not worth having a program, if it doesn't reflect the ideas of all of us, beginning with Fidel. I see nothing positive in isolated actions that mean little and help encourage caudillism and split us even more. . . .

I hope you'll like the copy of *Revolución:* it's our best answer to the censor and to the negative climate produced by the false rumor that Fidel is dead and that the expeditionary force was crushed after the disastrous landing and the battle at Alegría del Pío so effectively exploited by the press and the regime to isolate us.

Two important things about the publication: it must appear regularly and it must have good distribution. That's the only way it can be an effective instrument for agitation, orientation and organization.

You can write to me in care of the magazine.

REVOLUCIÓN

Article   Santiago, January 20

The 26th of July is sabotaging public utilities, burning sugar-cane fields, and setting fire to large estates.

Fifty days after November 30, there is tremendous tension in Santiago de Cuba and all of Oriente Province. Unable to control the situation, the authorities have unleashed a general massacre. There have been more than fifty known murders. The people are protesting against Batista's insane fury and fighting back.

The most important of the intense and continued acts of sabotage these last days was the destruction of the underground cables in the new and powerful Regla electrical plant in Havana. Losses were estimated at half a million dollars, and the light and power failures affected Havana and the rest of the country. In Portugalete, trains carrying sugar were derailed.

CHE GUEVARA   January–February

On January 31, we camped at the top of a hill overlooking some planted fields in what was probably La Cueva del Humo. We explored the area without finding anything.

On February 1, we stayed in our small camp, practically in the open, resting up after the long hike the day before.

A few hours later, we heard some noise and got ready to defend ourselves, not knowing if someone had double-crossed us, but it was only Crescencio coming with a long column made up of almost all our own men, besides some new recruits from Manzanillo, led by Roberto Pesant.

We went down again to the Ají Valley, and on the way we distributed some supplies the men from Manzanillo had brought, including surgical equipment and a change of clothing for everyone. We were touched by the initials embroidered on the clothes by the girls of Manzanillo. The next day, February 2, two months after the *Granma* landing, we had a close-knit, orderly group, increased by ten men from Manzanillo, and we felt stronger and in better spirits than ever.

After the surprise air attack, we left Caracas Hill; we tried to retrace our steps to familiar territory, where we could be in direct contact with Manzanillo, get additional help from the outside, and have a better vantage point to size up the situation in the rest of the country.

So we crossed the Ají Valley, over familiar ground, till we came to old man Mendoza's house. We had to use our machetes to cut new trails on the ridges of the hills, and we made poor progress. We spent the night on a hilltop, with almost nothing to eat. We went on again, till we got to the house to "the right of Caracas Hill," where old Mendoza would prepare some food for us. He was always afraid but, like most country people, he loyally welcomed us each time we came through, because of ties of friendship with Crescencio Pérez and some of the other peasants in our group.

It was a painful march for me; I had malaria and it was only thanks to the efforts of Crespo and my unforgettable friend Julio Zenón Acosta that I was able to get through that excruciating day's march.

We had left Florentino's place and were camped in the dry bed of a stream. Ciro Frías had brought some chickens and some other food from his home, which wasn't far away; that morning hot broth and other nourishment made up for a long rainy night out in the open without raincoats. We found out that Eutimio had been around there too. He was free to come and go; we trusted him. He had caught up with us in Florentino's house and had explained that on his way back, after going off to visit his sick mother, he had followed our tracks and had seen what happened on Caracas Hill. He told us that his mother was better. He really had a lot of gall. We were in a place called Altos de Espinosa, near a series of hills—El Lomón, Loma del Burro, and Caracas—constantly strafed by planes. He would put on a prophetic air and say: "I told them to strafe Loma del Burro today." The airplanes would attack it, and he would jump up and down with glee because he had predicted it.

On February 9, 1957, Ciro Frías and Luis Crespo went out to forage for food as usual; everything was quiet until 10:00 a.m., when a young peasant named Labrada, who had recently joined us, captured a man close to the camp. He turned out to be a relative of Crescencio's who worked in Celestino's store, where Casillas's troops were billeted. He told us there were 140 soldiers in the building, and sure enough, from our position, we could make out some of them far off, high up in a clearing. The prisoner also said that Eutimio had told him that our sector would be bombed the next day. Casillas's troops had been shifting from place to place; we never knew which way they were headed. Fidel started getting suspicious about Eutimio's odd behavior, and we began to go back over it. At 1:30 p.m., Fidel decided we should get out, and we went up to the summit, where we waited for the men who had gone scouting, Ciro Frías and Luis Crespo, who arrived shortly after. They had seen nothing unusual; everything was normal. We were still talking to them when Ciro Redondo thought he saw something moving, told us to be quiet, and cocked his rifle. In a moment the air was filled with the sound of gunfire and explosions. The spot we had just camped in was being attacked full blast. We got out of there fast. Later I found out that Julio Zenón Acosta had been killed up on the hill. The rough, uneducated peasant had understood the enormous tasks waiting for the Revolution after the final victory; he wanted to be ready and as a first step, had started learning his ABCs, but he would not be able to finish the alphabet. The rest of us scattered in all directions; the knapsack I was so proud of (filled with medicines), a few extra rations, books, and blankets were left behind. I managed to grab one blanket, a trophy taken from Batista's army at La Plata, and ran off with it.

A short while later, a group of us got back together: Juan Almeida, Julio Díaz, Universo Sánchez, Camilo Cienfuegos, Guillermo García, Ciro Frías, Motolá, Roberto Pesant, Emilio Labrada, Yayo, and myself. We took a circuitous route, trying to keep out of range of fire; we had no idea how the others had come out.

On February 12, after being separated for three days, we caught up with Fidel near El Lomón, in a place called Derecha de la Caridad. There the whole story of Eutimio Guerra's treachery came out. It began when he was captured at La Plata by Casillas; instead of having Eutimio killed, he offered him a reward for Fidel's life. We found out that Eutimio had given away our position on Caracas Hill and had told them to attack Loma del Burro (which was originally on our route, but had been dropped at the last minute). And he had also organized the concentrated attack on the riverbed at Cañon del Arroyo, where we had suffered only one casualty thanks to Fidel's order to retreat.

All the peasants had cleared out; only Prieto had stayed. We overheard one peasant talking to another: "Listen, aren't you leaving? I'm getting out of here fast. These sonsabitches are going to wipe out everything in these hills, down to the last field mouse."

Soon after we got there, Celia, Frank, and Guerrita Matos arrived; Armando Hart, Haydée, Faustino Pérez, and Vilma came the following afternoon.

Fidel, Celia, and I had gone looking for a small house we had seen the night before; Crespo had started out with us but we had lost him along the way. When Ciro announced that Matthews* had arrived, Fidel told us to look sharp, like soldiers. I looked at myself, then at the others: shoes falling apart, tied together with wire; we were covered with filth. But we put on an act; we filed off in step with me in the lead.

VILMA ESPÍN

Yes, it was in February 1957 that I first met Fidel. Then in April, I had to go into hiding and work with the underground. You know that we were rewarded for our work with trips to the Sierra; when one of us was tired out, he or she was given a few days' vacation up there. Whenever a message had to go there, it was given to the one who was the most run-down, so he or she could have a few days rest in the Sierra. They were always telling me: "Okay, it's your turn next," because I was already burnt-out.

FIDEL CASTRO   Sierra Maestra, February 20

I am writing this manifesto in the Sierra Maestra, after eighty days of fighting. Unable to defeat the Revolution with arms, the regime started spreading the most cowardly lie that our expeditionary force and I had been exterminated. After almost three months of sacrifice and effort that words fail to describe, we can tell the country that the "exterminated" force smashed a siege of more than a thousand soldiers between Niquero and Pilón; that the "exterminated" force stormed the garrison at La Plata at 2:40 a.m., Thursday, January 17, forcing it to surrender after forty-five minutes of fighting; that the "exterminated" force destroyed Lieutenant Colonel Sánchez Mosquera's column on the hills of Palma Mocha at noon, Tuesday, January 22; that the "exterminated" force broke through the ring of three companies of special troops commanded

---

* Herbert L. Matthews, correspondent of *The New York Times*.—ED.

by Colonel Barrera, at 3:15 p.m., February 9, on the Altos de Espinosa; that the "exterminated" force, whose ranks were steadily reinforced by the peasants of the Sierra Maestra, bravely resisted the attacks of the air force and the mountain artillery; and it fought successfully almost every day against more than 3000 men equipped with all kinds of modern weapons: bazookas, mortars, and several types of machine guns. Their desperate but powerless efforts have converted the Sierra Maestra into a hell, where falling bombs, the rattle of machine guns, and bursts of rifle fire are heard incessantly.

It is painful to have to say this, but after the battle of Palma Mocha, the dead soldiers were devoured by vultures. The enemy column retreated without taking its dead, and the battlefield was ours; but the air force kept us from burying the enemy dead that lay all around us.

Can Batista go on hiding from the country and the whole world what is happening here? The interview we had in the heart of the Sierra with the *New York Times* correspondent will be published with photographs any minute now.

The 26th of July Revolutionary Movement issues these guidelines to the country.

1. Step up the burning of sugar cane in the entire sugar region to stop the tyrant from getting the money he uses to pay soldiers to be killed and to buy planes and bombs to murder dozens of families in the Sierra Maestra.

To the slogan, "Without sugar there is no Cuba," we reply with a far nobler slogan: "Without freedom there is no Cuba."

2. The sabotage of all public utilities and all modes of communication and transportation.

3. The summary and immediate execution of: the lackeys who torture and kill revolutionaries; the regime's politicians whose stubbornness and inflexibility have brought the country to this situation; and all those who stand in the way of the Movement's success.

4. The organization of civil resistance in every city in Cuba.

5. The intensification of the economic campaign to cover the rising costs of the Movement.

6. A general revolutionary strike as the capstone of the struggle.

EDITOR'S SUMMARY   Sierra Maestra, February 17, 1957

Herbert Matthews' first interview with Fidel Castro appeared in The New York Times *on February 24, 1957. Castro acknowledged to Matthews that its publica-*

tion would be important: "The Cuban people hear on the radio all about Algeria, but they never hear a word about us or read a word, thanks to the censorship. You will be the first to tell them."

Matthews reported that Castro asserted that the morale of Batista's troops was poor, and many were taken prisoner. Castro's forces treated them with kindness and freed them quickly. He emphasized that this was because the 26th of July harbored no antimilitary feelings and respected many of the officers.

He displayed "bitterness" in discussing the U.S. government's role in supplying arms to Batista, but he declared: "You can be sure we have no animosity toward the United States and the American people."

Matthews concluded that Castro "has strong ideas of liberty, democracy, social justice, the need to restore the Constitution, to hold elections. He has strong ideas on economy too, but an economist would consider them weak."

In regard to both the battle situation and the future government of the country, Castro declared that "time is on our side."

COMMENTS

Che Guevara: Once our little army had regrouped, we decided to leave the El Lomón area and move to a new sector, and make new contacts with peasants along the way and set up the bases that we would need in order to survive. We also wanted to leave the Sierra Maestra and reach the plains, where we would be closer to our organization in the cities. We wanted to be closer as our nomadic and clandestine life made it impossible for the two sectors of the 26th of July Movement to keep in touch.

We were practically two separate groups, with different tactics and strategy. There was no sign yet of the grave differences that would endanger the unity of the Movement several months later, but it was already clear that we had different concepts.

This little island in the woods was the scene of other events. A reporter was to visit us for the first time, a foreigner, the famous Herbert Matthews. All he brought was a small box camera, which he used to take the pictures that became widely known and were later stupidly challenged by one of Batista's ministers. The interpreter was Javier Pazos, who would eventually join the guerrillas and stay with them for some time.

From what Fidel told me (I wasn't there), Matthews asked only straightforward questions, nothing insidious, and he seemed to be sympathetic to the Revolution. I remember Fidel saying that he had answered yes to the question of whether he was anti-imperialist; he had objected to the delivery of arms to Batista, pointing out that they would be used not for intercontinental defense but *solely* to oppress the people.

Matthews' visit naturally was very brief. We were soon alone and ready to move on. But we were told to be on our guard because Eutimio was somewhere in the neighborhood; we told Almeida to bring him in.

It was Ciro Frías's job to guard Eutimio, and he did so easily. He was brought to us and we found a .45 pistol, three hand grenades, and a pass signed by Casillas on him. He had been caught red-handed and knew what to expect. He fell on his knees before Fidel and asked to be killed, saying that he deserved it. He seemed to age before our eyes; his temples were gray, which I had never noticed before. It was an extremely tense moment. Fidel tongue-lashed him for his treason and Eutimio admitted his guilt and just wanted to be shot. All of us there will never forget the moment when Ciro Frías, his old friend, started talking to him; he reminded him of all the things he and his brother had done for Eutimio and his family; he accused him of betraying them—he had turned Ciro's brother in to the police and they had killed him a few days before, and finally he had tried to have our whole group wiped out. Eutimio listened silently, with lowered head, to this long, pathetic denunciation. He was asked if he wanted anything and he said yes, he wanted the Revolution, or, better yet, he wanted us to look after his children.

A terrible storm broke out just then, and everything got very dark; in the midst of a tremendous downpour, the sky was criss-crossed with lightning, the thunderclaps were deafening, and in the burst of a ray of lightning and in the rumble of thunder that followed, Eutimio Guerra's life ended; even those who were nearest to him did not hear the shot.

Fidel Castro: Eutimio had instructions to kill me but couldn't make up his mind, although he was on the verge of doing it two or three times. He slept next to me, with two hand grenades and a pistol ready. One night I covered myself completely with a cape someone had sent me. I heard him asking, "Where are the advance guards?" It was unbelievable; instead of killing me himself, he seemed to prefer to have us all wiped out by enemy troops without leaving any telltale signs. He kept asking Almeida where the advance guards were. Then he did something incredible; when the soldiers were supposedly heading in our direction, he asked to be put on guard duty, and he stood watch, but a heavy rainstorm kept the enemy away that day.

This gave us time to pump a prisoner who had been captured by a sentry, despite my orders to keep an eye on the enemy but not to take any prisoners—where would we put them? He said they knew exactly where we were. We asked him where the troop was and he pointed to a certain place. I went with him a little way and saw through the telescopic sight on my gun where the troop was; it was lined up, ready to march on us. I said: "What did you do yesterday?" "Well, we went out yesterday. Some of us went that way and the others went that other way." Which put us right in the middle. Right then I knew that Eutimio was a traitor. That's why he had volunteered to stand watch the day before; he had expected the soldiers to come into our camp.

Che Guevara: Frank País promised to send us a group of men in early March: we were to pick them up at Epifanio Díaz's house, near El Jíbaro.

When we left Epifanio's house, we had seventeen of our original men and three who had recently joined us: Gil, Sotolongo, and Raúl Díaz, who had all arrived on the *Granma*. They had been hiding near Manzanillo but came to join our group when they heard where we were. Their story was like ours; they had managed to elude their pursuers, and had stayed first in one peasant's house, then in another's, finally reaching Manzanillo and going into hiding. Now they were throwing in their lot with us.

We traveled slowly for several days, without a set route; we were simply marking time till March 5, when the armed men sent by Frank País were to arrive. We had decided to fortify our small front before making it any bigger, and so all the armament available in Santiago had to be sent up to the Sierra Maestra.

On February 27 or 28, censorship was lifted, and the radio broadcasts, almost nonstop, reported what had been happening in the last few months. There was news of terrorist actions and of Matthews' interview; at this time the minister of defense made his famous statement that the interview had been trumped up and challenged Matthews to publish the photograph of Fidel and himself.

Around four in the afternoon, Luis Crespo and Universo Sánchez were watching the roads, when Universo saw a large troop coming along the road from Las Vegas to occupy the area. We had to make a dash for the hill and cross over to the other side before the soldiers cut us off. This was not hard to do because we had seen them in time. The mortars and machine guns were firing in our direction; Batista's troops knew we were there. We were all able to get to the hilltop and over it easily, but it was an excruciating task for me. I managed to get there. My asthma made it very difficult for me even to take one step. I remember the hard time Crespo had trying to help me; whenever I just couldn't go on and asked to be left behind, he would say in our special army lingo: "You goddam Argentine, you'd better get a move on or I'll help you with this rifle butt!" Then he would have to drag his own load, my body, and my knapsack and we would go on walking over the rough terrain while a heavy rain beat down on us.

We had to make up our minds; I just couldn't go on. Fidel generously handed me a Johnson repeating rifle, one of the jewels in our arsenal, to defend ourselves. We made as if to leave all together in the same direction, but a few steps later, a companion (whom we called the

Teacher) and I went into the woods at a prearranged place to lie low and wait. That day we heard that Armando Hart was in prison, accused of being the second in command of the Movement. It was February 28.

The peasant did his job, supplying me with plenty of adrenaline. For me, the next days of the struggle were the most bitter in the Sierra. I walked, leaning on my rifle and stopping to rest from tree to tree, accompanied by a frightened soldier, who trembled every time he heard a shot and almost had a nervous breakdown each time I coughed where someone might hear me. It took us ten long days to get back to Epifanio Díaz's house, when ordinarily it would have taken about one day. March 5 had been the date set for the rendezvous, but we couldn't make it. The army's encirclement and our slow progress kept us from reaching Epifanio's hospitable house until March 11.

Several things had happened that people in the house already knew about. Mistakenly thinking that they were about to be attacked again, Fidel's eighteen men had become separated in a place called Altos de Meriño; twelve men had gone with Fidel and six with Ciro Frías. Ciro had run into an ambush, but they had gotten away unharmed, and were back in the neighborhood. Only one of them, Yayo, who had come back without his rifle, had stopped at Epifanio's place on the way to Manzanillo. He told us everything. Moreover, the troops we expected Frank to send were ready, although he was in prison in Santiago. We talked with the troop's leader, Captain Jorge Sotú. He hadn't made it on the fifth, because news of their coming had leaked out and all the roads were being watched. We took every precaution to make sure the men, about fifty of them, would get there as soon as possible.

CARLOS FRANQUI   Havana

The *Revolución* workshop was in a good location now. I had moved it from my home to a house that we rented in San Carlos, and we installed a large family with lots of children in it—they were members of the Movement, the Peréz de Guanabacoa. Only our Dominican printer, Julio César Mártinez, went there. From the garage the newspaper was taken out for distribution in a car trunk; we kept the printing separate from the distribution.

A high-ranking police officer lived across the street and this made the place safer.

One Sunday, Bauta, Aldo Vera, and I were on the Vía Blanca in a car loaded with newspapers, on our way to the Vedado, when two patrol cars stopped us. We had no guns and we couldn't escape. They made us pull up in a side street; but instead of arresting us, they began stopping other cars and forming a long line. They were taking in people whose license plates had expired, and we had been caught accidentally.

I told Vera to help me and we started unloading the bundles of papers onto some benches in the park, while the police went on looking for other cars. We called a cab and Vera went off with the newspapers. I got back into our car feeling as relieved as I had been scared before.

Although we were members of the press, I had not been able to convince the police to let us go. The chief said we'd have to leave the car in the pound, pay a fine, and come back with new license plates to get the car.

They finished their work and the long line of cars set out for Station 10. Mine and a squad car behind it were the last ones. When we stopped for a red light, I glanced back. There was a copy of *Revolución* with the headline FIDEL IN THE SIERRA in the back seat.

I got out, scared stiff, opened the back door, folded the paper, took it and went over to the squad car. As I was asking the officers if they had my driver's license, I dropped the paper. As the light turned green and we started off again, the wind blew it to the sidewalk.

Half an hour later, I left one of the worst police stations in Havana, free but without a car. Luck had been with us twice that Sunday.

The story of the Auténtico Party's arms, hidden all over Cuba, was incredible. They were always offering us some without ever coming through. This time Ofelia Gronlier, whose house at Eighth and Nineteenth in the Vedado was the Movement's headquarters, made sure we'd get them. They were at the home of a lawyer, who was terrified to have them there.

Since the police had my car, we called up a friend who had an old car and went to our rendezvous with the lawyer at the corner of Paseo and Zapata. The man was a nervous wreck and asked us to go with him to his home, a small house just beyond Sans Souci.

When we got there, he showed us some huge crates in his garage. We opened a couple and saw the marvelous arsenal: .30-caliber machine guns, modern rifles, ammunition. More than fifty guns. The lawyer couldn't wait for us to get them out of there, but all we had was the old jalopy and no place to store the shipment.

It took us hours of hard work, help from the militants at Fifth and A streets (where we had the sabotage workshop on the second floor), and fantastic luck to move those arms that were so vital to the guerrilla war.

Sabotage to U.S. and Cuban companies was becoming effective in Havana too. The Movement was studying the best places and times to carry out sabotage without harming civilians. We all agreed with Sergio González that we must first warn people in the streets. It was dangerous but it was the humane thing to do. The electric and gas plants were our main objectives.

Batista's police had just received an old hunting dog from Machado's time, who had worked with the FBI in the United States—Colonel Mariano Faget. With Ventura and other henchmen, he began an efficient and continuing repression.

EDITOR'S SUMMARY   Havana, February–March

A few days after Herbert Matthews' interview was published, Batista lifted press censorship in Cuba. Jules Dubois, Latin American correspondent of the Chicago Tribune, *interviewed Batista a few weeks later and attempted to get his pledge that he would not reinstate censorship. During their talk, Batista told Dubois that Castro was a Communist. As proof, he cited the fact that "he killed six priests in Bogotá during the Bogotazo." Dubois assured Batista that no priests had been killed in Bogotá at that time, but Batista insisted and as "proof" sent Dubois crudely forged documents that had no bearing on the charge. Batista repeated his accusation in a public speech on March 10, the fifth anniversary of his coup, adding that Castro was a "tool of Moscow." Dubois comments: "He might have persuaded American Ambassador Arthur Gardner to believe this, but not an overwhelming majority of the Cuban people, including the Roman Catholic Church."**

---

* Jules Dubois, *Fidel Castro: Rebel–Liberator or Dictator?* (Indianapolis and New York: Bobbs-Merrill, 1959), pp. 151–152.

8. MARCH: TO THE PRESIDENTIAL PALACE

REPORTS

Faure Chomón   Havana, March

Once the Revolutionary Directory and Menelao Mora agreed on a strategy, they combined their forces to embark on a concrete objective: the physical liquidation of the tyrant in the Presidential Palace. The thesis of "striking a blow at the top," as the Directory publicly describes the concept, was put in motion. But this time it would be very different from previous attempts, whose only objective had been to strike a blow at the dictator, without any longer-range purpose, since it had not been possible to count on the decisive factor of the people to insure the final outcome.

Our plan was to attack and capture the fortress where Batista lived and assassinate him, thus both eliminating him and buttressing the Revolution by seizing the very stronghold of absolute power. The decapitation of the regime would be complete with the death of Batista and the occupation of the seat of his government, where he held council sessions with his corrupt ministers, received the diplomatic corps, the members of his spurious Congress, the representatives of the ruling classes which paid him court, his officials, his police, and the informers who constituted the lofty inner circle of his intimates. By eliminating the dictator and taking into our hands all the threads that made possible the functioning of that apparatus of oppression and exploitation, we would put the machinery of the tyrannical government out of action and obtain the time necessary for the Revolution to make headway.

Part of the plan was to incorporate the people in the revolutionary struggle. On the radio, José Antonio Echeverría would issue a call to the people to gather at the university, where, once Batista was dead, the General Staff of the Revolution would be installed, and from where all other operations would be carried out with all the weapons we could seize, until we had completely crushed the tyranny.

Once the Presidential Palace was taken, the entire sector of the city that surrounded it would be in our hands. The next objective would be to attack the Maestre Police Barracks, and then one by one, all the other police barracks that did not surrender. At the same time, militiamen would set out from the university to occupy all the radio stations and newspaper offices and, through them, call for a revolutionary strike and issue instructions about where the people should go to get arms.

At this time, the forces of the 26th of July Movement were spread thin. However, despite the gigantic plan in which we were involved, the Directory made its actions felt in the streets of Havana (the attempt on the life of Colonel Orlando Piedra, the burning of the squad cars at Ambar Motors). At the end of January Eduardo García Lavandero left the country secretly to carry out a mission for the organization.

The operations to launch the action would be threefold: first, the assault on the Presidential Palace by a commando squad of fifty men; the second, an operation to back up this commando squad, in which more than a hundred men would take part; and third, the taking of the Radio Reloj radio station in order to broadcast news of Batista's death and address the people, while the commando squad that had taken the station would go on to the university, where our general headquarters would be installed.

Julio García: The first thing I did was to head for Sixth Street to pick up the people there. At 3:05 we set out for the other base on Nineteenth Street, where José Antonio was waiting. At 3:10 we left there in three automobiles and went as far as B Street, then turned toward Seventeenth and continued straight along this street as far as M Street, made another right turn until we reached CMQ, where the Radio Reloj studios were. There were fifteen of us. Armando Hernández and a comrade from Camagüey, Lorenzo, who had brought Léon Llera with him, also from Camagüey, had set out directly for the university, in Carlos Figueredo's convertible. They were to wait for us so that we could transport most of the weapons together through the entrance to J Street.

There were five of us in each car. The first one was to arrive two minutes in advance. José Azzef and Pedro Martínez would get out there. With their weapons concealed, they would get into the elevator, like two peaceful citizens, and take it up to the control floor and wait there for José Antonio Echeverría to arrive. The other three people in this car (Rodríguez Loeches, Humberto Castelló, and Néstor Bombino) would go on to the corner of Twenty-third and M in order to seal off this intersection and prevent access to the station.

The second car would drop off José Antonio Echeverría, Fructuoso Rodríguez, and Joe Westbrook, who would go up to the studio. The

other two, Otto Hernández and Carlos Figueredo, would take up positions in the doorway of the CMQ building guarding the entrance.

The third car would stop at M and Twenty-first streets to bar access
to the CMQ from that intersection. Juan Nuiry was to be the driver and
the four passengers would be Mario Reguera, Antonio Guevara, Héctor
Rosales, and I.

We were familiar with the interior of the radio station building.
There was a cell of the Directory there and its members were Jorge
Martín, Reinerio Flores, Floreal Chomón, among others. Besides, not
even a week before, Loeches and I had gone inside and cased the terrain
where José Antonio and his comrades would be carrying out their
action.

Everything went as planned. We arrived at CMQ at 3:14. We had
allowed ten minutes for Echeverría to speak on the radio. During that
time, we would block any police patrol cars that might show up from
entering the street. After addressing the populace, we planned to throw
a hand grenade into the control room as we withdrew, and set out for
the university. Neither the two comrades who went up first nor those
who accompanied José Antonio, met with the slightest trouble. The only
incident was coming across a soldier in the corridors of the station; he,
surprised to see a gun pointed at him, gave his revolver to Echeverría
without putting up any resistance. Thus, José Antonio and his men arrived at the broadcasting studio at 3:21, and they produced the previously prepared "communiqué," which gave an account of the
beginning of the uprising . . . the death of Batista. . . . All of this was read
by the announcers on duty, Héctor de Soto and Floreal Chomón. The
news reports we had written read as follows:

Radio Reloj reporting! Attack on the Presidential Palace. A few minutes ago, a large group of unidentified civilians opened fire on the
Presidential Palace using rifles and automatic arms. . . . A fierce
exchange of shots took place with the palace garrison. . . . The attackers, taking advantage of the element of surprise, managed to
break into the interior of the palace, where, it is reported, the president of the republic, Fulgencio Batista, was at his desk. . . . There
are numerous civilian and military casualties. . . . New contingents
of civilians have arrived at the site and are firing on the palace from
nearby vantage points. . . . We will continue to report. Radio Reloj
reporting! . . .

A minute later, Floreal Chomón was reading an "Official Communiqué from the Army General Staff," which stated:

Our correspondent at military headquarters, Luis Felipe Brión, reports that a few moments ago, noncommissioned and commis-

sioned officers of the army, navy, and police gathered in the Cabo
Parrado Barracks at Camp Columbia have taken over command of
the armed forces and have issued the following official communiqué: "In view of the profound crisis confronting the nation, the
noncommissioned and commissioned officers of the armed services
of our country, faithfully carrying out their sacred duty to safeguard
public peace and order and acting on behalf of the majority of its
members, have relieved General Tabernilla of his command, as well
as other high-ranking leaders and officers, supporters of the dictator Batista."

The supposed "Official Communiqué from the Army General
Staff," which was read at 3:22, was repeated a minute later. While our
news was being interrupted by all kinds of advertisements, José Antonio
in the broadcasting booth and we in the street waited patiently. We
could hear the announcer saying: "Ask for genuine codfish from Nor-
way," and he went on to plug a certain brand of Cuban cigar, an academy for the study of English (giving the name of the place in that
language, of course), the name of a furrier, another brand of cigars (this
time North American), and even an advertisement for some foodstuff
with a chocolate base "for perfectly balanced nutrition."

A little later, the announcers would again deal with the "events"
happening in the capital, which, literally transcribed, stated the following: "Radio Reloj report: Concerning the important events taking place,
we shall now broadcast an address to the people of Cuba by the president of the Federación Estudiantil Universitaria and the leader of the
Directorio Estudiantil José Antonio Echeverría."

Then José Antonio Echeverría began to read a proclamation, which
was never finished. The people of Havana were able to hear for the last
time the unmistakable voice of their greatest youth leader, who addressed his countrymen in the following words:

People of Cuba! At this moment the dictator Fulgencio Batista has
just been executed in revolutionary fashion. The people of Cuba
have gone to his very lair in the Presidential Palace to settle accounts. And it is we, the Revolutionary Directory, who, in the name
of the Cuban Revolution, have administered the coup de grâce to
this opprobrious regime. Cubans listening to me: We have just
liquidated. . . .

FAURE CHOMÓN   Havana, March 13

We scarcely noticed the dawn's coming on the thirteenth because we
were so busy trying to tie up all the loose ends and deal with last-minute
details. Our main fear was that Batista would be able to escape us dur-

ing the few hours that remained until the sun rose on the day that we had planned to be our rendezvous with history.

We had a comrade with earphones constantly on duty. The radio gear was spread out on a chair, the top of its case open so that another comrade could see the code pasted inside. Sitting next to it and leaning against a table, he wrote down in a notebook everything he heard and the time he heard it. The man on duty would constantly leap out of his chair to interrupt us in order to communicate some news he considered interesting, almost always provoking the same comment: "Batista is still in the palace."

All through the early morning this went on, endlessly, while we carried on our discussion in a whisper—Carbó, Machadito, Pepe Wangüemert, Abelardo, Osvaldito, Leoncito, Briñas, Tony, and myself.

We talked about the operation but also about unrelated matters, war and politics, which were almost the same thing, plans for the future, the shape our Revolution should take, revolutionary justice (which should be implacable), American interference in our affairs, personal anecdotes, and even art.

This was the last meeting in that house, which, until it became a center for the attack on the palace, had been the general headquarters of the best action group ever known; they had given invaluable help to the weak, disorganized insurrectionary movement in the capital.

Here were the prototypes of the men who would go to the palace to die for liberty—men of twenty and men of forty alike formed that glorious group of commandos. Older men, like Norberto Hernández, a veteran of the Spanish civil war, a member of the Cayo Confites* expedition, a great chess player, active in the struggle from March 10, 1952 on, one who, though not very optimistic about the chance for success in the attack on the palace, nevertheless marched forward to meet death, alongside youths like Osmani Arenado, whose unshakable determination I will never forget—an architecture student, with a beardless, simple, serene face—he greeted me at the headquarters as if he were doing the most natural thing in the world.

At the first light of day, I decided to take a tour around the neighborhood of the palace, along with Pepe Wangüemert. We had gotten little sleep during the last few days and were very tired, so we stopped in the Plaza del Vedado to have some coffee and clear our heads. A few minutes later, while passing one side of the palace, we noticed some SIM cars parked in the neighboring streets, and a couple more that were constantly patrolling the area. We stopped at the Bellas Artes building; Wangüemert went to "take a look," and chatted with the police guards

---

* Site of a camp in Oriente Province from which an attack on the Trujillo dictatorship in the Dominican Republic was planned in 1947 with the support of Cuba's President Ramón Grau San Martín. The assault was called off.—ED.

in an effort to get some information from something that might slip out. He returned and told me that everything was normal, and that the dictator had not abandoned his den. We soon lost confidence when, during one of our rounds, we discovered that the streets leading to the palace had been closed off with wooden barriers.

We immediately returned to our headquarters, where we discussed the new situation with Carlos and Menelao. This upset all our plans, for it would be impossible to carry out an attack without bringing our vehicles up to the very entrance of our objective; besides, these measures were an indication that our plans had leaked out, and that the dictator had been alerted. We could expect the worst in the hours to come. We went back toward the palace for another look, accompanied by Carlos. Everything was exactly as we had left it. The barriers were still there, sealing off the streets; when he saw them, Carlos intoned a popular song of the day that included the words "Esto pinta mal."* But back at headquarters, everything suddenly was cleared up, when one of the comrades—Armando Pérez Pinto—told us that it was perfectly normal for these barriers to be set up. He worked on one of the bus routes that normally go through these streets and knew that whenever Batista was in the palace at night, these barriers were put up to block off traffic noise while the dictator slept; when he woke up in the morning, they were removed.

We took our weapons and cartridge clips, along with some extra ammunition. The assault group, some fifty men, was now ready and armed. We had about twenty-five Thompson guns, M-2 and M-3 rifles; the rest were M-1 carbines, all perfectly oiled and loaded, ready for firing.

Comrade Enrique Rodríguez Loeches, who would later participate with José Antonio Echeverría in the attack on Radio Reloj, was with us then but left to tell the others to get ready for this other operation.

Julio García Oliveras, who had been chief of operations at Radio Reloj and at the university, was to remain with us until the moment we set out, when he would join his own comrades and, after twenty minutes, would strike at his objective.

At three in the afternoon, Carlos Gutiérrez's car led the procession; behind it came the truck, and behind the truck, our automobile. We passed the half block of Twenty-first Street that separated our strategically located general headquarters from the busy street, full of people and vehicles, in the Vedado quarter. We proceeded on to Twenty-sixth Street, and then to Seventeenth, where we turned to head toward Havana.

I remember riding in the back seat, looking at the streets and the people walking along them. How remote the events that were about to

---

* "This doesn't look too good."

occur and that would stir the entire nation seemed! And the truth was that on this particular afternoon we were the destiny of our nation, the destiny of each one of those people.

The men in the convoy must have surprised many people, including some Batista types, who thought we might be agents of repression, since there were four of us in each car, and we were carrying our arms practically in the open, our grenades hanging from our belts, and although we talked and even smiled once in a while, we carried ourselves with a certain martial air, our bodies stiff with tension and the same expression on all our faces. In the truck, which bore a painted sign reading "Fast Delivery," the men were pressed against one another, in total darkness and asphyxiating heat. From the back of the truck, Menelao was making encouraging remarks. He and some others were glued to the back door of the truck to make sure it did not open, and also to be ready to jump out first, to protect the rest of the comrades in the "landing."

We knew that our attack on the palace was an act of far-reaching, historic dimensions, which would free our people; we were going to assassinate the tyrant and set a formidable example to the world. It was, besides, the great moment of which we had dreamed, during the whole time we had been constantly chased like vermin by the murderous Batista police.

Carlos's automobile was in the lead, while I covered the truck's rearguard. It had been agreed beforehand that if any obstacle turned up, Carlos would stop and deal with it, while I kept on in the second car, along with the truck, toward our objective. If, on the other hand, some difficulty occurred in the rearguard, the four of us in our car would deal with it, while Carlos continued on, followed by the truck. In case the obstacle was such as to make it nearly impossible to reach the palace, or in case we received some warning en route to stop, we had an emergency plan; we were to head for the Main Police Barracks, capture it, and then go on with the same type of operation against the rest of the police stations, once we had armed enough men with the weapons taken at the Main Barracks.

At times, the truck would get slightly ahead of us because of the heavy traffic and we would have to speed a bit to catch up. Finally, on Monserrate Street, all three of our vehicles were together, one behind the other, and we reached the Parque Zayas, from where we looked anxiously at the Presidential Palace.

Once again, the heavy traffic at this hour forces our car to fall behind a bit. I can see Carlos's car beginning to turn the corner of the park into Colón Street. I tell Abelardo to speed up, so that we can arrive at the same time. Abelardo, a splendid driver, skillfully threads his way around the cars in our path. We turn at the same time as the truck. On we go: Carlos's car stops in front of the entrance to the palace. Our car brakes to the left, between Carlos's car and the truck. I jump out, fol-

lowed by Wangüemert, Abelardo, and Osvaldito, and advance toward
the entrance. But Carlos's speed is unbelievable and he is already standing in the middle of the arcade of the entrance from Colón Street. The
surprise is so complete that the guards have no time to do anything but
watch Carlos's machine gun mow them down. There, in front of the entrance, in the very center, under the arcade, Carlos Gutiérrez Menoyo
looks like a Cyclops, under whose power the soldiers fall, as if struck by a
bolt of lightning. Wangüemert and I, advancing toward the entrance,
have to fire on two soldiers, who, in turn, are firing on Carlos from behind. We put them out of action. Castellanos, Almeida, and Goicoechea
join up with Carlos, firing their machine guns. I am already at the arcade and feel Wangüemert beside me. Carlos goes in through the open
iron grille; through this conquered breach we will take the palace. Ricardo Olmedo goes toward the entrance from the truck, where he had
sat next to the driver. I jump toward the grille and my hand grasps an
iron bar; I want to leap behind Carlos. I feel shaken, weak, as if I were
made of paper, lose consciousness, all the while under the impression
that I am being hurled through the air by a gigantic hand, feeling as if I
am dreaming, thinking only: Have they killed me?

Several seconds must have passed until I regain consciousness. I am
lying on the sidewalk, dazed. For a moment I don't know what to do,
but the bursts of gunfire are biting into the pavement around me; I don't
understand why they don't hit me. I drag myself to the palace wall. I
have a very clear recollection of what has happened to me; strangely, I
can remember exactly where my body was hit, the impact of the bullets.
I feel as though I have a cramp in my arm from the bullet wound there.
Another bullet wound burns in my hip, and my liver feels as if it is being
pounded by a load of rocks. At that moment, I am sorry that I haven't
been killed, as I think of my destroyed liver. I put my hand on the spot
and find no sign of a wound, but it still hurts there. Then I realize that
the four grenades I had hanging from my belt have disappeared, and
that the bullets must have hit the grenades, which protected me from
the impact and deflected the bullets. My security belt is open and the
M-3 cartridges have also disappeared, along with the pistol in my belt.
The bullets must also have torn the M-3 out of my hands and hurled it
out of reach. The only thing left me is a box of .45 bullets in my back
pocket, fifty rounds. I feel weak and my sight constantly clouds over. I
realize where I am, and I see some comrades beside the truck in the
middle of the street, firing at the upper floors of the palace. They are
committing the error against which they had been warned a thousand
times. I try calling out the order to advance, but the noise of the shooting
is deafening and my voice could not have been heard six feet away. Between the place where I am lying and these comrades is the entrance to
the palace, and on the sidewalk, next to me, I see the bullets falling like
hail. I decide to make my way toward those comrades, and I take ad-

vantage of a moment when the firing seems to let up around me to drag myself behind Carlos's car, parked at the entrance. Awaiting my chance, I get as far as a bus in front of the truck. But by making that very movement I am discovered, and they open up against me from the top floors of the palace. I hide behind a wheel of the bus as best I can; pieces of metal, paint, and asphalt hit me in the face. I can no longer see the place where the comrades had been. I think they have gone in or pulled back. I realize that I have committed the same error, drawing away from the walls of the palace and turning myself into a target. The firing from the top floors of the palace becomes more intense, and the bullets are hitting the pavement like rain. I realize that from time to time they are concentrating their fire against me, and I am resigned to die, since I can't move anywhere and I am sure that the bullets will soon hit me. Still, I am under the impression that we are winning and that victory will be ours; and I bewail my fate, which has taken my weapons away and laid me out flat, so that I am missing the triumphant battle within the palace.

I look around the wheel, my covering parapet, toward the palace arcade and catch sight of Ricardo Olmedo flung down there, wounded, and waving his arms. The bullets are landing around him, too, and I am upset to see that he doesn't have the strength to move. I see that from inside Comrade José A. Alfonso is firing his machine gun. I am struck by his confident attitude, as if he were immune to the retaliatory fire.

Our attack caught the garrison by surprise, our commando squad hit them hard, and our automatic weapons kept up an incessant barrage. In the face of that, although a fierce battle was raging on the ground floor, the palace defenders began to give way, taking refuge in the upper stories. A .30-caliber machine gun was abandoned, unused, in the patio. The soldiers had been wiped out on the ground floor, which was now in the hands of the comrades assigned to it, who did not let up their fire. Meanwhile, others reached the second floor, going up the stairs on that side. Once there, they had divided into two groups and continued their advance. Heading toward the left wing were Carlos Gutiérrez, Pepe Wangüemert, Luis Almeida, Pepe Castellanos, Luis Goicoechea, advancing through the passageways and rooms until they burst into the Hall of Mirrors. There, they surprised three servants, who, with fear written all over their faces, raised their hands in surrender. Carlos begins to ask questions, but it is a waste of time, for they can scarcely speak. This group gets as far as the north terrace, where they can see some policemen in the distance, along Avenida del Puerto; our men had created the impression that the palace had been taken, and the police open fire on the entire building for a while. Our comrades continue their cleanup operation and reach Batista's office. They have to use several clips of bullets on the lock to open it; at last they succeed and go in, where they make a fruitless search. The other group has advanced toward the right wing, in an operation identical to the first, and begins a clash with the garrison, which is firing on them from the third floor. Menelao fires without stopping and moves with as much agility as the youngest in the group. Delgado and Esperón, protected in the passageway that opens onto the patio, fire their M-1's continuously in answer to the fire coming at them from the top floors. Machadito hurls several hand grenades against these upper floors, where the defenders of the palace have entrenched themselves. Next, he takes out some bombs, made of seven charges of dynamite—which we had brought along in case we needed them to blow open some door—he lights their fuses one by one, and he hurls them. When these bombs blew up, they shook the entire palace, making a terrifying racket, and the disconcerted Batista garrison stopped firing. Later we learned that they had thought they were under mortar fire. One of those bombs struck a column and landed at Machadito's feet—luckily it did not explode. The same thing happened to Carbó, who threw a grenade into a room made of glass and wood, realizing only after he had let go of the grenade that it was a trompe-l'oeil room, but it also did not explode; it would have killed him if it had. Abelardo and Osvaldito appeared and disappeared in one place or another, without letting up in the search for the enemy, who had grown cowardly and fled. Esperón and Delgado fall dead, next to each other. Machadito is wounded in the thigh. Bullets rebound off the walls and shatter the windows. Menelao remains sitting on the floor in a faint, apparently hit. Carlos's group, which has advanced on the left, makes contact with the others, and they identify each other, shouting [the code words] "Directory, Viva the Directory!" From the roof, some soldiers shout "Viva Batista," in answer to our comrades, and this convinces our men that Batista is now on the roof, for these soldiers have remained silent until that moment.

Carbó has a bullet wound in the sole of his foot, which he received getting down from the truck with Tony Castell, León Llera, and Machadito, when they had opened fire on the official parking area in front of the palace. Carbó could not fire, for as he jumped off the truck he was hit and the burst of fire had wrenched his Thompson gun from his hands and knocked off his glasses, and several shots came so close to his head that they left numerous burns on his face. Carbó did not know what to do, but just then he had heard Carlos calling out: "Forward, Comrades, this place is ours," and he had run into the palace, where he found another machine gun. Though he could walk, he was just one more of our wounded. Wangüemert ran from place to place using his M-2 against the dictator's defenders. His face and shirt were covered with blood, perhaps from cuts made by the fragments of glass that shattered in the firing. Wangüemert was a thoroughgoing fighter, a true revolutionary who knew how to use his head and how to act: when the telephone rang, he stopped firing and answered the call. They asked if it was true that the president had been killed, and he answered at once: "Yes. You are talking to a member of the armed militia of the Directory. We've just taken the Presidential Palace and we've killed Batista." Such an answer had as much impact as if it were true, for the call could have been coming from Camp Columbia, from one of Batista's generals or ministers, and in consequence it could have paralyzed all help for the dictator, caused many of his allies to flee, and made the fall of the regime more likely.

Briñas falls, with a bullet in his chest, into the arms of Carbó, who carries him next to Menelao, who tries to help but Briñas dies immediately. Carlos goes up some stairs and takes a look around the third floor. He comes down and says: "Boys, we're already on the third floor, let's go." Machadito, who has made a quick estimate of the situation, reports to Carlos and tells him we need reinforcements. Carlos agrees and, accompanied by Pepe Castellanos, goes down the corridor toward the stairs to call down to the comrades on the ground floor.

We have to cross the same spot where Briñas and Carlos and Castellanos had been shot down. Machadito makes himself heard and announces: "I'll cover the rear; when I begin to shoot, all of you get out of the way, I'll be the last." And, with supreme courage, he emerges in front of the snipers on the third floor, his machine gun rattling in an unceasing burst of fire, while all the other comrades slip down the stairs to the first floor. There is little doubt that Batista's soldiers didn't dare expose themselves to Machadito's machine gun. As our men retreated down the stairs, projectiles from what must have been a heavy-caliber weapon tore chunks out of the wall along the way. We and the comrades on the ground floor began to withdraw. We all set out in different directions, but Machadito lost sight of Carbó, and went back into the palace to look for him. Machadito was a true hero of the attack on the palace. He left by way of Monserrate Street, with Evelio Prieto and another comrade, firing to the left and right.

In our planning we had calculated that a retreat from the palace was impossible unless our supporting operation functioned, and that anyone who tried it would not get very far or stay alive, once he left the palace walls. And though some comrades fell in this attempt, others miraculously managed to get away alive. Each one of our successful retreats involved daring, decisiveness, and a lot of good luck. We were convinced that retreat was impossible without outside help. Carlos had gone as far as to suggest—were the second operation to fail—that we lock ourselves in the palace and throw the key away: if we were going to be killed in any case, each of us might as well try to find Batista and die while looking for him rather than die in a doomed retreat. The way in which the attack took place made this hunting party impossible, because when we retreated, there were too few men left, they were wounded, and there was not enough ammunition left.

Our confidence in the support operations was based on the fact that the men in charge of it were considered highly competent marksmen and leaders because some of them were veterans of the Spanish civil war. That absolute confidence was also based on the friendship between those men and Carlos Gutiérrez Menoyo and Menelao Mora, which made everyone believe that they would rather die than go back on their word.

I remember proposing that this supporting operation be led by our comrade Pepe Wangüemert. I knew he had the qualities necessary to carry out the operation: intelligence, courage, decisiveness, the true spirit of sacrifice, and, naturally, strong reasons for the success of the plan we proposed to accomplish. Besides, I had observed some skepticism in the person who was in charge of the plan, and a lack of coordination with his lieutenants. And all this made me recall that these men, though veterans of the Spanish civil war, were already years away from that heroic struggle of the Spanish people, and that they were now elderly, logically enough; many of them had taken part in undertakings of this type, which always failed, beginning with the action at Cayo Confites, up to the one at Luperón, and now in the fight against Batista, and had never succeeded in any of the many plans in which they were involved.

Carlos and Menelao agreed with me, but they raised the objection that if we named Wangüemert chief of this second operation, the support mission, it would antagonize those who had already committed themselves to the Movement, and they would consider themselves released from their pledge of secrecy and start talking, endangering everything we had accomplished, possibly aborting our attack on the palace.

At the time the commando assault was begun on the palace, 3:20 in the afternoon, Ignacio González, posted on the Paseo de Prado with a group of comrades awaiting his orders, turned out to be incapable of issuing them, and was terribly indecisive. He went from one place to another without knowing what to do, despite the fact that men were available to him, and there was a truck loaded with arms close by, driven by our comrade Domingo Portela, which was ready for the supporting operation. Meanwhile, his lieutenants Valladares, Morales, and others positioned in Luyanó with a strong contingent of men assigned to this operation had heard over the radio that the attack on the palace had begun, and although they were urged by some of their men to go to the palace to fulfill the task entrusted to them, they were incapable of giving the marching orders and go where they had pledged to go. Later, they gave a host of baseless reasons for not doing so: they would not move until they received a telephone call from Ignacio; the truck mounted with a .50-caliber piece and other weapons could not be used. Those in charge later claiming that the machine gun was not properly mounted, that the truck had been caught in a traffic "jam," or that they had arrived too late and the army tanks were already in action.

Luis Goicoechea: The group that was supposed to support us never showed up. We had to retreat as best we could.

I saw Machadito with Juan Pedro Carbó and a peasant from Pinar del Río who, I understand, also survived that day on the second floor of the palace. We tried going down the stairs. The first landing was continuously being swept by fire from a machine gun up above. Castellanos was the first to hurl himself through it. We heard a burst and saw him turn around to fire back at the enemy. He fell right there, riddled with bullets. Carlos Gutiérrez, enraged at Pepe's death, leaped onto the landing, firing upward. He also fell lifeless. By then, those of us behind them had spotted the soldier shooting from above. We concentrated our fire on that spot and momentarily silenced the sniper, giving us enough time to cross, one by one, the "deadly landing." I was the last to reach the guard post, which was littered with dead and covered with blood.

I saw the street filled with shells of different calibers. Farther on, Parque Zayas, with men splayed out on the ground. We would have to cross the street and the park to escape. Gómez Wangüemert was the first to make up his mind. He rushed off as swift as a gazelle. Juan Pedro and Machadito went next. I could see the bullets following in their tracks. When I began to run toward the park, I heard someone shout "Luis!" I turned, without stopping, and saw Luis Almeida still standing in the entrance to the palace. I had lost sight of the peasant from Pinar del Río. Now, only my instinct for self-preservation was working. I ran like a deer, feeling missiles landing all around me. I reached the fountain in the center of the park and hunks of cement, torn up by the bullets, fell over me. I threw myself headlong on the grass, between some bushes and lawn, clinging to the fountain wall, scarcely a foot high. My shirt was sticking to my body with sweat. All I could smell was gunpowder, blood, and death. That terrible odor clung to me for two weeks. Then I felt my machine gun firmly against my body; my finger was on the trigger. Suddenly the firing stopped.

A sinister calm invaded the place. I didn't think twice; I jumped up, and ran at an angle from the fountain toward Villegas Street. When I reached the intersection at Villegas and Tejadillo, I heard a man shouting at me from a doorway: "Here! Get in here!" I pointed my weapon at him and yelled: "Get out of sight or I'll shoot you down!" Perhaps that man saved my life; I had intended to go down Tejadillo and on that street I would have fallen into the hands of the police reserves coming from headquarters.

Juan Nuyri: The only failure in our plan was that José Antonio's proclamation was not broadcast in its entirety, due to a technical detail. We forgot that there was a "relay" that shut off transmission automatically whenever there was any loud noise close to the microphones. While we waited in the street outside the radio station, tension was very high. A police sergeant routinely covering his beat, without noticing what was happening, pointed to our lead car that it was occupying a space reserved for taxis. The comrades inside the car said that they were about to leave, and the policeman continued on his beat down Twenty-third Street. No more than two minutes elapsed before Echeverría and his comrades got out of the car and a tremendous exchange of fire began. The policeman probably had little heart for a fight, but in an attempt to do his duty, he came back with his hand on his holster only to find the barrel of the M-1 that Rodríguez Loeches was carrying pointed at his head. He made a move to take out his gun when a well-aimed shot, from Chino Figueredo, sitting in the car, struck him in the leg and knocked him to the ground. Loeches, still covering him, took away his service weapon.

We had to continue toward the university. The order was for each of us to return in the car in which he had gone to the radio station. We were to go up M Street to Jovellar and there turn into the university by the entrance at the end of J Street. The convertible and the four cars were to be waiting there to get safely inside the precincts of the "alma mater." But the unexpected happened. On M Street, between Twenty-third and Twenty-fifth, a number of trucks were parked, because of the construction work on the old Havana Hilton. This created a traffic jam that separated our three cars. The lead car set out in second place, behind Echeverría's, and continued all along M Street as far as San Lázaro; its occupants entered the university by the great staircase. Echeverría told his close friend José Azzeff: "Moor, now I can die in peace!" How unaware he was that death was awaiting him so soon. Azzeff got into his car, which went up M Street and turned into Jovellar, while those in the third car were obliged to turn in on Twenty-fifth Street.

Carlos Figueredo: We continued along M Street as far as Jovellar, crossed L Street, and as we passed alongside the university, we came face to face with an enemy automobile. Since we had orders to interfere with any police reserves that might be going to the Presidential Palace, we stopped our car in the middle of the street, crashing head-on into the squad car. Almost simultaneously with the crash, I fired on the other car and we received a burst of machine-gun fire that cut diagonally through our windshield. No one was wounded. Crouching, we got out of the car on the right-hand side. The first to get out was José Antonio Echeverría, who advanced firing on the squad car.

With absolute disregard for his life, he went toward a squad car and shot the policemen through the window. He fell to the ground and then got back up on his knees and, drawing out a revolver (which he had taken from a soldier), he again shot through the window; at that moment, a burst of machine-gun fire finished him off.

Julio García Oliveras: Those of us who had attacked Radio Reloj began to enter the university. In the Plaza Cadenas, we found Lorenzo and Armando Hernández unpacking the heavy arms. We all asked each other about the rest of the group. Fructuoso arrived at that moment. Everyone asked the same question: "Where is Echeverría?" The reply paralyzed us for a few moments: "They wounded him, and he was carried off in an ambulance."

Nevertheless, despite the bad news, we could not stand still; it was a time of action, of feverish activity. We set up the heavy weapons where their range of fire would be most effective. A .30-caliber machine gun was placed on the staircase; the other two were also placed strategically: one covered the entranceway to the university by J Street, and another was placed on the roof of the Faculty of Architecture building.

We had no news of what was going on at the palace. But less than three-quarters of an hour after we reached the university, Faure Chomón, who was seriously wounded, arrived from the palace bearing bad news. Our assault had failed. Already we could hear very little firing from the hill. We decided, nevertheless, to stay at the university until we could see what happened. Juan Nuyri took Faure away from the university precincts. I was in charge of the .30-caliber gun on the Faculty of Architecture roof when Rodríguez Loeches came up and, pointing down Twenty-third Street in the Vedado, said: "Look at what's going on there." There was a long column of tanks and armored cars, reinforcements sent from Camp Columbia to the palace garrison. I tried to change the position of my Marsden so I could fire on the column, but I didn't have time, and when I had it at the right angle for firing, the tanks were already going down behind the construction at the Havana Hilton.

It got to be 5:30 in the afternoon. We had no news of events at the palace. Echeverría's address over the radio had been cut off and only one volunteer showed up at the university—a mechanic who had been able to get through the police cordon that was slowly closing around the university hill. We held a meeting in the basement of the Rectory Building and counted up the number of those of us left and surveyed the general situation. It was logical to assume that very soon fewer than fifteen men would have to face the armored cars and tanks of the dictatorship. Some of us thought that we should stay there, put up resistance, and die. The majority thought it would be best to leave while there was still time and carry on the fight under better conditions. We began to withdraw as best we could. I went with Fructuoso and Armando Hernández down J Street, and later, holding the driver at pistol point, we continued on in a National Coffee Shop's delivery truck.

CARLOS FRANQUI

On March 6, in Ernesto Vera's café, at Aguila and San Lázaro, the police arrested our propaganda group. Later they attacked the underground workshop of *Revolución*. They pursued us very intensely, and after the arrest of the group at Fifth and A streets, I took special measures. A gangster turned informer, who had infiltrated into the Movement, led the police thugs to all our known hideouts in the city. Once again I was lucky and used my wits when I ran into him accompanied by several agents. Before he had the chance to say anything, I told him that we were holding a meeting at 3:00 that afternoon at the entrance to the Havana cemetery and everyone was to attend. He figured that he would nab us all at the rendezvous and let me go. At the hour I had given him, the police mounted a gigantic operation at the cemetery, and, needless to say, found no one there.

I moved and did not give my address even to my family or to anyone in the Movement. I made my contacts in the street, and every day at a different place.

That day Vera did not attend either of the two appointments. Cheché Alfonso and I were looking for a new place to house the newspaper. That night the radio reported that the newspaper's premises had been occupied and Vera and the others arrested. I did not hear the news. The comrades on *Carteles* tried to warn me, but they didn't know my address; I went off peacefully with my wife to a clinic and to see a movie starring Burt Lancaster.

On the other hand, it was the first time I lived in a safe house. At three in the morning, police cars deployed all around the block and attacked the apartment where I was living. The lock on the door got stuck, and the police were about to blow it open with their guns, which meant endangering my family. When I was finally able to open and the thugs saw I was alone and unarmed, they lost their jitters and began their big talk.

On the way down the stairs, my mother tried to tell them I was a good man, and they understood her to say simply that I was a man. Right there the blows began. Once out on the street, there was an argument between those in two armored cars as to which one would take me away.

When I saw Sergeant Calzadilla, the same man who had showed me around the Moncada Barracks in December, I was as frightened as I have ever been in my life—and there have been many times when I was really frightened—each time I've been part of an action—and I thought that Calzadilla would never let me reach the police station alive. But the occupants of the other armored car, the famous torturers of the Bureau of Investigations, Sarmiento and Bencomo, were the heads of this operation, and they shoved me into their car.

They took me to their headquarters, and there Colonels Faget and Piedra showed me the four comrades they had arrested, the multilith, the printing equipment, copies of the newspaper, etc.

They said that I was the man in charge and that they knew a lot. . . . I answered that yes, I was the chief, the one and only; they now had everything in their hands.

Those were very hard days. The police knew I was the editor of the paper, the one responsible for propaganda, and a member of the 26th of July leadership. Following our tactics, I limited myself to saying that my contacts were the Harts, prisoners in the El Príncipe and outside police jurisdiction, and other comrades who were in the Sierra.

I discovered that the hardest blows make one insensitive to pain and that one's own body seems like someone else's. But Faget was a technician of torture. A scientist of the North American school: continuous blows on the head, leaving no marks, but producing tremendous pain and tension. To my inveterately poor memory was added in those days an almost total unconscious amnesia. I had the good luck to put an end to the chain of arrests by saying nothing.

I endured hours of peril as if resigned to death. I did not react. Some absurd things happened. Someone had declared that I had hidden a truck full of dynamite. And the police wanted to know where it was. The only trouble was that the truck had never existed. We had merely been talking about attacking a mine, and I was supposed to find someplace to hide the dynamite, but the scheme had never been carried out.

Another matter was the photos of Fidel and Matthews in the Sierra, which I had given to Miguel Quevedo, the editor of *Bohemia*. Those pictures were supposed to appear in the magazine about that time. And they did appear.

I don't know how much time had passed while I was nearly unconscious from the blows, and the torturers kept yelling that I should stop looking at them that way—considering my state of fear, I don't know what they saw in my eyes—and eventually my brain started to function.

I calculated that I had to resist until ten in the morning of that day, which was a Saturday, and in the middle of an interrogation, pretend that the address of the phantom truck of dynamite had simply slipped out: it was in the building where *Carteles* was published, almost an entire block. I would pretend to weep, pleading that I didn't want to go there, proposing an enormously complicated plan to them, and thus get them to take me there so that my newspaper colleagues would see me and give the alarm. And it happened that way. They took me to *Carteles,* and I led them to the center of the editorial offices, and pointed to a typewriter, and said the truck was there.

Our people at *Carteles* were in a state, thinking that if I talked, our entire cell would be arrested; my silence was rewarded by real comradeship, for they did my work for nearly two years and supported my family during that period.

I had a marvelous opportunity to escape while the thug Bencomo was escorting me to the proofreading room, which opened onto the roof. I used a heavy bar of lead to keep my papers from blowing away. If I had hit him on the head with the bar and seized his machine gun, I could have escaped. But that day the bar wasn't there, and my strength was so far gone that I couldn't even lift my arms. We went back to the Bureau of Investigations, where Faget, in a fury, told me I had pulled his leg, that now the journalists had seen me, and the news had been cabled out. But I should get ready to die. Jorge Quintana, dean of the journalists, mobilized everyone, including the Inter-American Press Association, and thus my life was saved.

On the afternoon of March 13, they led us out to the patio of the bureau. A lot of buses were there. An agent called Pistolita was yelling: "They're attacking the palace." There was enormous confusion. The police went crazy and wanted to murder the prisoners. The commander, Major Medina, ordered men with machine guns to be placed in front of our cells, and to wait for the bureau to be attacked. Suddenly someone shouted: "They've killed Batista!" The police panicked, they were more frightened than we were. For the moment, that cry had saved us. It had come from Luis Gómez Wangüemert, who in the middle of the battle had answered the telephone in Batista's office, and replied: "Yes. You are talking to a member of the armed militia of the Directory. We've just taken the Presidential Palace and we've killed Batista." He had sown panic among the police.

The torturers were running from one place to another; they did not pay any attention to the commands of their officers and refused to go to fight at the palace.

The officers had forced the agents to get in their vans and go to the palace. In order to avoid fighting, the agents arrested anybody they found in the streets. Dozens of innocent people who had no notion of what was going on, some of them arrested in their own homes, filled the cells in no time. They were frightened out of their wits.

A little later, we learned that the attack had failed. The minions of the law were swaggering again. Thirsty for blood and cowardly, they wanted to kill all the prisoners, but Major Medina forbade it.

Those were very uncertain hours, especially that night. Piedra and Faget had me brought to their office. On the way over, the other thugs—including Bocanegra, a sergeant from my hometown, who personally had not behaved badly toward me—told me my situation was growing serious. In the office, I found the bureau's top brass.

Faget told me that because I had not talked, the palace had been attacked, and I was responsible for the dead and everything that had happened. I maintained that I was ignorant of any such plans and cited Fidel's words against tyrannicide. I added, sotto voce, that I had already told them I was a combatant without hatred, with no wish to die and even afraid of dying, but ready to die, because that was the risk I ran in the fight for my ideals of liberty. And that if they wanted to kill me for that, I would not ask for clemency—but of the attack on the palace I knew nothing.

Faget then asked me how I could explain my meeting with Norberto Hernández,* on the night of my arrest in the Pasteur Clinic, on Santos Suárez Street.

I immediately surmised that Norberto had participated in the palace attack, and realized the seriousness of Faget's question. I knew absolutely nothing about the assault on the palace, but obviously the police could not believe it.

I answered Faget that I had been at the clinic to visit a patient and that on my way out I had greeted two or three people in the corridor, and that if he had such exact information, he must know that I was telling the truth.

Ironically, Faget answered: "And at Cayo Confites, you also didn't know Norberto Hernández, Carlos Gutiérrez Menoyo, or Luis Gómez Wangüemert, either?"

"There were fifteen hundred people there and it was impossible to know them all." Then Faget took out a photo and said: "Do you know him or not?"

"But that's the doorman of the Cine Niza, and the whole of Havana knows him by sight. He was at the clinic that night, and we had waved to each other but did not speak.

"Colonel, how can it be, since you were following me that night and found my house six hours later, that you found it necessary to torture the private chauffeur who moved my things? And how can it be that you followed this man and let him escape and he participated in the attack on the palace, as you say?

"Don't blame me for the attack on the palace. Blame the police for their inefficiency.

"If my responsibility is a moral one in fighting against the regime, I'll take responsibility for everything that takes place in Cuba, in which case I'm guilty. I'm a helpless prisoner and I can't stop you from killing me. My only consolation is that you are more frightened than I am. And this time you won't be able to blame Ventura for my death."

---

* Norberto Hernández was a friend of mine, a veteran of the Spanish civil war, whom I had met in 1947, in the anti-Trujillo expedition at Cayo Confites; in July 1956, through me, he had proposed to Fidel an attempt against Batista's life—an idea that did not interest Fidel.—C. F.

As Piedra and Faget went out, I saw several prisoners pass by covered with blood, terribly tortured.

Major Medina, who in the afternoon had prevented our being murdered, led me to my cell again; on the stairs he told me: "We'll kill you in a little while, but before we do, we're not going to leave a piece of your body whole." I had no reason to doubt him.

Later I heard that they had killed the Ortodoxo political leader Pelayo Cuervo Navarro. I thought it must be an act of bravado to frighten us and make us talk. It seemed impossible that it should be true, but it was. That was the measure of the madness and fright of Batista and his paid assassins after the assault on the palace.

At three in the morning, they took me from my cell. They led me to the courtyard, where some vans were waiting. They brought the other four imprisoned comrades from *Revolución,* who told me with a certain satisfaction that they were taking us to El Príncipe, a prison under the control of the courts for prisoners awaiting trial, where the repressive bodies could not intervene; they told us it was known as "Paradise."

The day before they had brought a confession of guilt for me to sign before they opened a file on me; I had refused to sign, and that was why they had neither taken my photograph nor my fingerprints.

I asked the comrades if they had their police dossiers drawn up. They told me they had not, and we looked at each other, knowing well enough what that meant. The police vans set out from the bureau and, instead of heading for El Príncipe, went toward the Havana woods and the Almendares River. It was the night of the assault on the palace, and here we were out in the open, and without dossiers. There was no room for doubt.

In a voice that didn't seem like my own, I encouraged the comrades to face death, crying: "Viva the Revolution! Viva the 26th of July!"

In my heart I knew I didn't want to die. I thought of many things, including some quite absurd. I recalled a Chaplin film and the unveiling of a statue. But I would not be there to boo. I had always detested statues and the speeches that would be made later by cynics—in those days, confidence in a radical revolution of the type I wanted was unimaginable. My voice, encouraging the other comrades, just did not sound like my own. Outwardly, I was getting ready to die. But not inwardly. I could encourage the others with my voice; but for myself nothing would work.

The vans stopped at the edge of the Almendares River. I had figured out a plan. The instant they opened the door, I would run to the bank of the river yelling "Viva the Revolution!" I didn't think of escaping. Only of dying from a shot and not being tortured to death.

They were talking on walkie-talkies, receiving orders. They set off again. And once again they stopped. And did the same several times. There was another message, and the cars sped off at full speed. We returned to Twenty-third Street and set off toward El Príncipe. Minutes later we were climbing the stairs in the Castillo del Príncipe.

I thought they would shoot us at any moment and later say we had tried to escape. It was the only explanation I could find for the precipitate transfer that night, and without our having been registered. I could feel death at my back.

The gates were opened, and seconds later we were ushered into one of the large cells of El Príncipe, where we found numerous comrades under arrest. Among them was Alberto Mora, a leader of the Directory, who, a few days before the assault on the palace, had been arrested with his father, Menelao, and had fought with the police in order to give his father a chance to escape. And now Alberto was alive and Menelao was dead.

I think that was the longest day of my life. I had to prepare myself to die six times. The heat, the smell, and the sensation of death pervaded my entire body.

JOSÉ ANTONIO ECHEVERRÍA

An address   March 9, 1956

The American era opens abruptly with United States expansionism. The northern lands of Mexico are plundered; there is intervention in Cuba by means of the Platt Amendment; the independence of the people of Puerto Rico is appropriated; there is intervention in Nicaragua and Sandino is murdered; there is intervention in Santo Domingo, and as a terrible fate, they leave behind that scourge Rafael Leónidas Trujillo; the repressive forces in Guatemala are encouraged and the worst of volcanoes erupts for that nation: Castillo Armas. After the politics of intervention comes the creation of a zone of influence, faithfully defended by the new gendarmes who sustain foreign enterprises that exploit and destroy the national resources.

RENÉ ANILLO

An address

In 1955 Echeverría is again elected president of the FEU.

On June 9 Commander Jorge Agostini* was the victim of an assassi-

---

* A veteran of the Spanish civil war and of the abortive Cayo Confites expedition against General Trujillo of the Dominican Republic, Agostini was minister of the navy during the administration of Ramón Grau San Martín (1944–48). He was a member of the AAA, led by Aureliano Sánchez Arango, when he was killed, in June 1955.—ED.

nation carried out by Laurent.* Echeverría leads the mourning and courageously accuses the murderer by name.

In August he participates in an abortive revolutionary plan to attack the Presidential Palace. He manages to escape before the police arrive.

On December 4, at the Stadium del Cerro, a group of students occupy the grounds to protest the treatment of their jailed comrades, and again they are subjected to cruel repression, which was viewed on the television screens, for the clash with the police took place while the baseball game was being televised.

Far from being frightened by the police forces, the students issue a call for the people to congregate on December 7 in front of the monument to Maceo on the Avenue of the Malecón; from here a demonstration sets out for the university. This was intercepted by the police, whose bullets wounded more than a dozen of the numerous participants.

The student struggle is linked with the sugar-workers' strike, begun at the end of December, both movements acting mutually and equally repressed, thus constituting the firmest and most sustained popular action carried out thus far against the tyranny.

During these final days of November and the beginning of December 1955, the Revolutionary Directory is founded by Echeverría, Fructuoso Rodríguez, Faure Chomón, Joe Westbrook, and other comrades; it was this body that, together with the FEU, headed by Echeverría, directed the actions just described.

In 1956 Echeverría is re-elected president of the Architectural Students' Association and of the FEU.

He goes to Chile, to a Congress of Latin American Students, and travels through several countries explaining the struggle of the Cubans against Batista. He arrives in Mexico City, where in the name of Cuban youth he signs a pact together with Fidel Castro that pledges them to fight until victory or death.

Shortly after his return to Cuba, Echeverría is subjected to continuous harassment, which forces him to live clandestinely.

On March 13, 1957, the Revolutionary Directory assigns him to command the assault action on Radio Reloj, which is synchronized with the battle in the Presidential Palace. He is killed when he returns to the university. The Cubans lose one of their most dedicated fighters, the students their greatest leader, and the Revolutionary Directory its secretary general.

Shortly before his death he had written a manifesto:

---

* Lieutenant Julio Laurent was the chief of Batista's Naval Intelligence Service.—ED.

People of Cuba! Today, March 13, 1957, a day on which we render homage to those who have devoted their lives to the worthy profession of architecture, for which I am studying, at 3:20 in the afternoon, I will participate in an action in which the Revolutionary Directory has placed all its efforts, together with other groups who also fight for Liberty.

This action involves great risks for all of us, and we know that. I am not unaware of the danger. I do not seek it, nor do I shrink from it. I simply try to do my duty.

Our commitment to the people of Cuba was established by the Mexico City Pact, which joined our youth in conduct and action. But the circumstances necessary for our youth to carry out its assigned role were not forthcoming at the right time, forcing us to postpone the fulfillment of our obligation. We think that the moment has now come. We are confident that the purity of our motives will bring us God's favor so that we may achieve the rule of justice in our country.

If we fail, let our blood mark the road to liberty. For whether or not our action is crowned with the success we expect, the shock it will generate will send us forward along the road to triumph.

But it is the action of the people that will prove decisive. For that reason, in this manifesto, which may become my last will and testament, I here exhort the people of Cuba to demonstrate civil resistance, to refrain from actions that might in any way support the dictatorship that oppresses us, and to give effective support to those of us who bear arms so that we may gain freedom for the people. For this purpose, we must keep alive the faith in the revolutionary struggle, even though all the leaders fall, since there will never be a lack of determined, capable men to occupy our places, for as the Apostle Martí said, "Whenever there are no men, the very stones shall rise" to fight for the freedom of our country.

We ask our comrades, the students of all Cuba, to organize, since they constitute the vanguard of our struggle, and we ask the armed forces to remember that their mission is to defend their homeland, not to oppress their brothers; and that their task is that of the *mambí* army which fought for THE LIBERTY OF CUBA, as they affirm at the end of all their writings.

Viva Cuba Libre!

9. APRIL–MAY
THE CRIME AT 7 HUMBOLDT STREET

ENRIQUE RODRÍGUEZ LOECHES Havana, April

The retreat from the palace and the university by the survivors of the events of March 13th is replete with dramatic details. José Machado Rodríguez, with a bullet going through his thigh, from side to side, escaped from the palace with Abelardo Rodríguez Mederos, Evelio Prieto, and Juan Gualberto Valdés.

Abelardo was felled by a burst of machine-gun fire during the flight—near the Parque Zayas—and Evelio, shot through the face, also clear through, managed to reach the house of his friend the magistrate Elio Alvarez. He was discovered there and murdered in cold blood by agents of SIM that same night. Machadito then set off toward Mantilla. He sought refuge in a church, but the priest turned him down. His wound was still untreated and he spent the night of the thirteenth seated on a bench beside the church, and then in a vacant lot. The next day he made his way to Colón and Consulado, to the house of a friend who also failed him. He started off to the Vedado, where a good woman comrade, María Cobiellas, treated his wound as best she could and put him up for several days. Somewhat revived, he left the Vedado for Guanabacoa. One night he slept in the town's famous school, later he stayed with a friendly family, and then he slept in a house under construction. Finally Julio García found him in the house of a bus driver and took him to a basement on Nineteenth Street where there were already some comrades. Machadito, charged with the death of Colonel Blanco Rico, had been sought for months by the police.

Fructuoso Rodríguez was taken by Javier Pazos to the house of Enrique Menocal, a member of the 26th of July. From there he went to the house of Pepe Garcerán, a leader in the organization, who was later killed when he tried to dynamite the bridge at Ceiba Mocha on the

Central Highway. Fructuoso was never out of contact with us for more than a few days at a time. Joe Westbrook, together with his cousins Hector Rosales and Carlos Figueredo y Reguerita, got out of the university on the thirteenth. They went to the house of journalist working for *Carteles,* and here they separated: Joe ("Gilberto" in the underground) went to live in the house of Dr. Primitivo Lima in the Vedado. Days later he came to join us in the basement on Nineteenth Street, between Avenues B and C.

Juan Pedro Carbó Servía's escape from the palace with two bullets in his body is straight out of Dostoevski. An ambulance took him to the first-aid station at Corrales. There, a police lieutenant interrogated him while the doctor treated his wounds.

A corporal went through his clothes and found several bullets from the pistol he had thrown away. "How do you explain this," the policeman asked, "if you were traveling on a Route 14 bus?" "It doesn't matter," Juan Pedro answered. "We killed Batista and that's what matters."

The officer, far from becoming irritated, left the place and didn't come back. Maybe he went to verify what he had been told.

From here, where they took his picture, and he gave his name as "Juan Faite," they transferred him to the emergency hospital; there, some friends gave him emergency treatment and took him out through the front door, while through the back Masferrer and the son of Justo Luis Pozo were coming in. Juan Pedro was moved then to the Edificio Pentágono, facing the Ninth Precinct Police Station, where Mérida Guillén put him up. Four days later, Chomón, Julio García, and I went to see him. The place was awful. That night Julio took him away to Nineteenth Street.

Tony Castell and Faure Chomón had participated in the attack on the palace. Tony emerged unscathed and set out for his grandmother's house on San Lázaro and Perseverancia, where he stayed four days. The place was not very safe. Tony was also being sought for the death of Blanco Rico.

Faure Chomón escaped from the palace alive, but he had two bullets in his body. He took Ricardo Olmedo, along with José Alfonso, to the Calixto García Hospital. Then he went to the university. And from there to my father's house—9 Ronda—and then Felipe Pazos's wife, Sara, took him to La Víbora, to the house of her uncle, Nené Mediavilla. After two more stops, he went with Julio to the basement on Nineteenth Street. Chomón was the first to go to live in this basement.

Once contacts had been re-established, the Executive Committee of the directory met on March 24 at Cheo Silva's house in the Vedado. We all vowed to keep up the fight despite our losses, and not to abandon Havana. Only Chomón was to leave Cuba in search of arms. From that point on, Chomón was to take over the secretary general's job in place of Echeverría.

Our comrades' situation became virtually untenable. With the help of the architect Aquiles Capablanca, Julio managed to have Machadito granted asylum in the Brazilian embassy. Everything was arranged so that on the following Monday, the twenty-second, Machadito was to be taken there. They arrived at 7 Humboldt Street after midnight on the nineteenth. And in the time between leaving General Lee Street on the night of Tuesday the sixteenth, until they arrived at Humboldt Street, they never spent twenty-four hours in the same place. From Zapata they went to Las Alturas del Vedado, on Thirtieth Street between Thirty-fifth and Kohly Avenue. From there, to the Pharmaceutical College, on the Malecón between Galiano and San Nicolás. An unforeseen event made them leave this place, where they intended to remain until the end of Holy Week. The college president had managed to see to it that the janitor who did the cleaning should not go there during that time, but a nephew of the janitor suddenly put in an appearance and found himself apprehended by three unknown individuals who began to interrogate him. It was the nineteenth. From morning until night, they held him prisoner until they knew exactly what the situation was. After light had been shed on the intrusion, they did not dare spend the night there and they went off to Ricardo Bianchi's house to see Chomón. At that point, contact was made with Joe, who had found the apartment at 7 Humboldt Street. At Bianchi's house, Chomón took leave of his comrades and drove off in Vilella's car. Vilella left him at the corner of my house, near La Tropical. Julio García Oliveras, the hero of a hundred battles, again led his three comrades to Humboldt Street, where Joe and a friend were waiting for him. Before entering the building they nearly had a mishap, for standing in the doorway to the building was the man detailed to be on watch by the district police captain. Since there was nowhere else to go, they took a walk around the block amid the jokes and jests of Juan Pedro and Fructuoso, who insisted on teasing Machadito, who was in no mood for games.

On the night of the nineteenth, Julio García agreed to fetch Joe the next day at his fiancée's house, where he was living, to take him to his comrades. All that was there was a bed and a sofa. On the morning of the twentieth, Julio went out with Gustavo Pérez Cowley to buy our comrades a target game and a basket of food. At one o'clock, he brought them lunch and the bed. That afternoon he was to return to bring them some clothes and some brilliantine that they had left behind in the house on La Víbora. He also had to meet Joe. The house on General Lee Street and the basement on Nineteenth Street were apparently safe. Julio had circled them both and found nothing suspicious to indicate they were under observation. But clandestine life has complications. There are houses to be feared and houses that inspire confidence. The comrades were very much afraid in some houses that later proved to have been "problem-free" at the time.

After lunch, Julio took a longer than usual siesta. When he went to pick up Joe, his fiancée, Dysis Guira, had already taken him to Humboldt Street; Joe had become impatient waiting and did not want to wait for Julio. Julio thereupon headed for La Víbora in search of clothes and the other belongings for the comrades, and he was a little behind schedule because of the overlong siesta. On his return from La Víbora, he stopped at the house of Delia Coro, a woman comrade, in Hospital Street, where she told him the latest news broadcast. It must have been about 5:50 in the afternoon when Esteban Ventura Novo and his assassins began to break down the door to the apartment with the butts of their guns. The comrades, only half-dressed, did their best to escape. They were not all armed. Joe Westbrook gets as far as a ground-floor apartment and asks the woman living there if he can stay. She agrees, and Joe calmly sits down on the sofa in the living room, pretending to be paying a call. The woman is trembling with panic. Minutes later they knock at the door. He realizes he is lost, and continuing to behave like a thoroughgoing gentleman, even on the threshold of death, he tries to reassure the woman, and opens the door himself. The woman, aware that he is scarcely more than a boy, asks the murderers out of humanity not to harm him. He walks only a few yards up the stairs when a burst of machine-gun fire knocks him down. His face was untouched, so he looked as if he were resting and dreaming in his coffin. Joe was unarmed when he was killed.

His other comrades, barely dressed, leaped down the air vent in the apartment's kitchen, which led to a house below. They warned the woman whose house they had fallen into not to be alarmed and set off in different directions. Apparently, they did not know that they were completely surrounded, outside as well as inside the building. Juan Pedro Carbó raced for the elevator but was intercepted and gunned down point-blank.

Machadito and Fructuoso ran in another direction along the corridor and then jumped from a window to the ground floor. They fell into an alley next to an automobile agency, Santé Motors Co. It was a long, narrow passage, and at one of its ends, there was an iron gate with a padlock preventing any exit. When the company's workers heard the noise of the falling bodies, they ran over thinking they were the fellow workers who had been fixing a television antenna and had had an accident. Our comrades had jumped from such a height that Fructuoso was lying unconscious, while Machadito had broken both ankles. Still, he was making supreme efforts to get up but not succeeding. One of the Santé employees signaled them to wait, while he went off to get the key to the padlock. But at that moment, the "dogs" arrived. While all this was happening, another policeman headed for the café on the corner to get a hammer with which they broke the padlock. Once through the gate, the police finished off Fructuoso and Machadito.

The exchange of fire was so heavy that the people in neighboring buildings peeped out of their doors and balconies. Filled with euphoria, triumphant, Esteban Ventura, a captain, came and went from 7 Humboldt Street issuing orders and taking care of every matter. If the scene of the massacre seemed macabre, the work of carrying the corpses from the various places they had fallen was even more grisly. Those were not men. Luis Alfaro Sierra, the police agent Mirabal, Corporal Carratalá, later promoted to lieutenant, whose brother was a colonel, dragged all the bodies to the sidewalk by the hair, in full view of everybody. And then they dragged them again, the same way, to the next corner. The people on the balconies began to protest loudly. A burst of machine-gun fire scared them off.

The events at the palace had nearly destroyed us. Almost without arms, without houses, without money, without automobiles, we survived solely on courage and dignity. The only two cars in which we "moved" our comrades were not much good. Julio's black Oldsmobile was the one used in the attempt on Orlando Piedra's life. Comrade Teresa Fernández-Arenas's brown Pontiac, which I drove, had belonged to Pepe Wangüemert.

I had returned from Miami on Monday, the twenty-second, with the news that on Wednesday Faure Chomón could leave on the boat to Miami. That night, Julio and I, despite a thousand vicissitudes, got him there and he was able to embark.

CHE GUEVARA   Sierra Maestra

March and April 1957 were months of restructuring and apprenticeship for the rebel troops. After receiving reinforcements from a place called La Derecha, our army numbered some eighty men.

Toward the middle of April, we returned with our army to train in the regions around Palma Mocha, near El Turquino.*

Guillermo García and Ciro Frías came and went from one part of the Sierra to the other with patrols of peasants, bringing news, exploring, requisitioning stocks of food; they were the true mobile vanguard of our column.

On April 23 the reporter Bob Taber and a photographer arrived among us; along with them, Comrades Celia Sánchez and Haydée Santamaría and the envoys from the Movement in the plains: Marcos [Delio Gómez Ochoa],** and Nicaragua [Major Carlos Iglesias], who was in

---

* The highest peak in Cuba, 6561 feet high.—Ed.
** When underground names are used by the writers, real names have been supplied in brackets by the editor.

charge of our action in Santiago, and Marcelo Fernández, coordinator of the Movement.

Comrade Nicaragua brought news that more arms were available in Santiago, remnants of the assault on the palace: 10 machine guns, 11 Johnson guns, and 6 short carbines, according to his count. There were some more, but we thought of establishing another front in the zone of the Miranda sugar mill.

The entire column climbed Pico Turquino, and up there, we finished the interview that Bob Taber did on the Movement in preparation for a film that was televised in the United States.

MANUEL FAJARDO

When all of us joined up again, we once more went in search of Che and an armed troop commanded by Frank in the name of the Santiago Movement.

The idea of attacking El Turquino was born there, although Che thought we should first assault a garrison close by, near where we were. Others of us thought we should first train the new troops by taking them on long hikes, give them some training, and familiarize them with guerrilla life.

Then Fidel had the idea we should attack El Uvero; he thought that the troop was sufficiently trained. The garrison at El Uvero was chosen for the troops' baptism of fire.

At that time, because of our presence, there were no local people in the Sierra. We got supplies for the first time after the battle in a shop at El Guayabo. We returned to the Santo Domingo area, near where Lalo Sardiñas lived. There, we met up with the group under Delio Gómez Ochoa, who had brought some things from Santiago, and we got some clothes.

CASTELL [CARLOS FRANQUI]

Letter to Frank País   El Príncipe Prison, Havana, April

Here in prison we have lively discussions: talk of tactics and even ideology. Armando's talk is impressive. Faustino cheers up. Enrique is caustic. Actually, El Príncipe is a permanent assembly. I need only tell you that there is even a "securities market" run by Miralles, who in moments of tension sings out the "liquid and the solid assets," in the so-called diarrhea of war. The guards say we are mad.

Sometimes, at three in the morning, we play imaginary baseball, all the motions carried out in pantomime, and since the umpire Maestri is in prison with the workers from the electricians' strike, he himself calls the plays, just as in the Stadium del Cerro. There are two hundred of us in prison. Over a hundred from the 26th of July, about forty from the RD,* about twenty from Menelao's Auténtico groups, and about ten Communists.

The Communists do not believe in insurrection. They criticize sabotage and guerrilla tactics. They say we are playing the game of régime terrorists. They say the 26th Movement is putschist, adventurist, and petit bourgeois. They cling to their hypothetical "mobilization of the masses" and their classic "unity, unity."

In the discussions here, Ursino Rojas, of the Central Committee, and Villalonga and Armas, Communist workers' leaders, take a big part. We are represented by Armando, Enrique, Faustino, and myself. The Communists do not understand the nature of tyranny and do not believe in the possibility of the revolution; yet they call themselves its only representatives. They evidently believe that Batista will return to legality and elections, as happened in 1939. They are the same Communists he killed in 1935, and who formed an alliance with him and voted for him in 1940. The party is bureaucratic, reformist, and politicking and it will never outgrow its limitations.

It is curious that while they declaim rhetoric against the bombs, repeating all the old saws, as prisoners they are delighted by the noise of sabotage in the city, which we can hear perfectly from here. Our differences with the Communists are insurmountable; it's better that way, for they are contaminated with the "Soviet virus." And the Cuban people are right in not supporting them, not merely because of their ideology but because of their history.

The Auténticos are a mixed group: revolutionaries, adventurers, and political types.

There are a good many from the Directory. They were badly beaten up after their attack on the palace. They are like us, except for certain differences: on the importance of Havana (which they overestimate and we underestimate), on striking at the top, on the battle in the Sierra: they are concerned with Fidel's bossism and his criticisms of the assassination of Blanco Rico—about which Fidel was wrong.

What creates the most problems is that they could not take part in the landing because of faulty contacts with Pepe Suárez and the arrest of Aldo; and the fact that Faustino, Miret, Armando, and Haydée were out of Havana, which was left without leadership—a serious mistake Fidel made while he was in Mexico.

At the time of the attack on the palace, Soto and a group of comrades were in hiding nearby; they waited and waited but nobody gave them the word. Later they were arrested right there. And Faustino went

---

* Revolutionary Directorate.

to the airport to bring reinforcements from the cell there for the attack that Calixto Sánchez did not carry out because some weapons were hidden in Sans Souci.

The story of the weapons is incredible. They belonged to the Auténticos, and were in the hands of a lawyer, who had agreed to give them to us. We took them to Quinta and A, our bomb factory, and from there to the outskirts of Havana, to the small house Juan Misterio was building. The Bureau of Investigation seized them there; they had traced the address through an electric-light receipt found when the sabotage group was arrested at the airport.

On March 13 Calixto Sánchez went to look for them and, naturally, did not find them. Faustino did not know anything about them. When the group from the airport was taken prisoner by Ventura, he took them to the place where the weapons were, to kill them there. They were saved because the weapons were not to be found. As Enrique says, this war is a race between cripples. Fortunately, they are more crippled than we are.

We will have to achieve unity with the Directory through action. Apart from ourselves, they are the only serious fighting, revolutionary group in the country. Ideological agreement is almost total; the discrepancies are minimal. Alberto Mora and almost the entire Directory are prisoners here with us, and the daily contact means a great deal. Orders are almost better transmitted from here than from the underground.

A few days after one gets out of the hells of the repressive forces, the tortures are forgotten. Our collective feeling here is so strong that we are actually in charge: we prisoners are free and the guards are captives.

Really, Batista's police are a gang of imbeciles, who are only good for torturing and assassination. When the police vans take us to court, we sing anthems and cry out "Viva the Revolution! Viva the 26th of July!"

We put on some fantastic shows in the courthouse. When the people in the street hear us singing behind the bars of our cells, they applaud us.

You know I am always criticizing and am no optimist: I fight and analyze. But this prison shows me clearly that we are not a vanquished generation, but a vanquishing one.

And to see it, one need only walk around anywhere in Cuba: they have the weapons; we have the youth and the people.

GUILLERMO Sierra Maestra

The arms arrived, and the "30s" really are there. Almeida went to pick them up, with ten men; in the consignment there were also ten M-1's, along with forty or fifty rounds.

I took a "30" and Celia took an M-1, and then and there, they gave us a little training in the use of those arms. That was when Joel Iglesias arrived with two other kids, and Fidel did not want them to stay. One left, and two stayed—Joel and his cousin Hermes. Che took another "30," and we gave a "30" to Crescencio.

FIDEL CASTRO   Sierra, April

The government is using the arms furnished by the United States "against the entire Cuban people." Bazookas, mortars, machine guns, aircraft, and bombs. But we are secure in the Sierra; they have to come and find us.

To Jacinto [Armando Hart]: The National Directorate of the Movement can count on our complete trust; it should use all its powers in accordance to what the circumstances require; often, it is virtually impossible to consult each other ahead of time. I trust its ability to sort out the difficulties and take the most convenient steps leading to the ultimate triumph of our cause. In short: it may act as the representative of our Movement. I think as it does: nothing can stop the Cuban Revolution.

CHE GUEVARA

At that time, I had to attend to my duties as a doctor and in each small village or hamlet we reached, I carried out consultations. It was monotonous, since I had few medicines to provide and the clinical cases in the Sierra were always the same: prematurely aged, toothless women; children with enormous bellies; parasitism; rickets; general vitamin deficiency—those were the typical diseases of the Sierra Maestra.

It was while we worked there that we began to become aware of the need to bring about permanent changes in the life of the people. The idea of agrarian reform became clear, and the communion with the people ceased to be theory and became part of our very beings.

There, also, Guillermo García was promoted to the rank of captain, and he took charge of all the country people who joined our columns. Perhaps Comrade Guillermo does not recall that date; it is written down in my combat diary: May 6, 1957.

The next day, Haydée Santamaría went off with specific instructions from Fidel to make the necessary contacts, but a day later, we received the news of the arrest of Nicaragua [Major Iglesias], who was in charge of bringing us arms. This upset us all, since we could not figure out how the arms would get to us; however, we resolved to proceed toward our goal.

That day we heard on the radio the news of the sentencing of our comrades from the *Granma;* in addition, we heard that one judge had cast his vote against the sentence. This was Judge Urrutia, whose honorable gesture would later lead to his being asked to be the provisional president to the republic.

Around then, a contact from Santiago, Andrés, arrived; he had definite information that the arms were safe and would be brought in a few days.

Finally, on May 18, we got word of the arms and also, more or less, what kind. The news produced an uproar throughout the camp, for it was immediately common knowledge, and all the comrades wanted better weapons and secretly hoped to get the new ones or at least get those that were discarded by the men who got the new weapons.

We also received word that the film that Bob Taber had made in the Sierra Maestra had been shown with great success in the United States. This news made everyone happy except Andrew St. George, who, despite being an FBI agent, had a touch of journalistic ambition in his heart, and he felt robbed.

The arms arrived that night: for us it was the most marvelous spectacle in the world. The weapons, those instruments of death, were laid out before the greedy eyes of the fighters as if at an exhibition. There were 3 machine guns on tripods, 3 Madsdens, 9 M-1 carbines, 10 Johnson automatic rifles, and a total of 6000 rounds.

On May 25 we heard that a group of expeditionaries led by Calixto Sánchez had landed from the launch *Corintia* near Mayarí; a few days later we were to learn the disastrous results of that venture.

April–May

Guillermo García went to look for Fidel in the Caracas region, while I made a short trip to pick up Ramiro Valdés, who was partly recovered from his leg wound. On the night of March 24, Fidel appeared. His arrival was impressive: he was accompanied by a dozen comrades who had faithfully remained with him. And there was a notable difference between the bearded men, with their improvised knapsacks, made of whatever had come to hand and tied on any which way, and the new soldiers with their uniforms still clean, their knapsacks all identical and fresh, and their shaven faces.

New platoons were formed; the entire troop was divided into three groups under three captains, Raúl Castro, Juan Almeida, and Jorge Sotú; Camilo Cienfuegos was to command the forward troops and Efigenio Amejeiras, the rear; my mission was that of medical officer to the General Staff, and Universo Sánchez was chief of the General Staff.

Our troop took on a new importance through the incorporation of this many men, and moreover, we now had two submachine guns—although of dubious efficacy, due to their age and poor condition. Nevertheless, we were now a considerable force. We discussed what we might do immediately. I thought we should attack the first possible post, to give some battle experience to the new comrades. But Fidel and all the other members of the council were of the opinion that it would be best to have them march for a while so they could get used to the rigors of life in the forest and mountains, and the long hikes over the steep terrain. It was decided that after some basic schooling on the rudiments of guerrilla life, they should go eastward and walk as long as possible, but still be on the lookout for an opportunity to attack a group of guards.

FAUSTINO PEREZ, ARMANDO HART, AND CARLOS FRANQUI

Letter to Pepe Prieto*   El Príncipe Prison, Havana

Relations with the other sectors and leaders should be studied, above all else: the electrical sector, transport, telephones, banks, sugar refineries, etc., and also all other revolutionary and political organizations. Consider the possibility of creating a central committee to direct the general strike: and similar committees, for the same purpose among the laboring sectors and centers.

The Conrados, the Auténtico labor leaders, and those in the above-mentioned sectors should be visited in the name of the Movement and its leader. The workers' commissions should be as broadly based as possible.

FIDEL CASTRO   Sierra, May 28, El Uvero

On May 28, 1957, we were one hundred men, many armed with shotguns and .22-caliber rifles. The enemy garrison was composed of sixty soldiers strongly entrenched and fortified, most of them with automatic arms. At 5:15 a.m., at the first light of day, the command and a platoon under its orders opened fire on the enemy from a height, some 300 yards from the barracks. The platoon under Jorge Sotú attacked on the right flank, while on the left flank, the squads led by Camilo, Efigenio, Che, and Crescencio Pérez went into attack. Almeida's platoon had the most difficult mission.

The situation seemed difficult, the reports furnished by the guides had little resemblance to reality; the distances they gave were totally at variance with what we found. I called Captain Juan Almeida over and told him: "The situation is difficult, the information does not correspond with reality, but El Uvero must be taken at any cost. Advance with your

---

* Director of the 26th of July Movement in Havana; he was killed by Batista's men.—C. F.

platoon under cover of our fire and don't open fire until you are on top of the enemy trenches." Almeida carried out his mission: he advanced and advanced until he hurled himself upon the fortifications. His men began to fall, he himself was wounded, but he continued advancing. The various platoons carried out similar actions from all angles: one by one they assaulted and took all the outer defenses at El Uvero. The enemy was entrenched and protected by thick pine trunks, invulnerable to bullets. In many cases, combat was a matter of man-to-man action. Our machine guns were moved forward from their original emplacements and brought closer to the enemy's last positions. Casualties continued to mount in our lines. One of the first was Julio Díaz, a veteran of Moncada and of the *Granma*. Finally, the barracks, where sixteen men were still holding out, surrendered under the cross-fire of two .30-caliber tripod-mounted machine guns, which never stopped firing and answered every enemy shot with a hail of bullets.

The field of El Uvero was covered with the corpses of enemy soldiers and rebels. Our forces took 46 rifles, 2 machine guns, and 6000 rounds, and thus began a new phase in the Sierra Maestra.

The 19 wounded belonging to the regular army were carefully attended by our medical corps—Che—and left there in the care of their own doctor, so that the army might pick them up and move them to their own hospitals, thanks to which none of them died. A wounded rebel, Mario Leal, was too badly hurt to be moved. The army doctor, touched by the behavior we showed toward our military foes, asked us to leave him under his care, and said that he would be given medical treatment and his life would be spared.

Meanwhile, the same day that we freed 16 prisoners and saved the lives of 19 wounded men, the dictatorship killed the 16 prisoners from the *Corintia* expedition in cold blood. Calixto Sánchez and his comrades heard their death sentences over the radio.

June

Our method of attack began to soften up the enemy. You know what it's like: a troop of 350 men beside the sea, delighted with themselves, and then . . . a hailstorm of bullets from nowhere! Fire away! Because all our shooting took place at two in the morning, or at two-thirty, or at one; no one could sleep. When night fell, the shooting began. This kind of thing lowered their morale; they really respected us.

Now we realize that all these many soldiers meant little to us, because we began to discover possibilities and more possibilities.

We lined up very few people before firing squads, very few indeed, during the entire war; we did not shoot more than 10 guys in twenty-five months. Over in the Escambray, 33 were lined up and shot by Carreras alone, and he was not even at war. The truth is that for us it had to be something very serious, a matter of treason or a very serious offense, a spy, for instance. For Carreras, it was not a matter of firing squads, but of murders.

We had firing squads really only for traitors, but sometimes we used them for someone who had committed a very serious offense, like rape, a man who had taken the wife away from her peasant husband. That was the case with the Teacher, who went over to El Jigüe, pretending to be Che, the doctor, and began to examine women who came to him. Che, who had been with us for a few days, was going back there and told us: "I'll send you the Teacher." At that time a kind of contagious banditry broke out, people demanding money, a whole series of things, 30 men who had run into a group of prostitutes around there, and all 30 had forced themselves on the prostitutes. . . .

So then the Teacher showed up at that moment, just as I was lining up a batch of men for the firing squad. He got there and I said to him: "Follow me." He went there directly, he wasn't even brought to trial, for he had already been pardoned from a death sentence.

He was a picturesque type, a character. How did we come to know him? When we arrived in the Sierra, we were told of a schoolteacher, "the Teacher who was with you at Moncada." "What teacher was with us at Moncada? I'm positive I didn't know any teacher there."

He had spent about two years in the Sierra, and one day we ran into him. He was a strong, healthy man and he joined us. I said to him: "Come here, Teacher. Were you at Moncada?"

He says: "Yes, I was at such and such a point."

"But come now, are you going to tell me that story? Listen, buddy, tell me the truth. Whatever you did or didn't do, we're not going to take it into consideration now, but let's begin by telling the truth."

"The truth is," he told me, "I stole two cows and came here to the Sierra."

"Well, okay. We'll forgive you for the two cows. But now that you have the opportunity, behave yourself." And we gave the Teacher a chance. He was an orangoutan; he grew a huge beard. He was also a born clown and carried loads as though he were Hercules, but he was a bad soldier.

Besides, his habit of stealing things did not seem to have left him.

The worst thing he did was when Che had a terrible asthma attack and we had to leave him behind. We assigned the Teacher to take care of him. The Teacher knew the area, was very strong, but we didn't know him very well then. He behaved abominably toward Che, who needed some medicine for his asthma. The medicine was to be picked up somewhere, but Che had to lead the way while the Teacher followed behind him.

He liked being a doctor more than being a teacher! What stupidity to pretend he was Che, in that area, where we had spent a long time, where everyone knew all of us, especially the Teacher and Che. Still, some people knew Che by name only. And now, with the new beard, the Teacher was passing himself off as Che: "Bring me women. I'm going to examine them all!" Did you ever hear of anything so outrageous?

We shot him.

10. JUNE–JULY: SANTIAGO IN REVOLUTION

ALEJANDRO [FIDEL CASTRO]

Letter   Sierra, June 15

Norma [Celia Sánchez]: You and David [Frank País] are our essential pillars. If you and he are well, then all goes well and we are easy in our minds. Why bother to tell you of our anguish and sadness when we heard the news of your arrest? There was such a coincidence between your leaving and the news that it could scarcely be doubted! I began to recover some hope only when I heard Matthews' report to *The New York Times*.

I'm forwarding the letters you want: (1) for the patriotic clubs, (2) for my sisters, and (3) for the gentleman in Miami. But I am not sending the letter to our people in Havana, because I consider it unnecessary, given the fact that David is sufficiently accredited to transmit it as a national executive.

All your news is good. How anxiously we await news of the Second Front!

We are racking our brains here in dealing with all our needs and trying to find out how we are to take care of such a large family.

We received the $1500. For the time being, that part of it is doing well. We have not paid the bearer here. The sum total comes to $1328.30. We owe two other debts, much smaller sums, to two other people.

The powdered milk was a great disappointment. They told us there would be 5000 cans and less than 1000 arrived. You can imagine all the headaches this entails: we counted on a certain quantity in our plans and then received something quite different. I don't know what I'll do when the 50 come! We've just gotten the previous 30.

CARLOS FRANQUI

Letter to Frank País   El Príncipe Prison, Havana, June

Stick to your plan for opening a Second Front in Oriente.

In order to win, we must make total war from Oriente to Occidente, as in 1895.

Each action marks the limits of a tactical struggle. For Santiago, you took the naval police station and burned the national police station, you had the people of the city in your power for a day, with only three dead and without losing a weapon.

The *Granma*, between the dead, lost, and captured, forfeited seventy of its eighty-two members and its battle equipment.

But while the mountain multiplies, the city annihilates. The twelve survivors of the *Granma*, along with the reinforcements you sent from Santiago, added up to about a hundred men, and they have been strengthened with the action at El Uvero. Meanwhile, we in the city are fewer every day. From the Directorate alone, the following are in the hands of the police: you, Daniel, Faustino, Armando, Haydée, Cheché, and myself, and the best action units of the entire island.

The Sierra cannot exist on its own. Without the men, the arms, the money, the medicines, the propaganda, and the help we gave the Sierra, it would have gone under.

And without the struggle in the cities, the army would have liquidated the Sierra. But there, in the mountains, guerrilla activity grows.

Like you, I do not share the thesis of some comrades of the National Directorate who think the Sierra is a focal point, a passion, an example. Those comrades underestimate the possibilities of guerrilla warfare, and do not properly evaluate the decisive role it has played throughout our history. Fidel is altogether right in this. He is not right when he underestimates urban combat and the importance of Havana and Santiago.

I also do not share the idea that an almost spontaneous general strike can bring about the fall of the regime. That is a dangerously utopian idea.

On the possibility of your opening the Second Front much depends, much that affects the future of our struggle, the Movement, and the Revolution, as well as the equilibrium and integration of the Sierra and the plains.

EDITOR'S SUMMARY

In May members of the 26th of July Movement had carried out their most important sabotage to date: a dynamite explosion that destroyed a gas and electric station in

Havana. The center of the city was blacked out and paralyzed for fifty-four hours; no business or other activities could be carried on.

Jules Dubois, Latin American correspondent of the Chicago Tribune, *reported that on a visit to Santiago de Cuba, he found that José M. ("Pepín") Bosch, head of the Bacardí Rum Company, Judge Manuel Urrutia, and many leading businessmen were out-and-out supporters of Fidel Castro. Even the head of the Catholic Youth Movement commended Castro for asking that chaplains be sent to his troops, and he flatly rejected the notion that Castro was a Communist.*

In June Herbert L. Matthews, correspondent of The New York Times, *confirmed his own observations that a broad spectrum of people in Santiago—university officials, businessmen, religious leaders, workers—opposed Batista and welcomed Matthews' reports on Castro's activities.*

Matthews observed that not just the city of Santiago but Oriente Province as a whole was striving to oust the dictator. He pointed out that Oriente, Cuba's richest and most populous area, had been the launch site for Cuba's previous liberation movements.

Despite Batista's objections, the United States finally replaced Arthur Gardner, its long-time ambassador and a crony of Batista's, with Earl E. T. Smith, a stockbroker.

FRANK PAÍS

Letter to Alejandro [Fidel Castro]   Santiago, June 26

As you must know, what happened to the 40s was a disaster. Sierra sent in a group of young boys who, at the last minute, refused to obey; besides, they got lost and wandered around for twelve days, they had no decent guides, and this was more than they could stand. On the one hand, I am happy, because those who were useless left, and those who were worthwhile remained; but I'm sorry about the ammunition and food that went by the board, as well as the messages they had that were delayed—not to mention the danger that both good men and good weapons were exposed to. A delegate of ours will leave for Manzanillo to find out who was responsible.

Perhaps by the time this letter arrives, National Plan 7 and the Second Front will have begun—with great success, I hope.

A key comrade for the Second Front—Daniel [René Ramos Latour] was freed today by the Emergency Court: this will advance the work greatly.

I hope you've already received Bienvenido's reports (the military ones) and let's hope the 40s also got them. I trust that letters are now reaching you sealed; I had heard that they were arriving open and many people were reading them. From now on, I'm going to close them with sealing wax.

Don't forget what Faustino and Pedro asked. We have already planned what we're going to do on the thirtieth.

We received three letters here from Che, and we are sending him what he asked for.

CHE GUEVARA   Sierra Maestra

The entire month of June 1957 was spent treating our comrades wounded during the attack on El Uvero and organizing a small outfit with which we were to join Fidel's column.

My asthma took a turn for the worse during these days and the lack of medicine made me almost as helpless as the wounded; I was able to get some relief by smoking dried sweet-pea leaf, which is the usual remedy in the Sierra, until medication arrived from civilization. Thus I was in fit condition for the departure, but day after day, it was delayed. At last, we organized a patrol to go out and search for the weapons that the enemy had dumped as unusable after the attack on El Uvero; they would be useful to our guerrilla band.

Under these new conditions, all those old rifles with more or less serious defects, including a .30-caliber machine gun without a pin, were potential treasures, and we spent an entire night searching for them. We finally set June 24 as our departure date. At that point, we were an army consisting of the following: five convalescent wounded, five escorts, ten enlisted from Bayamo, two recently enlisted "on their own" (so to speak), and four from the area: a total of twenty-six. The march was organized with Vilo Acuña in the lead, then, what could be called the command, led by me, since Almeida was still recovering from a wound in the thigh and he had trouble walking, and then two small squadrons led by Maceo and Pena.

We didn't leave on the twenty-fourth because of a combination of small difficulties; sometimes we had word that a new recruit was arriving with one of the guides and that we had to wait. At one point, we had to look for a new cave to store our food, because at long last, our contacts with Santiago had crystallized, and David [Frank País] had brought us a fairly important shipment, which was impossible to transport, given the marching conditions of our convalescent troops and rookie recruits.

On June 26 I made my debut as an oral surgeon, although in the Sierra they gave me the more modest title of "tooth puller." My first victim was Israel Pardo, and he turned out pretty well. The second one was Joel Iglesias, who really needed a charge of dynamite to extract his eye-tooth but he made it till the end of the war with the tooth still in place, since my efforts had been in vain. Added to my meager skill, was a shortage of "shots," so that anesthesia had to be hoarded carefully, and, instead, quite a bit of "psychological anesthesia" was applied, such as calling people pretty tough names, when patients complained while I worked in their mouths.

With merely the threat of a march, some of the men showed how weak their commitment was, and off they went; but new ones replaced them. Tamayo brought us a new group of four men. Among them was Félix Mendoza, who came with a rifle and explained how he and his companion had been surprised by some army troops; while the other fellow had been stopped, he dashed along some cliffs and ran off without the army doing anything about it. Later we learned that the "army" in this case was a patrol led by Lalo Sardiñas, who had met up with the other fellow, and that now he was one of Fidel's troops.

With Evelio Saburit and Félix Mendoza and his group, we were now thirty-six men, but on the following day three took off, and then others joined the group, and we were thirty-five. However, when we began our march, our numbers again dropped. We were climbing the hills of Peladero, on very short marches.

The radio reports a pattern of violence all over the island. On July 1 we heard the news of the death of Frank's brother, Jossué País, along with other comrades, in the long battle that broke out in Santiago.

We were twenty-eight when we left the following day, but two new recruits joined up, ex-soldiers, who came to fight for the freedom of the Sierra. They were Gilberto Capote and Nicolás. They were brought by Arístides Guerra, another of the contacts in the region, who was later of inestimable value to our column. We called him the "King of Grub," and throughout the war, he performed enormous services many times more dangerous than actually fighting the enemy. For instance, moving troops of mules from the Bayamo zone to our area of operations.

Gilberto Capote, then a lieutenant, died heroically at Pino del Agua.

We left our camp at the house of Polo Torres, on a plateau that later became one of our centers of operations, and walked, guided now by a peasant named Tuto Almeida. Our mission was to get to La Nevada and then meet up with Fidel, by crossing the north slope of El Turquino. We were walking in that direction when we saw at a distance two peasant women, who tried to flee as we approached; we had to run to stop them. They turned out to be two black girls surnamed Moya, and by religion they were Adventists. Though against all types of violence because of their religious beliefs, they gave us their open support at that moment and throughout the entire war.

We refreshed ourselves and ate magnificently there, but when we were about to cross through Malverde (we had to cross Malverde in order to get to La Nevada), we learned that there were army troops everywhere in the zone. After a short period of deliberation between our reduced high command and the guides, we decided to backtrack and go over El Turquino, a rougher way, but less dangerous under these circumstances.

We increased our pace as much as we could in order to reach Fidel. We set out at night and stayed with a peasant (nicknamed El Vizcaíno [the Basque] because of his birthplace) who lived right on the slopes of El Turquino. He lived entirely alone in his little hut; his only companions were a few Marxist books, carefully hidden in a small hole under a stone, far from his hut. He proudly displayed his Marxist militancy, which few people in the region knew about. El Vizcaíno showed us which road to take, and we continued on our slow march.

It was very hard to maintain the morale of the troops without arms, without direct contact with the chief of the Revolution, practically groping our way along, without any experience, surrounded by enemies who grew to gigantic proportions in our minds and in the tales the peasants told us. And there were continual crises in our guerrilla band caused by the inadequate preparation among the new men who came from the plains and were unused to the thousand and one difficulties of mountain paths.

After difficult, short marches, we reached the region of Palma Mocha, beyond the western slope of El Turquino, around Las Cuevas, where we were very well received by the peasants and where we established a direct contact through my new profession as "tooth puller," which I practiced very enthusiastically.

We ate and patched up our forces in order to continue rapidly to old familiar places, such as Palma Mocha and El Infierno, where we arrived on June 15. There a local peasant, Emilio Cabrera, informed us that Lalo Sardiñas was encamped with his troops in a nearby ambush, whose location, Cabrera complained to me, put his house in danger in case of an attack from an enemy patrol.

On June 16, a meeting took place between our small new column and the platoon from Fidel's column led by Lalo Sardiñas. We learned that, once more, the obstinate Sánchez Mosquera had made his way into the Palma Mocha region and was almost encircled by Fidel's column, but that he managed to elude the encirclement by crossing El Turquino on forced marches and reaching the other side.

We had had some inkling of troops nearby, because a few days before, when we had reached a hut, we saw trenches that soldiers had occupied until the day before. But what we didn't suspect was that what seemed to be a sustained offensive against us was, in reality, evidence of the flight of the repressive columns. This marked a total change in the quality of operations in the Sierra. We already had sufficient forces to encircle the enemy columns and put them to flight by threatening them with annihilation.

At this time, a new column was formed, of which I was in charge, holding the rank of captain, and some other promotions were made as well: Ramiro Valdés was promoted to captain, and he and his platoon joined my column; Ciro Redondo was also promoted to captain, leading another platoon. The column consisted of three platoons, one led by Lalo Sardiñas, who brought up the vanguard and, at the same time, was the second in command of the detachment; and two others led by Ramiro Valdés and Ciro Redondo. This column, which was called "the Evicted Peasants," contained seventy-five men, heterogeneously dressed and heterogeneously armed. Nevertheless, I felt very proud of them. Much prouder, more closely tied to the Revolution, if that were possible, more eager to prove that my chevrons were merited—I would feel this some nights later.

We sent a letter of appreciation to Frank País, who was living his last days. All the officers in the guerrilla army signed it, that is, those who knew how (the peasants in the Sierra were not very experienced in the art of writing and they had become an important element of the guerrilla forces). The letter was signed in two columns and when those in the second column were to write in their ranks, Fidel simply said, when my turn came: "Put down major." In this informal, almost offhand fashion, I was named major of Column 2 of the guerrilla army (which would later be called Column 4).

We were in a peasant's house—I don't recall which one—when we wrote our message to our brothers in the city who struggled heroically to provision us and to relieve the pressure from Santiago itself.

The vanity that we all share made me feel the proudest man on earth that day. The symbol of my commission, a small star, was presented to me by Celia, together with one of the wristwatches that had been ordered from Manzanillo.

ALEJANDRO [FIDEL CASTRO]

Letter to Norma [Celia Sánchez]   Sierra, July 5

Raúl Chibás, Robertico [Roberto Agramonte], and Enrique Barroso have now joined forces with us. It is of the utmost urgency to communicate to Havana so that it can be published.

I think it would be extremely advantageous to form a revolutionary government presided over by Raúl Chibás, but after the first efforts in this direction, I think it would be very difficult to overcome his personal scruples; he fears that in such an event, his trip to the Sierra might be interpreted as furthering his own interests. The best arguments are dashed to smithereens in the face of his belief about this. Only time will tell what we can do in this direction.

I am enclosing rolls of his photographs for you to take to *Bohemia*, which would be terrific material for an exclusive picture story.

I must send a copy of Raúl Chibás's statements to Herbert Matthews. This thing is going to have great national and international repercussions.

Today is Friday, the fifth. The rolls of film should be sent to *Bohemia* by air from Manzanillo, right away, carried by a person you can trust, so that they will be there Sunday or Monday at the latest, and can appear next Friday.

The impact caused by the news of the death of Jossué and the other comrades was tremendous. To think that we were at the point of cutting off and destroying a column of 140 men—which would have been a great retribution—but at the last minute, less than half a mile from the trap, they changed their route! How David [Frank País, Jossué's brother] must feel about all this, together with the blow to the plans for an imminent Second Front! I know he has more than enough fortitude to bear these terrible trials. But in any case, we've thought a lot about him. I don't want to write precipitously because I have a lot more to say. Let him know that, as far as I'm concerned, I think his answers concerning the matter of the military people* are completely correct. I have nothing to add or object to concerning his answers. I am absolutely confident that he is very clear in his approach to the possible situations; he interprets our duties perfectly, and I want to delegate full powers to him, without any need for consultation, so that he can transact everything pertaining to this matter on his own. He should only report to me about what is going on.

I want to tell you about the trip of the last contingent and its results: it was really disastrous. I am told that they wasted an endless amount of bullets. It's monstrous! And a lot of other kinds of material was lost. They tell me that half-filled cans of condensed milk were thrown out, and other things like that. It really hurts when things like this happen! The ones who are guilty can't expect forgiveness! The result: we don't even have a doctor, or nurse, alas, because Vierita, who made the rounds, had to remain behind because of sickness. We've received a total of *fifteen hundred* .30–'06 rounds here, including those for the machine gun, which arrived on cartridge belts, another few for the Mendoza, and about a thousand cartridges of .44s and other calibers. Not more than *forty-two hundred* in all.

As for the rest, in other respects, we're marvelously well off. Our troops have become more and more skilled and effective. Through careful selection, discipline, and the weeding out of the unsuitable, we're bringing together a real army.

We here are full of admiration for the enormous impetus the Move-

* The navy conspirators from Cienfuegos and Havana.—C. F.

ment is gaining in the rest of the island. And we also admire, above all, the heroism being shown by our men in the underground. At times, one feels ashamed of being in the Sierra. It is much more commendable to be there than to be here.

I advise David not to become disheartened about the Second Front. We must persevere in this strategy whatever the obstacles. It does not matter that the beginnings are modest and more limited than what he had planned.

I understand why he insists I do an article for *Bohemia* as soon as possible. I haven't been able to do anything these last two days because of the crush of work incorporating the new contingent, selecting men, bullets, weapons, and then going immediately to meet Raúl Chibás; I've hardly slept at all the last two nights. The physical effort here is added to the huge mental effort: attending to security and supplies, friends and enemies, the latest news from here, as well as from the outside world. In short, so many things, that the human organism would not be able to bear it all, if it were not for the many illusions that keep one incredibly strong.

I received the pistol; it's a beauty. I've lent it to Raúl Chibás. Out of the last money (1050 dollars), we received 600 dollars. The bearer explained the run-ins he had with troops at El Turquino.

A big hug.

ALEJANDRO [FIDEL CASTRO]

Letter to Norma [Celia Sánchez]

Except for the powdered milk, the synthetic Knorr-Swiss foods seem very practical, especially the cream-of-pea soup with ham, which makes four cups of thick, delicious soup. I received six packets; we need quantities.

The messenger tells me that your sister who works in Casa S would like to visit me and wants written permission. I leave it to you. As far as we're concerned, there's no problem. We have such pleasant memories of your presence here that one feels your absence has left a real vacuum. Even when a woman goes around the mountains with a rifle in hand, she always makes our men tidier, more decent, gentlemanly—and even braver. And after all, they really are decent and gentlemanly all the time! But what would your poor father say!

I agree to possibly taking in the other group that David [Frank País] mentions. Besides, we always have to have reinforcements ready to replace the wounded and sick.

FIDEL CASTRO   Sierra

Our forces are taking on the characteristics of a small army, a disciplined, devoted, and trained army; every day it improves and expands its fighting tactics and, above all, its aggressiveness, along with high combat morale.

Support from the peasants is almost absolute; some of us are in the process of developing their qualities of leadership and we have an ever-increasing knowledge of the terrain, which makes us more and more masters of the situation.

The Sierra is not growing in size, but our knowledge of it is and it is as if it has become immense.

The number of our present combatants can be obtained by multiplying by ten the figure in Matthews' interview.

Whatever equipment has reached here and whatever we've taken from the enemy is being used by somebody here. Even a machine-gun tripod with missing legs, which didn't work in El Uvero is being taken with us in the hope that you'll be able to get the legs for it. In the last shipment, the mortar arrived, also the M-2 butt end, and the three rifles, but these are of no use at all as they don't work with ordinary .30–'06 bullets.

We are forced to plan encounters with the enemy in such a way that their ammunition and weapons will fall into our hands. Actions in which we limit ourselves to causing casualties would mean a dangerous lowering of our supply of ammunition, even if actions of that type could be carried out almost constantly.

I assure you that if we had a good supply of ammunition, the enemy columns would not be able to set foot on the Sierra.

Besides, when we take bullets, we also take the corresponding rifle, so the average number of bullets per rifle remains the same or drops.

I calculate roughly—and perhaps optimistically—that this front costs the Movement at least *six thousand* pesos monthly, and the costs will probably increase. One of the reasons for our success with the peasants is that we pay them generously for the things they provide, and we exercise discretion the many times we help them.

We need approximately 100 uniforms, 100 pairs of good shoes, and 50 strong knapsacks every month.

That they don't even contemplate the folly of planning a landing at Santa Clara. This is a matter of strategy. Besides, our experience gives us the right to decide about this struggle. *Order them* to come to the Sierra Maestra.

I am enclosing a message to you to be sent to Mexico; it has a quality of desperation, so that it may actually get them to hand over funds.

Make a point of telling them that they need not think about sending a huge contingent of men; twenty, if they're good, are more than enough. There are plenty of men here; what we need are weapons.

I sincerely feel they've done a great job in the plans for the next months. Armando Hart knows how often I insisted, when I got out of prison, that this was the correct strategy, rather than a military coup or putsch in the capital. I see this so clearly today that given a choice between a victory on November 30 or thereabouts and our landing, or a victory a year later, I'd unquestionably choose the victory now taking shape through this incredible awakening of the Cuban nation. Still more: I feel that the fall of the regime in a week's time would be far less fruitful than four months from now. Here, as a joke, I usually assure the comrades that we don't want to give birth to a *seven-month* revolution. The spirit of renewal, the desire for collective excellence, the awareness of a higher destiny, are at their apogee, and can reach incomparably further. These abstractions, these words—we've heard them many times and we have imagined their lovely meanings, but now we are *living* them, they throb in all our senses. They are truly unique. We have seen them evolve in amazing fashion in this very Sierra, which constitutes our little world. The word *people,* which is spoken so often with a vague and confused meaning, is here transformed into a living reality—marvelous, dazzling. Now I know what *people* means; I see it in this invincible force surrounding us on all sides, I see it in those caravans of thirty and forty men, illuminated by torches, as they descend muddy slopes at two or three in the morning carrying 60-lb. loads on their shoulders to bring us provisions.

Where did they come from? Who organized them so marvelously? Where did they acquire so much ability, cunning, bravery, and self-denial? No one knows! It's almost a mystery! They organized themselves on their own, spontaneously! When the animals get tired and fall to the ground, unable to make another trip, the men appear, from who knows where, and carry the goods themselves. From now on, force is impotent against them. They'd have to kill all of them, down to the last peasant, and that's clearly impossible: the tyranny simply cannot manage that. The people realize this, and they are becoming more and more aware of their enormous strength.

Our armed force is minuscule, insignificant, when compared to the vast and terrible army that we have among the people: men, women, old people—even children, who are in awe of revolutionaries as if they were characters out of fairy tales.

FIDEL CASTRO

Letter to Frank País

I'm very happy—and I congratulate you—that you so clearly saw the
necessity of formulating working plans on a national and systematic
scale. We'll keep fighting here as long as it is necessary. And, we'll finish
this battle with either the death or triumph of the *real Revolution*. We can
now say this word. Old fears have disappeared. The danger of a military
regime decreases because the organizational strength of the people is increasing every day. And if there is a coup and a junta is formed, we'll
insist from here that our basic demands be met. And if we continue this
war, no junta will be able to maintain itself. To maintain ourselves here,
we need only the support of the peasants. They won't give up until the
Sierra is really their property, furrowed with highways and covered with
hospitals and schools. This is what is referred to as our little world, the
Sierra; it is really our big world: all of Cuba and its inspirational awakening. Your letters speak for themselves.

I don't see why we should raise the slightest objection to the U.S.
diplomat's visit. We can receive any U.S. diplomat here, just as we
would any Mexican diplomat or a diplomat from any country.

It is a recognition that a state of belligerence exists, and therefore
one more victory against the tyranny. We should not fear this visit if we
are certain that no matter what the circumstances may be, we will keep
the banner of dignity and national sovereignty flying.

And if they make demands? We'll reject them. And if they want to
know our opinions? We'll explain them without any fear.

If they wish to have closer ties of friendship with the triumphant democracy of Cuba? Magnificent! This is a sign that they acknowledge the
final outcome of this battle. If they propose friendly mediation? We'll
tell them no honorable mediation, no patriotic mediation—no mediation is possible in this battle. And this doesn't even need saying; it has
already been said in the Sierra Maestra Manifesto.*

After carefully analyzing the pros and cons of establishing a revolutionary government in the Sierra Maestra, we came to the conclusion
that this was not the most positive and intelligent step. Your reports and
the letter from Justico confirm my opinion about this. Therefore, we
wrote the manifesto as you know it and hope it will now achieve the
most fruitful results.

The present revolutionary wave is cresting at a moment when the
morale of our men is at its highest; the men are strong and well fed,
besides.

---

* Issued July 12, 1957, by Felipe Pazos, Raúl Chibás, and Fidel Castro. See
p. 216.—Ed.

I confess that I'm in a state of suspense whenever I hear over the radio that a young boy is found murdered in Santiago. Just today I heard that the corpse of a young man, about twenty-four, mustache, etc., etc., had been found, but he was still unidentified. I'll be anxious for hours until I know his identity. You can't make worries go away, however absurd they may be. We are really living through rough times.

DAVID [FRANK PAÍS]

Letter to Alejandro [Fidel Castro]   Santiago, July 5

I suppose you have already heard the latest news. Even my pen shakes when I have to remember this terrible week. It was our *Fernandina:** everything planned in such detail, everything so well distributed, and it all turned out badly, absolutely everything went awry, one thing after another.

The time bomb, so meticulously prepared and placed, did not go off because it got wet a few hours before; the hand grenades did not work; the Second Front, organized in such secrecy, was aborted and we lost weapons and equipment worth more than 20,000 pesos, as well as the life of a comrade. And we lost three more comrades here; they were taken by surprise as they were carrying out a delicate operation. They preferred to die fighting rather than allow themselves to be arrested. The loss of the youngest among them has left me with emptiness in my heart and sorrow in my soul.

Our key communications and intelligence man became seriously ill with what turned out to be an embolism, and he is now unable to speak or write. We sent out the information for the national sabotage order as well as we could. Just as well the Movement in the rest of Cuba conducted itself so well, showing that all the communications and insistence on discipline and organization were not in vain. And to top off our troubles, Bienvenido [Léster Rodríguez] could not leave Cuba.

The idea you proposed to us is a good one if a meeting takes place with the opposition—not with the government. The latter came in full battle gear, and the meeting was held with the backing of tanks, three thousand armed soldiers, and more than two hundred of Masferrer's thugs. There could have been a massacre, except that we couldn't risk playing that card yet. We had arranged things in such a way that *they* would be the victims of the massacre, not us. We did interrupt Masferrer when he was broadcasting—and that only for the rebroadcast to Havana—in which we cheered for the 26th of July, the Revolution, and Fidel Castro. Batista heard this quite well.

---

* The *Fernandina* was José Martí's boat, which was seized by the Americans in 1895.—C. F.

The people behaved well; no one went, and there were only about five thousand people present, and they were brought from all over the republic. The fiasco was such that the government has outlined plans for Oriente. Masferrer is moving to Vista Alegre, and his men are also moving; we now have discovered two houses used as barracks.

I think it is necessary for you to have a General Staff with certain outstanding personalities to give it prestige and an even greater aura of danger for all the sectors of the nation who look upon you—romantically, perhaps?—with certain reservations. But when they see you surrounded by people of this kind, they will think you are trying to establish programs and concrete government projects, and, at the same time, a civilian-revolutionary government which will provide our Movement with still more prestige and enhance its militance. You must have heard the tendentious statements that attempt to portray you as an ambitious man, surrounded by immature boys who are trying to stir up trouble and take advantage of the existing situation, but without concrete ends, or support from serious and responsible elements. Propaganda that would identify you with Raúl Chibás, Felipe Pazos, and Justo Carrillo would change things and would irritate the regime. It would also arouse fear in the ailing factions of the opposition schemers and, at the same time, enhance the Movement in the opinion of all the social and economic levels, making it the only faction capable of solving the crisis.

What do you think of Armando Hart's escape? Isn't it really terrific?

Twenty-five weapons, the best, were salvaged from the Second Front, and a truckload of food, boots, uniforms, and knapsacks that they didn't manage to seize. Yesterday I saw René and he explained what happened, and we got into a fatalistic mood. Sometimes the things done offhandedly turn out better than those planned down to the last detail. The army is searching for René and twenty other comrades who left the occupied sector and marched on foot for miles, in order to save the weapons I spoke to you about. They were spotted at a distance by many peasants who offered to help, but they got carried away and their joyous and loud voices were heard by the army which immediately began an active search for them. They're here now and so are the weapons, safe—for the moment.

Funds are down a bit (it would have to happen right at this moment!), so we'll have to find a way of getting more. Havana spends too much: 4000 pesos a month, sometimes more. This is exorbitant and, according to María [Haydée Santamaría], the culprit, that is, the person who spends almost all the money is "the Thin Man," René El Flaco.

Things in Manzanillo aren't going very well. The Galician Morán stool-pigeoned on the whole Movement. Then I warned Norma [Celia Sánchez] and Sierra that the enemy was profiting by what Morán was regaling them with and that they had better execute him before he did more damage, but Sierra is irresolute by nature. Now the damage is done, and I think the least Sierra deserves is to be expelled from the Movement for his constant negligence and incompetence. He was responsible, to a large extent, for the goods that went astray. He said he had a sure-fire, rapid route and urged me to send men (forty); I sent him twenty men with twenty-three weapons. He took advantage of them and used them to carry a large quantity of ammunition and food. I also sent more than thirty uniforms and more than thirty pairs of boots. He said that he had thirty men already outfitted from Manzanillo, and I told him he could keep the best twenty. The final result: you hadn't asked for these men; he had no safe route to convey anything; he had contacted no one; he ignored discipline; he welcomed some "little boys" from Bayamo, Holguín, and even as far as Camagüey, and didn't even have equipment for them. Imagine ninety-three men with a little over twenty weapons and a little over thirty uniforms and boots. A disaster. I'm not trying to excuse them, but it's natural that there would develop indiscipline, fear, and even desertion, in men who are led like that and under such conditions. It took long enough to produce the hetacomb—some fifteen days they had to endure this, lost, without word from you, and not even knowing if they were going to reach you, hemmed in by the army. I really don't envy them the moments they lived through, especially since I always classify men as normal, not as supermen or superheroes.

You probably know that, at long last, after so much work, El Gordito [Fatso Léster] Rodríguez left today for the United States. The very meritorious and valuable American embassy came to us and offered any kind of help in exchange for our ceasing to loot arms from their base. We promised this in exchange for a two-year visa for El Gordito and for them to get him out of the country. Today they fulfilled their promise: the consul took him out personally, and the papers, letters, and maps that he needed were taken out in the diplomatic pouch. Good service. In exchange, we won't take any more weapons from the base (anyway, security there is now so tough, we couldn't possibly get away with it), so we will only take ammunition (they didn't mention that). The weapons, if all goes well for us, will be brought directly from the United States.

After this one, I'll be sending you three more mortars in a little while. I think that with four of them, and the four hundred grenades, you'll be able to do enough; if El Gordito can line up a better bazooka, even better—we'll save ammunition and no machine gun will need to fire 700 shots.

I'm thinking of using the other mortars on the Second Front and Third Front, as soon as they are established (if the grenades don't arrive before, and if they do arrive, then, immediately).

On the tenth of this month, we're going to start National Plan No. 2, which will consist of a month of sabotage, coordinated on a national scale. We're going to tighten up little by little.

P.S.: Did you receive the radio equipment?

CARLOS FRANQUI

Caudillism—bossism—is one of the fundamental problems of Latin America.

It is the end result of myriad causes in the Hispano-Arabic-Roman heritage. The Spanish Conquest in America happened in a Spain that had not gone through the Renaissance, the Industrial Revolution, the bourgeois revolution, the Reformation, the republic. The metropolis, Spain, had not created institutions, ideas, doctrines, ideology, capitalism. It was a semifeudal and precapitalist monarchy.

The caudillos: Christopher Columbus, Cortes, and Pizarro were all great personages who left powerful marks.

Economic causes: dependence on a single crop, vast property holdings, slavery, sugarcane, coffee, cacao bean, and other raw materials requiring a foreign market—Spain, the United States—colonialism.

The Wars of Independence were more a revolt than a revolution: a reaction against Spain. They were started by great caudillos, whose armies were obedient to them. The military prevailed over the civilian, action over ideas. Once Spain was defeated, each caudillo built a fief in his own image, which was called a republic. The zeal of these caudillos blocked Bolívar's dream of the creation of a single great Latin American nation.

The new power was: the army, caudillism, oligarchism, monoculture, and dependency on foreign nations.

The world was divided into two parts: one capitalist and the other the producer of raw materials or simply colonial. And it coincided in America with the advent of the most powerful modern empire, the United States.

Spain's colonial domination was followed by that of the United States, sometimes by direct occupation of territories—Texas, California, Mexico—at other times, indirect, but always by economic domination.

In Cuba, forces alternated: military occupation and economic control. José Martí's efforts, like Agramonte's before him, did not survive the republic.

The Cuban Revolutionary Party, the driving force and organizer of the Wars of Independence on new bases—popular, democratic, and anti-imperialist, and its military instrument, the *mambí* army—was liquidated with the military occupation by the United States, from 1898 to 1902.

José Martí and Antonio Maceo were dead; Máximo Gómez, Calixto García, Bartolomé Masó, Julio Sanguily, Juan Gualberto, and other anti-imperialist civilian patriots were impotent when the Yankees "withdrew" and left the republic in the hands of their puppet leaders— Estrada Palma, José Miguel Gómez, Mario García Menocal, Gerardo Machado—second-rate colonels and doctors.

The army was the repressive body, and sugar the economic base of colonialism.

Then came other caudillos: Fulgencio Batista, a military man; Ramón Grau San Martín, the false heir of 1933, cheated the revolutionary feelings stirred up by Antonio Guiteras's heritage during the Auténtico period between 1944 and 1952.

Eduardo Chibás, a romantic caudillo, after creating the Ortodoxo movement, committed suicide to give people faith in his words and moralizing ideas: "Honor versus money."

And then Batista got another chance at a barracks coup. Batista was not born of a war, or of a revolution, like other Cuban and Latin American caudillos. He was born of a barracks.

The 26th of July is against caudillism. To end it, the material, political, and cultural reality of Cuba must change: the single-crop sugar industry, the single-market dependence on a foreign power—at present the United States. The army as the decisive instrument of power. The feudal oligarchy, the vast rural estates, the imported neocolonial bourgeoisie, as well as the cultural and political elements that go with it.

Economic liberation, industrialization, diversification, and self-sufficiency in food production, development of the nickel mines and other minerals, the freedom of commerce, "commerce with the whole world and not with one part of the world," wherever it may be, as Martí said. The impetus of a new, free, popular culture: "culture at the service of liberty."

The creation of new institutions, products of new ideas, in order that the people can participate and decide on their acts. The elimination of neocolonial capitalism and of state capitalism (which is dangerous because it presents itself as socialism), the search for a new form of property that is held neither privately nor by the state but by the people—all these elements are fundamental for the disappearance of caudillism, the symbol and reality of all the past and present evils in Cuba.

Only by strengthening the 26th of July Movement all over the country and integrating it into a single civic and organic body (today we are two movements: the rebel army and the organization in the city), forcibly developing new unions, organs of opinion—press, radio, TV (some of them are already burgeoning), organizing student, youth, and professional sectors—civil institutions—the peasantry, women, Negroes. All this would be a future guarantee of a new revolutionary power, in which the people would be the protagonist in the victory against tyranny, and also the protagonist of the future.

If the Movement predominates over the people, the military over the civilian, caudillism is inevitable.

New institutions must be created before our triumph, or else they will be swept away later. If triumph is obtained by a heroic minority in the vanguard, with popular support, but without popular participation, as is happening now, a single military chief will again impose himself above everyone, with all the incalculable consequences of total power.

"A republic, a people, is not created, Generals, in the same way as an army camp is commanded," José Martí wrote in a letter to Generals Gómez and Maceo. A revolution cannot be born from an army camp, an army, a caudillo, no matter how much of a genius he may be. Free republics were not born from the great generals in the Wars of Independence. And real revolutions will not be born from military rebels.

It is the old Cuban polemic. Céspedes and Agramonte. Gómez, Maceo, and Martí. We cannot deny the role played by personality in history; that would be to deny an obvious reality. It is much more than obvious here.

There is a difference between a leader and a caudillo. The caudillo, the all-powerful, a kind of god on earth, conqueror or hero, Cortes or Bolívar, represents the past with all its present consequences. We hope that a leader may emerge as the result of the new, the leader of a collective movement—not to command but to obey the people. The people must be the supreme and permanent leader of the new, the leader of a collective movement; not to command except by popular power. From now on the people must be the protagonists of the struggle and not its passive supporters.

At the head will be the most outstanding, the most capable of the leaders. Not the only one. The representative of a collective leadership, of a collective organization, and of a people who decide by means of appropriate instruments. We hope that Fidel Castro, who is the strongest personality, the most capable, and the best revolutionary warrior, will be a leader and not a caudillo. Beyond his personal will, and ours and the Movement's, it will depend on whether we can eradicate the past, as well as all its economic, political, social, military, and cultural causes.

Economic dependence, misery, hunger, monoculture, militarism, personality cults, heroics, the one-party system, bureaucracy, the monopoly of the economy, force, and ideology—if we could only get rid of them all!

Now, that would be a real revolution.

FRANK PAÍS

Letter to Alejandro [Fidel Castro]   Santiago, July 7

The last time we spoke in Mexico, I told you that I did not believe in the existing organization in Cuba, in the workers' activity for the general strike, or in the efficiency of the Action groups, since they were defenseless, unprepared, and in disaccord. The events on November 30, in which we felt the reality of what I dreaded, left our organization in very bad shape, disoriented, and almost out of combat.

Your indomitable spirit and that of your comrades who persevere stubbornly, even under the harshest and most difficult conditions—and they have faced adversity in the most difficult conditions—have accomplished the miracle that all of us together would never have been able to achieve, even with our most desperate efforts and firmest conviction.

I thought, and many others did too, that the type of LEADERSHIP that operated before the thirtieth would never be able to produce results. *In a revolution one cannot always hold MEETINGS, nor can everything be centralized in one person either,* one cannot grant equal responsibility to a sometimes indefinite number of members of the National Directorate (I remember that some weeks before the thirtieth, there were twenty-five executive members, all of the same rank, whom I had to consult and deliberate with on just about every point, and naturally they knew everything and even wanted to add to it!), yet neither can one establish "taboo zones" that one cannot enter to find out what work is being done there.

The excess of democracy contrasted curiously with the action in some other areas that was at the whim of a single individual.

After the thirtieth I was disgusted to see that once more national and provincial directorates were being set up with too many members, many of them unqualified. Many directors and poor coordination led to little conscientious work; slipshod work began to recur. By chance, the same revolutionary situation offered the solution, acting as a distilling crucible. Out of diverse circumstances, all that was dross, everything that was ailing or disturbed the smooth functioning of affairs was consumed in it.

Jacinto [Armando Hart] (one of the revolutionaries with the clearest political ability, as well as an indefatigable organizer) and I discussed at length the turn things were taking, and we decided on an audacious move to revamp the Movement in its entirety. The leadership would be centralized for the first time in the hands of a few, the distinct responsibilities and tasks of the Movement would be clearly assigned, and we took on ourselves the job of making it more active and powerful. We managed to get everyone's acceptance, and slowly we began to make it a reality. We were taken prisoner. The Movement went through a moment of crisis, as Faustino was already a prisoner and the work was too great for the few men left to carry it out. But things were being arranged. When we came out, the state of the Movement was deplorable, but never as after the thirtieth, since much had been accomplished that would continue to go forward.

During this brief period, we had to work a little highhandedly, dictating orders and becoming rather strict, but now we are able to channel things in accord with prepared and carefully thought-out plans.

A general strike, but with well-trained people, has always been talked about, yet, again and again, the training was neglected or the plans were drawn up without conviction and so were ineffective. It was essential to give this sector the impetus it required and it began in Oriente.

This work had to be done all over the island and a National Workers' Directorate was established to set up the guidelines, as well as to decide on a day for the general strike to take place.

But we have decided that this is not the only decisive sector, so we have embarked on the task of enlisting professionals, businessmen, and industrialists in the strike. An executive director of civilian resistance was created, and provincial nuclei now exist in all the provinces. The task to be carried out goes hand in hand with the workers', although it is a bit simpler, as now all the provinces are functioning. The work of the executive committee is to unite all the provincial organizations and to create the National Directorate of Civilian Resistance. As did the workers, some have already started, although along different routes naturally, to Camagüey and Santa Clara, and, in the coming week, they will go to Pinar del Río, Havana, and Matanzas to establish a National Directorate of Civilian Resistance. An enormous number of people are carrying out these tasks; our efforts at rallying all social levels of the country to the Revolution are showing results.

Immediately after the National Boards of Workers and civilians have been established, special delegates from them will form a strike committee, whose work will be broader. Keep in mind that all the bodies that I have mentioned are part of the 26th of July or closely allied to it and that there are a series of bodies that do not want to or cannot become associated with us or with any particular faction, yet are in agreement on creating a paralysis of national life in order to overthrow the regime. The objective of the delegates of our organizations is to join all personalities, sectors, and organizations—civilian, political, religious, business, and workers—in a strike committee that would not appear to be an organ of the 26th of July, but would carry out the job at the time we consider propitious.

We need to have militia everywhere: active, disciplined, aggressive, daring militia. Practically speaking, this is what works best throughout the island. Only we must insist that all our cadres work in *coordination*. And with this as a goal, National Plan No. 2 is now under way; it will bring together all sabotage actions, and they will consequently have much greater psychological force and impact. It will also create collective confidence in action when the order is given, so as to maintain the state of insurrection, provide experience, and gradually increase the tension in the country according to our prearranged plans—until it becomes red-hot. That will be the moment when all the institutions and all the organizations grouped together in the strike committee will demand in unison that Batista must go! All Cuba will throw itself into the general strike with an accompanying wave of workers' sabotage, as well as of mechanical and revolutionary sabotage, never seen before. I wish to clarify one point which I forgot to mention: in all the workers' directorates there must be sections devoted to sabotage in order to back up the national action at the planned moment. Because of their importance and crucial role, these sections consist of militants from the 26th of July.

The national leadership of the Movement consists of Bienvenido [Léster Rodríguez], me, and a small group, who occasionally act as the executive committee.

The national treasurer, the new propaganda chief, the national workers' coordinator, the national resistance coordinator, the national coordinator, and the general coordinator of the Movement will form the executive of our leadership: the national directorate will be formed, moreover, by the six provincial coordinators.

We have tried to place revolutionaries who think and act in all these jobs—people tried and tested throughout all these days by severe trials and intense work.

Another of the defects from which we have always suffered is the lack of a clear and precisely outlined program, which is, at the same time, serious, revolutionary, and within the range of achievement. It is now being worked on intensely in order to unite it to our economic project and to create a revolutionary program for the Movement. The work is broken down into different sectors and distinct provinces, and if you have any suggestions or tasks to be done, tell me so. In any case, when the draft of the program is complete, I will send it for you to look over and give your opinion.

At this moment, the vagueness of the pronunciamentos, like the lack of plans and projects, causes many still to be distrustful about our intentions and our capacity for making the Revolution they all await. It is a fact that the Cuban people still do not aspire to overthrow the regime, nor do they wish to substitute one figure for the other; they seek fundamental changes in the structure of the country, and it is the concern of all sectors and all interests to know whether our leaders and directors are really capable of bringing about such changes, whether they can rely on us to do the task or not. No one doubts that the regime will fall; what concerns them is the quality of the engineers that the 26th can mobilize to construct the new edifice.

We aspire to do it, and we will make all the efforts necessary to achieve this end, so that the program of the 26th can be issued to coincide with the beginning of the final propaganda offensive that must be carried out in two months.

The situation of the Movement outside of Cuba, as you know, is very good, but unfortunately we lack unity. I think this will be resolved with the new delegate; for the moment, we are counting on patriotic clubs with their own leadership.

Very well, you will all decide on this, but I ask that your opinion be communicated to this Directorate as rapidly as possible. Likewise, I ask your opinion on the work that has been done. We have tried to do our best, and we are striving hard to accomplish our goals. Cuba and history are waiting, and the 26th of July cannot let them down or allow pages to be written that are anything but glorious, constructive, and patriotic.

DAVID [FRANK PAÍS]

Letters to Alejandro [Fidel Castro]   Santiago, July 11

We knew that certain personalities hold a favorable opinion toward us and the Sierra. I thought it would be a good idea to explore them and give them a slight "shove," if needed, quite subtly, to create the impression that the decision came from them. I sent María [Haydée Santamaría] and another group of young people on this mission, and that is why Raúl and Felipe, Robertico and Barrosito, Martínez Páez, etc., turned up, but I want to make it clear to you that we never said that you sent for them, or that they were going to form part of any revolutionary government. Carrillo says a number of things in his letter that Yeyé [Haydée Santamaría] told me she had not proposed to him. The only thing she mentioned concerned the possibility of forming part of a revolutionary government, but no proposal or personal commentary, nothing more.

Santiago, July 11

María A. told me very urgently at noon today that the American vice-consul wanted to talk with you, in the presence of some other man, but she didn't know who. I just went to Havana to ask for permission. I told her I would consult with you, but that we would first have to find out who the other man is and where they wanted to go and what they wanted to talk about.

She had already sent me a note on the third, which I enclose, but either they are tricking her, or she's exaggerating. I'm sick and tired of so much backing and forthing and conversations from the embassy, and I think it would be to our advantage to close ranks a bit more, without losing contact with them, but not giving them as much importance as we now do; I see that they are maneuvering but I can't see clearly what their real goals are.

DANIEL [RENÉ RAMOS LATOUR]

Letter to Alejandro [Fidel Castro]   Santiago

Among the papers David [Frank País] sent you are the instructions for operating the radio transmitter; however, he has not sent you the key, and I will have the pleasure of bringing it to you.

I have made several trips to the region of N with weapons and up to now we have had success.

I am sorry not to be with you. Once I learned to fight in the mountains, as well as on the plains, I now opt for mountain warfare. However, I can't be happy one minute without working for our country, and until I can return, I'll work in the underground.

DAVID [FRANK PAÍS]

Letter to Alejandro [Fidel Castro]

I'm keeping Daniel [René Ramos Latour] here against his will because I need him very much. He's very capable and very useful. Besides, I am not giving up on the Second Front. I'll postpone it for several days or weeks, but sooner or later, it will happen. Because of two brothers, and solely because of them, we lost everything, but we'll start again. I'm giving René the job of telling you (he's the one who has to deal with everyone arriving from there) of the quite unbearable state in which they arrive, absolutely babied, thinking we are all slaves obliged to wait on them. Let me explain: we have forty families to take care of here, of dead comrades or comrades who have been taken prisoner or are in the Sierra. They are given food rations and some money; we don't give them any more because we don't have any more. Some have come to us saying they must be given more money, that they are not being taken care of. Others ask for watches, money for movies or to buy something or other, or they tell us that the house we've found them is no good or they don't like it and that we should find them some other place. Others have rejected clothing we've given them, saying they want it with such and such a pattern or that they don't like the color. The last straw was Sabú, who told us that he couldn't take his medicine by himself, that we should find a house where his wife could give it to him (the medicine that is, which we had already provided!). René said you should tell those who have to come down that here they will be taken care of as best we can but not like "kings," nor better than anyone else; they will be treated the same as the other comrades. The things that we have to put up with here are something awful! René is dying to go to the Sierra—"to rest" he says. And even I . . . !

Las Villas, Havana, and Pinar were here this week discussing the plans for the future of the Movement.

When René el Flaco [the Thin Man] got to Havana, he said he was your personal delegate in order to make himself chief of the Movement. Then when Yeyé [Haydée Santamaría] arrived, fully empowered by the Directorate to organize everything, René said he was receiving instructions from Faustino, who was the man that you had told him to obey. When Faustino figured out the hoax, he then said he was receiving orders directly from me, and he pretended not to recognize anyone else.

He began by working in Action but soon tried to take it over completely. The chief of the Movement in a province is the coordinator. Yeyé is the coordinator in Havana. Then he issued circulars on his own, saying he was authorized by me (and was working in my stead) to restructure the Movement and also to put the other sectors under his orders. When Marcelo arrived, with orders from the Directorate to take charge of propaganda, he tried to put one over on him. Marcelo knew what he was up to and played along. He then ignored Marcelo and began to put out propaganda. Yeyé reorganized the cadres and tried to include René. He didn't want that. Then, when the funds arrived we chose a treasurer (Yeyé selected a great boy), and René was left out of things. While all this was going on, Yeyé had not told anyone anything about him as she thought that René wasn't all that bad and that she could bring him back into line. But he connived to come this far to intrigue against Yeyé, telling me that she did not want to pay the costs of the Action groups, that she was stealing money, living off the fat of the land, and that the boys who made and planted the bombs were going hungry and suffering great hardship. I sent for Yeyé and that's when I began to learn of René's disruptiveness. He got all the boys from Action up in arms against the Directorate in Havana. He didn't allow anyone to mix into his work and demanded ("demanded," mind you, not asked) for money.

René still respects me and has made his "boys" think that I am the national all-powerful chief of Action. We judged him and agreed on the following: I would write him a letter telling him I need to see him right away. Here, I'll tell him that you absolutely must see him personally to discuss certain plans about Havana. Yeyé is the coordinator and official from the Movement to whom he must listen. Then I'll write another letter to the other leaders of Havana's Action groups explaining their real functions and separating the work into three special sections. I'll put René in charge of one, Enrique Hart of another, and Marcelo Salado, of the third.

All this is an attempt to salvage the organization and to avoid a conflict, which would be fatal right now, and at the same time, to save the young people in Action from a kind of "gangsterism" that might result from René's leading them down a very bad path.

CRISTIÁN [FRANK PAÍS]

Letter to Alejandro [Fidel Castro]

I think that today we've taken a more solid step concerning the military operations.* You know that in Havana there are thousands of military men conspiring on all levels and from all ranks, and thousands of these conspiracies don't come to anything serious; what happens is mostly a waste of time. We've talked with some of these conspirators in order to get an idea of their opinions and to have some idea of what is being said about us. But some days ago we began something more serious that looks as if it will bring good results. I cannot give you the details because it would take too long, and be very *dangerous* besides. So I am going to try and sum it up for you.

There has been a navy conspiracy going on,** which was being somewhat held in check and was progressing very slowly. About the time of the Barquín business,*** they again began to close their ranks, and it is now monolithically structured. The key people in this group are recently promoted officers whose thinking is revolutionary and democratic. We started our contact with them some time ago and we've been slowly infiltrating them. Today, I received a special delegate, sent expressly by the leadership of this movement. He's a rather young officer, intelligent and cultured. I'll tell you briefly of what we talked about, but our conversation lasted for five hours.

First he told me that his mission was to speak openly and frankly with us. He gave me the history of their former alliances and the whys and wherefores of their former antipathy toward the 26th of July and especially toward you. They had unfavorable reports of your behavior at the university when you were a student and also of your role at Moncada; besides, they also had heard some unfavorable reports about you personally—as being an ambitious caudillo. They thought you were in cahoots with Trujillo and they broke their ties with the FEU when they

---

* With the navy.—C. F.
** See pp. 167–68.—Ed.
*** See p. 101.—Ed.

learned about the letter from Mexico.* Today, he went on to say, these things have been overcome and you are far beyond all that, but they still have misgivings regarding the caudillism and the lack of a program. I cleared up these points fully and described your real position, as well as that of the Movement. He then felt more reassured. He laid out the aspirations of the navy, which in great measure coincided with ours. I gave him a comprehensive outline of our program. He read it through and liked it very much, and he told me he would turn it over to his superiors and make an extensive report of everything that I had told him. He became more open then and told me how they are organized and what their ambitions are.

We understood each other very well and I made him see that we had always been in sympathy with their conduct, and he, for his part, excused himself for the Laurent and García Olayón affairs.**

He told me then that the object of his visit was to know if the navy could make a common front with the Movement. We talked at length about this. Convinced also that this was our desire, he told me then that he was going to make contacts with members of the army. He explained, at length, the mechanics of all the existing conspiracies. We agreed on everything. He told me that they were planning to create a movement of their own, but they thought that first, it would not be revolutionary and, second, that a great number of the officers believed they could come to terms with us and with the army. He told me that they were speaking with us first because they considered us better prepared and organized and more forthright. It seems that within the army there are five seditious groups; and that if we form a united front, we could incorporate into our ranks the best-intentioned and the most competent group, which, in his opinion, is Barquín's group (he had letters from Barquín and contacts to speak for them). He felt that we should propose a rapprochement with the army, something serious and in full agreement, as that between the Movement and the navy would be. I liked the idea. He judged our position quite accurately, also our possibilities. I think, moreover, that when we present the armed forces with a united revolutionary block from both civilian and military ranks, this would undermine them and destroy whatever morale they still have left. I also believe that a union of the navy and the 26th would be useful for both parties. (I consider it even more advantageous since I observe a communion of ideas and projects between them and us, including their view on the problem of the army.) We agreed to meet for further, more extensive conversa-

---

* The Mexico City Pact. See p. 110.—Ed.
** For Laurent, see p. 168. Captain Alejandro García Olayón, a member of the maritime police, had been charged with killing a navy officer in 1956. When the case was shifted from civil to military jurisdiction, the charge was dropped and he went free.—Ed.

tions; we also agreed on the strategy to work on with the army (I'm very pleased about the way it is to be done). This officer was in charge, together with Barreras, of operations in the Sierra and he told me about the army's weakness and low morale and that you could consider the Sierra yours. He told me how they messed up the work that had to be done, how they delayed and they didn't carry out orders, never any synchronization, etc.

He has gone now to Havana to explore matters with Barquín's high command; he was optimistic and thought they would be able to break down prejudices and come to an agreement. He spoke of the good effect caused by our freeing the prisoners at El Uvero and of the good treatment given them, and they also spoke very well of you and your comrades. He said also that your position in the Sierra was a thorn and goad to the army, that they no longer wished to destroy you (naturally, except in the case of a betrayal) and that the discontent of the troops, whom you force into retaliatory action, is very great. They make notarized charges, openly accusing the officers of robbing them of their pay and of living off their daily rations. They talk about this out loud among themselves.

We spoke at length about their plans and ours. They coincide in general and even on many details. If the army doesn't come forward decisively, they are ready to work only with us. I am not talking about the plans because it isn't prudent, and, besides, they are still vague. He left confident that from now on we could work closely together (I think so too). If he finally wins over Barquín's representative (which I think should be easy, given our previous conversations, about which I have already told you), then they'll both come to discuss our concrete plans at length. As soon as it happens, I'll let you know. The officer was up to date about many matters, aware of many details, and I found out other things that pleased me even more.

JUSTO CARRILLO

Letter to Alejandro [Fidel Castro]   Havana, July 25

Just as I was arranging for a personal interview with you to consult on the schedule, which will go with this letter, I received a visit from Yeyé [Haydée Santamaría], who brought me your offer of collaborating in the formation of a government, along with your request to accompany you—once the junta or council was established—in what you consider the last stage of the battle in the Sierra.

I spoke and I listened. I talked with friends whom I trust completely—as close to you, though they don't know you personally, as I am myself. One day you will be amused at the internal arguments of our group. And I also sounded out opinions—sounded out, that is, in theoretical terms, a certain person very close to you, the highly qualified Jules Dubois. From what I heard, I found not a single thought at variance to mine, which reaffirms my opinion.

Not only do I decline the honor you confer on me but in addition, I energetically oppose—and with arguments that I will add—the establishment, *for the moment,* of any kind of organization as the representative of a supposed provisional government.

I oppose it because to establish it is to define it and the simplest definition entails limitations. It would mean placing a limit on the very impetuous hope you have sparked in the Cuban people. Limiting the true hierarchy that one day will be your government team. Limiting the possibilities for the swiftest defeat of the despot. Limiting the wide and ample cooperation given to you, now centered totally in you, though restrained, in this case, by certain antipathies, sectarianism, or vested interests.

"The strong man is strongest when he is alone," someone said. And you, so alone in face of the government and in the face of certain opposition, without a radio, without the press, or TV, without a party, without a membership role, without power, you are stronger than any other Cuban political factor because of your solid invulnerability as the rebel chieftain. And also because you are—alone—with only the powerful company of a total national ardor, which longs for your victory. And it is this solitude, my dear Alejandro, that I do not wish you to share.

For you to appear before public opinion with a government that does not include representatives of all classes of society would permit the supposition that some of these classes reject you in totalitarian fashion; a judgment I do not share, even were it to apply to the highest bourgeois element of the nation. For you to appear before the country, without the presence in your government of well-known persons from all walks of Cuban life with vitality—and all, except the public sector, have it— would lead to the supposition that the Cuban people's desire for betterment is remote, or at least marginal, to the great insurgence that you represent today.

Rebels like you, even if they are not with you, are also the same elements that have made our Cuba of today progress during its entire republican course, from the astounding physician, to the farsighted financier, from the farmer to the sportsman, from the scientist to the sugarcane cutter, all of them dissatisfied with the operation of the Cuban state, impatient with its inefficiency; they dream wildly of its functioning better. And you represent all that, even though thousands upon thousands of them do not know it, are not part of the 26th of July, are not Fidelistas, and yet you represent them. Are you going to appear now with a government in which some "good people" show up—I among them—but who do not faithfully represent a total national cross section?

I oppose the establishment of a symbolic government because, along with the ideal, one must keep in mind that there is ambition, too—the two unique motivating forces that have engendered the marvelous deeds of history, and though I have the greatest respect for ambition, I tell you that I am essentially lacking it. I feel that any effort of setting up a government equals smothering ambition as well as discouraging efforts, negating and dashing the hopes of glory and thus the impetus of hundreds and hundreds of people who think themselves qualified for these tasks.

I refer to the possibility—for me still uncertain—of a military coup against the regime, and the possibility—equally uncertain, but not impossible— of not being consulted in advance.

It's for this eventuality that I have to be in Havana, and need to have your opinion.

Since I have continued working in the particular areas that you know, we could help produce a decisive coup which—if my participation were a controlling factor—would turn out as if it were your own, as far as the final objectives that unite us are concerned; in Oriente, it would be the blow that would trigger the final overthrow.

a. What must our position be vis-à-vis a strictly military junta that ousts the regime?

b. What is our attitude if civilian groups form part of such a junta?

c. Which people in the junta, military or civilian, would represent opinions contrary to ours or would engender confidence in the fulfillment of our final objectives?

d. What would our position be if the military elements did not form a junta and turned over power to a government of the "national consensus" type?

e. In one case or the other, what should be the terms—as far as the length of time—that should be granted this transitional government?

f. What should be the function of this government: to be strictly administrative in content or to draft major substantive legislation, with a view to taking over leadership in the future?

g. What should be this government's way of consulting the people: calling a constitutional assembly that would revise the Constitution and, naturally, the age at which one can be president, or holding general elections immediately?

"Whoever has garnered so many good points cannot fall into this error. That would make a mockery of a government."

CRISTIÁN [FRANK PAÍS]

Letter to Alejandro [Fidel Castro]   Santiago, July 26

The situation in Santiago is becoming progressively more tense. The other day we had a miraculous escape from a police trap. There were some comrades near the house we were in; one careless thing and some-one squealed on them, and then the block was surrounded. Three were picked up, one fled onto the roofs, and they chased him and there was an exchange of shots. He managed to escape, but they began a search of the rooftops and the streets, and when my comrade and I decided our turn had come to fight, they left. They searched the house next door, but they seemed to feel confident about our house and left again. However, there is a wave of searches going on, fantastic and absurd, but no matter how absurd it's dangerous. They no longer wait for a stool pigeon; now Salas systematically carries out searches anywhere, without any particular reason. We had to flee from three houses from Sunday to today, and yesterday they came to the block on which we are located but it was in order to search a house opposite us. Since then we've been taking turns doing guard duty.

I've got some .30–'06 ammunition, and I'll send it together with the other things. I've been waiting for a week for Norma [Celia Sánchez] to give me the green light. A big hug for one and all.

Vilma sends a hug, too.

I have two pieces of good news for you: we have a machine-gun tri-pod, which I'll send with the equipment going out now. Daniel told me that the special bullets for it were kept here, and since he didn't know what they were, he left them, so I'll also send them. I'll send all this with the thirty men you asked for.

Give my thanks to all the officers and comrades for their very sincere and brave note; it was especially meaningful to me.

VILMA ESPÍN   Taped interview by Carlos Franqui

I talked with Frank on the telephone eight or ten minutes before they killed him. You know, he said nothing about being surrounded and that Salas Cañizares was out there!

Yes, they were already there, but he didn't say anything about it; spoke to me normally, as if we were working.

For days, a North American had been asking for an interview and we had arranged Léster's trip at that time. Then, I don't remember what he told me; he wanted an interview with us, and I can't recall if it was to propose something to us, but for days, the North American insisted that he wanted to talk to us; that he had something important to tell us. Frank then said: "Well, go see him, talk with him, and find out what he wants." Days passed and Frank didn't call me. I called the house where he was, and he had already left it. His disappearing seemed strange and I was terribly worried.

He was in a house that I didn't like—the house where they killed him—because there was no way to escape from it, no back exit. We had vetoed that house, but he was so desperate because he couldn't find another place that he moved in there.

Finally I spoke to him on the telephone. He called me about twice. I asked him: "But why haven't you called, what's happened?" And he didn't tell me anything about what was happening at that instant.

But he spoke to me rapidly. I realized he was in a hurry. I hung up, and in about ten minutes I heard gunfire in Santiago: I got on the telephone immediately to learn what was happening and they said: "Over there, at such and such place, they say there's a young man on the roof, and they're firing on him."

I finally found out about Frank's death in the most awful way possible. The telephone company informed me that "There's a call on the line from Salas Cañizares." You know they gave me all the calls from those people. You know I had to listen to all the calls from Salas Cañizares, Río Chaviano, the entire bunch.

Then they informed me that Salas Cañizares was going to speak and also Laureano Ibarra. And do you know what I heard when they were talking? "We already finished off that——— What do I know, how do I know when?. . . It's done, we put a bullet through him. Look, I'm going to put Basol on." And Basol says: "Listen, Chief"—I think he was with Tabernilla— "Chief, the three thousand pesos you told me about, well, you know, I'm here and ready!" Three thousand pesos for killing Frank.

He didn't want to fight back in order to keep them from killing the family hiding him.

Imagine! But, in any case, he couldn't do much. Where was he going to escape to when he was surrounded by all of them? Besides, he couldn't fight back the way things stood: the little boy was in the house. Then what they tried to do was to get out. Pujol left the car on the corner—it was a rented car—he went around the block and reached the house, and then he said to Frank: "Let's go." They had to take the chance of seeing if they could get through.

Pujol came from the outside, and he conducted himself admirably. He left the hardware store with the car; then he went into the house and took Frank out. They were walking slowly along the street. Randisch, the stool pigeon, was there. He had identified Frank twice before and he had been brought along to identify him again (we later executed him). He pointed him out and they grabbed him. Then Pujol's wife began to scream. They put the men in a car, and two and a half blocks farther they let them out and killed them on the spot.

We knew how he died, because, even though everybody was ordered to draw their blinds, an old lady kept looking out, and she said they shot Frank in the back of the neck, with his arms out in front; Pujol the same. They killed them there.

It was in Callejón del Muro [Rampart Lane] that they killed Frank.

ALEJANDRO [FIDEL CASTRO]

Letter to Aly [Celia Sánchez]   Sierra Maestra, July 31

It's hard to believe the news. I can't even begin to express my bitterness, my indignation, the endless sorrow that overwhelms us. What barbarians! They hunted him down in the street in cowardly fashion, taking advantage of everything to pursue an underground fighter. What monsters! They have no idea of the intelligence, the character, the integrity of the person they've murdered. Not even the people of Cuba are aware of who Frank País was, what greatness and promise there was in him. It's painful to see it happen like that, finished off in his full flowering, when he was only twenty-five, and giving the Revolution his very best. I will keep his last letters, notes, etc., as proof of what talent the man had who was murdered in the prime of his life. There are many Guiterases, Abel Santamarías, Frank Países murdered. All Batista's collaborators, big and small, are guilty of treachery, high treason to humanity; they are accomplices to what is happening, they are stained with the past and present blood that this evil, gutless creature has cost our fatherland. We vow to fight to exterminate the perpetrators of this inhuman crime, and their accomplices in this treason! Just how long are the Salas Cañizareses, the Cruz Vidals, the Venturas, the Fagets, the Masferrers, the Alliegros, the Santiago Reys, people who have amassed fortunes, unscrupulous, gutless, soulless people, just how long are they going to sow death and mourning summarily without themselves being riddled with bullets by the just hand of our people? Haven't we seen our men advancing here under a shower of bullets to take an objective? Don't we see our prisoners resolutely facing the cruelest of deaths on a hunger strike? Don't we see our women marching in demonstrations on the street, defying bullets and beatings? Did we see Frank País abandon his post, despite the imminent danger threatening him? No. The hour has come to react as the circumstances dictate! The hour has come to demand that everyone do something! The hour has come to demand action from everyone who calls himself a revolutionary, from everyone who says he opposes, from every decent and dignified human being, no matter what institution he or she represents, or what party or organization he or she belongs to! Enough of this childish contemplation! Enough of these people who stand around with their arms crossed waiting for others to die and make all the sacrifices! And if they don't heed the reasons, or the sentiments, we'll force them to do their duty with our facts. We'll burn down the island from one end to the other. We'll make life impossible for everybody under the boot of this shameful tyranny. We'll make the entire nation confront this choice: either Batista is finished off—along with everything and everybody that signifies oppression, crime, banditry, and savagery—or the country will be ruined and will perish. I can't resign myself to the idea of seeing our best youth die while people are still dancing, partying, and politicking. Or aren't we capable of making this nation shudder?

I beg you to somehow get this exhortation to all the cadres of our Movement. It is not my personal message; it comes from all of us who are here, with weapons in hand, furious at not having been able to be at Frank's side when these cowards ganged up on him and murdered him, aching to be able to be in the streets of Santiago or Havana hunting down those thugs and at the point of committing some act of foolishness here. . . .

For the moment, you'll have to assume, for us, a good portion of Frank's work, especially as you know more about it than anybody else. I know that you will find the strength to add still one more obligation to those that already tax you beyond the limits of your physical and mental stamina. But in these extraordinary times, willpower and energy increase. As concerns the National Directorate, it seems to us that someone must assume Frank's functions, even if other people can do only part of them. For the essentials, it seems to us that our doctor comrade [Faustino Pérez] can take Frank's place and therefore you should bring him up to date on all the matters Frank had been dealing with.

Now there is greater need than ever for the discipline that Frank thought was so important. We don't want to have to listen to any more moans and complaints about this or that comrade.

Daniel [René Ramos Latour] has to come to the Sierra because I need to speak to him as soon as possible.

I beg you to report to me as quickly as possible on how they are facing up to this situation.

EDITOR'S SUMMARY

In July there were several plans in the air concerning the government of post-Batista Cuba—who would be at its head and what programs would be instituted. For the 26th of July, the most publicized discussion took place among Fidel Castro, Raúl Chibás, the head of the Ortodoxos, and Felipe Pazos.

The three issued a joint declaration, the Sierra Maestra Manifesto on July 12; it was published in the widely read Cuban magazine Bohemia *on July 28. It opened with a challenge: "Is the Cuban nation incapable of fulfilling its highest destiny or does the blame for its impotence fall on its public leaders with their lack of vision?"*

They then stressed the need for unity, observing that Batista had employed many stratagems to divide his opponents—with great success, so far. "To unite is the one and only patriotic course at this time. To unite all the political, revolutionary, and social sectors that are combating the dictatorship on the basis of what they hold in common . . . the desire to put an end to the rule of force, the violations of individual rights, infamous crimes, as well as the search for peace that we all yearn for, in the only possible way, that is, by guiding the country along democratic and constitutional paths."

Answering charges that the fighters in the Sierra Maestra did not "want free elections, a democratic regime, or a constitutional government," the text stated: "Because we are deprived of these rights, we have been fighting since March 10 [the date of Batista's coup in 1952]. Because we want them more than anyone else, we are here. To prove it, there are our fighters dead in the Sierra and our comrades murdered in the streets or locked in the dungeons of prisons, all of them fighting for the beautiful ideal of a Free Cuba, democratic and just."

The three leaders called on all who would back the Civic Revolutionary Front established by this manifesto to "declare publicly to the country and to the armed services and before international public opinion that, after five years of useless effort, of continual deceit and rivers of blood . . . the only solution is for Batista to resign." The front also rejected intervention by foreign powers, and requested an end to U.S. arms shipments to Batista.

It urged a boycott of elections under the aegis of the Batista tyranny, termed a military junta unacceptable, and spelled out alternate electoral procedures: the provisional government—whose head would be designated by "a group of civic institutions" to ensure "impartiality"—would hold "general elections for all state, provincial, and municipal offices at the end of one year under the provisions of the Constitution of 1940."

The manifesto concluded: "It is not essential to decree revolution: organize the front that we propose, and the fall of the regime will come of itself. . . . We hope . . . that our appeal will be heard and that a real solution will bring an end to the shedding of Cuban blood and will usher in an era of peace and freedom."

11. AUGUST–DECEMBER: FROM THE GENERAL STRIKE TO THE MIAMI PACT

DANIEL [RENÉ RAMOS LATOUR]

Letter to Aly [Celia Sánchez]   Santiago, August 1

I must tell you that I've been entrusted with the enormous task of temporarily substituting for our beloved David [Frank País]. This decision was made by our comrades from the National Directorate here, in the interim until it is convenient for all the members of the National Directorate and Alejandro [Fidel Castro] to be consulted.

You can imagine what a devastating loss this has been for us. During the last three months, I was very close to him, I saw him daily and we worked hard together. I was with him in his house a few minutes before he was killed. And so for me the loss of such a beloved person has come as a terrible shock. When I learned about it, I felt that a terrible blow had been leveled at the Movement. We were fully aware then, at that dreadful moment, that there was an enormous vacuum to fill, and we would have to increase our efforts and even our ability if our ship was not to founder. And the task of mobilizing the people, who were distraught at the loss of one of their finest sons, turned out remarkably well. Through the press and radio you must have heard that the impact of this was brutal for the people, who loved him dearly, that it broke down all barriers. There were no conservatives or radicals, rich or poor, blacks or white. No! They, the people, were determined to face every risk, to overcome every obstacle, great, heroic people who at the felling of their leader forgot everything—work, family, repression. All businesses, movies, cafés, banks, factories, professional people, in a word, all of Santiago shut its doors, and they came together in one of the greatest outpourings of sorrow in the memory of this city. Out of rebellion, patriotism, and courage, they sang—in fact, shouted—the hymn: "Revolution; Salas the murderer; freedom; death to the tyrant." The people of Santiago are ours and they meant to show that they no longer cared about being found out by their oppressors—and they let the dictatorship know it.

The latent spirit of rebellion dawned today, and we are maintaining it. As I am writing this, Santiago continues to be a "dead city," although this term is really not accurate, because it is truly a "living heroic city." Employers as well as workers are ready to prolong this work stoppage if necessary. The emotional shock has opened the flood gates of patriotism and the order of the day is: general strike.

I am planning to send men and also the equipment that couldn't be sent on the previous trip (the uniforms, armbands, kitchen equipment, and a few other things). I'll send you a list of everything, as you've asked me to do. Probably none of the young men will be able to leave tomorrow because of the situation here in Santiago. There is much expectation: in any case, I wouldn't want anything to be interrupted.

Concerning Frank's death, I want you to know that they did not get a single document of importance, only a tiny notebook with some telephone numbers in it. He had many important documents at home, among them, the famous forty-one page letter from Alex [Fidel Castro]. Luckily, everything has been recovered and is now in our possession.

You know, in that letter Alex talked about the ammunition he had taken. It was saved because when Frank found out they were searching the entire block, with two squad cars parked out in front of the house, he decided to leave. Apparently he thought he could slip out unnoticed, but he had bad luck. In one of the cars there was an ex-friend of his from Normal School who now is a henchman for the dictatorship. He recognized Frank, and grabbed him and then, after holding him, they killed him. This is the version we believe, and it is borne out by Pujol's widow, with whom David [País] had been staying since Sunday, barely three days. Before leaving, he turned the papers over to her and told her to keep them, saying, that they were as "valuable as her own life." Up to the final minutes of his existence, he maintained a high sense of responsibility, courage, and serenity.

They left his bullet-riddled body in the street. For the first moments, they didn't allow even his mother to go up to him. We soon managed to mobilize the women, asking them to dry their eyes and get themselves ready for work. They got the corpse, which the police had taken to the cemetery, and moved it to the place that we had selected: his fiancée's house, which was in the center of the city, quite far from the cemetery, so as to make the cortege as long as possible.

On his chest lay his beret and over it a white flower.

I assure you that a glorious page of the history of the Revolution has been written, although it has cost us dearly. Frank is continuing to win battles from the regime. At this moment the people of Santiago are still up in arms. The repression has already begun. You know we don't have sufficient means to counteract the violence that is being unleashed by the army. If this doesn't spread to other cities, it will be extinguished; but, in any case, we have won a new battle and the principal reason for this has been Frank, previously our leader, now our flag.

The government has suspended all rights and has imposed press and radio censorship.

I don't know if I will be able to write to Alejandro this evening. I have a lot of work to do. If I don't send you a letter for him, you can give him some news of what has happened here from what I've told you.

I'm anxious to have news from him. We need to know if we've really had a success in Estrada Palma and Bueycito. It seems so from the news.

FIDEL CASTRO

Letter to Aly [Celia Sánchez]   Sierra Maestra, August 11

I have just received your letter of the seventh, together with the last one from Frank, Jacinto's [Armando Hart] to him, Bienvenido's [Léster Rodríguez], etc. On the other hand, I haven't received the 1000 pesos you told me about. Three or four days ago I did get the 500 sent earlier. Our finances are in bad shape, although almost everything is paid for at your end.

The most important things I want to tell you are going to be relayed verbally. The same people will also give you details of the operations at Estrada Palma and Bueycito, the situation of our forces, and our tactics.

The proper order should now be: *All guns, all bullets, and all supplies to the Sierra!*

After El Uvero, when, in your presence, I suggested to David [Frank País] that it was the opportune moment to open the Second Front, this front had not reached the importance it now has. At that time it seemed dubious that large forces could be sustained here; now there are vast prospects. The breach that we opened up before the thought of other prospects were considered has to be filled. Perhaps later the opportunity will arise on other fronts.

By what I'm writing you'll be able to gather that we're getting ready for a long struggle. These moments strike me as similar to those days that followed the battle at El Uvero. The dictatorship will use its greatest strength to beat us back and we are oiling our weapons; we're ready to hold our ground.

Today I put on the new uniform that was sent to me, and I'm going to begin the fourth campaign in it.

Just like you, and like the people, I don't see the strike as a failure at all, but rather a rehearsal, an unmistakable proof, a lovely explosion of Cuban dignity in a well-deserved homage to our Frank. The realization of what a large void he has left is an incentive for us to redouble our strength and faith—to show that by assassinating our men, they are not going to beat us but will only die that much sooner. As for Frank, they'll have to pay for that here in the Sierra too. May the fight not be over until the whole nation is up in arms, so there won't be any more danger of juntas or deception in the process. May it truly be a victory of the people for the people, won with all the sacrifice and sweat of the people. And now to the hard work! We must prepare the strike on a very large scale, an organized, overwhelming strike. The virtue of this all-day demonstration is that everybody has started thinking about the strike, and that it is the people's weapon. Those who did not support it feel ashamed and will serve vigorously in the next one. So the army of the Sierra has to be prepared to advance resolutely to the cities and conquer them.

I believe our comrades in Santiago can continue Frank's work. They are inspired, and I'm certain they will do it well. I undertake myself to work harder and to help in any way possible from here. I urgently need to have news of the doctor [Faustino Pérez] and Jacinto: about their plans, their ideas, their immediate projects. I have great confidence in what they can do.

And you, why don't you make a short trip here? Think about it, and do so in the next few days, days of observation and expectation.

A big hug.

DANIEL [RENÉ RAMOS LATOUR]

Letter to Alex [Fidel Castro]   Santiago, August 14

I've waited until today for news from you. This prolonged silence really worries us.

We're trying to keep you informed of the course of events through Aly [Celia Sánchez].

We received your warm, inspiring exhortation and we've spread it to all cadres of our Movement.

We saw Frank develop his enormous capacity for action at every turn. We saw him come into his own shouldering responsibilities and enduring setbacks. We were always in close touch in our work that paved the way for the thirtieth of November. How can I ever forget his fortitude, his unfailing spirit in those terrible days when we had no news of you and your men!

Then I joined the battle in the mountains, and he was taken prisoner. When you entrusted that very important mission to me at a time that you had pointed out was difficult, as the facts later confirmed, I had the good fortune to find myself once again in the fray, freed from prison bars. I fulfilled my mission with the greatest success and I told him of your opinion that he ought to go with me and join our battle in the mountains. Despite the fact that the idea always appealed to him, his clear, unfailing sense of responsibility made him realize that his place was right here. And how well he would show it! His creative impulse gave shape and spirit to what is today the 26th of July Movement, a powerful organization that has taken root in the heart of every Cuban throughout the entire island; it carries out coordinated activities, and daily improves in the discipline and training of its cadres.

I worked at his side very closely for three months. Although he had always been secretive, he brought me up to date on all matters—perhaps he anticipated his tragic end. His situation in Santiago had become so difficult that he was scarcely able to go out or receive visitors, and it was through my being the go-between that he settled most matters. Only an hour before he was viciously murdered I had been working with him on the material that we had sent you.

He almost vanquished the dictatorship after his death. He did not manage to achieve it totally, but the enormous popular reaction has given the regime an idea of our power and has awakened the few consciences that were still asleep in these provinces. We are now in a position to accelerate all our tasks, in order to wage the final battle with the tyranny in a very much closer future.

Until now we have managed to carry on our activities at a normal pace in our organization. To do so, we have counted on unanimous support from all responsible comrades, who, from the very first, have redoubled their efforts and continue to cooperate in the same way as they did with our unforgettable David [Frank País].

Today I'm going to Havana, since it turns out the trip is easier for me than for Jacinto [Armando Hart], María [Haydée Santamaría], and Fausto [Faustino Pérez] who had a hard time coming here. I'm sending you Jacinto's letter in which he tells me about the matter. I hope to return within two or three days, and in accordance with the information I am expecting from you, I will arrange to send twenty or twenty-five men, armed as well as possible, now that they are making it more difficult for us to establish the Second Front. And we believe it is better to put at your disposal many of the things that we were holding in reserve for this undertaking.

We need to know if Che Guevara is operating in another zone, since Bayamo spoke to us of ways of supplying provisions and also about some contacts whom we don't know, and you know we've forbidden using channels other than those agreed upon between you and Aly.

The contact we made with the navy, which David spoke about, continues to hold, and although nothing could be done during the strike, work goes on in that department and we have been kept informed. I think David explained to you that it concerns very solid contacts with people who wish to work *solely and exclusively* with us.

ALEJANDRO [FIDEL CASTRO]

Letter to Aly [Celia Sánchez]   Sierra, August 14

I insist, as I did in my previous letter, that a directive must be given to the Movement right now concerning the war: "All weapons, all bullets, and all resources are for the Sierra."

Weapons must be sought everywhere. I assure you the prospects are marvelous.

What did they think we could do with so little help? I am taking inventory and I see that a large part of our arms and bullets, those of the best quality, are those taken from the enemy.* It is indispensable that we make a great drive of our own for equipment. Before, perhaps, it wasn't so necessary, but now it is, because everything is happening at a dizzying pace and the prospects are really marvelous. Now we have to have weapons of all kinds that will let us embark on a wide range of action and win resounding victories.

Tell me whom I should write and what I should do, to direct the military effort of the Movement to this goal. I am afraid of some people's whims and I become very impatient thinking about comrades a thousand miles from this reality who are busy formulating unworkable plans.

Finally, you know that with Frank gone, we'll have to be more directly involved in the work that he carried on so brilliantly. There is no shortage of courageous comrades, but one doesn't acquire that authority, that initiative, and that experience in a couple of days. For that reason, I'm ready to write whatever letters, papers, or recommendations are needed from here. Before, matters in the Sierra were my prime concern and they can wear anyone out and they are, besides, increasing day by day. Now I realize that I should help you where and when you need me in order to facilitate your work.

P.S. Take great care! I don't know why but I feel sure that nothing can happen to you. Our misfortune with Frank was too great for it to happen again.

ALEJANDRO [FIDEL CASTRO]

Letter to Aly [Celia Sánchez]   Sierra, August 16

When are you going to send me the dentist? If I don't receive weapons from Santiago, Havana, Miami, or Mexico, at least send me a dentist so my teeth will let me think in peace. It's the limit; now that we have food,

---

* There were approximately 200 arms in the Sierra at that time, of which more than 100, including the machine guns, had been sent by the Movement from Santiago and Havana.—C. F.

I can't eat. Later, when my teeth are all right, there won't be any food. I'm not blaming you. You do all you can already. But I really feel that I'm just not lucky when I see that so many people have arrived here, and not one dentist.

ALEJANDRO [FIDEL CASTRO]

Letter to Aly [Celia Sánchez]   August 17

Don't think I'm discouraged; exactly the opposite: it's simply the desire to do more, and then we find ourselves completely impotent; the fervor of battle, the need for weapons, the eagerness to hit the enemy harder. Before, we fought to keep our flag flying; today, we fight to triumph. The obstacles that have arisen make us feel that our strength and our will have increased. The morale, the experience, the enthusiasm, and the self-confidence of our men are greater now than ever before. These small bitter remarks that I give vent to are almost exclusively mine. The others enjoy a state of permanent joy, serene confidence, tremendous faith, and no worries. That's why they have gained so much weight. If you could see our soldiers, you wouldn't know them: they are more than fat; they seem swollen. They are strong, healthy, and tough. Among the people— the peasants—our control is absolute, our support unconditional and unanimous. I cannot remember having had so very many courageous collaborators. The entire Sierra is up in arms: everybody is prepared to vanish as soon as an enemy soldier shows up. The void is going to be total. The murder of peasants in Peladero, far from filling them with terror, has sown hatred and resolution in them. Death in the Sierra is now something that does not frighten anyone.

CHE GUEVARA

Letter to Commander Fidel Castro   Bueycito, August 31

I'm writing to you about two important matters. The first one you must have already heard over the radio and you must have felt its effects. My debut as a major was a success from the point of view of victory and a failure as far as the organizational part was concerned. Despite every-thing, we took the barracks at Bueycito, wounded 6, and took another 6 prisoners. We took a Browning (like the one at El Uvero), 5 Garands, and about 10 Springfields, some .45-caliber revolvers, and far more am-munition than we had used up (the battle lasted twenty minutes). Ra-miro and Raúl Castro Mercader won the day when they decided we should attack from the rear. We blew up two wooden bridges and burned the barracks (which is also made of wood) and we allowed our-selves the luxury of setting free a sergeant and a stool pigeon, a certain

Oirán, after a request made by a kind of popular assembly. The battle ended at 5:20 and at about 10 in the morning we took the hill without being bothered by their airplanes. A decisive factor in the success of the operation was the determined and enthusiastic cooperation of some of the neighbors whom I don't want to mention by name. They gave us three trucks to get to the combat site. There are a hundred of us now, and only about ten men are without a weapon of any kind. One man died in the battle, Pedro Rivero from Campechuela, and two were wounded, one rather seriously in his right shoulder, but he can walk perfectly well. I cannot say anything further and so on to the second point: Frank's death, as sad in itself as the consequences it could have for the movement in Santiago. Perhaps we are on the verge of Batista's final collapse after this latest suspension of rights. But, if not, I think you'll have to make a resolute decision and send a man to Santiago as a leader who would be a good organizer and who would have a pipeline to the Sierra. In my opinion, it should be Raúl or Almeida or, on the other hand, Ramirito or myself (which I suggest without any false modesty, but also without the slightest desire to be chosen). I stress this because I know the moral and intellectual qualities of the pipsqueak leaders who will try to replace Frank. I think that a man from the Sierra, not known to the enemy, would take far better care of himself than poor Frank did and could render immense benefits to our cause.

What remains is the important subject of our future activity: I am thinking of, if there is no specific counterorder from you, carrying out a diversionary maneuver on the beach and then quickly returning to try to attack some other town, which could well be Guisa.

Send any order, counterorder, or suggestion with the messenger to Polo's house in El Zorzal. To end, I want to remind you of the little troop of soldiers that should be in Palma Mocha, in which they say you have a cousin. In my opinion, they're not worth a damn (I mean the soldiers).

JULIO COMACHO   September 5, 1957

In July 1957 Frank designated me Action Chief of M-26-7* in Las Villas Province. In Cienfuegos, a conspiratorial nucleus from the navy was in contact with the Movement.

In Havana, the navy plotters were in touch with Faustino. Officers in contact with other groups from the army participated also.

The threads of the conspiracy were held by Miguel Merino, our leader in Cienfuegos, who got in touch with Lieutenant Dionisio San Román and Corporal Ríos, the leaders in Havana and Cienfuegos.

---

* The 26th of July Movement.—Ed.

We gathered at Manacas and decided on plans for the joint uprising of the navy and of the 26th of July.

Everything was set to carry out the action in Havana at 6:30 on the morning of September 5.

At 6:00 p.m. on the fourth, the three of us left together: San Román, who was to lead the rebelling navy men from Cienfuegos, and Merino and myself, who would be in charge of the 26th of July group. At Colón, we split up: they continued along the direct southern route to Cienfuegos, while I went to Santa Clara to meet the provincial leadership. The uprising was to be supported by a national work stoppage, which would come about when station CMQ broadcast an announcement of the insurrection, and which, in turn, the militia would back with a plan for national sabotage.

At one in the morning of the fifth, I left for Cienfuegos, accompanied by Osvaldo Acosta; the others involved left for the five zones that divide the province.

At the house of a 26th of July comrade in Cienfuegos, we met San Román, Corporal Ríos, the Calañas, and other navy people and those from the 26th of July: Miguel Merino, Raúl Coll, Totico Aragonés, and other leaders.

We agreed on the final plans: Cayo Loco, where the naval installation is located, is joined to land by a narrow strip of earth guarded by several sentry stations.

One of the Calaña brothers was to be stationed at the first post. At a determined time, the conspirators would overcome any guards who refused to join the insurrection. Then, Calaña would signal, waving his machine gun three times, for those of us on the outside to enter the stronghold.

Everyone took up his position.

At 6:20 we left in two cars. In the first were San Román and Merino; in the second one, Coll, Totico Aragonés, Acosta, and myself. When we reached the first post there was no signal. It was a tense moment. The drivers turned the corner, and we went around the block, and returned.

They signaled. We entered the installation, which had been taken over by the navy rebels without firing a shot; San Román woke up Colonel Comesañas, chief of the garrison, told him he was a prisoner, and entrusted him to Merino's care.

San Román ordered reveille to be sounded, and when the troops were drawn up, he spoke to them: "The navy of Havana and Cienfuegos has rebelled against the tyrant, and it is ready to fight for Cuba's freedom. Those in agreement step forward." The majority of them did, and those that did not, we took as prisoners, treating them all with due respect.

Once Cayo Loco was under our control, we sent for the civilian nucleus of the 26th of July, and we formed navy and civilian platoons.

Navy gunboat 101 and coast guard ship 47 joined us. The new weapons were distributed to the people. Our trucks attacked and we captured the navy police. Their chief, Commander Cejas, died. We formed new detachments with our captured weapons.

We concentrated our forces against the National Police headquarters. The commander, Major Ruis Beltrón, asked for a truce in order to gain time. We opened fire, and minutes later they surrendered.

The people asked for the execution of Beltrón, the murderer. We explained that prisoners' rights are respected and they are judged later.

At 8:30 the battle began against the rural police barracks, the last enemy stronghold.

San Román and I stationed men at the entrances of the town to deal with possible reinforcements. We surrounded the barracks. We fought. Lieutenant Rosell, an enemy leader, asked to negotiate the surrender when a navy plane flew over Cayo Loco without firing. Immediately we machine-gunned the barracks. The guards were all for surrendering.

At that moment, the army announced that the insurrection was limited to Cienfuegos* and that they were sending reinforcements. We learned of this through the telegraph operator from Cayo Loco.

We deliberated. The situation was critical. We agreed to continue the battle in the hope of assistance from Havana.

The first reinforcements that reached the city from neighboring barracks were beaten back and taken prisoners.

At eleven there was intense fighting in the barracks. Four army bombardiers attacked Cayo Loco, which answered with antiaircraft guns. Powerful reinforcements with tanks were getting closer. Cayo Loco is small, and enemy fire can be concentrated.

We thought of evacuating the position and heading for the Trinidad Mountains with 300 men, but some of the navy people were not convinced that this action would succeed.

The battle went on furiously. The air attack was pitiless.

For the first time, a town in America was being bombed.

At 3:00, the first military reinforcements from Santa Clara began to pour in. They came in full of confidence and were mowed down by our machine guns. Trucks with 30 soldiers in them were completely wiped out.

Then they retreated, and more reinforcements were brought in at different points of the city. A house-by-house battle began. Block by block. In the face of an infantry, tank, and aerial attack our situation was desperate. Our final redoubts were the school buildings of San Lorenzo and the National Police headquarters.

---

* The conspiracy had been postponed in Havana but the telegram never reached Cienfuegos.

By 5:00, our ammunition was beginning to run out. The sailors at San Lorenzo were asking for ammunition urgently. Only a small group of navy people and a few leaders remained at the Cayo Loco installation. Corporal Ríos and I decided to abandon it, and we left with 30 men in a truck, and took along all types of ammunition, other weaponry, and a jeep.

A group of sailors decided to stay on and defend Cayo Loco to the death.

Under an incessant fire, we got the truck as far as San Lorenzo, and a little later, we took ammunition to our comrades who were battling away at the National Police headquarters.

At 6:00 p.m., San Lorenzo and the police headquarters were besieged by large enemy forces.

In a large launch, our group tried going by sea to the Trinidad Mountains. But it was impossible. We saw a military plane alight near gunboat 101, and several prisoners were taken from it. That was how San Román and other navy men were carried off to be tortured and to die in Havana.

We hid our rifles and returned in the launch to Cienfuegos.

Cayo Loco had fallen.

At nightfall the group that had started together was still intact: Miguel Merino, Osvaldo Acosta, Raúl Coll, Totico Aragonés, and myself. Only San Román was missing.

In the city, we made a final effort to enter San Lorenzo and the National Police headquarters, which were still holding out.

Impossible.

The night was hair-raising. The streets were full of corpses and wails from the wounded. The aerial attacks had ripped houses and entire families into shreds.

We were stumbling over the dead.

Then there was silence. It was all over.

We hid in a fish store, and with the help of some people we escaped from Cienfuegos, one by one.

CARLOS FRANQUI   September

When the fighting ceased, and the rebels withdrew, bulldozers opened up ditches, and hundreds of unidentified corpses were thrown into them. Thirty-two navy men were buried. A number of fatally wounded were buried alive.

Soldiers from the tactical regiment at Santa Clara leveled the city. They pillaged. They stole goods, alcohol, and money. They shot up the Casino Español, and destroyed oil paintings, pictures, and lamps by using them as targets.

Lieutenant Dionisio San Román and Captain González Brito, imprisoned by Laurent and Ventura, were tortured and murdered. Navy and civilian prisoners were killed.

Cienfuegos was the first city in Cuba taken by the insurrectionary forces. At Cienfuegos the "monolithic" unity of the armed forces around Batista was broken. For the first time one of the branches of the armed forces—the navy—joined ranks with the 26th of July and the people to fight Batista. To recover the city that had rebelled, Batista had to bomb and massacre.

Cienfuegos was the fourth of the powerful blows dealt to the tyranny in 1957: the attack on the Presidential Palace, the taking of El Uvero, and the August strike.

DANIEL [RENÉ RAMOS LATOUR]

Letter to Alejandro [Fidel Castro]   Santiago, September 15

Luckily the delegate from the "Rebel General Staff" got here. He gave us a perfect picture of the real situation in the Sierra, a situation that we suspected without having imagined it had reached such extremes. However, we could do nothing. With Aly [Celia Sánchez] absent and we ourselves aware of the encounter at Palma Mocha and the five army companies blocking the way to the area that we had been using as a communication route, we tried to make contact with Guevara. To this end, we wrote Che and sent for the coordinator at Bayamo, who had met with him. In the letter, we reproached the new major for having written to everybody but us. Through various channels, the news of the column reached us. He had communicated with people from Palma, Bayamo, even from Santiago itself, but never with us. Then I asked him to have a permanent channel established and someone designated to serve as an intermediary between them and the Directorate in order to be able to send cash and some other things that they surely needed. However, the leader from Bayamo reported to us that he had lost all contact with Che after his column's incursions at Bueycito and Yao; and that security was extremely tight and it was necessary to wait a few days to make contact again. Then we tried to locate a girl here in Santiago, who, according to what was reported to us, was the person who had delivered the letters (we weren't really sure they were Che's, since the writing differed from one to the other). We couldn't find her anywhere. Then we hunted for the person who had replaced Aly in Manzanillo. He explained the difficulties that Aly had had and he told us that she still hadn't been able to meet with you. Desperate in such a situation, we were pleasantly surprised by a visit from Ulises [Jorge Sotú]. But even more than his visit, he surprised us by his initial attitude and the note signed by you, which essentially was an expression of mistrust toward us, tacitly accusing us of responsibility for the state of neglect in which our forces in the Sierra found themselves, as well as of holding back for the cities the supposed newly arrived weapons destined for you. We knew these unjust insinuations stemmed from a visit by a couple of gentlemen from Havana—one of them Aureliano's adjutant captain, the other one an ex-military man and mediocre soldier, both enemies of the Movement—who, in order to gain entry, had brought us four or five rifles and spread a series of lies and sowed false rumors just to get a letter from you and go on a special mission. No, Alejandro, we have never belittled the Sierra. We think the battle ought not to be limited solely and exclusively to the mountains; we must fight the regime on all fronts. Nevertheless, we have never used any money, weapons, ammunition, clothing, or food that was needed in the Sierra and that you requested; we always work with leftovers. We are fully aware that the Sierra is our primary bastion. With the scanty means that remain to us, we are trying to intensify the fight over the entire island, to show the army that our courageous men in the mountains are not alone, that there is also an enormous army on the plains ready to bring into being the slogan that serves as our motto: "Liberty or Death."

However, despite these unfounded judgments, we have never stopped working to solve the problem of the Sierra once and for all. We could not leave the matter to Ulises, because we feel committed to meeting and satisfying all your needs, and we know how little can be done by someone who spends so many months out of touch and unaware of all the difficulties we encounter here, which we are always trying to overcome. When he arrived, we were already preparing a group of men, uniforms, knapsacks, shoes, ammunition, etc., to send off to you, only waiting for instructions from Aly, who had promised to write as soon as she arrived. She came to see me on my return from Havana and was waiting to leave around the twentieth to be back at the end of August or sometime during the first few days of the month. Today I received this letter from her that I am enclosing; it is self-explanatory.

Regarding the weapons, we now have only a small quantity, which we brought four or five days ago from Mayarí and obtained from our people there. This, together with four or five rifles that we had here, is all that we can put at your disposal. There are ten Winchester .44s, with ample ammunition, three Winchester .30-'06s, one M-1, one .30-'06 with telescopic lens. We wrote to Fausto to send us 7000 M-1 rounds, which reached Havana from Miami, thanks to María's [Haydée Santamaría's] intervention. It is probable that we will continue to get ammunition and pistols by this channel. I also asked Fausto to gather all the rifles he could and send them to me. I don't think he will be able to get many, since almost all the material they managed to acquire lately has been retaken. What the airplane delivered came from some army people who were involved in the recent abortive conspiracy and they turned over the supplies to the Havana Action cadres, specifically to Aldo Vera and Armando Cubría. They also lost a lot of weapons that Enrique Hart had obtained in a daring attack on an estate of Feito y Cabezón during the strike.

Innumerable difficulties have arisen. You will be able to appreciate this because of the fact that it's now three days since I began this letter. Neither Ulises nor I can get a single word to you. But yesterday the horizon began to clear. Aly arrived and told us that she had given the $1000 that we delivered to her to El Vaquerito [the Little Cowboy, Major Roberto Rodríguez] to take to you. Besides, according to the news we are getting, we think you're moving toward the other zone, where it will be easier for us to make contact.

We have readied a good supply of uniforms, knapsacks, boots, etc., and hope to send the men over to you well outfitted.

As we are resolving the serious problems of supplying the Sierra, which we will never abandon, I also want to report to you on other matters of interest.

DANIEL [RENÉ RAMOS LATOUR], ALY [CELIA SÁNCHEZ], AND JORGE SOTÚ

Memo to Alejandro [Fidel Castro]   Santiago, September 20

In what follows, we are going to set forth a series of requests that we hope will be given special attention in view of the serious upheavals and troubles we have experienced in our work because of not having anticipated these small details that, at first sight, seem insignificant but nevertheless have caused very serious problems in practice.

1. Organization and control by the Directorate of the recruiting of men into our army of the Sierra: during the days following the battle of El Uvero, because of the irresponsibility and lack of organization of the leadership at Manzanillo, a group of very poorly equipped men was sent without having been requested by you.

The Rebel General Staff's acceptance of individuals who, for the most part, lacked the necessary physical and moral qualities has brought about a very serious breakdown in the discipline that we had striven to maintain. David [Frank País] and Aly agreed, with your approval, that in the future the authorities would strictly control shipments of men to the Sierra. A sharp watch must be kept on the quality of our soldiers in the mountains, since they must combine the best physical and moral standards in order for the Sierra to continue to be the principal bastion of the Revolution and a magnificent example of purest sacrifice for the people of Cuba and America.

All these standards have been rigorously observed. At present we have more than 60 men in Santiago from all over the island who feel very disgruntled after waiting, many of them for as long as three months, to be sent out.

2. Official channels of the 26th of July should be employed for all types of negotiations or missions initiated from the Sierra.

To our way of thinking, it seems more reasonable to place your faith in people who have been fighting for some time through the organization for the advancement of the Revolution, and who have demonstrated a sense of responsibility, than to accredit or confer overriding powers on many people who have gotten to you by disregarding discipline and acting irresponsibly. And so we ask that all individuals who are sent out on negotiations or special missions be sent to the Directorate, where we would gladly offer them our cooperation through an existing organization.

3. Correspondence outside official channels should be avoided. We are not asking that all mail be censored, but that all letters go through our hands so as to avoid spreading false or improper news. Iron control must be exercised on all correspondence from the Sierra.

4. Those dismissed for not meeting physical standards or with authorization from the General Staff must have an official statement to that effect or the Directorate must verify the condition in order that these people not be considered deserters.

5. Names of deserters must be reported immediately so that they can be circulated and prevented from causing further damage.

6. There are many cases of individuals who have taken advantage of Fidel Castro's signature on papers of no importance, which, however, have been used by irresponsible parties to pass themselves off as direct representatives of our leader, simply by flashing his signature.

For the triumph of the Revolution.

CHE GUEVARA

In the "Hombrito" valley, during October 1957, we were laying the bases for a free territory and setting up the primary rudiments for industrial activity in the Sierra, and for a bakery that was to be started during this period. In the same area, there was a camp that was like an initiation center for the guerrilla forces, where groups of young people arriving to join up remained under the authority of some trustworthy peasants among the partisans.

The head of the peasant group, Arístidio, had belonged to our column until some days before the battle at El Uvero, in which he did not participate because he had broken a rib in a fall and he seemed reluctant to continue with the partisans.

Arístidio was one of the typical cases of peasants who joined the Revolution without clearly understanding its significance, and after his own analysis of the situation, he found it more to his taste to sit on the "fence." He sold his revolver for a few pesos and began to make declarations around the district that he was no fool and wouldn't be caught at home, meekly waiting, and once the partisans left, he would make contact with the army. Several versions of Arístidio's declarations were brought to my attention. Those were difficult moments for the Revolution, and utilizing my prerogatives as chief of a zone, we made a quick investigation and executed the peasant Arístidio.

Today we wonder if he was really so guilty as to deserve the death penalty and if his life should not have been saved for the constructive stage of the Revolution. War is difficult and tough, and while the enemy's combativeness is on the rise, one cannot allow for even a hint of betrayal. Months before, because of much greater weakness on our part, or months later, because of our relatively greater strength, his life might perhaps have been saved; but Arístidio had the bad luck of having his weaknesses as a revolutionary fighter coincide with the precise moment in which we were strong enough to use drastic action, as was done, and not strong enough to punish him in another way since we had no prison or any other means of guarding him.

We left the zone temporarily and went with our forces in the direction of Los Cocos on the Magdalena River, where we were to join up with Fidel and captured an entire military band, which, under the command of the Chinese Chang, was devastating the Caracas region. Camilo, who had left with the vanguard, had already taken several prisoners when we reached the area, where we stayed about ten days in all. There, in a peasant house, he was judging and condemning Chang to death. Chang was the head of a band that had murdered some peasants, tortured others, and had taken on the name and goods of the Revolution by sowing terror in the district. With the Chinese Chang was a peasant who had been condemned to death for raping an adolescent girl and for exploiting his authority as a rebel army messenger. Along with them, a good part of the members of the group were sentenced. They consisted of a few city kids and some other peasants who had been tempted to lead a free and easy life, without being subject to any law and, at the same time, enjoying what the Chinese Chang offered.

Most of them were absolved, but we decided to teach three of them a symbolic lesson. First, the peasant rapist and Chang were executed. Both of them were serene, tied to posts in the hills, and the first one, the rapist, without being blindfolded, faced the firing squad shouting, "Long live the Revolution!" The Chinese faced death with complete calm, but asked for the religious ministrations from Father Sardiñas, who was far away from the camp at the time and so this request could not be fulfilled. Then Chang asked that we make it known that he had asked for a priest, as if this public testimony would serve him as an extenuation in another life.

Then we carried out a symbolic execution of three of the boys who had been involved in Chang's outrages, but whom Fidel thought should be given another chance. The three of them were blindfolded and subjected to mock execution. When the shots had been fired into the air, and the three of them realized they were still alive, one of them gave me the strangest spontaneous demonstration of joy—a noisy kiss, as if I were his father.

This system that we used for the first time in the Sierra, may seem barbaric, except that there was no other punishment possible for those men whose lives could be saved, despite the string of bad marks against them. The three of them went into the rebel army, and I received glowing accounts of the behavior of two of the three boys during the insurrectionary stage. One belonged to my column for a long time, and in the discussions among the soldiers, when they would describe their deeds in war and someone expressed doubt about what he related, he would always say very emphatically: "Me, I'm not afraid to die and Che is my witness."

Two or three days later, we took another group of prisoners. Their execution was painful; they were a peasant named Dionisio and his brother-in-law Juan Lebrigio, two men who helped the partisans at first. Dionisio, who had helped unmask the traitor Eutimio Guerra* and had come to our aid at one of the most difficult moments of the Revolution, had totally abused our trust, just as his brother-in-law had. He had appropriated all the provisions the organizations in the cities were sending us and had set up several camps where he slaughtered cattle indiscriminately, and from that had descended to murder itself.

At this time in the Sierra, a man's economic status was measured essentially by the number of women he had, and Dionisio, as a believer in this custom and also because he considered himself a mighty man, thanks to the powers bestowed on him by the Revolution, had established three homes, and in each one of them he installed one woman and an abundant supply of provisions. At the trial, in the face of Fidel's indignant accusations of the treachery he had committed against the Revolution, as well as of his immorality in keeping three women with money from the people, he maintained a peasant artlessness by saying that there were not three, but two, because he was married to one (and that happened to be the truth).

Two of Masferrer's spies confessed, were found guilty, and were shot with them. And there was also a boy named Echeverría, who had performed special services for the Movement. He belonged to a family of fighters for the rebel army, with one brother who had sailed in the *Granma,* and he formed a small troop while awaiting our arrival, but—

---

* See pp. 135; 138–42.—Ed.

giving in to I don't know what temptation—began to carry on armed attacks in partisan territory.

Echeverría's case was pathetic because once he acknowledged his crimes, he did not want to die by execution; he begged to be allowed to die in the next battle and swore he would seek death that way, but he did not want to dishonor his family. Condemned to death by the tribunal, Echeverría, whom we called El Bizco [Cross-Eye], wrote a long, emotional letter to his mother telling her to be loyal to the Revolution. The last person to be executed was a picturesque fellow called the Teacher,* who was my comrade at one difficult stage when I was wandering about sick through the hills, and he was my only company, but then he left the partisans on the pretext of illness and had also taken up an immoral life, topping off his exploits by passing himself off as me, as a doctor, and trying to take advantage of a peasant girl who needed medical attention for some complaint or other. They all died proclaiming the Revolution, except for the two spies from Masferrer, and although I was not there to witness the facts, they said that when Father Sardiñas—this time he was there—went to administer the last rites, one of the prisoners said: "Look here, Father, go see if someone else needs it, because the truth is I don't believe in all this."

These were the people with whom we made the Revolution. Rebels against all injustice at the beginning, solitary rebels, who had grown used to satisfying their own needs and could no longer conceive of a battle with a social character. When the Revolution wasn't on its toes for a second, their materialistic behavior would involve them in mistakes that would eventually lead them to crime with shocking naturalness. Dionisio or Juanito Lebrigio were no worse than any other of the few delinquents who were let off by the Revolution and are in our army now, but the moment itself demanded a strong reaction and exemplary punishment to deter any attempt at disregarding discipline and to eliminate elements of anarchy that seeped into these zones that lacked a stable government. Moreover, Echeverría could have been a hero of the Revolution, a distinguished fighter like two of his brothers, both officers in the rebel army, but by bad luck, he transgressed during this particular period and had to pay for his crime in this fashion. We were uncertain about including his name in these pages, but his attitude was so noble, so revolutionary, and he was so resolute in the face of death and so clearly acknowledged that the punishment was fair, that we thought his end was not to be disparaged. It served as an example, tragic, of course, but valuable in making certain that our Revolution was pure and uncontaminated by the banditry to which we had become accustomed from Batista's men.

---

* See pp. 143–44, 181–83.—ED.

DANIEL [RENÉ RAMOS LATOUR]

Letters
To Alejandro [Fidel Castro]   October 3

Two or three days ago I received a visit from two of Prío's envoys, who delivered the letter I am enclosing. They will wait in Cuba for your answer. It seems to me that these people are more interested in the propaganda that is being made, or can be made, on the basis of the much-desired "pact"* than in all the joint action they talk about.

In the letter that we wrote as an answer to the two reports from Bienvenido [Léster Rodríguez], we said: "The attitude adopted in the name of the Movement with regard to the Auténticos strikes us as correct. They would rather deliver weapons to the police than to us. And they waste time in conversations and sterile discussions, while courageous and worthy comrades are dying daily in the mountains and the streets.

To Alejandro [Fidel Castro]   October 4

This letter was interrupted yesterday by a tremendous search they made of the block. Fortunately, we were able to get out in time, and we've been going from one place to another since last night and have still not found a safe place. The circle is getting smaller by the minute.

The Hungarian-Yankee reporter Andrew [St. George] is with us again. He is definitely thinking of going to the Sierra as a war correspondent. We'll keep him here until we have your opinion about it.

As far as the organization is concerned, I can say that it is constantly improving. The new structure we've given the Action units has increased the effectiveness in this sphere. Both sabotage and action are on the increase, and it is likely that Plan No. 4, already in effect, will work more efficiently than the previous ones.

To date, Oriente, Camagüey, Santa Clara, and Pinar del Río provinces are well organized. In spite of the efforts of María [Haydée Santamaría] and the doctor [Faustino Pérez], Havana has not yet reached the level of the remaining provinces (except for Matanzas, where there is still much to do). We have used Movement workers from Oriente and Camagüey to push forward in Havana, and there has been fair progress. The Movement's civilian resistance in the capital has also improved and grown; the departmental problem in this province is that of Action. The doctor has promised to visit me in a few days and I hope to hear what has been done there lately.

---

* The Miami Pact, signed November 1, 1957, by various exile groups, forming a Junta de Liberacíon [Liberation Junta] to oppose Batista. See p. 427.—ED.

P.S.: I'm sending 1000 pesos with this letter and another 1000 in another way. Aly [Celia Sánchez] has 1000 more. That is, 3000 pesos, which brings the total sent to TEN THOUSAND PESOS. Is it possible you still don't have money?

To Che Guevara   Sierra, October

This is in answer to your letter of September 29. I had them look for Carlos,* and we agreed to send the material that he cannot obtain there and I'll get it all to you as rapidly as possible.

Your letter was well-timed, since I had been meeting then with the executive board members from Palma, who had brought some of your letters that really had alarmed them. It is impossible for them to get all the supplies you request. On the other hand, I want you to know that contributions for the expenses in the Sierra, from all the provinces and municipalities of the country, are reaching us in cash at the level set for each. Until now, only the municipalities of Manzanillo and Bayamo had been directed to keep all their funds in order to defray the costs of the columns operating in the bordering zones. All the others sent the major part of what they obtained to the National Directorate, which is in charge of paying for necessities. In short, if the people you sent had had orders to go to Santiago, they would have been much more useful to you, since Palma is only twenty minutes from Santiago. Any Movement member around these parts could have given them an address here where they could have found us, since they do it every day. But the most serious part of the matter is that one of your letters was addressed to Parmenio; he has been the problem person in Palma, and to such an extent that we've had to expel him from the Movement and take energetic steps against him. At the very time when he was being convinced he had to come to an agreement and respect the discipline of the organization, you write him that letter, which luckily did not reach him—if he had it in his possession, he would have used it as a weapon for his disruptive activities.

Another letter that was brought is one you wrote to André Menés. The leaders in Palma have had a lot of trouble controlling that fellow, who thinks he has plenipotential powers to do and undo things in that municipality, completely forgetting and overlooking all the work and organization in operation there. In such cases, the proper thing to do is to put these individuals under the direct orders of the leaders of the Movement in that particular area, since they know better than anyone else the work pattern of the area where they have been carrying on their revolutionary activities for a long time.

---

* Carlos Chain, a leader of the 26th of July.—ED.

As far as Bayamo is concerned, there are as many ways of thinking as there are people. Some who are unhappy with the organization, because they don't have a prestigious job—due to inability or bad faith—prefer to deal with you, who don't know them, and use your support to gain what they could not acquire through revolutionary work.

Lara is one of the boys who was in Paquito's group. Do you remember that group that fell apart? They wasted the food they were carrying, the ammunition; in short, a disaster. He went back to Bayamo to work in the Action Department. They say he's brave and determined; however, about a week ago Bayamo's Directorate informed us that he refused to work, according to norms established by the Movement, and that he wanted to work on his own without bothering about the plans put into practice by the Movement on a national level; he is trying to create his own treasury. All in all, he acted in such an anarchical fashion that it became infuriating. We then warned the Executive at Bayamo to put an end to this attitude in an energetic fashion, or we would put a person in there who would resolve the problem in the name of the National Directorate.

I imagine that by now you will have talked to this man. The best solution would be for you to allow him to stay in the column; on the other hand, if upon his return he persists in his attitude, we will be forced to take steps we would rather avoid.

I ask that in the future you do not give credence or confer powers on these people that come to you in defiance of discipline and organization, as they are usually disruptive elements who solve nothing. Merely by paying attention to them, we further burden and weaken the organization of the municipalities, which has been so hard to maintain.

We hope that in the future Bayamo will be able to cooperate with you more. If not, we'll replace the Executive, but we must never create factions that undermine the cohesiveness of the Movement in any specific place, since this leads to less effectiveness for the organization. The productivity of the work accomplished depends on the unity and harmony that our members observe.

I think that either you did not understand or we did not make ourselves clear in regard to authorized mail. We were referring to correspondence going out from the Sierra. The Directorate often has no news of the operations of our forces, the lists of dead or wounded, victories, etc. However, many of our soldiers take advantage of someone leaving for the city to send news to their friends and family. As a result, they start the ball rolling, and eventually the friends and families come to us trying to find out the truth, because they suppose that the Directorate of the Movement is bound to know what is really happening in the Sierra. And as months pass and we have no information at all about what is happening up there, we find ourselves unable to confirm or deny the rumors. Besides, sometimes they bring false or misinterpreted news, which harms all of you as much as it does us. All this can be avoided in two ways: *Either all letters coming from the Sierra should be censored there or they should be sent only through the Directorate, which can check them and send those that pass muster.* Some families are in mourning for relatives or friends who are safe and happy in the Sierra. Of course, the ideal would be that together with these measures, each column name an officer whose duties would be to see that we receive, in the shortest possible time, the information we need to ensure the proper functioning of the organization and for our propaganda.

We hope to send you everything you need in a short time. We are also striving to set up supply centers in the two zones already mentioned. A thousand pesos are enclosed.

P.S.: In Santiago, Manzanillo, Palma, and even Bayamo, there is only one Movement. All over the island, there are nonconformist elements, but in general, they are misfits who only try to harm our cause but cannot.

FIDEL CASTRO   Sierra, October 11

Since our arrival in Cuba ten months and nine days ago, we have not received a single rifle or bullet from the outside world.

The weapons and bullets that we have are those we have taken from the enemy. During the last battle, we captured a .30-caliber tripod machine gun, a machine-gun rifle, seven Garands, and 12,000 bullets.

DARÍO [ARMANDO HART]

Letter to Alejandro [Fidel Castro]   Santiago, October 16

When, over three months ago, I fled from the court the idea crossed my mind that it would be more prudent to go to the Sierra, because there was no doubt that, for me in particular, the danger was greater here.

A few days before David [Frank País] was killed, I had planned a trip there to discuss with him all the organizational problems of the Movement, which he was running in a way that had not been achieved since you left for Mexico. However, after what happened, I decided I was needed outside the Sierra and therefore had to take certain risks. These are my present circumstances.

A few days ago Fausto [Faustino Pérez] passed through here, and a national meeting took place at which the general organization of the Movement was decided. It was decided that I was to take on the responsibility of the Movement's general organization outside the Sierra, which would be based in Santiago.

a. Because from the point of view of internal organization, it is far easier to function from here, since the work in Havana itself would completely absorb the attention of the Directorate, and, as a consequence, general organizational matters would be neglected.

b. Also, in this way, the Directorate can maintain direct contact with the Sierra, and there have been, as you know, a series of problems that have arisen out of a lack of contact, an aspect we hope to overcome completely with the trip Aly [Celia Sánchez] and Daniel [René Ramos Latour] are making there.

1. I would be holding back something from you if I concealed the fact that I did not like the viewpoint from which you discussed relations between the Movement in the Sierra and the Movement outside the Sierra in your last letter to Aly. You said that Aly considered herself as part of the Sierra before but now she is thinking like them (referring to the Executive Committee of the Directorate outside the Sierra). I myself am certain that all our comrades here have always considered the Movement there and here as one single entity. Rest assured that supplying you up there is so vital for us that we consider it our foremost and fundamental revolutionary obligation. Not just for yourselves, whom I must regard as members of the Directorate here, but also because of the certainty that the very success of the Revolution itself is going to depend on the success of the forces in the Sierra and their maintenance.

2. If you add to this the large number of opportunists whom we have to deal with daily, especially in the capital, and the Johnny-come-latelies, who have joined the Movement, and are gaining strength, you'll understand how in the midst of the most brutal persecution in Cuba's history (300 have been taken prisoner because of underground work and there are many dead), you would have to come to the conclusion that this is an arduous, complicated task. Also, we are not sure what capabilities a revolutionary leader needs. But, unfortunately, there are few people with even our average capabilities and total sense of sacrifice to the cause, as well as minimal organizational ability. Besides, we have been losing the Abels, Franks, Cándido Gonzálezes, the Raúl Suárezes, and many more who could have given so much in this struggle had they been able to be with us.

Here are a few solutions for this situation:

a. That several comrades from the Sierra, chosen by Daniel, be considered members of the Directorate while he is on this trip.

b. All communications and relations between the Sierra and the plains should be conducted through a special department, which Aly will head, along with an officer of the General Staff designated by you.

3. I want to tell you something about the general situation of the Movement, the Revolution, and the fight against Batista. A year ago, I wrote you in Mexico saying that we were the best-intentioned group in

the country, the most highly organized, and with a unity of purpose and plan, but, after all was said and done, we were simply a group, no more. Now, thanks to the heroism of you and your men, as well as the sabotage, the agitation, and the entire series of achievements that have been carried out by comrades, who, as you well put it, have acted heroically, we are now much more than a group, now indeed, we are truly the Revolution.

On the other hand, the general conditions of the country are more than ripe. I assure you that Havana is as ready to work as Santiago. The cooperation of all sectors, the integration of the best elements with the Movement is total. We are waiting for the signal. We are ready to depose Batista within a few months, the time we need to consolidate workers' cadres and civilian resistance. I think the strike in Havana did not succeed—and I mean this quite sincerely—through a lack of popular readiness. I've managed now to send a very valuable comrade from Camagüey there—David Salvador—he has extensive experience in fully incorporating workers into the Movement. We are going to work toward the following goal:

To make the workers' cadres of the 26th of July Movement sufficiently strong before November 15 to assume the responsibility of forming the strike committees.

4. I attach the highest importance to this work—especially the organizing of the militia—among all the functions that the Committee outside the Sierra has to supervise.

The civilian institutions seem to be ready to take the step indicated in the Sierra Manifesto. At long last! They sent us a memorandum proposing the formation of a government-in-exile, which will be backed up by the Auténticos and the 26th of July Movement, and also controlled by both of them. We answered in a long letter, which I unfortunately do not have available to send you. We threw the ball back to them by saying that we, in accord with the Sierra Manifesto, revere the constitutional legality of a government supported or formed by civic institutions. That we had nothing against organizing the government-in-exile, and in fact, it even seemed better to us, but that it should not come about through the incorporation of several partisan groups, but rather through a spirit of independence and an apolitical stance.

And that all parties or political and revolutionary organizations, military groups, social sectors, etc., should be committed to this government.

I would like you to send me a letter in your own hand addressed to Herbert Matthews saying that Franqui, Llerena, and Léster [Rodríguez] are the only people who can speak in the name of the Movement outside of Cuba. The letter should ask that no one allude to our internal problems.

We need a person with acknowledged public prestige to be on the Committee abroad. I personally think if Raúl Chibás got out he would be the most suitable candidate. He has always acted through the organization's channels, without forfeiting his own personality and personal criteria, of course.

5. René Rodríguez will go with Daniel. You must bear in mind that all the members of the Directorate Committee outside the Sierra, as well as the Executive in Havana, consider him a disruptive character.

6. I have left a very important point for the end. As I said in my letters that Karín [Haydée Santamaría, Hart's wife] delivered four or five months ago, cordial relations with certain diplomatic circles have continued.

Everybody, that is, all the parties and organizations, went crazy trying to manage to see the U.S. ambassador. Luckily for us, we were not asked to any of the meetings. However, I have been in contact with people close to the embassy. These contacts have told me that people who are on our side—but who do not appear to be—have had conversations with the ambassador himself. I think this is the best policy, since we are kept up to date about everything happening there and of all the possible U.S. plans, and at the same time the Movement does not officially commit itself. It seems that the United States has taken advantage of Batista's difficult situation to obtain certain benefits from him: for instance, a concession for the abundant cobalt mines in Cuba, which will be the key to atomic industry in ten years. Just imagine what this means and the kind of problems they're going to leave for us when we take over. Of course, the ambassador's attitude is, after all, correct, and I would do the same if I were representing Cuban interests in the United States.

I think that when the work gets to a slightly more advanced stage, I should make a trip up there to discuss some fundamental questions with you. Faustino is still in charge of all the work in Havana, and we are taking care of the organization here.

EDITOR'S SUMMARY   Havana, October 28

The National Medical Association of Cuba addressed a statement to the presiding judge of the country's Supreme Court detailing incidents in which doctors were killed for activities carried out in the proper exercise of their profession, the sanctity of hospitals was violated, and wounded patients were forcibly removed and left to die unattended. The statement noted that frequent flouting of legal safeguards against such treatment by members of the army and police force had caused widespread alarm and insecurity among the members of the medical profession in Cuba.

FIDEL CASTRO

Letter to Mario Llerena   Sierra, October 30

Together with Daniel [René Ramos Latour], who is visiting us to deal with matters of the Movement in a broad fashion, I am writing you these lines, even though they may be quite brief—there's no time for anything here these days.

Daniel had already arrived when we received the news that Raúl Chibás had been released and sent into exile. To our way of thinking, this solves the problem that was up in the air about the person to be responsible for finance. All the members of the Directorate favor him for that post. Beg him, in our name, to accept. I know he will do everything in his power to help us.

The committee will be set up in the following fashion:

Propaganda and Public Relations: Mario Llerena
Organization: Carlos Franqui
Military Affairs: Léster Rodríguez
Finance: Raúl Chibás

Although the Committee naturally has to choose a president from among its own people, we propose it designate you, so that in any activity or meeting you will be able to represent the Committee with a big vote of confidence. This in itself would facilitate much of the work.

You will have a magnificent comrade in Raúl Chibás, because he is the most impartial and noble man I have ever known. Quite unlike others, he aspires to nothing, and one always has to struggle to get him to take on positions for which his prestige and standing make him eminently qualified.

None of you should become discouraged by anything. The 26th of July Movement is extremely strong at this time. It is operating with an awareness of being the representative of an unquestionable majority of Cuba's populace.

Daniel is tremendously impressed by the Sierra and by how much we have advanced. The territory is totally in our hands.

One hundred percent of the population actively backs us up, and we are preparing to resist what will perhaps be the last attack from the dictatorship.

Redouble your efforts to try and get some kind of assistance from abroad, which would help consolidate our situation. It is indispensable for the final and toughest battles.

EDITOR'S SUMMARY

October

In September, Jules Dubois, Latin American correspondent for the Chicago Tribune *and a leading member of the Inter-American Press Association, prepared a report for the association's Executive Committee on Censorship reviewing Cuban events from Batista's coup, March 10, 1952, to the present. Dubois concluded that Batista could never again permit a free press to operate, since it would be impossible then for him to rule with "virtually the entire country . . . opposed to him."*

In October, many Cuban exiles came to Washington for the association's annual meeting. By picketing, pamphlets, and talk, they publicized Batista's violations of human rights and freedoms, especially freedom of the press. Not even the editor of Batista's own newspaper, Pueblo, *"dared" to vote against the resolution condemning Batista's regime for its undemocratic treatment of the press.*

DANIEL [RENÉ RAMOS LATOUR]

Letter to Alejandro [Fidel Castro]   Santiago, November 4

Upon my return, I found that revolutionary action had increased to such a point that it aroused brutal repression on the part of the regime; they even brought tanks into the streets to intimidate the people.

During the Action Program for Revolutionary Justice week, nine informers were killed, among them the Galician Morán (in Guantánamo), which ended his career of cowardice and betrayal.

As was to be expected, we also lost men—three. The most painful was the killing of Armando García, the captain of a large group of Action people. He was taken from his house at about two in the morning and viciously tortured—his testicles crushed, his ears burned by cigars, his body and feet stabbed—and later shot in the street, where he was left to perish. His wife went to the police station to investigate her husband's fate. He had been arrested in front of her, and when she wanted to go with him, they told her not to worry, that it was only a routine interrogation. Later, in the station, they told her: "He's out there in the street, dead."

In Bayamo, the balance was unfavorable, indeed. Three known thugs were done away with, and as a reprisal, the regime's assassins dragged twenty-one people from their homes—the majority of them uninvolved in revolutionary activities—and unmercifully murdered them, and then machine-gunned several houses.

As a result of all this, the situation is tense in Bayamo and Santiago, and the streets are deserted as soon as night falls.

But the most unpleasant news I've heard since I returned is the consummation of the famous "unity," thanks to Felipe Pazos.

I think the political schemers have leveled their surest blow at us and have derived the best results since this process began, in which the 26th of July Movement has carried the entire burden of the bloody battle.

The political schemers, standing on our dead, think they can rise to our level and be equal to us.

Within two or three days I'll send an extensive report about everything, the unwanted "unity" document and the letters from Bienvenido [Léster Rodríguez] and Felipe [Pazos], also the letter Darío [Armando Hart] wrote in the name of the Directorate.

I only want to let you know in advance that the Junta de Liberación Cubana, which thinks it will lead the revolutionary struggle in the future, is composed of the *Auténtico Party, Ortodoxo Party, Student Revolutionary Directory, FEU, Auténtico Organization,* two *Auténtico Workers' Organizations,* and the 26th of July Movement. And so the Auténticos have four organizations in the *Unity* and the Directory, two.

A uniform is being sent. I don't know if it will be of use to you.

DARÍO [ARMANDO HART]

Letter to Alejandro [Fidel Castro]   Santiago, November 8

Herewith 2000 pesos. We'll send the remaining 3000 pesos for the month of November in the next few days.

Concerning the problem of unity, everything is made clear in these documents. I just want you to know that we learned of it through the same channels as the populace of Cuba. Perhaps we've been a bit hard on Felipe and Léster, but frankly we feel that this matter of unity shows a lack of consideration and even something more serious: a political shortsightedness. The organizations in Havana, or at least some of their leaders, are now ready to form a provisional government as outlined in the Sierra formula, but the false unity achieved in Miami has paralyzed such moves. Now, logically, the demand it come as a proposal from the Junta de Liberación.

We must maintain a discipline here, Fidel, as rigid and severe as you maintain, in exemplary fashion, up there. Particularly keep in mind that down here the Movement does not have the benefit of the force of your own persona in the Sierra. As many are opportunists and many want to work entirely on their own, we have to fight this insubordination if we don't want to perish as an organized institution.

CIRO FRÍAS

Report to the Commander [Fidel Castro]   Santiago, November 8
                                                Sierra, November 9

I am writing this to inform you that yesterday, on the eighth, at the appointed place, I gave Pablo García orders to set fire to the sugarcane plantations at 10:30 p.m. At midnight, eleven soldiers arrived in a truck, and when they confronted us, we fired. Only one was able to escape. The fate of the other ten was as follows: four dead, two mortally wounded, three others wounded but not dead, two I am taking along as prisoners, and the driver of the truck, who is also seriously wounded, as well as two peasants who brought the guards to put out the fire. We collected eight weapons in all: five Garands, three Springfields, and a revolver.

DANIEL [RENÉ RAMOS LATOUR]

Letter to Alejandro [Fidel Castro]   Santiago, November 9

I think that with these two shipments and the group of men I am sending, you will be well reinforced.

Among the best weapons the men will bring are two Winchester .30-'06, both with telescopic sights, two .30-'06 Remington rifles, several Springfields (one of them taken from a soldier in the middle of a street in Santiago), several old carbines, four Crackets, and a lot of Winchester .44s. Unfortunately, I did not receive the tripod that Fausto [Faustino Pérez] promised from Havana. The .30-'06 bullets are dribbling in. Today I received 2800, which I immediately sent off. The remainder will go out as they come in.

In addition, I am sending uniforms, boots, bandannas, woolen socks, and a variety of other things that will be very useful to you in the winter.

As I said in my previous letter, upon my return, I found out the sad news of the "unity" comings and goings. I think that Pazos himself, in his letter to Fausto of October 20, mentions what he should have kept in mind, but unfortunately forgot: the 26th of July Movement's undeniable and universally acknowledged supremacy—which is not reflected in any of the documents made public by the brand-new junta. He says: "When they arrived in Miami, the Ortodoxos had agreed to take part in the unity pact with the FEU and the PRC [Partido Revolucionario Cubano (Cuban Revolutionary Party)] and the Demócratas, *if the 26th would do likewise.*

Pazos adduces flimsy arguments when he says, "Or make us responsible for rejecting it, without valid reasons, and thus endanger the lives of our men in the Sierra, who urgently need the help that unity can give them, *and risk the very triumph of the Revolution.*"

It is a known fact that the Sierra front has daily become more established and has expanded without any help from revolutionary parties or sectors outside the 26th of July. Besides, the triumph of the Revolution is now so imminent that it is perhaps the fundamental motive that inspires most members of the signatory organizations to implement the unity pact.

We're sending 2000 pesos with this letter and in a few days we'll send 3000 more.

EDITOR'S SUMMARY   Miami, November 1

Representatives of seven Cuban political groups had agreed to join forces in the struggle against Batista. Their declaration of unity, the Miami Pact, was signed at the home of Lincoln Rodón, former Speaker of the Cuban Congress. The organizations represented were: the Auténticos, the FEU, the Revolutionary Directory, the Directorio Obrero Revolucionario (Workers' Revolutionary Directory), Partido Revolucionario Cubano, and the 26th of July Movement (although the exact status of Felipe Pazos, who signed for the Movement, was disputed).

The chief points of the declaration were:

Agreement to work to rid Cuba of Batista's "reign of terror" and to establish a democratic government there.

Creation of a Junta de Liberación Cubana (Cuban Liberation Junta) to organize and preside over these steps.

Release of political, civilian, and military prisoners and restoration of civil liberties.

Support for charges made in international bodies that Batista violated human rights.

Request that the United States stop shipping arms to Cuba under the hemispheric defense pact, since these arms were being used against Cubans themselves.

Request that the United States recognize the Junta de Liberación as a legitimate government body engaged in civil war in its own country.

Invitation to all Cuban groups in the intellectual, religious, commercial, and other spheres to join the effort against Batista.

Guarantee that the armed forces not participate in politics.

Maintain the democratic government after the triumph of the Revolution.

November

Jules Dubois reported two U.S. actions in November that "failed to enhance the popularity of the United States government . . . in the minds of the Cuban people." First, Colonel Carlos Tabernilla, commander of the air force, which had recently bombed the Cuban city of Cienfuegos, was awarded the U.S. Legion of Merit. Then, speaking "on behalf of my colleagues" on the Inter-American Defense Board, U.S. Marine Corps General Lemuel C. Shepherd responded to a toast from Batista: "I wish to thank you . . . because those words come not only from a great general but also from a great president."

RAÚL CASTRO

Letter to Fidel Castro   Sierra, November 20

I heard yesterday afternoon that you were still in the Altos de Limones, planning to go through the Mariño pass in order to reach us. My squadrons are well distributed, although there's no specific ambush, because there are no soldiers anywhere in the district.

My time these days has been almost entirely devoted to the communications received from the National Directorate regarding the infamous Miami Pact. I opened them thinking there might be some sort of urgent message that you should know about quickly. Even though I think you'll be here today or tomorrow, I'm sending these papers to you. Besides, I'd like to have news directly from you. Guerra will give you news verbally about the three zones of Operation Mariposa [Butterfly], for which reason Ulises [Jorge Sotú] went abroad. In a note to Daniel [René Ramos Latour] on the tenth, he said that within ten or fifteen days the equipment would be in our hands; ten days have already passed. Although there hasn't been an advance notice, I presume you will have men posted at the places specified, and they'll wait—thus my haste in reporting to you, since one of the points is some distance away.

To go back to the subject of the unity pact: I've read all the papers quite carefully, and I'm getting more and more furious. The very clever 26th of July Movement has ingenuously fallen into a clumsy political trap. Pazos's arguments are infantile at first glance, but upon closer examination, they reveal a kind of boundless ambition. He has been honest for a long time in his public life, but now an ambitious political finagler, heretofore dormant, has been awakened in him. This gentleman's only exploit was to come to the Sierra to sign a document that he originally opposed with *calculated premeditation,* and had blocked with endless obstacles. When he signed it, he acquired an important political personality in the present Cuban situation, thanks to the formidable support of the 26th of July Movement. Then he left with his friends and showed his true colors by reneging on the Sierra Manifesto in practice (he had used it as an instrument), and he pasted on the fig leaf of: "by inviting us to join the unity, they (along with other sectors) promised to accept all the fundamental tenets of the Sierra Manifesto, except that they will not specifically include our pronunciamentos in the public document (1) against intervention, (2) against the military junta, and (3) leaving the manner of choosing the provisional government open to discussion" (Pazos's exact words). These three points, all in one paragraph of his letter to Fausto [Faustino Pérez], are worth analyzing. I will point out only that perhaps the last point might have been his advice from behind the scenes, since it is easy to imagine that because he was the "inventor of unity," the much-sought-after choice should be his spoils.

You will observe the very "impressive" arguments he used, for instance, that he "had to take refuge and could not talk to Fausto," and that "much time had elapsed and the civic institutions did not respond" (as if this new force, given its internal formation, could reply to such an important proposal as quickly as it could to an individual work contract). Hart answered this point very well. Pazos also said that if he had not acted as he did it would have "endangered the survival of our men in the Sierra." ("We who twice came out of nowhere and are accustomed to defend ourselves all alone!") etc., etc. You can read the rest of the arguments, which are no less ingenuous than those I've pointed out. It's simply that the unjustifiable is always going to be unjustifiable.

As for Léster, I don't have much to say. He once abandoned a mortar against the army and the enemy captured it; this time he abandoned a mortar against the politicians, and they also captured it. We should leave him where he is, once and for all.

Our National Directorate answers Pazos and Léster; I think their answer is perfect, theoretically, but what cowardliness to accept the fait accompli! (at least from my humble point of view). A paragraph from one of Hart's letters to you: "Concerning the problem of unity, everything is made clear in these documents. I just want you to know that we learned of it in the same way as the populace of Cuba. Perhaps we've been a bit hard on Felipe and Léster, but frankly we feel this matter of unity shows a lack of consideration and even something more serious: political shortsightedness." First the *personal justification,* perhaps as "historical proof"; then what Hart calls being a little hard—a mere admonishment, more benign than what we do when a man lets a single bullet go astray; he goes on to say that *"this matter of unity shows a lack of judgment,"* when, in reality, it was a flagrant betrayal of the Revolution (undoubtedly, he's analyzing it from a personal point of view). And he ends, "and even something more serious: *political myopia,"* when it was actually well-calculated, ambitious political scheming.

Of course, from Hart's point of view, it seems an irrefutable, forceful, and overwhelming argument! To wit: "The American press welcomed the formula for unity with a great demonstration of sympathy." (At this point we have just shitted an inch short of the chamber-pot brim.) "And so, *it is not good tactics* to oppose the pact."

In the midst of all this, I don't want to talk about the signers of the pact (each and every delegate with a voice and vote in the brand-new Junta de Liberación). On the one hand, the Prío Auténticos and the Auténtico Organization, and on the other, the FEU and the Revolutionary Directory (four of them), later the Workers' Revolutionary Directory (unknown in Cuba). The historical Ortodoxos (historically disappeared, especially now that Raúl Chibás has joined our ranks; and thanks to the charm of "unity," they are now transformed into a "historical obstacle"), and, finally, to breathe life and flesh into all these political skeletons, our 26th of July appears.

Even shooting these two gentlemen (Pazos and Léster) would not be enough to repay them for what they've done.

Something definitely has to be done and I am partial to the scalpel, to slice off the tentacles that are winding themselves around us, and not only us, but the Revolution that we represent. I have faith that you know how to get us out of this mess they've gotten us into, and that you are determined enough to do it; thousands of our militants will most certainly share my faith, those who are now aware of and possibly furious about a pact between the putrid and painful past and the pure and promising future.

If we let this pass, later, on any given day, some of these delegates will sell the republic, and we will learn about it from international cables and won't be able to reject the deal because it pleases the American press.

DANIEL [RENÉ RAMOS LATOUR]

Letter to Alejandro [Fidel Castro]   Santiago, November 20

Within a few hours, I hope your column will run into the men I'm sending you—they're already on their way.

As you want us to send Ulises [Jorge Sotú] north, this group will be divided into four squadrons, each under the command of a chief: Horacio Rodríguez, César Lara, Rámon Paz, and Raúl Menéndez (the last has still not been able to leave).

I highly commend César Lara to you. He is very young, but he has given proof of extraordinary bravery on several occasions. He has been imprisoned twice, once in Miranda and then here in Santiago; he was brutally tortured but never uttered a word.

Rámon Paz was head of the Movement at La Mina de Charco Redondo. I think he's a serious and responsible man.

As for Horacio, he seems fully prepared to remake his past in the Revolution. In my opinion, he deserves this chance.

I hope to be able to send Sergeant Coroneaux out today. We've tried to send him out so often and yet have never managed it because of the difficulty of getting him out of Santiago. Uniforms, bandannas, blankets, shoes, and more than fifty shirts are being sent. They left the trousers, but they'll go out at the first opportunity, in order to complete the fifty uniforms.

Also the uniforms marked "for the veterans" are being sent—for those from the *Granma* and from the trucks.

In addition, I'm sending 4000 rounds of .30–'06 and 1350 carbine rounds, 1000 rounds of .22, 300 No. 12 cartridges, and 300 No. 16.

Today I'm leaving on a trip to try and step up the work in the other provinces.

We're starting to receive supplies from abroad (thanks to the last people we sent there), but we have been very unlucky. The car left the United States perfectly, got into Cuba and crossed most of the island without a hitch, but then crashed at Holguín and all the supplies were lost because of this cursed accident.

P.S.: Herewith, 2000 pesos.

EFIGENIO AMEJEIRAS

Report to the Commander [Fidel Castro]   Sierra, November

As you ordered, we laid an ambush in the Maestra; I put two men to watch the old road leading from Gaviro and another posted on the road leading from La Habanita, from which I was told Mora was to arrive with reinforcements for me. Meanwhile, we saw a platoon of guards advancing in close order from Gaviro, firing on us; we were quite pleased as our position was magnificent.

I picked six of our best men and at a run took to the old road and surprised a scout. We captured him and continued looking for a good position, but we couldn't find one. We heard noise and fell back as best we could; then another appeared. We signaled him to keep quiet, but he answered by shouting: "I'm alone! I'm coming!" I frightened him into keeping quiet and keep advancing toward us, which he did, quite slowly. When he reached us, I took off his pants and stretched him out at a turn in the road. Now the guards were on the alert, and fell back on both sides of the road. They sent out a vanguard of six or seven men who walked very slowly and quietly. I was stretched out in the road with Humberto on my left and Bayamo and Guapo on my right, waiting for Bayamo to fire the first shot, but he hesitated, thinking that I had a better position. I signaled to the guard and shot him from a yard away. In a flash, it was an inferno: bullets rained down everywhere; they had taken our right and left flanks. We kept them at a distance for fifteen or twenty minutes, and I am certain that four or five of them fell in the road, but we could not take their weapons because they were firing at us too fiercely from a position above our own. We retreated without firing a shot.

FIDEL CASTRO

Blockheads! What would you think if I told you that instead of guards, the people ambushed in the Maestra were Efigenio and his platoon, plus Luis Crespo and Fajardo, and that at 4:15 they had to do battle with the guards, killing some of them, but also against you, and luckily they killed none of you, but because of your attack, they had to retreat.

The combat began when one of Efigenio's sections shot at the enemy vanguard.

While I'm ensconced in the Espinosa peaks, I receive news of the guards in Gaviro. I ordered men to the Maestra immediately, so that the guards wouldn't get there first; then I went to the mines of Sariol, where Raúl was, and we quickly ordered a platoon to seize the road from Gaviro to Las Mercedes, at the enemy's rearguard, so as to cut it off. Another platoon was placed on the left flank.

When Efigenio had to withdraw from the Maestra, the guards went as far as San Lorenzo instead of retreating, which was the moment that we were going to take the Gaviro road and attack them. The result: the plan failed.

If you and Efigenio had made contact about defending the Maestra, the enemy would have had to surrender; perhaps it would have turned out that way if you hadn't attacked Efigenio.

To go into detail: it turns out that you were all forced to retreat or at least held in check by two rifles—Binto's and Roberto's—and by Vives's pistol; they didn't bring in the .30 machine gun. If instead of us, they had been guards, some showing this detachment would have made. But luckily it turned out this way!

DARÍO [ARMANDO HART]

Letter to Alejandro [Fidel Castro]   Santiago, November 22

I'm writing you just after receiving the news of the setting-an-example execution of Cowley.* For months our Action group carefully prepared this blow. Holguín had the reputation of being too peaceful. The Action men there had repeatedly asked the Movement to allow them to strike that blow rather than do anything else. We had allowed several consecutive delays, because it dragged on, and the last extension was up tomorrow. They fulfilled their promise perfectly. Holguín has vindicated itself. I don't have to describe to you the excitement and joy among the people when they heard the news. They are toasting the news in cafés and bars.

---

* Army Colonel Fermín Cowley Gallegos.

What a disgrace for a country to toast the death of one of its military chiefs!

I'm sending 1000 pesos with this. If you need more, tell me quickly.

About the problem of unity—we're already feeling uneasy about it. I don't know if we told you that we gave him until December 1 to resolve the question. We'll send you a copy of the letter to Llerena in which all our worries are spelled out. Along with this, if possible, I'll send a copy of the letter about extending the time to December 10; I can't remember whether we sent it before. I would like to talk to you personally about this, but with the volume of work here, I couldn't stay away for two weeks. And so, I beg you to tell me what you think about this matter. I believe if we can be responsible for important events, like the burning of sugarcane plantations and perhaps even bigger things, without unity interfering with what we originally planned, the time will have come to show that the responsibility for whatever failure there is lies with Carlos Prío and the other of the "patriots."

DARÍO [ARMANDO HART]

Letter to Che Guevara   Santiago, November 23

We received your lengthy letter addressed to Daniel [René Ramos Latour], and as it concerns some general matters of organization outside the Sierra, I must speak to you about this, and especially in reference to Camagüey.

The Cuban, as a worthy heir of the Spanish spirit, is extraordinarily individualistic, and it is difficult for him to understand the meaning of the word "organization." I even go as far as saying that this has been the primary difficulty that we, the people south of the Río Grande—which Martí called "Our America"—have had to face in order to overcome the traditional enemies of our freedom and of our higher destiny in the world. I leave this philosophical concept aside in order to deal with something more concrete, which is my main concern today: the necessity of keeping all the cadres of the organization outside the Sierra functioning at their peak.

There are many opportunists or many merely lacking in revolutionary sense who try to make contact with you directly or even with us in Santiago, going over the heads of the provincial or municipal leadership and basic structure—all of which have been worked out carefully and with great historic awareness for more than a year, and happily, today, thanks to our many comrades and especially to the extraordinary capacity of our unforgettable Frank País, have come of age for the fight against the tyranny. These organized cadres must be maintained, come hell or high water, because, together with your forces in the Sierra, they are the only hope left if the country is to have a revolutionary instrument capable of transforming it socially, politically, and economically. It is because of this that I've begged you, over and over, through Fidel, that no one be admitted to the Sierra Maestra without first letting the National Directorate outside of the Sierra and even the provincial directorates know about it. Naturally, I'm not talking about the legions of peasants in direct contact with you, who are not included among the organized units outside of the Sierra.

Fidel himself once told us that a revolutionary movement had to be a process of continuous purging of its units. In two years of organized work, or at least trying to organize, I've come to understand how right that statement was. Certainly, because of the pressure of events and the ever-growing risks of collective work, many people have been left by the wayside, but they still persist, and they accomplish their ends—but not through work and organization. Instead, they take advantage of our good faith to establish direct contact with the leaders of the Movement outside the Sierra or even with you. This creates a state of disorientation and all sorts of difficulties. We believe there is no dissidence in the Movement because we have a strict sense of organization, and we are not ready to admit people who call themselves representatives of this or that group.

Many revolutions have triumphed, but all of them, or almost all of them, have been betrayed. And it is for this reason that we must keep even closer check on those within the Revolutionary Movement than on its enemies.

This is what it's about, Che, and I assure you that if you talked to us at length, you would understand certain things that make you uneasy now, but of which we are very aware. For us, this is a revolution of the people and we have put our greatest energy into it because it is the mobilization of the people—specifically, the workers' sectors and the Civic Resistance Movement—who are trying to weld together the so-called middle classes and proletariat to bring about the definitive fall of the tyranny, so that you and the men of action can finish it off with one final blow. In Cuba, we have generated a complete mobilization of civilian and proletarian consciousness; it is the basis of all our strategy, and we work fervently for it. Rest assured that we and the Movement in general share your basic concern about the participation of the workers in the overthrow of Batista.

Because of all this, my dear Che, I beg that you reject any contact made with you that is not in the zone immediately around you. Simply show the organization circular that I am enclosing. Rest assured that things will function better this way. If you have any complaints about any comrade at all, or a feeling of lack of support at any time, remember that you can turn to us at once, and we'll try to solve the problem as effectively as possible. That way things will work better. I'm enclosing a report from the Workers' Section of the Movement that I'm sure you'll like. I'm also enclosing the second organization circular, which has been out for a few days in the province. I trust the first letter to the militants has reached you, and today I'm going to see if I can send the second. With this material you'll have ample information about our immediate plans and the organizational form we've decided to adopt. I hope you'll acknowledge receipt of all the documents and that you'll make suggestions about them, since I'm sure your ideas will be useful to us.

I do not want to end without congratulating you very sincerely on the strength your column has been gaining under your leadership, as well as on the bravery your men have shown throughout the zone. María [Haydée Santamaría] also sends her greetings.

CHE GUEVARA

Letter to Fidel Castro   Sierra, November 24

As so many other times, your excellency (isn't there a junior lieutenant colonel rank?) was right and the army got as far as our beards. Don't worry, nothing has been happening so far in any way.

Before I say another word, I must tell you it was impossible for me to send Pazos* because I needed him for the defense, and I still can't do it. That's why I'm sending someone else to report, so don't worry.

When I arrived here, I ran into a novel situation. The groups we left have now conquered the area, and the army respects them. We then decided to create a fixed base of operations in El Hombrito and in Zarzal and to establish our heavy industry there. We already have our armory functioning full blast, but we still haven't been able to make a mortar because Bayamo is not sending the necessary materials. I ordered the manufacture of two experimental models of grenade-throwing rifles that I think will turn out very well. They have already manufactured several very powerful mines but none has been exploded yet and the army got hold of one of them.

The shoemaking workshop is installed and ready to manufacture all kinds of saddles and shoes, but the materials have not been received.

We have two embryonic farms for raising pigs and poultry; we have constructed a bakery, which will probably turn out its first cake the day after I write this, in celebration of your embarkation. We've started constructing a small dam to supply hydroelectric energy to this zone. A permanent hospital has been established, and construction of another one, with excellent hygienic standards, is about to begin. The materials for it have already been donated.

The entire zone is covered with antiaircraft shelters. We intend to stand fast here and not give up this place for anything.

---

* Javier Pazos, son of Felipe.——ED.

Now comes the sad part: our failures. The guards attacked us at Caña Brava and California, where we dominated the heights with a practically invulnerable half-moon defensive position. There were several exchanges of fire, which probably caused them one wounded man. I ordered a slow advance, and the men cooperated with quite a bit of enthusiasm, but Camilo, in his zeal to reach them, took along two of our lookouts with binoculars, and as a result, he left a road easily defended by two men, unguarded. That was where the enemy sent in a mighty vanguard, forty peasants, in anticipation of the mines. The outcome was that they made a "triumphant march," passing through Santana and then returning to Caña Brava and burning two houses and some of Carlos Más's provisions that they discovered. They dumped some weapons, which fortunately were recovered. The army went through six of our ambushes, but we did not shoot. Some of the men say they didn't fire because there were children. I was 500 yards away, there were a lot of them, and I had lost contact with the other ambushes; I was behind a banana tree—not a very sturdy tree for the Sierra Maestra—and there were two darling P-47 planes hovering overhead constantly. As the intellectuals would say, we ate shit with hair in it. The army sped away, and with their usual coordination they began an advance to Pinalito and surprised Pazos, who meant to surprise them, which gave him a fright, but without any consequence so far. (Mitico is lost, but that's not serious.)

At this very moment, your messenger arrived with your letter. The part regarding Pazos is already answered. I'll send him to you immediately, no matter what condition we're in. The incident of Argimiro is solved, and in principle, another squadron was put in the place that can't be abandoned. About Camagüey: I have written to the National Directorate about it and let them know I had no authority to deal with them, but in any case, I asked for the materials for the homemade mortar, and they've arrived already. Calixto's nomination seems very good; he was useless, and he can't screw up Camagüey more than it already is and can contribute to the creation of centripetal expansion, which has been shown to be the only efficient way of solving our problems. Mabay was a mess: they didn't take the barracks and weren't even able to burn sugarcane plantations because they were damp. It was my fault, since I believed the people who assured me that with those few weapons (very poor ones) they could take the barracks. It appears the guards fled, but so did ours. This work was carried out by the patrol from Las Minas and I couldn't send anyone because I was involved in the ambitious operation of deballing all those guys from Caña Brava. That's why I didn't order any more operations than the ones we agreed on.

Reports are arriving as if in newsreel sequence. The guards are now in Marverde. We're going there full speed ahead. You can read the continuation of this interesting little story later. I forgot to tell you that the flag of the 26th of July is flying on the peak of El Hombrito, and we're trying to keep it there. We put another flag at Corcabá in order to set up a trap for the small plane; and the two volunteers had the P-47s turn on them, and their asses were shot up with shrapnel (it's true, but they were small pieces, and no further developments from either the volunteers or the small plane).

While the troops get ready, I'll tell you about other matters. A gringo newspaperman from the New York *Herald Tribune* came here. He wouldn't walk, because he's so fat and heavy. He sent them to tell me that he was not walking a step farther, and as I did not rush out to see him in due speed, he left in a huff.

I'm sending you the newspaper* and the declarations we've printed. I have hopes that the low quality will serve as a shock to you, since you are now contributing to something that bears your signature. The editorial in the second issue will be about burning of the sugarcane plantations. In this issue, the contributors are: Noda on agrarian reform, Quiala on the reaction to crime, the doctor [Faustino Pérez] on the real life of the Cuban peasant, Ramiro on the latest news, and I, to explain the name, do the editorial. The choice of subjects is mine. They urgently need all news of actions, crimes, promotions, etc., and regular communication for which a special corps can be created.

Also, I must talk to you about some important matters:

1. The necessity of creating a special permanent patrol on the heights of the Maestra over Palma Mocha, in order to secure our communications at this point, since it is vulnerable from the beach.

2. It is very important to set up a third column to operate the other side of Pino del Agua, under the command of a very able leader. Even with the lack of weapons, it can be done by taking people from this or that column. If we had had some kind of column in that location, we would now have been able to act without having to scatter the troops around so much and have taken the offensive against Las Minas. Think this over carefully. Raúl, Almeida, and Ramiro are there.

I still haven't told you something terribly important: Complying with your orders, although it was impossible to get patrols into action, I sent men to burn all the principal sugar mills in Oriente. They did not do anything in the vicinity of Bayamo because we had strict orders from the Movement not to start until the twenty-fifth of this month as they themselves were going to take charge of setting the fires; had we set the mills on fire, the region would have been full of guards, who would have prevented us from acting.

---

* *El Cubano Libre* [The Free Cuban], mimeographed at Che's camp, edited by two students, Leonel Rodríguez and Ricardito Medina.—ED.

I sent people to Mabay; the mission failed, but they will try again. Also Contramaestre, Preston, Boston, Chaparra, Manatí, Delicias, and other small villages. The men seem quite fine and they are all knowledgeable about the area. I'll send news as soon as there is some.

FIDEL CASTRO   Sierra, November

We have organized a disciplined, tough army, and it grows daily, winning important victories against the enemy. We are already in control of two-thirds of the southern coast of Oriente, and above all, or even more important, we have the total support of the civilian populace that occupies the territory.

My father has a large sugarcane plantation in Oriente, and it will be the first one burned by our underground organization, by way of example. When the North American colonists dumped tea into the sea, didn't they do exactly the same thing? Who can deny us this right of self-defense?

The U.S. ambassador was in Santiago de Cuba when the events that led up to the strike occurred. A group of women who went to visit the ambassador were beaten back by Batista's police in his very presence. The same day, 60,000 people who attended the burial of Frank País, leader of the 26th of July Movement, who had been killed the day before by the thugs of the dictatorship, put out the order for the general strike. It was a spontaneous strike and there was no advance organization; it was simply a public explosion against the chain of crimes being committed. The industrialists came to a standstill, as well as businessmen and workers. And although it was not organized, the strike spread all over the island and lasted for a week. The people are now preparing for an organized general strike, which the dictator will not be able to stamp out.

CHE GUEVARA

Letters to Fidel Castro   Sierra, December 1

I suppose that you must have heard the sad news on the radio. Ciro died of a bullet wound in the head, fighting in the front ranks, in a truly heroic act. Ciro had won his troops' admiration and love.

I think it would be simple justice that he receive the rank of major, if only for the sake of history, which is all most of us can hope for.

Sánchez Mosquera took the road to Agua al Revés, and I followed, after I had sent Camilo by way of La Nevada to block his route up El Cojo. Camilo arrived but too late to prepare anything and with very few men. He killed the guide, wounded someone, but had to retreat because of the very intense firing and because they tried to surround him, climbing several routes. When I arrived from behind, they had already left for La Nevada to pursue Camilo, but he got out with one of the Pardos, who was slightly injured in his shoulder. He took a Garand rifle with its ammunition from them.

The next day they went from La Nevada to Marverde, and in Tocio we managed to surround them. The orders were to shoot with deliberation and to keep them encircled for three days, if necessary, until they surrendered. The men directly under my command carried out the instructions and worked carefully. Ciro went too fast and wound up in the lion's mouth during an action in which all the others were wounded and he was killed. The injured are Fajardo, Reyes in an arm, and Pazos with a stone splinter. Joel was wounded while taking three prisoners, whom we captured; he's the most seriously wounded, but there's no danger. The action failed because a new troop of reinforcements was brought in. There was sniping at Dos Brazos by a little patrol, and the vanguard was surprised and beaten down in an ambush that we had prepared for them. We withdrew in orderly fashion but I have lost contact with three men who were in a remote spot, and two others went astray after leaving the danger zone. I hope they'll show up, though the news of the four dead weighs heavily on my mind.

The army lost three prisoners, and discounting their usual exaggerations, I figure a minimum of three to four dead and six to eight wounded, as a result of the action.

Sánchez Mosquera did not have a radio, bazookas, or mortars when they surprised him. We've used a great deal of ammunition. Now we're waiting for the enemy in El Hombrito, ready to fight another battle, but with different tactics. This fight lasted twelve hours, from sunup to sundown; if they want to come here, they'll have several days of battle ahead of them.

It would help if you sent us some new supplies of weapons, if there are any. It's impossible for me to send you Pazos now. On other things, it's important you send me the key points you want me to lean on, since I don't want to make any statements in the newspaper without your consent. It would be advantageous to have a declaration signed by you; we'd print several thousand copies. We'll soon be ready to do that. I've already taken precautions so that nothing will be lost if they enter El Hombrito, except our stupendous bakery, which is impossible to take with us. The guards are close by. They're fighting with enthusiasm, even though Sánchez has been deserted by twenty of his men and his column is decimated.

When we took the first truck, we found two dead men and one wounded, who was still making fighting gestures in his death agony. He was finished off without being given the opportunity of surrendering, which he could not do because he was only semiconscious. This barbaric act was committed by a combatant whose family had been annihilated by the Batista army. I reproached him severely for this action, without realizing that another wounded soldier, who had covered himself with blankets, was listening immobile on the stretcher in the truck. When he heard this, and the apologies our comrade was making, the enemy soldier made his presence known by asking that he not be killed. He had been shot in the leg, had a fracture, and remained at the side of the road while the battle continued on other roads. Every time a soldier passed him, he would scream, "Don't kill me! Don't kill me! Che says he doesn't kill prisoners." When the battle was over, we took him for emergency treatment, and he remained there until he could return.

CELEBRATION OF FIDEL'S LANDING   Santiago, December 2

On December 2, the first anniversary of the *Granma* expeditionaries was commemorated. In keeping with the main plan, the streets of Santiago de Cuba were bustling, reminiscent of past days of liberty. From ten to twelve in the morning and from four to six in the evening, a vast multitude of people moved about happily, visiting shops and the central area with the joyousness of other times. During the morning hours, traffic had to be detoured while a deployment of forces maintained a strict vigilance. At San Félix and Enramadas, a huge number of people met at the appointed time to cut the "anniversary cake" publicly and chatted between drinks and overt merrymaking. And so Santiago expressed its feelings and longing for freedom, shared by all of Cuba, which have been attacked by the bigwigs of the regime for a long time. In other words, the Revolution managed to bring the city back to a normal rhythm for a few hours, during which it recalled the heroic gesture that fired the entire country to rebellion, whose epilogue is very close at hand.

DANIEL [RENÉ RAMOS LATOUR]

Letter to Aly [Celia Sánchez]   Santiago, December 5

We just received a lot of news a few minutes ago. I'm profoundly sorry not to be able to enjoy these brilliant victories. On the one hand, the death of someone who was for me more than a comrade, a beloved brother, Juan Soto: the unforgettable—Juan, who stood at my side in the underground revolutionary struggle, and who later insisted on accompanying me when I decided to join the troops in the Sierra. And also the death of Ciro, who, besides being a brave leader, was extraordinarily valuable to the Revolution. And, on the other hand, those "three points that have infuriated Alejandro [Fidel Castro]"—analyzed like this, superficially, disregarding a reality that does not seem to get through to the rugged forest of the Sierra Maestra—they are more than enough reason for us to feel discouraged.

And I'm surprised that you, Aly, who knows about the gigantic and heroic struggle of the plains, have come to such inaccurate and mortifying conclusions.

You say that postponing the burning of the sugarcane plantations made it possible for the soldiers to invade the Sierra. And consequently, that the blame for the death of two brave comrades and for the consumption of so much material in the battles that have been waged so successfully since November 8 should fall on our heads.

1. I arrived in Santiago November 3, because the documents couldn't be obtained from Alejandro before, and he thought I should wait for them.

2. As soon as I arrived, I concentrated on the innumerable tasks that had accumulated during the eighteen days I was away. Mainly, this was organizing a group of men and equipment, that we had decided to ship to the Sierra before beginning any preparations to facilitate their arrival.

3. Here one doesn't have, as you do there, men who are poorly armed. On almost every occasion, we have to risk carrying out an action *without any arms* and in the *sure knowledge of what awaits us*. None of these circumstances existed in the action on the eighth in that zone.

However, on November 28, after six meetings, one in each province, the burning of the sugarcane plantations was begun. And with the burning of the sugarcane, the most brutal repression began. Because of this, scores of victims lie dead throughout the length and breadth of the country. They were also revolutionaries, they were also militants of the 26th of July Movement, but they did not have the good luck to die in battle, and instead were vilely assassinated because they had no weapons in their hands. But this reality is only seen from here, from below.

The results of the burning of sugarcane plantations, up until now, have been quite satisfactory, despite the victims, whose deaths grieve us greatly, though they cannot be attributed to a simple change in date.

We intend to send more concrete details in future reports, but we can say that enormous stretches of sugarcane plantations have been burned in Pinar del Río, Las Villas, Camagüey, and Oriente provinces. In Camagüey, there are several sugar mills that can no longer function, and in Oriente Province, the burning has extended to Banes, Mayarí, Contramaestre, Palma, Bayamo, Guantánamo, San Luis, and Tunas. The Soledad mill (in Guantánamo), the Santa Ana (in San Luis), and the Mabay (in Bayamo) can no longer process the cane. At this moment, the burning continues all over the country, and the number of dead is also on the rise. Many peasant houses in the plains have also burned down.

In addition, the battle in the cities is intensifying. All sorts of actions are planned to shake up the country until the desired climax is reached, paving the way for the general strike.

Cowley's killing was in line with a plan drawn up in August and carried out by the Action chief in Holguín, with two other militants. The four of them were able to flee with weapons. However, scores of people have been arrested, including the Finance chief, an extraordinarily capable man who made Holguín one of the municipalities that contributes most to the national Treasury. You can categorically discount the lies of the jokers whose only talent is to get up here and tell malicious tales, but who do nothing for the Revolution.

Elsewhere, our action units at Nicaro managed to interrupt the activities of the nickel plant for thirty-six hours. It is owned by the U.S. government. They did this by placing a charge of dynamite in the electrical cables, which caused an explosion that was heard as far as Preston (several miles away). This also took place on the twenty-eighth, at night. More than two hundred employees were arrested, among them some higher-ups in the company: engineers, technicians, etc. It has caused a big stir.

I won't go on about the pacts or unity with other political and revolutionary sectors, since I entirely subscribe to what Darío [Armando Hart] said in his letter to Alejandro. However, I wish to make it clear that I repudiate the pact as much as you and Alejandro, because in my short but intense political-revolutionary struggle I have served in the ranks of only one organization or party: the 26th of July Movement. Before the rise of the Movement, I could never imagine any group capable of enough moral force to sustain both the principles and aspirations in the heart of every young Cuban who loves his country and feels the need to transform our republic and its political, economic, and social system radically.

DARÍO [ARMANDO HART]

Letter to Aly [Celia Sánchez]   Santiago, December 6

I am tasting the bitterness of incomprehension. Every day I seem to have a better understanding of the reason for the failures of two great revolutions, the 1895 and the 1933. Never have I better understood Frank País than in a letter to Karín [Haydée Santamaría], written on the occasion of his brother Jossué's murder, he said: "Perhaps it's all for the best, because we don't know what fate has in store for any of us." We watch in sorrow as our finest comrades fall.

However, Aly, we thought you were going to keep your promise to return. Without your very able collaboration, they have had to make superhuman efforts to keep the supplies going to the Sierra. Because of this, Daniel [René Ramos Latour], who could have been doing other things, has had to put much extra time in to make up for your absence. Don't they understand that in the mountains? I, on the other hand, have been endlessly checking all the organized cadres of the Movement and urging them on. If you think all this work is unnecessary, then that raises the question of whether we should consider ourselves members of the present Directorate solely as the instruments for supplying the Sierra, and leave to the future Príoses and Hermidas to carouse about the island as they please, leading the people astray, and living off the Revolution. If such are the thoughts in the Sierra, then you would have to acknowledge that the Revolution will not occur during our generation, and I, to fulfill an obligation of conscience, would settle for being a simple soldier in the 26th of July Movement. We think we have a duty to organize the workers, to strengthen civilian resistance, to build provincial and municipal cadres with real revolutionaries, who, together with the Revolutionary Army of the Sierra Maestra, will guarantee the accomplishment of our program. We must also help the militia, which, outside the Sierra Maestra, without resources or arms (all that we have had were sent to you) have heroically succeeded in extending the Revolution beyond the boundaries of the Sierra Maestra and have created an organization that you, as much as ourselves, are duty-bound to protect.

Concerning unity, it would seem to be a serious political error to have broken publicly with what Felipe Pazos had subscribed to—since he is the very person Alejandro [Fidel Castro] had set so much store by, to endorse publicly, in the name of the 26th of July Movement, the most important political document of this stage. We would not dare make a public declaration of disagreement without first consulting Fidel, which is what we are now doing through your good offices. It is easy to say that we should have rejected it publicly when Herbert Matthews was in the picture, as well as the Inter-American Press Association, and international public opinion, but we depended on the sound judgment of the tough militants of the Movement, which had always rejected the pronunciamentos of unity. However, we would have done it, if it were not for the fact that we were assured that either this pact would become what was proposed by the Sierra Manifesto or we would be able, then, with greater reason, to reject it as pointless.

My opinion is now quite clear: if the basic tenets of the Sierra Manifesto are not accepted within a few days, we must put forth a barrage of propaganda against the Junta de Liberación.

I think I'm the most radical of all of us (circumstances force me to make this statement) in the area of revolutionary thought, and I take historical responsibility for what we've done. And I must beg Alex that if the propositions of the Movement are not accepted, then we must start a brutal onslaught against the Príoses and the other supernumeraries. If Alex is prepared to take this step, it will be one of the happiest days of my life. He has an extraordinary ability of knowing exactly the right political moment to make radical statements. We are ready to go beyond the proposals of the Sierra Manifesto and to return to the programmatic points of *History Will Absolve Me*. I tell you that only by doing this will we be able to liberate ourselves from the mistakes that Pazos and Bienvenido [Léster Rodríguez] have made.

CHE GUEVARA

Report to the Commander [Fidel Castro]   Sierra, December 9

We got full vengeance for the loss of El Hombrito by killing at least three guards on the Alto de Conrado. The victory didn't come gratis, since we could not capture a single weapon and a rifle was lost.

Alejandro Oñate was wounded in the shoulder, and I got a bullet in the instep of my foot, which is still there and prevents me from walking. For the moment, Ramiro [Valdés] is taking command of the column and is going with most of the men to a place that the person delivering this letter will reveal. Rapid help with .30-'06s and .45 automatics would be most timely. I'm safe here in a well-prepared ambush. I'm terribly sorry not to have heeded your advice, but the morale of the men was quite low, as a result of the useless comings and goings they were subjected to, and I considered my presence on the front lines absolutely necessary. For the most part, I took good enough care of myself, and the wound was accidental.

The beating we gave them was impressive; and it can be gauged by twelve definitive losses, among the dead and prisoners, not counting the wounded. The results were less brilliant in regard to taking arms.

If we see one another, or if I have a chance to write at length, I must tell you of my complaints about the Directorate. My suspicions have reached the point that I think there is direct sabotage against this column or, more directly, against me. I view of this fact, I think that there are only two solutions for me: to act sternly to prevent steps of this type, or to give up my command, pretending physical incapacity or whatever seems best to you. This consideration is not dictated by depression about the defeat that abandoning El Hombrito implies, since I had already spoken to Ramiro of the problem before our retreat. The facts are a little too subtle to be able to give you conclusive proof, but you'll have the chance to read the letters from there, in which my important, urgent requests are answered by three-page letters that latch onto one paragraph of mine, in which I did nothing but carry out orders given to me by passing visitors.

The situation has calmed down, and there is no news of other troops in the area, except for a small garrison at Marverde, which I dare not order an attack on because our ammunition is short. I'm enclosing the proclamations produced by the "genius" of Capote, which I had distributed as widely as we could manage.

FIDEL CASTRO

Letter to the National Directorate of   Sierra, December 14
the 26th of July Movement
to the Cuban Liberation Juntas

These weeks have been the most strenuous and busiest since our arrival in Cuba, because on Wednesday, November 20, our forces had to withstand three combats during one six-hour period—which gives an idea of the sacrifices and efforts our men have undergone without the slightest help from any other organizations. It was on that day that the surprising news and document containing the public and secret basis of the Unity Pact were received in our zone of operations. In this, we were informed that the pact was endorsed in Miami by the 26th of July Movement and these other organizations I now address.

The 26th of July Movement did not designate or authorize any delegation to discuss said negotiations.

If the organizations you represent had considered it essential to discuss bases of unity with some members of our Movement—especially because those bases fundamentally altered the positions endorsed by us in the Sierra Maestra Manifesto—such bases could not be made public in any way as a final agreement without the knowledge and approval of the National Directorate of the Movement.

While the leaders of the other organizations who endorsed the pact are abroad fighting an imaginary revolution, the leaders of the 26th of July Movement are in Cuba, making a real revolution.

To leave out of the unity document the express declaration rejecting any kind of foreign intervention in the internal affairs of Cuba is evidence of lukewarm patriotism and of a cowardice that is self-incriminating.

To state that we are against intervention means not only to demand that there be no intervention in favor of the Revolution—because it would be detrimental to our sovereignty, and even detrimental to a principle that affects all the peoples of America—but also to demand that there be no intervention in favor of the dictatorship, no sending of planes, bombs, and modern weapons to keep the dictatorship in power, and from which no one but ourselves, and most of all, the peasant population of the Sierra have suffered with their own flesh.

The unity document also omits the express declaration rejecting any type of military junta to govern the republic provisionally. In America, experience has shown that all military juntas eventually lead back to autocracy. The worst of the evils that have lashed this continent is the entrenchment of military castes in countries with fewer wars than Switzerland and more generals than Prussia.

If there is no faith in the people, if their great reserves of energy and fighting spirit are not to be trusted, then no one has the right to take their fate in his own hands and twist it and lead it astray at the most heroic and promising moment of their republican life.

Martí said that the methods of revolution are always secret, but the ends must always be public. In the same spirit, the 26th of July Movement cannot accept Secret Provision No. 8, which says: "The revolutionary forces will join the regular armed forces of the republic, with their weapons."

In the first place, what is meant by revolutionary forces? Can a police, navy, or army card be handed out to whoever shows up at the last minute brandishing a weapon? Can uniforms be issued to dress up agents of authority who keep their weapons concealed today, and pull them out and flash them only on the day of triumph, and keep their arms crossed while a handful of compatriots takes on all the forces of the tyranny? In a revolutionary document, are we going to make room for the very seed of gangsterism and the anarchy that were derided in the republic not so long ago? Our experience in the territory our forces control has taught us that maintaining public order is one of the country's major problems. Facts have shown us that as soon as the existing order is destroyed, a series of floodgates is opened, and crime, if not checked in time, flourishes everywhere. Severe measures if applied promptly, with full public consent, put an end to the outbreak of banditry. Before, the people were used to considering the agent of authority an enemy of the people and would give refuge to anyone pursued or to any fugitive from justice, simply out of hospitality. Today, they consider our soldiers the defenders of their interest, and complete order reigns and its best guardians are the citizens themselves.

Anarchy is the worse enemy of the revolutionary process. It is of fundamental importance to combat it from now on. Anyone who does not wish to understand that is indifferent to the fate of the Revolution.

The military importance of the struggle in Oriente has been badly underestimated. At this time in the Sierra Maestra, what is being fought is not guerrilla warfare but a war of opposing columns. Our forces, inferior in number and equipment, take maximum advantage of the terrain, and maintain a continuous watch over the enemy and the greatest possible mobility of forces.

The entire populace is stirred to revolt. If they had weapons, our detachments would not have to patrol any zone.

The leadership of the struggle against the tyranny is and will con-

tinue to be in Cuba and in the hands of the revolutionary fighters. Anyone who wishes to be considered a leader of the Revolution now and in
the future must be here in the country, directly facing the responsibilities, risks, and sacrifices demanded at this moment in Cuba.

The exiles must cooperate in this struggle, but it is absurd that they
should try to tell us from the outside what peak we ought to capture,
what sugarcane plantation we should burn, what sabotage we have to
carry out, and when and in what circumstances and manner we can
launch the general strike.

If our conditions are rejected—the disinterested conditions of an organization whose sacrifices are exceeded by no other, an organization
that is not even consulted, whose name is not mentioned in a manifesto
of unity that it did not endorse—we will continue the struggle alone, as
we have up to now, with no weapons but those we take from the enemy
in every battle, with no support but the long-suffering people, with no
sustenance other than our own ideals.

Because after all is said and done, it has been the 26th of July Movement alone that has been and is carrying out actions all over the country. Only the militants of the 26th of July have brought rebellion from
the wild mountains of Oriente to the western provinces. Only the militants of the 26th of July have committed sabotage, executed Batista's
thugs, burned sugarcane plantations, and carried out other revolutionary actions. Only the 26th of July Movement has been able to organize the workers all over the country for revolutionary action. It is also
only the 26th of July that has today been able to undertake the strategy
of strike committees. The 26th of July is the only sector that cooperates
with the organizations of the Civilian Resistance Movement, in which
the civilian sectors of almost all the localities of Cuba are united.

Let it be understood that although we relinquish any claim to position or power in the government, it must also be understood that the
militants of the 26th of July do not relinquish and will never relinquish
orientation and leadership of the people—from the underground, from
the Sierra Maestra, or from the tombs to which they are sending our
dead. And we do not relinquish our role because it is not merely we ourselves, but an entire generation that has a moral duty to the people of
Cuba to provide substantive solutions for their great problems.

And alone we shall know how to overcome or to die. The struggle
will never be tougher than it was when we were only twelve men, when
we did not have an organized, a populace inured to war throughout the
Sierra, when we did not have, as we do today, a powerful, disciplined organization throughout the country, when we could not count on the
support of the masses, now made evident at the death of our unforgettable Frank País.

To die with dignity, one has no need of company.

DANIEL [RENÉ RAMOS LATOUR]

Letter to Che Guevara   Santiago, December 14

I trust you have received most of the ammunition sent you. I think that as far as the .45, .22, and .12 and .16 cartridges go, you are well supplied. We are continuing our search for .30–'06s, .44s, and the other kinds requested. I assure you I have gotten to the point of desperation when I receive one request after another from you, and I find myself practically powerless to remedy the situation. From Havana, where I pinned my greatest hopes, I received only 450 shots of .30–'06; from Guantánamo, nothing. Everything I've sent you was acquired here in lots of 50, 100, or 200, paying whatever they asked. We are continuing to try to gather together a big quantity. If only all of it reaches you in time!

You know I'm a tenacious defender of organization in the strictest sense of the word. However, now that I've tried to get you the ammunition you asked for, and as swiftly as possible, I've come up against irresponsible people, delays, indecisiveness, etc., and I realize why you latched onto Piferrer and others, who could get you what the Directorate at Bayamo could not.

Within a few days, you'll be getting 200 coats, 75 pairs of woolen underpants, 150 pairs of socks, the new mimeograph, and some other things that we're sending you.

P.S.: Darío [Armando Hart] left for the Sierra. I suppose you'll see him.

CHE GUEVARA

Letter to Daniel [René Ramos Latour]   Sierra, December 14

I have to answer you to put some order into things, since I'd like certain murky aspects of our relationship to be cleared up. I beg you to consider all this as an attempt to improve and define our relationship. The good of the Revolution demands it.

From the—let's call it administrative—branch, only the 2000 pesos have yet arrived. As I told them in my previous letter, I was forced to follow a credit system, vouched for by one of our good backers, Ramón Pérez (Ramonín), whose signature is worth several thousand pesos. Right now, I am told that a messenger with bullets will arrive, and I have to wait.

Of what I received, basically only the 1000 .30–'06 bullets and some .45 bullets are of interest. The M-1 cartridges are also good. Everything else is necessary but not basic. The .44 bullets are missing and also those for the Cracket, which would put several more rifles into operation. But effort was made and quite rapidly; that's what we need.

As regards Piferrer, that letter was addressed to him. You say you don't know if it was good luck or bad that it fell into your hands. Neither can I know it yet; but I know that those things were to arrive, and we need them. If they come, nothing is lost, and if they don't, then it's a shame. I think I sent you the newspaper, even though it doesn't appear in the list I checked, but it seems to me I marked one margin in ink to call your attention to it. Nor do I know if I recommended it to you or only suggested it. One thing I'm sure of is that I thought Piferrer could act from Bayamo, and I didn't see how it could interfere with anyone. When I wrote, or rather, when I began to write, I had every intention of accepting all the objections that are constantly being made about "centripetal" activity. I did it because I was impelled by my spirit of discipline, but I was very disappointed by the turn things were taking in respect to the unspeakable pact signed with Prío and the others—a pact that you yourself laughed at in Los Cocos. This brings things to a point that I have determined to clarify with all of you. Fidel is aware of it, too.

Because of my ideological background, I belong to those who believe that the solution of the world's problems lies behind the so-called iron curtain, and I see this Movement as one of the many inspired by the bourgeoisie's desire to free themselves from the economic chains of imperialism. I always thought of Fidel as an authentic leader of the leftist bourgeoisie, although his image is enhanced by personal qualities of extraordinary brilliance that set him above his class. I began the struggle with that spirit: honestly without any hope of going any further than the liberation of the country, and fully prepared to leave when the conditions of the later struggle veered all the action of the Movement toward the right (toward what all of you represent). What I never counted on was the radical change that Fidel made in his basic ideas in order to accept the Miami Pact. It had seemed impossible, and I later found out that it was—that is, that the intentions of someone who is an authentic leader and the sole motivating force of the Movement could be altered that way and I thought things that I am ashamed of having thought.

Fortunately, Fidel's letter arrived during the intervening period, while we were waiting for the bullets, and it explained how what can be called a betrayal came about. Moreover, Fidel says that he has not received any money, only some bullets in poor condition and badly armed men. If things have come to that, why should I renounce contacts who offer me the opportunity to get supplies so as to get on with this? For the sake of a supposed unity, which is rotten at the core, and for the National Directorate that betrayed its agreements with the one I recognize as supreme leader? Piferrer may be a shady character, but the person who maneuvered the Miami Pact is a criminal; and I consider myself capable of dealing with Piferrer because I never sacrifice anything, although I receive little. In Miami, on the other hand, everything was sacrificed and nothing was received: all that happened was that an ass was yielded up in what was probably the most detestable act of "buggery" in Cuban history. My name in history (which I mean to earn by my conduct) cannot be linked with that crime, and I hereby put that on record.

Naturally, I am writing this so that one day there will be evidence to verify my integrity, but because of the common task that unites us and the sense of duty I have, this letter should not go beyond the two of us, and I am willing to cooperate in every way to achieve the common goal. If this letter pains you because you consider it unfair or because you consider yourself innocent of the crime and you want to tell me so, terrific. And if it hurts you so much that you cut off relations with this part of the revolutionary forces, so much the worse. One way or the other, we'll go forward, since the people can't be defeated.

You're right regarding the electrical tools: one was for the hydro-electric power and the motor was for the bakery and other things. It's not worth buying anything now, for El Hombrito is as flat as a board, with forty houses burned to the ground and all our dreams are broken. Since my last letter we had two more battles, besides several exchanges of fire of minor importance. In the first one, we killed a corporal and it seems there were a couple of wounded. Nothing happened to us, but we left El Hombrito. In the second encounter, we killed three or five. As for us, two were wounded, one of them myself, in the foot—it's not serious, but I can't walk at the moment. If José Márquez is the man from Palma, he's the one that came, recommended by the leaders there. If not, then I have to find out who he is. Send definite confirmation so that I can deal with him when he comes.

I am enclosing the newspaper and the proclamation. You will see what you want to do with them. They are the fruits of an intense sacrifice by many people. If you think it's worth the effort, we need paper galore, ink, stencils, and a stapler. If you are interested in a photograph of Ciro, let me know. I am enclosing some letters from militants.

Despite the tough tone of this letter, I'd be pleased if you would give me an explanation. It's up to you.

Greetings.

CHE GUEVARA

Letter to Fidel Castro   Sierra, December 15

They've now left El Hombrito to us, free, though somewhat reduced in value. Not one of our houses was left standing. I figure thirty houses were burned now, plus the forty that were burned before.

At this very moment, the messenger arrived with your note of the thirteenth. I confess that it, together with Celia's note, filled me with peace and happiness. Not for any personal reason, but rather for what this step means for the Revolution. You well know that I didn't trust the people on the National Directorate at all—neither as leaders nor as revolutionaries. But I didn't think they'd go to the extreme of betraying you so openly. That's why the confirmation of the news of a pact of this kind left me cold, but before I made a final judgment, I glanced through your letter, which, as I've said, is a great comfort to me.

I think your attitude of silence is not the most advisable at this time. A betrayal of such magnitude clearly indicates the different paths they're taking. The enlightening Welles* report that Ramiro [Valdés] is carrying in his knapsack will give you an idea of who is pulling the wires behind the scenes. We unfortunately have to face Uncle Sam before the time is ripe. But one thing is clear, the 26th of July, the Sierra Maestra, and you are three separate entities and only one true God.

I think a written document, with the invaluable help of the new mimeograph that's on its way (or even with the broken-down one we now have), sent simultaneously to political leaders and published in the press, will produce the necessary effect. Later, if it becomes more complicated, with Celia's help, we can fire the entire National Directorate.

If you have the written document, I promise to run off ten thousand and distribute them all over Oriente and Havana; it might even be possible to cover the whole island.

It's important you send all the facts of battles, promotions, etc.

As you will see, this issue of the newspaper turned out quite a bit better than the previous one, and its tone can be raised still more.

I was on the point of breaking off contact with Piferrer because of all the National Directorate's accusations, but keeping the contact seems an act of self-preservation, even if I don't rank him as one of my personal pets.

I sent Israel to carry out the mission you entrusted me with some days ago, and also to look for an electric detonator to mine the roads.

The position of the enemy troops is the same as ever, except for those from El Hombrito, which went as far as Las Minas, took ammunition, and are now at Yao. Sánchez Mosquera is in command and he has told anyone who will listen to him that he's not leaving the Sierra until he finishes me off. We'll see if we can't make trouble for him.

The bullets just arrived. More hullabaloo than anything else, but a thousand .30–'06s got here, which I appropriated in their entirety. You'll figure out how to distribute them.

I have thirty fighting men I've set up with the automatic 150s and Springfield 110s. I'm enclosing a photograph of Ciro, the last. It's very natural. Keep it.

I'm waiting for news of your latest victories and plenty of war mate-

---

* Sumner Welles (1892–1961).—ED.

riel. My foot is completely healed, but I still can't stand on it. The morale of my troops is magnificent.

A heartfelt embrace.

DANIEL [RENÉ RAMOS LATOUR]

Letter to Che Guevara   Santiago, December 19

I just received the letter that you yourself describe as "tough" and whose contents simply surprise me, but in no way hurt me, since I am so far from considering myself a traitor to the Cuban Revolution and so deeply satisfied with my short, but pure and correct, revolutionary life, that I would never be affected by any comments from people like yourself who do not know me well enough to judge me.

I must make it clear that I answer you because of the respect, admiration, and good opinion I have always had toward you, which has not changed in the slightest despite your words. However, essentially, I answer you for the same reasons that you gave—to provide proof in writing with this letter, so that when the day you mention comes, any servant of humanity, like you and me, will also have the "evidence to verify my integrity," and my revolutionary purity, which is no less than yours or Fidel's, or that of anyone else who is participating with a true spirit of sacrifice in this cruel struggle to liberate a people and lead them along paths that will speed their evolutionary progress and secure for them their higher destiny.

Be assured that never, no matter how painful or wounding the expressions used against me are, and no matter from whom, they will not be sufficient to deter me from my intention always to make the maximum effort—to the extent permitted by the difficult conditions prevailing here and of which you are unaware—to supply a revolutionary force comprised of Cubans of diverse origins, who are firmly united in a common ideal; a revolutionary force I respect and admire, and to whom we feel obligated, above and beyond any ideological or political differences there may be between us; in short, a force that is neither yours nor mine, but is the Cuban Revolution.

I also want you to know that whatever is sent here is considered to be addressed to the entire National Directorate of the Movement, which consists of a small group of comrades who vow to be integrated and united and not to make unilateral decisions. For that reason, your letter has been read by the other members of the Directorate, and my answer is from all of us.

As for the disparaging way you acknowledge receipt of the supplies, we must say that whatever reaches there is the result of an effort by a great many Cubans who work with enthusiasm and in the face of terrible risks—first, to acquire the money, and then the goods themselves, and finally to move them to the Sierra, while outwitting the vigilance of hundreds and hundreds of soldiers and knowing that if they are caught, they will be viciously murdered—because here we don't have the chance to die in battle, heroically; we don't have the weapons needed to give to the people who carry out these jobs. It is a pity that many comrades have had to give up the bullets from their pistols and revolvers, which are essential to them, since they would at least enable them to die fighting. And it is painful taking weapons away from comrades who are as revolutionary and as militant as anyone else in the 26th of July Movement, every bit as much as those who are fighting bravely up there. Though they obtained these weapons at much sacrifice, they turn them over to us out of an extraordinary sense of discipline and generosity, as in the case of the comrades from Mayarí, who, after overcoming a thousand obstacles, managed to take fourteen or fifteen rifles (some from an attack on a barracks full of guards, and others that had been lost by the murdered expeditionaries of the *Corintia*), all of which they brought to us for the Sierra. Now, completely unarmed, they are forced to burn sugarcane plantations and must confront an army that we all know is absolute master of the situation down here, an army that runs no risks and, consequently, is far more effective and its bullets much better aimed. But that does not matter, since this goes no further than ourselves, who stay here because we consider it necessary, though it runs counter to our desires. Our only wish is to share in the heroic battles in the mountains, and we will always be ready to do the utmost to supply our men, without considering whether or not they recognize our efforts, because we are aware that we are fulfilling an inescapable duty to the people and we are driven by our own convictions and principles.

I told you before that you did not know me well enough to form a real judgment about my ideological or political background. I am not the slightest bit interested in where you situate me, nor will I even try to make you change your personal opinion of us. Therefore, all I am writing here is by way of leaving this testimony of which we spoke at the beginning.

I've known your ideological background ever since I met you, and I never found it necessary to make reference to it. Now is not the time to be discussing "where the salvation of the world lies." I want only to make our opinion clear, which, of course, is completely different from yours. I believe there is no representative of the "right" on our National Directorate, but only a group of men who aspire to advance the liberation of Cuba. The Revolution based on the political thought of José Martí (who wandered through the countries of the Americas) found itself frustrated by the intervention of the U.S. government.

Our fundamental differences are that we are concerned about bringing the oppressed peoples of "our America" governments that respond to their longing for Liberty and Progress, governments that will be cohesive units that can guarantee their rights as free nations and make themselves respected by the big powers.

We want a strong America, master of its own fate, an America that can stand up proudly to the United States, Russia, China, or any other power that tries to undermine its economic and political independence. On the other hand, those with your ideological background think the solution to our evils is to free ourselves from the noxious "Yankee" domination by means of a no less noxious "Soviet" domination.

We believe that by overthrowing the dictatorship of Fulgencio Batista *through action from the people,* we will be making a step forward on the road we have outlined.

However, we know that you feel the same as we do about the necessity of fighting to rid our countries of administrative corruption, militarism, unemployment, poverty, illiteracy, poor health standards, lack of social rights, and a great many other ills of our peoples, and that the attainment of these objectives is of the essence to safeguard the progress of the American republics.

As for me, I can tell you that I consider myself a worker. I worked until I gave up my salary in order to join the revolutionary forces of the Sierra, and at the same time, gave up studying social science and constitutional law, which I had undertaken in the hope of preparing myself properly to serve my people better. I am a worker, but not like those in the Communist Party who concern themselves deeply over the problems in Hungary or Egypt, which they cannot solve, and are unwilling to give up their jobs to join the revolutionary process whose immediate goal is the overthrow of an opprobrious dictatorship.

And now let us talk about the *unity.* Before the 26th of July Movement, I never belonged to any political party or organization. I rejected all the Auténtico governments as immoral, and I thought little of the Ortodoxo Party as an organization capable of going anywhere or of bringing reality to the aspirations and longings of the people of Cuba. I saw in it only a group of men hovering around a more or less well intentioned caudillo, but a leader just the same, lacking a well-defined program and doctrine.

I think that the only positive aspect of the fatal coup of March 10 was to rid Cuban public life of the political schemers who made up those parties.

Since this is my point of departure, I never regarded Fidel's pact with Prío sympathetically before November 30, and much less now, after what Felipe Pazos has tried to do, which is far more negative because it attempts to crystallize a coalition just at a time when the 26th of July Movement—after a year of battle during which we have left many of our most solid revolutionary values by the wayside—has succeeded in unifying the majority of the populace and establishing itself as the basis for all possible solutions. And above all, at a time that Batista's govern-

ment, because of the increase in revolutionary action, has found it necessary to apply the most barbarous measures—suspending all rights, three
times in a row, not human rights, which were never respected by the tyranny, but invoking the most iron-clad press censorship in Cuban history—all of which is obvious proof of the weakness of the regime and its
inevitable demise.

This was and is my point of view, and if I had committed the crime
you accuse me of, I would have acted against my own way of thinking
and that of all the comrades of the Directorate, a way of thinking that
you and Fidel know very well, because I demonstrated it in El Coco and
it has not changed in the slightest.

When I came down from the Sierra, I found the documents of the
Unity Pact, which had been sent from Miami by Felipe Pazos and
Léster Rodríguez, asking the National Directorate's authorization to
sign them in the name of the Movement. At the same time, U.S. newspapers reached us; they reported that *Unity* had become a reality. I, likewise, saw the letter from the National Directorate to Pazos and Léster,
accusing them of having appropriated power that had not been granted
them and demanding that the conditions for unity come closer to the
formula of the Sierra Manifesto, which would put the government in the
hands of civic institutions and at the same time make it known to the
Auténticos and other signatory organizations that we would never permit the revolutionary process to be directed from abroad and that we
would accept a war pact only on condition that arms our soldiers needed
would be sent to Cuba.

I don't think my indignation during those first moments was any
less intense than what comes through in your letter. Only I was not able
to accuse any member of the Movement in Cuba of a crime that was
planned and executed by Felipe Pazos, who has been in the Movement
only during the time he spent in the Sierra, where the famous Manifesto
was signed. Nor did he ever belong to the National Directorate, nor was
he named by it to represent the Movement abroad.

As a revolutionary, I would have preferred a noisy, public break
with the so-called Unity and a barrage against Prío and all the signa-
tories of the pact. However, I considered the attitudes of the other members of the directorate correct. They thought it was neither good politics
nor good tactics to put into effect a type of radicalism that all the directors of the Movement supported, while the basic tenets of the Sierra
Manifesto still prevailed, since they were the basis on which the civic institutions of the country were working at that very moment.

Frankly, my desire is that Unity be irretrievably broken, but to do
that, it is necessary for us to decide, once and for all, where we are heading and what we propose. For that reason, Armando Hart went to the
Sierra, and I hope that he and Fidel will come to an agreement that will
satisfy everybody.

All the materials you asked for should have reached you by now. You can send us a list of what you're missing.

As you allude in your letter to some of Fidel's opinions, I think it is necessary to send him a copy of your letter to me, as well as my reply, in order that everything may be clarified.

I hope this letter will put an end to our sterile polemics, as we have both expressed ourselves with complete sincerity.

And let us continue to work together, as we have up till now, for the triumph of the Revolution.

With my esteem.

EDITOR'S SUMMARY

Sierra Maestra, Army–Confidential: Major Pedro Castro Rojas to President General Batista

The High Command decided to carry out its military operations in the Sierra Maestra, after the action failed in Belic to trap F.C. and his group, who had managed to take refuge in the Sierra Maestra.

Said operations began on January 29 of this year, when the High Command put a Joint Operational Plan into effect (Army, Navy, and Air Force), as a result of the events of La Plata and Llano del Infierno. When this was carried out, F.C. had only 26 men, and twice they were at the point of perishing in the zone of Caracas, according to information brought in by the spy Eutimio Guerra. Immediately afterward, the second phase of the plan was begun, in which a maneuver was executed from north to south, with boundaries from Manacal to El Turquino, troops leaving from Estrada Palma, and a Regimental Combat Team crossing the Sierra as far as the coast. The outcome of this maneuver was that the small group of rebels disbanded (information obtained from the prisoner Reinaldo Benítez, while General Cantillo witnessed the interrogation), F.C. and his General Staff remaining completely hidden and nonoperative. Meanwhile, it appears that the M-26-7 was working secretly on a policy of winning goodwill and operating actively, not in the Sierra, but in different urban zones. Immediately, the third phase of the plan began, in which sectors were set up from Manzanillo to Santiago de Cuba, in order to control the comings and goings of elements sympathetic to the rebel movement.

Once the inoperativeness of the rebels in the Zone of Operations was verified, the High Command decided to demobilize the troops and end operations, at the same time holding a press interview in which both the national and foreign press took part. When this happened, F.C. immediately felt called upon to give signs of life to different publications regarding his person. Taking advantage of the demobilization of the troops, he began to gather various elements around him, with the help of his sympathizers from the outside world and by using deceptive propaganda among the peasant population. He made contact with a North American journalist, managing to have a showing of a film made from El Turquino, which was highly propagandistic. This was extremely vital for him in order once more to build his personality up in both national and foreign spheres, since he and his personality had become almost totally forgotten.

UNDERGROUND ACTIVITY   Havana, December 24

Action militias of the Movement carried out a rapid and effective series of activities that brought the regime's euphoria to a sudden end. Twenty-seven bombs exploded in the city and neighboring areas, damaging houses, informers' automobiles, and public facilities.

The regime's hypocritical Christmas Eve could not be celebrated.

Trinidad, December
In reprisal for the intensive burning of sugarcane plantations in this municipality, Captain Guerrero of the rural guard arrested seven men from this city. They were found hanged a few days later on the highway to Cienfuegos, a little over a mile from Trinidad, at the place known as Puente Azul.

CARLOS FRANQUI

From a political standpoint, the Miami Pact was serious. The rupture of that "unity," nurtured by the U.S. State Department and the bourgeois sectors of the opposition, omitted two key points of the Sierra Manifesto in its text: no Yankee interference and on the refusal to accept military juntas. Fidel's document opposing it was quite to the point, in fact, extraordinary. The two people responsible for this pact of betrayal were Felipe Pazos and Léster Rodríguez. The Sierra and the underground units were equally responsible for designating them representatives.

Felipe Pazos, the former president of the National Bank, was a prestigious member of the Cuban bourgeoisie. Pazos made a brief visit to the Sierra in July 1957 and Fidel drew up and signed the manifesto with Pazos and Raúl Chibás, leader of the Ortodoxo movement.

The Sierra Manifesto was a step backward as regards the famous *History Will Absolve Me*, which had been more radical and anti-imperialist. This was intelligent temporizing on Fidel's part. Léster Rodríguez, one of the leaders of the attack on Moncada, whose group Raúl Castro commanded during the combat, was an able person with good contacts outside the Movement, and it was he who obtained almost all the weapons for Frank País's attack in Santiago, on November 30, backing up Fidel's landing from the *Granma*.

Caught inside the barracks, Léster abandoned the mortar and was taken prisoner. He was freed when his term was up, and by mutual agreement Frank and Fidel sent him abroad as military affairs representative because of his experience in acquiring arms. And there he did two extremely serious things: using his Moncada veteran's signature, and without Fidel's and the National Directorate's permission, he endorsed the Miami Pact and he let himself be inveigled into a phantom expedition by ex-President Prío, which cost the Movement and the Cuban people 200,000 pesos, because it was financed with revenues collected by extraordinary sacrifices for the purchase of crucial weapons. This loss affected the Sierra as much as it did the underground. The people who came out against the Miami Pact from the very beginning were: Raúl, Che, Evelio Rodríguez, Julio C. Martínez, and Carlos Franqui, in exile, Daniel [René Ramos Latour] and his comrades of the underground National Directorate.

FIDEL CASTRO

Order of the Day   December 31

Distribute cigars among your men in combat lines; it is a little painful to waste things on people who are not very secure, although I know there are many good people there. In any case, send twenty boxes.

1958

12. JANUARY–MARCH: FROM THE UNDERGROUND TO THE SECOND FRONT

FIDEL CASTRO

Letter to the Leaders in Santiago   January 13

On two consecutive occasions, I have categorically ordered the return of the four comrades, who right after the attack at Veguitas, went, without any justification, to Santiago de Cuba, and both times I have received the same answer: they cannot be sent.

I can't imagine what they hope to achieve by such irritating procrastination. It's necessary to get things straight, including the duties and prerogatives of each and every person in the Movement.

The weapons that these comrades have kept illegally have been out of action for a month, and we still don't know when we will get them. This is simply criminal, when the lives of men are constantly being risked in the search for weapons, and is particularly painful when one takes into account the complete lack of provisions and the total failure of every arrangement to remedy this. It is enough to make even the most imperturbable man lose his patience. Mine in particular, since I'm already at the end of my rope after a series of incidents that have occurred these last months, beginning with totally forgetting a list of things requested (from mortars to lettuce seeds).

I am at the point of asking the Movement not to bother about us any more and to abandon us to our fate and leave us on our own once and for all.

I'm tired of having my feelings misinterpreted. I'm not meanly ambitious. I do not believe I am the boss, nor do I want to be, nor am I irreplaceable or infallible. All the honors and responsibilities don't mean a damn to me. I'm disgusted by men when they set out to attain those offices; they stamp out any interest I may have in these chimeras. And I'm even more disgusted by stupid prejudice, the blindness of fanatics, who have no comprehension of standards, as well as the hypocritical zeal of the eternal pharisees.

Why go on? My poor country, so thick-headed, and incompetent! Yet, what big shots we think we are!

DANIEL [RENÉ RAMOS LATOUR]

Report to Alejandro [Fidel Castro]   Santiago, January 13

At 8:00 p.m., on the night of the tenth, the driver who had twice accompanied Darío [Armando Hart] and Tony [Javier Pazos] showed up. He told us that at about noon that day, as they were approaching Bueycito, their jeep broke down because of a damaged part. The five of them got out and went to a nearby house, where they were solicitously cared for by some peasants. He went on to say that at that point, Tony ordered him to go to Bueycito or Bayamo to get a new part and, once the car was repaired, to continue on to Santiago, while they would go by train, possibly arriving here before the driver himself. He did what he was told, and when he returned, the peasants told him that they had gotten a ride in a passing truck and had left in the direction of Bayamo. The peasants had advised them not to stay there, since five members of their family were prisoners.

When we saw the trains arriving that evening without Darío and the others, we became alarmed. We got in touch with Bayamo and asked them to begin investigating. We also sent the driver with two people who know our contacts in Bayamo, Yara, and Manzanillo, and we alerted all the people who keep us informed about the internal activities of the regime. A normal state was reported everywhere, but in spite of our intense search, they did not appear. At 1:00 a.m., on the twelfth, we learned that Javier Pazos and "another important person" had been arrested and that documents had been seized. From that moment on, we mobilized all the people who were in a position to keep the worst from happening. Havana was informed and from there the news was relayed abroad. At 8:00 a.m., on the twelfth, Felipe Pazos made an appeal that his son's life be guaranteed. Around 2:00 p.m., Chaviano* received an order from Batista himself to spare the life of Pazos' son, but that "Armando Hart was to be killed like a dog in a feigned battle on the outskirts of the Sierra." I don't have to tell you what that hideous sentence meant to all of us. It was extremely hard for me to keep calm and not do something idiotic. While we were pressuring the civic organizations, the consular corps, and the citizenry by telling them the whole truth and making Batista's *order* public, our men managed to take over a local

---

* Brigadier General Alberto del Río Chaviano, Commander of Oriente Province.

radio station that was broadcasting a meeting of liberals. They interrupted the program and reported that Armando had been taken prisoner and Batista had ordered him killed in simulated combat, and they exhorted the people to prepare for struggle.

With all this barrage of mass and institutional resistance, the assassin general saw that he was cornered, and he found it impossible to carry out the disgraceful action he had ordered.

This morning a radio station in Havana gave the news that "three outstanding revolutionary leaders had been arrested in Santiago de Cuba." I suppose this is in response to my request to Fausto [Faustino Pérez] that a national station broadcast the facts.

Now they tell me that the order has been revoked; that Chaviano will transfer the arrested men to Havana. This morning a person close to him, who has behaved with great skill, was able to talk with our flashy little "general," who said that "he had the three of them and that he would reject any intercession on behalf of the prisoners." He also said U.S. Ambassador [Earl E. T.] Smith had sent several telegrams asking to be informed as to their whereabouts and he had answered that he didn't have them, that it was all a fairy tale. Moreover, he admitted that Armando had been beaten a lot because he was "such a wise guy," but thought he was a "nervy fellow."

The Manifesto* has made an enormous impact nationally and internationally, and everyone has received it favorably, especially the very tough militants of the 26th of July Movement. The Ortodoxo Party supports the pronunciamento unconditionally. However, the Student Revolutionary Directory made some unfair declarations. Among all the leaders and responsible people here, the only ones who disagree and say that the letter has frustrated major operations with Prío, are Léster [Rodríguez] and Jorge [Sotú].

FIDEL CASTRO

Letter to Félix Pena   Sierra, January 15

After the arrest of Armando Hart, the courageous efforts made by our comrades in the Movement in order to save Armando's life—mobilizing civilian institutions and diplomatic bodies, taking over a radio station to broadcast Batista's order "to kill him like a dog," etc.—seem, for the moment, to have been successful.

It's essential they take great pains to bring this mission to the proper outcome.

---

* Fidel's rejoinder to the Junta de Liberación and the Miami Pact; see pp. 265–67.

We'll have to compensate for Armando's arrest, which seems to have given them a new impetus.

News on the radio has it that a battle occurred around California and El Hombrito, with twenty-three rebels dead. They were probably peasants.

We must give them a lesson, once and for all. It's enough to make one go mad merely thinking of the horrors committed by these people.

I hope the Browning you got has given the boys even more courage.

KARÍN [HAYDÉE SANTAMARÍA]

Letter to Aly [Celia Sánchez]   Havana, January 19

You can't imagine what the repression here in the plains is like! It's really frightening; I think we'll all end up prisoners, one by one, or something worse. Aly, even though it's impossible for you to be here, you can imagine the work. I can tell you that Daniel [René Ramos Latour], as well as everyone else, is trying as hard as possible to meet your requests. The dentist arrived, and he'll go where you ask.

We're sending 4000 pesos. We wanted to send more, but we're afraid.

They seized the notes Armando had on him, but so far can't make them out. He's the only one who can understand them.

RAÚL CASTRO

Letter to Fidel Castro   January

Thursday, the twenty-third, at 11:30 a.m., the boys told me that the radio station at Manzanillo, on the Masferrer program, had "accused me of plenty, also Che," and that they were referring to a letter that had been seized. The same day, on Díaz Balart's program, they devoted their editorial to the same topic (I'm explaining this to you because I don't know if you heard it). They attack me personally, just as they do Che; as for you, on the other hand, they say they don't believe you're a Communist. I heard this editorial, and I came to one conclusion: that the letter Armando Hart wrote to Che, which was not sent because of your order, had been seized in Bayamo. In this editorial, they said the letter was one I wrote to Che. I knew that was wrong, since the one I had written to Che had been sent with Antonio, his messenger, who left from Arroyones, and I didn't talk about Stalin or any other damn thing in it. I remembered, on the other hand, that Armando did say something on this topic. And last night on a program introduced by Díaz Balart himself on CNC, my suspicions were confirmed, and if you heard it, you'd have certainly come to the same conclusion. At first I thought that Armando, finding himself in this mess, had blamed me, but it was nothing more than a governmental distortion of the truth. Last night Díaz Balart's exact words, more or less, were "a letter confiscated from an arrested leader," and he makes no mention of me, which confirms everything. It seems that Armando wanted to keep the letter to show it to the other comrades on the National Directorate and that's where the shit hit the fan, with all the predictable consequences.

I'll keep advancing little by little.

FIDEL CASTRO

Letters   January 28

The dictator is starving ten thousand families living in rebel territory. Our answer was to confiscate the herds belonging to a number of army officers who have grown wealthy by cheating, and we have distributed the cattle among the peasants.

A certain English magazine asserts that we are receiving reinforcements from the Russians via submarines, which are landing weapons on the east coast of Cuba at night.

The magazine is very badly informed. The Russian reinforcements are received by means of remote-controlled intercontinental projectiles, and moreover, the little Russian dog "Laika" is on the Sierra Maestra, and they haven't mentioned that.

Sierra, January 30

We have an enormous quantity of TNT on hand that was taken from airplane bombs that did not explode because the fuses didn't go off. We have manufactured very powerful hand grenades with this material.

The idea has occurred to us, and it seems perfectly feasible from our knowledge, that we could manufacture mortar projectiles and a kind of bazooka.

We have a lathe here already, also a gasoline motor; but we need an oil motor, if it's possible to get one. And we need disks for the lathe.

In order not to get involved now in the work of casting, we can make projectiles from corrugated metal or aluminum sheets, or some other heavier metal that is also easy to handle.

Havana, February

New street demonstrations in Havana—at the corner of San Rafael and Galiano. The bulk are students. On the sidewalks and in doorways were scattered pamphlets from the 26th of July Movement calling on the people to overthrow Batista's tyranny.

February 2

We are overjoyed to learn that another group of Cubans is also fighting in this province.

Whatever its revolutionary affiliation may be, we have given instructions to extend all possible help.*

We want to know the situation where you are. At such a distance, there is little we can do for you, but we want to express our most sincere solidarity.

We consider it essential in this fight against tyranny that this front be held at all costs. We can imagine there will be obstacles to deal with initially. If the topography of the zone makes it impossible to hold out or if you run out of ammunition, we advise you to move in our direction, walking at night and taking cover by day in places where you can't be spotted by aircraft; follow a zigzag route. When the enemy has fallen into your ambushes once or twice, you will no longer be pursued; you can advance 15 to 20 miles every night. We have a patrol situated between Bayamo and Victoria de las Tunas that can be useful. We will try to intensify the campaign in order to relieve the pressure. The bearer of this message can inform you of details and experiences of interest to you. I await news. We wish you every success on this front and we send your brave combatants a fraternal greeting.

Pino del Agua

Pino del Agua is a sugar refinery on the top of the Maestra close to Pico la Bayamesa. It is defended by Captain Guerra's company, which is very well entrenched and armed. It is the most forward point on the Sierra Maestra. The objective of the attack was not to take the settlement, but to encircle it, which would force the army to send troops to its aid. The positions of the nearest troops were as follows: in San Pablo de Yao, Sánchez Mosquera's company, about ten miles away; in El Oro, Captain Sierra's company, some five miles away; and about twenty miles away is El Uvero, with its navy garrison; the other places from which reinforcements might come were Guisa and Bayamo. Our forces were posted on each of the roads that led from these points to Pino del Agua.

At 5:30 a.m., on the sixteenth, Column 4, under the command of Captain Camilo Cienfuegos, launched the attack. It was carried out with such force that the guard posts were taken without any difficulty, while occasioning eight enemy deaths, four prisoners, and several wounded men. From that moment on, the enemy resistance intensified, and our lieutenants Gilberto Capote and Enrique Noda were killed, as

---

* This was the expedition of Revolutionary Directory led by Chomón and Rolando Cubelas.

well as Comrade Räimundo Lien; Comrade Angel Guevara was so badly wounded that he died several days later in our field hospital.

The siege lasted all day. Forces moved up from El Oro—seventeen men in all—to reconnoiter in the direction of Pino del Agua. These forces were taken by surprise and totally wiped out; three badly wounded prisoners were left behind in peasants' houses because it was impossible to move them. The leader of the column, Second Lieutenant Evelio Laferté, was taken prisoner. Only two men, apparently injured, were able to escape; the rest died in the action.

The enemy had from eighteen to twenty-five dead, an equal number of wounded, five prisoners, and they lost thirty-three rifles, five machine guns, and a large quantity of ammunition. Our troops sustained the casualties mentioned, plus three wounded—one of them Captain Camilo Cienfuegos—all of them lightly.

The entire ambitious plan conceived by the General Staff of our army was not fulfilled in Pino del Agua, but a victory was gained over the regular army, which further damaged its already waning battle morale.

To Che Guevara

If everything depends exclusively on the attack on this side, without support from Camilo and Guillermo, I don't think you should take any suicidal chances because there's the risk of heavy losses and of not achieving our objective.

I seriously urge you to be careful. You are strictly forbidden to assume the role of a combatant. Take charge of leading the men well; that is indispensable at this time.

EDITOR'S SUMMARY

In February, forty of the fighters of the 26th of July, including Che, Raúl Castro, Ciro Frías, Félix Pena, Manuel Fajardo, Camilo Cienfuegos, Efigenio Amejeiras, Humberto Sori Marín, Universo Sánchez, and Calixto García, addressed a plea to Fidel to end his active participation on the battlefield, and to safeguard his presence for the fulfillment of the Revolution, of "the illusions and hopes that rest on you, of yesterday's generation, today's, and tomorrow's. In the full awareness of this, you must accept our plea. . . . Do it for Cuba. For Cuba, we ask one sacrifice more."

The kidnapping of world car-racing champion Juan Manuel Fangio, on February 23, 1958, by members of the 26th of July in Havana resounded throughout the world.

Fangio was to race on the highways of Havana the following day. He was ab-

ducted from his hotel, treated courteously, and freed after the regime had been held up to ridicule.

Fangio later declared that he had no complaint to make:

I wish to state officially that during my friendly kidnapping, my treatment was always warm and cordial. I was asked only to forgive them this situation, which had nothing to do with me.

This daring act could not be censored by the Cuban press, and the resulting national scandal seriously weakened the regime.

FIDEL CASTRO

Communiqué   February 27

Captain Raúl Castro Ruz has been promoted to the rank of major and named head of Column 6, which will operate in the mountainous territory to the north of Oriente Province, from the municipal boundary of Mayarí to that of Baracoa. The rebel patrols operating in said zone will be under his command.

FIDEL CASTRO

Letters
To Herbert L. Matthews, *The New York Times*

We have had the great pleasure of receiving your friend Mr. Ricart, who has made extraordinary efforts to fulfill his mission.

I do not want him to return without conveying an expression of our profound and everlasting friendship for you.

We have made great progress since you did us the honor of your unforgettable visit.

We eagerly await the opportunity for our people to be able to render national homage to all the brave journalists who, with their generous and noble pens, are helping us to regain our freedom.

You and your colleagues have performed a greater service for the United States than all its diplomats and heads of military missions.

The words written on behalf of the people in these terrible days of oppression will be eternally appreciated.

I believe that we will soon have the pleasure of saluting you in a free country.

To José Pardo Lladó, Havana   Sierra Maestra, February 28

You know my writing, so you will have no doubt about the authenticity of this letter.

Since I consider it a legitimate right of the Cuban press to be informed about all matters of national interest and for these matters to be loyally divulged to the people, I write these lines in order to ask publicly that all organs of our press, spoken and printed, send us a commission of journalists and then tell the Cuban people what they are interested in knowing: our attitude at this decisive moment through which our country is going.

People talk of peace, and it is said that the whole nation desires it; that thousands of families, whose sons are fighting on one front or another, long for it. It has been asserted that rebels on the Sierra Maestra have set specific conditions for peace. Our first condition toward peace is that all Cuban journalists be permitted to come to the Sierra Maestra.

Peace must be preceded by the truth: the right of the press to report the truth and the right of the people to know the truth.

With the request that you publish this letter without any delay or omission, I remain yours very fondly.

EDITOR'S SUMMARY   Havana, February 28

Six Cuban bishops, led by the archbishop of Santiago, issued an appeal to the country for an end to the upheaval the civil strife was causing:

The Cuban episcopate contemplates with profound sorrow the lamentable state of affairs to which our republic has been brought, particularly in the Oriente region. Hatred grows, charity wanes, tears and grief permeate our homes, the blood of our brothers flows throughout our countryside and in our cities. We do not doubt that those who truly love Cuba will know how to answer before God and before history, ready for any sacrifice to achieve the establishment of a government of national unity that can prepare for a return to a normal and peaceful political life in our land.

FIDEL CASTRO

Letters to the News Director   Santiago de Cuba, March 9
of Station CMKC,
Free Cuban Territory Sierra Maestra

The Cuban episcopate should define what is meant by a "government of national unity."

The ecclesiastical hierarchy should explain to the country whether it considers it possible for any honorable and respected Cuban to be ready to sit on a council of ministers provided over by Fulgencio Batista.

This lack of definition on the part of the episcopate is enabling the dictatorship to carry out measures that will lead to collaborationist and counterrevolutionary negotiations.

Consequently, the 26th of July Movement categorically rejects all contact with the conciliation commission.

The 26th of July Movement is interested only in expressing its thoughts to the people of Cuba and, therefore, reiterates its desire to do so before a commission of representatives of the national press.

To Father Sardiñas*   Sierra, March 9

You speak of a pistol that you learned of through reports. Just tell me if I am also supposed to know about all the offers of arms not brought to my attention.

I have never concerned myself with these details, nor am I able to do so. Ask me about the hundreds of weapons taken from the enemy and I can tell you where each and every one of them is.

Your mission is religious and humane, and I gladly offer you my help in it, although it has nothing to do with revolutionary activity.

RAÚL CASTRO

Letter to Fidel Castro   March 9

I'm leaving this evening and everything's ready. I'm about to leave Enrique's encampment in order to join the motorized team. I've given Almeida two days head start. Enrique will send you 200 detonators, wicks, and some mortar shells that they have stored here; I don't know the exact quantity. I'm taking along some dynamite charges, 100 detonators, and some Molotov cocktails.

I was really surprised by how much work Enrique had accomplished here, the seriousness and discipline in carrying out everything. All his gunners are good men, and the affection that all the civilian population feels for them is obvious throughout the zones I've crossed—all of which I've already told you in my previous note sent to Che. This zone has little forest covering, but actually it's not essential. The enthusiasm and collaboration shown by civilians is far greater than any we've experienced up to now. Although the shops here and in nearby villages haven't received provisions for a long time, there's still a good supply of merchandise. Only vegetables are scarce and they are brought in by mules. The economic position, the bravery and calm, even the mentality of the people is superior to the peasants over there. People here help the Revo-

---

* A priest who obtained permission from his archbishop to leave his parish on the Isle of Pines and join Castro's forces.

lution. Enrique is respected by everybody, and people anxious to help him come from everywhere. Communications are perfect and quick, the jeeps come up to the camp itself. Anything at all from Contramaestre, Palma, even Santiago, comes in a matter of hours. Yesterday, I talked here with the Action chief from the Movement in Palma. He impressed me greatly and offered his cooperation. I think that the trip I'll be starting this evening will go off without any hitch, since the contacts I made through Enrique were of vital importance. The gunners here outclass us in many aspects of technical organization. They even have connections with *owners of small aircraft,* who can carry any urgent message about troop movements in a few hours. Little by little, I'll tell you all that there is here. As for informers, not a one. Almeida is wild with joy about what he's seen here. Since he left two days ago, Enrique will catch up with him tomorrow after I go. The gringo here is a fellow about twenty-six years old (the other one went to Santiago), and he fought in the Korean War. He's brave in battle and gives military training to the boys. With Enrique's dynamite, we made an M-26 today and tried it out; the test was very satisfactory. They'll be able to make about 200 M-26s with it. The gringo was making a test for me with a battery that consisted of two small electrical wires. The dynamite, along with its detonator and wick, is set up, a resistor in the form of a cross is connected to the wick, which is connected in turn with two wires (positive and negative), one of them already connected to the battery, and when the second wire is connected, a current is generated in 3 seconds. The resistor in contact with the wick becomes red-hot, and this ignites and produces the explosion. In the test we made, it took 5 seconds from the time we placed the second contact until the explosion went off. The battery was automobile current. I still don't know the exact results of the battle at Estrada Palma, though I gather from the news that it turned out very successfully. Congratulations!

FIDEL CASTRO

Letters   Free Territory of Cuba, Sierra, March 9, Sierra Maestra

The National Directorate of the 26th of July Movement, meeting in the encampment of Column 1, General Headquarters, unanimously agreed to support Judge Manuel Urrutia Lleó as provisional president of the republic. They agreed also to communicate this information to the Committee in Exile and to Dr. Manuel Urrutia, expressing the recognition of our organization for the actions of the committee and the future president.

To Comrade H[ubert] M[atos]   Sierra Maestra, March 13, 5 p.m.

I have just received and studied your report of March 9. I'm enclosing a letter for the president,* which should be presented to him as soon as possible.

I must tell you there is not a single soldier on the coast between El Uvero and Pilón. At those two places, there are garrisons. The Sierra and a good part of the plains surrounding them are controlled by us. There are rebel patrols on all sides.

I prefer simplifying any operation.

The airplane should arrive after 5:00 p.m., preferably near 6:00 p.m., but with enough light left to be able to see the landing area. The Cienaguilla zone, which is very flat, could be the point of arrival. No troops are there, and there will be more than enough time to unload and transfer everything, with the neighbors' help. It is important to arrive after 5:00 p.m., in order to avoid any later encounter with the air force. But the distance must be carefully calculated, so as not to arrive at night.

The plane could take off for Jamaica, or be destroyed. We're able to pay any indemnity. I cannot guarantee refueling.

We need .30-'06 ammunition for rifles and machine guns. If the president is favorably disposed, do your best to get us mortar shells of .30-'06 caliber, since we have the mortars but no shells. We also need several bazookas with a great many shells and, if possible, at least two .50-caliber machine guns and the ammunition for them.

You should bring as few people as possible, as we have more than enough combatants here. What is urgent are weapons and ammunition. Don't start making plans that would delay things. Everything has to be here on or about the twenty-fifth. Not after the thirtieth, in any case, and, if possible, before the twenty-fifth, which would be still better. I'm giving instructions to send you 5000 pesos more. Don't hold up anything for lack of money. Borrow, and any debt will be settled immediately upon your arrival.

I hope you will make every effort necessary, considering how valuable help is at this moment, since we're so close to fighting the final battle.

EDITOR'S SUMMARY   Havana, March 15

Before word of the March manifesto had reached Havana, recognition of Batista's waning support came from a broad-based coalition of more than thirty Cuban civic,

---

* José Figueres, of Costa Rica, where Matos was readying an airborne expedition for a landing in Cuba.—ED.

cultural, fraternal, professional, religious, and sports organizations. The United Cuban Institutions issued a proclamation "to the people of Cuba" seeking to end "the serious crisis" and "chaos" in the nation:

The time has come. The government, deaf to all demands and taking refuge in force, has provoked a stream of young Cuban men and women to exchange their schoolbooks for the trappings of a rebel. And it is this generation that is setting the standards for the country and making all the social classes its wholehearted admirers and supporters. The forces of the regime have mobilized against them for six agonizing years. Until now, the United Cuban Institutions have proposed formulas for a tolerant, civilized understanding. Now aware that the nation is in the process of dying, we are today asking calmly, that the present regime resign, since it has shown itself incapable of carrying out the normal functions of government and of fulfilling the lofty objectives of the state.

The proclamation called for the creation of a provisional government of national unity and subsequent general elections for a democratic government. It urged the citizens to "unite so as to resist oppression by exercising the rights of the Constitution granted to free men."

FIDEL CASTRO

Letters   March 16

Just what are we going to do about these guys God sends us? Around here there's absolutely nobody who knows a thing about anything. I'm trying to get this boy to do something useful; he's certainly willing to work. My swearing is famous around here. When I'm worn out, dead, he follows me around talking constantly about a thousand and one things and doesn't give me a moment to breathe. The only thing is that I can tell him to go to the devil, and he stands for it without having an attack of apoplexy. He's always putting his foot in it, but it doesn't faze him. Besides, he's not a philosopher or a theoretician of the Revolution.

This is all I have to say, so you won't worry, but also so you'll go on feeling sorry for me.

Havana, March 16

A hundred bombs exploded last night in the city of Havana, causing several thousand dollars' damage. The groups were active, both in old Havana and in Luyanó and the Vedado section. In a shoe store at 703 Monte Street, the violence of the explosion destroyed all the shopwindows and caused extensive damage to the merchandise. Shoes were tossed about and strewn on the ground. At the same time, acts of sabotage were reported in sugarcane plantations in Camagüey and Las Villas, in tobacco plants in Pinar del Río, in a warehouse at Manzanillo; other similar acts were carried out in different municipalities of the republic.

Antonio Fernández León and Angel Espino Sarmiento lived in the Santa Barbara housing development in Santiago de Cuba. They were students at a private school and neither of them was more than sixteen years old. They left their houses Saturday night in order to pay a visit. They were found shot to death on the so-called Island Road. Their deaths aroused a general protest among the civic institutions of Santiago and later caused a total paralysis of educational activities in all schools throughout the country.

EDITOR'S SUMMARY   Miami, March

A "Survey of Prospects for Our Movement in South America and the United States" was compiled by Carlos Franqui for the use of Fidel Castro and the National Directorate in Cuba.

Drawing on sources throughout the hemisphere, he reported extensive popular support in Ecuador, Venezuela, Bolivia, Colombia, Costa Rica, and the United States. In Brazil, forty young people had signed up to go to Cuba to fight. Parades, demonstrations, and fund-raising meetings for the 26th of July were held in many of these countries, though in Colombia, a "supposed major from the Sierra . . . had started a campaign to gather thousands of pesos," obliging the Movement to disavow him and recover the money. In the United States, Franqui reported "Great sympathy from the entire press; there are possibilities of reaching universities, labor unions, outstanding personalities, and some political sectors. Sympathy among the youth."

Franqui suggested that a "congress of students, workers, institutions, personalities, intellectuals, and people" could quickly be assembled in the Americas to urge an end to arms sales to Batista, a break in diplomatic ties, and recognition of free unions in Cuba instead of the Mujal-dominated CTC.

FIDEL CASTRO

Letters
To Panchita   March 18

I'm wearing the uniform you sent me. I hope to finish the campaign in it, since I think victory is close. But if it doesn't turn out that way, I know that neither of us, you or our people, will flag in our efforts, because no matter what sacrifices are needed to end this sruggle, there can only be one outcome: the triumph of the country.

March 23

The felling of trees is prohibited. This measure has been taken for reasons of military tactics and also for the safety of both peasants and rebels.

To Che Guevara   March 25

This is a complete fuck-up. Despite the fact that I'm desperately short of bullets, they sent the entire two thousand they had in Santiago to Almeida. The six thousand they said were coming here from Havana, which were procured by I don't know whom, have not shown up anywhere. Now they tell me they're being delivered from there.

When you're ready to attack, they tell you the bullets are a thousand miles away. I'm going ahead with the plans, no matter what.

If, by chance, the bullets reach you, send me at least four thousand, since Crescencio has 25 rifles, and almost no bullets.

I'm going to keep the machine guns in any old place. The only tragic news is that it seems they killed Lieutenant Chinea, the officer I told you about in an earlier message. The official dispatch says it was an automobile accident and that Salas Cañizares was wounded.

I suspect they went to arrest him and he tried to resist. I don't think it could have been anything else. I had already picked up the patrols wandering around there.

I was insistent with his wife (she came to visit me) that she be very much on guard against any arrest warrant and go around with an armed escort.

EDITOR'S SUMMARY

Though Batista had vowed to uphold the constitutional rights he had returned to the people on January 25, he reimposed his ban on March 12. And he announced that an additional seven thousand men would be recruited to combat the Revolution as Castro reported with some pride. On March 14 the U.S. government announced that it would send no more arms to Cuba.

In the midst of this mounting opposition to Batista, Faustino Pérez, of Havana, and other members of the National Directorate of the 26th of July, went up to the Sierra to meet with Fidel. On March 12, Pérez, in the name of the National Directorate, and Castro, as commander of the Rebel Forces, issued a manifesto and strike call "to the people of Cuba."

They noted that Batista refused to permit Cuban journalists to come up to the Sierra Maestra and deplored the total intransigence he displayed in the face of national chaos and bloodshed. They described the growing strength of the Rebel Forces, and their support by the people of the Liberated Territory who had suffered ruthless attacks on their homes and fields by Batista's forces.

In twenty-two points, they explained the purposes of a "revolutionary general strike" and the organizational structure it would require. Each sector of civilian society would be in charge of its own group, the FEU, for instance, heading the student sector. The Rebel Forces would meanwhile continue their pressure—"even if a military junta tried to seize the government power. On this point, the position of the 26th of July Movement is unyielding." Other measures of noncompliance with the regime were decreed: citizens were forbidden to pay taxes to the government on all levels.

A ban was announced on travel into Oriente Province, "starting April 1, for reasons of a military nature." Both new recruits and veteran members of the armed services were warned that from April 5 on, their persons and their weapons were subject to seizure by the people of Cuba.

In conclusion, the manifesto declared: "The entire nation is determined to be free or to perish."

His conclusions:

Our Movement and Fidel Castro have produced an enormous impact on hemispheric opinion, especially in South and Central America. We must study seriously and calmly the possibilities of making the 26th of July Movement into a continent-wide organization. The need proclaimed long ago by Bolívar and Martí for all the nations of America to become united might well find an adequate instrument in us. Our responsibility is now much greater. No longer does it extend only to Cuba; it now reaches all the Americas. Our comrades should be assured that the entire continent has its eyes on Cuba.

FAJARDO

We reached the place destined to be the Second Front at dawn on March 10, in Cape Rey, near the Miranda Sugar Mill. The first encampment was in Piloto Abajo. We had no encounters on the road; only we were severely punished by the air force. Then we camped in Piloto Arriba, in Yaguasí, in the Mayarí zone.

There, Raúl began preparations for organizing the Second Front. There were rebels in that zone—many gunners and many individuals from Manzanillo.

We also met Tomassevich and Villa, who are the heads of well-organized rebel groups. Tomassevich had taken Mayarí Arriba, and Villa had taken Nicaro.

There were partisans from the 26th of July from Santiago, organized by Daniel [René Ramos Latour]. Aníbal had taken the barracks at Yaguas, seized arms, just as Villa and Tomassevich had done. There were hundreds of gunners. Practically speaking, Frank's Second Front existed and was battling to reach us.

13. APRIL:
THE APRIL STRIKE

ENRIQUE RODRÍGUEZ LOECHE   Havana, April

For weeks now, Havana has been a tinderbox. Batista's followers are terrified; the population is worried by the bloodletting; the tension throughout the island at the bursting point. News and rumors are rampant.

Following the meddling declarations of U.S. Ambassador Smith, in Washington, announcing that Batista was doing away with press censorship, the dictator obeys and lifts censorship, allowing the newspapers to print news of revolutionary activity—which makes the whole island tremble. Thousands of bombs go off from east to west. There is a hurricane of news after months of silence.

There is not a single municipality in which a bomb does not go off, where a train is not derailed, a sabotaged electrical cable does not paralyze work.

The reprisals are bestial. Mutilations, torture, mass hangings. During February, revolutionary agitation increased. In the hills of the Escambray, a dozen tenacious peasants had been hanging on to a bivouac with old rifles, when Faure Chomón brings them a shipment of 50 modern weapons.

The total for the Escambray came to 50 Italian carbines, 2 Sten guns and a Thompson gun, 2 M-3s, 2 Springfields, a Garand, and an M-1, 5 semiautomatic Remington rifles with telescopic sights. Ammunition: 11,000 rounds for the Italian carbines, 2000 for the M-1, 2000 of .30-'06 caliber, and 5000 of .45 caliber.

The Italian carbines are in the hands of Cubelas, Abrahante, and Guin. During the few days without censorship, Cuba learned of the front opened in the center of the island by the Revolutionary Directory. In the northern part of that province, Major Víctor Bordón of the 26th of July mounts an attack.

Once again the dictator clamps on censorship. It is impossible to permit anyone to publish what is actually happening. The hair-raising account of the torture of a teacher, Ester Lina Milanés, and the involvement of that butcher, Esteban Ventura, shake the regime to its foundation. On March 13, exactly a year after the attack on the Presidential Palace, a Batista minister, Raúl Menocal, miraculously escapes after having been hit by half a dozen bullets. Havana once again asserts its active presence. The news that at Nuevitas an expedition of the Revolutionary Directory has landed filters through to the capital of the republic. Toward the middle of March, two of the most daring leaders of the 26th of July die in Havana. At the end of this month, three young leaders of the Revolutionary Directory, denounced by an informer called Pitaluga, are arrested in Havana. Pitaluga, as if by chance, manages to hand over the entire arsenal of arms that the organization had brought to Havana for a new attempt against the tyrant. Capture of this equipment on the beach of Santa Fe leaves us with scarcely enough arms for our personal defense. Meanwhile, from the Sierra Maestra, Fidel Castro announces to the entire nation that in the first week of April he will overthrow the tyranny by means of a general strike. Substantial withdrawals of funds are noted by Havana banks.

With the strike date announced, Batista brings to the capital one of the regime's most ruthless killers: Pilar García. This cruel soldier quickly readies a defense against the armed strike. The old fox orders armbands to be manufactured with the sign M-26-7 and also March 13,* which, discovered in good time, are rendered harmless by the two revolutionary organizations. At the same time, he obtains hundreds of automobiles with license plates from various parts of Cuba, each conveniently outfitted with a siren. The "guard dogs" are on watch. They lie in wait for quite some time before they try a massive hunt in the capital. Like a pack of hounds, they swoop down on all the working-class centers of the island's cities. The youth of Havana come out into the streets defenseless, without adequate arms. They don't even have a tree trunk behind which to hide. The struggle in the city is face to face, and the rebels have everything to lose. In Sagua, Matanzas, Oriente, Camagüey, throughout the entire island, the blood spatters. The new chief of police has just assumed command in the capital. And when, at nightfall, the jails are filled up with prisoners and the morgues are filled with dead, the voice of the murderers—of Reynold García and of the other brave men who attacked the Goicuría Barracks—is heard. The voice of Pilar García, not

---

* I.e., the 26th of July Movement and the Revolutionary Directory, which had attacked the Presidential Palace in Havana, March 13, 1957 (see pp. 147–69ff.), and had added that date to its original name.

yet satiated with blood spilled, imperatively orders his minions: "I do not want wounded men or prisoners, only dead."

Sierra, April 8

In response to the call put out by our Movement, advising members of the judiciary and of parastate organizations to resign their offices, seven judges of the Supreme Court handed in their formal resignations, explaining that said legal body lacked the moral attributes that it was created to uphold, and that it had demonstrated its inefficacy due to the dictatorial apparatus that misgoverns us.

STRIKE NOTICE   Sierra, April 9

Strike, Strike. Strike. Everyone on strike. Everyone into the streets. People of Cuba, the hour has struck. We must stop the tyranny of Batista, backed by the terror of its thugs and the traitorous strike-breakers, from keeping the public services running. We must prevent shops from opening; we must prevent traffic on the streets; we must prevent every move by the dictatorship. If they can count on terror and crime to maintain themselves in power, we can count on our courage and the rightness of our struggle.
We honor the people.
Strike!   Strike!   Strike!

To All Cubans

Transit of all vehicles and of strikebreakers must be blocked in front of your houses. Put obstructions in the streets surrounding your houses. Strew the area with nails, spikes, glass—anything that could obstruct the passage of vehicles of repression. Throw stones at all strikebreakers from your windows. Throw ignited Molotov cocktails at the patrol cars and the other police cars in the streets.

Radio Rebelde Report   April 9

An official communiqué from the Batista regime reports that in the city of Havana, the naval armory has been attacked and an intense small-arms barrage has occurred at La Rotonda, on the highway to Guanabacoa. The old section of Havana was without light due to the breakdown of an electric transformer, and an attack was made on radio stations CMQ, CNC, and Radio Progreso. The dead in all these actions amounted to seven persons, although the army of the dictatorship sustained "no casualties" whatsoever. The official communiqué goes on to say that at no time was public order disturbed. That's the regime's version. Despite all these events, or rather, despite the words of the official communiqué, public order has not been disturbed! What then does the tyranny think that disturbing public order means? A naval armory is assaulted, a firearms barrage is exchanged between the repressive forces and several individuals, Old Havana is without light, three radio stations are stormed, and the dictatorship, grown accustomed to crime and terror, describes what has happened as *unimportant*. Our armed militia is already facing Batista's henchmen. Throughout the island, there is a heroic response to the summons of the fatherland that longs to be free.

FIDEL CASTRO Sierra, April 10

At dawn today, the Batista regime announced some of the events that occurred in the city of Havana and in other cities of the province, as well as offering vague details regarding other uprisings and work stoppages in different places in Santa Clara.

But the despot continues to insist that perfect order reigns. The official communiqué states that there are more than twenty dead. While they say that, the population knows, on the basis of earlier manipulations with figures performed by the dictatorship, that the dead in Havana alone exceeds one hundred.

It is not just a matter of the assault on the naval armory and the radio stations, the small-arms duels in the streets of the capital and suburban roads, it is not merely that light and telephones have been cut off in Havana. All Cuba burns and erupts in an explosion of anger against the assassins, the bandits and gangsters, the informers and strikebreakers, the thugs and the military still loyal to Batista.

Sierra, April 11

A few days ago, in the Cienaguilla zone, an airplane landed [from Costa Rica, commanded by Hubert Matos], bringing a shipment of arms and ammunition to our forces in the Sierra Maestra. Despite the irregular terrain, the plane made a magnificent landing, unloading the shipment of arms without mishap. But because of damage to the motor it had to be set on fire to avoid falling into the hands of the mercenary forces of Batista, who appeared moments later but were repelled by our troops.

Sierra, April 13

In the hamlet known as El Pozón, on the highway about three miles from Manzanillo, a rebel patrol attacked a group of mercenary soldiers who were engaged in burning the houses of defenseless peasants, six of whom they killed. When our patrol put the incendiaries and killers to flight, reinforcements for the tyranny arrived on the scene from the Yara Barracks. Batista's loyal soldiers came to the battle zone in trucks and jeeps, falling into an ambush we had set. They lost twenty-three killed, and eight were taken prisoner. Almost all their weapons were seized. Our forces suffered two dead and three wounded.

Once again, they were surprised by the rebel forces, and we left them with twenty-five dead. All of which added up to a total of forty-eight dead and eight prisoners for the tyranny.

FIDEL CASTRO

Radio Rebelde Broadcast   Sierra, April 13

I have walked without rest day and night from the operational zone of Column 1, under my command, in order to keep my appointment with Radio Rebelde Radio Station, and make this broadcast.

It was hard for me to abandon my men at this junction even though it is to be for just a few days. But to speak to the people is also a duty and a necessity that I had to fulfill.

We feel sorrow when any adversary falls, although our war is the most just of wars, because it is a war for liberty. The Revolution is constantly growing; it is well known that what was a spark scarcely a year ago is today a flame that cannot be extinguished; that we are fighting not only in the Sierra Maestra—from Cabo Cruz to Santiago de Cuba—but also in the Sierra Cristal, from Mayarí to Baracoa; in the Cauto Plains, from Bayamo to Victoria de las Tunas; in Las Villas Province, from the Sierra del Escambray to the Sierra de Trinidad; and in the mountains of Pinar del Río. Heroic battles rage in the streets of cities and villages, but, above all, the people of Cuba know that the will and tenacity with which we started the struggle are unshakable; the people know that we are an army that emerged from nothingness, and that adversity does not dishearten us; that after each reverse, the Revolution has surged ahead with greater force; they know that the *Granma* expeditionary detachment was not the end of the fight but the beginning; they know that the spontaneous strike that followed on the murder of our comrade Frank País did not bring down the tyranny, but it did point the way to an organized strike.

You can see how the American dictators use the arms given to them by their friend, the United States, in the interests of "continental defense." An announcement is made that the sale of arms to the government of Batista has been canceled by the American State Department. But the result is in no way altered. The United States sells them to So moza and Trujillo. Somoza and Trujillo sell them to Batista.

If the dictators help each other, why shouldn't the people give each other a hand? Don't we sincere democrats throughout America have the obligation to help each other? Haven't we paid heavily enough for the sin of our indifference toward the concert of tyrants who promote the destruction of our democracies? Isn't it understood that in Cuba we are fighting a battle for the democratic ideal of our entire continent?

We Cuban rebels do not ask for food, we do not even ask for medicine; we ask only for arms to fight, for arms to prove that in America the will of the people is more powerful than the alliance of dictators and their mercenary armies.

Let the people of Cuba be assured that this fortress will never be vanquished, and we swear that the fatherland will be free or not one combatant will remain alive.

COMMANDER FIDEL CASTRO

Communiqué   Sierra, April 16

Major Camilo Cienfuegos is hereby named military chief of the triangle of land bounded by the cities of Bayamo, Manzanillo, and Victoria de las Tunas.

The duties of Major Cienfuegos are those pertaining to his rank, and include coordination of the different guerrillas operating in the zone.

His command also extends to the urban areas of the cities of Bayamo, Victoria de las Tunas, and Manzanillo, since he is to coordinate supply and sabotage actions in the cities.

It will be his responsibility also to organize agrarian reform and modify the civil code.

FIDEL CASTRO

Letters to Celia Sánchez   Sierra, April 16

The strike experience involved a great moral rout for the Movement, but I hope that we'll be able to regain the people's faith in us. The Revolution is once again in danger and its salvation rests in our hands.

We cannot continue to disappoint the nation's hopes. There are many things we must do, do them well and on a grand scale; and I will do them. Time will justify me one day. The story of the strike has been a repetition of the story of the sugar harvests. No one will ever be able to make me trust the organization* again.

The 200,000 pesos lost outside Cuba; in Pinar del Río, the seizure of

---

* The National Directorate of the 26th of July, until then run by the urban wing of the Movement.—Ed.

arms that should have come here; the fact that they were on the point of diverting those from Costa Rica to another zone—all suggest to me that I can never again rely on the organization to supply us.

At this juncture, I do not know if I have any jurisdiction or whether I can give orders to the militia or not; and as regards the funds collected by the Movement throughout the island, I do not know if I have the right to use any part of them.

I am the supposed leader of this Movement, and in the eyes of history I must take responsibility for the stupidity of others, and I am a shit who can decide on nothing at all. With the excuse of opposing caudillism, each one attempts more and more to do what he feels like doing. I am not such a fool that I don't realize this, nor am I a man given to seeing visions and phantoms. I will not give up my critical spirit and intuition which have helped me so much to understand situations before, and especially, now, when I have more responsibilities than ever in my life.

I don't believe that a schism is developing in the Movement, nor would it be helpful for the Revolution, but in the future, we ourselves will resolve our own problems.

The trip I made was very difficult, and I became ill on the road. Right now I don't know how I will get back. The hospital must be readied in case I have to be operated upon in a little while; if this continues, there is no other solution.

Sierra, April 20

Mobilizing the populace for a strike involves a technique of its own to which we must adapt ourselves, and it is one that is at odds with the secrecy, strictness, and surprise required by armed action; for the security of these surprise actions we sacrificed the mobilization of the masses. The success of an armed action may depend on many imponderable factors; but the mobilization of the people, when revolutionary consciousness has been brought about by the proper methods, is infallible and does not depend on chance.

In a revolutionary struggle, the strike is a formidable weapon in the hands of the people. The people cannot be led to battle (nor can an army) unless they are mobilized at the moment of battle.

And that was not the case on April 9. Moreover, the day chosen did not coincide with the peak of tension, which had occurred at the beginning of the month. It was a very hard lesson, which must not repeat itself, but we have not renounced the general strike as a decisive weapon against tyranny. We know how to wait for and be ready for the opportune moment. Then, our Radio Rebelde will be much more powerful, the militia will be better armed and better trained; it will be able to give the strike decisive support throughout the country. A battle was lost but not the war.

For Havana and all the cities of Cuba, that sad night of April 9, the sad night after our failure, was one of the most difficult moments of the Cuban Revolution. I thought of the streets, I thought of the patrol cars, those vans loaded with criminals, those vans filled with corpses, and that moment of general skepticism that follows a great defeat. It was not the only setback the Revolution had to suffer.

The Revolution has endured many sad days. The Revolution endured the disaster of the attack on Moncada. The Revolution endured the disaster of the attack on Goicuría. The Revolution endured the disaster of the uprising in Cienfuegos, of the landing of the *Corintia,* of the attack on the Presidential Palace, of the dispersal of the expeditionaries of the *Granma,* and of the abortive strike of April 9.

FAUSTINO PÉREZ

We always thought that the struggle would culminate in a general insurrection and a strike; that is, as the guerrillas grew in strength, the necessary conditions and consciousness would also develop, and that when the thing took place, there would be no problem with the masses— which is what happened.

The very organizational structure of the 26th of July Movement included someone from the workers' organizations, which was one of the most important factors. In the work centers, on the provincial executives, in the zones, and so on, there was always someone from the workers' organization preparing them for the strike, along with those responsible for propaganda, finances, action, etc.

As we went on, the development of the workers' organizations had its ups and downs. At times we received terrible blows, for we had to face police roundups, in which a number of key comrades were caught. And then we had to begin almost from scratch. At the time of Frank País's murder in Santiago de Cuba, July 30, 1957, a spontaneous strike took place; it spread from Santiago de Cuba to the very gates of Havana. But the strike did not catch on in Havana, and it abated without major consequences.

From this point on, we thought that among the people, and among the workers, the conditions necessary for the strike existed, but that we must develop the organization of the 26th of July Movement further, and we gave ourselves over to that task. We even developed the actions that we knew would contribute to developing a state of consciousness and opinion among the masses. And then, beginning around February of 1958, following the kidnapping of Fangio, when clandestine actions in the cities had developed enormously, we were able to carry out the Night of the Hundred Bombs, the blowing up of the refinery reservoirs, and the execution of some informers—things which helped to turn the tide. On the other hand, the murders carried out by the tyranny increased, and corpses were everywhere. All this created a situation in which, possibly, we were victims of a mirage, in thinking that conditions were ripe for the strike.

A manifesto was then issued calling on the masses to strike. It was in the month of March—March 12 was the date on the manifesto—and total war was to begin April 1.

But then there began a series of coincidences: we were awaiting arms from different places, which we were to receive before April 1. A shipment coming from Miami was intercepted on the high seas and confiscated by the Yankees; a launch with another shipment en route from Mexico arrived in Pinar del Río on April 11 or 12—we had expected it at the end of March; a delivery that was to be made in a village in Oriente was also delayed.

In our judgment, another factor was the timing of the strike call. A strike can be called several days in advance. One can say: There will be a general strike in forty-eight hours; and the people will know about it, everyone will know about it, and then the conditions are created. It is possible that the wave we saw ebbing in those days could have crested again if we had called for a strike and announced it forty-eight hours in advance.

There was also the following consideration: if we announced the strike, then the army, the regime, would have taken protective measures at a series of points that we planned to attack. We had a plan, for instance, to paralyze transport, to storm the radio stations and broadcast an announcement and then put them out of commission, as well as blowing up the electrical transformers.

Those who were partisans of strike action pointed out that any advance announcement would mean that the regime would guard the key points, and we would lose the advantage of surprise.

The thesis then prevailed—and we all accepted it—that we should make a surprise strike call, and at 11:00 a.m., on April 9, we took over the radio stations and issued a brief call for strike action, without any previous warning, the strike to begin immediately.

But the citizenry had not been informed about any of this, and we made a strike call at a time when everyone was at work and was not listening to the radio. The people began to hear about the strike call, indirectly, but they were not even sure of the origin of the call, and so the whole thing was confused and support was spotty.

One of the important actions was to blockade Old Havana, by means of traffic jams, and then to attack the armory. But the sequence was reversed. The comrades at the armory acted before the traffic jams could be arranged, before the streets were closed to paralyze traffic, and buses burned, etc.—all calculated to prevent the repressive forces from entering; that is, those already inside would stay there, but no one from outside was to get in.

Among those of us in the capital, there was another point of view— with which I could not agree—on the unity of all factions. It was not that we thought that other organizations should not participate; that was not the case. But there was no conviction, no enthusiasm for rallying other organizations that could have contributed, because we believed that they would not be important factors. We did not incorporate them into the strike leadership.

In any case, there were meetings, and we considered it right that they support the strike, but in these talks, different points of view were expressed—on the matter of the strike call, on the opportune moment, on the question of organizing the workers to a greater or lesser degree. But we had already gone over these questions and had already formed another view of the matter; as a consequence, there was no mutual cooperation in the action. We can say this much for our relations with the Partido Socialista Popular [PSP, Popular Socialist Party] and the 13th of March Revolutionary Directory, with whom we held dialogues: we were unable to reach any agreement on the question of integrating them at this time. The same thing happened with other organizations, and we believe that all this contributed to the failure of the strike.

In short, a whole series of factors, among which we must include the earlier loss of numerous cadres in Havana. And the deaths of Sergio González, Arístides Viera, Pepe Prieto, Julián Alemán, and many others had a serious negative effect on our attempt to overthrow the Batista tyranny definitively.

VILMA ESPÍN   Interviewed by Carlos Franqui, April

I was in the Sierra when Raúl came by on March 10. Raúl went one way, Almeida another, but we went toward Estrada Palma; then, after the meeting in which the strike was agreed on, I left. After the strike, the day before the meeting called by Fidel, I wanted to go to the Second Front to find out if Raúl was going to go to the meeting, or whether there was any chance he would go, and also to see if there was anything important to report.

Another thing I wanted to talk to Raúl about was to ask him for a contact in the group that had sprung up at the time of the strike. We had remained with the boys of the Action group, since the situation was so difficult that those up there carried out their actions and then had to regroup behind Puerto Boniato, near La Gran Piedra. From there, they marched off to the Second Front, as a column or a platoon.

They were very successful. They took all the weapons, forced the soldiers to flee, and left many dead among the guards.

Two of the boys had a bad fall near La Gran Piedra; one of them had a swollen knee, and the other a broken arm.

CHE GUEVARA   El Hombrito, April–May

Our mission at the time of the April strike was to maintain the front occupied by Column 4, which reached to the outskirts of the village of Minas de Bueycito. Sánchez Mosquera was quartered there, and our combat consisted of brief encounters in which neither party risked anything decisive. At night, we would fire on them with our M-26s, but they were well aware of the limited power of this weapon and had simply rigged up a large stretch of wire netting against which our charges of TNT—placed in empty cans of condensed milk—exploded and set off nothing but a big racket.

Our encampment was set up about a mile and a half from Las Minas, in a place called La Otilia, in the house of an absentee landlord. From there, we could watch Sánchez Mosquera's every move, and day after day, we would engage in strange skirmishes. The regime's thugs left at dawn to burn peasants' huts—from which they first looted anything of any value—and then withdrew before we could intervene; at other times they attacked our riflemen scattered throughout the area, putting them to flight. A peasant suspected of being in contact with us was a dead man, killed immediately.

I was never able to figure out why Sánchez Mosquera allowed us to remain comfortably installed in a house, in the middle of a relatively flat area, devoid of vegetation, and did not call in enemy aircraft to wipe us out.

One day, I went with an adjutant to see Fidel, who was then at Jíbaro; it was a long trip, almost an entire day. After staying with Fidel for a day, we set out the next day to go back to our quarters at La Otilia. For some reason I no longer remember, my adjutant had to stay behind, and I had to take a new guide. One part of our route crossed an auto road and then went through undulating farmlands covered with pastures. In this last stage, when we were already close to our house, we were suddenly presented with a rare spectacle, brilliantly illuminated by the light of a full moon: in one of those undulating pastures, with a few scattered palm trees, there was a row of dead mules, some with their harnesses still on.

When we got off our horses to examine the first mule and saw the bullet holes, the expression on my guide's face when he looked at me was straight out of a cowboy movie: the hero of the film who arrives with his pal and sees a dead horse, usually killed by an arrow, and mutters something like "The Sioux," and puts on a face to go with the circumstances. That was how my guide's face looked to me, and perhaps my own wore the same expression—not that I was much concerned with looking at myself. A few yards farther on, the second mule, then the third, the fourth, the fifth dead mule. It had been a convoy with supplies for us, captured by a patrol sent out by Sánchez Mosquera; I seem to remember that a civilian had also been killed. My guide thereupon declined to accompany me any farther; he claimed he didn't know the terrain, and he simply got back on his horse, and we parted amicably.

I was carrying a Beretta, and I kept it cocked as I led the horse by the reins through the first coffee plantation. When I reached an abandoned house, a terrible noise startled me so much I almost fired at it; but it turned out to be only a hog, frightened, by *my* presence. Slowly and very cautiously, I crossed the few hundred yards that separated me from our position, which I found totally abandoned. After a lot of searching, I found a comrade asleep in the house.

Universo, who had stayed there in command of our troop, had ordered the evacuation of the house because he foresaw some nocturnal or early-dawn attack. Since our men were well deployed around the house, I lay down to sleep along with the solitary comrade. The only meaning this whole scene has for me is that of the satisfaction I felt at having overcome my fear during the course of a journey that had seemed endless until I finally reached the command post, alone. That night I felt brave.

But the toughest confrontation with Sánchez Mosquera took place in a small village or hamlet called Santa Rosa. As always happened, it was dawn when we were warned that Sánchez Mosquera was there and we hurried to the place; I was a bit down with asthma and so was mounted on a bay, with which I had made friends. The battle was being waged at several scattered sites. It became necessary to abandon my mount. My men and I took possession of a small hillock, positioning ourselves at two or three different levels. The enemy fired off some preliminary mortar fire, without really aiming. Then the fire on my right intensified, and I made my way to those positions, but when I was halfway there, it also intensified on my left. I sent off my adjutant somewhere, and I stayed alone between the shots. On my left, now, after some mortar fire, Sánchez Mosquera's men began climbing the hill to the accompaniment of some unbelievable yelling. Our men, lacking experience, managed to fire only an isolated shot, and then set off at a run downhill. Alone, in an open pasture, I could see nothing but some soldiers' helmets. One of the enemy guys began to run down the hill after our troops, who were running into the coffee plantations; I fired my Beretta without hitting him, and almost at once, several rifles sighted me and began firing. I began to run in a zigzag fashion, carrying on my

back a thousand bullets in an enormous leather cartridge box, greeted
by obscenities from the enemy all the while. As I reached the cover trees,
my pistol fell. My only worthy gesture of that dismal morning was to
stop, retrace my steps, retrieve my weapon, and start running again,
again greeted by the enemy, but this time amid little clouds of dust
caused by the impact of their bullets. When I decided I was safe, with no
knowledge of my comrades or of the result of the fight, I stopped to rest
behind a big rock in the middle of the hill. My asthma, showing great
pity, had allowed me to run a few yards; but now it took its vengeance
and my heart was jumping in my chest. I heard branches being broken
by people approaching. It was no longer possible to flee (which is what I
really felt like doing); but this time, it turned out to be another lost comrade, a recent recruit to our troop. His words of consolation were more or
less as follows: "Don't worry, Major, I'll die with you." I didn't feel like
dying and was tempted to tell him something about his mother. But I
don't think I did. I felt like a coward that day.

A magnificent comrade, whose name was Mariño, had been killed
on one of the skirmishes; the rest of the action turned out to be pretty
poor. The corpse of a peasant with a bullet through his mouth, killed for
who knows what reason, was all that was left in the positions the army
had occupied. The Argentine journalist Jorge Ricardo Masetti, who was
visiting us for the first time in the Sierra, took a photograph with a small
box camera of the murdered peasant; it was the beginning of a deep and
lasting friendship.

After these encounters, we withdrew a little way back from La Otilia, but then I was replaced as commander of Column 4: Ramiro Valdés
was promoted at that time. I left the zone accompanied by a small group
of combatants to take charge of the Recruits' School, where the men
destined to make the crossing from Oriente to Las Villas were to train.
We also had to begin preparations for what was now becoming imminent: the army's offensive. The following days—at the end of April and
the beginning of May—were spent preparing defensive points and trying to bring to the hills as large a supply as possible of goods and medication in order to endure what we could see coming: a large-scale
offensive.

At the same time, we were trying to arrange for tax levies from the
sugar planters and cattlemen. Remigio Fernández came up to us at this
time; he was a big cattleman who offered us the sun and the moon, but
he forgot his promises as soon as he got back to the plains.

The sugar planters likewise gave us nothing at all. But later, when
our forces were stronger, we took our revenge, though we had to go
through the offensive without material indispensable for our defense.

A short time later, Camilo Cienfuegos was called up to strengthen
the defense of our small territory, which contained incalculable riches:
a radio station, hospitals, munitions depots, and, best, a small air-

strip situated between the hills of La Plata, where a light plane could land.

Fidel maintained that the enemy soldiers did not matter; only how many men *we* needed to make our position invulnerable mattered, and that we must be guided by that. Such was our tactic then, and as a result, our forces were gathered together around headquarters to present a compact front. There were not many more than 200 usable rifles when, on May 25, the expected offensive began in the middle of a meeting that Fidel was holding with some peasants to discuss how to harvest the coffee, since the army no longer permitted any day workers to come up for the harvest.

He had called in some 350 peasants, all of them very much interested in resolving the problems of the harvest. Fidel had proposed: creating "Sierra money" in order to pay the workers; bringing in some palm fiber and sacks for packing and transport; he wanted to create work cooperatives, as well as consumers' cooperatives, also a tax commission. Moreover, he offered the cooperation of our guerrilla army for the harvest. Everything was approved, but Fidel was just bringing the meeting to a close when machine-gun fire began. The enemy had encountered Captain Angel Verdecia's men, and its aviation was punishing the surrounding area. Actually, when the circle around us tightened, hardly any peasants were left in the rebel zone, no more than a few of those most dedicated to the Movement.

FIDEL CASTRO

Letters
To Señor Manolo Arcas   Sierra, April 23

The tough battle we are waging sometimes imposes painful duties on us.

For more than a year, a tight blockade on food has been the lot of the inhabitants of this Sierra. This situation, which does not affect our forces, constitutes an inhuman and criminal action against the civilian population.

Despite the fact that the people are bearing this situation with heroic forbearance, in recent days, some of them, made desperate by hunger, have carried out raids on nearby cattle ranches in search for food. I had them brought to me, they have been stringently censured for these actions; they themselves are fully aware of their guilt and have asked for comprehension of their needs.

Compelled to take drastic measures in order to avoid a repetition and extension of such acts and to prevent civil disorder, I have determined on a humane and practical solution: to order our forces to requisition the large herds of cattle near the Sierra Maestra and make an equitable, reasonable, and orderly distribution of them among the neediest families, as well as to take a series of measures to guarantee provisions to the civilian population.

The bulls will be butchered and every single cow will be kept for milk production.

Among the more or less legitimate rights which an armed force must protect, the survival of its citizens is the most sacred and to this end, if necessary, others must be sacrificed. I cannot allow the population to die of hunger, nor will the tyranny be allowed to achieve that end. What I propose is not an act of force but an act of humanity; I am violating a venerable right, but only to serve a higher right. I take nothing for myself. I do not deprive others of what is theirs for my own gain, but simply to save the lives of thousands of our fellow countrymen. But since we are fighting for the triumph of justice and respect for all rights, I am writing to tell you that the measures I have ordered are of an exceptional nature and that as soon as the battle is won you will be reimbursed for the value of the cattle taken from you, as will others affected by these same measures.

I assume full responsibility for this measure, in the conviction that I am acting with honesty and justice, and I anticipate the most noble and just understanding from you.

To Bebo Hidalgo   Sierra, April 25

We are all deeply affected by the turn events are taking. And though the hour is one for self-criticism and strict measures, all of us united will go forward until we turn defeat into victory.

Yeyé [Haydée Santamaría] will leave here in a few days, and she, better than any letter of mine, will tell you of our position.

We have decided to organize our own supply apparatus for arms from abroad. After seventeen months without receiving the least help from the organization (what reached us some weeks ago was the result of an independent action), it is very difficult to have any faith in anything but our own efforts. Nearly 200,000 pesos have been spent without a single rifle or so much as a bullet reaching us here. What we expected from Mexico for over a year has fallen, in good part, into the hands of the enemy, and in no less a place than Pinar del Río. And how badly we need these weapons; but shipment after shipment has been lost because other comrades hold the view that other fronts should be opened rather than strengthening the one we have!

The time has come for us to show that from here the war could be extended as far as necessary, with men experienced through long combat of this type. I must tell you that I feel very bitter about the neglect of our needs, and it has been one of the gravest errors that could have been committed. Had this not been so, the Revolution would be much further advanced by now.

At this moment, the dictatorship is preparing to concentrate all its resources against us, drawing new breath from the defeat of the strike; for our part, with the second wind given to some men in the face of defeat, we are preparing to resist. The comrades of the directorate agree that the Movement must be strengthened militarily and that we must concentrate the greater part of our attention on this phase at the present time.

To Ricardo Lorié   Sierra, April 25

Receiving effective help immediately is a matter of life and death. Therefore, we have decided to organize our own supply apparatus. Counting in advance on your consent, we have decided to entrust you with this responsibility. You will act under my own direct orders, with full powers to carry out your mission.

Bebo will continue in the same post, but his task will be limited to supplying the militia with the funds available at the time, depending on the state of our finances.

You can count on the funds we send you directly from here via the friends you left here. We are working intensively on this aspect of the operation and we shall soon be able to observe the first results. You will also be able to figure on sums gathered abroad, in accordance with instructions I will send to the Committee-in-Exile. Besides, the funds that it can get from certain governments will be sent to you, in accord with the detailed, precise instructions that our pilots will get. You should speak to Bebo, informing him of the urgency of sending whatever he has gathered for us, asking him to hand it over to you, and if he has nothing on hand, that he offer help in any way possible. Every rifle arriving here will be one more possibility of victory. As you know, we make them multiply on arrival.

To Mario Llerena and Raúl Chibás, President and Treasurer of the Committee-in-Exile of the 26th of July Movement   Sierra, April 25

I have only one bitter complaint, and not because of anything that has happened to me personally, but because of the consequences that have followed. The Movement has failed utterly in the job of supplying us. Egotism, and at times trickery from other sectors, have combined with incompetence, negligence, and even the disloyalty of some comrades. The organization has not managed to send us so much as one rifle, not one bullet from abroad. The only shipment received here for several weeks was gotten by us from here. Despite everything, there are patrols of ours operating at the gates of Camagüey. And from Cabo Cruz to Santiago de Cuba, from Mayarí to Baracoa, and from Camagüey to

Victoria de las Tunas, the territory is totally dominated by our columns. But how are we to justify the expenditure of close to 200,000 pesos without our having received a single weapon?

But apart from all moral considerations, once again the task of saving the Revolution in one of its most profound crises falls on our men.

The danger of a military coup reaffirms the thesis that only the military can overthrow dictatorships, just as they first put them into power, a thesis that mires the populace in fatalistic apathy and dependence on the military—while the refutation of this thesis constitutes an objective of continuing importance in the politics of Latin America as a reaffirmation of the rights and power of the peoples; all this is now in the forefront as a result of the failure of the strike. *And the failure of the strike was a matter not only of organization but also of the fact that our own armed action is not yet strong enough;* and it is not because we must fight only with arms we can seize from the enemy, who is well armed, which exacts a painful toll in lives lost. If the entire island had already been invaded by rebel columns as is Oriente, no repressive measure could prevent the action of the people and the strike itself would be the inevitable consequence of the paralysis of the country by means of military action. No regime could endure the total and unlimited severing of its routes of communication, just as no living organism could endure the severing of all its arteries.

To Celia Sánchez   Sierra, April 26

They want to speak to me directly from Costa Rica today at 6:00 p.m., but they ask for the code. Damn the code! Where are the papers they brought me from Costa Rica by air? They tell me that Pedrito* knows the code, but where is Pedro? How come he isn't with his mortar? What kind of disorder is this? I am ashamed not to know what to tell them. I will have to resign myself to letting them simply send the message.

I need *cyanide*. Do you know any way to obtain it in some quantity? But we also need *strychnine*—as much of it as possible. We must get these very circumspectly, for if word leaks out, it will be of no use. I have some surprises in store for the time the offensive hits us.

To Camilo Cienfuegos   Sierra, April 26

The saddest thing that I have to report is the death of Ciro Frías in an attack on the Imías Barracks, in the Baracoa zone. This loss grieves me deeply. Ciro was intimately involved in the history of this struggle. I

---

* Pedro Miret, a veteran of the attack on the Moncada Barracks, was chief of the mortar battery for Fidel's operations in the Sierra Maestra.—ED.

don't know how his poor mother will be able to bear the news. Her only two sons have died.

To Che Guevara   Sierra, April 28

The pilots will tell you that yesterday was a great day. I spoke with Costa Rica and Venezuela. Everyone is working very hard. Even my sister is in Venezuela, and Gustavo told me her relations with them are very good. I had the feeling that they were taking our situation seriously. And what a coincidence! They were waiting to speak to me from both countries. Our people abroad tell me there is tremendous support for our cause, and arrangements are being made "not in one, but in several countries."

From Costa Rica, they sent me a family message for you, which they received by telephone after our conversation was begun; the lady (who sent the message) is in Peru. Thus I deduced it must be Hilda.

To Celia Sánchez   Sierra, April 28

Yesterday my tooth hurt terribly. I found I had no painkiller, and I could not find my toothbrush either. Not even a bottle of wine came in my package. Please send me some of these things.

To Celia Sánchez   Sierra, April 29

Our positions seem good, but we must set up a good defense for our planes, and move them around constantly so that the enemy never knows their whereabouts. We must try to avoid frontal attacks; our strategy will be different.

To Celia Sánchez   Sierra, April 30

It's enough to drive me mad. What the devil was I supposed to do with that woman who was brought here to me and whose talk clearly reveals she is in contact with our people living underground in Havana? I sent her to you because I don't know her and don't know what credence to give her words. Talk to her, and if she strikes you as suspicious, have her arrested and sent to jail. For my part, I didn't note any suspicious questions, though I did notice she is rather weird. This is the result of the confusion in the Movement outside the Sierra.

It is evident that there is a state of rebellion among the men at the lower echelons. Their problems must be resolved by moving the men; failure to do this would merely complicate the situation. I intend to be firm when these people show up. It is obvious we are overwhelmed with problems, and the work is exhausting, but we have no other recourse but to deal with it frontally.

The pilots take off constantly. Everything is their fault. My plan to have Ochoa call the American and Arcas, as he did a few days ago, and seize the plane *manu militari,* was the best. Then they started to complicate matters. If it is not settled there, they must go to La Plata, talk to the coast guard, and discreetly plan to seize a launch and leave for Jamaica at night.

Tomorrow I was going to start transmitting from the station, but I'm going to have to go there instead and talk to Daniel [René Ramos Latour] and the others. Bring them up through the mine as far as the Mompié's house at the top of the Maestra, so we can meet halfway.

I must also go to La Habanita in a few days to inspect the situation and position Crescencio's men, whom I ordered to assemble at Los Ranchos.

I heard that a 1000-lb. bomb had been dropped at Malverde, which scared all the neighbors. I think we are going to find that there won't be many of us when the party really gets going. I'm preparing all kinds of defenses around here. I am convinced they can't break through here. I already have fifty-one mines and I plan to use some 100-lb. bombs, as well. If the one I left there hasn't been sent to Crespo, send it back here. What we need are detonators for the mines and long fuses. We have only about twenty.

To William Gálvez   Sierra, April 30

The need to take someone's weapon is perhaps linked in my subconscious with an incident that occurred some time ago when an armed man brandished a rifle to show his defiance of an order. It became a reflex action on my part.

CHE GUEVARA   Sierra, April–June

During the months of April and June of 1958, two opposite poles of the insurrectional wave could be observed.

Beginning in February, after the battle at Pino del Agua, it began to increase gradually until it threatened to become an avalanche that could not be checked. The populace was rebelling against the dictatorship throughout the country, especially in Oriente. After the failure of the general strike decreed by the Movement, the wave receded until it reached its lowest point in June, when the troops of the dictatorship tightened the circle more and more around Column 1.

In the first days of April, Camilo Cienfuegos set out from the shelter of the Sierra toward the Cauto zone, where he was to be named commander of Column 2, Antonio Maceo, and where he achieved a series of impressive feats on the plains of Oriente. Camilo was the first commander in our army who went out to the plains to fight with the morale and effectiveness of the army of the Sierra.

CARLOS FRANQUI

The strike was launched in a climate of illusion, the illusion of victory.

Events had been going in favor of the opposition to Batista ever since the kidnapping of the auto racing champion Fangio, which had made Batista's police look ridiculous. There was also favorable news of bombings, sabotage, burnings of sugarcane plantations, and guerrilla advances in the Sierra Maestra and the Escambray. The Revolutionary Directory was also scoring successes in Las Villas. The struggle had reached a higher pitch, the highest since its beginnings at the end of 1956 and its development throughout 1957.

Three political events conduced to the illusion of victory:

The government of the United States decreed an embargo on arms to Batista.

The Catholic Church made an attempt at mediation.

The Civic Institutions—all the professional associations—called for Batista's resignation, and various magistrates of the Supreme Court resigned.

There had been months of ironclad press censorship when Batista eliminated it under U.S. pressure.

Then six television stations, seventy radio stations, and twenty-five newspapers and magazines endlessly repeated the events of the last few months. The impression was thereby created that the fall of the dictatorship was imminent.

But the workers' organizations were still in swaddling clothes. The militias of the 26th were unarmed: there were not a total of a hundred small arms in the entire country. The guerrilla forces, including the Sierra, the Second Front, and the Escambray, did not exceed three hundred men in the mountainous zones or in isolation.

Batista's army was intact. The national transportation system functioned perfectly. Some days before the strike was announced, Batista again imposed press censorship by cutting off news accounts and created the illusion that nothing was happening, and euphoria vanished. Under these conditions, the absurd radio announcement of a strike was heard by almost no one. And the militias in Havana and in the interior, poorly armed, were killed within a few hours.

The tactical error seemed to be the fundamental cause of the strike's failure. And certainly it contributed to the final disaster. But as would be demonstrated in January of 1959—when the general strike consolidated the revolutionary victory—in order to have an effective halt to all activity, we needed union organization, as well as an activist consciousness on the part of the majority of the people, the advance of insurrection throughout the island, the paralysis of transportation, the cutting off and isolation of the provinces, the demoralization of the army through defeats suffered on the field of battle. In short, a situation that did not exist in April 1958.

The false sense of victory was followed by a false sense of defeat. The Sierra blamed the plains for the setback, and the city and the Movement did not recover, despite their prompt reaction and the courage of thousands of militants who continued fighting clandestinely against the unrestrained terror unleashed by the tyranny.

14. MAY–JUNE: FROM ENEMIES IN THE SIERRA TO THE ROUT OF BATISTA'S ARMY

FIDEL CASTRO

Letters
To Che Guevara   Sierra, May 5

Apart from the many functions I am assigning you, after Ochoa leaves you will have to take charge of the platoons around Cuatro Caminos, Las Mercedes, and Jíbaro: we don't want them to be leaderless when they have their first encounters. You'll have to organize a means of quick liaison with each one of them.

Llerena informed me yesterday that the U.S. State Department had authorized the base at Caimanera to deliver 300 aerial rockets to Batista, which I imagine are for the jets to use. This report has all the earmarks of authenticity: the people there tend to be well informed about these things. I'll ask today for confirmation of the report; I don't want to start a row without being fully certain, because I am thinking up some effective measures.

To Celia Sánchez   Sierra, May 5

We had already decided to take measures in the zones of Moa, Nicaro, and Caimanera, when the first American rocket was fired here, one of those they say have been delivered to Batista. I spoke of this matter in very strong terms.

To Celia Sánchez   Sierra, May 5

If my pen was in the other shirt, as you say, it must have gotten lost, because that shirt is in the hands of the boy who travels with me, and the only things that turned up were a couple of pencils, which I've just thrown away because they don't work. I can't make any use of this junk; at every stroke, it scratches the paper without writing anything. I need a fountain pen; I hate being without one.

To Celia Sánchez   Sierra, May 7

Do you have some PSP papers that we received at the house last night? They were given me by Aguilerita [Pedro Aguilera] and I don't know what happened to them.

No other news around here, except that the employee who escaped from the prison has been recaptured on the plateau and he is en route here.

The 120-foot radio station is already broadcasting, and is beamed to Venezuela. Today I'm going to try to talk to Llerena.

To Celia Sánchez   Sierra, May 8

I rejected the resignation, the turned-in money, and armband, adding two or three other things, when he appeared with those packages. I claimed I couldn't abandon the store. After all the stupid mistakes every day, which could have already brought everything to an end, he doesn't understand why anyone should be in a bad mood and moaning all day. A virtuoso, who never makes a slip. He has a great explanation always at hand! They've just taken away for a firing-squad mission the only three men who know how to handle the two .50-caliber machine guns! If enemy planes were to show up, we couldn't fire on them. What these people have for brains is pure s---. So, though the fuses and detonators are in good shape, and the mines are so powerful that the smallest one blew up a 120-foot tree by the roots, I am discouraged when I think that the most of it will be wasted or lost, due to the imbecility of the people involved.

I'm eating hideously. No care is paid to preparing my food. By six in the afternoon, after twelve hours of running around, I'm completely bushed.

I won't write more because I am in a terrible mood.

To Ramón Paz   Sierra, May 8

It seems that the enemy has moved faster than expected, and I am worried by your delay. Fifteen minutes ago I received messages from the coast, saying that the army has landed troops in El Macho and probably in Ocujal. I believe that they will start to advance at any moment from different points. As soon as you get this message, advance in forced marches toward Santo Domingo, leave the men from Paco Cabrera's platoon there, so they can defend the road from Estrada Palma to Santo

Domingo, taking up positions downriver as far as Piedra's house. Suñol is at Providencia, and there he will put up the first resistance, and will slow them up as far as Piedra's house. At that point, Suñol will retreat, and then the road to Santo Domingo will be defended by Paco's men. At each bend in the road, resistance should be offered by small groups of snipers, posted at strategic points, where they can resist attacks from enemy aviation, mortars, etc. Give them a leader who is able and brave.

You, with your own platoon, can move to Palma Mocha and take the road there, near Emilio Cabrera's house. Remain there on the alert, ready to face the enemy, whether they come from Las Cuevas or from La Playa.

Lalo Sardiñas will be guarding the entrance to Los Lirios and Loma Azul. We'll take care of La Plata. We'll put up resistance on all the roads, pushing them back slowly toward La Maestra and trying to inflict as many casualties as possible.

If the enemy succeeds in invading the entire territory, each platoon should convert itself into a guerrilla force to fight, intercepting them where possible, until we flush them out again. This is a decisive moment. We must fight as never before. I'll try to stay in contact with you. Send all messages to La Plata, to the house where the boy from Villa Clara lives.

To Celia Sánchez   Sierra, May 8

We must immediately put all our advance forces in a state of alert along the roads to Las Vegas, Las Mercedes, and Jíbaro. You should read the message to Crescencio, make a copy, and deliver it to Che. I'll send a .50-caliber quickly to the La Plata road, as well as the mortar, mines, and some weapons, no more than four.

This afternoon two 100-lb. bombs were sent there, as well as mines and detonators. I plan to go there tonight.

I think that they will begin to advance from all sides at any time now. We must dog their footsteps with all our energy. I think they have already gotten ahead of us, but there is still time. It's a terrible shame that we have so few detonators and caps. But what can we do? I am sure that we will be able to fight them and beat them. We'll see if they advance right away, or whether they give us even two or three days more to prepare. I don't think they will.

To Celia Sánchez   Sierra, May 9

I'm at Río de la Plata, on my way down to the beach. Last night I was caught by the downpour at nightfall and couldn't move forward. This morning the river crested, and we are on the shore waiting for it to subside.

When I got here, I remembered something very important: we haven't got *a single drop* of rifle grease.

Another thing: We must start building up our gasoline supplies. At the moment, the plane has fuel for an hour and a half. But we must also prepare another camp for emergency use. The hospital never seems to get finished.

It's urgent to get some mules for use in this zone. I'll see if I can bring them from Ocujal.

To Celia Sánchez   Sierra, May 11

I don't think the reason the army gave for requisitioning mules is logical. To my mind, they are stockpiling them for a time when they need them, since that's one of the problems they'll have to solve.

Celia Sánchez   Sierra, May 11

The telephone!* It's very important to install it as soon as possible. That way I can keep in touch more directly with everything.

Though I know that Marcos doesn't have much confidence in the mine, I can't do anything about it; it would be a matter of trepaning the men's skulls, and I don't have anyone to place there.

To Che Guevara   Sierra, May 12

You must pick up the two 100-lb. bombs. In their place I'm sending a pair of the others for each of the points where the two big ones were. Since each 100-lb. bomb had two blasting caps, now instead of two explosions, four can be made, using the round bombs. As I see it, after the first mine blows up under the guards, they will be so rattled that you can do the same thing again with a big one. Of course, the first mine in each instance should be a double one, or one of the square ones. I don't expect to make use of the aviation until the decisive moment.

I think now you will be more satisfied with the use we'll make of the large bombs. Isn't that so? I was really going to sacrifice them because I am very worried about these two roads and because I wanted to give the guards a scare.

---

* The Movement in Manzanillo and Camilo Cienfuegos's column had sent wire and technical equipment from the plains for installation of the telephone. Roberto Pesant, who later died with a rebel patrol in a bomb explosion, built a telephone network several miles long, in a matter of days. It ran through rebel territory from Minas del Frío (Che's camp), as far as Las Vegas, Mompié, La Plata (general headquarters of Fidel and Radio Rebelde), to Santo Domingo and its suburbs, where Duque, Hubert Matos, Sardiñas, Paco Cabrera, and Ramón Valdés operated.—C. F.

To Celia Sánchez   Sierra, May 17

I have no tobacco, I have no wine, I have nothing. A bottle of rosé wine, sweet and Spanish, was left in Bismarck's house, in the refrigerator. Where is it?

To Che Guevara   Sierra, May 17

We've just found a solution to the problem of the factory-made electric fuses: use them with the current from five batteries directly, without the coil.

We've just exploded three grenades at the same time, from 15 yards. The result couldn't have been better.

In the future, we'll make blasting caps without coils so that we can use them with electric fuses. We have 78 of them at the moment. They'll serve our immediate needs, but we must keep on trying to get more, through Miami. Then, besides the large bombs, we'll be able to set off small grenades. The possibilities are endless.

Sierra, May 18

Now that journalists don't come here, they've discovered a new technique: the radio interview. Jules Dubois asked for one yesterday from Caracas. I asked for a list of questions and he immediately sent one, with all the well-known and tendentious queries. I answered them in writing at once, in order to send them out this afternoon. I'll send you a copy when they're typed up.

EDITOR'S SUMMARY

According to Jules Dubois, an interview with Fidel Castro was sought by two Cubans in Venezuela, Sergio Rojas, head of the Movement's activities there, and Justo Carrillo, an opposition leader in exile.

Dubois's lead question dealt with the charge linking Castro with Communism, dating back to his presence in Bogotá at the time of the riots in April 1948 generated by the murder of the Liberal Party leader, Jorge Eliecer Gaitán. Now, as before and after, Castro flatly denied the charge: "I have never been nor am I a Communist. If I were, I would have sufficient courage to proclaim it."

Dubois then probed the ideological positions of the 26th of July Movement. Castro asserted that the attempt to read Communist doctrine into the Movement's positions was a device that enabled Batista to pose as an anti-Communist in order to continue to receive arms from the United States. Castro warned that this policy linked the United States not only with Batista but also with the Nicaraguan and Dominican dictators, Somoza and Trujillo, and fostered "the increasing hostility of all Latin America."

While Castro maintained that the Movement has no intention of socializing or nationalizing industry of any sort, he observed that "certain interests are very much concerned that an economic right should not be violated, but they are not worried in the least about the violation of all the other rights of the citizens and of the people." Castro once again pledged to uphold the Constitution of 1940 and its guarantees to all sectors engaged in business activity.

In response to Dubois's comment that lack of unity had apparently hamstrung the efforts to overthrow Batista, Castro replied: "The 26th of July Movement is in itself the immense majority of the people, united under its direction." He dismissed the failure of the April strike as the result of a "tactical error," focusing rather on the military successes of the Movement. He also repeated his stand against taking direction from groups outside Cuba itself. Although he firmly rejected the possibility of a military junta, he continued to welcome any military support that might be offered. He reaffirmed the Movement's backing for Manuel Urrutia Lleó as provisional president and disclaimed any personal interest in office for himself after Batista's overthrow: "After the Revolution we will convert the Movement into a political party, and we will fight with the arms of the Constitution and of the law. Not even then will I be able to aspire to the presidency of the republic because I am only thirty-one years old."

FIDEL CASTRO

Letter to Che Guevara   Sierra, May 19

It's been too many days since we've talked, and that's a matter of necessity between us. I miss the old comrades here.

Yesterday I carried out an experiment with a tin grenade that produced terrific results. I hung it from a tree branch about 6 feet from the ground and set it off. It showered lethal fragments in all directions. A 9-foot tree, almost 50 yards away, was hit by more than thirty powerful impacts, from the roots to the branches at the top. It sends projectiles downward and on all sides, as if it were a sprinkler. I think that in open terrain it could kill you at 50 yards. So, along with the large mines, we can use tin grenades as aerial mines, with magnificent results. I'm going to order fifty of them made up for this purpose. Since the factory-made electric fuses are larger, the holes in these grenades must be enlarged. Today I'm going to try out a 700-foot cable, made from television antenna, to see whether the current reaches that far. You can't tell what effect a series of tin grenades exploded simultaneously from a single detonating box would have on a marching column. I've already written you how I exploded three simultaneously from a single detonating box, about 15 yards away from each mine.

The bombs for the plane are made in our workshop, and are really impressive.

FIDEL CASTRO

Commander in Chief: Communiqués   Sierra, May 20

Rebel troops of Column 1 sustained a violent battle yesterday against a battalion of the dictatorship, which was advancing toward the hamlet of Las Mercedes.

Las Mercedes is a tiny village of coffee growers and dealers who supply the agricultural zones of the region. It is situated some nine miles southwest of the Estrada Palma sugar mill. At one time, it was an important center of enemy operations. After the November offensive last year, when the forces of the dictatorship abandoned the zone under pressure by rebel troops, our advance patrols took possession of the place. As a consequence of a food blockade, its shops and warehouses have been totally empty for several months. Many of its inhabitants have left because of the bombardments and machine-gun fire. The army of tyranny, which has been massing troops for several weeks at Jibacoa, Roca y Alvarez, Estrada Palma, Canabacoa, Minas de Bueycito, and other points in order to mount a general offensive toward the Sierra Maestra, attempted an advance toward Las Mercedes, evidently intending to establish a new strongpoint. Starting yesterday, Sunday morning, using explosives and live phosphorus, they began to machine-gun and bombard the road from El Cerro to said point. When they thought that their intense aerial attack had cleared the road of any possible rebel forces, their infantry began to advance on foot and in trucks under aerial cover. But when they reached a place known as La Herradura, about a mile from Las Mercedes, rebel units—which had stoutly resisted eight hours of bombardment and machine-gun fire and held their positions along the route—greeted the enemy with heavy rifle and machine-gun fire, simultaneously detonating a 50-lb. TNT mine in the middle of the enemy column; its dense smoke and the explosion, which could be seen and heard for several miles, sowed panic and death among the enemy ranks, paralyzing its advance. Combat continued for the rest of the afternoon and the firing ceased only with the final light of day.

Last night, both sides mounted guard about 400 yards from each other. Las Mercedes remained in our hands. Today the battle was renewed.

The enemy high command appears disconcerted by the possible tactics of our forces.

I do not know if we will defend the terrain inch by inch or whether we will let them reach our most strategic defense points.

Sierra, May 26

Despite the fact that the Movement numbers many outstanding revolutionaries, proved in action, the naming of a commander from our forces,* which is a sacrifice for us from the military point of view, is essential in order to utilize the experience of our military campaigns in developing a new strategy of struggle throughout the nation. We also are seeking to achieve total homogeneity between the comrades of the militia forces and operational forces of the 26th of July Movement, coinciding with the establishment of a common high command to plan and direct all action by our military forces.

Havana, May

Thirty-eight civilians have been murdered by Batista's police in Havana: they were taken from their homes, and vilely mowed down right in the streets. The orders given by the chief of police, Brigadier Pilar García, to his thugs were clear: "I don't want prisoners, or wounded; I want dead men," and he got thirty-eight corpses in a single day.

FIDEL CASTRO

Letters
To Che Guevara   Sierra, May 28

Letters from Gómez Ochoa, Daniel [René Ramos Latour], etc. They give me the impression that the Movement is on the march again. Yeyé [Haydée Santamaría] wrote very interestingly on several matters.

Lorié already has more than 20,000 pesos. Our friends were going to send him a like amount from Cuba. Bebo handed over some two hundred rifles, among them twelve .30-caliber machine guns. As soon as I've reread the letters thoroughly, I'll send them to you.

To Pedrito Miret   Sierra, May 29

Don't let up for a minute in getting our defenses ready. When the bullets and the planes start in on us, that's when you'll know the value of this work. In Las Mercedes, a group of fourteen men put up resistance for 30 hours—against tanks, mortars, aviation, etc.—and they had no casualties.

We must keep knapsacks, reserve ammo, picks and shovels, etc., behind our lines so that they'll be safe.

---

* Fidel designated Major Delio Gómez Ochoa, a leading member of the 26th of July Movement, to reorganize the Movement and suspend underground activities. Actually, this military intervention put an end to the autonomy of the Movement.—C. F.

Be very careful not to take any chances with the bombs and grenades that I sent for the airplane. In case of evacuation, not a single one must be lost.

Greetings and be patient about all the shortages you're having to put up with!

To Che Guevara   Sierra, May 29

We've perfected a kind of fortified trench, in La Plata, which is impregnable. I was planning to talk to you about it today. I think it would be good to send forty or fifty men from the school to work on fortifications there. It's the army's favorite route. At least we should try to keep them from clearing their way to La Maestra, and consider the possibility of surrounding them, if their rearguard gets through along the road from El Frío to Las Mercedes. It's the logical point to use the personnel of the school, if weapons arrive, and I think if we can win ten additional days, we'll be receiving some.

To Pedrito Miret   Sierra, May 30

The entire shipment that arrived in the airplane with Franqui has to be here tonight.

The day after tomorrow there will be a reinforcement of ten armed men to fortify the position. I'll send five men to guard the beach at Palma Mocha, which has no protection, and six to reinforce El Macho.

I'll send the automatic weapons there because it's the critical point at this moment.

The shipment means a lot to us.

I'm sure there are some exciting things going on where you are, but it's essential that everything come here first to be distributed, without a single bullet missing.

To General Eulogio Cantillo   Sierra, May

I think highly of you. My opinion is not incompatible with my having the honor of recognizing you as an adversary.

I appreciate your noble feelings toward us, who are, after all, your compatriots, not your enemies, because we are not at war against the armed forces, but against the dictatorship.

I realize you are today the most prestigious and influential officer in the inner councils of the army, whose fate you can influence decisively for the good of the country, and it is to the country alone that the soldiers owe their allegiance.

Perhaps when the offensive is over, if we are still alive, I will write you again to clarify my thinking and to tell you what I think that you, the army, and we can do for the benefit of Cuba, on which the eyes of all America are focused at this moment.

But if the men who have taken up arms against the just principle that we represent are sufficiently inspired by the infamous cause they are defending to overcome the tenacious resistance that they will meet, and even if the last rebel is exterminated, do not be saddened by our fate, because we shall leave an example to the country that will make the most heroic pages of history pale. A day will come when even the sons of the very soldiers in battle against us today will look at the peaks of the Sierra Maestra with fervor.

To Che Guevara

If we manage to install a telephone before the army gets here, our possibilities of success will increase markedly. We must take advantage of every means of solving the problem of communications; trenches must be dug, explosives and detonators readied, and supplies stockpiled as much as possible.

FIDEL CASTRO

Reply to the Venezuelan Press   Sierra, May

At this time, the Rebel Army is holding out against the most powerful offensive the dictatorship has organized against us. I calculate that some twenty thousand soldiers are being mobilized to fight in Oriente Province. A fleet of fifty planes, thirty helicopters, and all the weapons the tyrant has been able to obtain from Santo Domingo, the United States, and Nicaragua. The dictator himself is directing the movement of his troops from Camp Columbia, on a gigantic, detailed map. Villages are being bombed incessantly. Although the North American State Department has denied the sale of three hundred rockets, these projectiles are being launched by the dictatorship's planes. One of the rockets has fallen into our possession; it is numbered 462594—it is of North American manufacture.

To crush the offensive, then, is our immediate military task.

There are many honorable military men in prisons for having conspired against the dictatorship. The dissatisfaction of the army, heightened by eighteen months of civil war, is on the verge of outright crisis.

The armed forces are now facing a very difficult task. The Sierra Maestra campaign is no longer a guerrilla struggle, but has become a war of columns and positions. Every entrance to the Sierra Maestra is like the pass at Thermopylae, and every narrow passage becomes a death trap. The Cuban army has lately begun to realize that it has been led into a real war, an absurd war, a meaningless war, which can cost it thousands of lives, a war that is not theirs, because after all, we are not at war against the armed forces but against the dictatorship.

These circumstances always have led inevitably to a military rebellion.

On the international level, I seek absolute sovereignty for the country in the face of all political and economic interference, solidarity with peoples oppressed by dictatorships or assaulted by powerful countries, and in the strengthening of ties with our fellow Latin Americans. As the path of all great ideals is strewn with obstacles, my only future aspiration is to continue battling. I will take up arms only when I must defend a just right in the face of force or aggression. I am an adherent of civilian rule. The only warriors I admire are those who like Bolívar fought to liberate the people.

CARLOS FRANQUI

Sometime in April, after the failure of the strike, I was asked to take charge of Radio Rebelde. My trip back to Cuba was to coincide with an arms shipment being prepared in Miami. Plans moved at full speed. A small Cessna was bought, and practice maneuvers, which were made to appear like aerial tricks, were begun on an abandoned landing field near Miami. The operation was repeated several times: the gliders are lifted up, and the cars arrive and join the group.

It was a way of putting the continual vigilance of the FBI and the North American police offguard and synchronizing the operation down to its minimum time. The airplane, with a sports registration, could legally leave Miami for Jamaica and return.

By flying low, we should be able to avoid the radar, and fly toward the Sierra, cross Cuba, between the north coast of Camagüey and the southern coast of Oriente, where we would land on a small bulldozed hill near La Plata, and then would continue immediately on to Jamaica, not very far from there. Three obstacles had to be overcome: the North American police, radar, and Batista's air force.

We had been told to leave at a specific time in order to reach the Sierra between the daily two bombardments and reconnaissance flight made by the enemy air force.

May 29 was the day chosen. We left Miami the night before and slept in a motel near the airfield, ready to leave during the first hours of daylight.

Díaz Lanz was to telephone us from the Miami airport at the last moment. The twenty-ninth dawned with bad weather, rainy. There were long hours of waiting. Around noon the weather cleared. Flights were resumed, and Díaz Lanz telephoned.

We drove the cars loaded with arms to the airstrip. The Cessna arrived immediately, and in a matter of seconds, we loaded on the weapons, the ammunition, the explosives, and gas, which along with Díaz Lanz and myself, comprised the entire cargo of the small plane.

We took off, waving to our comrades who remained behind, and in a few minutes, flying quite low, we left North American territory. We had evaded the police and the radar, and we now were over the Gulf of Mexico. After a half hour's flight, we ran into a violent tropical storm. Díaz Lanz thought that it would be very difficult for the plane to withstand the bad weather, apart from the risks of losing communication and also our way. To turn back meant losing everything except our lives. Díaz Lanz's decision, with which I agreed, was to continue. The storm over sea lasted for an hour, and only Díaz Lanz's extraordinary coolheadedness and skill, as well as good luck, saved us from the elements.

As we approached the Cuban coast, at Nuevitas, the weather was clear, the sky cloudless. Now that we were over the fright of bad weather, we were suffering the fright of good weather, which made us visible from land and air at a great distance.

The Cessna was slow, and it seemed as if we were always in the same place. It was almost twilight when we crossed over Las Mercedes, the hamlet at the entrance to the Sierra Maestra. The smoke coming from the burning peasant huts signaled the presence of Batista's army in the area.

After several anguished turns among the mountains peaks, the coast, and the Caribbean, the beach, and the canyons, Díaz Lanz's eagle eye spotted what had to be the tiny airstrip between some ravines. Shortly before, we had seen people running. We had been mistaken for one of Batista's small planes, which machine-gunned the Sierra at a low altitude.

Díaz Lanz's risky landing was successful. It was more a plowed meadow than a landing field. We unloaded the cargo swiftly and we were rather surprised not to see any rebels waiting for us. Díaz Lanz and I bid each other farewell. If landing was difficult, taking off was more so.

With his skill and proverbial daring, he managed to level with the peaks, and then the plane was lost among the clouds, in the direction of the not-too-distant shores of Jamaica.

Since no comrades appeared, I decided to hide the cargo among the trees and go away from the spot, in order to throw the enemy off the trail, since it was a place I did not recognize at all.

Years of fear began to fall away. I walked alone among the mountains and an unfamiliar sensation overcame me. It was the first time in six years of underground struggle that I felt free, like that rebellious nature around me. I felt that the city was enemy territory and the mountains free.

Afterward I met up with the bearded fellows, guided by a peasant boy on a horse, and then, with Pedro Miret, who was wearing a red-and-black armband of the 26th of July, and his squadron, with whom I set off on my first long walk in the mountains, to meet up with Fidel at his camp in La Plata.

His joy was such that it made me continue walking for hours, keeping up with his long strides, as far as Las Vegas, which I reached by sheer willpower, and the help that, according to writ, all saints offer.

Fidel's joy seemed disproportionate to such a small shipment. Later I understood that those twenty thousand bullets, the electric fuses for the mines, and the thirty flimsy Italian carbines were the last reinforcements to be received before the offensive, and they were vital to repulse the army.

In addition to the joy and satisfaction of the day; the certainty of triumph that emanated from the rebels, and Fidel; the marvelous welcome they gave me; the dream-come-true of ending my exile; the new responsibilities in the leadership and Radio Rebelde; Fidel's comprehension of my work—much more than that shown by the comrades in the city with whom I had worked—there was also a deep concern on a collective level: the underground which held the Sierra in its heart, the same underground which died unarmed in the cities and torture chambers while shouting, "Long live the Sierra Maestra! Long live Fidel Castro!" those in the Sierra held that underground responsible for all disasters, neglect, lack of understanding, errors, and abandonment the Sierra suffered, guilty of past difficulties as well as of present and future dangers.

I was accepted not only for the airplane shipment but because I was coming from Miami and not Havana or Santiago. There was a total lack of mutual understanding. It was a wall. A wall against which it was impossible to do battle.

But I would have been a miserable creature, and not a revolutionary if I had not fought to overcome such injustice; it was not overcome and would have serious consequences in the fight ahead.

FIDEL CASTRO

Letters
To Delio Gómez Ochoa   Sierra, June 1

I can visualize the extraordinary task ahead of you. I'm not surprised because I understand it perfectly from here. But I know that to carry it out, it is essential to combine the self-control and calm that you possess to a high degree. You'll find Havana immense, unknown, and complex, just as we found the Sierra to be during the first days. Here, as there, the enemy was master of the terrain, well informed, and in full control, but you'll conquer Havana as we conquered the Sierra. You must sow terror in the enemy ranks there, as we did here. You must take advantage of their smug confidence, give them surprises they don't expect; their wrath in the face of your first actions will be the usual and they won't change tactics until they have suffered their first disasters. If I were asked what would have been the ideal approach for us in this battle in the mountains, I would answer: to have caused the enemy large disasters, from the start, by taking advantage of that smug confidence and lack of worry with which they stalked about the Sierra. This is also the ideal approach for you there, if you can achieve it. We are not pressing you; on the contrary, it worries us that you might go too fast. Follow our instructions down to the last detail on preparing everything carefully, and invest the time necessary to study the ambience, the personnel, the terrain, and the circumstances.

I'm going to suggest acquisition of a type of uniform, practical weapon for you.

As for the money, I think we'll obtain the amount needed not only for ourselves but also to help you. Unfortunately, we must first get through the present crisis of our organization.

I sent a letter to a certain very prosperous group in a region that we are going to invade, and I asked for a million. There are several projects of this kind in the offing. What is the essential condition for them to become a reality? We must repulse the offensive. Even our most loyal contributors are waiting for us to do that!

The offensive seems to have begun, but it has become very hard on the guards. They were stopped a week ago at Las Mercedes. To enter, they had to wage a thirty-hour battle, using tanks and airplanes. The telephone is partially installed, and the installation is going ahead rapidly. Yesterday I armed the first forty recruits and sent them to the lines; they have already exploded two mines with destructive results. This weapon has reached perfection. It's impossible for me to send you your boys at the moment. I have them in key positions, and they're vital to me.

To Haydée Santamaría   Sierra, June 1

Your letter filled us with joy. You've done everything beautifully, and you fully justify the hopes we placed in you. You have no idea how the first fruits of your efforts have cheered us up! We're a little bit stronger now. The number of enemy soldiers advancing toward us is simply staggering. Daniel [René Ramos Latour] and Fausto [Pérez] and the others still haven't arrived.

P.S. I'm glad that Raúl's envoy is already there and in contact with you.

Remember, everything having to do with the forces in the campaign must be under your control.

Of utmost importance: the trips must be planned so that the plane arrives at approximately 6:30 p.m.

To Che Guevara   Sierra, June 1

If the line breaks, Crescencio has to stay on the other side so that all that territory is not abandoned. But they must not penetrate it, at least not easily.

JUAN CARLOS [Raúl Castro]

Report to Déborah [Vilma Espín] and Daniel [René Ramos Latour] Second Front Frank País, June 2

I'm sending you a report of the latest encounters and a summary of the general situation; from here, I can hear the noise of the battle, which is today going into its sixth day in the neighborhood of Bayate in Guantánamo.

I have made contact with Captain Demetrio Montseny (Villa), a splendid comrade from Guantánamo, who is determined, disciplined, and brave. He leads a platoon of twenty-five uniformed men, well disciplined and well armed. They attacked and occupied the barracks at Nicaro on February 27, and seized 12 Garands and M-1 Springfields; they also have Winchester .22-caliber rifles, 2 machine guns, and some pistols.

That same day, March 20, I made contact with Lieutenant Raúl Menéndez Tomasevich, who was authorized by the National Directorate to operate in this zone. At the beginning of March, he occupied the barracks at Mayarí Arriba, inflicting casualties and seizing some weapons; his command is made up of around a hundred men, poorly armed.

On Monday, April 7, some thirty well-outfitted, well-armed, and disciplined men arrived here under the command of Lieutenant Carlos Lite and Sergeant Zapata, sent by the Movement to the Caujerí zone; they had already seen action. Also in action is a force of thirty men from the Movement, under the command of Sergeant Wicho, in the Sierra Canasta.

Tomasevich and Totó arrived here; they had taken Caimanera on the thirteenth, seizing 5 machine guns, 10 Springfields, 2 M-1s, ammunition, and pistols, from the two barracks they had captured.

Captain Totó, chief of the Guantánamo militia, reached our camp with seventy well-armed militia men, all great fighters from Caimanera and Guantánamo, along with five prisoners, guardsmen they had captured in the fighting at Caimanera.

Rebel forces under the command of Major Aníbal Casillas attacked and captured the rural guard barracks at Ramón de las Yaguas, on April 28, capturing a heavy machine gun and many other weapons.

May 11: The Movement's troops under Aníbal's command made contact with the first rebel post at Cupeyal.

May 12: Major Aníbal made contact with Major Raúl Castro, and the former is named chief of the northern zone of Sagua-Mayarí.

I won't say any more about the number of riflemen and of those in arms, because the total of men already organized is more than a thousand.

During the month of May, two battles started in the Mayarí zone, in La Zanja and Corea. Comrades, armed with rifles with one cartridge and hand bombs, and only one M-1 in the possession of Lieutenant Ignacio Leal, who led these units, faced the enemy in an unequal fight against the army at the two places I mentioned. The army retreated, lashed by our valiant gunners.

May 12: Units from Company E (Baracoa and the one from Guantánamo) maintained contact with the army in Jagüeyes, inflicting eight enemy deaths. This company, under the command of Captain Félix Pena, held out for a month, and almost every day, often morning and evening, they withstood intense aerial raids—including incendiary bombs—on their positions and shelters, above all, on the strategic entrance to El Abra, in Caujerí Valley. Airborne shrapnel is punishing us; our comrade Pedro Hernández had a leg torn off and, disconsolate, committed suicide by shooting himself with his revolver.

At the same time, five hundred soldiers of the dictatorship advanced along several different points. Our men sustained several skirmishes, but because of the enemy's numerical superiority and, above all the action from the aircraft in a zone where there are nothing but cornfields, the men had to abandon their positions, breaking the front they had established in that zone and leaving a flank in the Yateras zone exposed. In a quick talk with Pena, we decided to attack from behind the enemy lines, employing guerrilla warfare of harassment and ambush, which is going on right now. Some platoons from this company are covering the Yateras flank (Fajardo), and the rest are dispersed from Guantánamo Bay to the Caujerí Valley, where the army is now (one of many places), with instructions to keep up constant harassment of the army, in order to make certain that these five hundred soldiers meet some resistance in that zone, and don't leave and hurl themselves on the weak positions of Company D at Yateras, which is under the command of Captains Manuel Fajardo and Roberto Castilla.

I don't know if I already told you that a patrol of this company attacked the plant at Guaso (the aqueduct for Guantánamo), killing a soldier, capturing another, who was given his liberty at the request of the people, who vowed he had behaved well toward them. They seized two rifles with ammunition. Sergeant Manolito Sánchez, from Felicidad, of this company, fell into an ambush with three other comrades, close to the sugar mill at La Isabel. His three comrades managed to flee, but he was wounded and taken prisoner; now Chaviano is demanding that his father, a rich coffeegrower in the zone, hand over 20,000 pesos for his son.

At this time, the company has a Mendoza machine gun with only 120 bullets and fifteen rifles of the same caliber with 20 bullets for each one. Do your very best and send ammunition before the offensive begins at Yateras.

May 13: The offensive through the north is under way. Combat in La Yuita, south of Casanova, at 11:30 a.m. We've suffered one casualty. According to reports from intelligence, the army has eighteen dead, and among them the lieutenant from Sagua, José María Fernández, and twenty-three wounded. Comrade Ricardo Cisneros (Jotor) lost an eye in this action. He had been decorated a few days before with the revolutionary order of the Frank País Legion of Honor as, on one occasion, he went down to Sagua, killed an enemy soldier, and returned with the dead soldier's rifle and, not satisfied with that, asked for permission and, with another comrade, went down to Cayo Mambí, killed two soldiers, and returned with two more rifles.

May 23: Three hundred soldiers coming from Sagua de Tánamo were stopped by gun patrols under the command of Lieutenant Pedrín Soto Alba, at a point called El Sitio. As their ammunition was running out, our gunner comrades started retreating. At the end of two hours, the only ones left fighting were the officer Soto and two other comrades. It was at this moment that Lieutenant Soto, with a spirit of responsibility and revolutionary honor, turned over his Garand rifle to one of his comrades so that he could get out and save the weapon, while Soto stayed on battling with a pistol, although he was practically surrounded and lost, and the men took refuge in safer spots among the nearby hills. At this moment, Major Aníbal arrived with reinforcements to do battle with the enemy, dislodging them from high positions and putting them to flight after a fierce battle. Rebel patrols pursued the enemy soldiers to about a mile from Sagua de Tánamo. The army withdrew from Casanova to Sagua where it is busily digging trenches. The colonel directing operations in this zone, Cañizares, said he was going to ask for four tanks in order to go farther up, even though the heavy rains during these last few days would seem to make any such action unfeasible. In their flight the soldiers burned some houses. The peasants shouted at them from a distance: "Fight now, you pimps!"

May 24: Several comrades from Company B, from Guantánamo, led by Major Efigenio Amejeiras, went down to Guantánamo to kill enemy soldiers and bring back arms. A few, after carrying out the mission, are missing; they went to the Pena zone. The ones who returned, since they are comrades with several worthy qualities and great moral rigor, were decorated with the order of revolutionary merit, the Frank País Legion of Honor.

May 28: In midmorning, the peasant observation service reported that enemy troops were advancing from Cuneira toward Marcos Sánchez, some four or five miles from the first point. A little farther on, between Marcos Sánchez and La Lima, is where our first outpost in that zone is stationed. The army burned several houses in Marcos Sánchez, and after looting a wine cellar, burned it. Several trucks arrived carrying knapsacks and tents, preceded by a large number of infantry troops on foot. They were drunk and guzzling more alcohol while singing a refrain to some old music: "We're going to burn La Lima, we're going to burn La Lima," and so on. As this group arrived, about a mile before La Lima, our men, under the command of Lieutenant Terry, opened fire, trying out a cannon Evans made that fires cartridges of 153 pellets and covers a distance of some 200 yards, at which point it explodes in a circle 21 feet in diameter. The first shot brought down four soldiers. A few moments later, Major Efigenio arrived with his mobile squad and also Captain Demetrio Montseny with his squad. One man was wounded, and after the battle went on for three hours, the army retreated, defeated, with its dead and wounded.

May 29: Patrols from the platoon led by Captain Roberto Castilla of Company D at Yateras carried out harassment operations on an encampment of one hundred and fifty soldiers, under the command of Díaz Campa, who were quartered at the La Isabel sugar mill.

Fajardo asked for a hundred letters signed by me but without the names of the addressees, assuring me that he can collect 70, 000 pesos; a pity the coffee harvest is going to be lost, and let us hope I have time to work out a letter. Fajardo's company has received the least supplies since Guantánamo. And it is the most economical of all the companies, about 350 pesos a month, and its food is only meat with vegetables.

Around noon, a report reached me that the Batista forces were again in Marcos Sánchez, when Efigenio's and Villa's [Demetrio Montseny's] reinforcement arrived. The enemy had already broken through the first line and were very close to La Lima. They came in fifteen trucks, which stopped farther back. In La Lima, Efigenio and Villa were attacked. Villa retreated to the right, Efigenio to the left, and they began typical battle skirmishes. During the night, a graphic report arrived, which I'll try to describe.

On the night of the twenty-eighth, there were several skirmishes, some provoked by us. And so, we were in the same position when day dawned.

Today, at about three in the afternoon, troops under the command of Major Aníbal successfully attacked the military station at Las Minas de Ocujal, near Mayarí.

The results of the action, in which we fortunately did not have a single loss on our side, were: the army of the dictatorship suffered three casualties—one dead, one injured, and one taken prisoner. The six soldiers remaining in the barracks fled precipitously. In the barracks, the following was seized: 4 Springfields, 2 .45-caliber revolvers, a .38, 250 .30-'06 cartridge shells, 9 antipersonnel grenades of American make, 4 cartridge belts of .30-'06, 5 uniforms, 5 knapsacks, 22 flasks, 5 army blankets, 3 pairs of boots, towels, and underwear.

And last, from the offices and workshops at the mines, the following was seized: 8 automobiles, 3 jeeps (1951 and 1952 models), 2 Power vans, 1 Willys amphibious vehicle, 1 International truck with four-wheel drive (1958 model); 5 drums with 55 gallons of gasoline; 2 drums of oil, 5 typewriters, 2 telephones, 9 acetylene soldering outfits, 3 cylinders of carbon dioxide, and automobile parts and machine tools.

May 30: At 5:30 a.m., the air force began the most furious attack we have ever seen. There were nine air raids in a row, without a break, for ten hours. Only at noon was there a respite. B-26s, pursuit planes, Catalinas, light artillery planes machine-gunned us, and mortar shells and grenades rained down on us. Even an airplane from Cubana (although there are certain disagreements concerning this last point), at any rate, a civilian plane did appear, machine-gunned us and flung clusters of mortar shells. When the soldiers spotted one of our troops, they communicated the location to the air force. They even went so far as to throw fire bombs! With all this aerial menace, the boys abandoned their high positions and hid in the gullies, but when the air attacks were over, they rapidly resumed their positions. The town of La Lima was bombed unmercifully; happily, not a single civilian had remained there. The fighting is now raging on the heights above the village. One of those big helicopters with twin propellers landed twice. On its second trip, Efigenio fired on it, forcing it to make a rapid departure and it did not return. Several attempts to take the hills were repulsed. They only managed to take a section of hill facing Efigenio, thanks to the constant support of the air force and the sparseness of the vegetation on the slope.

During the night, too, they carried out harassment operations and several more skirmishes. And so May 31 dawned, the fourth day of battle, with the enemy having advanced scarcely a mile or two and, even at that, quite slowly. Now the enemy rearguard has twenty-five trucks in all, not counting jeeps, the radio cars, etc. Part of the town of Cupeyal was leveled by flames. During the day Efigenio, who is on the strategic height of Cabeza de Negro, repulsed something like three enemy attempts to take the position.

In view of what happened at Cupeyal, the order was given for all our forces on the right wing and Bayate front to fall back. Panic spread like wildfire among the civilian population and people began to abandon their homes, carrying only their most essential belongings. Bayate looked like a ghost town. Hundreds of gunners slept along the road between Bayate and Bombí that night. Efigenio remained in Bayate. I called a meeting, but seeing the state of general fatigue—no one seemed to be able to make sense—I ordered everybody to go to sleep.

June 10: At dawn, Efigenio left for the zone of Loma Blanca, trying to stop the army, which will try to advance through there toward Bayate. Our patrols are stationed between Cupeyal and Bayate, along other roads. At night, observers were sent to the zones of Lima and Guanábana and they are to return in the morning.

June 12: The enemy soldiers are leery about walking on the roads, where they know that at any point they may be surprised by an ambush and so they advance through the fields. Efigenio, who went down again, said that he would try to intercept them again, between Guanábana and Bayate, but he managed to keep them back before that. In the middle of the afternoon, Lieutenant Eloy Paneque notified us that the enemy was apparently planning to continue advancing, and Efigenio left for that area, while Villa went up to Loma Blanca. Both are trying to stop the enemy from reaching the strategic zone of Aguacate and La Escondida, which along with Juba (where you were), form a strategic and easily defended triangle. At this moment, 5:30 p.m., Captain Hermes Cordero and Lieutenant Torre (the "Frenchman") between them have organized the defense of this triangle, from the church to here. We're going to make these swine pay in blood for every inch they advance. The day before yesterday, during one of the combats, an enemy sergeant or lieutenant shouted to his group: "Advance, you cowards, it doesn't matter if a hundred of you die, we survivors will be able to have more girls to rape in Bayate!"

Almost all of them are drunk, perhaps some are on marijuana, and they're a bunch of crooks! They rape, murder, and rob. Their planes hurl firebombs, delivered to them by the Yankees, on their naval base in Guantánamo, as has happened these past few days, and the Yankees order Trujillo and Somoza to give arms to Batista. While here, the cream of our youth die with a miserable rifle in their hands. These monstrous crimes must be revealed to the entire world.

Day dawned with a bombing and strafing from five planes in the space of one hour. Meanwhile, we'll continue fighting as long as the ammunition lasts, and we'll keep trying to hold the front, although we are ready to organize quickly to go over to guerrilla warfare. We are trying to hold the front in order to cover Aníbal's rear and Casillas's and Fajardo's flanks, so that they can gain time.

I am sending three notes: the first ones came from the front along with some reports (I'm enclosing the third) so that you will realize our lack of all kinds of ammunition.

Efigenio has fought marvelously. His mobile squad has borne the brunt of the battle, which today goes into the sixth consecutive day. It's the first time that we've been involved in such a long battle, with a front line and positional fighting. The slowness of their advance shows how frightened they are and how we have surprised them with our new tactics. In any case, until we have adequate weapons, we have the alternative of guerrilla warfare, but just imagine how many hamlets will be razed and peasants murdered.

Only Guantánamo knows how many dead and wounded they have sustained. At the first chance, I'll send a description of the second part of this battle; we would have won it a long time ago and the enemy troops would be back in Guantánamo if we had a minimum of adequate weapons. I hope they'll get here someday. This offensive worries me and also Operation Pepe, if this one goes on too much longer.

FIDEL CASTRO

Letter to Celia Sánchez   Sierra, June 4

I am at Mompié's house. I left the mine a moment before a bombardment. A note sent from there reports that they shot up Mario's house and destroyed several things, including a typewriter. There were no casualties. Bullets, bombs, and other things must be gotten out of here. Absolutely nothing has been done to the house. The tunnel is made, yes, but I'm going to order some further improvements against the rockets they're using as bombs.

The telephone is already in contact with the station. The technician there devised a small amplifier to hear one's voice over the telephone. Actually, we now have a long-distance, international telephone service. But from here to the mine, not a foot of line has been installed. Pesant is going around barefoot and he's not the only one. What a problem! If there aren't any espadrilles to be found, I'm ready to give him mine! I've already written everyone and sent the medicine and a doctor to the beach. Luis Orlando* put his foot in it yesterday with a eulogy of de Gaulle. May the devil take him!

I still look like a beggar.

P.S. With this, I am sending 120 M-1 bullets, plus 2 combs and a note for Lara.

---

* Luis Orlando Rodríguez was a member of the Ortodoxo Party, a newspaper editor, and, briefly, a member of Castro's government.—ED.

RAMIRO VALDÉS

Report to the Commander   Sierra, June

Yesterday the bullets you sent me through Che arrived. As there are so
many roads, even the Mausers have to be put into action; although
they're always placed at points where they are least likely to be fired. In
the combat on the second, in the Vega Grande zone, we had one man
wounded in the thigh and another dead; the wounded was Abigail
Pampa, and the man who died was Mezail Machado.

It's true that Almeida asked for money from Santiago, but he didn't
know about the agreement. I haven't asked Déborah [Vilma Espín] for
anything, nor have I ever even written her. Perhaps she is saying that
because in a letter to a provincial delegate who held up a shipment—on
the pretext that it was not going through the proper channels of the
Movement—I said to the gentleman in question: "I take the advantage
of already being in contact with the Provincial Directorate to make a
second request to you," and I sent a long note, but more in the spirit of
screwing him up than anything else.

FIDEL CASTRO

Letter to Celia Sánchez   Sierra, June 5

Franqui is working hard on propaganda and that relieves me from worrying about the radio station. The only thing I need is to have the telephone lines extended.

In the house that's going to be built up here, I need good light,
whether it's a lantern like I have or an oil affair; if it can be a lantern, so
much the better, because it means less work. So that people will know as
little as possible about the new house this one can also be kept in use.

It seems you forgot to send the few .30-'06 bullets that remained
there, as I had asked you in the note that I wrote after I left.

We need two rolls of fence wire. Mompié tells me that some is coming by mule for the Infierno mine.

I think our defense plans have been going ahead quite well. The
problem that worries me the most, day in and day out, is that the men
never seem to realize that in a plan of continued and escalated resistance, bullets that must last a month can't be used up in two hours.

People bore me so. I'm tired of the role of overseer and going back
and forth without a minute's rest, to have to attend to the most insignificant details, just because someone forgot this or overlooked that. I miss
those early days when I was really a soldier, and I felt much happier
than I do now. This struggle has become a miserable, petty bureaucratic
task for me.

When I saw the rockets that they fired on Mario's house, I swore that the Americans are going to pay dearly for what they're doing.* When this war is over, I'll start a much longer and bigger war of my own: the war I'm going to fight against them.

I realize that will be my true destiny.

RAMIRO VALDÉS

Report to the Commander   Sierra, June 6

Fighting is going on every day. The army is advancing, but slowly. They started from Las Minas on the twenty-ninth, and today, they've gotten as far as Caña Brava. They've been advancing along one flank. Their operations seem clear to me: by advancing along one flank they're forcing us to cover all the roads up to the Sierra, that branch out from the zone they occupy, and so we are forced to keep our men dispersed at different points. Once this is achieved, they can easily take Pico Verde and Pico de Agua, not to mention the beach. The ammunition is running out, and so the men can't do much. I don't know what your situation may be, but we are badly pressed and need help.

Guillermo has borne the brunt of the fighting. We've suffered seven casualties—one dead and six injured, two seriously. No danger of dying, but they can't walk. I hope you'll reply quickly.

The director of Resistance went back to Havana; he said he would be more useful there. He left a note for you, but the person he gave it to misplaced it.

FIDEL CASTRO

Letter to Pérez [Ricardo Lorié]**   Sierra, June 6

Among the material received was an Italian carbine without a bolt, but it provided parts for another one, which had broken a spring while it was being tested, and a Garand, which was missing a firing pin, but

---

* Although the U.S. government had suspended arms shipments to the Batista government March 14, 1958, some U.S. government arms reached him after this date. The embassy in Havana reported that "three hundred 5-inch aircraft rockets" that had been delivered in January were found to have "inert [non-explosive] heads. . . . Since there was a stock of the correct heads available at the U.S. Naval Base at Guantánamo, Cuba . . . the U.S. Department of the Navy directed the Naval Base at Guantánamo to effect the exchange." Jules Dubois reports that "final delivery of the correct heads was made on May 19, 1958." (Quoted in Jules Dubois, *Fidel Castro: Rebel—Liberator or Dictator?*, pp. 497–98.)—C. F.

** Fidel had recently named Lorié to head supply operations abroad for the rebel forces.—C. F.

which could be fixed by using the part of an old, broken one that we had around. And so, all, except for one, are already tested, in perfect condition for use, distributed to their combat positions, and in the hands of brave boys, who have been in special training for a long time.

The M-1 bullets came in very handy, since I only had 189 in reserve, and there are about 100 M-1 rifles. The .30–'06 reserves have dropped considerably because we have sent them to several combat fronts: Raúl, Almeida, Camilo, etc.

I was really sorry that the Italian carbine bullets couldn't be used in the Mauser rifles that Hubert Matos brought.

We urgently need bullets for these rifles and others of the same caliber, for which there are none in reserve, and we have very few left because of the latest combats, although we are very careful to place them where they expend the least number of bullets. They use standard 7-mm. bullets, the same as the Mexican Mendoza rifles and the European ones of that caliber.

It's extremely inconvenient that our weapons don't use the same kind of bullets as the enemy in these battles. We have often supplied ourselves with the bullets the guards leave along the road or what we can take off of them. Besides, with this diversity of ammunition, we must constantly take pains to avoid mixing them up.

The Italian carbines seem rather flimsy weapons. It's a pity to waste energy and space bringing this type of weapon, when Garands, M-1s, and automatic rifles could be sent, and they are so efficient, or, in any case, Springfields, which are sturdy and use .30–'06 ammunition. The expense should be the least of it, because the fundamental problem has always been the transport and not the money.

In the days to come, there will be a tremendous and decisive battle. The dictatorship has taken the first steps in a massive offensive. Until now their advance has reached Las Mercedes and Purial de Jibacoa.

I've reinforced and fortified Alfa, which will be defended by blood and fire. By radio, via Venezuela, you will be informed about any danger at this point. But it's terribly important that you keep this in mind: if Alfa falls, and that can happen in a matter of weeks, even days, we would still control the valley of the Río de la Plata, which goes from the beach to the Sierra Maestra; this territory will then be defended inch by inch, provided only that you can continue sending us arms. In this case, the only possible way of doing it would be by parachute.

In fulfilling your mission, you must distinguish between two different stages: the present stage, which is urgent, a matter of life and death, in which every rifle you send can mean the survival of the Revolution, and the later stage, which will involve provisioning us for victory.

When the offensive is repulsed—and to accomplish that we must fight desperately—the picture will change, the difficulties will be fewer, and it's possible that there will be more than enough resources, which would allow us to draw up plans for shipments on a large scale in order to extend the war all over the island.

Pay attention to Venezuela and don't forget the great friend* from the first country that helped us.

CARLOS FRANQUI   Sierra, June

There has never been a politician, a leader, or an ambassador who has been the target of so much hostility, so many catcalls, so many angry demonstrations, as the vice-president of the United States, Richard Nixon, during his recent tour through South America. In Uruguay, the very civilized Uruguayans, led by students, gathered in large demonstrations at Montevideo to protest North American support of Latin American dictatorships, especially the support of Fulgencio Batista's regime.

In Colombia, Nixon had a bad time, between jibes and popular protests. There were signs proclaiming: "In the name of the United Fruit Company, the landless farmworkers of Colombia salute you, Nixon." And others that bitingly reflected the ironic and rebellious spirit of a people who have suffered, as they all have in Latin America, from hunger and misery, while North American companies have reaped millions and millions of dollars from their land. It was impossible not to recall the barbarous Rojas Pinilla, stupidly supported by the United States, whom the brave Colombian people overthrew. In Peru, in an overt demonstration, the people remembered Odría, who was also supported by the U.S. government. The Aprista leader Haya de la Torre said: "The United States has harvested the fruits of its political obtuseness in South America." Then Nixon arrived in Venezuela. And again he was the object of catcalls, he was spat on, his car was overturned, his aids injured, in the most explosive protest of all. The Venezuelans had not forgotten Pérez Jiménez with his North American medals.

Paraguay was left for the last, the only dictatorship in South America, and there Nixon was applauded. But not by the people, by the military.

The vice-president returned to his country amid a great controversy over his trip and the politics of his nation. To justify the failure, the first tactic was to blame it on the Communists. But the truth was coming to the fore. *The New York Times* wrote: "There was something more involved in this protest against Nixon than Communists." The secretary of state [John Foster] Dulles, wanted to soft-pedal the facts so as to conceal the fiasco, for which he was mainly responsible. But Nixon, who was the target of catcalls, rotten eggs, and every kind of protest imaginable, was

---

* José Figueres, president of Costa Rica.

of a different mind, since he recognized that the North American policy was wrong in Latin America. The controversy brought to light the causes of this fiasco, pointing up, among other things:

First: the support of dictatorships;

Second: economic exploitation;

Third: opposition to the democratic governments in Latin America;

Fourth: absolute ignorance of the needs of Latin America.

What will this lesson mean to the government of the United States?

FIDEL CASTRO

Orders
To Major C [Camilo] Cienfuegos   Sierra, June 11

After carefully studying the situation and analyzing our plans as well as those of the enemy, I had decided to send you this urgent message.

I need you here with all the good arms that you can muster. A battle of enormous proportions is going to break out in the Sierra. They are going to concentrate the main body of their forces in order to try to deliver a decisive blow. The number of men they will be able to gather here has no connection with the final outcome; what does matter is that we have the essential minimum force available to make the most out of the extraordinary advantage of this locale, where we know they are going to wage this war. Your presence is part of this essential minimum.

Your move over here, besides the courage it requires to do it at this time, has the advantage that in a few days, when overall strategy requires it, you can return to your zone. Besides, the enemy has already drawn up his plans in the expectation that you will be there; we are going to make him fight the battle with you here. To get the most out of your stay here, you should leave a patrol of gunners to operate in the zone to mislead the enemy and to permit you to manage your move here without anyone knowing or guessing your route.

Go toward the Santo Domingo zone.

To Ramón Paz and Pedro Miret   Sierra, June 12

The enemy's main objective on the coast is to take La Plata, since they surely know that we have an airfield there. You're both very much aware that people unfortunately blab, and some forty recruits worked there and later went on to the school, and that is only one of the ways for information to leak out.

As a basic step, the enemy will try to take Palma Mocha either by land or by sea during the next few days.

It's a terrific spot for us to trap them.

Cuevas should position himself on the banks of the Palma Mocha

River, on the side closest to La Plata, by the footpath leading down to the river, and entrench himself there against frigates and airplanes, so as to control the banks and the plains of the river's mouth, where he will be able to surprise and drive off any troops that arrive. The reinforced Teruel squadron should be upriver from there, some 50 yards before the point where the road coming from Las Cuevas along the coast meets the one from Palma Mocha. The mission of this position is to fire on the enemy rearguard when it meets up with Las Cuevas.

Five men must be entrenched at the side of the river, which is toward Las Cuevas, also some 50 yards from the road. The object of this position is to prevent reinforcements from reaching the people down below, and at the same time to control the upper part of the Palma Mocha River. These men must not be between the road and the sea, rather on the upper part of the pass.

With emplacements like these, it would be better for us if they came by land, because something bigger than what happened in El Oro or El Pozón could occur there; I can assure you both that if they use that route, they will not be able to get out. If they come by sea, they will also be turned back, even if the possibilities of retreat would not be as great.

Sierra, June 12

Cuevas's squad held out yesterday for five hours against the troops at Las Mercedes, forcing them to backtrack, apparently with several casualties. At 10:00 p.m., in compliance with my order and in the rain, he was already here. Today he goes to Palma Mocha with the squad you sent. The landing was confirmed: the first troops arrived at 10:00 a.m. on the tenth and the second at 6:00 p.m.

Sierra, June 12

While El Turquino provides support to us on the left, we prevent their advance toward the Maestra from Las Cuevas on; and toward La Plata from the sea. This last area can be defeated effectively from the sea and along the coastal roads. I am certain the army plans to go there.

The fortification of the road coming through Ají de Juana, to the right of Caracas, and leading toward Arroyones and San Lorenzo is vital because it offers many more possibilities for resistance. There is a veritable sea of soldiers descending on us.

There are troop concentrations about a mile from Providencia. Those troops are bound to advance toward Santo Domingo. Now I understand the bombardments and shelling at Gamboa and the village of Santo Domingo, on the ninth, on the eve of the landing, and the attempts to advance through Las Mercedes and Las Minas. The route that they are going to follow, or rather, the route the troops in front of Providencia are thinking of following, goes as far as Piedra's house, higher than El Salto, and that is where they'll divide, one section to go along the Santo Domingo road and the other on the Gamboa Road, which will come out at Naranjo, where Crespo's workshop is, or they'll be able to continue toward La Maestra past Pepe's store. I'll give instructions to Suñol on how he, too, should divide his men: he along the valley that leads to Gamboa and Paco [Cabrera] toward Domingo.

Sierra, June

For six days, intense fighting has been going on in the Bueycito zone. The enemy has managed to advance only about four miles.

Until the twelfth, our forces had suffered only one dead, two seriously wounded, and four less so. All in all, seven casualties. From then on, the battle has continued. Yesterday, intense artillery fire was heard in that direction.

EDITOR'S SUMMARY   Havana, June

The Chicago Tribune *correspondent in Havana, Jules Dubois, reported on the case of two young Cuban girls brutalized and killed by the police. On the afternoon of Friday, June 13, an attempt was made on the life of Senator Santiago Rey, who had once been a minister of the interior in Batista's government.*

On Saturday, police searched an apartment building where the suspected gunmen were thought to be hiding. The Giral girls, who lived in that building, had left on Friday to spend Father's Day in Cienfuegos, with their father. Sunday evening their brother drove them back to Havana and dropped them at the door of their building. They were never seen alive again. Their employer, José Ferrer, became worried when they did not come to work Monday. He called their brother, and the two began a search. They found the half-naked bodies at the morgue. Both had black eyes and bullet holes in the chest and showed evidence of beating and of sexual assault.

The police asserted that the girls had been killed inadvertently Saturday night during the building search. They also said that there had been a large cache of arms in the girls' apartment, and "a book by Leon Trotsky."

An attempt was clearly being made to link them with Communists. But Ferrer said that the Giral girls were devout Catholics and had no ties with Communism. "The whole story was nothing but a tissue of lies," he declared. "Their only offense was that, like thousands of other women in Havana, they were members of the Civic Resistance Movement."

An officer of the U.S. embassy invited Ferrer to discuss the case at the embassy. At the end of Ferrer's narrative, Ambassador Earl E. T. Smith asked whether he had "gone to the police to file a complaint." "What police?" Ferrer demanded. "The same police who killed the girls?"

Though Ambassador Smith did not carry the embassy's initiative in the case any further, Dubois believes that the report of these killings unquestionably strengthened "the determination of many Cuban men and women to fight Batista to the bitter end."

FIDEL CASTRO

Letters
To the Underground   Sierra, June 16

Avoid becoming impatient and strictly obey orders; this stage is one of organization. Train yourselves and gather resources for the struggle. Do not listen to the voices clamoring for action at any price; our poorly armed and badly prepared militia would have to confront the forces of repression head-on. When action is begun again, our organization must be adequately prepared to confront these factors successfully and in a struggle leading to victory. Resources will be scarce in these first months, that is, until the Movement can overcome this difficult time.

The Rebel High Command is well aware that its immediate task is to turn back the offensive of annihilation. It is not interested in isolated actions in the cities; when the offensive has been repulsed, and our forces can launch a counteroffensive, it wants the militia units to be as well prepared and as highly organized as possible.

Sierra, June 17

I've suspended distribution of sugar to everyone, except to the men in the trenches. I also discovered that we don't have a grain of salt.

I'm told that a mortar shell hit Lara in his trench. If this had happened, it would have killed him outright. Try to find out what did happen, in order to protect the trenches as well as possible in the future.

To Ramiro Valdés, Juan Almeida, and Guillermo García

I am carefully planning for the strategy to defend the Sierra Maestra against the enemy offensive in the weeks and months to come, more than for the present moment. This offensive will be the longest of all. After it is over, Batista will be irretrievably lost, and he knows it, and for that reason he'll risk anything.

This is a decisive battle and it is being waged in precisely the territory more familiar to us than to anyone.

I am directing all my efforts toward converting this offensive into a disaster for the dictatorship by taking a series of measures destined to guarantee, first of all, organized resistance over a long period of time; second, bleeding and exhausting the army; and third, acquiring the necessary men and sufficient weapons to launch an offensive just as their forces begin to weaken. I am certain we will make the enemy pay a very high price for its actions. At this moment, it is obvious that they are very much behind schedule in their plans, and although I think that there is still much fighting to be done, considering the efforts that they must make in order to gain terrain, I don't know how long their enthusiasm will last. The problem is to strengthen the resistance; we can do that as they lengthen their lines, and we can backtrack and take over the most strategic points.

Since at this point I think it is possible that they will retake La Maestra, I am going to give the positions to take based on the following considerations:

1. In case they penetrate our lines in depth, two tactics can be followed:

a. You must remain at La Mesa, as a focus of resistance isolated from us, or

b. bring these two columns here.

If we put the first possibility into operation, it would mean that you would lose contact with us, and the enemy would then have two choices: they could encircle you, with little danger of your attacking them, and then they would be free to concentrate all their strength against us. Or just the opposite: they could take advantage of the weakness of your forces, encircle them and wipe them out, while we remain impotent.

Because of this I have chosen the second tactic, that is, concentrating the forces, which is consonant (1) with the general plan, (2) with the most strategic positions, and (3) with the necessity of maintaining a zone of territory as compact and solid as possible, providing cover for the rear of the columns on the El Turquino side, as well as those on this side.

These are bitter measures, like all measures taken in difficult circumstances.

As soon as you receive this communication, begin to move the entire La Mesa encampment toward Agua Alrevés.

Then you must immediately begin to move as many heads of cattle as possible, in order to salt and smoke them, and at the same time, seek out and prepare sites where as many animals as possible can be kept alive, in order to provide fresh meat first.

Likewise, you must take with you all the grain, provisions, and general supplies that you have. In the new encampment, which must be dispersed, you should immediately dig all kinds of antiaircraft shelters—mainly reinforced tunnels.

When the enemy manages to reach the hill at La Maestra by way of Santana, you must withdraw the squads protecting the area of El Hombrito and Alto Escudero. Order them at once to take the road from La Gloria to the little house the boy from Villa Clara lives in in the Maestra, and to dig trenches on the road from Santana up to La Nevada. Prepare the site at La Nevada, where the forest begins, and look for gun positions that will dominate the road. Also prepare trenches along the hill as far as the cemetery to protect the approach to Malverde, while on the south we'll defend the entrance of the Mula River, farther than the place where the river from Zoltar empties.

You must look for the best positions on those hills, about a mile from the little house that should be your supply depot and your headquarters, and you must firmly resolve that they will not capture it under any circumstances. Once you are situated at Agua Alrevés and your forces deployed, you will not have to retreat any farther. With El Turquino on one flank, and La Maestra on the other, and us protecting you from this side, it will be impossible for any army to advance through here at any point. For that reason, I am going to try to have the telephone installed that far away. You will have charge of covering points 1, 2, 3, and 4 on the enclosed map, and I, for your greater security as well as ours, will cover 5 and 6, which will make our positions impregnable. Once there, for that stage of the struggle, I can send you mines and electric fuses from the reserves.

The fundamental objectives of these plans are:

1. To protect and maintain the basic territory in order to provision ourselves with airborne weapons and munitions, a plan that is going well.

2. To keep the radio station functioning; it has become a key factor.

3. To hold out in organized fashion for three months, a time which I consider indispensable in order to be able to launch our offensive with ample men and equipment.

4. To meet the enemy with ever stronger resistance, as we find and occupy the most strategic points.

5. To have at our disposal a basic territory in which the organization, the hospitals, workshops, etc., can function.

As to the instructions I have given on the points where you should place the squads (El Hombrito, Alto Escudero, etc.), you can make the changes and additions you deem necessary. The essential idea is to continue to be able to concentrate forces of men at key points. If it seems a good idea, you can send some light advance forces ahead along these roads; they should stay on the lower roads to throw the enemy off guard and confuse them.

Communicate these instructions at once to Almeida, wherever he might be. Keep this message because I have not been able to make a copy.

I believe that, despite my insistence, you are neglecting the problem of trenches and defenses, and it is really strange, because I've had to fight to get people to make real excavations and prepare effective trenches that are a protection against anything, and not just ridiculous little holes, which is what the vast majority tend to do. With proper defenses, neither Sánchez Mosquera nor anybody else can advance, without subjecting their troops to a tremendous bloodletting. It's hard to think that even though this is the route the enemy will take, the ground has not been readied with every defense imaginable. After five and a half hours, without resorting to machine guns, seven men here turned back the second consecutive attempt to advance from Las Mercedes toward Las Vegas, using only 350 bullets. And still that seems a lot to me. The trenches played a decisive role in this; the day before they had to retreat from a forward height because there was no real protection. I had ordered them to dig trenches farther back days before we went down, because I saw they had neglected the defenses. If those trenches had not been there, they would have had to abandon the point immediately, since they faced almost a hundred soldiers, who took positions aggressively and fired countless mortars.

General Cantillo's Plan of Attack   Bayamo, June 16, 1958 *

I. SITUATION

A. Enemy Forces

1. The enemy may have small encampments in Llanos del Infierno (to the west of the Mocha River) and at points on the rivers Palma Mocha and La Plata, as well as in Naranjal and the area of El Jigüe.

2. At the source of one of the branches of the La Plata River there is a prison camp, in a recently constructed house situated near the foothills. The place is known as Los Bajos de Jiménez. Apart from the recently constructed house there is another in the shape of an inverted L, which almost forms a cross.

3. Weapons: The enemy has rifles, revolvers, M-1 rifles, .30-caliber NS, and Amt .30-caliber Liv, and homemade bombs.

4. Their morale has been low lately because of the air raids and the continual advance of our troops.

B. Friendly Forces

1. The 11 and 22 Inf Bns under the command of Lieutenant Colonel Sánchez Mosquera are advancing from Dos Bocas de Nagua in the direction of Santo Domingo, to the foothills.

---

* Enemy document seized in combat.——C. F.

2. The 19 Inf Bn is operating in Arroyón and will move in a southerly direction when given the order.

3. The 17 Inf Bn is situated at Las Mercedes.

4. The air force is working daily over the area and will offer direct support to the 18 Inf Bn, if requested.

5. The frigate continues protecting the forces from the southern coast, and will offer direct support to the artillery, if requested.

II. MISSION:

The 18 Inf Bn, with two companies, will operate in the area bounded by El Jigüe, Naranjal, and the rest of the Sierra hills.

III. EXECUTION:

A. You, along with two companies will start the movement at 0500 on the eighteenth of this month, going up the Palma Mocha River as far as the Alto or Loma de Palma Mocha and from there you will take a western route as far as the headquarters of La Plata River.

B. During the movement you will carry out the following missions:

1. Locate and take the small rebel encampment mentioned in paragraph I.A. 2. Try to free the prisoners; among them are soldiers.

2. As soon as the aforementioned prisoners are rescued, put them into your unit and report.

3. Keep to the heights in the Jigüe, Naranjal, and foothills area, until further orders are received.

C. The 3rd Co of your Bn, 48 hours after your departure, will move by sea to the mouth of La Plata River and there the provisioning outfit will be set up.

CARLOS FRANQUI

The Oriente Province Second Front, where Column 6, Frank País, of the Rebel Army is fighting, under the command of Raúl Castro Ruz, controls the points of Mayarí, Sagua de Tánamo, and Baracoa, in the northern part of the province, a mountainous region from the Sagua-Baracoa area to the end of the island, which is made up of the Sierra Cristal, the Cuchilla de Toa, and Moa. In the center, the municipalities of San Luis, Alto Songo, and Palma Soriano, and in the south Guantánamo and Yateras, which is covered by the foothills of the Sierra Maestra, east of Santiago de Cuba, where the Sierra Canasta extends from Gran Piedra as far as Punta de Maisí.

Eight municipalities in all, about 4000 square miles, almost a third of Oriente Province with some fifteen sugar mills and large sugarcane plantations, vast, rich coffee and banana lands, as well as other fruits.

Recently, Column 6 waged a victorious battle at the Experimental

Coffee Station in Oriente, which was reported by international news agencies.

In this brief campaign, the column led by Major Raúl Castro Ruz has inflicted approximately a hundred casualties on the army, seized dozens of weapons, a large quantity of ammunition and grenades, more than a hundred motorized vehicles, and engaged in more than fifteen victorious combats, in which we suffered twenty casualties, counting both the dead and wounded.

The Rebel Army has industrialized the zone, established several factories, shops for making M-26-7 bombs; hospitals, and first-aid stations, a medical and nursing staff; a tribunal that has organized the civilian life of the region; a public-works department, which builds roads and trenches; and the Rebel Army has established numerous schools that provide free education to the peasant population.

Five soldiers were attacked and their arms captured at the powder magazine in Lagunas. In an encounter with an army reinforcement that was heading there, five soldiers and a militiaman from the 26th of July perished. In another attack on soldiers, at Veguita, there were two enemy casualties. In an encounter at the Altamira Reparto, two of Masferrer's men died and another two were injured. There was large-scale sabotage at the Cuban Electric Company, in which twenty-three radio-equipped trucks were burned and a substation destroyed. Losses exceeded $100,000.

Santiago: Three militiamen of the 26th of July Movement, taken by surprise in a house, fought against several squad cars, killed an army lieutenant and a corporal, before dying themselves. The woman of the house was machine-gunned down by the Batista thugs. A 13,000-watt transformer and another, of 66,000 volts, were blown up in Santiago de Cuba, leaving part of the city in the dark, as was El Cobre and Contramaestre. Ten of Masferrer's agents and several of the dictatorship's killers were executed in Oriente Province.

Camagüey: Several of the tyranny's torturers were executed. Sabotage was carried out in several sections of the city. Student sabotage in Ciego de Avila. Rebel forces operating in Santa Lucía were bombarded but suffered no casualties.

Las Villas: Major Victor Bordón's partisans carried out several incursions through the central province of Cuba, after taking Quemados de Güines, fighting in Sagua la Grande, and fighting their way clear in the zone of the Escambray. Rebel forces of the Revolutionary Directory have been operating in this province and have sparked actions in Topes de Collantes and the hydroelectric plant at El Habanilla in the Sierra del Escambray.

Matanzas: Acts of sabotage continue in Matanzas, and in Cárdenas, Colón, Jovellanos, and other zones of the province. Numerous persons have disappeared as a result of an attempted murder* by a local student.

Havana: Captain Lima, the tyranny's famous torturer, and several agents were shot while leaving a cabaret in Marianao. The ex-minister of the interior, a well-known hawk, was injured in an attempt on his life on L Street, near Station CMQ.

Pinar del Río: Fires in tobacco warehouses continue in San Juan and Martínez, Los Palacios, as does sabotage in Artemisa, Guanajay, and Pinar del Río.

Across the island, from Oriente to Occidente, a people are fighting for their freedom, pounding away against terror, repression, savagery, and the crimes of the tyranny.

FIDEL CASTRO

Orders
To Che Guevara   Sierra, June 17

After the previous message, I just received another by telephone telling me that today, at 8:00 a.m., the guards are advancing over a hill called El Infierno, and they can now go either to Santo Domingo or to San Francisco.

This troop has been proceeding without resistance, but we cannot allow it to enter Santo Domingo, because that would put our advance troops from Providencia and El Salto in a precarious position.

Send me, besides the two men with Garands, Lionel with his Garand and five men armed with M-1s.

This will weaken our defense on the route to San Lorenzo, but it's far more important to prevent their entering Santo Domingo.

Carry out this order with the greatest urgency.

To Pedrito Miret   Sierra, June

If the news Cuevas sent is true—that enemy troops have infiltrated from Palma Mocha to here—the situation allows for no alternative. You must retreat from the beach and go toward El Jigüe with all your personnel, taking great precautions, as you have no idea where this troop will appear. Once in El Jigüe, leave a squad at a strategic position to keep an eye on all directions, and then advance toward the hospital by the footpath from El Jigüe. This movement has been decided upon because it will not only prevent them from attacking your rearguard but it will also protect this zone, where there is not one single rifle.

---

* Santiago Rey, ex-minister of the interior, was the intended victim.—ED.

On the other hand, Cuevas has been sent to another spot, in case the enemy advances toward Santo Domingo.

The situation is difficult but we have to face up to it.

To Ramón Paz   Sierra, June 19

You've no idea how valuable it is right now that you repulsed the guards on this road. I congratulate you, and the brave comrades accompanying you, both on your decision and your action. The situation would have been very precarious if the guards had gotten as far as Naranjal.

Your mission now is to continue to keep the guards from making that crossing.

CAPTAIN PACO CABRERA

Report to the Commander   Sierra, June 19

We have just finished our first combat against the army and have inflicted at least twelve casualties.

Hubert [Matos] and I counted eight dead; we exploded the mine very close to us, just after a group of some twenty-five or thirty soldiers had crossed over. The boys conducted themselves valiantly.

Nothing new otherwise.

FIDEL CASTRO

Orders to Che Guevara   Sierra, June 19

The soldiers are going down toward Lucas's house. Send the remaining seven men with automatic weapons to the Villa Clara road. Fighting has been going on since 7:00 a.m.

You'll also be hearing an airplane over the spot where Horacio is; mortar fire and sometimes machine guns can be heard. It seems the soldiers are advancing on that side.

Sierra, June 19

The situation at the beach is extraordinarily dangerous because of an enemy troop there; we can't even locate it. We're running the risk of losing not only the territory but the hospital too, the radio station, the bullets, mines, food, etc.

I have nothing but my rifle here to confront this new situation.

I'm not even sure that the messenger I sent to Paz this morning asking for men managed to reach him.

I absolutely need the men I asked you for this morning, if we're even going to make any attempt at saving the La Plata zone.

I'm going to order Pedrito Miret to abandon the beach and move upward—if the news turns out to be true.

Mobilize Crescencio's column and begin to move personnel from there in your direction to try to defend the Alto de la Vigia, as far as this zone; abandon the Habanita front.

At the same time, the men at El Macho and El Macío must withdraw so we can concentrate our forces.

While there's a hope of maintaining the Plata territory, we must not alter our strategy.

The main problem is that we don't have enough men to defend such a vast zone. We must try to defend ourselves by reconcentrating before launching into irregular action again.

If Las Vegas falls, divide the personnel between Las Minas del Infierno and Mompié's hill.

They reported that the pilot arrived safely. That's the only positive news all day.

CAPTAIN PACO CABRERA

Report to the Commander   Sierra, June 19

Despite our efforts not to permit the guards to enter Santo Domingo, after a battle in which we inflicted from ten to twelve casualties and suffered none ourselves, the soldiers divided into three groups: one along the river and the others on two slopes. We had to retreat as it was impossible to hold them. They are entering Santo Domingo at this very moment. We're in El Naranjo awaiting orders.

FIDEL CASTRO

Orders
To Celia Sánchez   Sierra, June 20

The news arriving from Las Vegas is shameful and disappointing.

Communicate my order to Che to investigate what has happened and to disarm everyone involved in this act of cowardice, and send boys from the school to recover those rifles.

Arrest and send to me the person responsible for the loss of the detonator cable, the bomb, and the other idiotic actions. Communicate the order to Horacio* to use whatever men he has to hold whatever terrain is left of Las Vegas, inch by inch.

---

* Captain Horacio Rodríguez came to Cuba on the *Granma*. He did not stay in the Sierra Maestra but was later sent by Santiago to the hills. He was the man in charge of the 196 Batista men who surrendered after the combat of El Jigüe in the Sierra Maestra. He died in combat near Manzanillo on January 2, 1959, one day after Batista had fled from the country.

Have Aguilera begin fortifying Las Minas del Infierno, and the road leading up to it, with good trenches.

Send me the reinforcements I asked Che for.

The evidence seems to confirm that Paco [Cabrera] and Hubert's [Matos] ambush was effective. They fired point-blank at the vanguard and used the mine effectively—more than ten soldiers were killed. Seven stretchers were seen passing Lucas's house, apparently going down.

To Ramón Paz   Sierra, June 20

How many messages I've sent you today! And always, even before the instructions reach you, the situation changes. Luckily you always make the right decisions when you have to resolve anything because you keep calm at all times.

You must do the following: Position yourself on this side of Naranjal to block the enemy from proceeding upward.

Considering the possibility that you may not have joined up with Pedrito, I am sending you seven men with automatic weapons as reinforcements.

To Ramón Paz

Make sure that the people from Palma Mocha and Las Cuevas who had taken refuge here don't go hungry. Have some cattle killed for them.

I am sending you two hundred more Beretta bullets, a little packet of tobacco for you, and a big one for everybody in your squad.

Cuevas should clean up the beach and destroy all the low stone walls that the guards erected on the shore, so they won't have anywhere to hide when you open fire on them. A little farther from the shore you can put a delayed-action mine that will rake the surface and spread terror.

To Eddy Suñol   Sierra, June 20

The guards have entered Las Vegas.* So take this into account when you take up your position. Your mission is to defend the entrance of the Maestra through the Tiendecita from the lowest point possible. Send me the four Berettas and two rifles, which I might need, and defend yourself well with your other weapons. Today there will certainly be fighting in this zone. Success depends on our acting calmly and quickly. Order them to aim a 100-lb. bomb at the troops who will try to penetrate the

---

* At that time, Che was calmly entering Las Vegas on his little mule. He was saved by meeting another rebel commander, Humberto Sori Marín, who was the last to leave for Las Minas.—C.F.

Naranjal zone; I have another bomb like it ready at the top of the Maestra. Report any advance from that direction. Everybody is in position. I have complete confidence in the squad's courage.

To Che Guevara   Sierra, June 20

Direct the defense of the Maestra from El Purgatorio to Mompié's hill. Move the line toward here, shift the squads toward that zone, which will be reinforced with the twenty men from Las Vegas.

The men from the Maestra zone should be ready to attack any troops that advance from the sea and should try to deliver a decisive blow if they get an opportunity.

Suñol made a perfect withdrawal, without losing a thing. He is now defending the entrance to the Maestra through El Cristo and El Toro. On the sea side, he repulsed and contained a very large force that was advancing from Palma Mocha toward Naranjal.

Lalo is also in Santo Domingo taking care of the road on that side.

A new factor that might crop up is that the troops who stayed in El Coco and El Verraco may advance toward Santo Domingo by the San Francisco road, through La Jeringa.

Right now some mortar shells are exploding very close to us; maybe the army has been able to enter Naranjal. Try to mobilize everybody tonight, even Crescencio's men.

RAMÓN PAZ

Report to Fidel Castro

I made contact with the army at 9:00 a.m. I repulsed them. I have two men wounded (from mortar fragments). I have taken the two roads that lead to Naranjal. I am waiting for orders; now the planes are punishing us, but we haven't given up an inch. I've already ordered Cuevas and Teruel to withdraw.

FIDEL CASTRO

Orders to Ramón Paz   Sierra, June 21

The enemy force from Palma Mocha will try to get to the top of the Maestra or the slope of Palma Mocha, or both. They must be prevented from achieving their objective.

The force that is in Palma Mocha, may, after crossing Naranjal, attempt to reach La Plata, either by the new road that goes up the hill at Palma Mocha, and then descend by some little path, or climb up the Maestra by way of Palma Mocha and Santo Domingo, and advance through the Maestra toward La Plata.

Another spot that raises a question is at a very steep little pathway that goes from El Jigüe to the Maestra, along the ridge; it should be investigated and guarded by posting one or two men, if the guards that are on the beach at La Plata advance toward El Jigüe. These guards must be watched at all times and harassed constantly if they attempt to advance.

The Alto de Cahuara remains. Che ordered the patrol that was in El Macho to go there, according to what he told me yesterday. I am going to check and confirm this.

Naturally, there are some places here that the guards might occupy; the best thing would be to let them stay and be wiped out, because no reinforcements can possibly come. We must wait for this chance; some guards have already been seen, but we couldn't be effective because we didn't have enough armed personnel.

From now on, we must kill the vanguard wherever they turn up. The line now, through the Maestra, from El Frío to the Palma Mocha–Santo Domingo road, will be very difficult to cross. We will make the big strike from the south.

If we manage to carry out these plans, it will be a great victory, apart from the fact that we'll be able to save the radio station and the territorial base for supplying arms.

We must prepare effective and well-protected trenches against mortars; they must be covered with logs and a yard-high stone wall; the roof should be a foot higher than the hole.

FIDEL CASTRO

Communiqué   Sierra, June 25

Monday, the twenty-third, in the early hours of the night, rebel forces attacked the enemy concentration at the mouth of the Plata River with mortar fire and .50-caliber machine guns; Tuesday, yesterday, at 2:00 p.m., those same forces of the dictatorship sustained twenty-one casualties in the place called Purialon while attempting to advance upstream by the Plata. In this combat, the rebel forces sustained three casualties.

For courage and skill demonstrated in confronting the enemy forces, special mention is merited by Rebel Captain Ramón Paz. This same Rebel officer destroyed an enemy detachment in El Pozón, and in the Caridad de Palma Mocha on April 10. He has just repulsed one of the most powerful enemy columns.

FIDEL CASTRO

To Andrés Cuevas   Sierra, June 25

Tomorrow have them fetch the cheese. Today they're bringing honey; it's for dessert. Sugar has to be divided. The box must last for two weeks.

P.S.: Let me know what size shoes are needed. They'll get them
tomorrow.

MANUEL FAJARDO   Frank País, Second Front, June

Those gentlemen* thought that we Cubans were savages; they looked at
us contemptuously, even though they were our prisoners.

There was a fat one who weighed about 250 lbs., who said that this
was the "Cuban jungle." He said: "My children will be wondering
where Papa is, and their papa is in the Cuban jungle."

There were all kinds—North Americans, Syrians, Puerto Ricans,
Mexicans—it was practically an international brigade, but they were all
cut from the same mold.

I showed them the unexploded bombs that we had retrieved, and
they denied that they came from North America.

Many of them wanted to leave, and one of them, a Mexican, asked
me how I was going to stop him from going. I said that I wasn't planning
to use just a pail of water to stop him. I remember that one day I took an
empty can of sausages and shot it from about 50 yards away. An American said: "Captain Beard, you're a good shot." I said that if they made a
move to leave, they'd see a real good shot.

I told them that it was dangerous for them to leave, because there
were mines around here that could explode. Once I bandaged up one of
our men as if he was wounded, and I made them believe that he'd been
hurt by a mine. That's how we held on to them.

One day, at 3:00 a.m., there arrived a North American vice-consul
who had been a colonel in World War II. With him came a Cuban who
was more insolent than the vice-consul. They had been ordered to see
Raúl. He didn't speak Spanish until the moment I told him he was
under arrest.

When I told him that Raúl wasn't here, he said, through the Cuban
who served as interpreter, that he was leaving because he had been
tricked. I said he couldn't leave because he was under arrest, and he
started to say: "That is very serious, that is very serious. Do you know
what you are doing?" I said I was well aware of what I was doing, and
that if this were serious, it was more serious that his government was
giving bombs to Batista. "Arresting a North American official is serious,
serious," the vice-consul repeated. I told him that to me he was the same
as one of Batista's recruits.

I brought him a bottle of Bacardi, and we began to talk in a more
friendly way.

---

* Marines, sailors, and civilians from the U.S. Naval Base at Guantánamo,
kidnapped in a daring, desperate raid by Raúl Castro's men.—ED.

He wanted to know the political ideology of all the officers of the Rebel Army. I answered that my ideology was that I had never been political, that I was only a revolutionary who was fighting for the true liberty of my people.

I had many schools operating in the mountains, and near here there was one where classes were going on right then, under some trees, with a little girl, a nurse from Río Toa district, giving classes. He asked me what doctrine she was teaching the children, and I answered that it was the same as the doctrine Carlos Manuel de Céspedes taught in the Wars of Independence.

I explained that I was very concerned about education, because I had never gone to school, and therefore I wanted to be sure that in the future this would not happen to any children in my country. He asked me to let him go to see the little school, and when he returned he said: "Good, good." Afterward, he sent five hundred notebooks and a lot of pencils.

He also asked me what I would do if Russia sent me two shiploads of weapons. I told him that I would take arms from Russia without reservations, and from him, too, if he sent any.

An interesting detail is that while the Americans were with us there, on the Alto de la Victoria, not a single plane ever flew over us.

Batista's soldiers were also encamped on the Alto de la Victoria, about 40 miles away, and I had Raúl's order to send the vice-consul to him. I had a telescope in Boquerón with which I could see all movements of the army as far as Guantánamo.

I told the vice-consul that there were enemy troops and that he would run the risk of being killed, and that was why I had not allowed him to go to Raúl. "And why didn't you tell me that before?" he responded.

He informed the naval base, and in twenty-four hours there wasn't a soldier in any of those places.

This was the most unusual military order given in our war; Raúl Castro gave it; it is a document for history.

VILMA ESPÍN

Raúl took the offensive with the Americans because we were lost; we didn't have anything to push them back with. Our bullets arrived in the middle of the offensive.

When the Americans left, they attacked again, but now Fidel's offensive was going into action in the Sierra, which kept the army from attacking on other fronts.

EDITOR'S SUMMARY   Northern Zone, Second Front,

Oriente, July

While Raúl Castro was still holding the kidnapped personnel from Guantánamo, Jules Dubois interviewed him. Uppermost among the subjects was the kidnapping. Raúl gave three reasons for it:

1. In order to attract world attention in general and that of the United States in particular to the crime that was being committed against our people with arms which the government of the United States of North America had supplied to Batista for continental defense.

2. In order to deter the criminal bombardments—with incendiary bombs, rockets, and even napalm bombs—which in those moments were being carried out against our forces and above all against the defenseless towns of the peasants without taking into account at all the fact that they were not military objectives.

3. Some equipment, like tractors and vehicles, of Moa and Nicaro were taken as strict war necessities, and for the construction of strategic roads within our liberated territories. It filled a social function but it also furnished us with greater facility in mobilizing reinforcements between zones.

Dubois wondered why the military personnel had been released sooner than Raúl had promised. Castro explained that it had been done "mainly because of the crisis that had arisen in the Middle East and the need which your government has for them. For it is not our intention to interfere in any of the domestic questions of your country or of any country." The crisis to which Raúl referred was the threat to overthrow the pro-Western government of President Camille Chamoun in Lebanon. President Eisenhower sent U.S. Marines there to deal with the situation.

CARLOS FRANQUI   Sierra, June

Sabotage, in the key points of cities and of communication routes, has been one of the most frequently used weapons of the Cuban Revolution. In Cuba, sabotage has a tradition dating back to the rebellion against the Spaniards. The first example recorded in our history is the burning of Bayamo, in the Ten Years' War [1868–78]. When Carlos Manuel de Céspedes, leading a handful of brave men, took that city, our anthem, "La Bayamesa," was sung for the first time, and the spirit of heroism and liberty inflamed the people of Bayamo.

In the Wars of Independence, the invasion columns of Máximo Gómez and Antonio Maceo announced their triumphant passage by setting fires. When someone asked General Gómez not to set fire to the cane fields, because that would mean the destruction of the riches of the country, he made the historic reply: "How can you talk to me about miserable sugarcane when so much blood is flowing?" And wheeling his horse about, he ordered that the fields of sugarcane be set to the torch.

Apart from those Cuban ancedents, sabotage is a universal weapon
that every people has used in its struggle for liberty. It was used in Boston Harbor, when the tea was destroyed, and in Europe, during World
War II, the clandestine resistance fighters found sabotage one of their
most effective weapons against the Nazis.

The objective of our sabotage has always been to reach the great
national and foreign enterprises, in order to damage and disorganize the
economic base on which the dictatorship depends—and by these revolutionary acts, to arouse and mobilize the people.

Sabotage helps to develop revolutionary consciousness, as the
Cuban struggle demonstrates. There is a great difference between sabotage and terrorism. Terrorism is an action with a nihilist origin; it tends
to spread panic and terror, without any revolutionary objective, but simply to destroy. Let us compare an act of sabotage with an act of terrorism. It was sabotage to produce a blackout in Havana for several days;
there we were seeking to produce a major upheaval, and it was accomplished; we succeeded in paralyzing a city of a million inhabitants. And
in addition, we caused severe economic damage as a result of the paralysis of industry, work, business, nightlife, and all the economic nerves of a
great city. The losses ran into many millions of dollars. The national and
international consequences of this sabotage harmed and demoralized
the dictatorship. Unquestionably, this was a revolutionary victory. A
terrorist act would have been limited to placing a bomb, without considering the position or the importance of its explosion.

One of the major concerns of the 26th of July Movement has been
that its acts of sabotage should not harm human life. Therefore, we have
carefully studied the site and the time to act before carrying out any sabotage, seeking the least busy location and the moment when there would
be the fewest number of people at the chosen site. But besides, fellow
militants were placed at the site so that before the sabotage occurred,
they could warn passersby, even at the risk of their own lives. That explains why despite the thousands and thousands of acts of sabotage
throughout the country, there have been an extremely small number of
victims.

The revolutionary actions in Santiago de Cuba, Cienfuegos, and the
experience of a year and a half in the Sierra Maestra have shown that
there are thousands of Cubans ready to take up arms in the struggle for
liberty.

But the people of Cuba—who have hidden, protected, and cared for
thousands of our militia while they were engaged in sabotage—realized
at once that the burning of schools and other similar acts of terrorism
were done by the agents of the tyranny. It could not be otherwise; dictatorships are the enemies of culture; revolutions are its allies. The fascist
Millán Astray shouted: "Long live death! Down with intelligence!"
Martí observed: "Being cultured is one way of being free." Evidence that

this is so is to be found in the schools that the Rebel Army has been building throughout the free territory of the Sierra Maestra and in the rest of the liberated areas, despite the incredible difficulties of the war. While the dictatorship destroys peasant classrooms with its bombardments and blows up city schools with bombs, we are bringing education to the people by constructing schools wherever we go.

HUBERT MATOS

Report to the Commander   Sierra, June 26

Three big trenches have been dug at Las Palmas, but only one has a roof; I expect to finish them today. That is why I am still here with twelve men.

Leonel has already gone with six men to the hill where Maracaibo was.

Unless you give me orders to the contrary, I will stay here today, and early tomorrow I will go with six men to the trenches at Ramón's house; I want to improve and enlarge them if I have time. Paco is sick.

CARLOS FRANQUI   Sierra Maestra, June 27

Some months ago, the tyrant, powerless to stop the growth of the Rebel Army, conceived a project to which he devoted the substantial resources of his power and attention and that of his General Staff. The project is to concentrate all the military forces of the tyranny in a supreme effort to annihilate the rebel forces.

The first step was to collect hundreds of millions of dollars to meet the expenses of such a task. He put the republic even further into debt with new loans, bond issues, and taxes. The expenditures have been so large that a few days ago there was a new loan issue for $100 million; $18 million were budgeted for army transport alone.

The second important step in the preparation of the offensive was to look for men who would attack the army of the Sierra Maestra. For more than a year, the dictatorship's regular army has been unable to wipe out the men led by Fidel Castro. The soldiers have obstinately refused to go up into the mountains, where the only thing that awaits them is death and the incredible difficulties of life in the cordilleras, while their chiefs enrich themselves by robbing and smuggling far away from the site where they have ordered their men to advance toward death. The soldiers had learned through experience in Oriente that the ideal of liberty cannot be destroyed with a few lies uttered by the General Staff to deceive them, and they refused to fight.

Batista finally concluded that the regular army, the soldiers whom he had sacrificed for six years to maintain himself in power, would not succeed in annihilating the men of the Sierra.

And so to replace the old soldiers, they opened a recruiting station and signed up thousands of new enlistees, whom they deceived with the same story that the rebels were little bands without any weapons. They gave military uniforms to all the juvenile delinquents in the country and to the most retarded of the unemployed. With these thousands of new recruits, Batista formed a new army, the new contingent that would eliminate the rebels.

The third step in Batista's plans for the big military offensive was to equip those thousands of men with the most modern weapons and abundant ammunition. In the United States, he obtained rockets and big bombs for the planes, and other military equipment manufactured nowhere else. According to evidence, Trujillo and Somoza, Batista's equals in crime and barbarity, sent the rest of the weapons the tyranny needed for its offensive, including hundreds of San Cristóbal machine guns, made in the Dominican Republic, and much other equipment came from Nicaragua.

Batista now had men, arms, and supplies in great quantities to finish off the Rebel Army.

The end of the harvest permitted him to reduce the guard in the 151 sugar mills in the country.

The failure of the April strike had had a strong psychological impact on the people and had left them feeling defeated, which encouraged the dictatorship to think that the propitious moment had come.

Sunday, May 25, the enemy offensive began with the attack on La Herradura. Day after day, there were bloody encounters in the various zones of the Sierra Maestra. More than thirty battles, some extremely savage, took place in this month of the campaign.

We were not going to ask the Army General Staff to report their dead and their defeats. But now, when they have succeeded in entering Las Vegas, after bitter resistance, why haven't they made any announcement of it?

Why has the General Staff issued no military communiqués? Why is the tyranny's biggest offensive being carried out in complete silence? There is only one reason that can conclusively explain the dictatorship's silence: It does not believe that it can defeat the Rebel Army.

Batista has had a year and a half of experience in which he announced that Fidel Castro had not landed, then that the rebels had been exterminated, later that they were a tiny band, then that they had been surrounded. Finally, false announcements began that inflated the number of dead rebels to more than a thousand, while they said, on the other hand, that there were only a few to begin with. After April 9 they said that they were turning themselves in, but the truth was forcing its way

out: Every day the liberated territories were growing, and the Rebel
Army was stronger and more ready for battle.

FIDEL CASTRO

Orders
To Lalo [Eduardo] Sardiñas   Sierra, June 29

I congratulate you on your tremendous victory. Tomorrow it will be
even bigger. I have already ordered Camilo and Duque to cut off the retreat at Piedra's house and ordered Almeida's column to take the Alto
del Cacao. They have to hold the positions all day tomorrow. At 8:00
p.m. tomorrow, the general attack will come if they don't succeed in
breaking out of the circle. That will be the end of the offensive and of
Batista.

Send me ten rifles from the extras to strengthen the attack on this
side and to prevent the reinforcements from coming.

To Guillermo García   Sierra, June 29

So far the enemy has lost some 20 dead, and 23 men were taken prisoner,
as well as a .30-caliber gun, a mortar, and about 50 weapons, almost all
automatic.

When it gets dark, proceed directly to Lucas's house; we are going to
try to cut them in half at that point, also, attacking from Naranjal, Santana, and Piedra's house.

So far, we don't have any casualties.

To Braulio Coroneaux   Sierra, June 30

I am sending you about 350 bullets I recently received. Some of them are
good; some have deteriorated.

Sort them from the new ones and use them when you want to make
noise. Don't use the others and the ammunition that you still have except in combat when the enemy tries to advance, since we now have to
husband them very carefully.

You and the .50-caliber machine gun have behaved marvelously
well. I congratulate you.

It seems to me that you should now return to the previous position.

FIDEL CASTRO   Sierra, June 30

Saturday, June 28, the 22d Battalion, consisting of three companies, left
its quarters in Santo Domingo for the Yara River zone, south of the Es-

trada Palma mill, where Lieutenant Colonel Sánchez Mosquera had been encamped for several days with another battalion under his command. This battalion had already tried to scale the slopes of the Sierra Maestra, but it was repulsed by rebel forces, who kept close watch on these troops of the dictatorship. When the 22d Battalion, under the command of Major Villavicencio, reached the banks of the Yara River, Sánchez Mosquera, according to information from prisoners taken by the rebels, ordered them to continue upstream to scale the slopes of the Sierra—this without informing them that the place was under surveillance by the 26th of July Movement guerrillas. The 22d Battalion, formed into its three companies, advanced in order toward the Sierra, but a powerful mine with more than 65 lb. of TNT exploded, almost completely destroying the formation of the first company, which was immediately subjected to intense fire from .30- and .50-caliber machine guns manned by the rebels stationed there. The first company was totally decimated by the rebel forces, and Major Villavicencio ordered the second company to render assistance to the first, but an attack by a new column of rebels on the right flank of the second company halted this effort, and the revolutionaries subjected them to heavy fire from machine guns and .60-caliber mortars. Meanwhile, new rebel columns were put on the alert to cut off the retreat of the third company of the 22d Battalion, which also was subjected to an intense attack from the rebels. When Major Villavicencio ordered the retreat, Batista's soldiers fled in complete disarray, abandoning large numbers of dead and wounded, as well as quantities of equipment, on the field of battle. The rebels captured 28 soldiers, who surrendered unconditionally, and they gathered the dead men and the equipment abandoned by Batista's troops. Meanwhile, Lieutenant Colonel Sánchez Mosquera, who has always been noted for his cruelty toward the rebels, did not send his battalion to protect the soldiers he had commanded to attack. Comfortably installed in his camp, Sánchez Mosquera sent a new company, commanded by a first lieutenant, to try to protect those who had been abandoned and surrounded by the rebel forces. But the rebels, who had seized the arms and ammunition abandoned by Batista's soldiers, prepared a new ambush, with a new TNT mine, which exploded in the middle of the advancing new company, annihilating the soldiers, who died or surrendered without putting up much resistance. A large part of this company abandoned its equipment and fled in disarray through the mountains, pursued by rebel patrols. Sánchez Mosquera did not budge from his position, abandoning to their fate the soldiers he had sent to a certain death. The rebel forces stopped their attacks because it had gotten dark, but their last shots were still heard Monday, the thirtieth, at 8:30 a.m., Cuban time.

15. JULY: EL JIGÜE, A DECISIVE BATTLE

FIDEL CASTRO

Letters

To Raúl Castro   Sierra Maestra, July 7

I have not received any direct information about the earlier and present situation of the North American citizens who are said to be in the hands of your forces. All I know is what has been published inside and outside Cuba. Although I was not completely certain of the veracity of these sources, several days ago I sent you the enclosed message by Radio Rebelde. I was very concerned about the international campaign that is being waged against us, about which I have direct news by radio from a friendly American country.

We must consider the possibility that elements of the dictatorship, exploiting this incident, are hatching a plan for physical aggression against North American citizens; given Batista's hopeless situation, this would turn international public opinion against us as it would react with indignation to the news, for example, that several of those North Americans had been murdered by the rebels.

It is essential to declare categorically that we do not utilize the system of hostages, however justified our indignation may be against the political attitudes of any government.

All this, in the complete absence of official information, puts me in the rather awkward position of not being able to answer any of the questions that the international press and officials of the U.S. government itself ask me concerning an affair of major importance inside and outside of Cuba.

Although I am sure that you are aware of this, and that you are managing the affair with great tact, you must keep in mind that in matters that can have weighty consequences for the Movement, you cannot act on your own initiative, nor go beyond certain limits without any consultation. Besides, that would give the false impression of complete anarchy in the inner circles of our army.

My view is explained in the message I sent by radio. The bearer of those lines will explain it to you in greater detail.

Since I am in the same situation as you are, and have no means of rapid communication to establish contact with you, I authorized a North American helicopter to land in this territory and pick up an officer of our army, who will be flown to you, so that I will be able to answer the questions that they ask me in diplomatic terms; I need what you have to report to me to give the necessary, strictly fair orders.

This has coincided with the greatest battle and the greatest victory our forces have achieved since we have been in the Sierra.

We are in an intense fight against fourteen battalions and seven independent companies. I heard about the unfortunate accident to the plane that was bringing you arms. We are making efforts that I am confident will strengthen all the fronts and extend the war toward Occidente Province. I am writing you this letter early to send it to the place from which Daniel [René Ramos Latour] will leave, because I am busy on a sector of the front. He will explain to you the military tactics and measures that we have adopted and that have had very good results. I am sure that Batista must be angry with those troops and feels it necessary to create in some way the impression that he still is governing Cuba by trying to destroy that column; in that case, he would have to withdraw the forces already committed here.

Use the tactic of concentrating your forces when you are obliged to fall back, so that each time you can offer greater resistance at the most strategic points at which you plan to locate your workshops, food, supplies, etc., and where units can be shifted rapidly from one point to another, as we have been doing. As soon as possible, it is absolutely essential for you to try to set up a way of communicating with us.

To Major José Quevedo*   Sierra, July 10

It was difficult to imagine when you and I saw each other at the university that someday we would be fighting against each other, despite the fact that perhaps we do not even harbor different feelings about the fatherland.

I have often remembered that group of young soldiers who attracted my attention and awakened my sympathies because of their great longing for culture and the efforts they made to pursue their studies.

I have used harsh words in judging the actions of many, and of the

---

* The enemy commander.—C. F.

army in general, but never have my hands or those of my companions been stained with the blood nor have we debased ourselves by the mistreatment of any soldier taken prisoner. In one of our battles, El Uvero, we took a total of thirty-five prisoners, including wounded and uninjured; today all are at liberty and some are even back in the service.

Not even the esprit de corps, which binds your units together—a feeling that has been exploited by those who have brought the army into an absurd and senseless war—exists today, because the most honorable soldiers can be arrested on mere suspicion, beaten, and hurled into the dungeon of a prison like a common criminal, which no army with a genuine esprit de corps will tolerate among its officers.

I have often asked myself about you and the others who were studying with you. I said to myself: "Where are they? Have they been arrested and discharged in one of the various conspiracies?" What a surprise to know that you are around here! And however difficult the circumstances, I am always happy to hear from one of you, and I write these lines on the spur of the moment, without telling you or asking you for anything, only to greet you and to wish you, very sincerely, good luck.

July 10

Why was the airport in Santiago de Cuba closed two days ago by order of the army? It must have something to do with the news transmitted by international cable that one of the tyranny's planes was shot down in the northern zone of Oriente and another damaged. A large number of dead and wounded, from recent battles here, whom the dictatorship wanted to conceal, were brought there. For the third consecutive day, almost every neighborhood of the capital remains without water.

FIDEL CASTRO

Messages
To Che Guevara   Sierra, July 11

In the attack this morning, one of the guards was wounded in the ankle. When they went to get the wounded man, who was guarded by three platoons, they fell into the first ambush, where Guillermo and Cordoví and the five recruits that were sent to us were waiting. Five guards were killed, one badly wounded is in our hands, and another is a prisoner. Through him I have been able to learn that they have three companies whose artillery weapons include an 81 mortar, a 60 mortar, and a bazooka. The attack this morning took place near Plana Mayor, where the radio was, and we took the building that houses it.

Since this morning, I have been waiting for Coroneaux with the .50-caliber.

Everything will be better when the eleven men I asked you for this morning arrive. Also order Acevedo (the one with the .30-caliber) to start marching at 4:00 a.m. in this direction with the bullets that he has, plus the little box I had in La Mina, and a full cartridge belt.

Tell Camilo to send 750 .30-'06 bullets to Mompié's hill and then bring them here.

Tell the men along the line that they must resist any attack at all costs. Don't forget to settle the problem of the plane with weapons and order Laferté to send the twenty best recruits that you can pick to Cahuara, to Mariano Medina's house, where we'll use them if we get more weapons.

Our strongest line (Lalo [Eduardo Sardiñas] and Cuevas with a total of 41 automatic weapons, including two machine guns) has not gone into action. They are in Purialón, waiting for the enemy reinforcements. Paz is hidden in an ambush beyond, ready to attack the reinforcements through the rearguard. We hold the hill at Naranjal at one of its best strategic points. We have managed to take all the high points that might let them escape.

Send an urgent order to Ramirito to place fifteen well-armed men on the Alto de la Maestra, where the Palma Mocha–Santo Domingo roads meet. We must concentrate our efforts on this operation: it is worth it.

Find the mortar crew and the 4 shells, which should be ready by now, and send them if they haven't left.

To Che Guevara   **El Jigüe, July 11**

We are trying to give the impression that we've retreated. For three hours we haven't heard a shot. No plane has passed over; their radio equipment seems to be damaged. I'm using the time to reinforce this impression. They seem to be perplexed. What I am trying to arrange is that tomorrow, when they come to explore, they will have a surprise, because they have to come and see what is happening, but they don't know what awaits them.

Besides, this way all the men get a good rest today. If there is any way of doing it, rush the .30-calibers to me so that they can be here early, ready to start out tomorrow, when the fight begins again, with the .50-caliber machine gun on one side and the .30 on the other. Everything seems to indicate that the high command has no idea of the location of this troop. Tell Camilo to send thirty salvo bullets. I am going to try the grenade-throwers.

I think our strategy must be to bleed and decimate the enemy reinforcements, while we weaken, reduce, and exhaust the encircled troops. The army is compelled to make a great effort just when it seems exhausted. I am a little worried about the Palma Mocha flank, which could be strongly fortified with only a few men. With reserves here in the Alto de Cahuara I am not worried about the Magdalena and El Mulato flank. I think it will be difficult for them to enter again through Meriño. They need more cables, more mines, and more blasting caps there. Camilo should send three cables, three mines, and the large detonator that stayed there.

I'm figuring that these troops will make some effort to escape. When they are driven back two or three times, their morale will be destroyed, and it will be easy to wipe them out. I'm trying to get out of the prisoner as much data and information as possible about the quality of the men and their leader. They seem to be for the most part regular soldiers and about 25 percent new recruits. The chief is the same commander who ordered retreat twice (at La Caridad and Naranjal), in the face of resistance from Paz.

To Guillermo García   El Jigüe, Sierra, July 12

I already have the .50-caliber here and a .30 is about to arrive. The tactic I've followed is not to fire a single shot so that the guards will think we've gone and will try to explore the road where you are; that's the least that they can do. If they attack you in force, I am going to order an attack from here on the flank, from the stream. Besides, we have taken the small slope that you explored the first day, and that's where I am going to put the .30.

Yesterday afternoon, the enemy came back from combat with you very discouraged. But I still don't want to use the .50 until they've gone through one more attack.

Encourage your men to resist unflinchingly whatever bombs and shells the planes may drop.

To Che Guevara   El Jigüe, Sierra, July 13

I'm fed up with waiting for the .30-caliber. The mortar, and its personnel (except Pedrito, who is here) are at the mine. So that hasn't come either. We have four shells ready and hope that some of them will go off.

These bastards aren't budging. Tonight we're going to try to tighten the circle.

To Ramón Paz   El Jigüe, July 13

If they don't move today or tomorrow, we're going to open fire with the .50, take the hills that are closest to them, and dig ourselves trenches there; that will keep them from breathing.

You have to wait there as long as necessary. I now have here the radio car that we took in Santo Domingo so I can intercept their communications and find out definitely if they are aware or not of their situation; it seems strange that no plane has appeared here.

The shipment of loudspeakers is also on its way and we intend to utilize them to the maximum.

To Che Guevara   El Jigüe, July 14

For an hour, there has been fighting around here. About a hundred guards tried to get out, and they again clashed with us on the shore road. I sent a group of men with automatics to cut off the retreat by a stream.

I still don't have any news of the situation down below. I have the .50 and the .30 ready for them whenever they return to their camp—if, as I expect, they are driven back.

To Che Guevara

Of the troops that tried to get out yesterday and were separated, fifteen more prisoners have been captured and fourteen weapons. There are in all, between yesterday and today, nineteen prisoners and eighteen weapons. They were captured before they reached the beach. I am going to see Guillermo to prepare an attack tomorrow from the other side.

Give this information to Camilo.

FIDEL CASTRO

Letter to Major José Quevedo   El Jigüe, Sierra, July 15

We are not at war with the army, we are at war with the tyranny.

They have sent you and your soldiers to die, leading you into a real trap, placing you in a pit with no escape, without sending a single soldier to try to save you.

Your troops are surrounded, they don't have the slightest hope of being saved. All the roads, hills, paths, and streams have been captured, fortified with trenches, and mined with 100-lb. bombs.

To sacrifice those men in a lost battle, on the altar of an ignoble cause, is a crime that a good-hearted man cannot commit. In this situation I offer you an honorable, dignified surrender. Accept it; it will not be a surrender to an enemy of the fatherland but to a sincere revolutionary, to a fighter who struggles for the good of all Cubans.

All your men will be treated with the greatest respect and consideration. The officers will be permitted to keep their weapons.

FIDEL CASTRO

Messages
To Che Guevara   El Jigüe, Sierra, July 15

The struggle continues to proceed favorably. Yesterday they took mules
from the troops who were trying to get out; from their packs so far alone,
they've brought me a thousand bullets for .30-caliber machine guns.
Also they took six mule drivers prisoner.

We have already placed the .30 about 450 yards away from the
enemy camp, but it has jammed twice. The .50 is 500 yards away. We
have a mortar under fire, and can't recover it. The enemy has no more
food.

For two hours the fucking planes have been at us. The bombs they
are dropping are napalm.

To Che Guevara   El Jigüe, Sierra, July 15

I congratulate you on your success in overcoming the crisis there; it has
raised our spirits considerably to know that there is no danger from that
direction. If they are in Meriño and try to come down in this direction,
send me a messenger by horse to warn me quickly. I ordered them to dig
trenches beyond El Coco and we can catch them between two fires. In
any case, when they are on the Roble road, they'll be hit on the flank.

If you can't keep Las Minas, be sure to divide the squads as I told
you, so that one group takes care of the Maestra and the other of the
Magdalena.

I hope that today there'll be clashes with troops coming from the
beach; it's the shortest road that they can take to help the surrounded
men. The air force is showing extraordinary interest in us. I think that
their radio car is broken, since it doesn't answer the airplane, so we are
going to use ours to give their planes false information about where to
bomb.

Tonight we are beginning to use the loudspeakers. Well-prepared
talks and careful slogans.

This very minute the plane has machine-gunned us. Pedro Miret
was wounded in the chest.

The doctor who just examined Pedrito found that the bullet apparently hit him on the rebound, on the breastbone, and did not
penetrate.

To Braulio Coroneaux   El Jigüe, July 15

I'm going to send you the radio car because theirs seems to be broken,
and when the planes come over, speak as if you were a guard and tell

them: "The rebels have taken our camp. They're shooting from the river. We are on the mountain. Hey, you're machine-gunning our own men. The soldiers are on the mountain. Please, fellows. . . ."

Repeat this and things in that style all afternoon, whenever a plane flies by. Speak as if you were afraid.

El Jigüe, July 16

It is of the greatest importance that we take the Manacas stream, which is on the part of the hill beyond where Pax is, so that they can't try to give us the slip that way.

The perfect thing would be for the guards to cross without running into Paz and for the fight to begin when they fall into Lalo and Cuevas's ambush, so that they'll be surrounded. You already know what happens in that case: no one comes to get them out. Lalo and Cuevas should hold all the slopes and heights they can secure and try to drive them back completely.

Keep on using the mines, especially the ones with 100-lb. charges.

I didn't want to move a single man from here because this is a decisive battle and our aims are very ambitious; not only to make the surrounded troops surrender but to destroy the reinforcements as well.

This could be the end of Batista.

Keep calm, keep up your spirits, and good luck.

To Braulio Coroneaux   El Jigüe, July 16

You were very good at not letting the plane know who you were. Tomorrow say the same things as you did today, in a desperate tone—that there are men who are starving to death in the mountains, that the rebels are still in the camp, and in the river next to the camp, that for God's sake, they should send reinforcements, that there are many wounded.

If they ask you strange questions, break off as if the equipment had gone out of whack.

Tomorrow, possibly, Guillermo will begin to fire from the marker that is behind the guards. When he opens fire from that side, open with the .50 from this side.

Here are two cigars as your reward.

To Che Guevara   El Jigüe, July 16

Today we are bombing the guards. The trick with the radio car worked out perfectly. We announced that the rebels had taken the camp, and the planes attacked it with napalm, bombs, and shells. The whole thing was very well timed, because the first two 100-lb. bombs that were used to launch the raid today were fired on the side where I am, on the hill at Caymara. Now the guards run like hell every time they hear the plane.

Of the four mortar shells, none exploded.

The loudspeakers keep functioning during the day. From noon to 3:00 p.m., we announced a cease-fire so that they could consider our conditions; then this morning, after the first transmission, they were assembling in the camp—an ideal moment to hit them with a speech and win their confidence, but, instead of doing the intelligent thing, our gunners, as usual, opened fire on them. Tomorrow it's going to be very tough for them as soon as Guillermo opens fire from a crag that dominates the side of the hill where they are hidden. We've hit them with everything we have, with the .50, and .30, and about twenty-five scattered rifles. I am keeping twelve men in reserve for any contingency. With Guillermo shooting at them with only part of his squad, the pressure is increased. I don't want to take one man away from the shore side. I still don't see where reinforcements can land.

As soon as the personnel requested from Almeida and Ramiro arrive, some men must be placed on the slope of the Maestra, between Palma Mocha and Santo Domingo and the others must go up via Palma Mocha, to the point where the hill at Naranjal starts, and entrench themselves there, making contact with a patrol on the peak of the Naranjal hill, where the Palma Mocha–Naranjal road begins to descend toward Naranjal.

To Che Guevara El Jigüe, Sierra, July 16

At dawn we intercepted a message from a light plane to the chief of a battalion, apparently situated on the beach, saying that it should advance, taking key points, that is the heights, and protect the mule team with a platoon. Tonight I have just sent a messenger to Cuevas, Lalo, and Paz to report the above. The three of them have seventy-six well-armed men, with the highest fighting morale, good locations, and they are forewarned. There have been few times before, perhaps none, when we've been in better condition to await the enemy. What attracts me most in this whole operation is destroying the reinforcements, whichever route they take. Since we have the troops surrounded and on the verge of collapse, with the government obliged to rescue them, we must try to make this operation a decisive battle. Already the army can't do any more; in these last days it has reached the limit of its potential. It can't use more bombs, more shells, more rockets, more napalm, or more mortars, not even more columns; it knows that it is impotent. With you situated on the top of La Mina, and Camilo in La Plata, and the reinforcements from Almeida and Ramirito at hand, we couldn't have better prospects for victory.

To Che Guevara   El Jigüe, July 16

I didn't receive your message on the capture of La Mina until now, when I've just gotten back from a conference with Guillermo.

It is obvious that you made a huge effort and I congratulate you all.

Tonight, at 1:00 a.m., we had a real radio meeting with the soldiers, with a message from me for Major Quevedo (who was with me at the university and turns out to be the chief of the encircled forces), a list of the surrender terms we offer, a message from Vallejo to Dr. Wolf (medical officer of the troops, whom he knew during his student days), and other instructions. A wounded prisoner spoke with extraordinary eloquence. It was really impressive and serious. At the beginning, it seemed as if they were frightened, and a lot of shots were fired, but in a few minutes there was absolute silence and from then on, there were no more shots. I don't have any illusions. We'll have to pressure them still more; but they are already in a very unfavorable situation. I sent men to the only place they still hold that is beyond our range of fire. They ran out of provisions days ago. They don't even have a grain of salt left. They are virtually dying of hunger. Tomorrow at daybreak we are going to fire our four mortar shells at them. Tonight, I'm going to make all the prisoners talk. I think that if we manage to keep the reinforcements from arriving they will surrender unconditionally.

The planes have been shooting a lot—from dawn until afternoon—but the men really don't pay any attention to them at all. I hope to hear from you soon.

To Che Guevara   El Jigüe, July 17

The reinforcements lost their balls. So far they have 12 dead, 18 prisoners captured, 1 machine gun, 10 San Cristóbals, 15 Springfields, 2 Brownings, 4 Garands, and 1 M-1.

I want you to tell Camilo to send twenty unarmed men from those with Ramiro and Almeida, but they should be good. You can also order them to send ten recruits from the best that remain.

GUILLERMO GARCÍA

Report to the Commander   El Jigüe, July 17

Now they really can't move, because I control them completely. They can't go down to the river; I have a post a hundred yards from the little house below. I guess they'll have to shit in their trenches.

FIDEL CASTRO

Reports

To Che Guevara   El Jigüe, July 18

The encircled troops are on the verge of collapse. Tomorrow we will take positions about 40 yards from the camp. We now have taken some bullets, which improves our situation greatly, since we were down to thirty bullets for the rifles. Tomorrow at daybreak there will be an attack from a much smaller circle with fifteen more weapons.

I had already sent a reply to the Red Cross. This can be utilized for propaganda to the army. Besides, the prisoners are already a headache.

To Lalo Sardiñas   El Jigüe, July 19

The commander of the encircled troops spoke with Ramirito and told him that he had given his word to resist until six in the afternoon today. If the reinforcements did not arrive at six, he would come to see me to agree on the surrender terms.

The army promised him that the reinforcements would arrive today. So it is a matter of not letting the reinforcements get through, even if there are two thousand guards.

Also, it seems that the army talked about sending in a lot of planes today.

Protect yourself, and if the reinforcements try to come, don't let them get through for anything in the world; victory is in our hands.

Our men went to the camp, spoke with the guards, and gave them cigars.

To Che Guevara   El Jigüe, July 19

There has been a tremendous fight with the new reinforcements. Cuevas was killed advancing against the soldiers. I have the impression that this time our plan was carried out completely.

I hope that the guards have been given a devastating defeat, but Cuevas's death has made everyone here very sad, and although victory is now almost certain, it will be a bitter one. We don't have news from Lalo and Paz, who were farther down. Cuevas destroyed the vanguard and took all its weapons.

To Lalo [Eduardo] Sardiñas   El Jigüe, July 19

This is a decisive moment. Our comrades must be resolute and courageous in spite of the casualties. If we yield, we will have lost the opportunity to write one of the most glorious pages in the history of Cuba; if our men resist, the army will not be able to advance and Batista will be lost. I am confident that you have the courage and intelligence to handle the situation. If the men are very close to the guards tomorrow, the planes won't bombard them; if they continue firing at the river, the men can leave the road, but they must take steps to cut off the guards if they try to advance.

I am sending some men; keep those you need to replace the casualties and send back those you don't need along with our wounded.

If you have to lose terrain for any reason, you must resist firmly a little farther on. Under no circumstances can the road be given to the enemy. I am sure that after the destruction you have inflicted on them today, those troops will not advance. Lots of luck and much courage— this is an opportunity for all of you to write a page in history!

To Braulio Coroneaux   El Jigüe, July 19

The bearer is a prisoner who carries my message to Major Quevedo. Send word to Acevedo, Ignacio, and El Vaquerito [the Little Cowboy] not to fire on the man who goes to the enemy camp with a helmet and white flag; there should be a cease-fire until 10:00 a.m.

FIDEL CASTRO

Letter to Major Quevedo   El Jigüe, July 19

I don't know if you have news of what is happening. G-4 Company of your battalion, which was on the beach, was destroyed by our forces when it tried to advance. The operator of the CRC-10, according to his own words, communicated with you at the start of the fight, and told you that they were meeting opposition, and you replied: "I knew that was going to happen to you." (I can vouch for the veracity of this completely.) He was gravely wounded, and in spite of the efforts we made to save his life, he died the next day.

Today, at 2:30 in the afternoon, there was a clash that resulted in an enormous death toll, and countless prisoners have been taken from another battalion that tried to advance from the beach. At nightfall they were still surrendering unconditionally, attacked from the front, the flanks, and the rearguard.

There are several messages to you from the prisoners taken from that second group of reinforcements: I enclose them.

You know that the road to La Plata is like the pass at Thermopylae, which thousands of soldiers could not breach. And I also have an interest: to save the lives of my men. Be assured that I need only order a mass assault—and our forces are twice the size of those that you still have— and we would take that position, however tenaciously you resist, because our troops are impassioned and all the tactical advantages are with us.

What hope can you have, Major, that justifies the sacrifice of so many lives, yours and ours? Military honor? And don't you believe that military honor demanded, above all, that the army of the republic and the officers of its academy should never have been placed at the service of crime, robbery, and oppression?

I hope that because you are an honorable military man, you will send back the bearer of this letter, which he carries solely in compliance with an order.

Fidel Castro, Commander in Chief: Radio Speech

El Jigüe, July 19

Soldiers: The Rebel Army, certain that all resistance is useless and will lead only to greater bloodshed in this battle, which has already lasted five days—and because this is a struggle among Cubans—offers you the following terms for surrender:

1. Only your weapons will be taken. All your remaining personal belongings will not be touched.

2. The wounded will be turned over to the Red Cross, as is being done with the wounded soldiers taken prisoner at the battle of Santo Domingo.

3. All the prisoners, enlisted men, and officers, will be freed within a period of no longer than two weeks.

4. Until the wounded are picked up by the Red Cross, they will be cared for in our hospitals by qualified doctors and surgeons.

5. All the members of the encircled troop will receive cigars, food, and everything necessary for their immediate needs.

6. No prisoner will be interrogated, mistreated, or humiliated in word or deed, and all will receive the generous and humane treatment military prisoners have always received from us.

7. We will send news at once by radio to your wives, mothers, fathers, and other relatives, who are weeping and desperate because they do not know what your fate is.

8. If you accept these conditions, send a man with a white flag shouting: "Negotiate, negotiate."

FIDEL CASTRO

Reports
To Che Guevara El Jigüe, July 20

After a three-hour truce, the guards are negotiating their surrender.

Yesterday's battle against the reinforcements was long and bloody. We had four dead and four wounded, two very seriously.

The men were heroic under a rain of bombs that caused the majority of casualties. Although the reinforcements were repulsed, there was still sporadic fighting this morning. We took seventeen prisoners, left many dead, and so far we have taken more than twenty weapons.

All we really needed was to have to put up with today's bombardments. Send those who need weapons to La Plata, where the hospital is. I am planning to collect all the Mendoza rifles, Springfields, Garands, and San Cristóbals from the people and distribute automatics to the oldest, and then immediately cut off the guards' retreat from Santo Domingo and Las Vegas. You will be in charge at Las Vegas. Tonight I think I'll pull back the troops and not give out the news of the surrender for forty-eight hours.

To Ramirito Valdés   El Jigüe, July 20

Have all the officers keep their side arms. Make sure that nobody tries to take them away from them.

To Che Guevara   El Jigüe, July 21

My silence hasn't been very long. Yesterday I sent you an urgent message as soon as the guards began the surrender negotiations. At 1:30 a.m. today, everything was concluded. They are totally defeated, after going hungry for a week, and with water rationed. We took 161 weapons, including 2 machine guns; an 81 with many missiles, and a .60 with approximately 70 missiles; and the bazooka with many rockets. Plenty of ammunition. You will understand how much work this has meant.

There are 146 guards, plus 70 from the previous days: a total of around 220. Here in the La Plata hospital, there are about 140 of those who surrendered; another group is in El Jigüe (at Santos's house) with the prisoners and wounded from other encounters. Those who are here in the hospitals are going to go to Las Vegas, where I promised to set them free tomorrow. We will turn them over to the Red Cross, because they are sick and undernourished, along with those wounded in the fighting at Santo Domingo. Tomorrow or the next day, we will deliver those who are in Santos's house and then the old prisoners, like Tunidor, Solís, et al. Tomorrow at 8:00 a.m., I will be in the Maestra, to speak with you by telephone.

Try to have them prepare lunch for the guards at Mompié's hill. I will tell you everything personally.

Not one photograph has been taken of anything. Could you do something about this? It's a pity!

EDITOR'S SUMMARY   July 24

The Rebel Army had taken more than two hundred of Batista's soldiers prisoner in the battle of El Jigüe. They were a burden to feed, and proper medical treatment was impossible because medicines were in short supply. The Rebel Army proposed a prisoner exchange through the International Red Cross, and Fidel put Carlos Franqui in charge of the arrangements. Through Radio Rebelde, contact was made with M. Pierre Jacquier, the IRC representative, and the route was agreed on for the fifteen ambulances coming from Havana over the mountainous terrain to Las Vegas de Jibacoa. While the details were being worked out, an additional hundred prisoners were added to the group the Rebel Army wished to turn over. On July 23 a forty-eight-hour truce went into effect to facilitate the exchange at Las Vegas. And on the twenty-fourth 253 of Batista's men, 57 of them wounded, were in the hands of the Red Cross.

"When the exchange was completed, Major Ernesto Che Guevara made a spectacular appearance mounted on a mule," Franqui reported.

RAMÓN PAZ AND DANIEL [RENÉ RAMOS LATOUR]

Report to Commander Fidel Castro   Santo Domingo,
                                                          Sierra, July 26

At 12:20 yesterday we opened fire on the main body of P Company of the 22d Battalion, which was heading for Santo Domingo with food and supplies.

At exactly 3:00 p.m. the enemy resistance was overcome, and they were ordered to advance to the river from different points. We took the first prisoners and large quantities of weapons. During the afternoon and night, soldiers of the Batista army continued to surrender, and their arms were taken.

There are twenty-four prisoners in all, including Sergeant Eladio García and Corporal Pedro Maffi; eleven were wounded, some of them severely.

Although the exact number of dead is not known, eleven bodies have been found, but the soldiers themselves estimate that more than fifteen of them were killed in the fighting. Among the dead are Lieutenant Alfonso Pérez Martínez and Sergeant Alfredo Pereda.

The rest of the company beat a hasty retreat.

FIDEL CASTRO

Reports
To Arturo Duque   Santo Domingo, Sierra, July 27

The guards are trying to escape. It seems that yesterday they captured
one of Guillermo's trenches, and they found a dead rebel in the trench,
judging from what I heard on the radio. Everything indicates that they
have captured the hill between Lucas's house and Brazón.

Your mission is not to attack the guards, but to prevent them from
getting out, especially now that their advance squad has taken that hill.
We are going to open fire with the .50, a .30, and a mortar as soon as the
main body of the guards tries to take the path to go up that hill.

To Ramón Paz   Sierra, July 27

I think that we must establish an impregnable line here, and since a
strong contingent of ours is coming from the rearguard, I have decided
to send you these forty-three men to strengthen your line. I believe that
with them no one can budge you from there.

Remember that it is very important to place two strong ambushes
on the roads that come from Estrada Palma in order to guard your rear.
Those ambushes must not be abandoned for any reason, and if you see
that any of those ambushes are being strongly attacked, reinforce them.

Sánchez Mosquera has a bullet wound in his head. If his troops
clash with you, they will be wiped out.

To Celia Sánchez   Sierra, July 28

We have made a titanic effort to catch up to and destroy Sánchez Mosquera's whole battalion, which is fighting desperately to save itself, leaving dead all along the road. Today they had the support of a battalion of
reinforcements from the outside, and they broke through our circle and
fled in every direction toward Providencia. They got Sánchez Mosquera
out some time before by helicopter. The .50 had not arrived, or the 81
mortar either. Fighting has been continuing all day.

See that they send me quickly what I requested from Ramirito.

Warn Che that we are going to carry out an encircling movement
from below to surround the troops who are advancing from Durajones
and Las Mercedes toward Las Vegas, and when they come by cut off the
escape route for the enemy in San Lorenzo, if that is possible.

We have taken weapons, bullets, mortar shells. Sánchez Mosquera's
people burned many of the rifles of their dead, as well as almost all the
ammunition for the mortar, and the mortar itself, so they wouldn't fall
into our hands. They fought like devils, I still don't have the complete

results. I followed all their movements with the Minipacks and the CRC-10.

What has been happening is like in a movie. Duque, lost last night with five men, was about to stop at a guardpost. He and they were both confused, since Duque was between their camp and the post. They began to talk, Duque thinking they were rebels and the guards thinking Duque and his men were guards. When the truth was discovered, Duque started to crank up his machine gun and the guards attacked. He struggled with them for more than ten minutes. We all had given him up for dead, until he appeared today with two bashes on his head and he's black and blue all over. Because of this experience and others like it, the battalion was not completely destroyed, though our men fought very aggressively. It was a real hunt for miles and miles. The messengers were terrible. Do you remember the message I sent Duque with Marcelo yesterday morning ordering him to intercept the guards between the house in Santiago Ríos and Providencia? Well, I got it back today, after thirty hours, without its ever getting into Duque's hands. A peasant was afraid of the planes, and didn't deliver it. Some of the things that have happened are galling enough to kill you.

To Che Guevara   Sierra, July 29

I have everything ready here for the attack since I learned by the microwave that there were two battalions en route to Las Vegas and that they were planning to attack tomorrow to free the two battalions now at Las Vegas. So I thought it would be best to attack them tonight.

I have placed Guillermo [García] and Lalo [Eduardo Sardiñas], with 130 men and a bazooka, between El Cerro and Cuatros Caminos (they will be there before daybreak) to attack the reinforcements.

I have the 81 mortar here, two .60 mortars, four .30 machine guns, and I am expecting the .50. Since noon, Hubert [Matos] and Pedrito [Miret] have been planning positions for the mortars.

When I arrived here and learned that Las Vegas had surrendered, I was worried whether there had been any communication between you and Finalé.* I need to know urgently in order to decide what to do.

The plan now is not to attack with the bulk of the forces but to send the 250 men in two columns to surround the forces at Arroyones from below and take the hill at La Herradura facing Las Mercedes. Meanwhile Lalo and Guillermo will be busy with the reinforcements that are coming from Estrada Palma, and they will attack them at Arroyones with mortars and machine guns to frighten them. On the one hand, this

---

* A Batista commander.—ED.

will provoke a retreat, and on the other hand, it will help to bring the surrender of those who are between Arroyones and El Mango; according to our information they are already negotiating. But I need to speak with you urgently, so I ask you to make an effort.

In the battle of Santo Domingo, we lost seven men in all, among them Paz. The operation netted us more than fifty weapons. We retrieved as many bullets as we used up chasing Sánchez Mosquera. During the chase, we left them with more than thirty dead, but it is really a shame that the men were overconfident and made a number of errors, so we didn't wipe out the battalion completely. The success today must be exploited to the hilt.

To Carlos Franqui   Sierra, July 29

I am sending you this war communiqué dealing with the battle of Santo Domingo.

Tomorrow we will give you the one from Las Vegas. So that makes two consecutive victories.

You should add to this communiqué the list of the twenty-four prisoners, which I don't have but you can quickly get it there.

We are trying to surround the reinforcements that came to the aid of Las Vegas.

I thought that the statement concerning the aqueduct was good. This matter and others will necessarily have to wait for a few days since I am extremely busy and don't have a minute to sleep or rest. Greetings.

Communiqué from Commander Fidel Castro

Sierra, July 29

As soon as the battle of El Jigüe was over, another sizable battle began against two battalions of the tyranny, which were operating from Providencia to Santo Domingo, under the orders of Lieutenant Colonel Sánchez Mosquera.

The struggle lasted four days. It began on the twenty-fifth at noon against the enemy troops that came to reinforce the 11th Battalion encamped in Santo Domingo, and ended yesterday at 2:00 in the afternoon at the site known as Peladero, near Nagua, several miles from the Estrada Palma mill. The pursuit of the 11th Battalion lasted forty-two consecutive hours. Sánchez Mosquera, severely wounded in the head, was evacuated in a helicopter yesterday, the twenty-eighth, at 7:30 in the morning. The fleeing enemy troops left a trail of dead along the road, and a long caravan of wounded followed behind them.

Since the rebel units are scattered over a broad front, they have not yet officially reported the final results of this battle; until yesterday the enemy had lost forty-six dead and twenty-four prisoners, and we had taken twenty-nine Garand rifles, sixteen Cristóbal machine guns, eight Springfield rifles, thousands of bullets, one bazooka with twenty projectiles, two boxes of .60-caliber mortar shells, fifteen 81-caliber mortar shells, more than a hundred knapsacks, and other gear. The area of Santo Domingo, El Salto, and Providencia is totally cleared of enemy troops. In this bloody battle, our forces suffered seven dead and four wounded.

Between the battle of El Jigüe and this new battle, the Rebel Army has suffered only thirteen dead and twelve wounded, almost all not seriously. Among the forces of tyranny, it has caused more than four hundred casualties, including dead, prisoners, and wounded, and has taken more than three hundred weapons and almost one hundred thousand bullets. No one can doubt the truthfulness with which we have always stated our casualties in all our war communiqués, and someday that will be fully documented. It is not necessary to say that it is never a cause for jubilation to state the number of enemy dead, and we will never exaggerate them, since these men are being sacrificed criminally and senselessly by the tyranny.

The Rebel Army has enormously increased the size of its fighting force and continues the struggle against the remaining enemy forces, which began the biggest military offensive imaginable in our republic, with fourteen infantry battalions and seven additional companies, supported by a fleet of planes and armored units. Now armed with the bazookas taken from the enemy, our columns can strike against the tanks of the tyranny. The offensive has been turned into a hopeless rout.

Since yesterday, even before the battle from Santo Domingo to Providencia was over, we were already waging yet another sizable action against other enemy troops, situated in Las Vegas, and the reinforcements who are trying desperately to save them.

FIDEL CASTRO

Letters
To Lalo [Eduardo Sardiñas] and Guillermo García   Sierra, July 30

When I reached the Alto de la Llorosa, I learned from Camilo that the guards at Las Vegas had surrendered. In light of that, since there was no point in attacking the reinforcements, I decided on something better: to surround the reinforcements, that is, all the guards at Arroyones and Las Mercedes. That will be the end of Batista.

I am going to divide the 250 men I have into two groups. Half are going to be placed below Arroyones, to keep an eye on the guards, and the other half are going to be placed on the hill at La Herradura, to prevent those at Las Mercedes from escaping.

In Las Vegas, a tank was captured. If we can get it working, we can attack from Las Vegas and push them toward the ambushes.

To Celia Sánchez   Sierra, July 30

I imagine that you also want to go down to Las Vegas; if I can, I'll get there at night or early in the morning.

I have the impression that everything will be finished soon, and in the midst of my happiness at the victories that are the culmination of so many sacrifices and efforts, I feel sad.

CARLOS FRANQUI

Memo to Fidel Castro and Faustino Pérez   Sierra, July 30

In the negotiations with the North Americans for their immediate withdrawal,* they are proposing that we give our word not to attack the pumping station, declaring it a neutral zone.

Batista withdrew his forces and asked the North Americans to take over the site—a desperate maneuver to provoke an incident between us and the Yankees. We informed El Primo, after having consulted with the rest of our companions, that the term neutral zone did not please us, since it leaves room for tortuous juridical interpretations, and since national territory cannot be a neutral zone.

He told us that in practice our standing as a belligerent is recognized, that Batista also pledges that his forces will not go there, and that only the civilian workers at the station would remain there and possibly an international observer from the OAS [Organization of American States] or from some American government.

The Unity Front [Frente de Unidad] has participated: it seems very interested, and it has accepted the formula.

We answer that not even for the sake of recognition as a belligerent is it possible to sacrifice, even subjectively, our national sovereignty and territory. We proposed the following solution: (1) the North Americans withdraw immediately; (2) the zone be declared free territory; (3) we give our word not to touch the plant.

We agreed that this afternoon, after communicating with you, we

---

* Batista had pulled out the guard he normally furnished for the aqueduct that supplied the U.S. naval base at Guantánamo, and U.S. Marines had taken over the job. Their presence on Cuban territory outside the boundaries of the base was viewed as foreign intervention by the 26th of July and many other Cubans.—ED.

would give our answer, and if it is affirmative, we would inform Raúl, who would carry out the decision.

Yesterday General A. S. de Quesada was arrested in Havana. It is reported that he went to the palace, without permission, to state that it was necessary to enter into negotiations with us, that the situation in the army could not last, etc.

We believe that we must announce the news of Daniel's [René Ramos Latour's] death because it will have repercussions in Santiago, and people there would not understand why they were not told.

To prevent the Unity Front from moving in undesirable directions, we should call the meeting here. Tell me if you think this is correct.

Fidel Castro

1. The zone where the Guantánamo aqueduct is located is Cuban territory and must be given up immediately by the North American forces.

2. We are ready to give guarantees that the water supply will not be interfered with because our objective is not to attack that facility but to have the government of the United States order withdrawal unconditionally, just as the leadership of the Rebel Army ordered the freedom of the North Americans,* without any conditions.

3. The presence of North American forces in there is illegal and constitutes aggression against Cuban national territory.

4. The continued presence of said forces at the aqueduct will be considered a conscious and deliberate provocation on the part of the government of the United States and a clear case of invasion of the national territory of the people of Cuba, who will be ready to repulse it at all costs.

5. The government of the United States will not be able to justify to the world this act of arbitrary and absurd aggression against a people of America who are fighting for their liberty against a tyranny that has been armed by that very government.

6. Well aware that the dictatorship of Batista is promoting this incident in a desperate stratagem to bring about the intervention of foreign forces into the Cuban conflict, the Rebel Army will act calmly and deliberately and will resort to other means only when it has had recourse to all legal and patriotic arguments and when it is shown before the eyes of America and the world that the United States has become an aggressor against our fatherland with its use of force.

---

* Kidnapped by Raúl Castro and released in July.—Ed.

EDITOR'S SUMMARY

Oriente, Northern Zone, Second Front, July

In his interview with Raúl Castro at the time he was holding personnel kidnapped from the Guantánamo base, Jules Dubois tried to elicit Raúl's views on Communism. Raúl said that his first trip behind the Iron Curtain, in 1953, had come about through his participation—at his own expense—in the World Youth Congress in Vienna, where as the result of "an argument [he had] with a Rumanian delegate on the floor," he was invited to visit that country and then went to Hungary. "I would travel to China," Raúl said, "if I had the chance, because I enjoy traveling and I want to see the world, but that doesn't mean I am a Communist." He scoffed at Batista's charge that he was a Party member, and added: "What does surprise me is the attention that is given to this matter, when everyone knows he doesn't do anything but repeat stupid accusations like a parrot." Raúl described himself as a disciple of Martí, like the others in the 26th of July. "If we cannot conclude it ['Martí's unfinished work'] we will nevertheless have fulfilled our historic role, sustaining until the end the standard of his ideological principles." Expressing his confidence in a free and prosperous future for Cuba, based on the valor and rectitude of the Cuban people, he concluded: "We sincerely believe that in 'our America'—as Martí called it—it would be more convenient for them [the USA] to have friends of the heart in an equality of conditions than false friends obligated by circumstances."

FIDEL CASTRO

Message to Che Guevara   Sierra, July 31

Since this morning the artillery and the .50, men have been ready. I am located on a hill from which the zone of combat is visible. But it is impossible to move the mules without their being seen by the planes.

It's hardly possible to rely on the .60 mortars since only one out of every five shells explodes. That's why I couldn't bombard them yesterday at dawn. But I have hopes that the 81 will give very good results.

We must keep the guards immobile until night. In the afternoon, I will have these troops guarding the entry point against whatever reinforcements are coming from Cuatro Caminos, and at night, I will mobilize to prepare an attack with mortar support. Last night I didn't move because physically I couldn't do any more, and the rest of the men were in the same state. I believe, besides, that the men are much less efficient than in previous days because of the general exhaustion and the deaths of several officers. Daniel's [René Ramos Latour's] death yesterday canceled out the value of the ambush.

Judging from communications we have intercepted, Corzo is the one who is surrounded in Las Mercedes. Their tank seems to have been struck three times. They have asked for bullets for the .30 machine guns and firing pins for the Cristóbal.

CAMILO CIENFUEGOS

Report to Che Guevara   Sierra, July 31

Two tanks are coming as reinforcement, although I don't know exactly where, but I suppose it will be by the Sao Grande road. One tank driver was telling the other to be careful, "especially when you reach the river."

If the reinforcements come and manage to get through, we'll have to use bazookas. I think that they should be placed at the place the reinforcements will have to come by. Tonight we can start the general attack, backed by the mortars.

FIDEL CASTRO

Orders to Eddy Suñol   Sierra, July

Stay in that position with the instructions I gave you. Perhaps tomorrow they might try to go down from Las Vegas.

Everything is going very well. So far we have taken 23 guards prisoner, about 30 dead, and 1 mortar, 1 machine gun, and more than 40 rifles, almost all automatic. One slightly wounded on our side.

Tonight we will attack them from five points.

16. AUGUST–OCTOBER: THE REBEL ARMY— LAS VILLAS

FIDEL CASTRO

Memos
To Che Guevara   Sierra, August 4

You with your mule and I with "my" tank. We hunted up gas oil, the gas oil came, and the tractor still didn't start. The tank was going well under its own power until it hit a snag and began to skid. Today I ordered some oxen to be yoked to pull it out. It is discouraging to lose all this time. There seems to be an enemy concentration at Estrada Palma. Tonight I am ordering it to be bombarded with the 81, and I am going to put an ambush between El Cerro and Estrada Palma. We are also going to reinforce the Herradura and Sao Grande line. Holding Cuatro Caminos is very advantageous for us, since it threatens the flank of the reinforcements that are coming by way of Sao Grande. There are other plans for the tank, if it ever gets here. Order a position prepared with good trenches for the .50, and with it, put the antiaircraft gun from the tank, which is Joel's and which fires, according to what I hear, at fantastic speed. With both machine guns in a good position, we can stop that ridiculous parachute business. But they have to be protected with good trenches. Order them to do this tonight. Two days ago I sent them to fetch the loudspeaker and its crew.

From two women, we took a batch of letters for the surrounded guards. We can make good use of them by reading out the names of the soldiers they were sent to, and the names of the relatives who wrote them, and invite the guards to send someone to pick them up.

To Camilo Cienfuegos   Sierra, August 4

Today I have mobilized even oxen to move the damn tank. If it arrives, I'll send it to you tonight.

To Che Guevara   Sierra, August 4

Angelito Verdecia's father received the news today that his sister, wounded in the fighting at Arroyones, died in Manzanillo. This is three relatives in a matter of days. Seeing him so sad and thinking that he still has two sons at the front, I asked if he wanted me to take them out of the line, and he asked if at least the youngest, Porfirio, who is not in good shape, could rest up for a few days. So send him to spend a few days with his father.

To Che Guevara   Sierra, August 5

At noon, fighting began with the reinforcements that came from Sao Grande. Earlier they had been heavily bombarding and machine-gunning the zone. From my observation post, I could see several centers of fire all along the route. What I am counting on most is the attack by the squad under Verdecia's command, which camped last night 300 yards from the guards, whom they are following closely.

At first sight, it is obvious that the advance was carried out. One of the tanks ran out of gas. I think they brought two more.

I told Camilo to rush a group to the rearguard with the bazooka and put another force with the 81 mortar to attack any new reinforcements.

Did you see the General Staff's communiqué on Las Mercedes? It looks like they really believed that we had withdrawn. At least they believed it for a while.

The idea of the antitank ditches is very good. We have to construct them also against the tanks in the interior.

To Che Guevara   Sierra, August 5

The guards got through. At approximately noon, they clashed with the ambush, which of course was no secret for them. The mine, a big one that I sent last night, didn't explode. Apparently the detonator was defective; everything else had been made here. The boy in charge of exploding it was wounded after trying in vain to make it go off.

Cordoví fired five rockets with the bazooka, disabling a tank. But another tank attacked him with cannon shot, killing him and destroying the bazooka as well. Suñol, Wizo, and another boy who were in the same trench were wounded: Suñol badly, although not fatally. Wizo and the other not badly. There are *seven* more wounded and one of Guillermo's men and another from the crew of the .50 was wounded during the siege. Among these wounded, there are at least three pretty seriously wounded. So our losses add up to thirteen or fourteen.

Since they didn't have a bazooka to use against the tanks, the men withdrew. The men were brave, without performing miracles, and they withdrew in an orderly way. Morale is high. I have just received the unwelcome news that they managed to get the tank out of the mud but in the operation the steering wheel broke and so it can't be steered. Hopes dashed. It has been a long time since I've had such great pipedreams.

To Camilo Cienfuegos   Sierra, August 6

I was going into your area, but stopped after getting your message telling me you have the impression that they have all left.

In case you are still en route and there are definite possibilities of success if you attack them, inform Che, who is coming by way of Sao Grande, and carry out the plan together.

If they have really left, the counteroffensive is over.

EDITOR'S SUMMARY   August 7

Within two weeks after the prisoner exchange at Las Vegas, the rebel forces had taken 160 more prisoners. Fidel addressed a message to General Eulogio Cantillo, the Batista commander in Bayamo, suggesting another exchange and again stressing the medical hardships: "in our modest hospitals rebel wounded must be treated along with wounded soldiers."

Fidel went on: Although I regret having to raise these considerations, I am doing so as a result of the impression made on me by the continued and deliberate strafing of the field hospital, where there were wounded prisoners under the flag of the Red Cross, and there are orders to kill our emissaries sent to negotiate this matter and other things pertaining to it; we have heard this in army communications we have intercepted and which fill us with profound sorrow because of the extent of dishonor that they reveal within the armed forces.

If you are in agreement, we can, as we did the previous time, designate a cease-fire zone that in this case would be the triangle bounded by Cuatro Caminos, Santo Domingo, and Las Vegas.

I write to you with the same spirit, free of hatred and prejudice, with which I would write to all the honorable officers of the army, who, in my opinion, are the vast majority, and to those who have lacked the moral courage to cease being instruments of the tyranny, but who have squandered physical valor in combat, dying to defend an ignoble and degrading cause. Sincerely.

ARMANDO HART   Príncipe Prison, Havana, August 10

Sabotage of electrical facilities in Matanzas produced a blackout that left a large part of the city in darkness and caused substantial economic losses. On the southern coast of Matanzas, a few days ago, a band of partisan gunners from the 26th of July Movement attacked and captured a small garrison near the marshes of Zapata.

FIDEL CASTRO

Conditions for peace   Sierra, August 13

The 26th of July Movement and the Rebel Army will agree to discuss a peaceful solution only on the following terms:

1. That the dictator be arrested and brought before the tribunals of justice, as well as all the political leaders who are guilty of having upheld the tyranny, who are responsible for the civil war, and who have enriched themselves with the wealth of the republic; and of all the military personnel who have been responsible for torture and crimes, in the cities as well as in the countryside; and of those who have become rich through smuggling, gambling, and crooked deals—whatever their ranks may be.

2. That the provisional presidency of the republic be entrusted to the person designated by all the sectors combating the dictatorship so that general elections can be called in the shortest possible time.

FIDEL CASTRO, COMMANDER IN CHIEF

Communiqué   Sierra, August 18

Major Camilo Cienfuegos is assigned the mission of leading a rebel column from the Sierra Maestra to Pinar del Río Province in order to fulfill the strategic plan of the Rebel Army.

Column 2, Antonio Maceo, as the invasion force will be called in homage to the glorious fighter for independence, will leave from El Salto next Wednesday, August 20, 1958.

The commander of the invasion column is granted the authority to organize rebel combat units throughout the national territory, until the commanders of each province reach their respective jurisdictions with their columns; to administer the penal code and the agrarian laws of the Rebel Army in the invaded territory; to collect the contributions set by military decrees; to combine operations with any other revolutionary force that may already be operating in any given sector; to establish a permanent front in Pinar del Río Province, which will be the base for specific operations of the invading column; and to those ends appoint officers of the Rebel Army up to the rank of column commander.

Although the primary objective of the invasion column is to carry the war of liberation to the western part of the island—and to this end it must subordinate every other tactical matter—it will strike the enemy as often as the opportunity arises during the journey.

The arms taken from the enemy will be preferably given to organizing local units.

To reward, emphasize, and encourage acts of heroism among the soldiers and officers of Invasion Column 2, Antonio Maceo, the Osvaldo Herrera Medal of Valor is created, honoring the captain of said column, who took his life in the prisons of Bayamo, after gallantly and heroically resisting the tortures of the henchmen of the tyranny.

FIDEL CASTRO

Communiqués   Sierra, August 19

The people of Cuba must cooperate with the Civilian Resistance Movement to provide increased supplies for the Rebel Army's invasion columns so that with the effort and sacrifice of all of us we can swiftly put an end to the tyranny.

Sierra, August

Comrade Pastora Núñez has been appointed to set up a commission, along with other members, to visit all the proprietors of sugar plantations in Oriente Province to inform them that, by military decrees of the Rebel Army, a contribution has been set of 15 centavos for each 250 lb. sack of sugar produced in the 1958 harvest, of which 10 centavos will be paid by the mill and 5 centavos by the tenant farmer, the latter sum to be advanced by the mill in order to facilitate collection of the contribution, and to be deducted by the mill from the farmer's share in due time.

Fulfillment of this obligation on the part of the contributor entitles him to the guarantees that only the Rebel Army can offer to the cane fields and to the industrial installations of all the mills of the province.

Failure to comply with this in the time and form indicated will lead to sanctions that will be irrevocable as of this date.

Fidel Castro, Commander in Chief

Radio broadcast   Sierra, August 20

Exactly four months ago, I made use of the microphones of our Rebel Broadcasting Station to speak to the people at a difficult time. It was after the April 9 strike.

I am speaking to the people again today from this station, which has not stopped broadcasting, even when mortars and bombs were exploding all around. I speak now not of a promise to be fulfilled, but of one entire stage of that promise which has been fulfilled.

After seventy-six days of unceasing fighting on the First Front of the Sierra Maestra, the Rebel Army has clearly repulsed and virtually destroyed the cream of the forces of the tyranny, bringing about one of the greatest disasters ever suffered by a modern army, trained and equipped with all the resources of war, facing nonprofessional military forces confined to an area surrounded by enemy troops, without planes, artillery, or regular supply routes for arms, ammunition, and food.

More than thirty clashes and six large-scale battles have taken place. The enemy offensive began May 24. Since Holy Week, the tyranny had been concentrating troops throughout the Sierra Maestra, and they were gradually approaching the foothills of the cordillera. The enemy command had managed to assemble fourteen infantry battalions and seven independent companies for this offensive.

The dictatorship's strategy was to concentrate the bulk of its troops against the First Front of the Sierra Maestra, the seat of the general headquarters and the Rebel Broadcasting station. After the enemy had disposed its forces and thought they had divided ours, the rebel command secretly moved all the columns from the south and center of the province to the First Front. Column 3, under the command of Major Juan Almeida, which was operating in the zone of Cobre; Column 2, under the command of Major Camilo Cienfuegos, which was operating in the center of the province; Column 4, under the command of Major Ramiro Valdés, which was operating to the east of Pico Turquino; and Column 7, under the command of Major Crescencio Pérez, which was operating in the extreme west of the Sierra Maestra, were moved immediately to the west of El Turquino. These columns and Column 8, under the command of Major Ernesto Guevara, and Column 1, under the command of the commander in chief, formed a compact defensive front some twenty miles long, whose principal axis was the upper ridge of the Sierra Maestra.

We have taken a series of measures designed to ensure disaster for the enemy offensive:

1. Organized resistance.

2. Draining and exhausting the army.

3. Assembling resources and arms sufficient to throw them on the offensive as soon as they begin to weaken.

The fundamental objectives of these plans are:

1. To have possession of a basic territory where the organization is operating, with hospitals, repair shops, etc.

2. To keep the rebel broadcasting station on the air, since it has become a factor of importance.

3. To offer increasing resistance to the enemy, as our forces become concentrated and as we come to occupy the most strategic points from which to launch our counterattack.

These plans were carried out precisely. The guerrilla stage of the war had ceased to exist, and it became a war of position and movement. Our squads were placed at all the natural entrances to the Sierra, to the north and to the south.

Between the troops that attacked from both directions, there was a distance of hardly four miles as the crow flies, but the morale of our troops was intact, and we retained almost our entire reserve of ammunition and highly destructive mines. The enemy had to expend much energy and time to gain terrain in the heart of the mountains.

On June 29, in Santo Domingo, the first crushing blow was delivered against the forces of the tyranny, under the command of Lieutenant Colonel Sánchez Mosquera, striking one of his most aggressive units. With the arms and ammunition taken in that action, which lasted three days, we launched the furious counterattack that in thirty-five days ousted all the enemy forces from the Sierra Maestra, and inflicted almost 1000 casualties, including more than 443 prisoners.

The battles of Santo Domingo, Meriño, El Jigüe, the second battle of Santo Domingo, Las Vegas, de Jibacoa, and Las Mercedes, occurred in uninterrupted succession. In the final stage of the struggle, the tyranny made a desperate effort to withdraw from the Sierra Maestra whatever remained of the forces employed in the offensive to avoid their being completely encircled and annihilated by our army. They evacuated the Pino del Agua camp without even waiting for the attack; it was a shameful flight from the field of battle.

The rebel forces had in their hands a total of 507 weapons, including two 14-ton tanks with their respective cannon, two 81-mm. mortars, two 3-inch bazookas, twelve machine guns with tripods, 142 Garand rifles, about 200 San Cristóbal machine guns, as well as M-1 carbines and Springfield rifles, more than 100,000 bullets, and hundreds of mortar and bazooka shells, six Minipacks, and fourteen microwave CRC-10 radio transmitters.

In the light of the eventuality of a military coup d'état, the 26th of July Movement wishes its position to be clear. If the coup d'état is the work of military opportunists whose objective is to protect their interests and to dissociate themselves from the tyranny as advantageously as they can, we are resolutely against it, even if it is disguised by the best intentions.

If the military coup d'état is the work of honest people and has a genuine revolutionary aim, then it will be possible to reach a peaceful solution on just bases beneficial to the fatherland. The interests of the armed forces and the Revolution are not and need not be antagonistic; together they can solve Cuba's problems.

The dilemma that confronts the army at this time is very clear: either it takes a step forward, ridding itself of the cadaver that is the Batista regime and redeems itself before the nation, or it commits suicide as an institution. What the army can still salvage today it will not be able to salvage in a few months. If the war is prolonged six months longer, the army will disintegrate completely. The army can master the situation that faces it only with the support of the entire population, but quite the opposite is the case: the entire population identifies with and collaborates with the rebellion.

The rebel columns will advance in every direction toward the rest of the territory of the nation and nothing and no one will be able to stop them. If a leader falls, another one will take his place. The people of Cuba must be prepared to aid our combatants. Any town or part of Cuba can become a field of battle in the coming months. The civilian population must be ready to endure the privations caused by the war. May the fortitude demonstrated by the people of the Sierra Maestra—where even the children help our troops— people who have endured twenty months of campaigning with incomparable heroism, arouse emulation of their example among the rest of the Cuban people so that the fatherland will be truly free, no matter at what cost, and fulfill the promise of the Titan* that "the revolution will continue as long as one injustice remains to be righted."

There is revolution because there is tyranny. There is revolution because there is injustice. There is and there will be revolution while a single shadow menaces our rights and our liberty.

FIDEL CASTRO, COMMANDER IN CHIEF

Communiqué   Sierra, August 21

Major Ernesto Guevara is assigned the mission of leading a rebel column to Las Villas Province from the Sierra Maestra, and to operate in said territory in accord with the strategic plan of the Rebel Army.

The invasion force, Column 8, will carry the name of Ciro Redondo,

---

* José Martí.—Ed.

in homage to the heroic captain killed in action. It will leave from Las Mercedes between August 24 and 30.

Major Guevara is named chief of all the rebel forces of the 26th of July Movement operating in the province.

The strategic objective of Column 8 will be to strike relentlessly at the enemy in the central territory of Cuba and to intercept them until it totally paralyzes the movement of enemy troops by land from Occidente to Oriente Province.

FIDEL CASTRO TO CHE GUEVARA   Sierra, August 24

I had the seven Garands with 100 bullets each turned over to you so that you would send me back the seven San Cristóbals without bullets.

I am not accommodating you in the matter of the antitank guns because I am going to need them very badly, and it seems to me that their only value is in concentrating their fire on one tank. I rather doubt that they can do anything to the Sherman.

As for the M-2, it can't possibly be for your personal use, since you already have one, and there is no ammunition so I'm keeping the two that arrived.

EDITOR'S SUMMARY

On July 20 Radio Rebelde had broadcast a "Manifesto of the Civilian Revolutionary Opposition Front" signed by leaders of political workers, and military groups opposed to Batista. The text, also known as the Caracas Pact, had been written primarily by Fidel Castro and Carlos Franqui.

The manifesto exhorted the Cuban people to join together to "create a great civilian-revolutionary coalition for struggle in which every sector, shoulder to shoulder, each contributing its patriotism and its energies, will hurl the criminal dictatorship of Fulgencio Batista from power and restore to Cuba the peace long sought and the democratic leadership that will enable our people to attain the full measure of liberty and progress."

Three stages were outlined: first the ouster of Batista through armed struggle, with many more Cubans under arms, as well as civilian resistance, and a nationwide strike; second, the establishment of a "brief provisional government" and restoration of "constitutional and democratic procedures"; and finally, a program of justice for the guilty and of "order, peace, and the economic, social, and political progress of the Cuban people."

Appeals were made to the United States for an end to aid of any sort, to the military to turn away from the tyranny, and to Cubans throughout the country to join in the common effort. In closing, Castro promised to "convoke a meeting of delegates from all sectors to discuss and ratify the bases of unity."

On August 15 an airplane landed at Mayarí Arriba with a shipment of arms from Miami; aboard the plane was Bebo Hidalgo, who was in charge of all military matters in exile; with him was Renato Guitart; the planeload was one in a series that, together with assaults on civil aircraft in flight, the capture of military planes, and the help of Orestes del Río and other aviators, was to lay the foundation for a rebel air force, which ultimately had an important role to play. Later, naval units were to be formed.

PEDRO LUIS DÍAZ LANZ

Letter to Commander Fidel Castro

A few days ago I had the pleasant surprise of receiving the news of my appointment as commander of the future rebel air force and why not actually say it, of the present force, which, although small, will very quickly increase to the dimensions that all the forces under your command have reached.

My profound gratitude. With this I wish to say that I will continue working tirelessly as long as necessary, I will never falter, I am wholeheartedly committed, and I have absolute faith that you will guide us to final victory, which is already becoming visible on the horizon of this struggle for liberty.

FIDEL CASTRO

Letter to General Cantillo   Sierra, September

The Revolution, which is a project of renewal, a people's aspiration for justice, could have been crushed two years ago if Batista had had some foresight, intelligence, and a sense of history. He could have relinquished everything, even his position, whose salary and juicy benefits he had already enjoyed for five years, in exchange for a single commitment: the inviolable position of the army cadres. We who want the most far-reaching changes in our public life would have found ourselves ignored.

Today there is a complete reversal. The army's very existence is in danger; the soldiers are waking up to reality; peace has turned into turmoil, and if the only way that peace can be achieved is by tearing down the tottering edifice, nobody will be ready to hold it up and die under its ruins.

The army is visibly falling apart. New recruits are deserting by the hundreds. However, the struggle has not entered its most severe stage. With no one now able to stop them, the rebel columns will spread through the entire territory; and it is known that wherever they go they quickly grow. Sixty men who left the Sierra Maestra six months ago to go to the northern part of the province today hold a territory extending thousands of square miles, which is a model of organization, administration, and order. Within its borders are the wealth of seventeen sugar mills and the most valuable mineral reserves in Cuba; and 95 percent of our coffee production is located in liberated territory. When we began, we did not have 81 mortars or bazookas, or hundreds of automatic weapons, which is what we took in the latest offensive.

The U.S. arms embargo will be maintained; the purchase of equipment from Israel has been prevented by our friends abroad, after 1 million pesos had already been deposited; the government is obliged to acquire arms without authorization like a common smuggler.

Batista has no way out. Does he decide to stay? So much the worse for him and for the army; rebellion and conspiracies would triple. Suppose he decides to turn over his power to the puppet opposition that plays ball with him? How could he relinquish power to Grau,* in the middle of a civil war, after telling the soldiers for seven years that the March 10 coup was necessary because of the anarchy and the attacks of the Auténtico governments against the armed forces?

And the people would never accept the results of any elections in which the major, uncorrupted political forces of the country could not participate because of the absence of guarantees, the campaign of terror, and the general lack of confidence.

We will not recognize the results of those elections; they are a bloody hoax. The Revolution offers Cuba something better and different, a hope of which even the soldiers they have led into a criminal and unjust war must be aware.

When the military speak of the regime's opposition to an abrupt change, perhaps they are thinking too much about the blood that the people, in their just vengeance, might spill when the tyranny falls. The spectacle of raging crowds is always unwelcome, and serves to discredit revolutions and blame them for the excesses. But those guilty of causing disorders are those who seek impunity for crime and offenses in general, and force the people to take vengeance into their own hands. They have never tried to prevent the mass murders of unfortunate peasants, the horrible tortures the revolutionaries suffer in the police torture chambers, the crimes committed in every city and town in the island by the henchmen of the regime and Masferrer's gangsters, convicts released from prison to exercise the functions of public order to the shame of the armed forces.

While we are analyzing our points of view, the following considerations must be kept in mind:

---

* Ramón Grau San Martín, leading member of the Auténtico Party; he was president from 1944 to 1948.—ED.

1. Our columns have orders to continue operating as though nothing had changed if a coup d'état occurs that is not the result of an accord between the military and the revolutionaries.

2. We will not accept the results of the November 3 elections.

3. We are absolutely certain that if the struggle continues to its ultimate consequences, the entire country will rise in rebellion, and the armed services will be powerless to resist.

I speak this way because I know that you will appreciate frankness much more than diplomacy. For you, this communication is risky, and it would not be in any sense honorable on my part, nor natural for me, to hide what I think. So you will be able to decide whether or not you consider it appropriate to pursue this contact. A meeting is almost impossible for you. Therefore, I am writing you at great length that which I could express to you in person. But if you think it imperative, I could invent something to facilitate our meeting, such as returning some officer who was taken prisoner (so long as it is not Major Quevedo) back to your zone.

If you decide to assume responsibility for a revolutionary movement within the army, in order to achieve peace on principles that are just and beneficial to the fatherland, you could count on several commanders of battalions; you know who they are, as you also know those who must be arrested without giving them time to react, those who definitely have the unanimous hatred of their troops. Your name is respected; it would work like a charm among officers and soldiers who are only waiting for a resolute man.

Besides, the army needs a gesture that would redeem it in the eyes of the nation from its complicity in the dictatorship. The officers need this especially, more than anyone else. Recall what happened to the army officers when Machado* fell; the soldiers themselves drove them out, asserting that they had no moral authority to lead them.

Although I know that you could depend on other chiefs and their units if you wanted to, I am sure that your battalion would be more than enough to seize operations headquarters. It is all a matter of surprise and speed. We can relatively quickly concentrate one to two battalions at any point between Manzanillo and Santiago de Cuba.

In your place, I would make contacts only with very few of the chiefs who offer the greatest security, and I would act with the troops directly under my command and let the rest follow. In one night, it is possible to take almost all the cities and towns between the two points mentioned

---

* The dictator Gerardo Machado was overthrown on August 12, 1933. On September 4, 1933, there was a revolt of sergeants and classes and Batista, then a sergeant, emerged as a colonel.

above. The next day you can be sure that the generals would have abandoned Camp Columbia.

If you do it, take every precaution and don't permit yourself to be arrested by men who don't have your courage, character, or intelligence.

I hope that these lines may be of some use. I, for my part, will certainly feel some nostalgia when this struggle is over.

TO MEMBERS OF THE ARMED FORCES

Communiqué   Sierra, September 7

Every enlisted man or officer of the armed forces who does not wish to continue defending the tyranny can come and live in free territory. He will not be obliged to fight against his own companions in arms or to carry out military activities of any kind.

He will continue to receive the same salary that he got from the state, so that he can support his family; the only requirement is that he bring his weapon with him.

He can also bring his closest relatives to the Free Territory, where they will be offered housing and board until the end of the war.

He need only come with his weapon and make contact with our posts or with the peasants, stating that he is accepting the hospitality of the rebels proclaimed in the declaration of September 15.

FIDEL CASTRO

Report   Sierra

Six columns that left from the First Front of the Sierra Maestra after overrunning the enemy lines are penetrating deep into the territory of the republic.

Before the dictatorship could recover from this military disaster, our forces began a rapid and unexpected advance, which has been proceeding without incident for several days. Our forces have already gone beyond the borders of Oriente and Camagüey after marching more than 130 miles. Neither the hurricane-force winds, nor the incessant rains of the last weeks slowed their movement. They crossed the Cauto River by boat at flood tide.

The rebellion that was kept up for almost two years in the mountains of the Sierra Maestra was more than something symbolic. The forces of the dictatorship are powerless to contain the rebel tide.

The situation of Batista's army is similar to that of an army, which, while defending its frontiers, sees its rearguard being overrun by enemy battalions brought in by air. Only in wars between nations, the units that descend on the rearguard encounter hostility from the civilian population, which cooperates with its national army in reporting and wiping out the invaders. The contrary obtains in this war, which is an internal struggle against a despotic and hated regime; the entire population helps the troops who are operating behind the lines. In these circumstances, no army can avoid collapse.

When Tabernilla, with all his usual baseness and shamelessness, declared that "There were only twelve rebels and there was no alternative for them but to surrender or escape if they could,"* we were in fact an insignificant handful, but we neither escaped nor surrendered. And today for each one of those twelve, there are two columns in the field, and if they could not defeat the Revolution then, today we can throw the phrase back at them and say that the tyranny has no alternative but to surrender or escape if it can, because the very soldiers they have been sending to die in the defense of illegitimate interests are going to cut off its retreat.

FIDEL CASTRO, COMMANDER IN CHIEF

Letters
To Sr. Julián de Zulueta   Sierra, September 16

The armed struggle waged by the Rebel Army against the tyranny has been made possible by the spontaneous and patriotic cooperation of the people of Cuba.

At the same time, the administration of the Free Territory, which is steadily increasing in size, has required us to devote great resources and energies to the establishment of essential public services. This decisive stage of the struggle demands expenditures of a magnitude that requires a mandatory contribution—although minimal in proportion to the total value of their holdings—from the most important economic elements of the nation.

The commander of the Rebel Army and the civilian administration of the Free Territory have decided to levy taxes on the various levels of the economic system in the sectors of sugar, coffee, cattle, rice, etc.

In consequence it has been agreed to set a contribution of 1 *million* pesos from the National Bank of Cuba, which should be divided in proportion to the value of the interests of each one of the national or foreign banking enterprises based in Cuba.

This war contribution is decreed by the Rebel Army. It has legal force because it represents the will of the people who have taken up arms against repression.

---

* General Francisco Tabernilla y Dolz, head of the Joint Chiefs of Staff for Batista, had scornfully dismissed Castro's landing from the *Granma* in December 1956.—Ed.

The carrying out of this order is, therefore, absolutely obligatory.

We entrust you with the delicate mission of communicating this accord to the banks and collecting the amount entailed, maintaining absolute discretion—on their part, yours, and ours—in carrying out the matter, for the safety of the people involved.

If the banks comply with this order diligently and patriotically, the Rebel Army is ready to request from the future president of the republic, Judge Manuel Urrutia, that said amount be deducted from the sums normally paid as taxes by banking enterprises.

Accept a fraternal salute from your sincere compatriot.

To Exile Groups   **Sierra, September 18**

Discipline is essential; without discipline, it is impossible to have a revolutionary organization. Our ideas and aims must be guided by a single responsible individual; with more than one chief, propaganda would be chaotic and at times contradictory.

It is necessary that funds be assigned by a single administrator. With more than one administrator, it is impossible to administer or control funds, and we have no right to ask our compatriots to sacrifice if funds are to be spent without plan or order.

It is the duty of all Cubans to fight that characteristic tendency, which so often leads us to dilute our efforts in useless and sterile conflicts, such as those that long ago in the wars of liberation frustrated the finest spirits in the struggle. The damage is done to those who are fighting and need the help of their compatriots, who must not be confused by various factions and personalities. There are more than enough reasons that will be clear to any sympathetic, honest companion, who is sincerely patriotic.

In the Movement, there is room for every kind of effort and every enthusiasm, and there is also risk and goodwill, when one struggles for ideals and not out of ambition, to overcome the shortcomings that are natural in every human organization. They can be cause for disagreement, but must never be an excuse for wasting energy in moments decisive for the fatherland.

The help from those who have emigrated has been great, but it can be greater still if more join every day. May the effort of those who have emigrated keep pace with the advance of our invasion columns, which at this time are moving toward the liberation of the rest of the fatherland.

FIDEL CASTRO

Report   Sierra, September 19

Invasion Column 2, Antonio Maceo, under the command of Major Camilo Cienfuegos, has crossed the borders of Camagüey Province, entering Las Villas after advancing more than 200 miles. The advance of Column 2 constitutes a remarkable feat. Only men endowed with an extraordinary spirit of combat could have covered such a vast distance in a modern war, without air or tank support, against an enemy who had access to those resources of war.

Invasion Column 8, Ciro Redondo, under the command of Major Ernesto Guevara, was involved in hard-fought victorious battles with the enemy, south of Camagüey Province. The column is continuing its advance.

Two of our best commanders are, then, at the head of the invasion columns.

A third invasion force, Column 11, Cándido González, composed preponderantly of Camagüeyans under the command of Captain Jaime Vega, has also crossed the borders of Oriente and Camagüey and entered the latter province.

The forces of the three columns that have moved west are made up entirely of veterans of the Sierra Maestra who participated actively in the victorious counteroffensive begun by the Rebel Army on the First Front. After inflicting a military disaster on the dictatorship, this army has placed its vanguard in the center of the island.

Invasion Column 9, Antonio Guiteras, under the command of Major Hubert Matos, moving east, took the village of Santa Rita on the Bayamo–Santiago de Cuba highway, and after completely destroying a radio car and wiping out all its occupants, continued its advance, having sustained only a single casualty.

Forces of Column 3, Santiago de Cuba, likewise advancing east, attacked some electrical installations in the town of Contramaestre, also on the Bayamo–Santiago de Cuba highway, wiping out the enemy sentinels.

Rebel troops of the First Front of the Sierra Maestra, under the command of Captain Víctor Mora, advanced on the town of Yara on the Manzanillo–Bayamo highway, fighting with the enemy troops.

EDITOR'S SUMMARY   Havana, September 24

The Rancho Boyeros International Airport was destroyed today by saboteurs, who set it on fire; the big airport clock stopped at 3:07 p.m. Flames could be seen more than three miles away. The main airport building, housing airline offices, the customs warehouse, and the control tower, was totally consumed. Flights were canceled, and electric power to the airport was cut off.

Communications by telephone, telegraph, and rail between the city of Trinidad and the capital were cut by rebel forces.

In the city of Marta, power was cut off at 8:00 p.m. and not restored until 6:00 a.m. Revolutionary militiamen invaded the city in the darkness and shot at soldiers of Batista, especially in the vicinity of the prison and bus terminal.

FIDEL CASTRO

Report   Sierra, October

Two important clashes and other lesser actions have taken place on the First and Third fronts of the Sierra Maestra. Major Juan Almeida announced that rebel forces on the Third Front had defeated a battalion of the dictatorship, capturing its commander, Lieutenant Colonel Nelson Carrasco Artiles, and five other soldiers causing twenty-five casualties, and taking ten weapons. At the same time, on the First Front, many miles away, another victorious clash was taking place against the troops of the tyranny. An enemy battalion was strongly entrenched at El Cerro, three miles from Estrada Palma. After a thorough study of the terrain and careful observation of the enemy positions, forces from Columns 11 and 12, supported by mortars and heavy machine guns, surrounded the spot, in the early evening of Friday, September 27, and emplaced the .50-caliber machine guns and the mortars. At 11:45 p.m. a .60 mortar and two .50-caliber machine guns, under the command of Captain Braulio Coroneaux, opened fire on the enemy camp; five minutes later, at 11:50, a battery of 81 mortars, under the command of Captain Pedro Miret, situated only 240 yards from the enemy positions, opened fire, launching a mortar barrage on a rectangular area 150 yards deep and 100 wide where the enemy battalion was located. For a full hour the 81 mortars kept firing; fifty-four shells fell on the camp. The field tents, the command post, and all the other enemy installations there were blown up. At 12:50 in the morning two squads of rebel infantry, under the command of Major Eduardo Sardiñas, throwing flares to signal their movements to the mortars, advanced toward a ditch a few yards from the enemy trenches; the rebels and the soldiers of the dictatorship were so close that they could see each other's faces in the glare of the explosions. There they discharged their automatic weapons at the enemy garrison, which was on the verge of collapse. The troops of the dictatorship fought desperately to keep the camp from falling into rebel hands, defending it with .50-caliber machine guns, mortars, and cannons. The moon was full and the planes came to their aid. From the Estrada Palma mill, the dictatorship's Sherman tanks fired their heavy 75 cannons at El Cerro. But not a single reinforcement was sent to assist the encircled battalion.

Since the enemy had been immobilized for the entire night without any troop movement, our forces returned to the mountains at dawn. Five of our combatants died heroically when Major Eduardo Sardiñas advanced right up to the enemy trenches. Saturday, one of the dictatorship's big helicopters put down six times to collect the wounded. According to information that reaches us in various ways, the enemy sustained sixty-seven casualties, including dead and wounded.

In the last clash at El Cerro, they justified their reputation as one of the bravest, best trained, and most effective units of our army. Captain Pedro Miret also distinguished himself there through his bravery and effectiveness; it was the 81-mortar battery he led that was responsible for the large number of casualties suffered by the enemy.

The Mariana Grajales Squad of rebel women went into action for the first time in this battle and firmly held its ground under shelling from the Sherman tanks.

FIDEL CASTRO

Orders
To Juan Almeida   Sierra, October 8

I have struggled to advance preparations for Operation Santiago as much as possible in order to make it coincide with the electoral farce, so that we can force the enemy troops into a large-scale battle at that time, which, along with other measures we're going to take, would make it impossible to hold elections. I had also been thinking of going myself to the territory this month with as much equipment and men as I could take, but after analyzing everything carefully, I decided that it was impossible for several reasons:

1. The supply of arms and ammunition has not yet reached its maximum rate;

2. The multitude of matters and tasks of every kind that must be faced this month would remain unresolved or would be half done if I go away on a long march.

Since I am, as you know, stubborn about my plans, it's been very hard for me to give up the idea of leaving. At the same time, to use all our forces quickly in view of the elections, I have initiated a series of movements toward different parts of the province, arranging that while they are meeting specific objectives geared to November 3, they will at the same time serve as a basis for the strategy in subsequent weeks. That is, the troops that I am sending today to Victoria de las Tunas, Puerto Padre, Holguín, and Gibara will also carry out important objectives in the final weeks of the year. I am replacing the plan to take Santiago de Cuba first with a plan to take the outlying parts of the province. Taking Santiago and other cities will thus be much easier, and above all, we will be able to hold on to them. First we will take possession of the countryside. Within about twelve days, all the municipalities will be invaded. Afterward we will take possession, and if possible, we will destroy all lines of communication by land (highways and railroads). If the operations in Las Villas and Camagüey progress simultaneously, the tyranny will suffer as complete a disaster in those provinces as it suffered in the Sierra Maestra. This strategy has turned out to be more foolproof for us than any other, and meanwhile—rather than concentrating the bulk of our forces in one direction, which takes time, requires a large accumulation of provisions, and involves considerable risks—we distribute our forces in such a way that they can keep the enemy under constant harassment everywhere. Columns 3, 9, and 10 are assigned, for the time being, to your front, the Santiago de Cuba front. You must make these troops a powerful and disciplined force that progressively controls and, especially, studies the region thoroughly in anticipation of the time when it will have to dig in at strategic points. *All the important cities are going to be isolated simultaneously.* And it must be done at the moment when we are sufficiently strong to resist and the enemy is weak, demoralized, and harassed enough so that he cannot free himself from the encirclement. Following the tactics used in the Sierra Maestra, our offensive will not only force them to defend themselves but also make them take to the trenches if they want to save themselves. (All the foregoing is strictly secret, for your eyes alone.)

Well now, this is the strategy that we are going to follow in the province. But meanwhile we have the elections, which must be prevented at all costs.

The plan will focus on these points:

a. Public prohibition against travel throughout the nation, possibly beginning the thirtieth of this month. It will be announced by every means of communication one or two weeks in advance.

b. Military operations on a broad scale that will force the enemy into a major troop mobilization and cause panic and general flight.

Military actions will intensify to the maximum starting in the middle of this month, and on the eve of the elections, we will make it look as though we are threatening to capture some large cities; the electoral farce will be a complete failure, and who knows what might happen.

I emphasize that we are going to simulate a threat, because it is going to be a threat only and not an actual attempt. But the enemy must believe that it is an attempt. In several cities, the fake threat will take place on election day, the third, because circumstances don't permit anything else, but in Santiago, the maneuver must take place earlier since it is the only way to make the enemy military commanders really uneasy. The ideal thing would be two days before, but that seems a little risky to me. Therefore, I think it is safest to do it twenty-four hours in advance. The point is to surround Santiago, intercepting all the lines of communication from the night of the first to the second, taking positions and digging in to intercept any force that tries to enter or leave. On the second, during the day, any enemy advance must be resisted. Since the Central Highway is the principal road the enemy would utilize, you must concentrate special attention there. It seems to me that the best area for the fortified line is between Palma Soriano and El Santuario, where the highway crosses the Maestra. But there must be patrols intercepting the exit routes as close as possible to the city of Santiago.

If the encirclement can be maintained from the night of the first to the second, even to noon on the third, it will be a complete success.

I am giving you the general idea, the objective: to make them believe that Santiago is going to be taken, to force the enemy to move and start the battle. You should study all the tactical details and, depending on the circumstances, carry them out according to your own judgment. You can count on the forces of the three columns and all the patrols that you have there. In all, I calculate that you have close to four hundred good weapons available.

We've had little luck with bullets. Besides that plane that could not drop the packages—remember?—another plane, which was bringing fourteen thousand M-1 bullets, eighteen rifles, one antitank gun, and one .50-caliber, did not find the landing field, and dropped the cargo at random in the Sierra. Of that only the .50 and two thousand M-1 bullets have turned up. Only twenty thousand .30-'06 bullets arrived a month ago; we have supplied the troops sparingly with them, and I am sending you the last two thousand.

You must organize people to try to buy bullets for the soldiers. If necessary, you can go as high as 1 peso for each .30-'06 or M-1 bullet.

After November 3 all your thoughts must be focused on preparations for the moment when we isolate and encircle all the cities simultaneously. Your forces will be responsible for isolating the cities of Palma Soriano and Santiago. You must keep thinking about destroying the highway, which means destroying bridges, digging antitank ditches, studying heights and strategic points around the road. You must gather as many pickaxes and shovels as possible, as well as cables and batteries to make detonators. Installing mines on the asphalt highways is a technical problem that must be solved. We must gouge out a great many pits and potholes, in which a mine can be placed. If the highway is completely smooth, we will be able to surprise them the first time with a mine planted in the asphalt, but after that any pothole will make them suspicious. As your control over the highway increases, you must make potholes with pickaxes—at least until you can make antitank ditches. What I mean is that after one or two mines explode on the highway, and a night patrol chops up the asphalt in several places, the tanks will have to stop to inspect them one by one. Also mines can be placed in dirt embankments, one on each side, facing each other, and be exploded simultaneously. The explosion will strike the sides of the tank, and if the tank is squeezed between two blasts, I don't think it can hold up. But it is a matter of distance and other details.

Meanwhile, before and after November 3, systematic warfare against transportation must constantly be maintained, as you already have been doing. The transportation companies must be ruined if they don't suspend travel on the highways and railroads.

But it is extremely important that these plans be kept absolutely secret. I emphasize this because experience teaches me that even commanders are not very discreet. I am not referring to you personally, since I know that you are an old fox about such things, but I remind you for your guidance.

Above all, we must keep the strategy after November 3 secret, so that the enemy never suspects our purpose and can't prepare himself to counteract it. I will continue moving and placing forces, and at the opportune moment, I will give the order. I think it is still some months away. I will reveal my intentions to very few. Each one will receive instructions for his part in it.

I am impatiently waiting for news of Che and Camilo. I have the impression that the advance has been hard for them but that it has turned out well.

I congratulate you on capturing the lieutenant colonel; that is an impressive feat. I received his stars and his identification card. When he is well, send him over here.

To Delio Gómez Ochoa   Sierra, October 9

They tell us a plane will arrive Friday, apparently with considerable war materiel.

See that the best possible defensive measures are taken.

Any day now the guards may try to get as far as the landing fields. The men must prepare some defenses here. Emilio and the mortars can reinforce them as long as they don't have another mission.

EDITOR'S SUMMARY   October 1958

The matter of arms supply became urgent as the offensive swept into high gear. On August 26 Dr. José Miró Cardona, from his temporary home in Miami, had written to President Eisenhower to assert again that the Batista government was not a dem-

ocratic regime and not a proper recipient of aid from a U.S. military mission. Although Dr. Miró Cardona had written as the representative of the Civic Revolutionary Front, the reply sent to him on October 13 avoided according him an organizational status, as Jules Dubois pointed out. The letter came not from the White House, but from the State Department's chief of Caribbean affairs, who explained that regardless of the circumstances, withdrawal of a U.S. military mission was only "permissive rather than mandatory." In short, nothing would be done.

CAMILO CIENFUEGOS

Report to Fidel Castro   The Plains of Santa Clara,
Las Villas, October 9

Since we left the Cauto region and set out toward Occidente, we've traveled without resting a single night, forty marches, many of them without a guide, using the south coast as our landmark and going by the compass. The trip along this coast was disastrous; for two weeks, we marched in water and mud up to our knees, and every night we had to dodge ambushes and troops at the fords where we had to cross.

In the thirty-one days it took us to go through Camagüey Province we ate only eleven times, even though this is our major cattle-raising area! After four days without food, we had to eat a mare, the best of our already poor cavalry. Almost all the animals had gotten bogged down in the swamps on the south coast.

For twenty-two days we have not had any news from Che; the last time we heard was on the sixteenth of last month, when eight comrades joined us and later another from his troop, right after a fight in a place called Cuatro Compañeros.

Yesterday we reached this rebel camp, where they've received us magnificently. The commander, Sr. Félix Torres—of the PSP [Partido Socialista Popular; Popular Socialist Party]—has showered us with kindness. In expectation of Che, they had sent scouts to the boundaries of the province. A 26th of July group is also operating in this region, and we've already made contact with it.

Today they tell me that Che has left the Baraguá zone but is proceeding very slowly because of the poor physical condition of his men. We know the place well: the sea and the swamps on one side; the Lituabo River opposite, with only one crossing point, the Cantarranas bridge, where there were three ambushes of twenty men each set up 500 yards apart; the Baraguá, Jagüeyal, and Stewart sugar mills to the north, with a great many soldiers, and many ambushes all along that line. The tyranny had placed about seven hundred soldiers there. The tactic followed by the army was to let us advance to the Lituabo River, block our retreat and give us the blow that would prevent the Antonio Maceo Invasion Column from reaching its goal.

While we were crossing Camagüey Province, we had a total of three encounters with the mercenary army of the tyranny, in which we sustained no casualties. However, we lost Lieutenant Zenén Meriño, taken prisoner, as well as Lieutenant Delfín Moreno, the one who went up with the messages when we were operating in the Cauto region, and the soldier Germán Barrero (El Abuelo [the Grandfather]), who managed to escape although he hasn't made contact again with his troops, and we lost a large number of documents, including the diary of the months when we were on the plain for the first time.

This happened the morning after we had taken the road from Júcaro to Morón, where we burned and destroyed the aqueduct and pumping station at Ciego de Avila, after a little skirmish in which an army corporal was killed and we took a soldier prisoner, and confiscated 2 Springfields, 2 cartridge belts, and 2 pistols.

We crossed the Jobabo River to the south September 7 before midnight; on the eighth, we avoided a small ambush that the guards had waiting at the Tara sugar mill for a group of bandits that were said to be operating in that region; Che had an encounter with this ambush when he passed through here. We reached the La Federal forest without any problem; early in the morning, we heard several sporadic shots for more than two hours, which made us think that the army was advancing by the road we had taken the night before.

A little while later, through a messenger from Che, we learned that they had already clashed with them, with the outcome two casualties and one wounded from our side and two dead and five prisoners from their side; we took seven shotguns.

After withdrawing the ambush prepared for the reinforcements, the Ciro Redondo Column, commanded by Che Guevara, met with us and together we left for the forest in the vicinity of the Francisco mill.

On the night of the tenth, we left our cavalry, which consisted of more than seventy beasts, and set out in trucks. When we reached the first kilometer marker of the Francisco mill railroad, the first scouting squad, under the command of Captain Guerra, encountered a car occupied by soldiers, which was coming from the Francisco mill. Immediately, the appropriate measures were taken by the rest of our troops, thinking that we had fallen into an ambush, since the army knew our location. That same afternoon, 250 soldiers had arrived from Camagüey. We cut the telephone wires and took combat positions, the car took flight, and the whole thing ended with our trucks crossing rapidly at the spot. The river was overflowing, which stopped us, so we made camp in the brush next to the Macareño mill. The next night, in other trucks, we again set out on our journey. After much effort to free the trucks mired in the mud on a trip that seemed endless, but was actually only about a mile from this mill, we got onto the highway that goes from Santa Cruz to Camagüey, which is always patrolled by enemy vehicles.

After going a mile and a quarter on this highway, we turned off to the road that leads to the village of Cuatro Compañeros, having to stop again because we found the Najasa River overflowing. The trucks went back and we camped nearby.

On the thirteenth we reached the Forestal woods, near Cuatro Compañeros. Very soon we got information that an enemy troop was on our trail, although it could not reach us; we had already taken the measures necessary in case of a clash: the railroad and telephone lines from Camagüey to Santa Cruz were to be cut when the first shot was heard. At 7:00 p.m. we left the woods, and in a few miles, we reached an embankment. We had just crossed the bridge there when we heard a strong explosion followed by machine-gun bursts and shots from automatic rifles. We quickly threw ourselves to the ground. The vanguard squad, led by Captain Guerra, answered the enemy fire and surrounded the house and the grounds from which the firing came. This was enough to make Batista's boys withdraw, taking several wounded with them.

It was already day when we camped. On the sixteenth we learned that Che's column had fallen into an ambush in that same village, Cuatro Compañeros.

That afternoon we picked up a group of nine men, three of them officers, who had lost contact with their troop; from then on, they stayed with us. With them came two young bandits; they had guided the group to us. It turned out that the bandits spent their time assaulting and robbing in the name of the 26th of July Revolutionary Movement. Edel Casañas, seventeen years old, and Maximino Quevedo, twenty-nine years old, were declared guilty of the crimes of assault and robbery, and since they could not deny their guilt, judgment was passed, and they were condemned to death.

On the eighteenth we went to the place where we were going to cross the San Pedro River, which had been scouted by the vanguard, who found enemy troops and two gunboats at the mouth, in addition to 200 soldiers and several ambushes on the Castillo property. We crossed the Altamira River, which was very high, so we had to make rope bridges and rafts, over which we passed the arms and equipment. We had intended to rest there for several days, but our position was discovered by two men who took flight when they saw us, and later we were able to verify that they were military personnel.

At dawn on the twentieth we reached a small forest on the Trinidad property, 2 miles from La Yegua River; on the journey, we crossed the highway that goes to Vertientes and passed the railroad line that goes from the Agramonte mill to the shore, to the post at Santa María, with its 2 gunboats. The Batista troops had ambushes on the road that leads to the shore, in the store at La Trinidad, in El Tres [Regiment] del Caney, and in El Seis [Regiment] de Agramonte; a total of 600 mercenaries.

On the twenty-first we crossed the lines of ambushes that they had prepared for us from Santa María beach to the Agramonte mill along the railroad line, with a round of flares every ten minutes; we moved in one of the intervals. When a comrade fell from a horse, a shot from his San Cristóbal went off. A few days later, when we stopped a soldier, we learned that a group of soldiers posted where we had crossed had seen us and heard the shot, but did not make the slightest effort to stop us. This is the most concrete proof that Batista's army does not want to fight and its weak, flagging morale gets lower every day.

The twenty-third, Wednesday, Lieutenant Zenén Meriño, accompanied by a prisoner named Fernández, went to explore the region to try to find some peasant who could guide us, since we were lost. That afternoon the aircraft heavily bombed a small mountain several miles away from us.

The situation became more serious as we had to continue the march without a guide. We marched for two nights, following the coast and using a compass to orient us. After traveling all night we camped in some woods—we were lost again. Lieutenant Delfín Moreno posted himself with a squad in a forest about a mile away from us; he had orders to stop anyone who passed on the highway that he was watching, to find out where we were, and to get us a guide. After waiting all morning without anyone passing by, he went off to the refinery on the rice plantation, where he managed to find three workers and explained to them that he was lost and needed someone to get him out of there. One of the three, Edilio Sanabria, a large black with a moon face, volunteered to go to look for a certain person who knew the area; he turned out to be an A-1 informer, and instead of bringing a guide, he brought the army, which kept us from having the last swallows of the mare we had slaughtered for food, after four days without eating. Lieutenant Moreno got back to us, but the soldiers of the tyranny kept up heavy fire on the woods for twenty-three hours, although there wasn't anyone in them.

Guided by the workers on the rice plantation, we left the place where the soldiers were fighting with unaccustomed valor against deserted woods, and we went to the house of some charcoal makers, where we got five men who weren't worth a damn and one of them began to cry; the situation was difficult and we had to take them with us to get us out of there. They took us to some woods. We camped there, while in the distance we heard constant firing against the besieged woods.

A scouting patrol located a house where, besides food, we found a guide, a guide good for about a mile; they were all worthless. That night we crossed the tracks that run from the Baraguá mill to its dock. A few miles from the tracks, we found another guide, who was rumored to be an informer, but he could take us to the bridge over the Lituabo River. The swamps on the coast are impassable, and you can ford the river.

Since we wouldn't reach a place to camp that night after we crossed the bridge, and since we had some misgivings about the crossing, we decided to make camp before crossing, and the next day send some men to reconnoiter the dangerous point. We stationed ambushes well away from the camp since we knew that the caretaker of this property was a real bastard who had turned in people in the August 5 strike, and the three days before we arrived, they were searching for signs of strangers. At 3:00 p.m., the lookout surprised three men who said they were peasants. After long, separate interrogations, they were trapped in numerous contradictions. And two of them were wearing military boots. They all denied that they belonged to the army. The youngest, Enrique Navarro Herrera, was the caretaker I mentioned. When we told them that they had to get us across the bridge and march ahead of us, two confessed; one was Corporal Juan Trujillo Medina, the other a private, Jesús Pino Barrios, of the 22d Squadron of the Rural Guard of the Second Regiment, Agramonte. The third, the caretaker, Navarro Herrera, with all the earmarks of an informer, was the guide for the spies.

Corporal Trujillo described in detail all the ambushes that five companies (more than five hundred soldiers) had waiting for us on the bridge, and along the whole line from the shore to the Baraguá mill, and from the mill to the Central Highway, and even if these lines of ambushes were broken, they had others all the way to Stewart and from Stewart to Júcaro.

Since Corporal Trujillo was the one who had mapped out the sites of the ambushes, because he was the one who knew the entire region best, a veteran of thirty years' service here, we explained to him that the only way he could save his life was to get us out of there without our firing a single shot. The corporal explained that the only way we could evade the ambushes was by going to the north and crossing the Central Highway about 15 miles away, between the small village of Gaspar y Colorado, not very far from Ciego de Avila. Unquestionably, Corporal Trujillo turned out to be the best guide: he led us successfully past an endless number of ambushes and the Baraguá Barracks, where there were more than 200 soldiers. After traveling more than 20 miles, because of all the detours we had to make, at dawn we came very close to the Central Highway and decided to stay in a cane field 200 yards from the highway and 16 miles from Ciego de Avila.

At daybreak we sent the doctor-captain of the Antonio Maceo Invasion Column to Ciego de Avila to make contact with the leaders of the Movement, in order to obtain the goods, medicines, guides, and trucks we would need to travel through the area in the direction of Las Villas, where we were anxiously awaited.

Under a heavy rain, we waited until twelve at night; by that time our presence was sure to be known in Ciego de Avila, and in view of the dangers we would face if we were discovered, despite the lateness and the flooded roads, we decided to take some trucks to carry us as far as possible from this inhospitable area, in spite of all the risks of weather mentioned before—the chief one being that the trucks would get stuck and would tie us down there.

Although it was late at night, 12:30, we went to a sugar mill in a little village to locate some trucks to transport us, but we were continually getting stuck on the terrible road, which slowed our trip tremendously. At daylight we were surprised to find ourselves at another sugar refinery, and we had to take the thirty houses there. The inhabitants were terrified because they thought the army might appear at any moment, but in a little while, they lost their fear and chatted with the rebels just like old friends. In the village, we placed lookouts and ambushes far enough away so that the inhabitants would not run any risk, but strong enough to drive off the enemy. Every man was aware of the danger he was running if the army entered the village and, committing one more act of sheer barbarity, destroyed all the houses and their inhabitants. In the school, there were more than forty children. At first they were all crying and they wanted to go home; that day the teacher did not come to give classes because the road was impassable. A rebel, Captain Antonio Sánchez (Pinares),* put himself in charge of giving classes, of handing out refreshments, candy, notebooks, pencils, and a bit of money to the children. There was general joy. We spent happy hours with the little ones, which made us forget our fatigue and recent hardships for a while. When it was time for them to go to their homes, one refused to leave and, crying, asked to go away with us or else that we should return the next day. They all sang the national anthem, and they promised us that every Friday, in the school, they would place flowers before the bust of José Martí, the Apostle of Independence, and they would ask the teacher to tell them about Martí, why he struggled and why he died. That night we had to cross the historic road from Júcara to Morón.** The men, full of patriotic fervor, were waiting impatiently for the march to begin. At exactly 7:00 p.m. we began the arduous task of pulling out the mired trucks; it was late when we crossed the highway from Morón to Ciego de Avila.

At 12:30 a.m., September 30, we crossed the road. All the men crossed on foot, the trucks coming behind. Since the trucks were almost out of gas, we went to look for some in the vicinity of the Ciego de Avila aqueduct. The plant that supplies water to Ciego de Avila had been destroyed and burned, and the city had been without water for several

---

* Killed in the campaign with Che in Bolivia, in 1967.—C. F.
** This was the route taken in 1895 by Antonio Maceo and Máximo Gómez, in the Wars of Independence.—ED.

days. The men immediately got back on the trucks, and set off on the road to Marroquí. A few miles beyond the place where the trucks had gotten mired, we had to abandon them, since it was almost day.

At seven in the morning a light reconnaissance plane appeared and discovered the abandoned trucks, which were about a mile from where we now were. At 11:30 a.m. a rebel reconnaissance patrol saw a large number of soldiers traveling along the banks of the river we had crossed a short while before. At the same hour, six trucks loaded with soldiers of the dictatorship crossed a dirt road about 800 yards from where we were camped. All our men were put on alert; they formed a defensive line the whole length and width of the cane field where we were camped. The sun beat down harshly, but the men did not budge from their positions so as not to reveal where we were. At approximately four in the afternoon, we heard heavy fire about two or three miles away; trucks were coming and going which meant that the soldiers were trying to discover our position at that moment, when the rebel column was at a disadvantage. The light plane passed over several times trying to locate us. When night came we had to cross a zone that was really dangerous because we had no idea where the enemy was. At seven sharp, we started to march; after several hours of walking, we were out of danger, but we all wanted to make contact with the companions who'd become separated from us. The shots in the afternoon had been fired against them. That had been it. A truckload of soldiers had reached the house where they were, surprising Lieutenant Moreno, who was machine-gunned by several of them. Barrero managed to escape because he was not in the house. This serious mishap cost the life of one of the bravest and most effective men in this column, and at the same time we lost documents and the diary of the campaign during the months when we operated in the Cauto region.

Everyone was eager to reach Las Villas, and the fact that it was near gave us the strength to continue the march. Night had fallen when we reached a house where we found a guide who led us a little farther on the way; that night we crossed the road that leads from Marroquí to Majagua. In that area, we met people who were more resolute and more ready to cooperate in one way or another. Many visited the camp, and there were three enlistments, which made a total of seven that we had gained in Camagüey Province. Later, when we crossed the border of the province, some men even had two rifles. There we learned that five youths who were traveling in a car on the highway from Marroquí to Majagua were killed by troops of the tyranny. On that same road, the night before, trucks loaded with troops got confused in the dark and mistook one another for rebels. They opened fire on their own comrades, killing five and wounding several; many scattered and fled in the panic and were turning up the following day. The official story was that a large group of rebels had attacked them, and they had asked the villagers to protect them and take them to the nearest barracks.

That night we didn't go far but ate enough. We reached so-called Los Americanos hill at 2:00 a.m. There the terrain began to be rough, which reminded us of our beloved Sierra Maestra. That night, at seven, we set out on the road that would bring us to Las Villas. Because of the cowardice of the guides, the trip was very long. One of them who came voluntarily, Jesús López, arrived armed like a revolutionary and rebel, but took flight when he found out that on the road that we had to cross there were two ambushes of forty soldiers each, and we had to pass between them. Because of a mistake by the guide, we almost landed in the village of Florencia. We had to cut a number of fences, which is why they discovered that we had passed through. We camped a mile or so from the hospitable province of Las Villas.

The day dawned cloudy and rainy. That was the only night that we rested, after forty days on the march. The Jatibonico River had risen, and we could not cross it, so we had to return to the previous camp under a torrential downpour with strong gusts of wind. We commandeered several houses and spent the night in them. On the following day we ordered food prepared. Contradictory reports came in, one after another: the army is approaching, the soldiers are moving in this or that direction, the roads are blocked, the soldiers from Los Ramones, Boquerones, and Florencia are moving together and forming a circle that would block us from going to Las Villas. Nothing would stop our crossing, not the swelling rivers or the hundreds of soldiers who were said to be moving in around us. The Jatibonico River! We put a rope into the water; it came up to our chests, and the current was strong. I kissed the soil of Villa Clara. All the men in the troop were overjoyed. A small part of our mission had been completed. Camagüey was behind us. Camagüey and its difficult times. Camagüey and its hungry times.

This was one of the greatest triumphs in the annals of military revolution; in spite of the numerous efforts of the army of the tyranny to exterminate us, we had made the long trip from Oriente to Las Villas with only three casualties.

It is afternoon now; the person who will bring the message has been waiting since this morning. Today the plane is dropping pieces of paper announcing that they are going to bomb us.

I'll write you as soon as I have news of Che, since I now have contacts, and you will have news more often of our march, which is taking longer than we thought. We tried very hard to shorten the time, but it wasn't possible. I am certain that we'll reach Pinar del Río; the men are determined, and their will and their spirit never weaken. The more they are hungry, in need of sleep, or faced with danger, the more determined they are.

This is an A-1 troop, this troop will reach its goal.

Although I promised Franqui and Eduardo to keep them informed of everything and often, it was impossible for me to do it. I'm going to collect all the latest information about the province I can and send it to the radio station.

FIDEL CASTRO

Orders to Camilo Cienfuegos   Sierra, October 14

I can't describe the emotion I felt in reading your report of the ninth.

There are no words with which to express the joy, the pride, and the admiration that I feel for you and your men. What you have done is enough to win you a place in the history of Cuba and of great military exploits.

Don't continue your advance until you get further orders. Wait for Che in Las Villas and stay with him. The politico-revolutionary situation there is complicated, and it is therefore essential for you to remain in the province long enough to help stabilize it solidly.

Gutiérrez Menoyo's action is inconceivable—disarming and arresting Bordón and his forces,* according to the news received here, which I hope is not correct, but if it is, you must demand the immediate return of the arms that belong to the Movement and the release of the men arrested. They have behaved disgracefully, concentrating on their own affairs instead of helping you and supporting you however they could when you were threatened with extermination, as true companions and revolutionaries would have done. When Calixto Sánchez** landed in the northern part of Oriente, we attacked El Uvero, with one of our aims being to alleviate their situation.

I believe that their actions will only discredit the perpetrators and make the mass of fighters mistrust them, because in a revolutionary process, very few can be rallied to defend someone's personal interests. Anyone who stops for such a thing in the middle of a revolution soon finds himself isolated or overwhelmed by the force of events. Che has been

---

* The dispute between Eloy Gutiérrez Menoyo and Víctor Bordón was rooted in controversies involving local guerrilla forces of the 26th of July Movement and the Revolutionary Directory in Las Villas Province, as well as groups with ill-defined allegiances, including Auténtico bands and Yankee "adventurers."

When the 26th of July's invasion columns, under Guevara and Cienfuegos, entered the province, they fueled the long-simmering disputes among the anti-Batista leaders there: Faure Chomón, of the Revolutionary Directory; Gutiérrez Menoyo, who had been expelled from the Directory; and Bordón of the local 26th of July. After Bordón went to confer with Castro about the role of Guevara and Cienfuegos, he urged his men to unite with Che's. Gutiérrez Menoyo promptly arrested him for "treason." Guevara persuaded Chomón to announce that he would cooperate with Guevara's forces, and in November, Che and Rolando Cubelas, for the Revolutionary Directory, signed the Pedrero Pact, pledging military and political coordination in the name of "the ideals of youth."—ED.

** Leader of the Auténticos' *Corintia* expedition (see pp. 179 and 181).—ED.

sent to Las Villas to fight the enemy and command the forces of the 26th of July Movement, not with any claims to command any other group. Now then, if they want to unite the forces that are operating in that province, it is logical that the command should go to the senior commander, to the one who has demonstrated the greatest military and organizational ability, to the one who inspires the most enthusiasm and confidence in the people, and those qualifications, which Che and you both have, no one will dispute, especially after the singular feat of having advanced from the Sierra Maestra to Las Villas against the opposition of thousands of enemy soldiers.

I won't accept any chief but Che, if the forces reach an agreement. If they don't, he must assume command of all the forces of the 26th of July Movement and those that spontaneously join with them and carry out our strategic plans.

It is a crime against the Revolution to incite quarrels and division; until today, they haven't emerged on the fields of battle, but they caused a great deal of harm in the liberation wars of the past. Anyone with merit, ability, and patriotism will find abundant opportunities in the Revolution to attain the highest glories and most exalted honors. The enemy is before us; this is the only area where all ambitions, all desires, and all dreams of glory are legitimate. The positions and honors that our commanders have attained are not the result of favoritism or of privilege but of merit, valor, sacrifice. It is in facing the enemy that our men will continue seeking rank, grandeur, and moral glories, without claiming them or coveting them, because the humble men who are today followers and leaders of the Revolution were not thinking about that when they enrolled in our persecuted, hungry, hunted, weak forces; nor did those who fell on this expedition think about it, as they gave their blood and their lives to lay the foundation for every victory of our army, which has been formed and organized on the basis of merit, sacrifice, and the purest disinterest. We began this war when nobody believed that anyone could stand up against a powerful, modern army. We managed it when there were only twelve of us, and no one offered the slightest support. We did not begin it in a spirit of rivalry or jealousy against anyone; envy has never inspired a single act of ours; we have not been pained by the triumph of others; solid unity and brotherhood have always prevailed among us; in two years of struggle, we have never heard the lips of a rebel speak of a public post or a petty ambition. That is the spirit that we must continue infusing into our Revolutionary Army.

Before continuing the advance it is necessary:

1. That your men recuperate physically.

2. That the struggle be intensified in the provinces of Oriente,

Camagüey, Las Villas, and Pinar del Río, to compel the enemy to use his forces to the maximum on all fronts and prevent him from concentrating the bulk of his forces against us, as happened in Camagüey.

3. That rebel operational centers be created all along your path.

4. That you study and prepare your plans for the advance in detail, collecting guides, making contacts beforehand, and carefully anticipating all the difficulties that you may encounter. In addition, you must use several very mobile patrols in different directions to disconcert the enemy and make it easier for you to get through.

5. Above all, this time, you must keep the route that you are to take strictly secret. The enemy must be induced to believe that you've given up the plan so that you can take him completely by surprise.

If you have any objections or suggestions concerning these instructions, I am willing to reconsider them, but I hope that you agree with me.

I am now more eager than ever for you to bring this endeavor to a victorious conclusion, reaching Pinar del Río and inscribing as glorious a page in history as the invasion of 1895; that is why I want to take all the measures necessary to ensure that that extraordinary episode will be written again.

An embrace of infinite admiration and affection for the heroic soldiers of your column.

In my name, thank the group of rebels who helped you to reach Santa Clara, and received you so hospitably. Greet Torres and his companions for us.

In regard to the politico-revolutionary problem there, although you and Che must energetically and firmly demand the return of the weapons and the release of the members of the Movement who were arrested, you must always proceed very tactfully and delicately, making all the parties understand the difference between our procedures and the procedures employed there. By this I mean that all diplomatic and rational means must be brought to bear to resolve the problems. Resort to force only in self-defense or when a vital revolutionary necessity is involved. But then, if you are obliged to act drastically the blow must be decisive and must resolve everything once and for all. Never be trapped into provocations or Byzantine conflicts. Always act with dignity. That's what will win the confidence and the support of the masses. The masses have to see that it was an act of unqualified treason to disarm the men of the 26th of July in Las Villas, leaving them powerless to support our columns as they were advancing arduously through Camagüey. That act here or in any other part of the world is treason, and the procedure by which, according to reports, Bordón and his men were disarmed was an act of common gangsterism.

Be on your guard against any form of treason, and—although I don't have to tell you this because anyone who has managed to outwit thousands of guards can't be a careless person—take all the measures necessary for security and protection while that atmosphere persists. You can count on all the support, weapons, men, and resources from us that you might need. With the invasion columns go our prestige, the justification for our cause, our history, and our people. I repeat that "nothing and no one can stop them."

FIDEL CASTRO

Statement   Sierra, October 17

Column 11, under the command of Captain Jaime Vega, suffered a serious reverse in its zone of operations in Camagüey Province.

Although this occurred more than two weeks ago, we did not announce it as we were awaiting the results of the investigations and exact data that were ordered concerning it. Any unit can suffer a tactical reverse in a war, because one cannot necessarily expect an uninterrupted chain of victories when the enemy has always commanded advantages in armaments and war materiel—although he has gotten the worst of it in this war.

We consider it a duty of the command of our army to report whatever setbacks may occur to any of our forces in operations, inasmuch as we consider it a moral and military principle of our movement that it is not right to hide reverses from the people or the combatants.

Reverses must also be publicized because useful lessons can be derived from them, so that errors one unit commits will not be repeated by another, so that the carelessness of one revolutionary officer will not be repeated by other officers. In war, faults are not overcome by hiding them and deceiving the soldiers, but by revealing them, always alerting all the commands, demanding new and redoubled care in planning and executing movements and actions.

Captain Jaime Vega, disregarding the tactical security measures contained in the precise instructions he received—measures that must always be taken in territory dominated by the enemy—advanced in trucks on the night of September 27/28 over the road that goes from the Francisco mill to the Macareño mill, south of Camagüey Province.

The 97th Company of the forces of the dictatorship, in ambush on the road, opened fire, surprising the column at 2:00 a.m. on the twenty-eighth. The enemy, supported by a barrage of heavy machine guns, fired against the vehicles and killed eighteen men in the column; eleven of the wounded were taken prisoner because they could not be recovered in the middle of the night under the fire of the enemy machine guns emplaced in favorable positions. The wounded rebel prisoners were taken to the Macareño hospital and attended by the local doctor and two doctors sent to Santa Cruz del Sur by Lieutenant Suárez, commander of the 97th Company. On the following day Colonel Leopoldo Pérez Coujil arrived by plane, and a little later Lieutenant Colonel Suárez Suquet, Major Domingo Piñeiro and his bodyguard, Sergeant Lorenzo Otaño, arrived by car. Colonel Coujil presented the company with 1000 pesos in cash, which was distributed to the soldiers.

The first thing he did after that was to strike one of the wounded prisoners on the face. The second thing was to instruct Lieutenant Colonel Suárez Suquet to have all the wounded killed. The latter designated Major Piñeiro to simulate a fight, while moving the wounded to Santa Cruz del Sur, and finish them off on the way.

They put mattresses on the trucks, placed the wounded on them, and set off. After traveling a few miles, they themselves began to shoot while Major Piñeiro shouted: "The rebels are attacking us," at which point Sergeant Otaño threw two hand grenades into the trucks where the wounded were. They, in turn, believing that their companions really were attacking, shouted: "Fellows, it's us and we're wounded; don't shoot." Sergeant Otaño climbed up into the trucks and finished off those who were dying with a submachine gun; the grenades had torn off arms and heads, and the inside of the truck was a mass of human flesh and blood.

They are losing the war and they are murdering the few wounded prisoners that fall into their hands.

Also in Camagüey, Columns 2 and 8, under Majors Camilo Cienfuegos and Ernesto Guevara, are marching victoriously and unchecked, and the massive forces that the dictatorship has hurled against them cannot halt their advance. The invasion vanguard has already penetrated more than thirty miles into Las Villas.

They will have to continue fighting until their total destruction, because the Revolution will not be deterred in the least by the nauseating farce that is being prepared for this coming November 3, or by a coup d'état unless it is based on the conditions set by the 26th of July Movement and its revolutionary program.

Sierra, October 17

We announce that the Agrarian Law of the Rebel Army will be proclaimed October 20, to bring into reality the promises of the Revolution to the oppressed peasant class of Cuba.

Here the Revolution will establish schools, hospitals, libraries, industries, sports fields, and hygienic, modern housing. These lands will forever belong to the peasants. And if today it is those who were the first to sacrifice who receive the first fruits, the law is national in scope and will be applied in all the territories controlled by our forces and those that are being liberated by the victorious thrust of our invading columns.

Wars are not won by those who have more weapons and more soldiers, but by those who are right. That explains why the army, which was thought to be invincible, is losing the war, because every day there are more rebels and more battlefields. Because every day the life of the soldier becomes more insecure and terrible. They have led them into an unjust war and they are losing that war.

FIDEL CASTRO

Communiqué   Sierra, October 17

When even the United States itself, which traditionally provides weapons to the Cuban Army, has placed an embargo on all military supplies to the Batista dictatorship, England is going to traffic in our tragedy and sell the tyrant seventeen planes.

In consequence, the commander in chief of the Rebel Army will promulgate a revolutionary law declaring an embargo on all the goods of English citizens and companies in the liberated territory; all their properties in the national territory will be confiscated as soon as the battle is over; and systematic sabotage of English industries and businesses in the national territory will be carried out while the war lasts, beginning at the very moment when the first of the seventeen planes arrives in Cuba.

Cubans! Don't feed Shell with your blood!

JULIO CAMACHO

Letter to Fidel Castro   Havana, October 20

As I advance further into matters relative to the army, situations are arising that really warrant my making another trip to the Sierra, but it is impossible for me to do it because I must attend to everything that comes up; that is why I have decided to write although I am aware of the grave risk that presents.

I have held important meetings with elements who until yesterday believed they could count on the force necessary to decide the situation. We have agreed on some points, like cleaning up the army; delivering the embezzlers and murderers, civilian and military, to justice; recognizing the Rebel Army as the national army, merged with what may remain of the present army; but we have not agreed on the method of establishing a government. They proposed a civilian-military junta, for a fixed period or until the elections; after rejecting this idea, I answered with Urrutia's proposal, which is not acceptable to them.

We need instructions on the possibility of reaching an agreement providing for Raúl Chibás as president and Barquín as commander of the army. That possibility was treated superficially, but I perceived a rather favorable atmosphere. I did not pursue it, but I await your ideas and those of the other comrades as soon as possible.

I have met again today, the twentieth, with the soldiers on active service. This time they gave more details; they are not so convinced that the agreement with their forces will hold in case of action in Havana. They have suspended certain rescue plans that they intended to carry out on the Isle of Pines. On the other hand, they propose to act in Oriente, or else for all of them to go to the Sierra Maestra, where they would form a military column attempting to rescue the morale and prestige of the armed forces, under the command of Raúl Chibás's friend and subordinate to our commander in chief, naturally. The captains who know about this and who are on active service, some of them in operations in the Sierra and others about to be sent there, would incorporate their companies into this column, assuring total control of Oriente Province.

Right now, there are large numbers of military men dissatisfied with the dictatorship, but they hesitate to desert and wonder how they would be received; in the plan I have just outlined, their fears would be eliminated and they would be incorporated into a column in the Sierra that would represent their own force, but with dignity, morale, and discipline.

At this time I am making closer contacts with groups who seem to have forces in places where the others need them, and as I have their authorization to offer their support to those who are in a position to produce the coup in a short time, I am waiting only to learn what they ask and what they accept, and if it is possible to reach an understanding, then I will join the forces together and the coup would be carried out.

I will devote all my efforts to reaching a definite, firm understanding, without loopholes, with these gentlemen in order to succeed in ending this horrible reign of blood in the capital and throughout the country. But if such an undertaking fails, perhaps that would be beneficial to our revolutionary ends, since a coup d'état without prior agreement with our organization presents certain obstacles. However, the formation of a column with the dissident elements would produce an impact on the armed forces that the dictatorship would be totally unable to withstand, and in the other sphere, in the political, these elements would have no influence, but would be completely subordinated to the Revolution. I await quick instructions.

CAPTAIN ANGEL VERDECIA

Report to Commander Fidel Castro   Bayamo, October 22

On the twenty-first, I went to the Manzanillo-Bayamo highway and I was ambushed less than a mile from the village of Barranca. At dawn on the twenty-second we fired at an army vehicle. I immediately shifted position, and at 12:25 p.m. we made contact with two patrol cars, a jeep, and a light truck, and fought with them almost hand to hand. The result of the encounter got us: three Garands, four Springfields, and six hundred .30–'06 bullets. We suffered one casualty: Comrade Ramiro Benítez, who was in charge of the Browning, killed in combat. On the dictatorship's side: eighteen dead.

CHE GUEVARA

Letter to Fidel Castro   Sierra del Escambray, October 23

I am writing to you from a terrain that is completely flat, with no planes and relatively few mosquitoes. I have gone without eating—by choice—because of the rapid pace of our march. I will give you a brief report:

We left at night, August 31, with four horses; it was impossible to leave in trucks because at Magadan they took all the gas, and we were afraid there might be an ambush in Jibacoa. On September 1 we crossed the highway and took three trucks, which kept breaking down with frightening frequency. We arrived at a ranch called Cayo Redondo, where we spent the day with the hurricane approaching. The guards came very close, forty of them, but they left without fighting. We went on in the trucks, helped by four tractors, but it was impossible, and we had to give them up by the next day, September 2, a day on which we continued on foot, leading a few horses, and reached the banks of the Cauto, which we couldn't cross at night because it was unusually high. We crossed it by day, taking eight hours to do it, and that night, we left the colonel's house and continued on the planned route. We have no horses but we can get more along the way, and I think everyone will be mounted when we arrive in the assigned zone of operations.

Nothing more for now; a big hug to the distant world that, from here, is hardly visible on the horizon.

Here is my diary:

September 8, 1958, 1:50 a.m.

After exhausting journeys at night, I am writing you finally from Camagüey, with no immediate prospects for accelerating our march, which averages eleven to fourteen miles a day, with half the troop mounted and half not. Camilo is in the vicinity, and I was waiting for him here, at the Bartles rice plantation, but he didn't arrive. It's terrific on the plain; there aren't so many mosquitoes, we haven't seen a single one of Batista's guys, and the planes look like harmless doves. It's very hard to hear Radio Rebelde from the station in Venezuela.

Everything indicates that the guards don't want war and we don't either; I confess to you that I am afraid of a retreat with 150 inexperienced recruits in these unknown areas, but an armed guerrilla band of 30 men could produce miracles in the area and revolutionize it. In passing, I left the groundwork for a rice workers' union in Leonero, and I talked about the tax, but it fell flat. It's not a matter of backing down before the bosses, but it seems to me that the quota is excessive. I told them that it could be discussed, and I left it for the next one who comes by. Someone with social consciousness could produce miracles here, and there are plenty of woods for him to hide in. I can't tell you anything about my future plans for the route, because I myself don't know it; it depends rather on special circumstances and chance. We are now waiting for some trucks to see if we can get rid of the horses, which were perfect for Maceo, where there weren't any planes, but they are very visible from the air. If it weren't for the cavalry, we could travel peacefully by day. I've been in enough mud and water to last me the rest of my life, and the Fidelisms that I had to devise in order to arrive with the shells in good condition are straight out of the movies. We've had to cross several streams by swimming, which was tremendously tough, but the troops behaved well—even though the disciplinary squad is still functioning at full steam and promises to be the largest one in the column.

Camagüey, September 13, 1958

After some rough days—I am still writing in the middle of Camagüey—today we are about to cross the most dangerous part, or one of the two most dangerous of the route. The night before last, Camilo crossed it, having a lot of technical difficulties but no military ones. Since the last report I gave you, we've had some unpleasant experiences: because of our lack of guides, we were caught in an ambush on the Remigio Fernández property, in La Federal, in which Marcos Borrero, who was captain, was killed. We subdued the guards—there were eight of them—killing three and taking four prisoner; we kept them with us until we found an opportunity to turn them loose, but the one who escaped gave the alarm. Some sixty guards arrived, and on the advice of Camilo, who was nearby, we withdrew, almost without fighting, but we lost another man, Dalcio Gutiérrez, from the Sierra. Herman was wounded lightly in one leg, and Enriquito Acevedo, seriously in both arms. Acevedo, Captain Angel Frías, and Lieutenant Roberto Rodríguez (El Vaquerito) distinguished themselves.

Very peculiar things are happening here that suggest it would be advisable for an experienced chief to come at once—someone who is savvy about these parts. He certainly wouldn't need more than thirty armed men, as he should be able to pick up what he needs—in all senses—here. It would be worthwhile to work in the area of Las Naboas; the climate is very favorable there because of the spoils from the Francisco mill. There are solid woods as far as Santa Cruz, and from Santa Beatriz, good cover for a number of men. They must wait to see what the command in Camagüey does because they are making promises to induct everybody and we are inundated with unarmed men asking to sign up.

September 13

Our contacts with the 26th of July Movement had assured us that the guides would arrive, but it didn't happen. In view of this situation, I decided to continue with a makeshift guide, no matter what. The result was that at daybreak he had led us straight to a guardpost at Cuatro Compañeros. We were completely unfamiliar with the area, but we ordered a march toward a thicket visible in the half-light of the dawn, but to get to it, we had to cross a railroad line with the guards advancing over it from two different directions. We had to fight so that the comrades in the very rear could get through. Captain Silva received a fracture in his right shoulder joint, but in spite of this, he has remained with exemplary stoicism at the head of his men. We had to continue fighting on the rail line, in a span of only 200 yards, to contain the enemy advance, since we were short of men. That situation lasted two and a half hours, until 9:30 a.m., when I gave the order to withdraw. We lost our companion Juan, whose right leg was blown off by a 100-lb. bomb; we had another wounded, but that was as the result of bombing and strafing by two B-26s, two C-47s, and two light planes, skimming the ground for forty-five minutes.

We spent the following days regrouping, and we confirmed finally that ten missing men had found their way to Camilo's column. Without allowing ourselves a single day of rest we went successively through Remedios, a rice plantation called Cadenas, and several less important spots. All this without a guide, sometimes finding a peasant and at other times going by the compass. The social consciousness of the Camagüeyan peasant in cattle regions is minimal and we have had to cope with the consequences of numerous informers.

September 20

Today on the radio we heard Tabernilla's report on Che Guevara's destroyed column. It happened that in one of the knapsacks they found the notebook that had the names, addresses, weapons, bullets, and supplies of the whole column, member by member. Besides, a member of this column, who is also a member of the PSP, left his knapsack with documents from that organization.*

September 29

We had left behind the last Aguilera rice plantation and entered the territory of the Baraguá mill when we found that the army had completely blocked the rail line we had to cross. The guards discovered us on the march, and our rearguard unit drove them off with a few shots. Thinking that the shots came from guards in ambushes along the line, according to their invariable custom, I gave orders to wait for night and cross them. When I found out about the skirmish, I realized that the enemy already had full knowledge of our position; it was too late to attempt the crossing, since it was a dark, rainy night, and we had no knowledge of the enemy position, which was very strongly manned. We had to go back by compass and stay in mud with only a thin cover of woods in order to throw the planes off our track; they actually were bombing the hell out of a leafy forest some distance from our position. The scouts led by Lieutenant Acevedo discovered a crossing point at the end of the enemy line; they had ruled out a lagoon, thinking we couldn't possibly cross it. We crossed this marshy lagoon, trying as much as possible to muffle the noise of 140 men splashing in mud, and we walked for over a mile until we crossed the line about a hundred yards from the last guardpost where we'd heard them talking. The splashing was impossible to prevent completely, and that, plus the bright moon, made me almost certain that the enemy was aware of our presence, but the soldiers of the dictatorship were so anxious to avoid combat by then that they were deaf to every suspicious noise.

October 3

In a spot close to the Baraguá mill, the local butcher was captured; his family was told that nothing would happen to him but that he had to stay with us as our guide for a couple of days. It seems that his wife must have wanted to change husbands for she turned in some juicy information, as a result of which we had a visit from the B-26s with their customary cargo. Nothing happened, but we had to travel all night in a lagoon full of plants with spiky leaves that cut anybody who had bare feet. The morale of the troops was suffering from the effects of hunger and filth. Every peasant looked to us like a possible informer; the psychological situation was similar to that in the first days in the Sierra Maestra. We couldn't establish contact with the 26th of July organization, since a

---

* Armando Acosta, a union leader in Las Villas, who defied the orders of the Communist Party to join Che's forces in the Sierra and entered the invasion column; he ended the war with the rank of major.—C. F.

couple of supposed members refused to help when I asked, and I only got it—money, raingear, some shoes, medicines, food, and guides—from members of the PSP, who told me they had asked for help from the groups in the Movement and received the following answer, which must be taken with reservations since I can't check on it: "If Che sends a request in writing, we'll help him; if not he can go fuck himself."

October 7

We made contact with three guides from Escambray, who brought a whole rosary of complaints about the behavior of Gutiérrez Menoyo, telling me that Bordón had been taken prisoner and a situation existed that came close to a pitched battle between the groups. It seemed to me that there was a lot of dirty linen being washed in public in this whole matter, and I sent one of them with an order for Bordón to come to meet me. Today, in order to try to clean out the scum in the column, I told them to discharge everyone who wanted out; seven took advantage of the "opportunity."

Since then the planes have systematically followed our path, bombing the woods that we left the day before and trying to cut off our crossing the Jatibonico River. In one of these bombardments, a retrojet exploded in the air; you must have heard the news on the radio. October 10 the planes caught us and strafed the woods where we were. They were light planes, and there weren't any casualties. The following day the vanguard took a sugar mill that was connected to an adjacent rice plantation, and through telephone conversations that we intercepted, we found out that the army knew our location. The "rats" were perfectly situated (although, expecting that, we had left the woods and hidden ourselves in a house surrounded with pasture, where we stayed all day without budging). According to the information we gathered from the army's conversation, they didn't think we could manage the seven miles that separated us from the Jatibonico. Of course, we did it that night. We swam across, although we soaked almost all the weapons, and we went another three miles until we reached the safety of a forest. The crossing of the Jatibonico was like the symbol of passage from darkness to light. Ramiro said that it was like an electric switch that turns on the light, and that was the exact image. But since the day before, the sierras of Las Villas appear bluish in the distance, and even the laziest hillsman felt a tremendous desire to reach them.

We then had an exhausting journey in swamps, we crossed rice plantations and cane fields, we crossed the Zaza, which must be one of the widest rivers in Cuba. We passed the last ring of guards on the highway from Trinidad to Sancti Spiritus on the night of the fifteenth, and then our wearisome political task began.

I heard about Vega's disaster. Obviously it was the result of inexperience—it would never have happened to Ramiro—but give us some time and we will show you that his presence here is positive for the Revolution.

FIDEL CASTRO

Letter to the Military Conspirators   Sierra, October 23

I have been kept informed about the contacts, although I have the impression that you have not yet drawn up a concrete plan. In my opinion, the important thing is to have an awareness of the possibilities. Almost all your efforts have failed because this awareness has been missing. You are discovered when you try to add to the possibilities. That would have some justification if a revolutionary process in an advanced state did not exist already. Today, a single company that rebels, a half dozen officers who embrace the cause of the Revolution would deal a disastrous blow to the morale of the dictatorship, and in the present state of discontent, it would not be difficult for the whole army to follow in a few weeks. I can assure you that countless members of the military are ready to join the revolutionary cause, but they are waiting for others to take the first step.

I am afraid that you are making the mistake of seeking to create a vast, secure movement; that is very difficult, and it is the wrong tactic.

Batista has managed to control the army with a dozen diehards and assassins. The commanders and officers of the army change, but the republic remains. The fatherland is permanent; the army can be reorganized, changed, cleansed, because its sole function must be to serve the country. What are the young officers waiting for to rebel? What historical or moral cord can bind them to Batista, Tabernilla, Chaviano, Merob Sosa, Ugalde Carrillo, Pérez Coujil, Pilar García, Ventura, and the other bosses of the armed services? Don't they understand that they have become instruments of the stupidest and bloodiest regime Cuba has ever been subjected to, and that the people and history also believe that they are accomplices? Why can't honorable revolutionaries and military men join together? Doesn't the same Cuban blood flow in the veins of military men and rebels? Haven't we embraced each other after a victorious fight as in El Jigüe?

Act in terms of real possibilities that you can rely on; don't delay your action, and above all, don't let yourselves be arrested without putting up resistance; to guard against this, you must take all the advance measures circumstances require. You cannot let yourself be stopped by Merob Sosa and his henchmen, men who have neither your courage nor your dignity.

FIDEL CASTRO

Communiqué to the U.S. State Department   Sierra, October 25

Three days ago, without any reason, the dictatorship withdrew its troops from the Nicaro plant.* Following their customary practice, the rebels occupied the installation and established a garrison, since the Batista regime had left it without military protection.** The rebels offered the personnel of the plant complete guarantees to continue operating. Today the Rebel Command intercepted an order from Colonel Ugalde Carrillo instructing his forces to land again.

All this is a maneuver by Batista and Mr. Smith, along with various officials of the U.S. Department of State, to bring about a landing of North American forces in said location.

The first attempt at this took place at the beginning of the month of July in agreement with Mr. Smith, and it resulted in the occupation of the Yateritas aqueduct by forces of the U.S. Marine Corps.

A major public-opinion campaign in Latin America, the responsible attitude of the Rebel Forces, and active steps taken by the Civilian Revolutionary Front resolved the problem.

Then an unimportant event provided a pretext for the plot against the sovereignty of Cuba: two North Americans and seven Cubans, employees of Texaco in Santiago de Cuba, were detained by rebel forces as a security measure. On the highway from the Texaco building to Santiago, which runs through rebel territory, a rebel detachment was in ambush, waiting for the dictatorship's forces, which were to pass by. Then a vehicle driven by these employees appeared, and they discovered the ambush. When civilians discover a military ambush, they must be detained in a secure place to prevent one of two possibilities: either the civilians do not want to reveal the rebel ambush and then they will be arrested and murdered by Batista's forces as soon as the troops fall into the ambush, or they reveal the ambush and the dictatorship dispatches a larger number of troops and surrounds the rebels before they have time to withdraw.

Lincoln White, spokesman for the U.S. Department of State, has made some insulting statements that constitute an overt threat against the integrity of our territory and the sovereignty of Cuba.

The Batista dictatorship has murdered more than one North

---

* A nickel refinery owned by the U. S. government.
** "It was reported that American civilians in Nicaro had been held by natives there as hostages against bombardment by Batista's air force. The Navy sent the transport *Kleinschmidt* from Guantánamo Bay to evacuate the civilians; the aircraft carrier *Franklin D. Roosevelt,* which was maneuvering off the naval base, was ordered to stand by in case its helicopters were needed for evacuation."— Jules Dubois.

American citizen and has arrested and executed journalists of other countries without the U.S. Department of State making any statement or informing the North American public so that it might form an opinion.

If Mr. Lincoln White considers the detention of two of his compatriots who were treated with absolute decency and consideration to be an offense against civilized standards, how would he classify the murders of thousands of peasants and civilians by planes and bombs supplied by the United States to the dictator Batista? We Cubans, Mr. White, are human beings just like North Americans. However, we have never killed a North American with Cuban planes or bombs. You, Mr. White, cannot accuse us Cuban patriots of these acts, of which we can indeed accuse you and your government.

The war that our fatherland is experiencing today is causing losses and hardships not only to North Americans, but to all the residents of Cuba. But this war is not the fault of the Cubans but of the tyranny that for seven years has oppressed our people and yet has been able to rely on the support of the North American ambassadors.

It is proper to observe that Cuba is a free and sovereign country. But if the North American Department of State continues to permit itself to be involved in the intrigues of Mr. Smith and Batista and makes the unjustifiable error of leading its country into an act of aggression against our sovereignty, be certain that we will know how to defend it honorably. There are obligations toward one's country that one cannot fail to fulfill, cost what it may. A country as great and powerful as the United States cannot feel honored by words and threats such as those contained in your recent statements.

CARLOS FRANQUI

To Fidel Castro and Comrades of the
National Executive of the 26th of July*   Sierra Maestra, October

A number of carefully pondered considerations oblige me to raise the following questions:

1. The Executive of the Directorate, created to operate and direct the Movement, is not fulfilling its mission as a collective directing organ. For example, it was agreed the other day to create a Civil Council, charged with drawing up a series of important revolutionary laws. And the members begin to work on some of those laws.

But suddenly I find out from an announcer on Radio Rebelde that

---

* Presented at the last national meeting in the Sierra.—C. F.

the agrarian-reform law is going to be read this afternoon, in spite of the importance of this question and the fact that I have not been given the courtesy of seeing it—although this is not in accord with the procedure agreed on.

Our comrade Fidel had simply forgotten or dispensed with the agreement creating the council and drafted the law with Sorí. The same process was followed with another law, I believe that one concerning electoral disqualification.

The other day an agreement was adopted stating that Luis Simón was to remain here, at the request of those responsible for the plains areas, because of the difficulties resulting from his direct participation in creating a superorganism coordinating the Unity Front, and his publication of 100 theses of a supposed program of the 26th of July without authorization.

One day, Luis Simón returns to Havana because of a personal problem. When the matter is raised, Fidel says: "That's your problem; everybody here has done things like that."

On the other hand, Fidel's attitude is very different when it is a matter of the discipline of the Rebel Army. He has been worried and taken strong decisions and positions with which we have all agreed.

I understand that military discipline has to be very strict but I believe that revolutionary discipline also has to be demanding. I have also observed that Fidel has a tendency to give public praise to figures who are not wholly committed to the Revolution, but he has not followed the same line with the rest of the comrades.

It is easy for me to say this because in these six years of struggle I have not been interested, nor am I now interested, in having my modest contribution be known to anyone. But the conversion of the revolutionary process into a political one makes it essential to think ahead to the role of these anonymous fighters. Obvious examples are the trade-union struggle, the students, all the masses, and the Movement itself.

What motivates his attitude—an unconscious lapse of memory perhaps? Perhaps a lack of faith in his comrades, as a consequence of the failure of the strike, or of the meager contribution and potentials of the Sierra?

I believe very strongly in the role of the leader in our Revolution. But I believe that his collaborators cannot be a group of extras who provide only the appearance of democracy, a chorus who praise his successes, or a group of men envious or resentful who question his function, but a group of men who contribute with their thoughts and their actions to the best progress of the Revolution, preventing the most likely and most dangerous mistakes; men who help to overcome the difficulties that custom and surroundings present to every being in exceptional conditions.

It has repeatedly been asserted that this is caused by Fidel's lack of a sense of organization. To me the problem seems very different and more profound.

How can there be such great organizational shortcomings in one who organized the formidable Rebel Army in the midst of the difficulties of the war; one who organized the assault on the Moncada Barracks in 1953; one who organized the *Granma* expedition?

Could it be that his organizational ability is greater in warfare than in civilian life?

Although I admit that the talents he has demonstrated in this struggle are primarily military, I don't believe it. It seems to me that if he would interest himself in the organization of civilian life, as he does in military organization, it would be very different. Since he is essentially a revolutionary, won't his demonstrated strategic and tactical ability be the same in civilian as in military matters?

It seems to me that it is not a matter of organizational shortcomings, but of something more serious. Of disregarding organization. Of lack of direct interest in anything that is not right in front of him. This is the only way that I can understand acts as significant as these:

That an extremely important report arrives from Zoilo.* That Fidel skims it and doesn't look at it again. That he is not informed about our publicity. That in the various cities near the Sierra, in spite of the revolutionary ambience, there is no 26th of July organization, a situation very different from that in other places.

That for such a long time he has failed to make vigorous demands for military and food supplies from the cities of the plains, that he has not taken a more active role as leader, and that, with all his persuasive powers, he has not helped to make those in charge there understand the outlook and potential of the Sierra. Failure to explain the outlook and potential that are greater, in my opinion, because the Sierra also fails to recognize these same things in the plains.

What does Fidel mean when he says that a problem is "yours" instead of "ours"? I have noticed also that Fidel absorbs everything with his personality, wherever he is, and that he is unconcerned about, he forgets about those he doesn't see or who are far away, and he grants them a liberty of action that sometimes can harm the organization.

It is evident that if much of the time wasted arguing and talking about minuscule things in the Sierra had been devoted to thinking about the organization and what is still out of reach, the situation would be different.

I believe that his acts are almost always greatly influenced by inspiration or reaction, that they depend on his good or bad humor.

---

* Marcelo Fernández, national coordinator of the clandestine work of the 26th of July.—C. F.

Despite what is observed of his inner struggle, and he is his own severest critic, it is very hard for him to accept the fundamental idea of criticism, which is perhaps why he always responds to anything at all, like a fighter who defends himself by counterattacking.

Furthermore, I don't believe that my function as a member of this Executive should consist basically in expressing enthusiasm over the enormous and repeated successes of Fidel. Triumphs and successes make me happy on the revolutionary level, as well as satisfying me on the human level, because if I am satisfied with anything it is with my capacity for admiration, without apple-polishing and without envy.

I have observed that many of our meetings are really a kind of consultation, or a conversation, almost always the prodigious conversation of Fidel, in which a decision is given as settled, although it is almost never an agreement reached after thorough discussion by all. A situation for which we are all responsible through commission and omission.

Fidel has another idea that seems wrong to me. He regards the Sierra as if it were his personal property. And although it is understandable that he feels that way because of his activity there, I don't believe that it is correct on the revolutionary level.

Nor should the Sierra be considered like a republic in normal times. The Sierra is the greatest force in the Revolution. It can't be a Jordan, a place of refuge.

The good manners that make him receive visitors politely, therefore, should not be permitted to outweigh the revolutionary consequences of these visits. Besides, those delicate attentions could never justify the lack of delicate attentions toward thousands of other revolutionary comrades.

In addition, I am very worried about some pessimistic statements by Fidel, who is always so optimistic and so full of the will to fight, since they reveal doubts concerning the outcome of the Revolution, a very dangerous thing for a leader to harbor.

In conclusion I propose:

1. That Fidel act as the only Executive of the Movement. This may not be the ideal solution, but at least it reflects reality.

2. That the total, complete Directorate, with all its members, and not the Executive Committee, continue to discuss any very important question.

3. That a position be taken on the provisional government as soon as possible.

4. That the Executive Committee be dissolved. That the members act in their respective capacities, coordinating with Fidel.

5. That a standard be established for enlistments, taking into consideration moral sanction and good faith in drawing it up. That a commission be named for this.

(At that time, Fidel denied that we would come to power upon Batista's fall, which was now very close. At a later meeting of the National Directorate, in the Sierra, only Raúl Castro agreed with me that there was no power other than us, that the chance to take power does not come twice, and that we had to take advantage of it, in addition to which the Revolution could be made only from a base of power.

The intentions of Fidel, always such a sagacious and astute politician, were incomprehensible. He maintained that we should not be part of the new government. And as always he didn't explain why. His intention, as he showed later, was to gain time and not to appear ambitious. Fidel knew that he was the real power, military and popular. We thought about the vacuum of power if it was not assumed immediately. He was talking about organizing a new political party. Of elections. The game was not really clear. Nor was it explained.—C.F.)

Lieutenant Colonel Suárez Suquet,   Camagüey, October
Military Commander of Camagüey:
Confidential Instructions for the Police

Search all the hotels, everywhere in the province, rooming houses, etc., note the appearance of strangers in the towns, bring them with extreme caution, never in groups, to the National Police Station.

Eliminate every action center of sympathizers or individuals who are known to have been arrested for belonging to the 26th of July Movement, and who are now free on probation; carry out registrations, roundups, interrogations, etc.

FIDEL CASTRO

Orders   Sierra, October

The citizenry must be on the alert and not let themselves be confused by the prevailing expectations and the rumors inspired by the desire to put an end to this nightmare as soon as possible. Neither the 26th of July Movement nor the revolutionary sectors have called for a general strike for November 3, nor do we think that November 3 will be the day to wage the final battle against the dictatorship. November 3 is a date for the dictatorship, not a date for the Revolution. The Rebel Army has not set November 3 as the date for launching decisive actions against the enemy forces.

And in the cities, in Santiago de Cuba, the people must be very cautious and not rush into the streets unless they are summoned to the struggle directly by the Movement and by the commanders of the columns that surround the city.

The basic task assigned to the Rebel Army and its militias for that date is to paralyze traffic on the highways and railroads throughout the national territory from October 30 to November 6, with orders to fire on any vehicle that moves, day or night, during that period, especially military transports. The instruction to the citizenry for November 3 is not to leave their houses.

EDUARDO SARDIÑAS

Commander, Column 12,   Oriente Plains, October 27
Simón Bolívar Report to Commander Fidel Castro

Seventeen days after we left our Sierra, I am making the first report to you on our campaign. I am writing this from Captain Concepción Rivera's camp, which is situated in the woods in Miquiabo. The rain, the mud, and the overflowing rivers made the march through the low, swampy terrain of the Cauto basin very hard. As we advanced, we kept making contact with the rebel bands; extraordinary numbers of them operate in that zone. The whole column advanced almost to the borders of Camagüey Province. We had scouted a large part of the terrain, so our fear of the plains had disappeared.

The army of the dictatorship is distinguished by its absence. It has abandoned the countryside and taken refuge in the cities. Even as I am writing these lines, we haven't had any encounter with them. The customary patrols and ambushes on the trails and roads have been withdrawn. We took the territory to the south of the Central Highway without firing a single shot.

At the same time as we were cleaning up and securing the area south of the Central Highway, I ordered regular rebel forces placed north of the highway to occupy the territory up to the border with Camagüey, taking the areas of Manatí and Puerto Padre, extending to the coast itself. The bulk of our forces surrounds the city of Victoria de las Tunas.

Tuesday, October 14, action elements in this column attacked the naval post in the town of Manatí. After half an hour of intense firing we captured the barracks and the weapons that were there.

We are working very hard to sabotage public and transport services. We hope to stop traffic completely on the Central Highway beginning on the thirtieth, as ordered by Radio Rebelde.

Within a few days, I expect to have a radio station operating, which will enable me to establish daily and direct communication with headquarters.

Electoral activity is nil. In the town of Guamo, we captured Sr. Armando Díaz, who was the council candidate for Bayamo, spending his time collecting voting cards. He is now a prisoner in one of our secure camps.

The cooperation of the peasants is worth mention, as well as Radio Rebelde's enormous audience and the definite influx of young elements who want to enlist in our column.

FIDEL CASTRO

Letter to Julio Comacho   Sierra, October 29

I am not favorably impressed with the results of the conversations concerning the plans for the coup d'état on the conditions they suggest.

We cannot make any concessions about the command of the branches of the armed services. Those responsibilities will have to be assigned according to the action and role of each of them. We are not going to participate in any business of commitments, ambitions, and divvying up.

The dictatorship may be very interested in provoking conflict on an international scale in Cuba, because it believes that with foreign intervention, as in the war of 1895, the traitors and murderers will save their skins and their ill-gotten wealth, but the Revolution, on the other hand, which is prepared to defend the sovereignty of the fatherland at all costs, does not have any interest in providing pretexts for those who are plotting against the liberty and sovereignty of our people.

I am sympathetic, however, to the other idea of forming a revolutionary military column. So much so, that for some days I have been taking steps toward that end, and it is possible that we will have good results very soon. If they come to a decision, they should act quickly; we can't wait for them.

How long are they going to keep on shilly-shallying? Batista is already falling, and they haven't made a move.

What is revolutionary is not the coup but the military's joining in the armed struggle.

Havana, October

A cable just received reports that nine officers of Batista's army have sought asylum in embassies: four in the Mexican, three in the Uruguayan, and two in the Brazilian. These refugees are linked to a projected conspiracy.

FIDEL CASTRO   Sierra, October 30

Orders

Five new rebel columns leaving from the First Front of the Sierra Maestra have invaded the central and western zones of Oriente Province and the east and north of Camagüey Province. They are the twelfth, Simón Bolívar; the thirteenth, Ignacio Agramonte; the fourteenth, Juan Manuel Márquez; the thirty-first, Benito Juárez; and the thirty-second, José Antonio Echeverría. A sixth rebel column, the sixteenth, Enrique Jara, under the command of Major Carlos Iglesias, left the Second Front and made contact with Company 3 of Column 14 north of Holguín. In this new advance, all the rural territory of Oriente Province is under the control of our forces. Column 13, under the command of Major Víctor Mora, has penetrated into Camagüey Province, reinforcing the forces of Column 11, Cándido González. The invasion columns, the eighth, Ciro Redondo, and the second, Antonio Maceo, under the command of Majors Ernesto Guevara and Camilo Cienfuegos, have taken strategic positions in Las Villas. Major Ernesto Guevara, member of the *Granma* expedition and hero of numerous victorious combats, has been named by this command to be military chief of all the forces of the 26th of July Movement in Las Villas Province.

All the fighters of the 26th of July Movement who have taken up arms in that province are instructed to place themselves under the orders of Majors Ernesto Guevara and Camilo Cienfuegos. This command wishes to explain that there is no force of any other revolutionary organization operating in Oriente Province. The only exception is the leaders of the FEU, to which we are linked by solid bonds of brotherhood, operating in Column 32, José Antonio Echeverría, of the Rebel Army, under the command of Major Delio Gómez Ochoa. In the territory of this province, as well as in Camagüey and Pinar del Río provinces, there is a completely unified, single command. In Las Villas Province, where there are units from several organizations, but no unified command, the forces of the 26th of July Movement under the orders of Majors Ernesto Guevara and Camilo Cienfuegos will carry out the parts of the strategic plan of the Rebel Army that involve that province.

The extension of the Revolution and the victorious advance of our forces westward, fighting with the bulk of the enemy forces, raise the problem of relations with the forces of other organizations that have been operating in Las Villas Province. These will be resolved in a meeting of representatives of the Frente Cívico Revolucionario [Civilian Revolutionary Front], which will shortly take place in Oriente Province, free territory of Cuba. Until that meeting, coordination of plans of a military nature between the Rebel Army and the forces of the different organizations operating in Las Villas Province will have to be arranged between Major Ernesto Guevara and the chiefs of the forces of said organizations.

EDITOR'S SUMMARY October

As the offensives against Batista mounted throughout Cuba, and political pressures intensified in the face of the approaching national elections, Cuban affairs in the United States, as described by Jules Dubois, continued to have repercussions on the island itself. Dubois reported that Ambassador Smith, using the letterhead of the Cuban-American Institute, had solicited contributions for a scholarship for a Cuban dress designer, an action that drew protests from Cuban members. Smith's wife, former television personality Florence Pritchett, followed this up with an elaborate fund-raising ball for the designer at the Waldorf-Astoria Hotel in New York. This struck many Cubans as extremely inappropriate in view of the turmoil in their country.

Dubois reported also that a 26th of July agent in the Cuban embassy in Washington obtained a copy of a letter from the air attaché, Colonel José D. Ferrer Guerra, to the Cuban General Staff. It related a conversation between Ferrer and two U.S. generals involved in Latin American affairs. Both deplored the embargo on military equipment to Cuba—especially since English manufacturers had jumped in to fill the void. One of the generals added that Ambassador Smith "now is a valuable cooperator with the American Armed Forces in his fight with the Department of State to approve the sale of arms to Cuba." This remark, Dubois stated, had "subsequent influence on Castro."

Dubois climaxed his reports with a description of a dinner at the Cuban embassy in Washington attended by Secretary of State John Foster Dulles. It took place on October 30, in time to permit reports of Dulles toasting Batista at the dinner to be published by Havana newspapers in their issues of November 2—one day before the elections.

BULLETINS October 30

Attention, attention, people of Cuba: In our editorial offices [at Radio Rebelde], we have just received a letter from one of our officials that brings this distressing news: David Salvador was arrested by the repressive bodies of the tyranny in Havana, October 18, at 2:00 a.m. That was twelve days ago. He had been tortured barbarously and is now in extremely serious condition. In view of this new instance of the tyranny's lawlessness, we make an urgent and heartfelt appeal to Cuban workers and to the people of Cuba to mobilize vigorously and remain alert and vigilant concerning the fate of this brave and valiant leader, head of our Workers' Section, promotor of the National Workers' Front, fighter in the Sierra Maestra, signer of the Caracas Pact, member of the Civilian Revolutionary Front and one of the most dauntless fighters for the defense of Cuban workers. We call on all the union organizations in America, on the International Red Cross and the Cuban Red Cross, who have been witnesses of our dealings with the prisoners of war, and on the Civilian Revolutionary Front to intervene so that our companion David Salvador does not come to the same end as Julián Alemán, Antonio Bernalles, Calixto Sánchez, and so many other union leaders murdered by the dictatorship. We also pledge with the lives of our comrades that we will safeguard the present representatives of the CTC.

Manuel Ray: Civilian Resistance Movement   Havana, October

Buy only essentials, so that gross receipts, imports, etc., will drop, and the dictatorship will have lower revenues and resources with which to pay informers, maintain gangs of murderers like Masferrer's, enlist police spies in goon squads, buy bombs to murder women, old people, and children in fields and cities.

Don't go to places of amusement or celebrate holidays. Cuba is in mourning. In sympathy with the grief of so many, don't go to movies, nightclubs, sports events, weddings or christenings, etc.; don't help the dictator who wants to give an impression of normality; contribute what you save to help the Revolution. Don't buy lottery tickets; the lottery is an instrument of political corruption; its revenues enable the government to bribe, buy, and corrupt consciences; when you buy tickets, you help the dictator to maintain his satrapy; gambling corrupts the people and keeps them from thinking about the horrors committed daily. The bankers pay juicy contributions to the commanding officers in every zone; don't enrich the thieves and murderers.

FIDEL CASTRO

Communiqué   Sierra, October 31

Powerful columns of the Rebel Army have surrounded the city of Santiago de Cuba.

The enemy forces are encircled by land and their retreat has been cut off. On the thirtieth, during the noon hours, an enemy force tried to leave by the highway from Santiago to El Cristo; it was intercepted and totally routed by forces of Column 9, Antonio Guiteras, commanded by Major Hubert Matos.

The fight began at 1:30 in the afternoon and lasted almost two hours. The only enemy vehicle to escape was a combat car. Three radio cars and an armored truck fell into our hands. Twelve enemy soldiers were left lying at the battle site. Another six fell prisoner. We took twenty-four shotguns, three automatic rifles and twenty-one Garand, M-1, and Springfield rifles.

Three valiant fighters of the Rebel Army fell in the violent action, but they won the laurels of victory for the revolutionary troops.

The enemy General Staff, in an effort to conceal their desperate situation from their own troops, issued a totally false communiqué, announcing twenty-nine rebels killed to the army's four killed and three wounded.

This is explained by the fact that, for troops surrounded as those of the dictatorship are in Santiago de Cuba, the defeat at El Cristo constitutes a tremendous blow to morale.

What produces real laughter among yesterday's communiqués is the way they try to explain the case of the officers of the Charco Redondo garrison, where all the men and weapons of the various units joined the Revolution. The General Staff communiqué asserts that a patrol of twenty soldiers was kidnapped by the rebels. But isn't it really absurd to declare that twenty well-armed soldiers can be kidnapped peaceably? Neither in Cuba nor in any other part of the world can twenty armed men be kidnapped without getting into combat. The General Staff of the dictatorship is not very flattering to the soldiers of the republic when it asserts that a patrol of twenty men was kidnapped by the rebels. The soldiers of the army are not at all cowardly; we have fought with them many times, and we know that they may surrender because of hunger and thirst, as they did in El Jigüe, or when they are pinned down under a deadly fire, as they did in Santo Domingo, Purialón, El Salto, etc. But they have always fought with valor.

The kidnapped soldiers the General Staff is talking about are those who rebelled, and there were not twenty but fifty-two in the Charco Redondo garrison, with two first lieutenants, all their weapons, eight thousand .30–'06 and M-1 bullets, and dozens of hand grenades. Can fifty-two soldiers armed with automatics and hand grenades be kidnapped?

CARLOS FRANQUI   Sierra, October 31

Three days before the electoral masquerade on Monday, what is the real situation in Cuba?

There are no constitutional guarantees, and none of the most minimal or elemental individual rights is respected.

The most severe press censorship in our history keeps even the most insignificant news from filtering out.

The prisons and jails throughout the country are full of men and women, youths and old people, Cubans of all creeds and ideologies.

Every day, in the main streets of big cities and towns, there are the corpses of dozens of Cubans, whose crime is loving liberty.

A peculiar electoral campaign, this one, without meetings, without opposition, without voters, without the most minimal guarantees. A peculiar masquerade, this, with voting cards confiscated, bought, and redistributed, with the attack on the electoral boards, with puppet candidates designated by the General Staff at Camp Columbia, coming from government gangs as well as from the parties in the pocket of the collaborationist pseudo-opposition.

Three days before the elections, many candidates, officials, and electoral judges resign, flee, and go into hiding; rural voting places—in which more than a million voters throughout the country vote—are eliminated, and the soldiers are trained to watch the voting places in the cities, as if they expect a pitched battle.*

Elections without voters, without votes, with shootings, deaths, fights, and revolution throughout the country.

With a people who make their complete rejection of that masquerade clear and obvious.

In the cities, thousands of fighters in the clandestine resistance are going into action: committing sabotage, attacking voting boards, holding soldiers, and taking over their arms in order to fight.

The twenty-two municipalities of Oriente Province have already been invaded by rebel columns.

From the First Front, in the glorious Sierra Maestra, revolutionary contingents are continuously emerging.

The Frank País Second Front, a model of organization and fighting spirit, is growing; it controls more than one-third of Oriente Province, including the major resources and properties of the country, national as well as foreign; their owners enter into relations with the new revolutionary power and receive guarantees and security for their development, the maintenance of order and of their property, and of industrial, agricultural, and commercial activities.

The Third Front is extending and concentrating its forces in the area of Santiago de Cuba, which is virtually encircled.

On the new fronts, the Fourth and Fifth in Oriente, the new rebel columns control the situation and harass the enemy unceasingly.

Land communications, highways as well as railroads, and telephone and electrical services are interrupted and under rebel control.

Rebel forces operating in Camagüey have been reinforced by the arrival of another rebel invasion column, the Ignacio Agramonte.

In Las Villas, where we have been fighting for several months, the

---

* In September the Superior Electoral Court ordered that the polls be concentrated in the urban areas and alongside army barracks—to avoid attacks and burning of documents.—C. F.

veteran columns of Ernesto Guevara and Camilo Cienfuegos have arrived, after duplicating the feats of Gómez and Maceo; in forty days, they crossed three provinces and outwitted thousands of soldiers who were supported by planes, tanks, and every kind of weapon.

The militias of the 26th of July defy the police terror of the tyranny in Havana, and sabotage and revolutionary actions mount from day to day.

Nobody believes in Monday's election farce.

Foreign missions report the terror, the U.N. refuses to send observers, and the people of America intensify their repudiation of Batista's barbarity.

The United States refuses to sell arms to Batista; Sweden, Israel, and other European countries break off negotiations on arms, and even the queen of England, worried, asks her government not to send Batista the rest of the planes he has bought.

Three days before the election farce of November 3, it can be asserted that a country never carried out its electoral deliberations in a climate of such violence.

But the tyrant is hopelessly lost, and November 3, instead of easing his crisis, will unleash it and hurl him toward his definitive and approaching end.

The Peruvian senate unanimously approved a motion to break diplomatic relations with the present government of Cuba, and urged other nations of the hemisphere to take the same action.

17. NOVEMBER–DECEMBER: FROM THE NOVEMBER ELECTIONS TO THE TAKING OF SANTA CLARA

FIDEL CASTRO

Orders to Majors Delio Gómez Ochoa   Sierra, November 1
and Lalo [Eduardo] Sardiñas

At any moment, there may be a military coup d'état in Havana or the collapse of the tyranny. If you see that something of this kind is happening, immediately seal off the exit from the province to prevent any of the troops in Oriente from leaving. Whatever happens, all the rifles and arms in general that are in the province are for us. We must let absolutely nothing leave here. I explain this to you because since the dictatorship is so weak, at any moment the military themselves may give it the final blow; but if that happens, that would not mean that the Revolution had triumphed yet. Military men always do that when they see that the regime that they have been defending is lost, but they try to preserve their prerogatives; they do not constitute any guarantee for the Revolution. The only guarantee for this is us, who have formed a true army of the Revolution, made up of the humble folk from the people.

It is also possible that the collapse will begin in Oriente if some units come over to us; in that case, as soon as you receive confirmed news that a company of the dictatorship has come over to our ranks, close off the province because the collapse will be very close.

If nothing like this happens, then our plans will continue unfolding in the way you know.

CARLOS FRANQUI

The tyranny's methods of torture surpass the most barbarous deeds of terror and barbarity in universal annals:

They insert iron objects into the genital organs of women. Girls who have been arrested are surrounded by circles of naked torturers.

They scar their breasts with pincers and violate and possess the bleeding girls collectively.

Day after day a mother goes to a police station or barracks, asking about her son who has been tortured there; finally she receives his clothes stained with blood. Or she is led to his beaten, whipped, almost inanimate body, and an officer arrives and says: "Look at him for the last time; tonight we are going to kill him."

Every day they try out new tortures.

In the past the paddy wagons stopped at the door of Military Intelligence, and when they shouted: "Get ready—the fresh meat has arrived!" dozens of agents got into position for the mass beating. They have now gone beyond that:

The telephone bell that breaks the eardrums.

Unremitting blows from a blackjack that mashes the skull.

The famous kick in the testicles, used by Esteban Ventura and Carratalá.

Sharpened instruments placed around the neck so that if you move, you risk cutting your throat, while the torturers whip you with bullwhips, bags of sand, rifle butts. This is called the Laurent torture.

Submersion in fresh cement, which slowly gets hard: the Sicilian torture.

This is the history of thousands of men, destroyed, maimed, driven crazy, or killed, who have passed through the hell of the tyranny's torture chambers.

Now they are using still more barbaric methods.

They insert sharp, pointed objects with electrical current into the male organs or the anus.

They drive nails into the body.

They hammer sharp, pointed objects into the head.

They burn the eyes with electric blowtorches.

They tear out the nose or other appendages with pliers.

They squeeze the testicles with pincers.

They drive stylets into the lungs.

They insert steel needles into the bones.

They tear out women's nipples with red-hot metal instruments. They remove a woman's hairs or down, one at a time, with scalpels.

They cover their wounds with acid, make them swallow ground glass, or implant broken bottles into their back.

FIDEL CASTRO Sierra, November 1

A Viscount plane of Cubana de Aviación that left Miami for Varadero, with sixteen United States and Cuban passengers, crashed at Punta de Cigarros, Oriente Province, killing nearly all the passengers and crew.

Although we have been accused of causing this mishap, we must point out that the place where they are said to have tried to land the plane is not even in rebel hands, which indicates that the sources of this information did not know the position of our forces.

We are the first to condemn such acts because they do not benefit the Revolution and serve only as a pretext for its domestic and foreign enemies to cast discredit and calumny upon the just cause that we are defending with infinite sacrifice. Anyone can well understand that in the midst of the whirlpool in which the republic lives there are countless cases of individuals who make desperate, often suicidal, decisions on their own, which they often, mistakenly, imagine will have beneficial results.

The Cuban is noted for his individualism. The fact that the 26th of July Movement is an important sector in the Revolution does not mean that it has to be responsible for the deed that any Cuban, *whether or not he calls himself a member of the 26th of July,* may make on his own initiative in any part of the world. It is essential to put an end to the series of risks the country is running, partly through irresponsible acts by people who have no idea of what an organized and planned struggle is and partly, and more fundamentally, through the provocations that the dictatorship is constantly hatching to produce clashes between the Cuban rebels and the United States or to discredit us in the public opinion of that country.

At any moment Batista's gunmen or those of the dictatorship's General Staff may start murdering U.S. citizens, blaming the rebels, and thereby getting the United States to suspend the arms embargo, or ultimately bringing about its armed intervention to rescue from the just wrath of the people the clique of assassins who govern this country.

Since an armed intervention into Cuba would harm the United States as well as Cuba, and would moreover be bloody, because it would encounter very determined resistance from our people, we hope that the United States agrees with us on the necessity of avoiding intervention at all costs.

We are not attempting to influence the government of that country; we are aware that we are a small people and that if we faced the forces of a powerful country, we would have no alternative but to die fighting, as in antiquity the men and women of Sagunto* chose to die before the Roman legions.

---

* A town in Spain known in antiquity as Murviedro, remembered for its citizens' resistance to Hannibal's forces in 219 B.C.—ED.

Fidel Castro, Commander in Chief

Report

The forces of the Frank País Second Front, who are being extremely active in the two days before the electoral farce, captured more than one hundred shotguns and enormous quantities of ammunition from the enemy. More than one hundred prisoners have fallen into our hands.

In the Holguín region, twenty of the dictatorship's soldiers have been killed, three wounded, six taken prisoner; twenty-seven shotguns, and thousands of bullets have been obtained.

Rebel troops of a company from Column 14 and forces from the Mariana Grajales women's squad won a resounding victory in Holguín. Only two soldiers in the enemy troop managed to escape, leaving their weapons. On the highway from Holguín to Chaparra, rebel forces under the command of Captain Suñol intercepted two trucks of enemy soldiers, touching off an intense fight that ended with the total destruction of the enemy unit.

Rebel troops from Column 1, José Martí, took the town of Baire at 8:30 last night. The enemy beat a retreat.

An important military action is unfolding for a distance of twenty-five miles along the Central Highway. There are many enemy garrisons whose only alternative is to surrender or be wiped out. For military reasons, we refrain from offering more details on the present state of those operations.

The victorious and ineluctable advance of our forces continues.

CARLOS FRANQUI

On November 4 the soldiers' last hope will start to fade: it was hoped that the elections would bring a peaceful solution.

What are the soldiers going to do with their last hope gone and hundreds of their companions dying every day in the invincible drive of the Rebel Army?

Three things may happen:

1. A military coup that would have to accept the conditions of the Revolution with no compromise.

2. A massive rebellion, with complete units going over to the rebel forces.

3. The total disintegration of Batista's army, if it has not already occurred, and the total triumph of the Rebel Army in the not very distant future.

Some may object that Batista has faced many difficult situations in his long career as dictator—general strikes, military conspiracies, military defeats, etc.—and has always emerged successful from them.

But now there is an essential difference: on all those occasions, Batista's strength was the army.

And besides, in none of those situations did he have to fight against an army that today numbers tens of columns and thousands of victorious fighters battling bravely in four provinces of Cuba.

COMMUNIQUÉ   Baire, Frank País Second Front, November 3

On the Frank País Second Front, in Oriente, in the action at the Santa Ana sugar mill, the forces of the Revolutionary Army destroyed a light tank, taking three hundred .30–'06-caliber rounds, and destroyed another light tank in a place known as San José, near the Santa Ana mill; Batista's army suffered fifteen to seventeen casualties, all dead.

Beginning at 9:00 p.m. November 1, mobile units of Column 17, Abel Santamaría, under the command of Major Antonio Lussón, made a synchronized attack and surrounded the rural guard barracks, the National Police station, and the Alto Songo town hall.

Troops under the command of Lieutenants Pena and Botello attacked and took the military post at La Araña.

In those actions, the following weapons were taken: from the police station in Alto Songo, nineteen shotguns; from the town hall, nine shotguns; from the military post at La Araña, three shotguns. It would be superfluous to add that in the Songo district no elections will take place.

CAPTAIN SUÑOL, COMPANY 3, COLUMN 14

Report   Holguín, November

Rebel troops blew up the water mains from Holguín aqueduct, leaving the city without water. Today is the seventh day that Holguín has been without electricity. Now there is neither water, nor electricity. Cities that have no light through the actions of this column are: Holguín, Gibara Velasco, Bocas, Auras, and Iberia; no water: Holguín and Gibara. Traffic in this region: completely paralyzed.

CARLOS FRANQUI

In spite of compulsory voting, threats, and frauds, the mass of the people did not vote. Eighty percent of the electorate obeyed the order to abstain.

The vast body of the people showed themselves to be participants in the struggle. From then on Batista's fate was sealed. November 3 was the first popular victory of the insurrection.

The 26th of July militias carried out sabotage, they cut electric cables, and with their actions paralyzed the principal cities of the country, setting fire to cane fields, strewing nails [on roads], taking weapons, and carrying out actions in every corner of the country.

RAÚL CASTRO   Frank País Second Front, November 7

The Soledad Barracks was captured along with twenty-nine shotguns and thousands of bullets. The garrison was taken prisoner. November 7, after seven hours of combat, rebel forces of Column 6, under the command of Major Efigenio Amejeiras and Captain Samuel Rodiles, captured the barracks of the rural guard in Soledad. They took twenty-nine shotguns, seventeen Springfield rifles, a Spanish .30-caliber machine gun, two Cristóbal carbines. The whole garrison, consisting of twenty-nine men, was taken prisoner.

The Barton Barracks is also in the hands of the rebel troops. Its garrison surrendered, and many weapons were taken.

The rebel columns of the Frank País Second Front have captured fourteen enemy barracks in recent days. The war communiqués from the headquarters of the Second Front, with their lists of weapons taken, prisoners of war, and the other details of actions, keep the announcers at our radio station busy all day. More than 250 enemy soldiers have already been taken prisoner.

Approximately 270 weapons have been taken. The troops of the dictatorship are abandoning many small garrisons without sending reinforcements. The General Staff of the tyranny is making no attempt to rescue them. One by one their barracks surrender unconditionally, in some cases after several days of fruitless resistance.

RECOLLECTIONS   Havana, November 8

On the morning of November 6, Norma [Celia Sánchez] inspected conditions in the new hideout. The one at O'Farrill and Goicuría had had to be abandoned a few days before, because it had gotten too "hot." For two hours Norma left the doors open, thinking that if the police had been alerted, they would come immediately when they saw the house open. Nothing happened. The next morning, the four revolutionaries moved into the place. Norma and Machaco [Angel Amejeiras], the Action chief of the Movement, left at once to make contacts in the Movement, which took them all day. After visiting the Vedado and the old

Plaza del Vapor, they came back at dusk. At eight in the evening they made a meal—rice, fried eggs, and chocolate ice cream—because the wounded Rogito's fiancée was coming to see him.

Pedrito was talking about his daughter's birthday, which was on the ninth. Norma was to go with him to see her, and he would give the girl a bathrobe he had made for her. At 11:00 p.m. they were all asleep; they had not slept the previous night, and had had a tense day. Norma and Machaco were in the first room, separated by the bathroom from the other room, where Pedro and Rogito were, along with the group's small arsenal. At 3:00 a.m. a burst of machine-gun fire awakened them. "Surrender, surrender," they were shouting in the street. Norma and Machaco jumped out of bed and pressed themselves against the wall. To get to the other room, they would have to pass in front of an open door through which bursts from the machine guns were coming. Machaco grabbed the pistol that he kept under his pillow and fired through the front door, which gave Norma a chance to get to the other room. Then the firing increased, concentrating on the rear.

More than thirty patrol cars were in the streets, and on the roofs of the adjoining buildings .30-caliber machine guns were set up.

In the midst of the shower of bullets, Machaco told them to shut the front door in case the cops used tear gas, which they later did. As soon as Rogito had shut the door, Machaco leaped from a window to the roof of the next building, quite a distance away. He shielded himself behind the water tanks from where he could fire against the cops who were at the back door of the house. Norma did the same thing.

When Machaco jumped, a cop shouted: "One jumped. . . . Fire at him." Norma recalled: "I saw the bullets fly by, one after the other. Then I told Rogito and Pedrito to help me jump. I wanted to be with him. We didn't have any way out of there. We had no escape. Machaco had said earlier: 'We don't have any way out of here. So we stay to the last bullet. We have to shoot at the cops and kill as many as we can.' "

When Norma moved away from the water tanks, she was shot in the chest. Machaco reported this to the other two, who were fighting in the apartment. They told them to come back to the apartment. On the way back, when they got to the open part of the little patio, Norma was wounded again. This time in the hip. Her legs wouldn't obey her, and she couldn't go any farther. Machaco stayed with her.

"I told him not to stay, to go back to the house. One way or another, we were going to die, and it didn't matter whether it was a little sooner or a little later. Machaco returned to the house and I stayed on the ground until it got light."

On the way, Machaco was wounded in the arm. Inside the apartment, his wound bandaged with a handkerchief, he kept on firing together with Pedrito and Rogito, until their bullets were used up. Then they began to throw TNT bombs and grenades outside. But then all the explosives were used up. They closed the windows, but they were shattered by the enemy machine-gun fire.

The fight must have gone on for four hours.

There was tear gas everywhere in the area. The neighbors were evacuated. The cops got ready to dynamite the building. But when they were convinced that the brave revolutionaries had no bullets or bombs or grenades to resist a minute more, and that the tear gas made it impossible to stay inside the apartment any longer, they went in and took them out.

The revolutionaries had caused about ten casualties among the police and had blown up a patrol car and prevented them from storming the apartment. The cops dragged them roughly down the stairs and put them in Military Intelligence cars. They were so savagely tortured that they died, and at eleven in the morning, their bodies were thrown on the floor of the clinic in Corrales. Colonel Ventura ordered them to be buried at night.

Norma was stretched out in the patio—at her side a Luger she couldn't use because her arm was immobilized, which also prevented her from turning over to reach it with the other arm. She had four wounds: in the arm, the chest, the hip, and the waist; as well as three fractured ribs.

When the master torturers realized in what condition she was, they came up to her from the back, lifted her up, and brought her to one of the patrol cars. An officer said: "Look, her hair is dyed. That's why we didn't recognize her."

She was taken to the military hospital at Camp Columbia, where the doctors did not want to be responsible for letting her die. After attaching a bottle of serum to her veins, they had her moved to the emergency hospital, where surgery saved her life. Then they took her to a cell in the basement of the police hospital. A couple of days later, she was brought to the Military Intelligence offices, where she was interrogated by Irenaldo García, who could not get her to say a single word that would implicate her companions in the organization.*

FIDEL CASTRO   November 9

Angel Amejeiras is the third brother to die fighting for the liberty of his people. The first gave his life July 26, 1953, in the action at the Moncada Barracks. The second, Gustavo, was arrested by Colonel Ventura's mob

---

* After a trial in the Urgency Court, she was confined in the Women's Prison at Guanajay. On June 22, 1959, her son, Angel Manuel ("Machaquito") was born.—C. F.

as he left prison some months ago, and he has disappeared without leaving a trace. The third, Angel, died yesterday in the streets of Havana. A fourth brother is in prison on the Isle of Pines, also for fighting against oppression, and the fifth, Efigenio Amejeiras, disembarked with the *Granma* expeditionaries on Playa Coloradas, December 2, 1956. He is one of the twelve who kept the banner of the Revolution aloft during the difficult days in the Sierra Maestra, and today, because of his bravery in innumerable encounters, he is a major in the Rebel Forces and the second in command of the Frank País Second Front.

Five brothers—three are dead, one is on the Isle of Pines and the other is fighting on the battlefield. The Amejeiras stock is a moving example of heroism that recalls the Maceo family. Those who have not yet understood the profound significance of this struggle and the sacrifices that our people are making to win their liberty should meditate on the example set by this family, which has already lost three sons in this epic struggle. Angel Amejeiras, dying in combat in the streets of Havana, a few days after elections that pretend to offer some cure for our misery, is one condemnation more of those who lent themselves to that disgusting farce.

Young people are pursued as if they were wild beasts, cornered, and forced to sell their lives very dear, criminal mobs who show no mercy, who destroy those who have the misfortune to fall into their hands—that is the only thing that the bloody despotism, imposed on our fatherland by force, can promise the country for another four years.

The death of three heroic youths, who for five hours fought off an attack by an entire police squad, that is the only thing—a melancholy trophy—that the tottering tyranny can offer.

Havana is still a fief of the henchmen. They are still encamped in Havana, but there too their hour will come. There too, as today in Santiago de Cuba, they will soon hear the echo of the rifles of the advancing rebels coming close. Santiago de Cuba was a fief of Chaviano and Salas Cañizares, and until very recently, the vile henchmen cynically exhibited their shameless strength there. But the hour of justice is coming near, when the blood of Frank País is still fresh on the pavement, and the pack of criminals who murdered him, and many others, tremble like caged rats. So too the Revolution will approach Havana, and also on a day not distant, perhaps long before the blood of Angel Amejeiras and his companions is cleansed from the pavement, the murderers will tremble and will hear the echo of our rifles.

Angel Amejeiras, a fighter for the Revolution. The valiant never die in the memory of their people—the valiant who fall continue fighting in every encounter—because our glorious soldiers bear them in their thoughts. All the heroes who fall become fighters in the front line who lead our men, and that is why our columns bear the names of heroes who have fallen. Major Angel Amejeiras, all the fighters of the Rebel Army stand at attention before you, and they will await your orders when they approach the streets of Havana.

MAJOR HUBERT MATOS   Santiago, November 8

Last night I was in the Vista Alegre section, moving in with a company from our Column 9, Antonio Guiteras. Our men felt genuine satisfaction as they passed through the beautiful streets of the city and this section. Captain José Antonio, Narciso, Lara, and Cabrera went with me. Our goal was to find the radio cars that usually cruise about the city at all hours, and we arrived at the San Juan barracks. We gave cheers for the Revolution and finally fired some shots in the air, but the enemy didn't appear. We withdrew to the tune of the national anthem sung by our companions from Column 9, Antonio Guiteras.

FIDEL CASTRO

To Juan Carlos [Raúl Castro]   Sierra, November 8

I propose the Carrasco Artiles–Borbonet exchange. I intend to demand a reply before you free prisoners. If the dictatorship refuses, release no one, and I will make a big campaign [about it].

I have a good plan.

EDITOR'S SUMMARY   Sierra Maestra, November 9

Fidel issued instructions to all the rebel commanders in Oriente Province to restrict movement of goods and people drastically. Bus and railroad travel was to be totally immobilized. Passengers were permitted to use the highways only on Mondays, Tuesdays, and Wednesdays; transport of commodities, including the coffee harvest, was limited to the same three days. Only milk could be supplied on a daily basis. Fuel deliveries were to be blocked and all fuel supplies requisitioned or destroyed. Civilians were warned not to travel with soldiers or convoyed by soldiers; they would thereby open themselves to the same treatment as the soldiers.

FIDEL CASTRO

Orders to Juan Almeida   Sierra, November 9

I have the impression that events might come to a head at any moment. I'm quickly taking measures to cut off entry and exit from the province completely. Raúl is successfully carrying out a series of operations that are going more rapidly than I had expected, but in any case, he's right to take advantage of this moment, when the enemy is in distress, to capture all those small barracks that had remained isolated in his zone.

The moment is approaching to execute the plan I mentioned in my earlier instructions. I'm in favor of carrying our encircling operations not in one specific city or sector but in the whole province, to prevent them from sending any reinforcements in the majority of cases and assuring their surrender. You must study your plans for the moment to begin the total encirclement of Santiago as part of the general plan. But that moment may come suddenly. I'm going to give you a code message so that in case there isn't time to communicate with you in writing, you can receive the order by radio.

The code message will be: *Immediately carry out Plan W-3-10-9.*

Plan W-3-10-9 is to surround Santiago de Cuba completely with the forces of three columns (3, 10, and 9) and not let anyone enter or leave the city. At the same time, you will be tightening the circle, more and more, until you confine them to their military installations, and increase the pressure until they surrender, whether they resist for a week or for a month. You must also think about the tactical details of the operation and resolve them.

You must think of the measures that you are going to take when Santiago falls. Among others, you must make sure that their weapons are not dispersed. Everybody is going to want to grab a rifle, and that is going to be a tremendous problem. The thing to do is to order the weapons to be put in one place, take the most essential for the men who have earned them, and await orders concerning the rest. Remember that in these situations, operations happen without pause, and once the men have reached one objective, they must be shifted immediately toward the next.

I'm waiting to see if any of the measures succeed regarding troops who might join up with us. If anything happens, we would immediately have to initiate the relevant operations.

We must be prepared, for at any moment the province may become a Sierra Maestra on a large scale.

With a little luck, you may even hook a general.

FIDEL CASTRO   Sierra, November 9

At 8:30 last night, this headquarters established radio communications with the Red Cross, requesting it to transmit to the enemy General Staff the proposal to exchange army Lieutenant Colonel Nelson Carrasco Artiles, prisoner of our forces, for Major Borbonet, imprisoned on the Isle of Pines.

Lieutenant Colonel Nelson Carrasco Artiles was wounded in combat and taken prisoner by troops of Column 3 several weeks ago.

With this exchange, the dictatorship could furnish comprehensive medical treatment to one of its officers who was wounded in combat, and it is equitable that another officer of the army, one of those who have been imprisoned more than two years for opposing the tyranny, should also regain his liberty.

FIDEL CASTRO

Letter to General Cantillo   November 10

Fine, General Cantillo! It doesn't matter! When your answer rejecting the exchange is drawn up, send two reliable officers to the Sierra Maestra, and I will turn over Lieutenant Colonel Carrasco Artiles without any conditions, because what the behavior of the General Staff arouses is not indignation but disgust and repugnance.

MAJOR HUBERT MATOS

Report   Third Front, Santiago, November 10

Yesterday afternoon, Monday, November 10, forces of Column 9, Antonio Guiteras, under the command of Major Hubert Matos, intercepted and repulsed an army column that was going from Palma Soriano to San Luis; it consisted of three light tanks and several radio cars. The first tank was totally destroyed by a mine, forcing them to retreat after we had inflicted more than fifty casualties. Be informed that this movement of the army forces involves a violation of the truce, since it was an attempt to bring troops into San Luis.

A. P. BULLETIN   New York, November 11

Batista has decreed the death penalty for doctors who treat wounded rebels. It is reported that hundreds of Cuban doctors have left for Mexico and the United States, since their own government punishes doctors who help wounded revolutionaries.

FIDEL CASTRO

Letter to Luis Crespo   Guisa, November 20

I am in Guisa right now, where a big battle is being waged.

If a plane with weapons arrived, Faustino was to send them to Providencia with some boys from the recruits' school. As soon as they reach you, send them here with all the bullets and weapons that might have come.

CAMILO CIENFUEGOS

To Carlos Franqui   Yaguajay, November 23

We took Zulueta Barracks after a two-and-a-half-hour fight, from three in the morning until five-thirty.

At five in the morning, a plane appeared and strafed the town.

COMMUNIQUÉ   Cabaiguán, November 26

Rebel troops under the command of Major Ernesto Guevara, chief of the Revolutionary Forces of the 26th of July in Las Villas, entered the city of Cabaiguán, where they remained for several hours. In this action, the equipment from the Cubanacán radio station and from the telephone company was taken, as well as a large amount of fuel from the RECA refinery. Our forces withdrew without incident.

FIDEL CASTRO

Communiqué   Guisa, November 30

Last night at 9:00 p.m., after ten days of combat, our forces entered Guisa. The battle took place within view of Bayamo, where the command post and the bulk of the dictatorship's forces are located. It was fought against nine groups of enemy reinforcements that came in successive waves, supported by armored tanks, artillery, and planes. The Guisa action began at exactly 8:30 a.m. on November 20, when our forces were intercepted by an enemy patrol that travels every day from Guisa to Bayamo. They were put out of combat in a few minutes. At 10:30 a.m., the first enemy reinforcements arrived at the site of the action, and we fought against them until 2:00 p.m. in the afternoon, when they were driven back. At 4:00 p.m., a land mine destroyed one of their T-17 tanks.

On the twenty-first, the enemy advanced, supported by Sherman tanks, and succeeded in entering Guisa and leaving reinforcements in the garrison.

On the twenty-second, our troops, recovered from the fatigue of two days of continual fighting, took up positions again on the Bayamo–Guisa highway.

On the twenty-third, an enemy force tried to advance over the road from El Corojo but was repulsed.

On the twenty-fifth, an infantry battalion preceded by two T-17 tanks advanced again on the highway from Bayamo to Guisa in a convoy of fourteen trucks. A mile and a quarter from this point, rebel troops opened fire on the convoy from both sides of the highway; meanwhile, a mine immobilized the forward tank. Then began one of the fiercest battles ever fought in the Sierra Maestra.

It was necessary to surround not only the Guisa garrison but also the whole battalion that had come to reinforce it. They were in the interior of the circle with more E-17 tanks.

At six in the afternoon, the enemy had had to abandon all the trucks grouped closely around the 2 tanks.

At 10:00 p.m., our 81-mortar battery attacked the enemy force, and revolutionary teams armed with picks and shovels dug a trench in the road next to the tank destroyed on the twentieth. The trench and the ruined tank would bar the exit of the two remaining T-17s inside the circle.

At 2:00 a.m., a rebel company advanced; they fought fiercely against the tanks, which had no food or water.

At dawn on the twenty-seventh, two battalions and the vanguard reinforcement, preceded by Sherman tanks, reached the site of the action. We fought against them all day.

At six in the afternoon, the units of the enemy infantry began a general retreat. The Shermans got out, thanks to their new caterpillar treads; they dragged one of the T-17 tanks but the other could not be moved.

The battlefield was covered with enemy bodies, and quantities of weapons were left: 35,000 bullets, 14 trucks, 200 knapsacks, and a T-17 tank, in perfect condition, with abundant ammunition and a 37-mm. cannon. But the action was not over: a rebel column, advancing rapidly on the flanks intercepted the enemy retreating toward an intersection of the Central Highway, attacked and inflicted many casualties, and took more arms and ammunition. The tank was quickly readied to go into action.

At night on the twenty-eighth, two rebel squads, preceded by the tank, advanced boldly toward Guisa. At 2:20 a.m., on the twenty-ninth, the T-17 tank, manned by rebels, stood right at the doors of the Guisa Barracks, and it began to fire its shells at the center of the many buildings where the enemy was entrenched. When it had fired fifty shots, two direct hits from enemy bazookas stopped the tank's motor. The crew of the damaged tank continued firing the rest of the bullets against the barracks. They left the tank and began to withdraw.

An act of unparalleled heroism then took place. Lieutenant Alfonso Prieto, who had manned the machine gun in the tank, jumped to the ground, grasping the gun. Although he was wounded, he crept off, taking his heavy weapon with him and not letting go of it for a second.

That same day, at dawn, enemy troops advanced from three different points: the road from Corralillo to El Corojo, the highway from Bayamo to Guisa, and the road from Santa Rita to Guisa. All the enemy forces were repulsed between the Yara River, Estrada Palma, Baire, and other points in that zone.

The column advancing on the road from El Corojo was repulsed after two hours of fire. The battalions advancing on the highway from Bayamo to Guisa were harassed for the entire day and during the night at a mile and a quarter away from Guisa.

Those coming on the road from Corralillo were also driven back, and then went around the northeast of the town.

The last actions took place in Santa Rita. The battalions that had taken up positions a mile from the town tried repeatedly to advance all day long without being able to achieve a breakthrough.

At four in the afternoon, while units were fighting the reinforcements, the Guisa garrison abandoned the town in a precipitate retreat, leaving behind all their supplies and weapons.

At 9:00 p.m., our vanguard entered the town. That same day, seventy-one years before, members of the liberating army, under the command of General Calixto García, had taken the town of Guisa.

At the time that this war communiqué is being written, the equipment taken from the enemy totals the following: a T-17 war tank, taken, lost, and recaptured; 94 weapons, including Garand and Springfield rifles, and San Cristóbal machine guns, two .60 mortars, one 81 mortar, one bazooka, seven .30-caliber machine guns, 55,000 bullets, 130 hand grenades, seventy .60-caliber mortar shells, twenty-five .81-caliber mortar shells, and 20 bazooka rockets.

More than 200 casualties—dead and wounded—were inflicted on the enemy in the ten days of combat. Eight of our companions fell heroically in the course of the action, and seven more were wounded.

The battle was fought principally against the troops quartered in Bayamo. It was a struggle of men against planes, tanks, and artillery. The most outstanding rebel officer was Captain Braulio Coroneaux, veteran of many actions, who fell gloriously defending his position on the highway from Guisa, where the rebels saw the enemy tanks go by.

The Mariana Grajales women's squad also fought valorously for the ten days that the action lasted, resisting the aerial bombardment and the attack by the enemy artillery. Guisa, eight miles from the command post at Bayamo, is now liberated territory.

CARLOS FRANQUI

Note to Fidel Castro   Sierra, November 29

The following message has just been received by telegraph from Zoilo in Havana: "Military coup imminent. Officers proposed by Alejandro [Fidel] to Julio Camacho are participating. Request immediate instructions."

Since I had to answer at once, I sent him the following reply: "Proceed if still accept 5 points Alejandro. Be ready event collapse to take positions, weapons, cities, newspapers, etc., etc."

CARLOS FRANQUI

To Fidel Castro   Sierra, November

If a military coup takes place, Radio Rebelde must go on the air at once to give instructions to the Movement and the people.

We have the disadvantage of being far away; we would lose precious time if we were to meet. So transmit the instructions that we have discussed so many times.

In moments like this, one man must make decisions on his own, but it is worse not to make them. Give us some guidelines.

I think:

1. Sealing off Oriente: Your instructions to Ochoa.

2. Che advances toward important cities of Las Villas.

3. Camilo approaches Havana or reinforces Che, depending on the situation there.

4. The forces in Camagüey should occupy and seal off the province as much as possible.

5. Escalona should reinforce Havana or Pinar del Río. All the rebel forces must occupy the cities and positions most vital for maintaining order, arresting cops and informers, preventing looting, arson, anarchy, etc. This is how we'll take weapons and barracks.

6. The militias and the Movement must do the same in the rest of the cities.

7. As soon as it happens, I will try to make contact with you; I will order that the closest radio transmitter be sent to you; I will announce to the people, army, the Movement rebels, et al., that they can expect to hear your instructions very quickly.

8. And they should supervise banks, property, newspapers, etc.; and take over newspapers, radio, government property, city halls, etc.

9. I will try to make contact with Urrutia, who must take over the government.

If there is fighting or any resistance to the coup, we will call for a general strike by the Movement and the people. And call on the Rebel

Army to seize cities and positions and reinforce the military men who rebel, and call on the army to join with the people, taking natural precautions in keeping with circumstances.

Of course, although this or another coup may occur, I will believe it when I see it, and although we have advanced quite far, I would be happy if this were, like other times, only one more rumor.

Why don't you direct them to bring the transmitter and operator of Radio Llano Rebelde* to you? They have another one.

EDITOR'S SUMMARY   Frank País Second Front, November

At a meeting of the Congress of Revolutionary Workers, it was agreed that the union leaders who supported the corrupt leadership of the Cuban Workers' Confederation, headed by Eusebio Mujal, and followed the orders of the tyranny were henceforth disqualified from their posts in workers' organizations.

At the same time, a Commission of Free Workers was established to handle the affairs of the twenty-five sugar mills that had been liberated in Oriente Province. The commission stated that it would replace the Official Directorship of the Cuban Workers' Confederation and the National Federation of Sugar Workers in discussions with landowners and tenant farmers concerning conditions of labor for the coming harvest of 1958.

In addition, the commission announced that it would take over offices and records of the previous unions and assume responsibility for day-to-day matters.

Drafts of revolutionary laws were drawn up in November. They provided for freedom of expression, abolition of union dues, and union democracy. They sought to restore honesty in ownership and management of property by taking over lands and other assets, illegally obtained. They attacked corruption by cleaning up the bureaucracy and denying civil rights and professional degrees to those who had collaborated with the Batista regime. Wages were to be increased, profits to be held down, gambling prohibited, and racial discrimination outlawed.

VILMA ESPÍN

Recollection

All the commanders were mobilized for the capture of Nicaro, at the end of November. That was fantastic. When we arrived, the whole town was there. There was a Chinese ship in the port, and we greeted the Chinese on the dock. We went all over the town. I went to see some friends of mine who are engineers, and we ate at their house.

---

* The rebel radio operating from the cities, on the plain.——Ed.

We were camped in Levisa, in a hotel. At daybreak the shooting began, when I was brushing my teeth. Do you know that the bombardments always caught me when I was brushing my teeth? They never let me finish brushing them!

This time they were bombarding with everything, frigates and everything. And those shells from the frigate, they really whistled!

You know, it wouldn't have been hard to catch us. We were in Levisa, and the guards came around from behind. They were Sosa Blanco's men.

We were with Raúl, in a house in Levisa, and we were directing the fighting from there, and getting news from everywhere. We had left the hotel and settled ourselves there after the big bombardment was over. Suddenly we heard firing near where we were.

We had to leave, running through the streets of Levisa, and Raúl told me to get into a jeep and take the radio. I was going with another comrade. In the middle of all that, with the planes encircling and firing, the jeep got stuck in a swamp without any trees or anything. You know, I lifted that jeep with one shoulder!

We reached the hills of Corea; all the men were arriving there. Finally everybody got there, and we turned back.

In Songo, almost the same thing happened; after we captured it we had to go away. Songo fell into our hands, then into theirs, and then into ours, and so on, until the end came.

You know the problem in the last towns that remained in that area of Songo and thereabouts was that the remaining traitors kept fighting harder and harder, because they knew that the day they were caught . . .

In La Maya, there were still about four hundred of that Batista mob, and not one was shot. They were getting more and more concentrated, and that barracks just wouldn't fall, because they had put even the families inside, and we didn't dare set fire to it or anything like that. There were children.

That was when "Pompón" Silva first bombarded, December 7. It was our first bombardment with a napalm bomb on the Second Front. The plane's route was prepared at night, and at dawn Pompón dropped it, and they surrendered immediately.

CARLOS FRANQUI

Books and records that should come on the plane for Che, Fidel, and Franqui

The Story of Philosophy (Will Durant); *Remembrance of Things Past* (M. Proust); *The Sound and the Fury* (William Faulkner); complete works of Hemingway; *Paradise Lost* (Milton); *Solitudes* (Góngora); Works of Graham Greene; *Materialism and Revolution* (Sartre); *Residence on Earth* and other poetic works by Neruda. Records of Beethoven, Bach, Stravinsky.

FIDEL CASTRO

Orders   Sierra, November

Traffic in Oriente Province must be immobilized again, totally. All the men and all the rebel units must be at their posts. All the roads in and out of the cities, as well as throughout the province, must be cut off.

The columns of the Second Front Frank País must continue their advance, surrounding and obtaining the surrender of all the barracks possible in the triangle bounded by Mayarí, San Luis, and Guantánamo, while the columns that surround Santiago de Cuba must tighten the circle to prevent any movement of enemy troops.

The rebel troops who are operating in the center and the east, guarding the entrance to Oriente Province, must fight tenaciously against whatever enemy reinforcements they try to send in.

The urban centers that fall into the hands of our forces should be declared open cities, and consequently no rebel troops should encamp in them, to prevent the bombing of defenseless cities. In that matter, we will request the participation of the Red Cross.

Invading Columns 2 and 8 of the Rebel Army, situated in Las Villas, receiving support from all the revolutionary forces that are fighting there, must in turn intercept the highways and rail lines and prevent enemy troops from crossing into Oriente and prevent those that still support the tyranny from getting out and continuing to fight at this end of the island, which our forces are now sweeping through virtually unimpeded.

The people must be the chief guardians of order in each city liberated, in order to prevent any kind of looting, destruction of property, unnecessary bloodshed. No one should take revenge on anyone else. The spies and the elements known for their inhuman acts against the people should be arrested and interned in prisons to be later judged by revolutionary tribunals.

In the decisive hours that are approaching, the people must give the loftiest evidence of civic feeling, patriotism, and desire for order so that no one will someday be able to make dishonorable accusations against our Revolution, which we must keep free of any stain because it is the loftiest achievement of the Cuban nation and its most extraordinary proof of love of country and civic dignity.

MAJOR HUBERT MATOS

Report   December

Although soldiers who escaped from the attack on the barracks in El Cristo are still hiding in the cane fields and pastures, we are giving a report on the weapons and ammuniton taken and the casualties among the enemy army. Weapons taken: 81, including 42 Springfield rifles, 2 Dominican rifles, 2 M-1 carbines, 8 Garand rifles, 15 Browning submachine guns, a .30-caliber tripod machine gun, 16,400 bullets. The tripod machine gun and 28 additional weapons were captured from an army column that was trying to help the soldiers who were fleeing. The casualties are the following: 13 dead and 82 prisoners. On our side we had 2 dead and 7 wounded. The barracks was taken by our forces. The situation in San Vicente is the following: In the last three days, enemy activity had been limited to strafing by planes and some long-range shelling by tanks.

CHE GUEVARA   Fomento, December 6

At dawn on November 29, troops of the army of the dictatorship, coming from Santa Clara, reached Fomento. There were several companies, making a total of more than a thousand men, supported by eight caterpillar tanks and various kinds of equipment, including cannons, bazookas, and mortars. The same day, November 29, advancing from Cabaiguán, they took the village of Santa Lucía, and they reached Punta Gorda, having started at Fomento.

Our troops put up flexible resistance, gradually giving up terrain that the enemy conquered at great sacrifice, relying always on the help of the tanks. On November 30 the enemy left flank advanced to a place called Conuco, supported by tanks and planes, but there they were stopped by the forces of Captain Joel Iglesias, which forced them to withdraw back to Santa Lucía. Their center went as far as the village of Mota; with the help of two caterpillar tanks on the right flank, they reached the village of Sitiados. These were the most advanced positions their tanks reached, evading our defenses.

On December 1 the enemy forces were blocked in their efforts to advance on every combat front, suffering many casualties. On December 2 the right flank of the enemy was defeated and routed. We took considerable ammunition from the enemy and a caterpillar tank with a 37-mm. cannon. We pursued them to the edges of Fomento, where they took shelter, although they were forced to abandon the village of Mota. In the defense of our left flank, Major Camilo Cienfuegos personally participated, at the head of a select group of veterans from his column. Before withdrawing from the village of Sitiados, the enemy set fire to twenty-one peasant houses by shooting at them with their tank cannons. On December 4 the enemy tried to retake Mota, but its forward squad fell into our ambush with the following result: eight dead and thirteen seriously wounded on the army side. We took a tripod .30-caliber machine gun and 1000 bullets, 3 Browning automatic rifles, 8 Garand rifles, and abundant ammunition for both. We remained in possession of the invasion route—Cabaiguán, Conuco, Sancti Spíritus. The bridge on the Central Highway over the Tuinicú River was rendered useless by the actions of Captain Silva, and as a result the Trinidad–Sancti Spíritus highway could not be used, and Major Camilo Cienfuegos's blockade in the center left them only one route—a local road going from the village of Guayo and passing through the Tuinicú mill, and this was very soon cut by our forces. On that road only light vehicles can pass.

CARLOS FRANQUI

To Celia Sánchez   La Miel, December 6

Che left with his radio. Things are going well for him and Camilo. You know all about it from Radio Rebelde. I'm enclosing some very recent messages.

Fidel should make a statement on the sugar harvest.

Raúl is going to turn over five hundred prisoners before the twentieth, in Santiago and Guatánamo.

It's reported that El Primo* has improved the situation with the U.S. a little.

There is a message from Gustavo Arcos; he mentions a conversation November 27 with Monsignor Pérez Serantes, in Santiago. They wanted to know what the Movement would do if a government other than the one proposed by us was in power, or if it was a military junta, or if Batista made a peaceful exit, resigned.

There were conversations with a general: [Gustavo] reports that it was Cantillo. They agreed to send a commission to the Sierra to talk with Fidel. This could be a preliminary to the conspiracy. I answered that I would transmit the message, I talked with Gustavo and Raúl on the five points of the coup d'état, and I told them to expect an answer.

One of Urrutia's men is coming. He says he is coming by plane, between today and Sunday, from Venezuela, with Luis Orlando and a big shipment of arms sent by Larrazábal.**

---

* Luis Buch, one of the members of the Committee in Exile.
** Admiral Wolfgang Larrazábal-Uguerto, president of the Venezuelan junta.—ED.

I'm sending them a radio to communicate with us. There are lots of questions that I can't decide. They operated on Faustino, and they report he's doing well.

Send me a copy of the codes you have.

Camilo and Che: radio conversation

Camilo: Tell me what the enemy movements are there and let me know if there is anything new. By the way, tell me what kind of tank you captured. The messenger who was there told me he had seen it but he couldn't explain what kind it was. Now, over to you, Guevara.

Guevara: Well, Camilo, I see that it's bothering you, eh? It's a caterpillar tank. Its markings are slightly burned, but it's very pretty. It's American-made and I think it's going to be very useful. I don't know if it's called a C-37 or not, although the C-37 is somewhat different. That's all I can tell you about the tank. The mechanics are working on it here because there's been a little damage. Now, about the problem that concerns us. Well, the enemy is concentrated in the usual places. Right now there are no problems on our lines. I think that there will be problems in a very short time. I heard you telling Fidel that you were going to take Santa Clara and I don't know what the hell else, but don't butt in there because that's mine. All you have to do is stay over there, where you are.

Camilo: Okay. I overheard you saying that they should communicate with Radio Rebelde. As far as that business about Santa Clara, okay, fine, we are going to make plans for later on, and we are going to do them together; I want to share some of the glory with you, because I'm not ambitious. I'm going to give you a little chance to grab the iron ring since we're going to put seven thousand riflemen in the attack. Those guys are crazy to get into that action, and in the past few days they have disarmed all the soldiers at the mills; it's really fantastic what those boys do to get rifles. Imagine, when I told them they couldn't join up without rifles, they captured the soldiers at the refineries and took their rifles away.

PEPE ECHEMENDÍA *

To Fidel Castro   Havana, December 13

Confidentially we have learned that decrees decommissioning Cantillo, Sogo, Sosa Quesada, and Díaz Tamayo await the signature of the tyrant.

---

* Coordinator of the 26th of July in Havana.—C. F.

Salas Cañizares and Sánchez Mosquera will both be promoted to general.

RAÚL CASTRO

Communiqué   Frank País Second Front, Oriente, December

Hundreds of weapons taken, more than a hundred prisoners! Today the La Maya garrison capitulated! Hundreds of weapons and prisoners captured!

After fourteen days of siege and after repulsing the reinforcements from Guantánamo, our forces took La Maya. Very soon we will give more details about this great triumph of rebel arms.

FIDEL CASTRO TO RAÚL CASTRO   Maffo, December 15

A hard fight is being waged here. Today is the fifth consecutive night of attack on Maffo. The planes have leveled the town. After this, we have the job of dealing with Jiguaní, which is surrounded, with two hundred and fifty men inside. A troop of two hundred guards has managed to infiltrate, trying to help the forces in Maffo. We have located it north of Baire, which is in our hands, and I expect to intercept it tomorrow. The troops in Maffo are defending themselves like wild animals, and they've already cost us thirteen casualties (two dead and eleven wounded, some seriously, some not), but we have them in a hopeless situation. I'm worried that the operation afterward in Jiguaní is going to take me a long time. So I need you to give me air support with some incendiary bombs. I can use some 81 shells in place of bombs.

We've captured the Central Highway from the Cauto River to near Palma Soriano. The only point they hold is Jiguaní. We have Baire, Contramaestre, and América. They are holed up in some Banfaic* building in Maffo.

I'm so fucking mad at those guys in Maffo that it will be a miracle if I don't shoot them all when they surrender.

---

* The Banco de Fomento Agrícola e Industrial de Cuba, a national bank that advanced credit for the development of agriculture and industry.—Ed.

CARLOS FRANQUI

Coordinator of the 26th of July,   Santiago, December 17
Santiago; to Fidel Castro and Carlos Chain

I have received an urgent communication from Santiago in which I am asked to inform Fidel or Raúl that the sailors on the frigate *Máximo Gómez* want to come over to our side.

These men spoke with Dr. Chibás and Major René de los Santos, in a place called Goderich, last Thursday. Present were Lieutenants Jorge Salvá and Carlos Jiménez, and they await instructions. Someone named Michel would be their leader.

They want a quick answer as they are desperate, and they say that if they have to wait much longer, they will go AWOL. They are bringing the boat with them; it is loaded with weapons and ammunition.

There are sixteen officers, and eleven of them are already in agreement. The crew has one hundred and twenty men.

I hope that you will answer this before three in the afternoon and have the message delivered to me in Santiago.

RAÚL CASTRO

Commander in chief of   December 17
the Frank País Second Front of Oriente:
instructions to the frigate

1. Everything is progressing; we are planning to coordinate the rebellion with the attack of Santiago de Cuba.

2. Wait until tomorrow, December 18, when you will receive definite instructions from Fidel Castro.

3. Meanwhile, since you are running the risk of being discovered and arrested, you must stay on the alert and be ready, in case of an emergency, to sail out to sea, keeping the decks cleared for action and not permitting yourselves to be captured under any circumstances.

4. In case of emergency, we inform you that we hold the port of Baitiquirí, under the command of Major Félix Pena, chief of Column 18 of the Frank País Second Front of Oriente, who will receive instructions in case the frigate wants to leave the crew's surplus weapons there, as well as the largest possible amount of supplies and whatever equipment may be useful on land. In case you need water and food, use the port mentioned. All this is provisional until we can work in coordination.

5. You should approach said port at night, giving intermittent signals with your lights, once you are close to the coast.

It must be clearly established that these instructions will be in effect only in the eventuality that you are discovered and forced to act before you receive definite instructions from Fidel Castro, tomorrow, December 18. In sending said instructions, the same route will be utilized.

COMMUNIQUÉ

Last night the Caimanera Barracks was taken by the forces under the command of Captain Villa. Dead and wounded. Twenty-eight shotguns were taken. Attack imminent from Holguín, Guantánamo and Santiago.

CHE GUEVARA   December 22

The city of Fomento,* Las Villas, has been captured by forces of the Ciro Redondo Column, the militiamen of the 26th of July, and troops of the Revolutionary Directory. One hundred forty-one of the dictatorship's troops were taken prisoner, the Rebel Army took 139 shotguns from the enemy, 98 Springfields, 21 Garands, 1 .20-caliber machine gun, 1 Thompson, 1 81-mm. mortar, 2 radio cars, 3 jeeps, 2 trucks (one of them armored), 15 grenades, and a large amount of ammunition for all these weapons. After our forces withdrew the enemy planes carried out a merciless bombardment against the civilian population of the city, killing two children and wounding several civilians.

FIDEL CASTRO

Memo to Che Guevara   Maffo, December 22

I consider it harmful from the military point of view to return prisoners at this time.

The dictatorship has obtained great quantities of tactical arms, but it lacks personnel to use them. Under these circumstances, if we return prisoners we are helping them to solve one of their biggest problems. Although they don't send them to fight again, they use them in garrisons where there are no combat fronts to replace troops who are sent on operations.

---

* The capture of Fomento was a key point in the campaign for Las Villas. Fomento was the first city to surrender, with a strong barracks, a revolutionary population, two sugar refineries, many unions, and it was well situated on the line that goes from the center to the south of the province. From that moment on, the situation of Trinidad, cut off from behind, became untenable, and farther on, Placetas and the highway toward Santa Clara were threatened.—C. F.

Except where the surrender terms have involved an express commitment, the prisoners from Fomento should not be returned.

CARLOS FRANQUI
Placetas, December 23

Arms taken: 159 rifles, 7 light machine guns, 2 .30-caliber machine guns, 1 81-mm. mortar, grenades, ammunition. More than 100 prisoners, later freed.

After a big battle, which began today at 4:30 a.m., Placetas was captured; it surrendered to the combined forces of the Revolutionary Directory and the 26th of July, under the command of Major Ernesto Guevara.

The city of Placetas was under cross fire all day from rebel machine guns and those of the forces of the dictatorship, in a duel without quarter that reached the far corners of the city. The rebel soldiers, who were waiting in their positions, took as their points of resistance the Central Highway, the gates of the cemetery, and all the places adjoining the police station, the town hall, and the army barracks.

All day long, the city was under the fire of rebel arms; snipers were on the roofs of the highest buildings, aiming their fire at all the mobile patrols that moved in the streets.

At 5:00 p.m., after two hours of intense shooting, fire from .30-caliber machine guns, mortars, and hand grenades, the police garrison opened negotiations with Major Guevara. It surrendered at 5:30 p.m. A few minutes later, at the headquarters of the 26th of July and the Revolutionary Directory, a petition was received for the surrender of the army garrison, trapped in the town hall, and minutes after, the soldiers who were fighting in the army barracks did the same. When the people of Placetas learned of the surrender of the tyranny's troops, they rushed out into the streets; the church bells peeled, and everywhere the cry rang out "Long live free Cuba!"

Placetas is the key to Santa Clara, center of important communications on the island, divided in two by the offensive of Che's troops in the center of Cuba.

MAJOR ANTONIO LUSSÓN
December 23

Sancti Spíritus is now free Cuban territory. Column 8, Ciro Redondo, as it surrounded the city, forced the tyranny's forces to retreat toward Jatibonico. Sancti Spíritus has gained its freedom.

At 9:30 a.m. today the important city of Sagua de Tánamo fell to the rebels, as a result of a combined action from Columns 19 and 17, led by Major Aníbal. One city more incorporated into the free territory of

Cuba. In future editions, we will give more details of this victory of the rebel armies.

The cities of Ranchuelo and Cruces, in Las Villas, have fallen into the hands of the rebels.

FIDEL CASTRO

Orders to Belarmino Aníbal   Maffo, December 23

Congratulations on the victory at Sagua de Tánamo. Lussón just reported everything to us. Now your objective is Mayarí. Send forces as quickly as possible to take the road from Mayarí to Preston. Send enough men to prevent the garrison from retreating. As I understand it, the reinforcement coming from Preston went toward Mayarí, and its objective is to replace the troops at this point. Under the present circumstances, I don't think they can contemplate anything but retreat from Mayarí.

After you have secured the only road on which they can retreat, you'll have time to prepare a systematic attack against their position.

All goes well here. Raúl is with me today, and we've already dealt with this matter. To save time, I'm sending you the instructions directly, as he's not here at this moment and I want the bearer to leave at once.

PEPE ECHEMENDÍA

Report to Alejandro [Fidel Castro]   Havana, December 23

Today I had a meeting with Colonel Florentino Rosell Leyva, chief of the Corps of Engineers of the tyranny's army in Las Villas, who acted as a representative of General Cantillo, General Río Chaviano, and Colonel Pérez Coujil. He proposes that all weapons and troops in Oriente, Camagüey, and Las Villas be made available to the Rebel Army and that both army and rebel troops invade the western provinces together. They suggested establishing a civilian-military junta that would include Cantillo, another military man to be chosen from among Barquín, Varela, and Borbonet, and three civilians, who would include Urrutia and two others selected by you. They offer airplanes with sufficient troops to free the military and civilian people you select. They commit themselves to turning over all those responsible for the March 10 coup, including Batista, but they would let Río Chaviano and Pérez Coujil get away. They want us to blow up the bridges connecting Matanzas with Las Villas. Colonel Rosell adds that this plan has been discussed with the North American embassy, and when it comes to fruition, they would immediately recognize the proposed junta. They want an interview with you or with Major Che Guevara within the next twenty-four hours. I've limited myself merely to listening to their propositions in order to communicate them so that you can decide what you deem appropriate. I await instructions, since together with what has already been outlined, we also know that small groups led by Aureliano Sánchez Arango, Justo Carrillo, and others are planning to kill Batista in order to seize power. I've also been informed that Pilar García, Ventura, and the Tabernillas are preparing a coup d'état. These are decisive moments.

CARLOS FRANQUI

To Pepe Echemendía   Maffo, December 24

North American–supported junta unacceptable. Turning message over to Fidel.

ANTONIO NÚÑEZ JIMÉNEZ   December 24

The capture of Fomento was important for the operations that culminated in the battle of Santa Clara. In Fomento, there was no rebel withdrawal; it was the first town taken and kept by rebel troops. Civilian authorities were elected at a meeting with representatives of the unions and civilian institutions, in collaboration with the troops from the 26th of July and the Revolutionary Directory, an example of unity against the tyranny. This example was repeated in the actions at Placetas, Cabaiguán, Sancti Spíritus, Remedios, Caibarién, and other cities in Las Villas. Three days after Fomento was freed, on December 21, simultaneous attacks at Cabaiguán, and Guayos on the Central Highway were carried out, in the violent December campaign led by Che Guevara.

A few hours after Víctor Bordón's troops attack Guayos, it surrenders; they seize new weapons, and the offensive continues. In Cabaiguán, the tyranny's B-26 aircraft strafe the populace and our positions. The following day, at dawn, the defender of the Batista barracks, Captain Pelayo González, surrenders, along with sixty-six men. His army comrades, freed and shipped to Placetas, take flight. All this contributes to the demoralization of Batista supporters. Cabaiguán is in the hands of men from the 26th of July and the Revolutionary Directory, the latter under Cubela's command. Che plans a frontal attack on Placetas December 22. Hours later, another bastion of the tyranny falls into our power. The ninety soldiers from the garrison are freed.

The taking of Placetas on the Central Highway, with its thirty thousand inhabitants, and only some thirty-two miles from Santa Clara, turns out to be of prime importance for future plans. Che, contrary to what Batista's men may expect, does not attack Santa Clara. He takes Remedios and Caibarién. The capital of Las Villas is surrounded by liberated cities: to the north, Encrucijada; to the south, Manicaragua; to the southeast, Fomento; to the northeast, Remedios and Caibarién; to the east, Santo Domingo, not to mention towns of lesser importance. Sancti Spíritus falls on December 23 to troops led by Captain Armando Acosta. With this action, a populace of more than 115,000 inhabitants becomes part of the Free Territory. The Revolution grows stronger by the hour. The fall of the tyranny is imminent.

ALEJANDRO [FIDEL CASTRO]

To Echemendía   Maffo, December 25

Conditions rejected. Arrange personal meeting between Cantillo and me.

ECHEMENDÍA

To Commander Fidel Castro   Havana, December 26

I returned from Las Villas, but I'm going back there immediately. Colonel Rosell reports that General Cantillo is establishing contact with you, using a priest as intermediary. Rumors persist that Batista will simulate a military coup with groups he trusts. On my return, I'll report more fully.

FIDEL CASTRO

Letter to Che Guevara   Maffo, December 26

I haven't time at this moment to write a long letter, nor do I have the means—the only light is from a flashlight.

The war is won, the enemy is collapsing with a resounding crash, we have ten thousand soldiers bottled up in Oriente. Those in Camagüey have no way of escaping. All this is the result of one single thing: our determined effort.

It's essential for you to realize that the political aspect of the battle at Las Villas is fundamental.

For the present, it is supremely important that the advance toward Matanzas and Havana be carried out exclusively by the 26th of July forces. Camilo's column should be in the lead, the vanguard, to take over Havana when the dictatorship falls, if we don't want the weapons from Camp Columbia to be distributed among all the various groups, which would present a very serious problem in the future.

At this moment the situation at Las Villas is my main worry. I don't understand why we're getting into the very same difficulty that I sent both you and Camilo there to resolve. Now it turns out that when we could finally overcome it, we're only aggravating the situation.

FIDEL CASTRO

Bulletins   Maffo, December 27

The walls of the Banfaic building in Maffo are crumbling under fire
from our batteries. This is the last enemy position in the territory between the cities of Bayamo and Santiago de Cuba. About 70 miles along
the Central Highway are in our hands. These battles have cost our army
27 lives and some 300 wounded, but we have caused the enemy more
than 600 casualties—dead, prisoners, and wounded. Numerous battalions have been decimated or destroyed, and the towns of Jiguaní, Contramaestre, Palma Soriano, etc., have fallen into the power of our
invincible columns, and more than 450 weapons have been captured.
We are heading toward the final destruction of the enemy army in
Oriente Province, where 2000 of the tyranny's soldiers are surrounded.

The enemy forces at Camagüey are likewise threatened by our invading columns.

Nothing can any longer stop the overwhelming and victorious advance of our forces.

Palma Soriano, December 28

Rebel troops from Columns 1 and 3, supported by units from Companies A and B of Column 17, marching on Santiago de Cuba, today
stormed the city of Palma Soriano, after five days of violent combats,
while Columns 9 and 10 transported all the equipment from Santiago de
Cuba.

The enemy army defended itself in Palma Soriano with some 350
men; almost half of them were besieged in buildings in the city, while
the rest were entrenched in the barracks, which is near the Central
Highway, at the entrance of the bridge that links it to the city.

The action began December 23 at 2:30 in the morning, when a rebel
company attacked the police station west of the city with bazooka fire.
At the same time, units were ambushed in the airport and on the roads
leading to the barracks at the aforementioned point. During the morning hours an enemy patrol went to the airport to meet a military airplane and was beaten back by our forces. Immediately afterward they
surrounded the Palma sugar mill, where an enemy force had taken
cover, while rebel companies, under the command of Major Universo
Sánchez, took up positions south and east of the barracks.

On the twenty-fourth our troops captured the sugar mill, while the
enemy forces managed to fall back in orderly fashion in time.

That night a rebel company crossed the Cauto and entered the city
from the south, capturing residential blocks on the west edge of the city,
thereby dividing the enemy forces in two.

Simultaneously the units that attacked from the west advanced toward the center of the town, after taking the police station. On the twenty-fifth a battery of 60 mortars pounded at the main enemy barracks from morning to dusk.

On the twenty-sixth the general attack against enemy positions was begun. At 7:00 a.m. the 81 mortar battery joined in the action. The concentrated fire from our batteries had a devastating effect on the garrison. The heavy shells began to fall exactly on the roof of the building and into the enemy trenches.

The soldiers manning the .50-caliber from the top of the building were put out of action by a direct hit. When the tenth shot from the 81 was fired, the white flag was raised and 250 enemy soldiers defending the place were taken prisoner, and we took 213 rifles and 65 pistols.

While this was going on the battle continued in the interior of the city. The buildings taken by the enemy were recaptured one by one. At one in the afternoon a very important structure, defended by 35 soldiers, was taken by our forces. But still Infantry Company 104 continued to hold out in the middle of the city, under the command of Major Sierra. The combat lasted all afternoon, during the night, and through the first hours of the dawn, today at 5:00 a.m., when we were finally able to capture the garrison building, its troops, and even take the major himself prisoner. All in all, 256 enemy soldiers were taken prisoner and 357 weapons seized. In the face of these successes won by our victorious Rebel Army of the 26th of July, the tyranny's General Staff ordered the liberated cities to be bombarded. This particular practice on the part of Cuba's tyrant is not at all new. Innumerable cities in Las Villas and Oriente and rural zones in Pinar del Río, Las Villas, and Camagüey bear witness to the criminal bombardments and strafings the tyranny's air force has perpetrated.

FIDEL CASTRO

Orders to Major Delio Gómez Ochoa   Maffo, December

The barracks at Cueto and Guaro have fallen into the hands of the rebels, so you should move toward the zone indicated upon leaving the Sierra Maestra and order Captain Suñol to be ready to back you up with all his men.

Inform all the forces under your command to be prepared to accomplish their basic objective as soon as the order is received.

EDITOR'S SUMMARY   Havana, December

Correspondents for the U.S. wire services were sending dispatches to their home offices that were more and more ominous for the future of Batista's regime. The rebels

*were reported to have captured Manicaragua, Zaza del Medio, Cifuentes, and Ca-
labazar de Sagua, and they had surrounded Santa Clara. Apparently, the correspondents concluded, the government was unable to counter these moves because of
insufficient weapons; reverses loomed in Las Villas Province that could signal a decisive shift in the fortunes of the two-year-old rebel movement.*

*It was unofficially reported on December 26 that the General Staff had de-
manded the resignation of Brigadier General Alberto del Río Chaviano and had
named Colonel Joaquín Casillas Lumpuy to succeed him.*

*On December 27 it was announced that Batista had organized a military com-
mand in central Cuba and had shipped another two thousand soldiers to Las Villas
to contain the campaign of the revolutionary forces.*

*Informed Havana circles reported on December 27 that it was widely believed
that decisive events were imminent in Fidel Castro's rebellion.*

ANTONIO NÚÑEZ JIMÉNEZ

At noon on Christmas Day we accompany Che as he places a vanguard
of his troops in Remedios, under the command of Captains Vaquerito
[Roberto Rodríguez] and Alfonso. Firing is concentrated on the military
barracks and the town hall, which houses the police station. Molotov
cocktails explode against the old walls of the building, and it is turned
into a ball of flame. Its occupants surrender. The barracks surrender the
following day. One hundred fifty rifles are seized and a large quantity of
ammunition—material utilized in the final battle against the dictatorship in Santa Clara. The military barracks at Caibarién, as well as the
navy quarters, are taken easily.

After the liberation of Caibarién, Che's strategy prevents military
reinforcements from reaching the besieged city of Santa Clara, reinforcements that could only arrive by sea at the ports of Cienfuegos and Caibarién to the north and to the south. Santa Clara could not be entered
from Cienfuegos, since the rebels had captured the towns on this highway. And as for Caibarién, that port was also in rebel hands. From
Sagua la Grande and the port of Isabela de Sagua, they could not enter
either, because the revolutionary command of Column 8 had cut the
principal bridges along this route.

Che asked that a road be found for him to arrive with his troops at
the gates of Santa Clara, without being discovered by the enemy. He
could not utilize the Central Highway, from Placetas, or the highway
from Santa Clara to Camajuaní, on whose side roads we were stationed.
Both routes were known and our march through them would have been
immediately reported to Batista's troops in Santa Clara and Batista's air
force would attack us. The neighboring La Vallita road, little fre-
quented, went as far as the outskirts of Santa Clara, along the University
City, through Caridad, Sabana Nueva, San Antonio, and Callejón de

Casas, and so that was finally chosen by Che for his advance on the capital of Las Villas. The forces set off in trucks and jeeps at night. It was December 29. The Revolutionary Directory Column under Cubelas's leadership was informed that it would attack the positions in the city itself. As the sun came up, we reached the university buildings at Las Villas, some five miles from Santa Clara.

Che established his general headquarters for the assault on Santa Clara at the university. He divided his forces into two columns, and they walked in the ditches of the highway going from the university to the city. The first news that Batista's men had of the rebel presence in Santa Clara came when an armored government detachment, composed of two tanks and infantry troops, had an encounter with them; and the rebels put them to flight. The invasion force reached the junction of the highway and the railroad tracks that divided the city in two.

Colonel Joaquín Casillas Lumpuy, murderer of the workers' leader Jesús Menéndez, defended Santa Clara with forces from Regiment 6, Leoncio Vidal, composed of 3500 soldiers, as well as police and an armored train, which Batista's generals had just sent, with all the technical resources the army had at its disposal, in hopes of maintaining communications and turning back the rebels.

FIDEL CASTRO   Maffo, December 31

During the last three days the forces of Columns 1 and 3 intensified the attack on Maffo. A T-17 tank that we seized during the offensive of the Sierra Maestra was moved from the outskirts of Manzanillo as far as Maffo; a 37-mm. cannon and an 81 mortar, arms all seized in battles against the dictatorship, maintained an incessant battering of fire against the enemy position. Today at 5:30 p.m. the holdouts at the Banfaic Building finally yielded to us. Major Leopoldo Hernández Ríos was made prisoner, along with five lieutenants and 124 enemy soldiers; 130 weapons were seized: 24 Garands, 42 Springfields, 46 San Cristóbal machine guns, 4 Browning automatic rifles, 1 Manin automatic rifle, 7 M-1 carbines, 1 Thompson machine gun, 2 mounted machine guns, 1 81 mortar, a .60 mortar, 42,000 rounds of .30–'06, and an M-1 with 100 cartridge belts, knapsacks, flasks, etc.

Our forces suffered 4 dead and 20 injured in the battle. With the fall of Maffo, only a single enemy troop remains between Bayamo and Santiago de Cuba.

HUBERT MATOS

Report

The battle of Santiago de Cuba will begin at any moment. Five thousand enemy soldiers are defending the city. Our troops, who have liberated the cities of Jiguaní, Baire, Contramaestre, Maffo, Palma Soriano, and Cobre during these last twenty-five days, will also take Santiago de Cuba, where a decisive battle will be waged.

In our advance, forces from Column 9, Antonio Guiteras, under the command of Major Hubert Matos, from the Mario Muñoz Third Front, took the main broadcasting station for the radio cars at 4:30 p.m. The garrison, consisting of 100 men who were waiting for reinforcements that never arrived, fled from the deadly and continuous rebel cannonfire, which ripped enormous holes in the walls of the building. The broadcasting station in Santiago de Cuba is situated at the highest point in the Boniato Cordillera, on the outskirts of the city. From the very beginning of the Christmas holidays, the people of Santiago have had the moving experience of seeing the immense 26th of July flag flying over Puerto Boniato, as a sign of freedom and of complete rebel control.

Yaguajay, December

Rebel forces under the command of Major Camilo Cienfuegos attacked the barracks at Venegas. The garrison put up some tough resistance, the majority were injured, but they surrendered to the thrust of our men. The results: 15 injured soldiers, 15 prisoners; numerous weapons taken.

On the twenty-third the barracks at Zulueta was taken. The combat lasted for over two and a half hours—from 3:00 a.m. to 5:30. We seized 2 San Cristóbal machine guns, 4 M-1 carbines, 7 Springfield rifles, cartridge belts, bullets, uniforms, etc. At 5:00 a.m. an airplane appeared and strafed the town.

Today, at 6:00 a.m., the powder magazine at Guanabacoa, in Havana, was blown up. The soldiers at Topes de Collantes surrendered.

The Revolutionary Directory, under Faure Chomón, captured all of Trinidad. "Six Fierce, Bearded Men" and the Red Cross coordinated activity in turning over a numerous group of prisoners.

CHE GUEVARA

As the enemy retreated from Camajuaní without putting up any resistance, we were ready for the final assault on the capital of Las Villas Province—Santa Clara, with its 150,000 inhabitants, the hub of the island, its railroad and communications center. It is surrounded by small, barren hills, which had previously been taken by the dictatorship's troops.

At the moment of the attack, our forces had considerably increased their rifle power as a result of capturing various points, and had some heavy arms that lacked ammunition. We had, for instance, a bazooka without projectiles, and we had to fight against a dozen tanks. But then we also knew that to do what we had to effectively, we needed to reach the populated neighborhoods of the city, where the tank loses much of its effectiveness.

While the troops of the Revolutionary Directory were trying to take the barracks of the 31st Squadron of the rural guard, south of the city, we concentrated on surrounding almost all the strong points of Santa Clara; although, basically, we were settling in for our fight against the defenders of the armored train, situated at the entrance of the road from Camajuaní; the positions were tenaciously defended by the army, with excellent equipment for our purposes.

On December 29 we went into battle. At first the university had served as a base of operations. Later we established our headquarters closer to the center of the city. Our men were pounding away against troops supported by armored units, and they put them to flight, but many of them paid with their lives for their daring, and both the dead and the injured filled our improvised cemeteries and hospitals.

I remember one episode that demonstrated the spirit of our forces in those final days. I had admonished a soldier for falling asleep during the height of battle, and he answered that they had taken his gun away because he'd fired a bullet by mistake. In my usual dry way, I told him: "Go to the front lines without a gun and get yourself another one—if you can." In Santa Clara, as I was cheering up some of the wounded in the field hospital, a dying man touched my hand and said: "Remember, Major? You ordered me to go and get that weapon at Remedios . . . and I got it here." It was the fellow who had fired off the bullet by mistake; a few minutes later, he died, and it seemed to me that he was happy to have showed his bravery. This is our Rebel Army!

The hills of Capiro would not yield and we fought there during all of the thirtieth, and at the same time, we gradually took different points in the city. They had already cut communications between the center of Santa Clara and the armored train, whose occupants, finding themselves surrounded in the hills of Capiro, tried to flee along the railway tracks. With all their magnificent cargo, they reached the branch previously destroyed by us, derailing the locomotive and some coaches. Then, a very interesting battle ensued in which Molotov cocktails drew the men out of the magnificently protected train, although they were only ready to fight from afar, from cozy positions, and against a practically unarmed enemy, in the style of the settlers of the North American West against the Indians. Harassed by men who were hurling bottles of flaming gasoline from nearby points and adjoining coaches, the train was transformed—thanks to its armor-plate veneer—into a veritable oven for the soldiers. In a few hours, the whole group surrendered with the twenty-two coaches, antiaircraft guns, machine guns, and a fabulous quantity of arms (fabulous in contrast to the scarcity of our supply, naturally).

We had managed to take the power station and the entire northeast of the city, and the news that Santa Clara was almost in the hands of the Revolution was released to the radio. During the broadcast that I made, as the major in charge of the armed forces at Las Villas, I remember the grief I felt in announcing the death of Captain Roberto Rodríguez to the Cuban people. "El Vaquerito," as he was known, was slight in stature and age, the chief of the "suicide squad," who played with death a thousand and one times in the struggle for freedom. The "suicide squad" was an example of revolutionary morale, and was made up of selected volunteers. However, every time a man died—and this happened in every combat—and a new candidate was named, the others were grief-stricken, to the point of weeping.

Later the police station fell, and the tanks that had defended it surrendered, and in rapid succession, Major Rolando Cubelas received the surrender of the jail, the courthouse, the palace of the provisional government, the Grand Hotel, where the snipers continued to shoot from the tenth floor almost to the end of the battle.

At that time only the Leoncio Vidal Barracks had not yet surrendered; it was the largest fortress in the central part of the island. But it was already January 1, 1959, and there were symptoms of increasing weakness among the defending forces. During that morning we sent Captains Núñez Jiménez and Rodríguez de la Vega to arrange the surrender of the barracks. The news was contradictory and extraordinary: Batista had fled that day, the leadership of the armed forces was crumbling. Our two delegates made radio contact with Cantillo to inform him of the surrender offer, but he replied that it was not acceptable because it constituted an ultimatum, that he had taken up the leadership of the army, following precise instructions from our leader Fidel Castro. We contacted Fidel immediately, telling him the news, and also telling him our opinion about Cantillo's treacherous attitude, an opinion that coincided exactly with his.

A battle is under way in Guantánamo; fighting is intense.

The Red Cross at Cienfuegos answered Che Guevara's message seeking its aid for the sick and wounded in Topes de Collantes, with the following (Lieutenant Colonel Alemany is speaking): "I believe the Red Cross will be very proud to take over the administration and running of the Topes de Collantes Hospital, and we are also very proud of the trust you grant us."

ENEMY DOCUMENT

Colonel Rego Rubido
to Major General Cantillo   Moncada Barracks, December 31

I enclose the answer to your note of yesterday. It can be seen that they insist on stressing unilateral action and that they are worried that because of an unjustified excess of scruples, it will help those who bear the greatest guilt, etc., to escape.

And it says: "What is obtained by duplicity and deceit can never be called triumph." According to the messenger, he requires that you or I go see him [Castro] and clarify matters.

1959

18. JANUARY:
BATISTA FLEES—VICTORY

GENERAL CANTILLO, CHIEF OF THE ARMY Havana, January 1

Flash! Batista, Guas Inclán, and Alliegro have resigned. The presidency
has been assumed by the senior judge, Dr. Carlos M. Piedra y Piedra.

They have all left. Colonel Daniel G. Martínez y Mora has been
designated chief of operations.

CARLOS FRANQUI Palma Soriano, January 1

During all these events, Fidel was at the Palma sugar mill, where a jeep
was sent to inform him of the gravity of the situation: of Cantillo's
attempt at a military coup, with the support of the U.S. embassy and
several conservative sectors of the country, in order to snatch the revolutionary triumph from the people, the 26th of July, and the Rebel Army.
In view of his absence I prepared a proclamation, to be read on Radio
Rebelde, to alert the people, the Movement, and rebel chiefs.

It announced:

We will never accept any government but one of civilians.

The people must prepare to declare a general strike.

The flight of the murderers must be prevented.

We demand the immediate liberty of all political prisoners.

The Rebel Army and the 26th of July Movement must continue to
advance on the cities, key positions, barracks, police stations, and at the
same time, seize arms.

The Revolution cannot be snatched away. It is now stronger than
ever.

Wait for Fidel Castro's words, which will be transmitted shortly.

Viva the Revolution!

EDITOR'S SUMMARY Camp Columbia, Havana, January 1, 1959

Batista spent New Year's Eve 1958 at Camp Columbia receiving reports from his advisers that the military and civilian situation was irretrievably lost. Church and business officials joined the military in urging him to resign and permit new men to try to deal with the country's desperate condition. Early on January 1 Batista signed a deed of resignation. He turned military power over to Major General Eulogio Cantillo y Porras. The senior justice of the Supreme Court, Carlos Manuel Piedra, became Batista's "constitutional substitute" as president, since those in direct constitutional succession had resigned.

About 2:00 a.m. Batista made his way from his private quarters at the base to the airfield, gave Cantillo some parting advice from his plane's doorway, shouted "Salud! Salud!" to a crowd of abandoned supporters, and flew off to refuge in the Dominican Republic.

Cantillo then met with the men Batista had advised him to consult—the members of the Conciliation Commission formed by Batista in 1958, but rejected by Castro—and sought to carry on the government.

At the same time Cantillo ordered Rego Rubido to contact Castro and try to arrange a nationwide cease-fire in the name of the new president.

Colonel Rego Rubido to Commander Castro

Official Radiogram
Ciudad Militar 010500 January 1959
Col Rego Rubido
1st Military District
Santiago de Cuba

Establish contact through persons known to you and try to obtain a cease-fire throughout the Republic on condition it be officially requested by the Hon. Sr. Pres. Dr. Carlos M. Piedra. This cease-fire is of the greatest importance in order to avoid useless loss of lives. SOP NS NS-959. Cantillo Porras, Chief of the High Command.

I CERTIFY that this is a faithful copy
of the original. J. M. Rego MM. Col Insp
Terr JPSR 1st Military District

Dr. Castro:
Happy New Year.   J.M. Rego

CARLOS FRANQUI   Palma Soriano, January 1

When Fidel reached the transmitter, we announced:
"Now coming to the microphone of Radio Rebelde, is the supreme

leader of the Cuban Revolution, Doctor Fidel Castro Ruz, to broadcast declarations of the utmost importance."

Fidel Castro: It has just been announced from Camp Columbia that the tyrant Batista has fled. General Cantillo, in the name of the army, announces that he has taken command of the military junta. In his declaration, he has spoken cynically of the patriotism of the tyrant, who has consented to resign, and to grant exit to the main thugs of the tyranny's repressive forces. I am ordering a rebel advance on Santiago and on Havana, and I am now proclaiming a general strike. We will never accept any solution other than a civilian government. This long and arduous battle will not brook any outcome other than the triumph of the Revolution. Let no one be deceived. We will not accept a military junta. The flight of the assassins must be prevented. We demand immediate liberty for all political prisoners.

A military junta, in connivance with the tyrant, has taken power to secure his flight and that of the country's main assassins, as well as attempting to halt the revolutionary tide in order to snatch away our victory.

Seven years of heroic combat and the blood shed by thousands of martyrs all over Cuba are not going to be used so that those people who until yesterday were accomplices of the tyranny and responsible for it can continue to govern Cuba.

The people and the workers of Cuba must immediately prepare for the general strike, which will take place tomorrow, January 2, all over the country, as a way of supporting the armed revolutionaries and thereby guaranteeing total victory for the Revolution.

The Rebel Army will continue its sweeping campaign; it will only accept the unconditional surrender of military garrisons.

I order Major Víctor Mora, chief of Camagüey Province, to advance on all cities, and to obtain the surrender of their arms, with the cooperation of the people and honorable military chiefs from the enemy army, using the troops under his command. Major Mora must close off all means of access to the towns, especially those on the Central Highway and the highways from Santa Cruz del Sur and Nuevitas to Camagüey. Major Camilo Cienfuegos and his glorious Invasion Column 2 must advance on to Havana, to take charge of the surrender and to assume command of the Camp Columbia military base.

Major Ernesto Guevara has been given the position of chief of the military camp at La Cabaña and, in consequence, must advance with his forces to the city of Havana; on his way, he must obtain the surrender of the fortresses in Matanzas.

Instructions have also been issued to Major Belarmino Castilla to obtain the surrender of the forces at Mayarí; Majors Raúl Castro and Efigenio Amejeiras are to obtain the surrender of Guantánamo; and

Majors Sardiñas and Gómez Ochoa, those of Holguín and Victoria de las Tunas.

These commanders are also instructed to maintain complete order in the cities that surrender and immediately imprison all those who are guilty for the present situation, and try them as soon as possible.

Major Escalona, military chief of Pinar del Río, should act, therefore, according to the preceding instructions.

Meanwhile, Columns 1, José Martí, 3, 9, and 10, under the direct command of the commander in chief, Fidel Castro, and of Major Juan Almeida, are already advancing on Santiago de Cuba.

MEMO   Havana, January

A great number of young people wearing 26th of July armbands and who form the militia, have appeared. They are occupying police stations. However, their clothing is quite inadequate, and it is cold outside. They have been called in and are being given a supply of winter clothing, which was to have been sent to the Sierra del Escambray.

CARLOS FRANQUI

The revolutionary general strike, which was an extremely important factor in the ouster of the dictatorships of Rojas Pinillas in Colombia and of Pérez Jiménez in Venezuela, was a decisive cause of the fall of Machado's tyranny in our country in 1933.

The people of Cuba and Cuban workers have more than proved their love of liberty. Cuban workers and all the people will join their strength to the forces of liberation, declaring themselves ready at the crucial moment in this battle.

Against oppression, against crime, against torture, against the dictatorship of Batista—the revolutionary general strike.

CONRADO BÉCQUER, JOSÉ PELLÓN

Bulletin   Palma Soriano, January 1

The Cuban workers, directed by the Workers' Sections of the Revolutionary Movement of the 26th of July, must today take over all syndicates dominated by Mujal and his henchmen, and organize themselves in the factories and labor centers so that the total paralysis of the country will begin at dawn tomorrow.

Batista and Mujal have fled. But their accomplices have remained in charge—in the army, as well as the unions.

A coup d'état to betray the people—no! That would mean prolonging the war. Until Camp Columbia surrenders, the war will not be over. This time, nothing and no one can prevent the triumph of the Revolution.

Workers: This is a moment when you must act to assure the triumph of the Revolution.

Laborers: For liberty, for democracy, for the full triumph of the Revolution.

On to the revolutionary general strike!

Palma Soriano, January 1

At this moment, when the tyranny is crumbling, the leaders of the 26th of July in every locality must provisionally assume the powers of government of each municipality.

Later, after investigation by a committee designated by the General Staff, municipal and provincial commissioners will be named.

FIDEL CASTRO

Broadcast   Palma Soriano, January 1

Fellow citizens of Santiago, the garrison at Santiago de Cuba is surrounded by our forces. If, by 6:00 p.m., it has not laid down its arms, our troops will advance upon the city and will take the enemy's key points by storm.

From 6:00 p.m. on, all air and maritime traffic in the city will be forbidden.

Santiago de Cuba: the thugs who assassinated so many of your sons will not escape as did Batista and the most guilty, who were aided by the officers who led the cunning coup last night.

The people involved in the military coup are attempting to keep rebels from entering Santiago de Cuba. They forbid our entering a city that we can take with the usual bravery and courage of our combatants; they want to forbid those who have liberated the fatherland to enter Santiago de Cuba.

You will be free because you deserve it more than anyone, because it is intolerable that the defenders of the tyranny still walk on your streets.

MAJOR DIEGO, CHIEF OF THE 26TH OF JULY MILITIAS

Report to Fidel Castro   Havana, January

The navy, army, and national police have surrendered totally. A large number of automatic arms, ammunition, patrol cars, jeeps; and the 26th of July has taken over patrol activities from these forces.

Strike continues until your orders are received. All state offices occupied. Total paralysis. Militias on constant alert, well organized, and determined to continue fighting if circumstances require it. Matanzas and Pinar del Río fair, unable to know for sure about conditions there, because of lack of time. We'll keep the strike going until Urrutia takes power. Workers' units functioning very well, same for the propaganda units.

Havana, January 1, 1959

11:00. Judge Piedra installed at 1 Refugio Street, the executive seat of the nation.

1:00. A diplomatic commission, presided over by Ambassador Smith of the U.S. embassy, meets with General Cantillo at the palace.

7:05. Colonel Ramón Barquín orders the tanks to withdraw from the military city.

7:25. Aldo Vera, one of the action and sabotage chiefs of the 26th of July Movement, who was in El Príncipe Prison, enters Camp Columbia.

Groups from the 26th of July demand Eulogio Cantillo's arrest.

12:00. Political prisoners from the 26th of July arrive at the Camp Columbia airport in a civil aircraft. They come from the Isle of Pines, fully armed and organized.

January 2

6:00 a.m. Revolutionary groups coming from different places in the republic begin to arrive at Camp Columbia.

8:00. The officers named by Barquín to take command report that the Rebel Army is in control of the respective units.

2:00. The vanguard of the Invasion Column Antonio Maceo appears in Camp Columbia. Its members fraternize with the soldiers.

3:30. Barquín affectionately greets the first of Fidel Castro's bearded men.

11:30. Major Camilo Cienfuegos, flanked by Captain Pinares, an aide-de-camp, Major Aldo Vera, and René López, speaks to reporters.

CARLOS FRANQUI

On December 28 General Cantillo, chief of the army, met Fidel in the América sugar refinery in Palma, which served as a makeshift office.

Contact had begun months before with the exchange of messages. Cantillo was a general with prestige, he was not one of the regime's big thieves, and he was not a murderer. A large group of high- and medium-ranking officers who obeyed orders, believed in the army, fought the rebels, did not murder or rob, but allowed others to murder was part of the contradiction of the Batista army. Cantillo was their unquestioned leader.

In contrast to Casillas, Ugalde Carrillo, Sosa Blanco, Sánchez Mosquera, and other chiefs of operations in the Sierra, who were known as killers of peasants, prisoners, and underground fighters, Cantillo conducted a humane campaign, strictly military, without murdering anyone. If he failed as a strategist and tactician, he retained the stature of a decent man. Conversing with families of soldiers taken prisoner in the Sierra, he praised Fidel's patriotism. Fidel's numerous letters and suggestions to Cantillo and his fellow officers displayed extraordinary talent.

This interview took place when the regime was falling apart, the rebel columns invading the country, the people as a whole repudiating the recent elections, and the army no longer willing to fight, yearning for peace. It was then that Cantillo, with the help of the U.S. embassy and the bourgeois sectors, the political elements and clergy, decided to talk to Fidel and to lay plans for the new military coup.

At the meeting in Palma, Fidel was explicit and skillful. He said he agreed to unite the rebel forces with the units led by Cantillo and his friends, on condition that Batista and the war criminals were not allowed to escape, and that no military junta or coup d'état be attempted, or foreign interference be permitted. Before leaving for the meeting, Fidel told me that he was concerned about the delicate question of discussing Cantillo's personal position. In the new army, there must not be any generals. The top rank would be that of major. Cantillo was a major general. Fidel said he would try to save the situation by offering him the job of defense minister. I suspect that this did not come up in the interview.

It was decided to suspend operations for two days and to act jointly beginning at three in the afternoon of the thirty-first. The rebels and military personnel would occupy the three eastern provinces together, while Cantillo would occupy Camp Columbia and arrest Batista.

On the thirty-first, before the operations were to begin, Colonel Rego Rubido, chief of the Santiago garrison, sent word to Fidel, in Cantillo's name, that the joint operations would be postponed temporarily.

Fidel immediately became suspicious. Cantillo was playing double politics. In Havana, in a deal with Batista, his generals, and ministers, whom he let escape, advised by the U.S. embassy, he maneuvered to have an old, discredited judge from the Supreme Court named president. This maneuver of putting the judge, Piedra, in office, supported by a military junta, would salvage the army and make it appear to the public as the architect of a peaceful solution. The army would thereby preserve its prestige, as well as keep the support of the embassy, the politicians, the bourgeoisie, and the clergy, while swindling the people out of their triumph, and everything would remain as before. But Cantillo had never deceived us, neither in war nor in peace.

Days before we had been warned by the leaders of the Movement in

Havana of an attempt at a coup with Yankee support. Leaders of the 26th of July, Julio Camacho and Echemendía, were in constant contact with all the conspirators and were on guard. Cantillo ran more risks than Fidel. If he let Batista get away and brought about a coup, it sufficed not to accept the coup and denounce his betrayal in order to stop the army from fighting any longer. It was not Cantillo but peace that the broken, weary army longed for.

On the other hand, all the people were with us: the organized workers, the civic institutions, the militias, and the underground fighters with their prestige in both big and small cities, and the Rebel Army, with its tremendous aura of triumph, with thousands of seized arms and numerous cities.

And above and beyond everybody else, Fidel was a figure of enormous prestige. The general strike would be complete, total.

And in the hypothetical event some military unit might resist, our forces multiplied by thousands would decide the outcome militarily.

And that's how it was.

Unwittingly, Cantillo gambled in Fidel's favor, instead of the opposite. As a general he had lost the war, as a politician he lost the peace.

FIDEL CASTRO

Bulletins   Santiago, January 2

In Camp Columbia a "mini coup" was prepared behind the people's back, behind the Revolution's back. It was meant to be an ambitious and treacherous coup. General Cantillo betrayed us.

The leaders of the coup called on the oldest of the judges of the Supreme Court—he, who until today had been president of the Supreme Court of Justice, where there was no justice of any kind. This Sr. Piedra, who, if he has not yet resigned, should get ready, because we're going to make him resign. I don't think he will last twenty-four hours. It will break a record.

The most criminal act of the Camp Columbia coup was allowing Batista, Tabernilla, and the other master crooks to escape. They let them escape with their millions of pesos, three or four hundred million that they had stolen, and it's going to prove very expensive for us because now they'll be making propaganda against the Revolution from Santo Domingo and other countries.

All the positions and ranks conferred by the military junta at dawn today are null and void, and whoever accepts a position designated by the military junta will be guilty of treason, and it will be considered a sign of a counterrevolutionary attitude.

In the face of this betrayal, we gave orders for all rebel commanders to carry on military operations and to continue marching toward their objectives. Consequently orders have immediately been given for all columns destined for the operations at Santiago de Cuba to advance on the city. Our forces are resolutely determined to take Santiago de Cuba by assault.

As soon as we have achieved that, we will march to the capital with veteran troops from the Sierra Maestra, and their tanks and artillery, in order to consolidate the Revolution.

Che Guevara is marching to the nonprovisional capital* of the republic, and Major Camilo Cienfuegos, chief of Column 2, Antonio Maceo, has received orders to march to the outskirts of Havana and take command of the Camp Columbia military base.

Efigenio Amejeiras has been recommended for the post of chief of the National Police. He has lost three brothers in this battle; he was an expeditionary on the *Granma* and is one of the most capable men in the Revolutionary Army. Amejeiras is involved in the operations at Guantánamo, but tomorrow he will arrive here.

Santiago, January

At last we have reached Santiago. The way there has been long and tough, but we have arrived. Santiago de Cuba has been the most solid bastion of the Revolution. The Revolution begins now.

The Revolution will not be an easy task. The Revolution will be a very difficult undertaking, full of danger. This time, luckily for Cuba, the Revolution will truly come into power. It will not be like 1895, when the North Americans came and made themselves masters of our country; they intervened at the last minute, and afterward, they did not even allow Calixto García to enter—he who had fought for thirty years. They did not want him to enter Santiago de Cuba. It will not be like 1933, when Machado was ousted and the people began to believe that a revolution was taking place, but then Batista took over the reins and instituted a dictatorship lasting eleven years. It will not be like 1944, when the multitudes were fired with the idea that at last the people had come to power, but those who had really come to power were the thieves.

Neither thieves nor traitors, nor meddlers; this time, it will really be the Revolution.

In order to put an end to coups d'état once and for all, freedom must be won through the sacrifice of the people. Because here, the ones who have the final say about who is to govern are the people and no one but the people.

What interests us is not power in itself, but that the Revolution fulfill its destiny, and we are concerned that the master crooks are being

---

* Fidel had designated Santiago de Cuba as the country's provisional capital.—ED.

permitted to escape and go off to foreign countries with their huge fortunes, so as to wreak as much damage as possible to our country from there.

At this moment we must consolidate power before anything else. The first thing to do is to consolidate power. Let the people have confidence in us: this is what we ask because we know how to fulfill our duty. When we were twelve men, we did not lose faith.

The Revolution will not be made in two days, but now I am sure that we are making the Revolution; that for the first time the republic will really be entirely free and the people will have what they deserve. Power has not been the result of politics: it has been the result of the sacrifice of hundreds and thousands of our comrades. There is no commitment except to the people and the Cuban nation. I know that it is the same hope, the same faith shared by an entire people, people who have risen and have patiently endured all sacrifices, even hunger; they richly deserve to achieve the happiness that they have not known in the fifty years of the republic; they richly deserve to become one of the foremost countries of the world.

This war was won by the people. And I say so in case there is any one person who thinks that he has won it alone. Therefore, the people come first of all. But something more: the Revolution is not in my personal interest, nor in the interest of any other major or captain. The Revolution is in the interests of the people. It is the people who win or lose with the Revolution; and it was the people who suffered the horrors of these seven years, and who must decide if in ten, fifteen, or twenty years from now, they, their sons and grandsons are going to continue suffering the horrors that the people of Cuba have suffered under the dictatorships, such as those of Machado and of Batista. Our organization was the first, the one that launched the first battle at Moncada, which landed with the *Granma* in the month of December, and the one who fought alone for more than a year against the tyranny, when there were no more than twelve men keeping the flag of freedom flying. Here, everybody was conspiring: the corporal, the sergeant, etc., until we came along to demonstrate that this was not the real battle, that it had to be otherwise, that tactics had to be invented, and we were the ones who led it most effectively to achieve its ideal, and I want the people to tell me honestly if this is true or not.

There is also another matter. The 26th of July Movement is a majority movement. Is that not so? And how did the struggle end? When the tyranny fell, we had taken all of Oriente, Camagüey, and almost all of Las Villas, Matanzas, and Pinar del Río. The struggle ended with the forces that had reached Las Villas, because we rebels had Major Camilo Cienfuegos and our Major Guevara in Las Villas on the first of January, the day of Cantillo's treachery. Because Camilo Cienfuegos had been ordered to advance on the capital and attack Camp Columbia, and because Major Ernesto Guevara in Las Villas also had been ordered to advance on the capital and take over La Cabaña, every military stronghold of importance remained in the hands of the rebels. And lastly, because it was our strength, experience, and organization that made us win. Does that mean that the others did not fight? No! Does that mean that the others did not have their merits? No! Because we all fought, as the people fought. In Havana, there was no Sierra and yet the general strike was a decisive factor in making the triumph of the Revolution complete. This is the only Revolution in the world from which not one single general emerged. Not one, because the rank I gave myself, I gave to my comrades, the rank of major, and I have not changed it; even though we have won many battles, I want to remain a major. The first thing we who made the Revolution must ask ourselves is what were our aims in making it; whether personal ambition or an ignoble purpose was hidden within any of us.

When I hear talk of columns, combat fronts, troops, it always makes me think. Because our staunchest column, our best troops, the only troops capable of winning the war alone, are the troops of the people.

No general can do more than the people can. No army can do more than the people. I was asked what troops I preferred commanding, and I answered: I prefer leading the people. Because the people are invincible, and it was the people who won the war. Because we did not have an army.

MANUEL FAJARDO

At the end of December we had some mobile columns, as a reserve corps, in the zone of operations in order to cover the army. I had some 130 well-armed men with me.

It had been agreed to leave the zone of operations and form battalions—this was part of the invasion plan for Oriente. I handed over the command of Yateras to a captain, and selected the best group, with which I formed Battalion 18.

I was ordered to replace Efigenio's column, which was close to Guantánamo. The only access to Guantánamo was through Camagüey, and we did not want them either to enter or leave through there.

We went toward "Cecilia," where we were to meet Efigenio, Villa, and Pena, to come to an agreement about the plan of attack on Guantánamo.

When we came to a sugar refinery, the people were already in the streets screaming: "He's gone, Batista's gone!" When I reached "Cecilia," Major Pena and other comrades were there, and I heard the news that Batista had fled.

I stood there with my head down, thoughtful, and a woman asked if the news didn't make me happy. I told her that the battle was going to be much more difficult for us, because before we had been fighting against an enemy face to face, but from now on, it would be against hidden enemies. Besides, the blood of the fallen comrades was still not dry, those men who dreamed about this day and had a thousand plans, and yet had not seen this triumph.

Then Fidel made his speech about continuing to advance on the objectives. We had to attack Guantánamo that night, in any case, and my job was to enter by the San Justo bridge, Pena from the Yateras zone, Efigenio from the Santiago de Cuba zone, and Villa from the Camagüey zone toward Guantánamo.

Guerrilla warfare without the direct help of the peasants is not successful. Peasant help is of fundamental importance in the kind of battle we were carrying out in the Sierra Maestra and on the Second Front.

At the beginning, we went through difficulties, because we did not have direct help from the peasantry. But as soon as we won the trust of the peasantry, and they took direct action in the fight with us, our conditions improved 100 percent. It's not the same for us to go down to the plains to search for food as to have the peasants themselves bring it up to where we are, and it is important to have peasants everywhere keeping watch over the enemy and warning us of their movements.

In the type of war we were involved in, no triumph is possible without direct peasant help. And without the assistance of the urban population, there is also no triumph. The people's involvement was decisive.

EDITOR'S SUMMARY   Holguín, January 3

Castro's "first postvictory interview" was granted to Jules Dubois of the Chicago Tribune, *in Holguín, January 3. It began at 8:30 p.m. and was apparently a wide-ranging, lengthy interview, with many of Castro's soldiers present, as well as Celia Sánchez. Despite the avalanche of unsettled problems he faced, Castro gave Dubois his thoughts on the future of relations with the United States: "If I have had to be very cautious about my statements in the past, from now on I am going to have to be even more careful."*

Dubois, as a veteran journalist and active member of the Inter-American Press Association, brought up the fact that newspapers had not appeared in Havana since January 1, although radio and television had been permitted to continue reporting.

Castro promptly borrowed Dubois's ball-point pen and wrote a decree recognizing the service rendered by the press to the Revolution and its consolidation, and urged that publication be resumed by noon on Sunday, January 4. He also promised to order an end to the general strike as soon as Camilo Cienfuegos was able to report that all the armed services were under his control, "because then the triumph of the Revolution and the first obedience to the civil power of the Revolution will be totally assured."

FIDEL CASTRO

Letter to David Salvador*   January

The triumph of the revolutionary leadership is now assured all over the country. Since Judge Urrutia has taken office as president of the republic, military command, which I represent, is now wholly subordinated to his powers. As full civil powers and liberties are restored in the republic, I request that all workers' leaders and the workers themselves, as well as all the entire working population, put a halt to the Revolutionary General Strike, which culminated in the most beautiful victory of our people.

At this hour of triumph, I bow to the memory of the fallen heroes and offer my heartfelt and profoundest gratitude to the people of Cuba, who are today the pride and shining example of America.

FIDEL CASTRO   Interviewed by Carlos Franqui

When Bob Taber and Wendell Hoffman, North American reporters from CBS, arrived for a television interview, I suggested it be done on El Turquino because, among other things, it might provoke a reaction from the troops of the tyranny, and they would have to pursue us and face the forces of nature up there on El Turquino, and secondly, because it is the highest peak in Cuba. It was the first time we went up. We were encamped in El Joaquín, and we climbed El Turquino this time for the TV interview. The next three times we went up were during military operations, sometimes while retreating, other times when we were pursuing the forces of tyranny.

Our headquarters at that time April 1957—had no fixed base, because we couldn't establish one during those first months. We could only establish a fixed fighting base when we had at least 300 men available to defend it, and that was when the Sierra campaign evolved, when the Rebel Army evolved, when our tactics were perfected, when we managed to increase our forces. Only then were we able to establish this fixed base, which was at the root of the failure of the strike in April 1958, when we knew after the strike that they were going to attack us with all their forces. As we then had three hundred rifles at our disposal, by joining together almost all the forces we had in Oriente, we opened the Second Front. Raúl was there, and we now knew the terrain better. There were many of these places, for example, where columns had gone through; they had mounted approximately five offensives against us. Afterward I would analyze the places where they had crossed, and since

---

* Workers' leader of the 26th of July and of the CTC.—C. F.

this army followed habitual patterns and really did not change its habits, I studied their habits, the paths, and lookout points. Then, I remember that when I had a hundred men, at the most, I said, "When we have two hundred or three hundred men, those people will never cross here again." That is, when we'd have sufficient forces, we'd be able to change the course of the war. . . . The war was first a war of guerrillas, then of columns, and finally of positions; that is, we established a front and defended it when we could count on three hundred men.

And so, we eventually established a fixed base in the month of April 1958, and it lasted till the end of the war.

During recent years, after the great wars of 1914 and the last World War, with the improvements in modern arms and resources available to armies, the use of aircraft, artillery, radio, etc., almost everyone agreed that guerrilla warfare was no longer possible. Among other things, it seemed much more difficult in Cuba, because Cuba is an island without frontiers. Frequently in this type of war, help has arrived across frontiers, even troop movements back and forth are possible. For instance, troops could retreat behind the frontiers of a friendly country and then, later, return to their territory for further combat. We lacked, for example, the advantage of frontiers, and we were totally isolated, that is, there was no retreat for us, nor was there any possibility of receiving aid by land. In other words, the conditions of guerrilla warfare in one of the most difficult settings imaginable was in Cuba.

I think ours was almost a unique case of guerrilla warfare. We fought a guerrilla war under the worst conditions possible. That is, territory in Cuba for this kind of warfare is extremely limited; the Sierra Maestra is only a corner of Oriente Province, and besides, with the plains facing the Sierra Maestra, we were surrounded by air, sea, and land, which is to say that jungle conditions, often present in other Latin American countries, did not exist here. Not having frontiers, because this is an island; few mountains, because our country isn't really mountainous; few forests, because in reality, there aren't many forests in Cuba; and then, no frontiers. The worst military conditions for guerrilla warfare and yet, virtually without any outside help, with the strength of our own guerrilla forces, the Rebel Army continued to grow until columns were organized, and after the columns, there were positions. It was almost only in the first months that we fought a guerrilla war, in which we struck a blow and withdrew, we struck a blow and we stayed; after, there were more columns, and still later, it was a war of positions, and still later occupation of territory. Because with only eight hundred men, we began the counteroffensive from Oriente to Las Villas—only eight hundred men! That is, we had three hundred men when they began to attack in the month of April and we ended that battle with eight hundred armed men, because more than five hundred weapons were seized, and with these five hundred weapons, we began the counteroffensive, and in five months, Batista's army was virtually wiped out.

That means that guerrilla warfare, given the right political conditions, is invincible. Do you understand? Naturally, that means that guerrilla leaders must use correct military tactics; if they don't then they really fail. Two conditions are necessary: to defend, in the first place, a just national cause, seeking social justice and national liberation; second, to employ correct military tactics. And it was precisely under these conditions that guerrilla warfare was waged in Cuba; it was the most difficult kind of guerrilla war to fight, yet victory was achieved. In any other setting, with the same political conditions as ours, guerrilla warfare is invincible. Well, they begin by being guerrilla wars, and later they become wars of columns, and end up by being wars of positions and the battle is over the occupation of the country's territory.

Guerrilla wars are difficult: destroying small, dispersed nuclei requires a great deal of effort, because frontal encounters are avoided. It requires a great deal of work, as well as the use of many men. No professional army in any of the Americas could conquer the forces of revolutionary guerrillas, no matter which country in America it might be.

No professional army in America would have the force to counter the activities of revolutionary guerrillas.

We fought without other weapons than those we seized from the enemy in every battle waged in this cruel war, against a large army, well armed with tanks, cannons, airplanes, and modern weapons. They said an army of seventy thousand men was invincible, but even though our people were defenseless against 500-lb. bombs hurled from airplanes, we achieved a fantastic victory.

Without training, without war tactics, we managed to beat that army, which they wanted to make us believe was invincible.

It was said that a revolution against the army was impossible and that only a revolution within the army itself would succeed.

All these concepts were shattered. All the lies that they had invented to keep the people subjected were shattered.

And the tanks and planes are now in our hands.

We have lived for some time under great emotional stress; we have become somewhat accustomed to exceptional circumstances. Also, for example, from the time we left Mexico, the crossing, the landing, when we landed in the swamp—I thought it was a shoal until we finally discovered it wasn't. It took a lot of effort to get out of there; the first reverses, leaving me with two men and two guns for almost two weeks, trying to re-establish contact, and regroup the first fighters, look for the weapons that had been lost, all the vicissitudes of battle; the first victories—from the smallest to the biggest—from the battle of La Plata to scarcely six months ago, when we were obliged to battle against fourteen battalions of rather well-armed infantry men, and we had only three hundred men and five thousand rounds in reserve.

For two years and thirty days we have been living through all sorts of emotional moments. Naturally, the first of January was also a terrible day. We were betrayed, and an attempt was made to snatch victory from the people. We had to act very swiftly. The military junta in Camp Columbia attempted a counterrevolutionary coup, in order to avoid the inevitable. If it had lasted two weeks longer, we would have taken all of them prisoner. At that time, we had ten thousand soldiers cornered in Oriente Province; we were about to attack Santiago, when Cantillo came along with his proposals. I, for one, thought—analyzing the situation coldly—that it would be best not to accept any kind of help because the war was already won, yet when one makes such calculations, it is essential to consider whether the same objective can be achieved without shedding another drop of blood. But the deaths of the men who fell at the end of the war cause me the greatest sadness, men dying after they had survived all the dangers of countless battles. After a victorious battle, there is always tremendous sadness because one thinks about those who did not live to see the fruits of victory.

This happened to some of our commanders, to Major Cuevas, during the battle of El Jigüe, a few hours before it became our first victory, because it involved more than three hundred enemy casualties and two hundred sixty weapons seized. It was a battle that lasted ten days. And this comrade, who had been one of its heroes, did not survive and could not see the victory. It happened to Major Daniel [René Ramos Latour] and Major Paz; it also happened to another comrade, Major Coroneaux, who was the hero of the battle of Guisa, which lasted ten days and was the fiercest battle we ever fought.

We began the combat at El Jigüe with a hundred and twenty men, and we fought against two battalions. Each one of our men exacted three casualties from the dictatorship. The battle of Guisa was waged at the gates of Bayamo, against all those Sherman tanks, and we had no artillery, we had nothing, and yet two hundred and twenty men fought against three thousand. This is what happened in these combats: We began fighting with a fixed number of men, but as the days passed, we had more and more rifles, because each time the enemy suffered a reverse, we took twenty or thirty rifles.

Our advance from Guisa to Santiago de Cuba was a continuous battle along the Central Highway. They had said that we were in the Sierra because we could control the situation there. And yet, we fought against troops in the middle of the Central Highway, against troops from Bayamo and all the garrisons between Bayamo and Santiago de Cuba. And once we were in control of the highway, they couldn't get a square inch of it back.

In those days, we took more than seven hundred weapons, and the forces of Column 1 and also Column 3 caused more than a thousand casualties. It was no longer a matter of columns; all our troops were working together: those situated at one position backed up the others to prevent the reinforcements from arriving. That was when the battle of Santa Clara was under way. After the battles in Guisa, I contacted Major Ernesto Guevara, who was our commander in that province, and informed him (because he knew the plans) that we were going to advance on Santiago. And that was very important; when he left the Sierra Maestra, the strategic objective of the advance of the columns as far as Santa Clara was exactly that of supporting us when we advanced on the capital.

It was a plan that was made and executed with such precision that Batista fell practically on the day we thought he would fall, and Santiago de Cuba was taken more or less on the day that we thought we would take it.

They attempted to snatch the triumph from us, and if there hadn't been swift action, the consequences would have been serious.

Constantly in dread of this danger, I had repeatedly said that we would not accept a military junta and that our conditions, should we reach an agreement with a military movement run by the military, were that they had not been involved with the crimes, immorality, thievery, vice, and all the other depraved acts of the regime.

I was in the América sugar mill, preparing troops to advance to Santiago, when I was told that Radio Progreso had announced Batista's departure. Of course, it didn't come as a total surprise, because the day before I had sent him an ultimatum saying that hostilities would resume, and I had sent it to the garrison at Santiago de Cuba so it could reach Cantillo.

I was aware of Cantillo's betrayal about twenty-four hours before December 31, at 3:00 p.m., the date and the hour designated to begin the joint action, along with their unconditional support—because any other kind of support offered to the Revolution was unacceptable. And realizing this, I immediately wrote him, and some of our letters crossed. I later read them on the radio—documents that absolutely prove Cantillo's betrayal.

In the ultimatum, I told him that when this hour had passed—3:00 p.m. on December 31—we would advance on Santiago. A very tough battle would have been waged in Santiago de Cuba, because there were about five thousand soldiers there, artillery, tanks. We were accustomed to fighting against all this, and besides, I was sure that we would take Santiago; the plan was already drawn up, and the tactics that we were going to use seemed almost infallible. Cannons were already being set up at the entrance to Santiago harbor, in order to cut off communications by sea. We were going to use cannons from tanks that we had destroyed;

all the rest we had manufactured. I would say that not even the famous Krupp factories turned out better cannons than our armorers. The mortars were being emplaced against the airport, and we had an enormous supply of mines that we were going to place between the airport and the city. The scheme was to cut off communications first—that was how our plan was designed: take the airport and block the harbor. We also had means of sinking a boat there, but that could have provoked an international incident and the loss of many, many millions. The cannons were going to be placed three hundred yards from where the ships had to pass. The troops were occupying their positions; first we were going to strike the advance posts they held near Santiago de Cuba.

And that's what we were doing when in the morning they told me that Radio Progreso had announced that Batista had fled to Santo Domingo. But so many lies are spread that there are times when someone hears something (and when it's news, one usually hears about it right away), and the first thing to do is to try to verify it.

In a half an hour, it was confirmed that Batista had fled, and that there was a junta, and that Carlos Manuel Piedra was president. Immediately, without wasting a second, I drew up declarations. In less than an hour I had drawn them up and left for Palma, where our mobile transmitter, Radio Rebelde, was located. It was then that we announced that a very suspicious coup had taken place and that it was unacceptable to us; it was then that I ordered the columns to advance on the towns, to attack, and to permit no respite unless it was to surrender.

I contacted Major Camilo Cienfuegos, and ordered him to advance immediately and take Yaguajay: within two hours at the latest he had to have his men on the march to the capital. And, quite easily, he took Camp Columbia.

I gave Camilo the following order: that he march with five hundred men, armed with automatic weapons, take Camp Columbia, and that he contact me again when he was there. Then I told Che, who was winding up the battle at Santa Clara—two hundred soldiers were still holding out—not to worry about them, to leave some troops there to maintain the encirclement, and to advance, immediately also, to back up Camilo; that Camilo was going to take Camp Columbia and he was to take La Cabaña. We immediately moved our troops to Santiago de Cuba.

Santiago had to be attacked in any case that very day, because otherwise the coup might be consolidated. Around two in the afternoon, I was very worried by the news coming in from Havana; the international press might be misinformed, public opinion might be confused. But my proclamation had already been read over CMQ and Radio Progreso; and besides, I immediately met with the comrades from the directorate of the 26th of July Movement, and we agreed to give the order for a general strike to begin on the following day—except in Santiago, where it would begin at 3:00 p.m., and we gave the city an ultimatum: if they didn't lay down their arms, we would attack at 6:00 p.m.

When I was moving on Santiago, I was very thankful because I heard on the radio that the people were jubilant, that flags of the Movement were flying in the streets, and the women were dressed in red and black, as a sign of triumph, for the triumph of the leader of the Revolution, for the triumph of Fidel Castro.

I said: But how will the triumph be for my men, since there are five thousand soldiers in this city? A very curious situation was shaping up; but actually, the garrison of Santiago de Cuba, which was headed by Colonel Rego Rubido—of whom I hold a very high opinion, as sometimes one knows one's adversaries better than one's friends, and he is an honorable soldier and a brave man—could have put up some resistance. We had already been in communication: I had told him the day before what Cantillo and I had agreed on, and what Cantillo was now up to. Then Rego Rubido's decision was to make contact with us.

Also, the navy was similarly disposed: the frigate *Maceo* contacted us and said that it placed itself unconditionally under our orders, the frigate *Máximo Gómez* immediately seconded this; police headquarters in Santiago said it supported us, and at the same time, the chief of the garrison flew in a helicopter to Palma to find me. He could not find me because we were continuing to advance on Santiago, and we were preparing the attack. As soon as we made contact with a captain situated in El Caney, we contacted Colonel Rego Rubido, and we had a discussion. Then I told him that I wanted to meet with all the officers of the garrison, and he said I was right, and that he would speak to them in terms relevant to what was best for the republic and for them. And so, in fact, the meeting was held at 7:00 p.m. I told them that Cantillo had come to speak to me in the name of the army. But what he had done was to betray me right from the start, and had also betrayed the soldiers, because he had acted on his own, had not consulted any of them. I said that I didn't want a coup, but wanted to meet with all the officers and, if need be, with all the soldiers, too, in order to speak to all the soldiers. That this was no conspiracy, that it was a democratic decision, that the generals didn't have the right to decide on this; normally, a soldier has to carry out orders and obey, but when there are questions as vital and fundamental as these to work out, to decide on the attitude and position of an army at a historic moment, the officers must be consulted.

And I also told my family, using other words: "Look we caught them off base—baseball language—between first and second, they didn't make it to home. . . ."

The history of these two years of fighting is the history of a series of errors on the part of our enemies; they underestimated the adversary. They thought they were going to pull the wool over the people's eyes, and they found that the Revolution became much stronger because of their betrayal than it would have been without it. I don't know if this man thought we were going to sit back with our arms crossed; we had scarcely begun to take basic measures to deal with the situation when, in less than ten hours, it was entirely under control; an extraordinary event has taken place in Cuba.

I had often thought that revolutions had to be carried out in two stages, that the first stage would consist of achieving part of the victory and that, later, new clashes would arise. But a revolution has taken place in one fell swoop, all the enemy troops have been disarmed in a matter of hours. The troops weren't really disarmed; rather, they really offered us their support at that moment of confusion, and besides, I count on those troops. Yesterday, I met with two thousand soldiers who were in Bayamo, and their enthusiasm was the same as that in the crowds; because, among other reasons, they had been abandoned to their own fate, to our mercy, in a certain sense. The circumstance of having backed us up worked in their behalf, and as far as we're concerned, they deserve every consideration. And later, young people, career officers, who were there, showed such enormous attachment to us that I have absolute confidence in those troops. In Bayamo, we have fourteen companies and in Santiago de Cuba, we also have a great many troops. At this moment we can count on thirty army companies ready for action and I am thinking of taking several units from the army.

When I began to hear broadcasters speaking freely, when everyone was suddenly in the streets, I realized that the regime was totally demolished, that the Revolution had triumphed; that was what had been missing. The service provided by the radio was extraordinarily useful in the final battle, which was the last victory of the Revolution, a victory in which not only military combatants participated but also the people, laborers, the working classes, the press.

It's absurd not to concern ourselves about the people; we have to be very concerned. I had a meeting with Camilo yesterday at dawn, and I was waiting for the results of the instructions given him simply to assume control over all military forces, and I was waiting for his answer that I have now received: "Confirm that all military installations in the country are totally in the hands of revolutionary authority." And then Dr. Urrutia took over yesterday. He named a cabinet, the Revolution has really triumphed, and this very afternoon, I am eager to inform the workers and their leaders that the strike should cease.

I want to do what I say, and until now I have done it: I said that on such and such a day I would do such and such, and I did it on that day. I once said, in 1956, that I would come if Batista did not resign within two weeks, and we were in Cuba two weeks later. I think I keep my word.

Although dictatorships can't hold out against anyone, there is no

one who can hold out against the people. And the people are on their
way and I must go with them; that's why I can't really set the day, it
depends on the people. I hope that with the cooperation of the people,
we will reach Havana on Wednesday. You must also understand that
our men are making an extraordinary effort, they are going in trucks;
there are no comforts; they travel hours and hours at a very slow pace,
long hours on their feet. And we have all gone for days on end without
sleep, I think we've learned not to sleep.

But I hope that our men will rest at some point at least. It's easy to
understand their joy at going to Havana. Almost all of them are peasants from the Sierra Maestra, and they visualize Havana as the realization of their dreams. And they are enthusiastic—that's why they can
stand all that; they're piled into trucks, uncomfortable, but no one com-
plains. And, besides, it takes a tremendous effort to keep going, to keep
order in the column, because automobiles are parked everywhere, people are everywhere, and I think it's just as well that we don't have to
fight, because if I had to order a mortar to shoot, a journalist would
shoot off his flash bulb instead. . . . I don't know if the person next to me
is a soldier, a rebel, a journalist; I no longer know who is manning the
cannon or driving the tank. I just don't know. . . . Everything is completely mixed up.

CARLOS FRANQUI

On December 31, the end of the year, we met in the house of some comrades from Palma Soriano, with some of the Santiago revolutionaries in
attendance. It was the first time during the war that I slept in a bed in a
hotel. We had installed Radio Rebelde in the broadcasting station at
Palma. I went to sleep January 1 about 3:00 a.m., and awoke at dawn as
usual, peasant style. I began to walk along the streets toward the radio
station. I kept walking. I heard voices and I realized that something important was happening. I asked and was told that it had been announced on the radio that Batista had fled. I hurried to Radio Rebelde,
and there, with the help of a technician and other comrades, I tried to
make radio contact with Havana. Minutes later we had it, and we spoke
with Vicente Baez, one of the leaders of the 26th of July in the capital,
who had seized several radio and TV stations with the help of our militia. Vicente confirmed Batista's flight and General Cantillo's attempt to
create a military junta.

It was almost nightfall when we went into Santiago de Cuba. The
encounter with the people was indescribable. The columns of bearded
rebels were literally swept off their feet by the overjoyed people. It was
the hour of freedom after a long tyranny and a very tough fight.

We installed Radio Rebelde in the CMKC station in Santiago de

Cuba. From there, we made contact with the entire country. Among the voices heard on the air was one called Columbia Rebelde. It turned out to be Armando Hart and Mario Hidalgo, leaders of the 26th of July, who had been freed from the Isle of Pines prison and were at the Camp Columbia military base. I told Hidalgo that Cantillo was a traitor. Hidalgo answered: "Cantillo's here beside me." I thought that would be the end of Hidalgo because there were twenty thousand soldiers at Camp Columbia and fewer than twenty revolutionaries.

A little later there was new radio contact; the person in charge was not Cantillo but Colonel Barquín, chief of the so-called pure military personnel, who had been imprisoned on the Isle of Pines after his April 1956 conspiracy failed. Barquín had now taken command of the army and was giving orders to the police; but as a prestigious figure of the opposition, he could be potentially dangerous to the revolutionary triumph. At midnight Fidel reached the station. Barquín repeatedly asked to speak to him. Fidel refused.

A little later, it was Armando Hart who called from Columbia. Fidel said to me: "Tell Hart that if he wants to talk to me, he has to leave Columbia." And as Barquín insisted, Fidel told me to ask Barquín if he wanted to speak to me.

I took the speaker and said: "Colonel Barquín, Major Fidel Castro cannot talk to you. If you wish to speak to me, I am Carlos Franqui, director of Radio Rebelde and a member of the Directorate of the 26th of July."

Barquín said that he did and he asked me what I wanted to tell him. I said: "One single thing, Colonel Barquín. Turn over the base at Columbia to Major Camilo Cienfuegos and La Cabaña to Major Che Guevera; they are advancing there on Fidel's orders."

Barquín answered, ironically, that if I wanted, he would turn over the base immediately. I replied that I was sorry not to be able to take it over the radio, but not to worry, because Camilo and Che would be there shortly. Barquín wanted to turn over Columbia to Hart, and I don't know why Hart did not agree. It would have been truly extraordinary for an unarmed civilian to take Columbia, with its thousands of soldiers. In fact, Columbia was already taken. A few hours later Camilo arrived. Che, carrying out orders, went to La Cabaña.

I remember pondering at length the reasons for this order of Fidel's: Camp Columbia was the heart and soul of the tyranny and of military power; La Cabaña was a secondary post. Che had taken the armored train and the city of Santa Clara, he was the second most prominent figure of the Revolution. Camilo was an extraordinary warrior, second only to Che in the province, and he had had to wage a furious combat against the Yaguajay barracks, sixty-odd miles farther away from Havana than Santa Clara. Che was the most obvious candidate to take

Columbia. What reasons did Fidel have for sending him to La Cabaña, a secondary position?

On January 2, at the University of Santiago, Urrutia was proclaimed president, and that night Fidel made a speech in which he said: "Now the Revolution is a reality."

The situation was still confused. To nullify the coup in Havana, Fidel declared Santiago the capital of Cuba and named Colonel Rego Rubido, chief of Moncada, head of the army; Colonel Izquierdo, chief of police in Santiago, head of the national police. Before that, Majors Raúl Castro, Hubert Matos, and Maro had gone into the Moncada Barracks, and later Fidel himself, and they had convinced the Santiago garrison and their leaders to join the Revolution. I remember that while Urrutia was being proclaimed president at the University of Santiago, the students and people screamed: "Izquierdo assassin!" Izquierdo, who had led the repression in Santiago de Cuba as chief of police, was shot three days later.

Urrutia, who had the mentality of a municipal judge, did not know what to do, and among the bizarre things that occurred to him was to keep two armies: the Rebel Army and Batista's. With some difficulty, we convinced him of the absurdity of that, and in a minute, by radio, we named the ministers of the new government, with the exception of the prime minister and the ministers of the interior, public works, agriculture, and education, whom Fidel had told me to leave to him to designate later. Raúl Castro was named minister of defense. Urrutia selected only one minister, the minister of justice. Luis Buch was named to head the treasury. The minister of foreign affairs was the Ortodoxo Agramonte. The rest we named. I remember that the ministry for the Recovery of Illegally Acquired Property was created by my writing a name on a note and ordering the radio announcer to read it out. The people who were there gave an enormous ovation in favor of this ministry, which was going to be the first revolutionary instrument of the new government, as well as to the minister of recovery, Faustino Pérez. Urrutia asked that no one ministry or minister be singled out for applause but, rather, all of them be applauded together. In reality, this was a radiophonic government. Later, Fidel named Hart, Ray, Sorí Marín, and Luis Orlando Rodríguez, and he surprised everyone by choosing as prime minister Dr. José Miró Cardona, who was the secretary of the Civic Opposition Front.

Miró Cardona's designation was a bombshell. He was president of the Havana Bar Association, the representative of great capitalistic enterprises, and one of Cuba's most pro-North American politicians. Years before, he had defended the biggest thief among Cuban presidents, in the celebrated case of Grau San Martín, who had stolen 84 million pesos. He had defended Captain Casilla, the murderer of the black sugar workers' leader, Jesús Menéndez, who was a well-known Communist. We did not understand Fidel's choice. It was understood by those whom Fidel wanted to understand it. It was actually an intelligent move, which confused the North Americans, the bourgeoisie, and the politicians. Miró Cardona was prime minister for only forty-five days. On February 16 he was replaced by Fidel Castro himself. Fidel separated himself from the government and set out on his spectacular march from Oriente to Havana, taking all the barracks, designating three mayors for each city, speaking to the people at huge rallies, consolidating military and political power. In Santiago, we published the first issue of *Revolución,* which had been the underground organ of the 26th of July. But that very evening, Raúl Castro took military control of the newspaper, fired Euclides Vázquez Candelas, and replaced him with one of his trusted men, José Causse. Fidel had wanted me to be minister of labor, but I rejected the post, making it clear that I was of no use as a bargainer between bosses and workers, and that if it was a matter of socializing the factories and putting an end to capitalists, then I would accept with great pleasure, but that this did not seem to be the case. Paradoxically, it was I who had Fidel's confidence in naming ministers and deciding many things, but I was not able to convince him that my function and desires were to stimulate culture, to create a real cultural revolution, without establishing bureaucratic organizations. There was only one way to fight for the ideas I thought just. We were a very heterogeneous movement. Each one had his own ideas, sometimes quite at variance from those of others. As far as the majority of the 26th of July Movement was concerned, I was a Communist. To the Communists, I was a leftist opponent, which is the worst. To Raúl, I was the same. To be sure, I fought for a free, humane, and revolutionary socialism, neither of Soviet nor bureaucratic style.

I went through Camagüey, and there I saw Fidel with his column, spoke with him, and took a plane for Havana, where I arrived on January 4. The gloomy Camp Columbia, mother of the tyranny and of crime, which I had known as a prisoner, was now almost a picturesque theater, impossible to imagine. On the one hand, the bearded rebels with Camilo, no more than five hundred of them, and on the other hand, twenty thousand army soldiers intact—generals, colonels, majors, captains, corporals, sergeants, and privates. When they saw us walk by, they stood at attention. It was enough to make you burst out laughing. In the commandant's office was Camilo, with his romantic beard, looking like Christ on a spree, his boots thrown on the floor and his feet up on the table, as he received his excellency the ambassador of the United States.

Afterward Che arrived with his bohemian getup, his pipe in his mouth, and his air of a revolutionary prophet. There were difficulties at the Presidential Palace. The Revolutionary Directory had installed themselves there. Che had not found Faure Chomón, and Rolando Cubelas had not wanted to receive him. The Directory had attacked the Presidential Palace on March 13, 1957, and, sentimentally, felt that it was a bit theirs. On the other hand, the Directory never got along with Urrutia and they were right about that. There was no lack of suspicion, intrigue, and other differences on either side.*

We had now been without a government for a week, and the country could not go on in this fashion. Urrutia was the president and the Presidential Palace was the seat of the government.

Camilo, half joking and half serious, said a couple of cannonballs should be fired off as a warning to Cubelas, in case he wouldn't give up the palace. As I was not an admirer of the palace, I said it seemed a good idea, but Che, with his sense of responsibility, told us it wasn't the right time to waste cannonballs, and he patiently returned to the palace, met Faure Chomón, and matters were straightened out. Camilo always listened to Che.

On the eighth, Fidel arrived. The entire population of Havana was in the streets to receive him and accompany him to the Presidential Palace and Camp Columbia, where Fidel, with an improvised dove of peace on his right shoulder and Camilo's beard on his left, made his well-known speech: "Arms, what for? This Revolution was won by the people and not by any major," and he finished with the famous "Am I doing okay, Camilo?"

In contrast to Cantillo, who betrayed the agreement with the Rebel Army, let Batista escape, and tried to frustrate the Revolution with a new military coup, Ramón Barquín, who, in spite of his ideas, was anti-Batista, created no difficulties, and from the moment of the initial radio conversation, he accepted Fidel's instructions. His group was merged into the new army, and he was sent on a technical military mission to Europe.

The conduct of the people was admirable. There was not a single act of vandalism, looting, or robbery. No government thug was killed, thousands of dollars found in various places were turned over to the state, there was perfect order. The people had been told that justice would be done, real justice. And so it was.

The Cuban people gave a demonstration of their revolutionary ability. They showed that their moral and civic reserves were intact, despite the difficulties they had gone through. In order to understand the signif-

---

* Troops from the Directory had fought with Che's troops when he took Las Placetas, Santa Clara, and other cities in Las Villas; Cubelas, though wounded, led the 31st Squadron attack in Santa Clara. Chomón had taken Trinidad. During the advance on Havana, Fidel ordered Che to march only with the troops from the 26th. The Directory then took the Presidential Palace and the University of Havana.—C. F.

icance of the strike, one has to remember that when General Cantillo attempted the military coup—with the support of the always powerful U.S. embassy, the Supreme Court, the well-to-do and wealthy classes, the old politicians, the Church, the traditional press, and the conservative sectors of the country—he also had the army, police, and repressive corps of the tyranny at Camp Columbia, and they could count on several tens of thousands of men in possession of all kinds of weapons, while the Rebel Army and the people's militias throughout the country could not count on more than five thousand armed men, a good part of them armed only with pistols.

The strength of the strike was a decisive factor in psychologically disarming the army. As had been the people's action when great numbers refused to turn out for the vote in the November 3, 1958, elections. The general strike was the instrument of their victory. And the 26th of July Movement all over the country was the backbone of the triumph.

And Fidel the unquestioned leader.

NOTES

CARLOS FRANQUI

The university: The university—in Havana and Santiago—was the laboratory, the home, and the mother of the insurrection.

Struggle was traditional: against Machado and Batista, from 1925 to 1944. For nationalism (the ouster of the imperialists), socialism and its heroes—Mella, Martínez Villena, Guiteras, Chibás—who established the revolutionary government of 1933–34.

Like other European and Latin American universities, the university in Cuba was by tradition an autonomous enclave, whose precincts government security forces were forbidden to enter; it had extraterritorial immunity somewhat like that possessed by churches and foreign embassies. This autonomy facilitated contacts, meetings, the formation of groups, an underground press, conspiracies, target practice, a youthful vanguard, fuel for the struggle. The universities also assumed importance because of the ineffectiveness of other opposition groups—the legal parties, Communists, bureaucratized labor unions, and others—against Batista.

From the universities—and from the secondary schools—the vanguard took to the streets and to the people, inciting them to join the struggle, to combat the police. Innumerable militant demonstrations had their origins in the university, from 1952 to 1956.

On January 15, 1953, a demonstration was organized to protest the desecration of Mella's bust; Rubén Batista Rubio was wounded in the course of this demonstration and died a few days later, becoming the first martyr in the struggle against Batista.

These demonstrations created the right conditions for the struggle, showed the true nature of the tyranny, and forged the basis of a unity between the university and the masses, between the students, the youth, and the people.

But these demonstrations had their limitations. We could not overthrow the tyranny with demonstrations, nor could we do so from the university. It would cost too much in blood and the arrests would expose our forces to easy identification by the police—who ultimately violated the university's autonomy.

Two attempts at other kinds of political action showed the ineffectiveness of such means: one was the forging of a union between the students and military conspirators; the other was to wait—armed with the weapons sent from Miami to the Prío Socarras followers—for the "zero hour," which never came.

Zero Hour: This was the watchword of the Auténtico groups of ex-President Prío Socarras and of his minister Aureliano Sánchez Arango, who, recalling Normandy, announced at every turn during the years 1952–1955 that a landing of armed men would take place from the United States. It never did take place, despite their enormous resources and the countless weapons they sent into Cuba through the underground. Meanwhile, in Santiago, Frank País, with a group of young people, attacked some small barracks, as Guiteras had done in the fight against Machado.

The organization of the 26th of July Movement, together with the attack against the Moncada Barracks and the Bayamo Barracks, led by Fidel Castro, represented a qualitative leap forward in our struggle. These actions gave rise to the strategy, the impetus, the leadership, as well as the libertarian and anti-imperialist ideology needed by the youth in the vanguard and by the people as protagonist in the victorious struggle against the tyranny.

The university—with José Antonio Echeverría, the president of the FEU, the Federation of University Students—also made its qualitative leap by creating the Revolutionary Directory, which was to participate actively in the sugar strike in December 1955, and which would give a continent-wide dimension to the struggle when it brought in the Latin American student organizations. In September 1956 the Mexico City Pact was signed by Fidel and Echeverría, and major attacks and other actions were carried out at the end of that year, and then, in March 1957, the extraordinary attack on the Presidential Palace took place. In 1958 came the landing of the expedition under Faure Chomón's command and the creation of a guerrilla front in the Escambray.

If the 26th of July Movement was the principal organization in the fight against Batista, the Revolutionary Directory was the next most important. It carried out spectacular actions that affected the entire country and led to the death of Echeverría and about 90 percent of its leadership, and contributed tremendously to the victory of the insurrection.

Underground Action: The 26th of July organized and fought in an underground struggle in the 126 municipalities of Cuba, from the large cities to the smallest towns, in the fields and plains, where our snipers harassed the rural guard and the police, and where they committed acts of sabotage and set fire to the sugarcane fields. Because the struggle was used in every part of the country, the regime was paralyzed, the regular army demoralized, and the participation and confidence of the populace in our victory greatly enhanced.

Lacking sufficient arms, dynamite, and explosives, the thousands of underground fighters made use of simple but effective sabotage. The principal act of sabotage was to throw metallic chains across electric circuits, thus causing blackouts and paralyzing factories and cities because of the lack of electricity.

Constant activities were: setting fire to sugarcane fields and warehouses, cutting telephone lines, throwing Molotov cocktails, smashing aqueduct conduits, firing on small barracks, and attacking soldiers and police with knives in order to seize their weapons.

Informers were executed and their rifles and pistols seized.

These anonymous actions, collective and clandestine, which occurred daily, were not officially recorded. Consider that on a single night, November 8, 1957, the Action and Sabotage Section led by Aldo Vera and Sergio González set off a hundred bombs. The militia in Santiago de Cuba, led by Frank País and "Daniel" [René Ramos Latour] carried out more than a thousand acts of sabotage, attacks, and other underground activity. Some weeks, more than five hundred acts of sabotage were reported in the anti-Batista press—*Bohemia, Prensa Libre*—which were free to speak out because there was no censorship at that time.

The minimum tally showed more than thirty thousand acts of sabotage up to the time of Batista's fall.

The Revolutionary Directory: There were four stages in the work of the Revolutionary Directory. 1955: foundation and sugar strike; 1956: underground attacks and actions; 1957: attack on the Presidential Palace; 1958: exile, landing, and establishment of the guerrilla front in the Escambray.

The Second Eastern Front, Phase 1:   To extend the guerrilla war to the fields and mountains of Oriente, in conjunction with the struggle in the cities, was urged by Frank País, René Ramos Latour, and the 26th of July Movement in Santiago and Guantánamo.

Simultaneously, with the opening of the First Front in the Sierra, where Fidel was operating, some comrades in the militia who had taken part in the battles November 30, 1956, at Santiago and Ermita, went into action on the neighboring mountains.

The first objective was to reinforce and consolidate Fidel's position in the Sierra. That fundamental task took almost a year and involved some of our best men and weapons from the Oriente front; meanwhile, sending armed relief to the Sierra and carrying out the underground struggle in the cities.

The strategy prevented Batista from concentrating his forces against a single point and wiping it out. It would have been a fatal error to have divided our small guerrilla forces—an error that Frank did not commit; the opening of the Second Front awaited an opportune moment.

The Second Front developed slowly, with ups and downs. After the death of Frank País on July 30, 1957, Fidel took a critical attitude toward the underground movement and also toward the Second Front, which the Movement never abandoned.

At the beginning of 1958, there were about a thousand men with shotguns and rifles, as well as three well-organized guerrilla units ready for combat on the Second Front.

When Raúl Castro, with his Column 6, Frank País, composed of some eighty veterans from the Sierra Maestra, reached the Second Front region, where Fidel had sent him at the beginning of March 1958, a month before the April strike, he found an organized guerrilla front: four guerrilla units, regulars who had already captured barracks, more than a thousand riflemen in organized formation, and a countryside ready to support the Movement and the insurrection.

Raúl's column reinforced the Second Front and made it possible for the Rebel Army and Fidel to control the forces that the Movement had already brought together in rebellion.

Frank País Second Front, Phase 2: The arrival of Column 6, Frank País, constituted a qualitative leap forward in the war. Raúl reorganized his forces into various companies (they would later be columns), under the command of his officers from the Sierra—Efigenio Amejeiras, Manuel Fajardo, Ciro Frías, Gilberto Cordero, Félix Pena—and those already operating there: Tomasevich, Villa, Totó, Aníbal, Lussón.

The most important battles waged during the time of the April Strike were Nicaro, Mayarí Arriba, Moa, Imías (where Ciro Frías died), Jamaica, Caimanera, Soledad, Yateritas, San Ramón de las Yaguas. The riflemen were distributed throughout the fourteen municipalities of the Second Front terrain, half of it in Oriente Province. Raúl could count on nearly three hundred regular guerrillas and a thousand riflemen, the same number as Fidel had in the Sierra.

In May, Batista's army launched an offensive against both the

Sierra and the Second Front simultaneously. The thirteenth of May, fighting raged north of the Sagua de Tánamo zone, and on the twenty-eighth, south of Lima.

While the guerrillas under Lussón captured the barracks at Las Minas de Ocujal in Nicaro, Fajardo took the waterworks of Guaso, which supplied the North American naval base at Guantánamo. Meanwhile, Raúl Castro was fighting a week-long battle in the zone of La Lima. In June the enemy intensified its offensive. Fighting at La Lima, Cupeyal, La Guanábana, El Dajao, San Antonio, Limonar, La Juba, La Escondida, Zanja de Mayarí, Imías, Santa Ana, where the rebels took the barracks, Cayo Mambí, Sagua, Songa, La Maya, Caujerí, Guantánamo, Baltony.

Batista's air force bombed the Second Front's zone, razing fields and villages, and causing numerous victims among the civilian population.

Batista's planes carried rockets and napalm from the North American base at Guantánamo—despite the arms embargo decreed in March by the U.S. government—and the planes took off from the base to bomb the agricultural zones directly.

On May 22 Raúl Castro made a historic decision: "The anti-aerial operation, Military Order Number 30," in which he decreed the detention of all North American citizens residing in the Second Front zone. Twenty-nine American Marines from the Guantánamo base were imprisoned, along with ten technicians from the Moa Bay mine, as well as functionaries of the United Fruit Company at Nicaro and Caimanera.

Raúl gains precious time.

The Second Front's weapons and ammunition supply is re-established and the enemy is harassed. The enemy offensive comes to an end.

Second Front, Phase 3:   In August Raúl organizes columns of regulars that operated in the following zones: Guantánamo, Songo, San Luis, Yateras, Baracoa, Sagua, Mayarí, Guantánamo, Santiago de Cuba. They prepare to launch an offensive, first against the small garrisons and then against the cities just mentioned.

Civilian, farm, and workers' organizations, the communications facilities of the Second Front, and the discipline and strength of the Movement's militia in that region, plus the organizational sense of Raúl, the presence of Vilma Espín, a member of the Directory in Santiago, make for a model relationship between the city and the country.

On the thirtieth of November, Raúl Castro proposes that three hundred military prisoners be returned through the Red Cross. Weapons taken so far surpass five hundred in number and much ammunition. The Rebel Air Force is now composed of ten planes.

December: Caimanera is captured, along with Cueto. Sagua de Támano is totally liberated. San Luis and Baracoa fall. Mayarí is cleaned up.

For the first time in this war the three fronts are lined up together: 1, 2, and 3 under the command of Fidel, Raúl, and Almeida; the respective chiefs attack and take Palma Soriano; after three days of combat, the city falls on December 29; taking part are the columns led by Universo Sánchez, Guillermo García, Hubert Matos, René de los Santos, Calixto García, Antonio Lussón, Tomasevich, Vilo Acuña, Diocles Torralba, Carreras, and others.

The Escambray: The Escambray front, opened by the Directory at the beginning of 1958, had a difficult and contradictory history at the outset.

The Directory did not have the time to create a genuinely national and underground organization to support the battlefront. It was an organization that could boast some extraordinary cadres; like many of those who made up the 26th of July Movement in the underground, they did not think in terms of guerrilla warfare as a strategic factor for achieving victory. Decimated after the attack on the Presidential Palace and after the Humboldt Street massacre, operations in which they lost most of their men and their true leader, José Antonio Echeverría, only the courage and the willpower of its few survivors made the reorganization of the Directory possible.

The 26th of July Movement, with Fidel's genius, had three years in which to reorganize and develop after Moncada. The Directory was greatly hampered by the fact that the regime intensified its repression in the final six months of 1957, the period the Directory needed to launch the last phase of the struggle.

Rounding up resources and arms within a few months' time, and transporting them from New York to Miami under the scrutiny of the FBI and other U.S. authorities, was very difficult. To buy a yacht, organize an expedition, dodge both the Yankees and Batista, land, and cross the hundreds of miles from Nuevitas to the Escambray was a real feat that really tested the capabilities of the Directory.

In March 1958, Batista's fall seemed imminent, and the April strike a final act in the insurrection. The Directory divided up the arms between Havana and the Escambray. The arms sent to Havana were lost in Santa Fe a few days before the April strike. The strike was a failure, and the politicians in Las Villas, the Auténticos in Miami, and the adventurers who infiltrated the Movement in the Escambray (William Morgan, Carreras, Fleitas, and others) joined forces with Eloy Gutiérrez Menoyo, whom the Directory had to weed out from the organization.

Chomón and Cubelas, with a small group of men and minimal resources, created an authentic guerrilla force that fought the enemy and simultaneously dealt with the bands taking over the region.

Che's arrival in the Escambray was made difficult by those same groups; they arrested Bordón, chief of a 26th of July guerrilla unit that was to have served as guides for Che.

From February on, the Directory fought in the Escambray. They resisted the offensive mounted by the tyranny in the battles of Cacahual, Lindero de Borges, La Diana, Hanabanilla. They came down to the plains and took the small villages of Guinia de Miranda and El Condado. The guerrillas under Cubelas and Chomón penetrated Sancti Spíritus, Placetas, and Fomento.

The honest and combative attitude of the Directory won Che over, and he signed the Pedrero Pact, with Chomón and Cubelas, and he incorporated their forces into the campaign in Las Villas; the men from the Directory fought alongside the guerrilla veterans from the Sierra until the fall of Batista.

On Fidel's order to Che: At this stage of the war, when the defeat of Batista was in the offing, Fidel's greatest political concern was to avoid a confrontation with the United States before the time was right. To this end he had to neutralize opposition from the Cuban bourgeoisie. This explains the Caracas Pact, of July 20, 1958, which joined the 26th of July Movement, the Directory, the military, the Auténticos and the Ortodoxos, civic institutions, and working-class leaders. Miró Cardona (the political candidate the U.S. State Department preferred) was secretary general. Fidel cleverly chose him for prime minister in the first month of the Revolutionary Government. Fidel juggled them all: Pardo Llada, Carlos Rafael Rodríguez (the Communist leader), Jules Dubois (the North American), General Cantillo (the military personnel) without committing himself to anyone.

Raúl Castro, slyly and without a word, introduced numerous Communists into many sectors of the civil administration, into the rural committees, into the syndicates and into other auxiliary bodies of the Second Front.

At Yaguajay, Camilo incorporated the small Communist group led by Félix Torres.

Fidel's note to Che clearly disapproved of the importance given the Directory; the latter organization had always been against Fidel's caudillism. For his part, Fidel showed his lack of trust in the Directory's leaders, with whom he had had serious student encounters.

Moreover, Fidel had, rightly, opposed the Directory's thesis of striking from above; and there was a certain amount of jealousy and partisan friction between the 26th of July Movement and the Directory. Che, for his part, was trying to forge unity from the left. At this time, he saw a guarantee for the radicalization of the process in the Communists.

The Directory—Cubelas and Chomón—were excluded and shelved. They marched on Havana on their own. They occupied the university,

the Presidential Palace, and the capitol building from whence they re-
treated under pressure after two days. Fidel's speech on January 8, at
Camp Columbia, "Arms, what for?" marked the political death of the
Directory.

Exile: The organization of the forces in exile followed the pattern established in the Wars of Independence: it constituted the rearguard of
the Cuban insurrection, and sent men, arms, ammunition, money, medicine, journalists, radio communications, and all manner of other help.

The centers of operation were Mexico, the United States, Costa
Rica, and Venezuela. It also extended to South America, Canada, Central America, the Caribbean, and even Paris. There were nuclei of the
26th of July in twenty-five countries. The principal tasks carried out by
those in exile were public denunciation of Batista's crimes, spreading
word of the underground struggle and guerrilla efforts, campaigning for
a halt in arms sales to Batista and for severing relations with him, collecting funds, purchasing and sending arms, ships, and aircraft.

It was from outside Cuba, from our people in exile, that the *Granma*
and the *Corintia* expeditions came, as well as those of the Revolutionary
Directory and other smaller movements, the weapons for the attack on
the Presidential Palace and for the underground struggle. From Costa
Rica, we sent a plane (a gift from President José Figueres and his suc-
cessor Daniel Oduber, and their party) with fifty weapons and men
under the command of Hubert Matos; this plane landed in the Sierra,
some days before the April strike. From Miami, in May, a plane with
Pedro Díaz Lanz and Franqui arrived in Cuba; in August, a plane dis-
patched by Bebo Hidalgo landed on the Second Front. At the time of
the rebel offensive (August to December), at least fifteen planes loaded
with rifles, machine guns, ammunition, and explosives landed in the
Sierra, in the Second Front area, and in the Escambray.

A conservative estimate would show a total of a thousand weapons
sent by the people in exile—the chief organizers in exile were Juan
Manuel Márquez, Pablo Díaz, Barrón, Angel Díaz, Fidel Castro, Gus-
tavo Arcos, Pedro Miret, Hubert Matos, Julio César Martínez, Evelio
Rodríguez, Léster Rodríguez, Mario Llerena, Raúl Chibás, Carlos
Franqui, Luis Buch, Manuel Urrutia, Bebo Hidalgo, Haydée Santa-
maría, José Llanuza, José Pellón, Ricardo Lorié—all from the 26th of
July.

From the Revolutionary Directorate: Rodríguez Loeche, Faure
Chomón, Luis Blanca, Orlando Blanca, Cubelas, García Lavandero,
Carlos Figueredo, Héctor Rosales, Antonio Castell and Jorge Robreño,
José Naranjo, Guillermo Jiménez, Alberto Blanco.

From the opposition Ortodoxo and Auténtico parties and other
groups: Miró Cardona, Bisbé, Agramonte, Toni Varona, and Justo
Carrillo.

The last plane from abroad to land on the Sierra, in December 1958, carried an enormous cargo of arms sent by the president of the Venezuelan junta, Admiral Larrazábal; in it were President Urrutia, the Dominican Jiménez and Luis Orlando Rodríguez, who had left the Sierra at the time of the June offensive.

The Ortodoxo Party: This was the progressive wing of the PRC Auténtico movement; it was led by Eddy Chibás, who opposed the corruption, the defeatism, the gangsterism and the line of Grau's and Prío's governments, and who, with the slogan "Honor before money," tried to reawaken the country's moral sense. He committed suicide romantically during the course of a radio broadcast which put an end to the Prío government, guaranteed the victory of his party in the elections to be held in June 1952, an election aborted by Batista's military uprising on March 10.

Fidel Castro, Abel Santamaría, Nico López, Jesús Montané, the two Amejeiras, and the majority of the attacking forces at the Moncada Barracks, and, after that, the militants of the 26th of July Movement, all came from the Ortodoxo movement. The student body and the Ortodoxo movement were the source of the insurrection.

Raúl Chibás, brother of Eddy, and the symbol of the historic role of the Ortodoxos, climbed up to the Sierra and signed the Sierra Manifesto, with Pazos and Fidel, during July 1957, while he was one of the 26th of July leaders.

The Communist Party of Cuba: Founded in 1925, it drew together the vanguard of the student body, the workers, and the intellectuals. It was one of the decisive factors in the fight against Machado, in the organization of the workers' and students' movements, and in the development of anti-imperialist and Marxist ideas. Its main figures were the student leader Julio Antonio Mella and the poet Rubén Martínez Villena.

Mella's ouster from the Central Committee, his exile and murder in Mexico in 1929, and the lengthy illness, exile, and death in 1934 of Martínez Villena, also in Mexico, deprived the Party of two revolutionary leaders of stature, who would not be matched until the emergence of Antonio Guiteras, in 1933, and, later, Fidel Castro.

The vanguard of the workers' movement, both popular and revolutionary, the Communist Party organized a general strike that paralyzed the country in August 1933, and was the principal reason for the fall of Machado's tyranny.

At the decisive moment in the strike, however, the Party leadership decided to have a meeting with the tyrant Machado—and they offered him a truce and called off the strike. The order was not heeded by the masses, but it marked the downfall of the movement, of the radical forces, and of the Party, and it opened the way for negotiation by the U.S. embassy, the army, and the conservative opposition headed by Batista.

The second grave error of the Party led by Vilar, Blas Roca, Joaquín Ordoqui, and Aníbal Escalante, was its opposition to the progressive forces in Grau's government led by Antonio Guiteras in 1933 and 1934. That group had succeeded in having the Platt Amendment abrogated, lowered the rates for electricity and telephones, both controlled by U.S. companies, and instituted the eight-hour day, the minimum wage, and other workers' benefits.

Grau's government was blocked by North American ships, which threatened to intervene, and their allies, the forces of reaction and the army led by colonel Batista. In January 1934 Batista, supported by these forces, overthrew Grau. At that time, the Party, following the directives of the Communist International, went from a right-wing position, exemplified by the truce with Machado, all the way to an ultraleft position, and proclaimed Soviets in Cuba.

The Party was savagely suppressed by Batista in 1934 and 1935, along with the followers of Guiteras and other progressive forces. But in 1938, following Soviet orders to form Popular Fronts, the Party veered toward Batista, after its union with the Auténticos failed. Batista, reacting to militant popular demands, and to the change in North American policy initiated by Roosevelt, attempted to carry out a pseudo-democratization.

The Party was legalized at that time and actively participated in the promulgation of the 1940 Constitution, one of the most democratic documents in the entire continent. The same year, the Party supported Batista for president, along with a conservative coalition that won the election in fraudulent fashion, stealing votes from the Auténticos who represented the majority of the country.

Through its influence in the government, and through the Ministry of Labor, which it was given and controlled under Batista, the Party set out to organize the working-class movement. It obtained many economic benefits for the workers, who were led by Lázaro Peña; while Juan Marinello and Carlos Rafael Rodríguez—also Communists—were ministers under Batista.

In 1944 Batista's candidate, supported by the Communists, was overwhelmed by an avalanche of votes for the Auténticos.

The workers' organization was strong in numbers, but the structure was top-heavy, overloaded with bureaucrats. The workers' gains were not the result of mass struggle, but came about because of the Party's influence in the government. This artificial bureaucracy opened the way for Eusebio Mujal and his gangs; Mujal, making use of the government's influence, divided, corrupted, and destroyed the working-class movement, so that it wound up supporting Batista's tyranny from 1952 to 1958.

Failing to understand the nature of Batista's tyranny and the emergence of a new opposition fighting throughout the country, the Party launched the slogan of "united opposition and mass struggle for elections and democratization." The Party criticized the armed student struggle, and in 1952, it called Fidel and the attack on Moncada "putschist," and the participants "adventurers" who played the tyranny's game.

At a gigantic opposition meeting in Havana during 1955, the political elders shouted "Elections," the Communists clamored for "Unity," and the youth from the 26th of July Movement and the Revolutionary Directory retorted by calling for "Revolution! Revolution!"

The Party fought against all underground actions, against sabotage and against the burning of sugarcane fields, and against the 26th of July Movement and the Directory, accusing them of being gangsters, petit bourgeois, and anti-Communist. They did not even agree among themselves on the strike in April 1958.

In July 1958, when the Caracas Pact came into existence—uniting all opposition groups in a common group—the Party then sent its leader, Carlos Rafael Rodríguez, to the Sierra Maestra and announced support of the armed struggle; it formed a group of riflemen in Yaguajay, under the orders of Félix Torres, who helped Camilo when he arrived there.

Armando Acosta, a workers' leader in Sancti Spíritus and local Communist leader, had already joined Che's column on his own and had taken part in combat and the taking of various towns when the invasion took place.

During those months at the end of the war, the Party made frantic efforts to infiltrate the Second Front in Oriente, with the help of Raúl Castro, who had been ousted from the Party for having taken part in the attack on Moncada in 1953, but who continued to think that the Party was the Revolution, and through contact with Che and Ramiro Valdés, who, for their part, although they had not been Party members, sympathized with Party aims and felt that it represented socialism.

At the National Congress of 1959, through the voice of its general secretary, Blas Roca, the Party made a self-criticism of its erroneous role in the struggle against Batista.

Weapons in the war: Weapons were acquired in three ways: taken from the army in combat; bought by our exiles in clandestine foreign markets; obtained or stolen on the island itself by the underground.

They were always in short supply and of poor quality. In 1958, for each armed combatant, there were approximately one hundred unarmed men.

The better part of these weapons were rifles, shotguns, and semiautomatic carbines, old Springfields, defective Dominican carbines, Garands, and more modern North American M-1s, and rather fragile Italian carbines.

We also had some .30-caliber machine guns mounted on tripods, a few heavier .50-caliber machine guns. We had a few mortars and, following our victory at El Jigüe and the defeat of the offensive against us in the Sierra, we had some antitank bazookas.

In our underground struggle, we could count on a minimum of pistols and revolvers, a hand-held North American machine gun plus Molotov cocktails or homemade grenades, which went off at the slightest touch. Hunting rifles and revolvers had to satisfy the irregulars, the riflemen who operated in the hills and plains, usually close to communications lines which they frequently destroyed. They also took part in attacks on towns and villages.

At the time of the *Granma*'s landing and the subsequent disaster at Alegría del Pío, when enemy forces surprised the expeditionaries, we lost almost all our equipment—more than a hundred weapons. All that remained were ten shotguns with telescopic sights, which Fidel had bought in Mexico, and these served for surprise attacks, such as those in La Plata and during the first stages of the guerrilla warfare. In the last six months of action, better weapons were captured: the famous tank in Las Vegas. On the Second Front, some small planes were seized and Raúl organized them into an improvised air force that bombed enemy garrisons. Che took the best arms, when, on December 29, 1958, he captured the armored supply train sent by Batista with three hundred officers and a large supply of ammunition. Another source lay in defusing bombs that the enemy dropped from the air and that failed to explode; they made mines for the rebels. At El Hombrito, Che invented the legendary M-26, which, placed over the barrel of a rifle, made more noise than it did harm.

In the cities sabotage was the rule: the damage was done with stolen dynamite; small iron chains were thrown over electric or telephone lines, producing short circuits, or blackouts.

We set fire to sugarcane fields, warehouses, shops, storage areas, yachts, and refineries.

Molotov cocktails were used against police stations and we used powder to make bombs.

Our sabotage of gas and electric lines proved most effective. The most spectacular was the one perpetrated at 222 Suárez Street, in May 1957, in Havana.

In 1957 the Rebel Army seized about a hundred weapons in combat in the Sierra. Approximately another hundred were sent by our people in exile, in four batches. In June 1958 there were about three hundred weapons in the Sierra. The Second Front had fewer.

In the course of the enemy offensive, the official army lost the battle, and we took 507 weapons.

The planes from Costa Rica and from Miami that landed in the Sierra prior to the offensive carried some one hundred weapons. Later, about fifteen planes landed in the Sierra and Second Front areas, bringing in about a thousand weapons and ammunition. The arms were either purchased or obtained in some other way in the United States, Mexico, Costa Rica, and Venezuela.

Beginning with the rebel invasion of the island, many garrisons were taken along with about five thousand weapons.

In the final days of the war, the twenty rebel columns, initially composed of fewer than a hundred men, consisted of six thousand or seven thousand men, all well equipped.

The Camp Columbia base in Havana had twenty thousand soldiers; the total number of men in the tyranny's armed forces was about fifty thousand.

The rebel irregulars, who numbered in the thousands, armed themselves by capturing small garrisons. They took their arms from surrendering police stations all over the island.

Camilo and Che entered and took Havana, despite odds of twenty army men to one rebel. The downfall of the tyranny was brought about by the general strike, the physical occupation of the territory by rebel forces, the collapse of the regular army, and the decisive support of the people, all of which frustrated the pro-North American coup planned by General Cantillo, while the army was still physically intact.

Strikes: The first strike against Batista was the bank strike in Havana, led by José Maria de la Aguilera. The sugarcane strike in December 1955 constituted a nationwide rebellion: the cities were dead; the students and the revolutionaries joined the workers; Echeverría, Chomón, Fructuoso Rodríguez, Blanco, David Salvador, Conrado Bécquer, Conrado Rodríguez, Lominchar, Salas, Faustino, Cervantes (the last, assassinated at Ciego de Avila).

The electrical strike in 1957 was limited to Havana. When the police assassinated Frank País on July 30, 1957, the people in Santiago replied to the murder by a general strike which spread throughout Oriente. The entire province was completely paralyzed. In the rest of the island, where public consciousness had not sufficiently matured, the strike was spotty.

This was a powerful blow to the regime. And the idea that a spontaneous strike was possible became firmly fixed.

This heritage proved fatal for the strike staged in April 1958, which was born with an illusion of victory and ended with the feeling of false defeat; it wiped out the underground movement.

As usual, the strike was complete in Oriente Province; it was strong in the interior of the island—Sagua, Güines—and practically nonexistent in Havana.

On November 3, 1958, the populace sabotaged the "elections." This move demoralized the tyranny's army.

The strike in January 1959 was decisive. The army remained intact: a military unit, teleguided by the U.S. embassy, and by the conservative elements. General Cantillo's coup, and the officers who replaced him, represented an enormous danger.

The strike against the coup paralyzed the island, disarmed the army and the enemy forces, and gave the people a more important role to play, that of protagonist.

The rebel radio and the underground press: We all knew that a newspaper could serve as agitator, organizer, and educator. We also knew that action—however intense—in itself, without organization and consciousness, is nothing. And many youths were thinking: It's enough to write the word Liberty on the butt of a rifle. Not at all. It was our belief that everything should exist in our heads, in our minds, and that all of us should know what the action was for and against whom. Thus we created *Liberación* in 1952; it was most impressive for its great size among newspapers; it was continued by the Dominican Julio César Martínez, Abel Santamaría, and Jesús Montané; we also founded *Son los mismos,* a mimeographed sheet, which was merged with Fidel's *El Acusador* that same year.

The Communist paper *Hoy,* which was shut down by President Prío, reappeared legally under Batista, and was published until Fidel attacked Moncada.

In 1952 and 1953 we took over *Alma Mater,* a FEU (student) newspaper, edited by Manuel Carbonell; the issue on the death of Rubén Batista caused a great stir. Beginning in 1952 a small radio broadcasted irregularly from the FEU. *Aldabonazo* appeared in 1955, and in 1956, *Revolución,* which became the organ of the 26th of July, during the struggle and after the triumph. *Sierra Maestra* appeared in Oriente. Later Vicente Báez and the propaganda section of the 26th of July published: *Vanguardia/Obrera, Resistencia Cívica,* and several provincial papers.

The Revolutionary Directory published: *El 13 de Marzo.* The Communists published *Carta Semanal* and a theoretical sheet. The exiles published *Sierra Maestra* and *Cuba Libre* for the 26th of July Movement and others.

In September 1957, with the collaboration of Julio César Martínez, and thanks to the help in Costa Rica of Daniel Oduber, a small shortwave radio station was set up, and President Figueres and then Fidel broadcast on it. At the end of this year, and with the help of the Barbachano Ponces, another transmitter was set up, this time in Yucatán, Mexico; it was the second station in our chain. Frank first, and then the

Movement sent two radio transmitters to the Sierra along with technicians for the rebel radio. One of these—Radio Rebelde—was inaugurated by Che at La Mesa, in February 1958. Che also edited a mimeographed paper, *El Cubano Libre*. After April, Radio Rebelde moved to La Plata, which was in Fidel's territory; it was run by Luis Orlando Rodríguez until May, when he left the island to join the exiles. From June until the end of the war, I was the director. Technicians: Eduardo Fernández and Bofill. Announcers: Martínez, Valera, Casal, Mendoza, and others. We also made use of loudspeakers, which demoralized the enemy soldiers in the battles of El Jigüe and at Santo Domingo.

Later on we built a chain of stations for the rebel columns, and these were also used for military communications.

La Cadena de la Libertad, which had ample stations in Latin America, rebroadcast our programs. The stations were: Radio Continente, Venezuela; Radio Caracol, Colombia; Nuevo Mundo, Bogotá; La Voz del Cauca, Medellín; La Voz de Antioquía; Radio El Mundo, Buenos Aires, Argentina; Emisora Central, Quito, Ecuador; WKVM, San Juan, Puerto Rico; Radio/América, Honduras; and other South American and U.S. stations.

Radio Rebelde was the Trojan horse of the insurrection, sending the truth into the garrisons and psychologically disarming the soldiers.

Radio Rebelde shattered Batista's censorship, informing the people of each episode of the struggle, the defeats inflicted, the victories gained, and it gave the masses an anti-imperialist consciousness; it informed the world of our cause, and of the liberty we defended.

Radio Rebelde was still playing a decisive role as late as January 1, 1959, when, joined now to the national radio and TV network, which were taken over by the propaganda sector, the Movement was able to denounce General Cantillo's treacherous coup plans before the eyes and ears of the people and to call for a general strike, which consolidated the victory of the insurrection.

BIOGRAPHIES

Gerardo Abreu Fontán: black youth leader; director of the 26th of July Movement in Havana; chief of the militia; murdered in 1958.

José María de la Aguilera: general secretary of bank employees; led the organization's anti-Batista strike; one of the foremost workers' leaders of the 26th of July Movement and member of its Directorate; treasurer of the revolutionary CTC after the victory; later in prison and afterward in production.

Cheché Alfonso: coordinator of the 26th of July Movement in Las Villas; murdered by the tyranny in 1958.

Juan Almeida: a black construction worker from Havana; participated in the Moncada attack; on the *Granma* expedition; a major and leader on the Third Front of Oriente; one of the veteran chiefs of the Sierra Maestra; aviation chief of the armed forces and head of other military sectors after 1959; is now part of the leadership of the Central Committee and the Party in Oriente.

Efigenio Amejeiras: transport worker from Havana; three brothers—Juan Manuel, Machaco, and Gustavo, a leader of the 26th of July Movement—all died fighting Batista; on the *Granma* expedition; a major in the Sierra; second in command to Raúl Castro on the Frank País Second Front; first revolutionary police chief; hero at Playa Girón* in 1961; dismissed at the time of sectarianism; demoted in 1965; reinstated into production as local agricultural delegate in the Escambray.

Gustavo Arcos: member of a petit-bourgeois family from Caibarién; student; accompanied Fidel in the second car in the attack at Moncada;

---

* The Bay of Pigs.—Ed.

wounded in the spinal column; Dr. Posada prevented the military from taking him from the hospital, thereby saving his life; rescued by Faustino Pérez at the Havana Orthopedic Hospital; later caught and sent to the Isle of Pines; organizer of the 26th of July Movement in Las Villas and in exile; one of his brothers died in the *Granma* landing; two others fought in the underground; ambassador to Belgium; in prison.

Conrado Bécquer (*El Guajiro, the Peasant*): leader of the sugar workers; organizer with Conrado Rodríguez, David Salvador, Isidoro Salas, and Luis Bonito of the December 1955 sugar strike; leader in the 26th of July Movement, he was in the Sierra and in the underground; named secretary-general of the Federación Obrera Azucarera [Sugar Workers' Federation] at the time of victory; replaced; in agriculture.

Julio Camacho: participated in the attack on Ermita, November 30, 1956; one of the leaders in taking Cienfuegos; a military leader with the 26th of July Movement, spent the final months of the struggle traveling from the Sierra to the military base at Camp Columbia, where, with the 26th of July coordinator, Echemendía, and the defecting officers, he prepared the military conspiracy; minister of transportation; presently a major in the army; a leader in Pinar del Río.

Juan Pedro Carbó Serviá: student leader in Havana and in the Revolutionary Directory; executed Colonel Blanco Rico, along with Rolando Cubelas and José Machado; one of the heroes of the attack on the Presidential Palace; killed by Colonel Ventura at 7 Humboldt Street on April 20, 1957.

Justo Carrillo: economist and ex-president of the Banco de Fomento y Crédito (Banfaic, which provided agricultural credit) at the time of Prío's government; personal friend of Fidel Castro, he always maintained contact with the "pure" element among the military; his thesis: "There can be no revolution against the army, nor without the army"; headed one of the economic organizations at the triumph of the Revolution in 1959; exiled in United States.

Raúl Chibás: member of a bourgeois family, brother of the founder of the Ortodoxo Party, Eduardo Chibás; went up to the Sierra in 1957, and signed the Sierra Manifesto with Fidel and Felipe Pazos, as the Ortodoxo leader; sent to be an exile organizer, he was arrested with Roberto Agramonte, and tortured by Colonel Ventura; freed from prison; treasurer of the Committee-in-Exile in the United States, he returned in 1958 to the Sierra with the workers' leader José Pellón and a load of weapons; he paved the way for military units to come over to the rebels; chose not to participate in the first government with Urrutia; in exile in the United States.

Braulio Coroneaux: machine-gun sergeant at Moncada Barracks, one of those who repulsed Fidel's attack, July 26, 1953; his lower-class background, as well as the crimes of the tyranny, impelled him to join the 26th of July Movement; arrested, freed from Boniato Prison in November 1956 by Frank País's militiamen, and then sent with a reinforcement of men and a .30-caliber machine gun to the Sierra; his coolheadedness, control of his weapon—the .50, which he discharged one bullet at a time to save ammunition—his bravery, and infallible aim all made him a pillar of the war, and his machine gun its hero; a decisive factor in innumerable battles, he trained a group of machine-gunners who all died in battle; died with the rank of major during the battle of Guisa, November 1958, battling against the tyranny's tanks.

Luis Crespo (El Guajiro, the Peasant): on the *Granma* expedition; one of the twelve who survived; chief of the weapons and repair workshop in the Sierra; major and head of a column; since 1959 a technical official of the National Institute of Agrarian Reform.

Rolando Cubelas: university student from a petit-bourgeois family; leader of the Revolutionary Directory; participated in the killing of Colonel Blanco Rico at the end of 1956; major on the Second Front of the Escambray of the Revolutionary Directory; joined his forces to Che's in the Las Villas campaign, took important barracks; occupied the Presidential Palace in January 1959; first president of the FEU; later went into the army and then into civilian life as a doctor; arrested in 1966 for having met, while traveling in Spain, with a group of exiles who were said to have been preparing an attempt on the life of the prime minister, which Cubelas was to lead; as a result, he was sentenced to twenty years in prison.

Pelayo Cuervo Navarro: one of the most famous Cuban politicians; a minister in several governments; one of the leaders of the Ortodoxo Party, along with Chibás; an opponent of Batista's dictatorship, he was killed in reprisal for the attack of March 13, 1957, on the Presidential Palace; his bullet-ridden body was thrown into the lake at Havana's Country Club; his death caused apprehension and nationwide protest.

Andrés Cuevas: a worker from Vueltas, Las Villas, he went up to the Sierra, and became one of the heroes of the war; his rapid marches, his astuteness and bravery—he fought standing up—in positional warfare, helped him, with only 8 or 10 men, succeed in escaping the advance of powerful, well-armed enemy columns; Cuevas, Ramón Paz, and Lalo [Eduardo] Sardiñas, along with a few men, destroyed the Batista columns that were trying to rescue the battalion at El Jigüe from the sea; a major, he died in the July 1958 campaign, in a combat that destroyed one of the reinforcements.

Jules Dubois: Havana correspondent of the Chicago *Tribune;* president of the Inter-American Press Association; former U.S. army colonel, attached to the State Department; favored replacing Batista with members of the bourgeois opposition, his reports denounced the tyranny's crimes; his interviews with Raúl Castro and Fidel, who declared himself "against nationalization," led Dubois away from his ties with the top professionals and bourgeois elements; and his views influenced the State Department and North American public opinion, and resulted in a halt to sales of arms to Batista in 1958; in April 1959 Fidel accepted his invitation to visit the United States, in an extraofficial capacity, and to answer questions from the American Society of Newspaper Editors; there, he defended Cuba's right to economic independence from the United States; author of a biography of Fidel that includes numerous war and underground documents.

Arturo Duque de Estrada (Chucho): secretary to Frank País in the underground; captain and leader of the Cuban Communist Party in Oriente.

Vilma Espín (Deborah): from a middle-class Santiago family, student, with an engineering degree; founding member and leader of the 26th of July Movement in Oriente, along with Frank País, José Tey, Félix Pena, Jorge Sotú, and René Ramos Latour; fought until the war ended on the Second Front in Oriente; married Raúl Castro in 1959; president of the Federation of Women and member of the Central Committee of the Communist Party; her sister Nilsa—Mme. Curie—an independent Marxist, university leader, and 26th of July member, committed suicide in 1965, with a burst of gunfire—in Raúl Castro's office—when she learned that her friend, Captain Rivero, had taken his life at a military base.

Ciro Frías (El Moro): peasant from the Sierra Maestra; Rebel captain; in March 1958 he was with Raúl Castro in the Second Front invasion; died in April in the combat at Soledad.

Rafael García Bárcenas (El Professor): held the chair of philosophy at the University of Havana; a left-wing Catholic, he organized the Movimiento Nacional Revolucionario [MNR, National Revolutionary Movement] in 1952–53; it sought to join the student element to the segment of "pure" military personnel from the army, in order to overthrow Batista in a civilian-military conspiracy that ultimately failed; died while ambassador of the revolutionary government in South America; the outstanding leaders of his movement—Faustino Pérez, Armando Hart, Frank País, Gustavo Arcos, José Tey, Vilma and Nilsa Espín, Enrique Oltuski, and Mario Llerena—became part of the 26th of July Movement.

Sergio González (El Curita): called "the little priest" because he renounced the priesthood when he was about to be ordained, in order to participate in the struggle; printer of *La historia me absolverá* [*History Will Absolve Me*] and other underground materials; one of the Action leaders from Havana; devised new forms of sabotage: milk carts that distributed white "bottles" containing bombs and explosives, push carts of "fruit" to sabotage Batista activity; famous for the March 13, 1957, Castro brothers' sabotage: in the hotels surrounding the Presidential Palace, members of the 26th of July registered with the name Castro, filled mattresses of the beds with bullets, set them on fire, which exploded and caused loud reports; the terrified Batista fled in ridiculous fashion; a week after the attack, Batista held a "vindication" on the balcony of the palace; Sergio was one of the fighters most concerned about maintaining the standards of the 26th of July, in making the underground fight humane, using all sorts of precautions to avoid injury to innocent victims and damage to the people, thanks to which the number of dead and injured was minimal; Sergio, who had organized a spectacular escape from El Príncipe Prison, was imprisoned by Batista's police in March 1958; brutally tortured, he maintained his silence and was murdered.

Armando Hart (Jacinto, El Abogado): a lawyer and the son of a Supreme Court judge, he belonged to a petit-bourgeois family from Havana; leader with Faustino Pérez of the MNR, joined the 26th of July with him after the events at Moncada, and was one of its principal figures; creator with Manuel Ray, Enrique Oltuski, and Osvaldo Dorticós of Civic Resistance; was arrested in 1957, but made a spectacular escape from the court in Havana; married to Haydée Santamaría; defended the underground in a discussion with Fidel and argued with the Communists on sectarianism and attacks on insurrectional struggle; arrested with Javier Pazos, a leader from Havana, upon coming down from the Sierra; his life was saved thanks to the mobilization of the Movement, which seized a radio station, sounded the alarm to the people, and brought pressure from civic institutions; spent the remainder of the war in the Isle of Pines Prison and entered the Camp Columbia military base with Colonel Barquín on January 1, 1959; minister of education in the first revolutionary government, organizational secretary of the Cuban Communist Party, and later of the Politburo; the only leader from the underground with a job of importance in the Castro government.

Melba Hernández (La Doctora): from a petit-bourgeois family of Caibarién, and creator with Abel Santamaría, Jesús Montané, Haydée Santamaría and Fidel of the initial nucleus of the 26th of July Movement, she participated with Haydée at Moncada; liberated at the time of amnesty, she married Montané, member of the National Directorate of the 26th of July in Havana; was in Mexico and on the Third Front of Oriente; president of the Pro-Vietnam Committee.

José Machado: fighter of the Revolutionary Directory and the university; took part in killing Blanco Rico and the attack on the Presidential Palace; killed at 7 Humboldt Street, April, 20, 1957.

Jorge Masetti: Argentine journalist, interviewed Fidel in January 1958 in the Sierra Maestra; director and founder of the Cuban news agency Prensa Latina; replaced at the time of sectarianism, he went to work with Che; went to Algeria; died while organizing guerrillas in Argentina.

Hubert Matos: professor, Ortodoxo Party member from Manzanillo; a small landholder in the Sierra; lent his trucks to the guerrillas; took refuge in Costa Rica; from there led the air expedition in March 1958 to the Sierra; chief of the guerrillas during the offensive of Column 9, Antonio Guiteras, which besieged Santiago de Cuba; he entered the Moncada Barracks on January 1, 1959, with Raúl Castro; major and military chief of Camagüey; in October 1959 sent a private letter of resignation to Fidel; arrested and accused of conspiracy and condemned to twenty years in prison; he was in La Cabaña Prison until his release on October 21, 1979.

Pichirilo Mejías: Dominican navy captain in exile; fought against the tyrannies of Trujillo, Somoza, Pérez Jiménez, and Batista; captain of one of the boats of the anti-Trujillo expedition in 1947; helmsman on the *Granma;* hero of the opposition to U.S. occupation of Santo Domingo in 1965; murdered in Santo Domingo.

Pedro Miret: engineering student at the University of Havana; wounded at Moncada; prisoner on the Isle of Pines; first Action chief of the 26th of July Movement; arrested in 1956, went to the Sierra in Hubert Matos's expedition at the beginning of 1958; chief of the mortar fighters, a tank fighter; major in the Sierra; minister of agriculture and engineering and a technical chief of an army department; member of the Central Committee.

Jesús Montané (Chucho): high official, an Ortodoxo-Chibás follower, he was the organizer with Abel and Fidel of the attack at Moncada; treasurer of the 26th of July and one of the major leaders; taken prisoner during the *Granma* landing; sent to prison for the second time on the Isle of Pines; freed in 1959; director of the tourist industry; minister of communications and organizational section of the Central Committee and the Cuban Communist Party.

Víctor Mora: peasant from the Sierra Maestra; guerrilla leader; commander of the column that invaded Camagüey; chief of that province when Batista fell; in La Cabaña Prison.

Enrique Oltuski: member of a middle-class family from Brest-Litovsk; engineer employed by Shell; went with Faustino Pérez and Hart from the MNR to the 26th of July Movement; organizer of Civic Resistance; member of the National Directorate; coordinator at Las Villas during the final months of the war; the youngest of the government ministers in 1959, in communications, handled the government takeover of the U.S.

electric and telephone companies; replaced as well as Faustino and Ray at the time of the Hubert Matos crisis; later worked with Che, and in Juceplan (the Central Planning Board); director of Fidel's cattle plan in Matanzas; was sentenced to six months' labor on the Isle of Pines; later accepted back in the Party in a sugar zone of Matanzas and became minister of sugar; at present in the Institute of Fisheries.

Frank País (David, Cristián, Salvador): son of a poor Baptist minister from Santiago; schoolteacher; attacked small barracks of the region in 1952; from the MNR entered the 26th of July Movement, which he organized in Santiago and Oriente; prepared the *Granma* landing with the militias from Manzanillo, while personally directing the attack on the city of Santiago de Cuba, November 30, 1956, the day Fidel was to have landed, but Fidel did not land until two days later because of the over-loaded yacht and lack of power of the craft; taking Santiago was the first victory of the Cuban Revolution; País created the militias, the workers' movement, the Civic Resistance Movement, and the national organiza-tion of the 26th of July Movement; he provisioned the Sierra Maestra, sending men, weapons, medicines, money, and food; murdered at the age of twenty-five on July 30, 1957, in Santiago; his death provoked a spontaneous general strike, which paralyzed Oriente and other parts of the country; the strike shook the tyranny; his loss was irreparable for the underground; he was the only figure respected by the people, the Move-ment, the Sierra, and Fidel, whom he counterbalanced; Frank País was a unique leader in the underground.

Felipe Pazos: member of a bourgeois family from Havana; a renowned economist; president and creator of the National Bank of Cuba; he re-signed with Justo Carrillo at the time of Batista's coup; signed the Sierra Manifesto with Fidel and Raúl Chibás; in November 1957, without the authority of the 26th of July, he and Léster Rodríguez, the military dele-gate of the 26th of July Movement abroad, signed the Miami Pact, the "creature" of the U.S. State Department and the bourgeois Cuban op-position; this meant the displacement of the leadership of the struggle from Cuba to Miami, and it eliminated two key points from the 26th of July Movement program which were included in the Sierra Manifesto: "No North American intervention and no military junta"; the Miami Pact was rejected by the 26th of July Movement in Fidel's well-known letter; president of the National Bank after Batista fell, was replaced by Che Guevara in October 1959; in exile in the United States.

Crescencio Pérez: patriarch and peasant leader in the Sierra Maestra; with dozens of children and personal "relations," he had connections with the leading families who controlled the mountains and who had fought against eviction, large estates, and the rural guard; Crescencio was the natural leader of the Sierra; Frank País, Celia Sánchez, and Dr. René

Vallejo organized the militias of the 26th of July Movement in the mountains, with Crescencio as the go-between, incorporating the Garcías, the Fajardos, the Tejedas, the Sardiñas, the Fríases, the Verdecias, the Moras, the Acuñas, and others to gather around Fidel, Almeida, Che, Raúl, and the group of *Granma* survivors, saving them from the army blockade, bringing them to Purial de Vicana to Mongo Pérez's house, and leading them on January 1, 1957, to the hills of Caracas; they established contacts between the guerrilla group and the city; they taught them about the Sierra, joined their ranks, and put them in touch with mountain families who would lend them support; the Sierra was an extremely inhospitable zone, impenetrable, rebellious, populated with miserable, persecuted families, who grew and developed like one big family; the Sierra Maestra—the site of the slaves' struggle in the Wars of Independence, of anti-imperialist uprisings, and of struggles against peasant evictions and abuses of land grabbers and the rural guard—was in physical and human terms, suited for guerrilla warfare, and the incorporation of the ancient and prestigious Crescencio opened all doors; his sons all fought with the rebels, and Ignacio died with the rank of captain; at present, a greatly revered retired major.

Faustino Pérez (Fausto, El Médico): member of a middle-class peasant family from Cabaiguán, a physician, leader of the 26th of July in Havana; on the *Granma* expedition, a major; signed, with Fidel, the 26th of July Manifesto, at the time of the April 1958 strike; named to head the Ministry for the Recovery of Illegally Acquired Property in 1959; replaced at the end of that year along with Manuel Ray and Enrique Oltuski, also ministers, because of disagreements over the arrest of Major Hubert Matos; participated in 1961, as unit chief, in the campaign against the insurrectionists of the Escambray; later made minister of water resources; member of the Central Committee of the Cuban Communist Party, local leader in Las Villas; ambassador to Bulgaria.

René Ramos Latour (Daniel): worker from the mines at Charo Redondo, Oriente; second to Frank País in the underground; chief of the militias; creator of the Second Front of Oriente; at the beginning of 1957, went up to the Sierra with a reinforcement of men and weapons; replaced Frank País when he died and led the August 1957 strike that paralyzed Oriente and a large part of the country; his anti-imperialist feelings were expressed in his repudiation of the Miami Pact and in his historic letter to Che, in which he condemned North American imperialism, defended the radical character of the Cuban Revolution and rejected Soviet intervention in Latin America because of the inherent dangers; partisan of organization and a critic of caudillism, he vehemently defended the role of the underground in its continuing support for the men, weapons, ammunition, money, and supplies in the Sierra, thereby rejecting Fidel's claim that the underground had abandoned the guerrillas; called to the Sierra at the time of the 1958 offensive, he brought up a group of men from Santiago and led one of the rebel columns with his comrade Ramón Paz; winner of victories; died in combat July 30, 1958, a year to the day after Frank País's death; next to País, he was the most important leader of the July underground.

Manuel Ray: engineer, principal organizer of the Civic Resistance, which gathered together professional organizations and sectors of the middle class to work against the tyranny; the resistance group was autonomous but linked with the 26th of July, of which Ray was a leader; named minister of public works by Fidel in 1959, he protested against the arrest of Major Hubert Matos and was replaced by Osmani Cienfuegos in October 1959; at odds with line of the revolutionary government, he organized an underground movement; from the United States, he came and went clandestinely to the island; his movement was later destroyed, and Ray tried other actions that failed; lives in the United States.

Ciro Redondo: founder of the 26th of July in Artemisa; one of the participants at Moncada; on the *Granma* expedition; a rebel captain; died fighting beside Che in November 1957; posthumously elevated to the rank of major.

Carlos Rafael Rodríguez: member of a petit-bourgeois family from Cienfuegos; economist; leader in the Cuban Communist Party for about forty years; treasurer, along with Jules Dubois, of the Inter-American Press Association; minister in Batista's government 1944; went up to the Sierra Maestra as the Party representative in August 1958; editor of the Communist newspaper *Hoy* in 1959; president of the National Institute of Agrarian Reform, in which he succeeded the prime minister; responsible for economic affairs and relations with the socialist countries; member of the Politburo and one of the vice-premiers; officially fourth in the official hierarchy—in reality third, and even on a par with Fidel and Raúl, given the influence of the Soviet Union in Cuba; in his shadow are other Communists, not very well known, but no less important: Flavio Bravo, Malmierca; vice-president of Cuba, June 1978.

Fructuoso Rodríguez: vice-president of the FEU and secretary of the Revolutionary Directory when José Antonio Echeverría died; organized student demonstrations, protests, and strikes; arrested, beaten, and injured several times by Batista police; participated in the attack on Radio Reloj with Echeverría; murdered at 7 Humboldt Street, April 20, 1957.

Léster Rodríguez (El Gordito, Fats): participated in the Moncada attack; 26th of July military delegate in the United States, signed the Miami Pact without authorization from the National Directorate and joined with former President Prío Socarras; lost weapons bought with savings of the underground on an abortive expedition, weapons earmarked for the April strike; later returned to the Second Front; captain in the army.

David Salvador: sugar workers' leader in Camagüey; organizer of the December 1955 strike; left-wing socialist, he split away from the Communist Party because of its lack of combativeness in the struggle against Batista; principal workers' leader in the 26th of July Movement and member of its Directorate; fought in the Sierra, was arrested and tortured by the Batista police, freed January 1, 1959; elected secretary-general of the CTC in the first free union elections; persecuted during the period of sectarianism by the Communists and their instrument in the Ministry of Labor, Major Augusto Martínez, he fell into disgrace when the new workers' movement was destroyed; tried organizing a left-wing opposition and was imprisoned in 1961; in prison.

Celia Sánchez (Norma, Aly): daughter of a petit-bourgeois doctor from Manzanillo, she, along with René Vallejo and the peasant leader Crescencio Pérez, organized the 26th of July Movement in the cities and in the Sierra; was responsible for provisioning and communications to the Sierra; accompanied Fidel in the mountains (during the war) and was his chief collaborator and leader of the guerrilla forces; minister of the presidency; her office, at the time of the triumph, and her apartment on Eleventh Street in the Vedado, is home, office, and working quarters for the prime minister.

Universo Sánchez: peasant from Matanzas; on the *Granma* expedition; the only combatant who stayed with Fidel after the rout and scattering of men at Alegría del Pío, December 5, 1956; then at nightfall, Faustino Pérez joined them; for several days, they fled from army pursuit, hiding in sugarcane fields; days later, the peasants of the Movement—Tejeda, Guillermo García, and Fajardo—led them to Purial de Vicana, where the nucleus of the *Granma* regrouped; veteran of the Sierra campaign, head of a column, one of the leaders in the battle at Palma Soriano, and one of the veteran majors; in the army.

Haydée Santamaría (Yeyé, Karín, María): one of the two women who participated in Moncada; sister of Abel and fiancée of Boris Luis Santa Coloma, both of whom were killed after the battle—the soldiers showed her the eyes of one and the testicles of the other; given amnesty in 1954, became an organizer and leader of the 26th of July, member of its National Directorate; married in 1956 to Armando Hart; treasurer, coordinator in Havana, and official of the exile groups; founder and president of the Casa de Las Américas and of the Latin American Solidarity Organization, in 1967; member of the Central Committee of the Cuban Communist Party.

René de los Santos: leader of the underground in Guanabacoa; headed one of the sabotage groups of the 26th of July during the April strike; went up to the Sierra as chief of the René Ramos Latour Column on the Third Front of Oriente; major in the army.

Eduardo Sardiñas (Lalo): peasant from the Sierra, one of the first in the war; captain; on trial because of an incident in which he killed a rebel soldier, his life was saved in a dramatic decision by Fidel's defense, but he was deprived of his rank; in June 1958, during the most difficult days of the war, Fidel gave him a group of men for an extremely dangerous action in the battle of Santo Domingo, which was decisive in the downfall of the enemy; one of the commanders who, along with his men, prevented enemy reinforcements from entering and rescuing the besieged battalion at El Jigüe; chief of the Simón Bolívar Column and the Fourth Front of Oriente; major.

Jorge Sotú: led the capture of the naval station at Santiago November 30; went up to the Sierra with the first reinforcements sent by the 26th of July Movement; captain in the Rebel Army; fought at El Uvero; sent abroad on military affairs, he broke with the 26th; with Léster Rodríguez, worked on an expedition for Prío which failed; returned with Léster at the end of the war to the Second Front of Oriente; sentenced in 1959, escaped from prison; entered Cuba clandestinely; died in an accident in Miami.

Jesús Suárez Gayol: student leader from Camagüey; member of the National Directorate of the 26th of July Movement; leader of the Havana militias; was in the underground, abroad, and guerrilla warfare; vice-minister under Che Guevara; died in Bolivia in 1967.

Cosme de la Torriente: colonel in the War of Independence, in 1955 he organized the Society of the Friends of the Republic and tried to achieve a peaceful arrangement, called "civil dialogue," among the opposition parties and Batista; it failed completely.

Ramiro Valdés: from a poor Artemisa family; along with José Suárez and Jesús Montané, took the Moncada guardpost; on the *Granma* expedition; major; one of the leading veterans; chief of a column; second to Che Guevara in the invasion campaign; head of security until 1969; member of the Politburo and high in the leadership hierarchy.

Aldo Vera: organizer and main Action and Sabotage chief of the 26th of July Movement in Havana; led and participated in innumerable underground actions, the most important, the sabotage at 222 Suárez Street, in May 1957, which cut off Havana's electrical power for three days; injured by the bomb explosion, along with a workers' leader, Alvarez de la Campa, was arrested by Batista police; chief of one of the police-investigation groups in 1959; later replaced, fled to the United States; entered Cuba secretly and organized acts of sabotage; killed in Puerto Rico.

Joe Westbrook: one of the youngest leaders of the Revolutionary Directory; killed at 7 Humboldt Street, April 20, 1957.

INDEX

The names with asterisks denote men belonging to Fulgencio Batista's regime.